EVERYMAN,
I WILL GO WITH THEE,
AND BE THY GUIDE,
IN THY MOST NEED
TO GO BY THY SIDE

JOSEPH CONRAD

Nostromo
A Tale of the Seaboard

EVERYMAN'S LIBRARY

88

First published 1904
First included in Everyman's Library, 1957
Introduction, Bibliography and Chronology © David Campbell
Publishers Ltd., 1992

ISBN 1-85715-088-0

A catalogue record for this book is available from the British Library

Published by David Campbell Publishers Ltd., 79 Berwick Street,
London W1V 3PF

Distributed by the Random Century Group Ltd.,
20 Vauxhall Bridge Road, London SW1V 2SA

Printed and bound in Germany

CONTENTS

INTRODUCTION

I was just then giving up some days of my allotted span to the last chapter of the novel *Nostromo*, a tale of an imaginary (but true) seaboard ... for twenty months, neglecting the common joys of life that fall to the lot of the humblest on this earth, I had, like the prophet of old, 'wrestled with the Lord' for my creation, for the headlands of the coast, for the darkness of the Placid Gulf, the light on the snows, the clouds in the sky, and for the breath of life that had to be blown into the shapes of men and women, of Latin and Saxon, of Jew and Gentile ... The whole world of Costaguana ... men, women, headlands, houses, mountains, town, *campo* (there was not a single brick, stone, or grain of sand of its soil I had not placed in position with my own hands), all the history, geography, politics, finance; the wealth of Charles Gould's silver mine, and the splendour of the magnificent Capataz de Cargadores, whose name, cried out in the night (Dr Monygham heard it pass over his head – in Linda Viola's voice), dominated even after death the dark gulf containing his conquests of treasure and love...

(A Personal Record, 1912)

On 23 October 1902, Conrad wrote to his friend John Galsworthy: 'with my head full of a story, I have not been able to write a single word – except the title which shall be I think: NOSTROMO'. Certainly, as the revolutions in Conrad's South American republic come and go and one regime gives way to another, Nostromo is crucially active from start to finish. Yet it is a strange 'word' with which to start, or on which to ground, this most ambitious and panoramic of Conrad's novels. In Italian – and Nostromo is an Italian ('I am placing [the novel] in Sth America in a Republic I call Costaguana. It is however concerned mostly with Italians', wrote Conrad as he was some way into writing the novel) – the 'word' means 'boatswain' but little or nothing is made of this in the novel in which the word itself is a matter of some contention. In the Author's Note which he added as a preface to the novel in 1917 (see pages xxxvi–xlii), Conrad stresses that Nostromo is the 'Man of the People'. Indeed he uses the phrase, or variants of it, four times within two pages: 'he is

vii

content to feel himself a power – within the People ... He is a man with the weight of countless generations behind him and no parentage to boast of ... Like the People ... he is a Man of the People, their very own unenvious force, disdaining to lead but ruling from within.... dying betrayed he hardly knows by what or by whom, he is still of the People, their undoubted Great Man – with a private history of his own'. We do not hear a great deal of, or from, 'the People' in the novel precisely because they are voiceless, the permanent, inevitable victims as armies and ideologies come and go – the 'people, suffering and mute, waiting for the future in a pathetic immobility of patience'. To the European, though kindly, eye of Mrs Gould, the faces of the local people 'looked all alike, as if run into the same ancestral mould of suffering and patience'. They are the field-fodder, the cannon-fodder, the mine-fodder, the everything-fodder as the varying tyrannies sweep across the land. (Remember how Ezra Pound started his Pisan Cantos: 'The enormous tragedy of the dream in the peasants' bent shoulders'.)

Conrad's novel is not *about* the People – it is part of their doom to remain somehow beneath the reach of narrative. But it *is* – centrally – about Nostromo, and it is worth looking a little more closely at that 'word'. We first hear of him from Captain Mitchell who has a very proprietorial attitude to him – 'my Capataz de Cargadores, as they called him in the town ... a fellow in a thousand ... a man absolutely above reproach'. Many people are under 'the spell of that reputation' which is Nostromo's proudest possession. He receives and basks in 'extraordinary adulation'; it is said that 'his prestige is his fortune'; he is capable of 'absurd fidelity' and is often said to be 'incorruptible' – a word used also of the silver from the mine. The irony of this becomes increasingly obvious as we watch the incorruptible silver 'corrupt' the hitherto incorruptible man. On the narrative level, he performs many brave feats, saving men and women and doing the state – and the European capitalists – a great deal of service: in all this he is a rather traditional, even stereotypical hero. But the adulation is sometimes interrupted by mockery – from another Italian. Teresa Viola, who is almost a mother to him, taunts him: 'To be first somewhere – somehow – to be first with these English. They will be showing him to everybody. "This is our Nostromo!" ... What a name! What is that? Nostromo? He would take a name that is properly no word from them.' She berates his appetite for 'the praise of people who have given you a silly name – and nothing besides – in exchange for your soul and body'. Since we have already heard Captain Mitchell boast that Nostromo is 'devoted to me body and soul', and since we have been told that he is guilty of consistent 'mispronunciation' of 'Nostromo', Teresa's taunts seem uneasily close to the mark. Nostromo's defence is a classic one: 'A good name ... is a treasure, Padrona'. Iago who, like the Devil, has many of the best (and truest) lines in *Othello*, pertinently reminds Othello that 'Good name in man and woman, dear my Lord,/Is the immediate jewel of their souls' and it is Cassio's grief in that play that this is just what he has lost: 'Reputation, reputation, reputation! O, I have lost my reputation! I have lost the immortal part of myself, and what remains is bestial.' Nostromo would have understood all these lines well and may indeed be unconsciously echoing them. But Teresa is not convinced by the old argument and thinks that 'reputation' only masks exploitation – 'They have been paying you with words.'

So what about this 'name' which 'is properly no word'? Presumably, given how possessive Captain Mitchell (and the other Europeans) feel about him, it is a crude running together of 'nostro uomo' – 'Ourman'. Well might Teresa ask 'What is that?' Names are very important in Conrad. It is one of Marlow's worries as he tries to recount the doings of Kurtz in *Heart of Darkness* that 'I do not see the man in the name any more than you do.' Why should Conrad use 'a name that is properly no word' as the title for his immense novel of politics, war, and the spread of capitalism? And if we don't see the man in it, what *do* we see?

Nostromo's 'real' name is Giovanni Battista Fidanza, but he never uses it; he is 'the miscalled Capataz de Cargadores'. Later, when he has become 'the enigmatical patron of the new revolutionary agitation, the trusted, the wealthy comrade', he *is* called by his 'rightful name', Captain Fidanza, and is considered the 'undoubted Great Man' of the People. Yet with the silver hidden on the island and 'the knowledge of his moral ruin locked up in his heart', he now has what Conrad calls 'a private history of his own' which makes a mockery of 'the admired publicity of his life'. By the end, there is thus a complete split between the private history and the public name, between the mortal, ruined man and the enduring, spotless reputation. It is his 'rightful' name which rings out in the last paragraph of the book, seeming to fill and dominate the whole Gulf and beyond – and this Conrad calls his most 'sinister triumph'. Sinister, perhaps, because it shows how utterly the power of names can be divorced from the reality of things. It is as if Conrad is implying how hollow *all* reputations are, if we did but know it. You can't, really, trust *any* names.

Nostromo himself thinks of 'his personality' as being 'the only thing lost in that desperate affair'. For 'personality' we might now want to think of 'identity' or perhaps 'true self', since he is doomed to a life of stealth, secrecy, bad faith, and the maintaining of false appearances. He has somehow – he never quite works out how it has happened – been condemned to inauthenticity. And in general one could say that the whole novel is, among many other things, a study of how selfhood and identity can be lost. Specifically, in the differing relationships people have with the local source of wealth, the silver of the mine: more generally, in their overall relations to matter, materiality, and to those attempts to manage matter which go by the names of politics and economics. In this connection the notion of 'treasure' is of vital importance. What do you value? What do you value *most*? Ruskin once advised that you must put your gods where your treasure is or *vice versa*, and if you follow that it becomes crucial to decide what is real treasure, *real* wealth? Identity – Conrad sees this as clearly as Ruskin – can come to depend on what you value. If you make a mistake as to what constitutes 'treasure' and put your gods into that, the result can be a complete loss of self, and matter may make you over. The wrong kind of *dei*fication may lead to *rei*fication – as we might say that, in his way, Gould deifies the mine and the mine, in its way, proceeds to reify him.

There is, in fact, a lot of more or less unconscious self-reification going on in the novel with people manifesting an increasing immobility, and a growing tendency to take on the qualities of things. Nostromo depends on publicity, reputation, prestige, admiration, audience – what we now call the gaze of the other; for him validation is inseparable from vanity, and so his identity is completely dependent on externals (solitude and secrecy are effectively fatal for Nostromo precisely because of his reliance on publicity and externality). He is thus permanently and equally vulnerable to appropriation and adulation, the latter all too often an easy cosmeticization of the former. He is indeed paid with words – and, to all intents and purposes, with words only. He saves the state and is the strong right arm of the powers that be – and the powers that are becoming. His reward is a 'silly name'. To the extent that he is *The* Man of the People, and thus in some way at once the representative and distillation of the People, he is indeed the paradigmatic figure of the book – entitled to entitle it. *Our* man is by definition not his own man. He is used, and used, and used again. But then who, one way or another, is not? We are dealing with degrees. The whole book offers a study of what can possess people and take them over, and of how it happens – it may be with utmost brutality, or with insidious subtlety. Mitchell says Nostromo is 'his' man: the silver mine would say that Gould was *its* man. Who owns who, and what owns what? Whatever else, the mine itself could, by the end, look out over Costaguana, perhaps over the world, and, with one or two exceptions, silently say of the inhabitants – 'mine, all mine'. You may be sure that Conrad would have taken a grim satisfaction at the pun yielded by the language whereby the substantive is also the possessive. It is very much to his purpose.

And, of course, the novel is indeed very centrally about the silver and the mine. Just one month after finishing the book, Conrad seems to be backing off a little from his eponymous hero. Thus to his friend Cunninghame Graham: 'I don't defend Nostromo himself. Fact is he does not take *my* fancy either ... truly N is nothing at all – a fiction – embodied vanity of the sailor kind – a romantic mouthpiece of "the people" which (I mean "the people") frequently experience the very feelings to which he gives utterance. I do not defend him as a creation.' Be that as it may – you shouldn't always trust the teller commenting on his own tale – some people *have* found Nostromo a rather romanticized figure. And this statement, to a Swedish professor, Ernst Bendz, in 1923 sounds fairly definitive:

> *Nostromo* has never been intended for the hero of the Tale of the Seaboard. Silver is the pivot of the moral and material events, affecting the lives of everybody in the tale. That this was my deliberate purpose there can be no doubt. I struck the first note of my intention in the unusual form which I gave to the title of the First Part, by calling it 'The Silver of the Mine', and by telling the story of the enchanted treasure on Azuera, which, strictly speaking, has nothing to do with the rest of the novel. The word 'silver' occurs almost at the very beginning of the story proper, and I took care to introduce it in the very last paragraph, which would perhaps have been better without the phrase which contains that key-word.

The phrase he alludes to describes the far horizon 'overhung by a white cloud shining like a mass of solid silver' which perhaps too portentously tries to suggest that the entire world is now under the dominion of silver and is doomed to go the same way as Charles Gould who comes 'to dwell alone within a circumvallation of precious metal'. Certainly, once the silver has, as it were, been released, or torn, from the mountain, it is always described as rushing down the mountainside, through the town onto the boats, at a torrential, unstoppable rate – destination everywhere, with unlimitable ramifying effects and influences. This, certainly, is Conrad's vision of the unarrestable, irresistible, spread of capitalism. It is worth noting that when the mountain starts 'pouring its stream of treasure' the actual waterfall on the mountain dries up ('filled up with the refuse of excavations') and exists only as a memory and an image in one of Mrs Gould's water-colours. Conrad is making an ecological point with which we have become only too familiar.

In earlier days, before Charles Gould took over the mine, we are told that there had been a primitive attempt to work the mine using Indian slaves, but that it had 'ceased to make a profitable return, no matter how many corpses were thrown into its maw'. Later, the metaphor is repeated as we read a description of how the mine 'would swallow' the gangs of workers going on shift. And of course, one of the great achievements of the novel is the way it traces how the mine gradually 'swallows' the seemingly masterful Charles Gould (and you may hear 'ghoul' as well as 'gold' in that name). Mrs Gould watches helplessly as the mine grows from being an 'idea' to becoming a 'fetish' and finally 'a monstrous and crushing weight' for her husband. He is said to be guilty of a 'subtle conjugal infidelity' whereby his passion has been transferred from wife to mine. Indeed, Gould is last heard from in the form of a telephone call from his office in the mine – 'the master remains to sleep at the mountain tonight'. He has been definitively 'swallowed'. I will just note that the other main actor in the novel, the sceptical, ironical, bantering Decoud, may seem the opposite of the grimly pragmatic Gould. Yet when he finally commits suicide by shooting himself and falling into the sea, making sure he will sink by putting silver bars in his pockets (silver can be used for all kinds of deaths), he is said to be 'swallowed up in the immense indifference of things'. Gould by earth, Decoud by water – both terminally 'swallowed' by the material world they had, in their different ways, sought to master. The moral has no limits to it.

One final irony concerning the operations of the silver might be noted here. Old Viola, 'the venerable Garibaldino', is a passionate republican idealist. That there might be something anachronistic and inefficacious about his Garibaldian idealism is sufficiently intimated very early on when we learn that a coloured lithograph of Garibaldi, which he keeps on the wall of his little inn, habitually 'paled' when the door opened, letting in the sunlight; as much as to say, these admirable ideals simply fade away when exposed to the searching light of common day. In his Author's Note Conrad speaks of the novel as concerning 'events flowing from the passions of men short-sighted in good and evil'. By the end of the novel, old Viola is, literally, very 'short-sighted' – indeed, almost blind. Yet he is installed as the keeper of the new lighthouse built on the Great Isabel (where the silver is hidden). This is irony enough: the almost blind in charge of ambiguous illumination, or 'enlightenment'. But the irony is compounded. Mrs Gould has given Viola two things – a Bible, and a pair of 'silver spectacles'. He tries to read the Bible while tending the lighthouse. He gets no 'illumination' either from the new glasses or the old religion. In the event, this passionate spokesman for 'the people' shoots and kills the Man of the People, Nostromo, whom he loved like a son (mistaking him for an unsuitable suitor of his daughters). 'Short-sightedness' could hardly have more bleakly ironic results. There is not much to see with – or by, or through – round here.

Mention of Viola's 'idealism' raises an issue crucial to the book, and I can best introduce it by quoting one of the key passages. It concerns Mrs Gould's reaction to the first silver brought from 'the dark depths of the Gould Concession':

She had laid her *unmercenary hands*, with an eagerness that made them tremble, upon the first silver ingot turned out still warm from the mould; and by her *imaginative estimate* of its *power* she endowed that lump of metal with a *justificative conception*, as though it were not a *mere fact*, but something far-reaching and impalpable, like the *true* expression of an emotion or the *emergence of a principle*. (my italics)

The silver in itself is simply a lump, a mere material fact. Inert in the earth, it has neither value nor menace, nor power. Everything depends on the 'imaginative estimate', the 'justificative conception', the 'principle' which the handling humans endow it with, or bestow or project on it. At first the idealization of the silver seems justified – 'security seemed to flow upon this land from the mountain gorge'. But it turns out to be a very equivocal asset. Gould's uncle fought with a sword, an honest blade of steel. His nephew fights with the metal deemed to be wealth – 'more dangerous to the wielder, too, this weapon of wealth, double-edged with the cupidity and misery of mankind, steeped in all the vices of self-indulgence as in a concoction of poisonous roots, tainting the very cause for which it is drawn, always ready to turn awkwardly in the hand'. One way or another, the silver does for all the main protagonists. The tyranny of Guzman Bento which preceded the reign of the Goulds was a crudely bloodthirsty affair. But by the end Mrs Gould perceives a subtler but more powerful tyrant. 'She saw the San Tomé mine hanging over the Campo, over the whole land, feared, hated, wealthy; more soulless than any tyrant, more pitiless and autocratic than the worst Government; ready to crush innumerable lives in the expansion of its greatness.' And yet, at the start, she herself had 'idealized' the silver. We must look more closely at this word.

Any reader of the novel will become aware of a spectrum of terms, a vocabulary, relating to the myriad aspects of the phenomenon of 'belief': faith, devotion, religion, cause, fanaticism; idea, ideal, illusion – any number of ways of gesturing towards some notion of 'spiritual' value, or 'ideal meaning' to be set against, or offset, the claims and exactions and imperatives of those 'material interests' which echo insistently throughout the book. In the Casa Gould there is a Madonna figure in a niche, reminder of an older, simpler world of communally-shared belief. Now, everyone seems to have his or her own more or less idiosyncratic 'conviction' on which to act. Decoud, the sceptical observer, has his own views about this. 'It seemed to him that every conviction, as soon as it became effective, turned into that dementia the gods send upon those they wish to destroy.' This takes us to the heart of an absolutely central, and cruel, Conradian paradox. Briefly and crudely summarized, he shows that man cannot act in this life without the support or inspiration or goad (call it what you will) of some ideal or illusion or conviction (words not easily separable in his lexicon): *yet* illusions, ideals, and convictions are inherently corruptive and flatter or mislead us to madness or doom. In particular, there is the special danger of that 'misty idealism of Northerners, who at the smallest encouragement dream of nothing less than the conquest of the earth'. But in this novel, Conrad shows *all* the main characters to be acting under the illusion of some kind of ideal – even, or rather particularly, those who pride themselves on being most practical. Gould is the most obvious case of a man 'haunted by a fixed idea'. And Conrad comments: 'a man haunted by a fixed idea is insane. He is dangerous even if that idea is an idea of justice.' As Decoud says, 'he has idealized the existence, the worth, the meaning of the San Tomé mine.' Gould thinks he is a simple pragmatist, but is shown to be a dangerous idealist, because he has made an ideal of 'material interests'.

But this is also Conrad: 'action is consolatory. It is the enemy of thought and the friend of flattering illusions. Only in the conduct of our action can we find the sense of mastery over the Fates. For his [Gould's] action, the mine was obviously the only field ... its working must be made a serious and moral success'. As Decoud says of Gould, 'those Englishmen live on illusions which somehow or other help them to get a firm hold of the substance.' It may indeed be that those illusions are subtly corrosive of character, but what of Decoud? Arguably, his trouble is that he doesn't, finally, believe in anything sufficiently to enable him to get hold of substance at all. He thinks he is a pure materialist rationalist, free from all ideals and illusions. But he has made an ideal of his detachment – one more illusion. When he is left alone on the island, he suffers from an extreme form of stimulus-starvation. With nothing to vent his irony on, he becomes nothing himself and simply ceases to be, effectively dissolving back into the sea. (It is yet another irony that he should have formulated the – successful – plan for the secession of Sulaco, under the slogan 'Separate!' Yet he dies from a personal, creatural 'separation' from his kind which proves to be unbearable.) There are many other ideals and idealisms in the book; and when we read that Dr Monygham 'had made himself an ideal conception of his disgrace', we realize that, for Conrad, idealism in one form or another is ubiquitous. It has to be. Without *any* ideals or illusions or convictions, man relapses from passivity to a sort of paralysed evaporation (Decoud's end is surely exemplary). With no action there is no getting hold of matter, and thus no possibility of living. *Yet*, ideals and illusions corrupt and action degrades. For two simple reasons. 'It was impossible to disentangle ones activity from its debasing contacts.' And, as Mrs Gould comes to realize, 'there was something inherent in the necessities of successful action which carried with it the moral degradation of the idea'. In Conrad's world it can seem as though you are damned if you do (act), and damned if you don't. Taken to an extreme, it can become a very pessimistic vision.

When Conrad spoke of putting every brick of Costaguana in position with his own hands, he was probably alluding to the immense effort it had required to assemble the materials for his imaginary (though true) South American country; as he wrote to Edmund Gosse, 'Sulaco is a synthetic product'. And it was synthesized more from books than from personal experience. Until the writing of *Nostromo*, Conrad had drawn on his own experience for a lot of his most ambitious work. This was different; he had almost nothing to go on. 'All my memories of South America seem to slip away. I just had a glimpse 25 years ago – a short glance. That is not enough *pour bâtir un roman dessus*. And yet one must live.' When he wrote, critically, of another book that it was 'Too easy. *Trop inventé*; never *assez vécu*', he might have had his own work-in-progress in mind, for he had a continual worry that *Nostromo* might be, indeed, 'too much from invention and not enough from experience'. He 'synthesized' his imaginary world primarily from other books, though we must include contemporary events and newspaper reports and leaders.[1] In that same letter to Gosse, Conrad also said of his novel: 'The historical part is an achievement in mosaic too, though, personally, it seems to me much more true than any history I ever learned.' Whether drawing his material from so many and such disparate sources to some extent prompted Conrad to lay out the 'mosaic' of his historical narrative in the novel way he did, we can only speculate. But it is time to say something about the narrative method of *Nostromo*.

Writing in 1914 of a later novel (*Chance*), Henry James spoke of Conrad as 'a votary of the way to do a thing that shall make it undergo most doing'. Memorably, he noted 'the baffled relation between the subject matter and its emergence which we find constituted by the circumvallations of "Chance".' He might have said the same of *Nostromo* (in which, curiously enough, 'circumvallation' is an important word). Indeed, if one wanted to identify one of the most important distinguishing characteristics of that whole move towards innovation and experiment which we designate as Modernism, one could hardly do better than to fasten on that 'baffled relation between the subject matter and its emergence'. Certainly, a first-time reader of *Nostromo* will be 'baffled' enough as he is plunged into the middle, or end, of events for which there has been no contextual preparation; confronted with a bewildering range of characters for whom there has been no biographical introduction; exposed to discontinuous scenes, places, voices, without any explanation of why he should be watching or listening and given no clue as to what might be the connection, or indeed, narrative relevance of all this. Late in the novel, we are told how a visitor to Sulaco would be 'stunned and as it were annihilated mentally by a sudden surfeit of sights, sounds, names, facts, and complicated information imperfectly apprehended' as Captain Mitchell gives his version of the 'history' of recent events. And very late in the book we are told that Decoud spent his last days 'beholding life like a succession of senseless images'. Clearly Conrad wants his reader, initially at least, to experience something of the visitor's initial confusion and something, too, of Decoud's terminal incomprehension.

Partly he achieves this, not only by presenting us with material without any positioning of the reader by the proffering of an explanatory introduction, but also by disrupting or inverting what we think of as proper chronological succession. For instance, there is President Ribiera who, as we learn in due course, succeeded the tyrant Guzman Bento; who is 'the embodiment of the best elements of the state', and who stands for 'the establishment of legality, of good faith and order in public life'. Fine. But by the time we hear his well-intentioned speeches as the railway and the mine are beginning to be developed, we have *already* observed him fleeing for his life on a lame mule, barely escaping the clawings of a mob. Indeed this is almost the first event we, incomprehensibly enough, are told about. So when we come to him in his optimistic prime, we have seen him defeated, crippled, and in flight. His brief reign of confidence is therefore sadly, or absurdly, ironic to us, since we have already seen how it ends. Similarly, we – with Nostromo and Dr Monygham – come across the mysteriously suspended corpse of the hapless Jewish trader, Hirsch, long before we learn the details of his torture and murder; or again, we are introduced, courtesy of Captain Mitchell, to a medallion commemorating Decoud some time before we are told how he died. Why this mystification? Why not – first this happened, then this, then this, as narratives usually, and as we think sensibly, proceed? Well, for one thing, we might think of Conrad as wishing to effect what might be called the redirection of curiosity, so that we don't continually concern ourselves with what happened next, because quite often we *know* what happened next, or anyway subsequently. Instead, Conrad, invites, or forces us to concern ourselves with *processes* – not so much the 'what' of things as the 'how'.

But there is a more important consideration. Conrad wants to scatter any possible gathering impression of a slow but inexorable logic of progress. The last thing he wants to do is to start with a given chaos (Guzman Bento's barbaric and primitive tyranny) and end with an achieved modern order (the American world hegemony promised, or threatened, by Holroyd). He wants no reassuring hints of necessary development, inevitable melioration – no Whiggish complacency or evolutionary optimism can stand up to his withering scepticism. He wants to show changes, certainly – and a very definite historical chronology can be reconstituted from the events of the book[2] – but he wants to depict them in such a fractured and scrambled way that we will not be lulled into assuming that such changes inevitably constitute improvements. At a time when capitalism and imperialism were making the highest claims for themselves as civilizing forces, Conrad was very determined that none of his readers should accept the notion of progress uncritically.

The man who *does* see everything that happens as constituting significant stages in the orderly progress of 'history' is, of course, Captain Mitchell who – deep irony here – 'prided himself on his profound knowledge of men and things in the country'. Mitchell is a 'narrator' *within* the larger narrative which is in the control of the omniscient narrator who is, as it were, responsible for the fragmentation and chronological shuffling of events. Mitchell effectively starts the book with his narration (Chapter Two), and he concludes Part First informing some unnamed auditor with his usual pompous confidence – 'It was history – history, sir!'. He is forever seeing events as

'marking an epoch': the random to-and-froings of cruel and
rapacious armed mobs, or the more subtly insidious encroach-
ments of Western expansionary capitalism are alike all part of
the solemn onward-marching, forward-looking, parade of
history. Any disastrous interruption to this stately progression
is hastily marginalized – 'Ah, that sir, was a mistake.' He is, of
course, deeply (happily?) 'ignorant of the real forces swirling
uncontrollably around him', another of those amiably imper-
meable, impercipient and myopic characters (short-
sightedness here, indeed) used by Conrad for strong, ironic
effects.

It is Mitchell who takes 'distinguished visitors' on a narrative tour of Sulaco and the 'historical events' which preceded
the establishment of the modern state. Mitchell is a 'public
man' and he believes in the publications, the publicity, of
history – monuments, memorials, medallions, everything that
constitutes what might be called 'the official version'. But by
the time he gives his orderly narrative tour – Chapter Ten,
Part Third – we have seen and experienced how *very* disorderly
and haphazardly constituted it has all been. Mitchell is last
seen – by Mrs Gould – living in isolated obscurity back in
England – 'He rambled feebly about "historical events" till I
felt I could have a cry'. Such, we might infer, is the fate of the
conventional narrator. In the world of this book – in the
modern world – conventional narration disqualifies itself.

As with time in the novel, so with space. The shifts and
switches are sudden and unpredictable. There are passages of
what we might call long perspective when we are given an
overwhelming sense of the vast, permanent (relatively speaking) natural background – the mountains, the Isabel islands,
the sea; and then we are suddenly forced to focus on a small,
human detail – for example, a man twitching his eyebrow
during a threatening cross-examination. Some of the details
are extraordinarily minute and thus take on a slightly halluci-
natory vividness – 'I remember looking at the high French
heel of her little shoe'; or, when a priest suddenly turns round,
'the skirt of his soutane was inflated slightly by the brusqueness of his movements'. And some of the panoramic evocations
are correspondingly vast – 'the precipitous range of the

Cordillera, immense and motionless, emerging from the billows of the lower forests like the barren coast of a land of
giants'. There is also what we have come to call 'defamiliar-
ization' – 'Those dark, shifting patches, alternately catching
and eluding the eye, altered their place always away from the
harbour, with a suggestion of consecutive order and purpose.
A light dawned upon him. It was a column of infantry . . .' The
effect of these sudden shifts between proximity and distance –
they are ruptures rather than 'cuts' – is to 'ephemeralize' the
insect-like, short-sighted squabblings of fallible, feeble man,
while at the same time making the cruelties he inflicts, the
follies he perpetrates, the sufferings he undergoes loom terrify-
ingly close. In a word – an ungainly word, I grant – Conrad
'de-perspectivizes' his material. There is no one, assured and
reassuring vantage point from which we, as readers, can view
the characters and events, the sequences and places, the
territory and the time.

There is one other aspect of the atmospherics of the book to
which I wish to draw attention. I know of no other novel in
which the light-source – literally, the way and extent to which
things are 'illuminated' – is so often, and so specifically,
designated. We are invariably told where whatever light there
is, is coming from – matches, candles, lamps, torches, street-
lights, fires, windows full of stars, patches of moonlight, dawn,
and so on: these fitfully, flickeringly, illuminate the scenes, or
do not – as when Nostromo suddenly puts out the candle on
the boat in the Gulf and Decoud feels that it is as if the whole
world has been destroyed. This is clearly not just dutiful
realism on Conrad's part:

And now the windows of the Amarillo Club were dark. The last
spark of resistance had died out. Turning his head at the corner,
Charles Gould saw his wife crossing over to their own gate in the
lighted patch of the street . . . As she passed in all the lights went out
in the street, which remained dark and empty from end to end. The
houses of the vast Plaza were lost in the night. High up, like a star,
there was a small gleam in one of the towers of the cathedral; and the
equestrian statue gleamed pale against the black trees of the Alameda, like a ghost of royalty haunting the scenes of revolution.

There are many such passages: the fire which flares up and

then suddenly collapses to 'an enormous heap of embers' aptly reflects the life and fate of Don Avellanos, that spokesman for 'enlightenment', who is even then dying, 'vanquished in a lifelong struggle with the powers of moral darkness'. There is something Manichean in Conrad's handling of light – if, simplifying, we take Manicheanism to involve a belief in a cosmos comprised of an ongoing battle between the forces of light and the forces of darkness, which the forces of light were by no means certain to win. This, even in apparently casual descriptive details – 'the daybreak struggled with the gloom under the arcades on the Plaza'. Conrad never takes light for granted. One powerful effect of this is to make reality seem, at times, astonishingly solid and material; and then, quite suddenly, utterly insubstantial. It looms up into overwhelming proximity, and then vanishes. We feel at once the force and the futility of things, the actual pain and – perhaps – the ultimate pointlessness. Nothing lasts. 'Then out went the candle and we were left darkling' says the Fool in *King Lear*. That now seems a very Conradian line.

When there is sufficient light, there are many other things to see, a *lot* of things. And they come from all over. The Gould household is full of 'knick-knacks' – 'tables loaded with knick-knacks' are mentioned more than once. There is a rocking-chair from the United States, straight-backed chairs from Spain, and an assortment of other European furniture. Charles Gould combines local attire with an English riding-whip and dogskin gloves: his book-cases are half-full of books and half-full of firearms. Everywhere there is a 'slight European veneer', and we surely know exactly what Conrad is talking about when he refers to 'the material apparatus of perfected civilization which obliterates the individuality of old towns under the stereotyped conveniences of modern life'. As well as local people, the town contains English, Germans, French, Italians, Basques, as well as figures from other Latin American countries. It appears as the simple truth that 'Sulaco seemed on the point of being invaded by all the world'. By people; by things. This is the local porousness, the omni-availability of goods, the giddy eclecticism, all alike ensuant on the commercial spread which attends triumphant capitalism. How much is gain, and how much might be loss, Conrad does not presume to say. But one feels there is a kind of madness in the randomness of the international clutter.

A key figure in all this, though he is seldom mentioned by the critics, is Anzani, who keeps the local general store, until he is murdered, fittingly perhaps, in front of his safe. He is only ever, but always, in the background. He provides loans to rebels, furnishings for Goulds, imported Swedish punch for tippling Generals and thirsty engineers, and even a rather horrid-sounding brown suit from London for Nostromo when he aspires to respectability. He is the generic purveyor. Mr Knick-Knack. You name it, Anzani will get it. Progress? Change, certainly. And, very pregnantly, Conrad puts a new newspaper office next to Anzani's store:

It was next to Anzani's great emporium of boots, silks, ironware, muslins, wooden toys, tiny silver arms, legs, heads, hearts (for ex-voto offerings), rosaries, champagne, women's hats, patent medicines, even a few dusty books in paper covers and mostly in the French language. The big black letters formed the words, 'Office of the *Porvenir*'. From these offices a single folded sheet of Martin's journalism issued three times a week; and the sleek yellow Anzani prowling in a suit of ample black and carpet slippers, before the many doors of his establishment, greeted by a deep, sidelong inclination of his body the Journalist of Sulaco going to and fro on the business of his august calling.

August calling? The contiguity of the Journalist (even so good a one as Decoud) and the Merchant (immensely successful in his own line of business) is hardly fortuitous. Are they perhaps *both* purveyors of only apparently different assortments of variegated trash? Writing tends to fare badly in Conrad – his work is littered with torn, ruined, or abandoned texts of one kind or another – and nowhere more so than in *Nostromo*. There is a lot of writing in the novel – diaries, letters, newspaper articles, state papers, histories. Decoud's diary-letter to his sister survives (he is the other main narrator *within* the narrative and 'better' than Captain Mitchell because more private, sceptical, ironical, incredulous) but a great deal of the other writing does not. The new press office of the paper, *Porvenir*, for instance, doesn't last long – 'the mob has thrown my presses out of the window and scattered the type all over the Plaza'. What happens to the noble attempt to write a comprehensive and enlightened account of the country's recent history by Don Avellanos – called 'Fifty Years of Misrule' – may be taken to be representative and admonitory:

> ... and hasn't he seen the sheets of 'Fifty Years of Misrule', which we have begun printing on the presses of the *Porvenir*, littering the Plaza, floating in the gutters, fired out as wads for trabucos loaded with handfuls of type, blown in the wind, trampled in the mud? I have seen pages floating upon the very waters of the harbour.

That last touch has, perhaps, a personal resonance. Conrad, the sailor-turned-writer, referred to his books as 'paper boats', and he seems never to have got over some deep sense of, finally, the profound futility of writing; as if all literature was, one way or another, doomed to end up as litter – litter-ature, he might rather grimly have punned.

But if writing fares badly in the novel, public speaking – 'oratory' – fares worse. Conrad was extraordinarily sensitive to the noises that come out of our mouths, from the quietest whisper, to the loudest scream; the shortest grunt, the longest howl. And thus, particularly aware of all the various ways in which we use words – or let words use us. He is nowhere more suspicious of 'eloquence' than in this novel:

> What's it to me whether his talk is the voice of eloquence or simply a bit of clap-trap eloquence. There's a good deal of eloquence of one sort or another produced in both Americas. The air of the New World seems favourable to the art of declamation. Have you forgotten how dear Avellanos can hold forth for hours here?

At this point Charles Gould's irony is hardly separable from Conrad's. From all sides there pours out 'pompous discourse' and 'grandiloquent phrases', most of which we do begin to register, along with Gould, as more or less extreme forms of 'deplorable balderdash'. Guzman Bento is simply a brute; when he gives his grotesque exhortations on 'democracy' and 'forgiveness', fittingly enough, because his front teeth have been knocked out, 'his utterance was spluttering and indistinct'. When the opportunistic Don Juste Lopez attempts to recruit Gould for the rebel side: 'Don Juste's eyes glowed dully; he believed in parliamentary institutions – and the convinced drone of his voice lost itself in the stillness of the house like the deep buzzing of some ponderous insect.' The English and Europeans use words more sparingly and to more effect – pragmatists as they are, who fix their eyes uninquiringly on the job in hand. But taciturnity and loquacity alike come in for undercutting irony – different kinds of insect. One way and another, there is a deep suspicion of language – its claims and pretensions, its mystifications and misrepresentations, its sheer breathtakingly shameless mendacities – running right through this novel.

It seems, indeed it is, in many ways a pessimistic book and one might ask if any one unassailable positive value is recognized in the course of it. We hear quite often of 'moral disgrace', 'moral misery', 'moral degradation', 'moral darkness', 'want of moral sense', but only once do we hear the following:

> There is no peace and no rest in the development of material interests. They have their law, and their justice. But it is founded on expediency and is inhuman; it is without rectitude, without the continuity and the force that can be found *only in a moral principle*. (my italics)

This is Dr Monygham, speaking very near the end. This sardonic, bitterly ironic figure, is a man apart – tortured beyond endurance during Bento's tyranny, he inhabits a realm of pained disillusion beyond the reach or comprehension of any of the other characters. He is quite beyond the influence of the silver of the mine; instead, he is silently devoted to the lonely, mine-widowed Mrs Gould – 'living on the inexhaustible treasure of his devotion drawn upon in the secret of his heart like a store of unlawful wealth'. The wording perhaps makes too obvious the comparison and contrast with Nostromo who at that time is, of course, secretly living and drawing on the unlawful wealth of the silver hidden on the island. But it would seem that Monygham has put his gods with a better 'treasure' than the other characters in the book. It is hard not to feel Conrad endorsing Monygham's one and only speech in defence of 'moral principle'. But hard, too, to envisage how he thought it might ever be active and efficacious – truly recognized and honoured – in the world of politics and ideology, capitalism, empire and revolution, which he has so panoramically exposed in this novel.

In 1905, a year after completing *Nostromo*, Conrad wrote two essays which serve as powerful postscripts to the novel. In 'Autocracy and War' he discussed 'the incredible infatuation which could put its trust in the peaceful nature of industrial and commercial competition'. In 'Henry James' he wrote: 'from the duality of man's nature and the competition of individuals, the life-history of the earth must in the last instance be a history of a really very relentless warfare. Neither his fellows, nor his gods, nor his passions will leave a man alone'. And yet, he says in the same essay, the 'voice' of 'the imaginative man' will never be silenced, even on the last day of creation:

For my own part, from a short and cursory acquaintance with my mind, I am inclined to think that the last utterance will formulate, strange as it may appear, some hope to us now utterly inconceivable. For mankind is delightful in its pride, its assurance, and its indomitable tenacity. It will sleep on the battlefield among its own dead, in the manner of an army having won a barren victory. It will not know when it is beaten. And perhaps it is right in that quality.

Nostromo is a pessimistic novel; but the writing of it was a victory, and not a barren one. It is, cumulatively, a stupendously powerful work – evidence, if evidence is needed that, indeed, while there is art, there is hope.

Tony Tanner

NOTES

———

1 A great amount of work has been done on the sources for *Nostromo*. Anyone wishing to read about this in a convenient form should consult: *A Preface to Conrad* by Cedric Watts (Longman, 1982); *Landmarks of World Literature – NOSTROMO* by Ian Watt (Cambridge University Press, 1988); and *Conrad's Western World* by Norman Sherry (Cambridge University Press, 1971). Watts lists four main books as contributing to Conrad's own imagined country and its characters: *On Many Seas: The Life and Exploits of a Yankee Sailor* by F. B. Williams, 1897; *Seven Eventful Years in Paraguay* by G. F. Masterman, 1869; *Venezuela* by E. B. Eastwick, 1868; and *Wild Scenes in South America* by Ramon Paez, 1863. In addition Watts notes Conrad's deep interest in the Spanish-American War, during which Spain lost Cuba and the Philippines; and in accounts of the United States' intervention in Colombia at the secession of Panama in 1903. Watts also comments on the high level of interest in all aspects of imperialism in the newspapers of the day, in which one recurrent cliché in political debate was, apparently, the phrase 'material interests'.

2 I think it is important to succumb to the initially confusing experience of reading the novel. But, for what it is worth, a more conventional chronology of the main events of the book would run roughly as follows (I take the tentative dates from Ian Watt's little book on *Nostromo* mentioned in note 1.) From 1852 to 1868, Guzman Bento maintains a ruthless dictatorship and unites Costaguana. In 1885 the Goulds reactivate the mine with backing from Holroyd. In 1888 Gould and Holroyd back Ribiera as the new President of Costaguana; the National Railway is inaugurated. In 1889 General Montero revolts; the revolt gains ground, and in 1890 Ribiera is defeated at Socorro. Many of the events of the novel, centred on Decoud and Nostromo taking the silver to the island, and the general foiling of the Montero revolution, take place between April and June of that year. In 1891, the war is ended by an international naval demonstration off Sulaco. Montero is assassinated, and the Occidental Province becomes the Occidental Republic. In 1900 Nostromo is killed by Viola. The Goulds return from a European tour. They have no children which is appropriate enough – British imperialism had no significant political heirs. The future belongs to the American capitalist, Holroyd ('Time itself has got to wait on the greatest country in the whole of God's universe. We shall be giving the word for everything ... We shall run the world's business whether the world likes it or not.'). The only likely challenge will probably come from the forces of Communism, as represented by the pale photographer, 'small, frail, bloodthirsty, the hater of capitalists', who hovers round Nostromo's death-bed, hoping to learn the whereabouts of the silver. This may not rank as full prophecy on Conrad's part, but it's not bad for 1904.

SELECT BIBLIOGRAPHY

BIOGRAPHIES

BAINES, JOCELYN, *Joseph Conrad*, Weidenfeld and Nicolson, 1960.

SHERRY, NORMAN, *Conrad and His World*, Thames and Hudson, 1972. Useful short illustrated introductory biography.

KARL FREDERICK, *Joseph Conrad: The Three Lives*, Farrar, Straus and Giroux, New York, 1978, and Faber, 1979.

NAJDER, ZDZISLAW, *Joseph Conrad: A Chronicle*, Cambridge University Press, 1983, Generally reckoned to be the best full life.

MEYER, BERNARD, *Joseph Conrad: A Psychoanalytic Biography*, Princeton University Press, Princeton, NJ, 1967. By a psychoanalyst; an interesting and intelligent investigation, quite out of the general run of such studies.

LETTERS

JEAN-AUBRY, G., ed., *Joseph Conrad: Life and Letters*, Doubleday, New York, 1927.

KARL, FREDERICK and DAVIES, LAURENCE, eds., *The Collected Letters*, Cambridge University Press, 1983–. Will print every known letter when complete.

CRITICISM

AMBROSINI, RICHARD, *Conrad's Fiction as Critical Discourse*, Cambridge University Press, 1991.

BERTHOUD, JACQUES, *Joseph Conrad: The Major Phase*, Cambridge University Press, 1978. One of the most important critical studies.

DARRAS, JACQUES, *Conrad and the West*, Macmillan, 1982.

FORD, FORD MADOX, *Joseph Conrad: A Personal Remembrance*, Little, Brown, Boston, 1924. Must be read critically, but absolutely essential for an understanding of Conrad.

FLEISHMAN, AVROM, *Conrad's Politics*, Johns Hopkins Press, Baltimore, 1967.

GEDDES, GARY, *Conrad's Later Novels*, McGill-Queen's University Press, Montreal, 1980. Stimulating discussions of the later novels.

GUERARD, ALBERT, *Conrad the Novelist*, Harvard University Press, Cambridge, Mass., 1958. A useful study along psychoanalytical lines.

HAWTHORN, JEREMY, *Joseph Conrad: Language and Fictional Self-Consciousness*, Edward Arnold, 1987.

HAY, ELOISE KNAPP, *The Political Novels of Joseph Conrad*, Chicago University Press, 1963.

JOHNSON, BRUCE, *Conrad's Models of Mind*, University of Minnesota Press, Minneapolis, 1971.

KIRSHNER, PAUL, *Conrad: The Psychologist as Artist*, Oliver and Boyd, 1968.

MOSER, THOMAS, *Conrad: Achievement and Decline*, Harvard University Press, Cambridge, Mass., 1957. An influential study.

SCHWARTZ, D. R., *Conrad: The Later Fiction*, Macmillan, 1982.

SHERRY, NORMAN, *Conrad's Eastern World*, Routledge, 1966.

SHERRY, NORMAN, *Conrad's Western World*, Routledge, 1971. Both the Sherry books are essential for their revelation of Conrad's sources.

STALLMAN, R. W., ed., *The Art of Joseph Conrad: A Critical Symposium*, Michigan State University Press, East Lansing, 1960.

WATT, IAN, *Conrad in the Nineteenth Century*, University of California Press, Berkeley, 1979.

CHRONOLOGY

DATE	AUTHOR'S LIFE	LITERARY CONTEXT
1853		Charlotte Brontë: *Villette*.
1856	Marriage of Apollo Korzeniowski to Ewelina Bobrowska in Oratów.	Bernard Shaw born.
1857	December 3: birth of their son, Józef Teodor Konrad Korzeniowski (later to be known as Joseph Conrad).	Flaubert: *Madame Bovary*. Baudelaire: *Fleurs du mal*.
1859	Family moves to Żytomierz.	Dickens: *A Tale of Two Cities*.
1861	Apollo Korzeniowski arrested in Warsaw for patriotic conspiracy.	Dickens: *Great Expectations*.
1862	Conrad's parents exiled to Vologda, Russia: he accompanies them.	Turgenev: *Fathers and Sons*. Ruskin: *Unto This Last*.
1863	Family moved to Chernikhov.	Thackeray dies.
1865	Death of Conrad's mother.	Birth of Kipling and Yeats.
1866	Stays with uncle at Nowochwastów.	Dostoevsky: *Crime and Punishment*.
1869	Death of Apollo Korzeniowski; Conrad becomes ward of relatives.	Tolstoy: *War and Peace*.
1870	Taught by Adam Pulman in Kraków.	Charles Dickens dies.
1871	Also taught by Isydor Kopernicki.	Dostoevsky: *The Devils*.
1872	Resolves to go to sea.	George Eliot: *Middlemarch*.
1874	Leaves Poland for Marseille to join French merchant navy.	Hardy: *Far from the Madding Crowd*.
1875	Sails Atlantic on *Mont-Blanc*.	Thomas Mann born.
1876	Serves as steward on *Saint-Antoine*.	Death of George Sand.
1877	Possibly involved in smuggling arms to Spanish royalists.	Tolstoy: *Anna Karenina*.
1878	Shoots himself in chest, recovers, and joins British ship *Mavis*.	Hardy: *The Return of the Native*.
1879	Serves on clipper *Duke of Sutherland*.	Ibsen: *A Doll's House*.
1880	Sails to Australia on *Loch Etive*.	Dostoevsky: *The Brothers Karamazov*.

HISTORICAL EVENTS

Crimean War begins.
Crimean War ends. Freud born.

Indian Mutiny.

Darwin's *Origin of Species*.
Emancipation of Russian serfs.
American Civil War begins.
Bismarck gains power in Prussia.

American slaves freed. Polish uprising.
American Civil War ends.

Gandhi born. Suez Canal opens.

Franco-Prussian War. Lenin born.

Paris Commune.

Mazzini dies. Bertrand Russell born.
Winston Churchill born.

Bakunin dies.

Russia declares war on Turkey.

Afghan War. Congress of Berlin.

Zulu War. Einstein and Stalin born.

DATE	AUTHOR'S LIFE	LITERARY CONTEXT
1881	Second mate of *Palestine*.	Death of Dostoevsky and Carlyle.
1882	Storm-damaged *Palestine* repaired.	Birth of Virginia Woolf and James Joyce.
1883	Shipwrecked when *Palestine* sinks.	Nietzsche: *Thus Spake Zarathustra*.
1885	Sails to Calcutta on *Tilkhurst*.	Birth of D. H. Lawrence.
1886	Takes British nationality; qualifies as captain.	Stevenson: *Dr Jekyll and Mr Hyde*.
1887	Sails to Java on *Highland Forest*.	Birth of Marianne Moore.
1888	Master of the ship *Otago*.	Birth of T. S. Eliot.
1889	Resigns from *Otago* and settles in London, writing *Almayer's Folly*.	Death of Robert Browning.
1890	Works in Belgian Congo.	Ibsen: *Hedda Gabler*.
1891	Officer of *Torrens* until 1893.	Hardy: *Tess of the D'Urbervilles*.
1894	*Almayer's Folly* accepted by Unwin. Meets Edward Garnett and Jessie George.	R. L. Stevenson dies; Aldous Huxley born. Kipling: *The Jungle Book*.
1895	*Almayer's Folly* published.	Crane: *The Red Badge of Courage*. Hardy: *Jude the Obscure*.
1896	*An Outcast of the Islands*. Marries Jessie George. Meets H. G. Wells.	William Morris dies; Scott Fitzgerald born.
1897	Corresponds with Cunninghame Graham. *The Nigger of the 'Narcissus'*.	Kipling: *Captains Courageous*.
1898	*Tales of Unrest*. Enters collaboration with Ford Madox Hueffer (later known as Ford Madox Ford). First son, Borys, born.	Wilde: 'Ballad of Reading Gaol'. Wells: *War of the Worlds*. Rilke: *Advent*.
1899	*Heart of Darkness* serialized. Serialization of *Lord Jim* begins.	Birth of Hemingway.
1900	*Lord Jim* (book). J. B. Pinker becomes Conrad's agent.	Death of Ruskin, Nietzsche, Oscar Wilde and Stephen Crane.
1901	*The Inheritors* (co-author Hueffer).	Kipling: *Kim*.
1902	*Youth* volume.	Gorky: *The Lower Depths*.
1903	*Typhoon* volume. *Romance* (co-author Hueffer).	James: *The Ambassadors*. Birth of George Orwell.
1904	*Nostromo*.	Chekhov: *The Cherry Orchard*.
1905	*One Day More* (play) fails.	Wells: *Kipps*.

CHRONOLOGY

DATE	AUTHOR'S LIFE	LITERARY CONTEXT
1906	*The Mirror of the Sea* (with Hueffer). Second son, John, born.	Samuel Beckett born. Ibsen dies.
1907	*The Secret Agent.*	Birth of W. H. Auden.
1908	*A Set of Six* (tales).	Bennett: *The Old Wives' Tale.*
1909	Quarrels with Hueffer.	Death of Swinburne.
1910	Moves to Capel House, near Ashford.	Yeats: *The Green Helmet.*
1911	*Under Western Eyes.*	William Golding born.
1912	*A Personal Record. 'Twixt Land and Sea* (tales). *Chance* serialized in *New York Herald.*	Patrick White born. Pound: *Ripostes.*
1913	Meets Bertrand Russell.	Lawrence: *Sons and Lovers.*
1914	Book of *Chance* has large sales. Conrad becomes prosperous at last.	Joyce: *Dubliners.* Birth of Dylan Thomas.
1915	*Within the Tides* (tales); *Victory.*	Lawrence: *The Rainbow.*
1916	*The Shadow-Line* serialized.	Henry James dies.
1917	*The Shadow-Line* (book).	Anthony Burgess born.
1918	Borys Conrad wounded in war.	Death of Wilfred Owen.
1919	*The Arrow of Gold.*	Woolf: *Night and Day.*
1920	*The Rescue.*	Lawrence: *Women in Love.* Katherine Mansfield: *Bliss.*
1921	*Notes on Life and Letters.*	Huxley: *Crome Yellow.*
1922	*The Secret Agent* (play) fails.	Eliot: *The Waste Land.* Joyce: *Ulysses.*
1923	Visits USA to acclamation. *The Rover.*	Yeats wins Nobel Prize. Huxley: *Antic Hay.*
1924	Declines knighthood. Dies of heart attack; buried at Canterbury.	Forster: *A Passage to India* Shaw: *Saint Joan.*
1925	Publication of *Tales of Hearsay* and the unfinished *Suspense.*	Eliot: *Poems 1909–25.* Shaw wins Nobel Prize.
1926	*Last Essays.*	Kafka: *The Castle.*
1927	*Joseph Conrad: Life & Letters,* written and edited by G. Jean-Aubry.	Woolf: *To the Lighthouse.*

CHRONOLOGY

AUTHOR'S NOTE

Nostromo is the most anxiously meditated of the longer novels which belong to the period following upon the publication of the *Typhoon* volume of short stories.

I don't mean to say that I became then conscious of any impending change in my mentality and in my attitude towards the tasks of my writing life. And perhaps there was never any change, except in that mysterious, extraneous thing which has nothing to do with the theories of art; a subtle change in the nature of the inspiration; a phenomenon for which I cannot in any way be held responsible. What, however, did cause me some concern was that after finishing the last story of the *Typhoon* volume it seemed somehow that there was nothing more in the world to write about.

This so strangely negative but disturbing mood lasted some little time; and then, as with many of my longer stories, the first hint for *Nostromo* came to me in the shape of a vagrant anecdote completely destitute of valuable details.

As a matter of fact in 1875 or '6, when very young, in the West Indies, or rather in the Gulf of Mexico, for my contacts with land were short, few and fleeting, I heard the story of some man who was supposed to have stolen single-handed a whole lighter-full of silver, somewhere on the Tierra Firme seaboard during the troubles of a revolution.

On the face of it this was something of a feat. But I heard no details, and having no particular interest in crime *qua* crime I was not likely to keep that one in my mind. And I forgot it till twenty-six or seven years afterwards I came upon the very thing in a shabby volume picked up outside a second-hand bookshop. It was the life story of an American seaman written by himself with the assistance of a journalist. In the course of his wanderings that American sailor worked for some months on board a schooner, the master and owner of which was the thief of whom I had heard in my very young days. I have no doubt of that because there could hardly have been two exploits of that peculiar kind in the same part of the world and both connected with a South American revolution.

The fellow had actually managed to steal a lighter with silver, and this, it seems, only because he was implicitly trusted by his employers, who must have been singularly poor judges of character. In the sailor's story he is represented as an unmitigated rascal, a small cheat, stupidly ferocious, morose, of mean appearance, and altogether unworthy of the greatness this opportunity had thrust upon him. What was interesting was that he would boast of it openly.

He used to say: 'People think I make a lot of money in this schooner of mine. But that is nothing. I don't care for that. Now and then I go away quietly and lift a bar of silver. I must get rich slowly – you understand.'

There was also another curious point about the man. Once in the course of some quarrel the sailor threatened him: 'What's to prevent me reporting ashore what you have told me about that silver?'

The cynical ruffian was not alarmed in the least. He actually laughed. 'You fool, if you dare talk like that on shore about me you will get a knife stuck in your back. Every man, woman, and child in that port is my friend. And who's to prove the lighter wasn't sunk? I didn't show you where the silver is hidden. Did I? So you know nothing. And suppose I lied? Eh?'

Ultimately the sailor, disgusted with the sordid meanness of that impenitent thief, deserted from the schooner. The whole episode takes about three pages of his autobiography. Nothing to speak of; but as I looked them over, the curious confirmation of the few casual words heard in my early youth evoked the memories of that distant time when everything was so fresh, so surprising, so venturesome, so interesting; bits of strange coasts under the stars, shadows of hills in the sunshine, men's passions in the dusk, gossip half forgotten, faces grown dim ... Perhaps, perhaps, there still was in the world something to write about. Yet I did not see anything at first in the mere story. A rascal steals a large parcel of a valuable commodity – so people say. It's either true or untrue; and in any case it has no value in itself. To invent a circumstantial account of the robbery did not appeal to me, because my talents not running that way I did not think that the game was worth the candle. It was only when it dawned upon me that the purloiner of the treasure need not necessarily be a confirmed rogue, that he could be even a man of character, an actor and possibly a victim in the changing scenes of a revolution, it was only then that I had the first vision of a twilight country which was to become the province of Sulaco, with its high shadowy Sierra and its misty Campo for mute witnesses of events flowing from the passions of men shortsighted in good and evil.

Such are in very truth the obscure origins of *Nostromo* – the book. From that moment, I suppose, it had to be. Yet even then I hesitated, as if warned by the instinct of self-preservation from venturing on a distant and toilsome journey into a land full of intrigues and revolutions. But it had to be done.

It took the best part of the years 1903-4 to do; with many intervals of renewed hesitation, lest I should lose myself in the ever-enlarging vistas opening before me as I progressed deeper in my knowledge of the country. Often, also, when I had thought myself to a standstill over the tangled-up affairs of the Republic, I would, figuratively speaking, pack my bag, rush away from Sulaco for a change of air, and write a few pages of *The Mirror of the Sea*. But generally, as I've said before, my sojourn on the continent of Latin America, famed for its hospitality, lasted for about two years. On my return I found (speaking somewhat in the style of Captain Gulliver) my family all well, my wife heartily glad to learn that the fuss was all over, and our small boy considerably grown during my absence.

My principal authority for the history of Costaguana is, of course, my venerated friend, the late Don José Avellanos, Minister to the Courts of England and Spain, etc. etc., in his impartial and eloquent *History of Fifty Years of Misrule*. That work was never published – the reader will discover why – and I am in fact the only person in the world possessed of its contents. I have mastered them in not a few hours of earnest meditation, and I hope that my accuracy will be trusted.

In justice to myself, and to allay the fears of prospective readers, I beg to point out that the few historical allusions are never dragged in for the sake of parading my unique erudition, but that each of them is closely related to actuality; either throwing a light on the nature of current events or affecting directly the fortunes of the people of whom I speak.

As to their own histories I have tried to set them down, Aristocracy and People, men and women, Latin and Anglo-Saxon, bandit and politician, with as cool a hand as was possible in the heat and clash of my own conflicting emotions. And after all this is also the story of their conflicts. It is for the reader to say how far they are deserving of interest in their actions and in the secret purposes of their hearts revealed in the bitter necessities of the time. I confess that, for me, that time is the time of firm friendships and unforgotten hospitalities. And in my gratitude I must mention here Mrs Gould, 'the first lady of Sulaco,' whom we may safely leave to the secret devotion of Dr Monygham, and Charles Gould, the Idealist-creator of Material Interests whom we must leave to his mine – from which there is no escape in this world.

About Nostromo, the second of the two racially and socially contrasted men, both captured by the silver of the San Tomé Mine, I feel bound to say something more.

I did not hesitate to make that central figure an Italian. First of all the thing is perfectly credible: Italians were swarming into the Occidental Province at the time, as anybody who will read further can see; and secondly, there was no one who could stand so well by the side of Giorgio Viola the Garibaldino, the Idealist of the old, humanitarian revolutions. For myself I needed there a man of the People as free as possible from his class-conventions and all settled modes of thinking. This is not a side snarl at conventions. My reasons were not moral but artistic. Had he been an Anglo-Saxon he would have tried to get into local politics. But Nostromo does not aspire to be a leader in a personal game. He does not want to raise himself above the mass. He is content to feel himself a power – within the People.

But mainly Nostromo is what he is because I received the inspiration for him in my early days from a Mediterranean sailor. Those who have read certain pages of mine will see at once what I mean when I say that Dominic, the *padrone* of the *Tremolino*, might under given circumstances have been a Nostromo. At any rate Dominic would have understood the younger man perfectly – if scornfully. He and I were engaged together in a rather absurd adventure, but the absurdity does not matter. It is a real satisfaction to think that in my very young days there must, after all, have been something in me worthy to command that man's half-bitter fidelity, his half-ironic devotion. Many of Nostromo's speeches I have heard first in Dominic's voice. His hand on the tiller and his fearless eyes roaming the horizon from within the monkish hood shadowing his face, he would utter the usual exordium of his remorseless wisdom: 'Vous autres gentilshommes!' in a caustic tone that hangs on my ear yet. Like Nostromo! 'You *hombres finos!*' Very much like Nostromo. But Dominic the Corsican nursed a certain pride of ancestry from which my Nostromo is free; for Nostromo's lineage had to be more ancient still. He is a man with the weight of countless generations behind him and no parentage to boast of ... Like the People.

In his firm grip on the earth he inherits, in his improvidence and generosity, in his lavishness with his gifts, in his manly vanity, in the obscure sense of his greatness, and in his faithful devotion with something despairing as well as desperate in its impulses, he is a man of the People, their very own unenvious force, disdaining to lead but ruling from within. Years afterwards, grown older as the famous Captain Fidanza, with a stake in the country, going about his many affairs followed by respectful glances in the modernized streets of Sulaco, calling on the widow of the *cargador*, attending the Lodge, listening in unmoved silence to anarchist speeches at the meeting, the enigmatical patron of the new revolutionary agitation, the trusted, the wealthy comrade Fidanza with the knowledge of his moral ruin locked up in his breast, he remains essentially a Man of the People. In his mingled love and scorn of life and in the bewildered conviction of having been betrayed, of dying betrayed he hardly knows by what or by whom, he is still of the People, their undoubted Great Man – with a private history of his own.

One more figure of those stirring times I would like to mention: and that is Antonia Avellanos – the 'beautiful Antonia'. Whether she is a possible variation of Latin-American girlhood I wouldn't dare to affirm. But, for me, she *is*. Always a little in the background by the side of her father (my venerated friend) I hope she has yet relief enough to make intelligible what I am going to say. Of all the people who had seen with me the birth of the Occidental Republic, she is the only one who has kept in my memory the aspect of continued life. Antonia the Aristocrat and Nostromo the Man of the People are the artisans of the New Era, the true creators of the New State; he by his legendary and daring feat, she, like a woman, simply by the force of what she is: the only being capable of inspiring a sincere passion in the heart of a trifler.

If anything could induce me to revisit Sulaco (I should hate to see all these changes) it would be Antonia. And the true reason for that – why not be frank about it? – the true reason is that I have modelled her on my first love. How we, a band of tallish schoolboys, the chums of her two brothers, how we used to look up to that girl just out of the schoolroom herself, as the standard-bearer of a faith to which we all were born but which she alone knew how to hold aloft with an unflinching hope! She had perhaps more glow and less serenity in her soul than Antonia, but she was an uncompromising Puritan of patriotism with no taint of the slightest worldliness in her thoughts. I was not the only one in love with her; but it was I who had to hear oftenest her scathing criticism of my levities – very much like poor Decoud – or stand the brunt of her austere, unanswerable invective. She did not quite understand – but never mind. That afternoon when I came in, a shrinking yet defiant sinner, to say the final good-bye I received a hand-squeeze that made my heart leap and saw a tear that took my breath away. She was softened at the last as though she had suddenly perceived (we were such children still!) that I was really going away for good, going very far away – even as far as Sulaco, lying unknown, hidden from our eyes in the darkness of the Placid Gulf.

That's why I long sometimes for another glimpse of the 'beautiful Antonia' (or can it be the Other?) moving in the dimness of the great cathedral, saying a short prayer at the omb of the first and last Cardinal-Archbishop of Sulaco, standing absorbed in filial devotion before the monument of Don José Avellanos, and, with a lingering, tender, faithful glance at the medallion-memorial to Martin Decoud, going out serenely into the sunshine of the Plaza with her upright carriage and her white head; a relic of the past disregarded by men awaiting impatiently the Dawns of other New Eras, the coming of more Revolutions.

But this is the idlest of dreams; for I did understand perfectly well at the time that the moment the breath left the body of the Magnificent Capataz, the Man of the People, freed at last from the toils of love and wealth, there was nothing more for me to do in Sulaco.

October 1917   J. C.

To John Galsworthy

So foul a sky clears not without a storm.

Shakespeare

PART I
THE SILVER OF THE MINE

CHAPTER ONE

IN the time of Spanish rule, and for many years afterwards, the town of Sulaco—the luxuriant beauty of the orange gardens bears witness to its antiquity—had never been commercially anything more important than a coasting port with a fairly large local trade in ox-hides and indigo. The clumsy deep-sea galleons of the conquerors that, needing a brisk gale to move at all, would lie becalmed, where your modern ship built on clipper lines forges ahead by the mere flapping of her sails, had been barred out of Sulaco by the prevailing calms of its vast gulf. Some harbours of the earth are made difficult of access by the treachery of sunken rocks and the tempests of their shores. Sulaco had found an inviolable sanctuary from the temptations of a trading world in the solemn hush of the deep Golfo Placido as if within an enormous semicircular and unroofed temple open to the ocean, with its walls of lofty mountains hung with the mourning draperies of cloud.

On one side of this broad curve in the straight seaboard of the Republic of Costaguana, the last spur of the coast range forms an insignificant cape whose name is Punta Mala. From the middle of the gulf the point of the land itself is not visible at all; but the shoulder of a steep hill at the back can be made out faintly like a shadow on the sky.

On the other side, what seems to be an isolated patch of blue mist floats lightly on the glare of the horizon. This is the peninsula of Azuera, a wild chaos of sharp rocks and stony levels cut about by vertical ravines. It lies far out to sea like a rough head of stone stretched from a green-clad coast at the end of a slender neck of sand covered with thickets of thorny scrub. Utterly waterless, for the rainfall runs off at once on all sides into the sea, it has not soil enough—it is said—to grow a single blade of grass, as if it were blighted by a curse. The poor, associating by an obscure instinct of consolation the ideas of evil and wealth, will tell you that it is deadly because of its forbidden treasures. The common folk of the neighbourhood, peons of the estancias, vaqueros of the seaboard plains, tame Indians coming miles to market with a bundle of sugar-cane or a basket of maize worth about threepence, are well aware that heaps of shining gold lie in the gloom of the deep precipices cleaving the stony levels of Azuera. Tradition has it that many adventurers of olden time had perished in the search. The story goes also that within men's memory two wandering sailors—Americanos, perhaps, but gringos of some sort for certain—talked over a gambling, good-for-nothing mozo, and the three stole a donkey to carry for them a bundle of dry sticks, a water-skin, and provisions enough to last a few days. Thus accompanied, and with revolvers at their belts, they had started to chop their way with machetes through the thorny scrub on the neck of the peninsula.

On the second evening an upright spiral of smoke (it could only have been from their camp-fire) was seen for the first time within memory of man standing up faintly upon the sky above a razor-backed ridge on the stony head. The crew of a coasting schooner, lying becalmed three miles off the shore, stared at it with amazement till dark. A negro fisherman, living in a lonely hut in a little bay near by, had seen the start and was on the look out for some sign. He called to his wife just as the sun was about to set. They had watched the strange portent with envy, incredulity, and awe.

The impious adventurers gave no other sign. The sailors, the Indian, and the stolen burro were never seen again. As to the mozo, a Sulaco man, his wife paid for some masses, and the poor four-footed beast, being without sin, had been probably permitted to die ; but the two gringos, spectral and alive, are believed to be dwelling to this day amongst the rocks, under the fatal spell of their success. Their souls cannot tear themselves away from their bodies mounting guard over the discovered treasure. They are now rich and hungry and thirsty—a strange theory of tenacious gringo ghosts suffering in their starved and parched flesh of defiant heretics, where a Christian would have renounced and been released.

These, then, are the legendary inhabitants of Azuera guarding its forbidden wealth ; and the shadow on the sky on one side with the round patch of blue haze blurring the bright skirt of the horizon on the other, mark the two outermost points of the bend which bears the name of Golfo Placido, because never a strong wind had been known to blow upon its waters.

On crossing the imaginary line drawn from Punta Mala to Azuera, the ships from Europe bound to Sulaco lose at once the strong breezes of the ocean. They become the prey of capricious airs that play with them for thirty hours at a stretch sometimes. Before them the head of the calm gulf is filled on most days of the year by a great body of motionless and opaque clouds. On the rare clear mornings another shadow is cast upon the sweep of the gulf. The dawn breaks high behind the towering and serrated wall of the Cordillera, a clear-cut vision of dark peaks rearing their steep slopes on a lofty pedestal of forest rising from the very edge

of the shore. Amongst them the white head of
Higuerota rises majestically upon the blue. Bare
clusters of enormous rocks sprinkle with tiny black
dots the smooth dome of snow.

Then, as the midday sun withdraws from the gulf
the shadow of the mountains, the clouds begin to roll
out of the lower valleys. They swathe in sombre
tatters the naked crags of precipices above the wooded
slopes, hide the peaks, smoke in stormy trails across the
snows of Higuerota. The Cordillera is gone from you
as if it had dissolved itself into great piles of grey and
black vapours that travel out slowly to seaward and
vanish into thin air all along the front before the
blazing heat of the day. The wasting edge of the
cloud-bank always strives for, but seldom wins, the
middle of the gulf. The sun—as the sailors say—is
eating it up; unless perchance a sombre thunder-
head breaks away from the main body to career all over
the gulf till it escapes into the offing beyond Azuera,
where it bursts suddenly into flame and crashes like a
sinister pirate-ship of the air, hove-to above the horizon,
engaging the sea.

At night the body of clouds advancing higher up
the sky smothers the whole quiet gulf below with
an impenetrable darkness, in which the sound of the
falling showers can be heard beginning and ceasing
abruptly — now here, now there. Indeed, these
cloudy nights are proverbial with the seamen along
the whole west coast of a great continent. Sky, land,
and sea disappear together out of the world when the
Placido—as the saying is—goes to sleep under its
black poncho. The few stars left below the seaward
frown of the vault shine feebly as into the mouth of a
black cavern. In its vastness your ship floats unseen
under your feet, her sails flutter invisible above your
head. The eye of God Himself—they add with grim
profanity—could not find out what work a man's hand

is doing in there ; and you would be free to call the devil to your aid with impunity if even his malice were not defeated by such a blind darkness.

The shores on the gulf are steep-to all round ; three uninhabited islets basking in the sunshine just outside the cloud veil, and opposite the entrance to the harbour of Sulaco, bear the name of " The Isabels."

There is the Great Isabel ; the Little Isabel, which is round ; and Hermosa, which is the smallest.

That last is no more than a foot high, and about seven paces across, a mere flat top of a grey rock which smokes like a hot cinder after a shower, and where no man would care to venture a naked sole before sunset. On the Little Isabel an old ragged palm, with a thick bulging trunk rough with spines, a very witch among palm trees, rustles a dismal bunch of dead leaves above the coarse sand. The Great Isabel has a spring of fresh water issuing from the overgrown side of a ravine. Resembling an emerald green wedge of land a mile long, and laid flat upon the sea, it bears two forest trees standing close together, with a wide spread of shade at the foot of their smooth trunks. A ravine extending the whole length of the island is full of bushes ; and presenting a deep tangled cleft on the high side spreads itself out on the other into a shallow depression abutting on a small strip of sandy shore.

From that low end of the Great Isabel the eye plunges through an opening two miles away, as abrupt as if chopped with an axe out of the regular sweep of the coast, right into the harbour of Sulaco. It is an oblong, lake-like piece of water. On one side, the short wooded spurs and valleys of the Cordillera come down at right angles to the very strand ; on the other, the open view of the great Sulaco plain passes into the opal mystery of great distances overhung by dry haze. The

town of Sulaco itself—tops of walls, a great cupola,
gleams of white miradors in a vast grove of orange
trees—lies between the mountains and the plain, at
some little distance from its harbour and out of the
direct line of sight from the sea.

CHAPTER TWO

THE only sign of commercial activity within the
harbour, visible from the beach of the Great
Isabel, is the square blunt end of the wooden
jetty which the Oceanic Steam Navigation Company
(the O.S.N. of familiar speech) had thrown over the
shallow part of the bay soon after they had resolved
to make of Sulaco one of their ports of call for the
Republic of Costaguana. The State possesses several
harbours on its long seaboard, but except Cayta, an
important place, all are either small and inconvenient
inlets in an iron - bound coast — like Esmeralda, for
instance, sixty miles to the south—or else mere open
roadsteads exposed to the winds and fretted by the surf.

Perhaps the very atmospheric conditions which
had kept away the merchant fleets of bygone ages
induced the O.S.N. Company to violate the sanctuary
of peace sheltering the calm existence of Sulaco. The
variable airs sporting lightly with the vast semicircle
of waters within the head of Azuera could not baffle
the steam power of their excellent fleet. Year after
year the black hulls of their ships had gone up and down
the coast, in and out, past Azuera, past the Isabels,
past Punta Mala — disregarding everything but the
tyranny of time. Their names, the names of all
mythology, became the household words of a coast
that had never been ruled by the gods of Olympus.
The *Juno* was known only for her comfortable cabins
amidships, the *Saturn* for the geniality of her captain

and the painted and gilt luxuriousness of her saloon, whereas the *Ganymede* was fitted out mainly for cattle transport, and to be avoided by coastwise passengers. The humblest Indian in the obscurest village on the coast was familiar with the *Cerberus*, a little black puffer without charm or living accommodation to speak of, whose mission was to creep inshore along the wooded beaches close to mighty ugly rocks, stopping obligingly before every cluster of huts to collect produce, down to three-pound parcels of indiarubber bound in a wrapper of dry grass.

And as they seldom failed to account for the smallest package, rarely lost a bullock, and had never drowned a single passenger, the name of the O.S.N. stood very high for trustworthiness. People declared that under the Company's care their lives and property were safer on the water than in their own houses on shore.

The O.S.N.'s superintendent in Sulaco for the whole Costaguana section of the service was very proud of his Company's standing. He resumed it in a saying which was very often on his lips, " We never make mistakes." To the Company's officers it took the form of a severe injunction, " We must make no mistakes. I'll have no mistakes here, no matter what Smith may do at his end."

Smith, on whom he had never set eyes in his life, was the other superintendent of the service, quartered some fifteen hundred miles away from Sulaco. " Don't talk to me of your Smith."

Then, calming down suddenly, he would dismiss the subject with studied negligence.

" Smith knows no more of this continent than a baby."

" Our excellent Señor Mitchell " for the business and official world of Sulaco ; " Fussy Joe " for the commanders of the Company's ships, Captain Joseph Mitchell prided himself on his profound knowledge

of men and things in the country—cosas de Costaguana. Amongst these last he accounted as most
unfavourable to the orderly working of his Company
the frequent changes of government brought about by
revolutions of the military type.

The political atmosphere of the Republic was generally stormy in these days. The fugitive patriots of
the defeated party had the knack of turning up
again on the coast with half a steamer's load of small
arms and ammunition. Such resourcefulness Captain
Mitchell considered as perfectly wonderful in view of
their utter destitution at the time of flight. He had
observed that " they never seemed to have enough
change about them to pay for their passage ticket
out of the country." And he could speak with knowledge ; for on a memorable occasion he had been called
upon to save the life of a dictator, together with the
lives of a few Sulaco officials—the political chief, the
director of the customs, and the head of police—
belonging to an overturned government. Poor Señor
Ribiera (such was the dictator's name) had come pelting
eighty miles over mountain tracks after the lost battle
of Socorro, in the hope of outdistancing the fatal news
—which, of course, he could not manage to do on a
lame mule. The animal, moreover, expired under him
at the end of the Alameda, where the military band
plays sometimes in the evenings between the revolutions. " Sir," Captain Mitchell would pursue
with portentous gravity, " the ill-timed end of that
mule attracted attention to the unfortunate rider. His
features were recognised by several deserters from
the Dictatorial army amongst the rascally mob
already engaged in smashing the windows of the
Intendencia."

Early on the morning of that day the local authorities of Sulaco had fled for refuge to the O.S.N.
Company's offices, a strong building near the shore end

of the jetty, leaving the town to the mercies of a
revolutionary rabble ; and as the Dictator was execrated by the populace on account of the severe recruit-
ment law his necessities had compelled him to enforce
during the struggle, he stood a good chance of being
torn to pieces. Providentially, Nostromo—invaluable
fellow—with some Italian workmen, imported to work
upon the National Central Railway, was at hand, and
managed to snatch him away—for the time at least.
Ultimately, Captain Mitchell succeeded in taking
everybody off in his own gig to one of the Company's
steamers—it was the *Minerva*—just then, as luck would
have it, entering the harbour.

He had to lower these gentlemen at the end of a
rope out of a hole in the wall at the back, while the mob,
which, pouring out of the town, had spread itself all
along the shore, howled and foamed at the foot of the
building in front. He had to hurry them then the
whole length of the jetty ; it had been a desperate dash,
neck or nothing—and again it was Nostromo, a fellow
in a thousand, who, at the head, this time, of the Company's body of lightermen, held the jetty against the
rushes of the rabble, thus giving the fugitives time to
reach the gig lying ready for them at the other
end with the Company's flag at the stern. Sticks,
stones, shots flew ; knives too were thrown. Captain
Mitchell exhibited willingly the long cicatrice of a
cut over his left ear and temple, made by a razor-
blade fastened to a stick—a weapon, he explained, very
much in favour with the " worst kind of nigger out
here."

Captain Mitchell was a thick, elderly man, wearing
high, pointed collars and short side-whiskers, partial to
white waistcoats, and really very communicative under
his air of pompous reserve.

" These gentlemen," he would say, staring with
great solemnity, " had to run like rabbits, sir. I ran

like a rabbit myself. Certain forms of death are—er —distasteful to a—a—er—respectable man. They would have pounded me to death too. A crazy mob, sir, does not discriminate. Under providence we owed our preservation to my Capataz de Cargadores, as they called him in the town, a man who, when I discovered his value, sir, was just the bos'n of an Italian ship, a big Genoese ship, one of the few European ships that ever came to Sulaco with a general cargo before the building of the National Central. He left her on account of some very respectable friends he made here, his own countrymen, but also, I suppose, to better himself. Sir, I am a pretty good judge of character. I engaged him to be the foreman of our lightermen, and caretaker of our jetty. That's all that he was. But without him, Señor Ribiera would have been a dead man. This Nostromo, sir, a man absolutely above reproach, became the terror of all the thieves in the town. We were infested, infested, overrun, sir, here at that time by ladrones and matreros, thieves and murderers from the whole province. On this occasion they had been flocking into Sulaco for a week past. They had scented the end, sir. Fifty per cent. of that murdering mob were professional bandits from the Campo, sir, but there wasn't one that hadn't heard of Nostromo. As to the town leperos, sir, the sight of his black whiskers and white teeth was enough for them. They quailed before him, sir. That's what the force of character will do for you."

It could very well be said that it was Nostromo alone who saved the lives of these gentlemen. Captain Mitchell, on his part, never left them till he had seen them collapse, panting, terrified, and exasperated, but safe, on the luxuriant velvet sofas in the first-class saloon of the *Minerva*. To the very last he had been careful to address the ex-Dictator as " Your Excellency."

" Sir, I could do no other. The man was down—
ghastly, livid, one mass of scratches."

The *Minerva* never let go her anchor that call.
The superintendent ordered her out of the harbour at
once. No cargo could be landed, of course, and the
passengers for Sulaco naturally refused to go ashore.
They could hear the firing and see plainly the fight
going on at the edge of the water. The repulsed mob
devoted its energies to an attack upon the Custom
House, a dreary, unfinished-looking structure with
many windows two hundred yards away from the
O.S.N. offices, and the only other building near the
harbour. Captain Mitchell, after directing the commander of the *Minerva* to land " these gentlemen "
in the first port of call outside Costaguana, went back
in his gig to see what could be done for the protection
of the Company's property. That and the property of
the railway were preserved by the European residents ;
that is, by Captain Mitchell himself and the staff of
engineers building the road, aided by the Italian and
Basque workmen who rallied faithfully round their
English chiefs. The Company's lightermen, too,
natives of the Republic, behaved very well under their
Capataz. An outcast lot of very mixed blood, mainly
negroes, everlastingly at feud with the other customers
of low grog shops in the town, they embraced with
delight this opportunity to settle their personal scores
under such favourable auspices. There was not one
of them that had not, at some time or other, looked
with terror at Nostromo's revolver poked very close at
his face, or been otherwise daunted by Nostromo's
resolution. He was " much of a man," their Capataz
was, they said, too scornful in his temper ever to utter
abuse, a tireless taskmaster, and the more to be feared
because of his aloofness. And behold ! there he was
that day, at their head, condescending to make jocular
remarks to this man or the other.

Such leadership was inspiriting, and in truth all the harm the mob managed to achieve was to set fire to one—only one—stack of railway-sleepers, which, being creosoted, burned well. The main attack on the railway yards, on the O.S.N. offices, and especially on the Custom House, whose strong-room, it was well known, contained a large treasure in silver ingots, failed completely. Even the little hotel kept by old Giorgio, standing alone half-way between the harbour and the town, escaped looting and destruction, not by a miracle, but because with the safes in view they had neglected it at first, and afterwards found no leisure to stop. Nostromo, with his cargadores, was pressing them too hard then.

CHAPTER THREE

IT might have been said that there he was only protecting his own. From the first he had been admitted to live in the intimacy of the family of the hotel-keeper, who was a countryman of his. Old Giorgio Viola, a Genoese with a shaggy white leonine head—often called simply " the Garibaldino " (as Mohammedans are called after their prophet)—was, to use Captain Mitchell's own words, the "respectable married friend " by whose advice Nostromo had left his ship to try for a run of shore luck in Costaguana.

The old man, full of scorn for the populace, as your austere republican so often is, had disregarded the preliminary sounds of trouble. He went on that day as usual pottering about the " casa " in his slippers, muttering angrily to himself his contempt of the non-political nature of the riot, and shrugging his shoulders. In the end he was taken unawares by the outrush of the rabble. It was too late then to remove his family ; and, indeed, where could he have run to with the portly Signora Teresa and two little girls on that great plain ? So, barricading every opening, the old man sat down sternly in the middle of the darkened café with an old shot-gun on his knees. His wife sat on another chair by his side, muttering pious invocations to all the saints of the calendar.

The old republican did not believe in saints, or in prayers, or in what he called " priest's religion." Liberty and Garibaldi were his divinities ; but he tolerated " superstition " in women, preserving in these matters a lofty and silent attitude.

His two girls, the eldest fourteen and the other two years younger, crouched on the sanded floor, on each side of the Signora Teresa, with their heads on their mother's lap, both scared, but each in her own way—the dark-haired Linda indignant and angry, the fair Giselle, the younger, bewildered and resigned. The Patrona removed her arms, which embraced her daughters, for a moment to cross herself and wring her hands hurriedly. She moaned a little louder.

" Oh ! Gian' Battista, why art thou not here ? Oh ! why art thou not here ? "

She was not then invoking the saint himself, but calling upon Nostromo, whose patron he was. And Giorgio, motionless on the chair by her side, would be provoked by these reproachful and distracted appeals.

" Peace, woman ! Where's the sense of it ? There's his duty," he murmured in the dark ; and she would retort, panting :

" Eh ! I have no patience. Duty ! What of the woman who has been like a mother to him ? I bent my knee to him this morning ; don't you go out, Gian' Battista—stop in the house, Battistino—look at those two little innocent children ! "

Mrs. Viola was an Italian, too, a native of Spezzia, and though considerably younger than her husband, already middle-aged. She had a handsome face, whose complexion had turned yellow because the climate of Sulaco did not suit her at all. Her voice was a rich contralto. When, with her arms folded tight under her ample bosom, she scolded the squat, thick-legged China girls handling linen, plucking fowls, pounding corn in wooden mortars amongst the mud outbuildings at the back of the house, she could bring out such an impassioned, vibrating, sepulchral note that the chained watch-dog bolted into his kennel with

2

a great rattle. Luis, a cinnamon-coloured mulatto
with a sprouting moustache and thick, dark lips, would
stop sweeping the café with a broom of palm-leaves
to let a gentle shudder run down his spine. His
languishing almond eyes would remain closed for a
long time.

This was the staff of the Casa Viola, but all these
people had fled early that morning at the first sounds
of the riot, preferring to hide on the plain rather than
trust themselves in the house ; a preference for which
they were in no way to blame, since, whether true or
not, it was generally believed in the town that the
Garibaldino had some money buried under the clay
floor of the kitchen. The dog, an irritable, shaggy
brute, barked violently and whined plaintively in turns
at the back, running in and out of his kennel as rage
or fear prompted him.

Bursts of great shouting rose and died away, like
wild gusts of wind on the plain round the barricaded
house ; the fitful popping of shots grew louder above
the yelling. Sometimes there were intervals of unaccountable stillness outside, and nothing could have
been more gaily peaceful than the narrow bright lines
of sunlight from the cracks in the shutters, ruled
straight across the café over the disarranged chairs and
tables to the wall opposite. Old Giorgio had chosen
that bare, whitewashed room for a retreat. It had only
one window, and its only door swung out upon the
track of thick dust fenced by aloe hedges between the
harbour and the town, where clumsy carts used to
creak along behind slow yokes of oxen guided by boys
on horseback.

In a pause of stillness Giorgio cocked his gun. The
ominous sound wrung a low moan from the rigid
figure of the woman sitting by his side. A sudden outbreak of defiant yelling quite near the house sank all
at once to a confused murmur of growls. Somebody

ran along ; the loud catching of his breath was heard
for an instant passing the door ; there were hoarse
mutters and footsteps near the wall ; a shoulder
rubbed against the shutter, effacing the bright lines of
sunshine pencilled across the whole breadth of the
room. Signora Teresa's arms thrown about the kneeling forms of her daughters embraced them closer with
a convulsive pressure.

The mob, driven away from the Custom House,
had broken up into several bands, retreating across
the plain in the direction of the town. The subdued
crash of irregular volleys fired in the distance was
answered by faint yells far away. In the intervals the
single shots rang feebly, and the low, long, white
building blinded in every window seemed to be the
centre of a turmoil widening in a great circle about its
closed-up silence. But the cautious movements and
whispers of a routed party seeking a momentary shelter
behind the wall made the darkness of the room, striped
by threads of quiet sunlight, alight with evil, stealthy
sounds. The Violas had them in their ears as though
invisible ghosts hovering about their chairs had consulted in mutters as to the advisability of setting fire
to this foreigner's casa.

It was trying to the nerves. Old Viola had risen
slowly, gun in hand, irresolute, for he did not see
how he could prevent them. Already voices could be
heard talking at the back. Signora Teresa was beside
herself with terror.

" Ah ! the traitor ! the traitor ! " she mumbled,
almost inaudibly. " Now we are going to be burnt ;
and I bent my knee to him ! No ! he must run at
the heels of his English."

She seemed to think that Nostromo's mere presence
in the house would have made it perfectly safe. So far,
she too was under the spell of that reputation the
Capataz de Cargadores had made for himself by the

waterside, along the railway line, with the English and
with the populace of Sulaco. To his face, and even
against her husband, she invariably affected to laugh it
to scorn, sometimes good-naturedly, more often with a
curious bitterness. But then women are unreasonable
in their opinions, as Giorgio used to remark calmly on
fitting occasions. On this occasion, with his gun held
at ready before him, he stooped down to his wife's
head, and, keeping his eyes steadfastly on the barricaded door, he breathed out into her ear that Nostromo would have been powerless to help. What
could two men shut up in a house do against twenty
or more bent upon setting fire to the roof ? Gian'
Battista was thinking of the casa all the time, he was
sure.

" He think of the casa ! He ! " gasped Signora
Viola crazily. She struck her breast with her open
hands. " I know him. He thinks of nobody but
himself."

A discharge of firearms near by made her throw her
head back and close her eyes. Old Giorgio set his
teeth hard under his white moustache, and his eyes
began to roll fiercely. Several bullets struck the end
of the wall together ; pieces of plaster could be heard
falling outside ; a voice screamed, " Here they come ! "
and after a moment of uneasy silence there was a rush
of running feet along the front.

Then the tension of old Giorgio's attitude relaxed,
and a smile of contemptuous relief came upon his lips
of an old fighter with a leonine face. These were not
a people striving for justice, but thieves. Even to
defend his life against them was a sort of degradation
for a man who had been one of Garibaldi's immortal
thousand in the conquest of Sicily. He had an immense scorn for this outbreak of scoundrels and leperos,
who did not know the meaning of the word " liberty."

He grounded his old gun, and, turning his head,

glanced at the coloured lithograph of Garibaldi in a black frame on the white wall ; a thread of strong sunshine cut it perpendicularly. His eyes, accustomed to the luminous twilight, made out the high colouring of the face, the red of the shirt, the outlines of the square shoulders, the black patch of the bersagliere hat with cock's feathers curling over the crown. An immortal hero ! This was your liberty ; it gave you not only life, but immortality as well !

For that one man his fanaticism had suffered no diminution. In the moment of relief from the apprehension of the greatest danger, perhaps, his family had been exposed to in all their wanderings, he had turned to the picture of his old chief, first and only, then laid his hand on his wife's shoulder.

The children kneeling on the floor had not moved. Signora Teresa opened her eyes a little, as though he had awakened her from a very deep and dreamless slumber. Before he had time in his deliberate way to say a reassuring word, she jumped up, with the children clinging to her, one on each side, gasped for breath and let out a hoarse shriek.

It was simultaneous with the bang of a violent blow struck on the outside of the shutter. They could hear suddenly the snorting of a horse, the restive tramping of hoofs on the narrow, hard path in front of the house ; the toe of a boot struck at the shutter again ; a spur jingled at every blow, and an excited voice shouted, " Hola ! hola, in there ! "

CHAPTER FOUR

ALL the morning Nostromo had kept his eye from afar on the Casa Viola, even in the thick of the hottest scrimmage near the Custom House. " If I see smoke rising over there," he thought to himself, " they are lost." Directly the mob had broken he pressed with a small band of Italian workmen in that direction, which, indeed, was the shortest line towards the town. That part of the rabble he was pursuing seemed to think of making a stand under the house ; a volley fired by his followers from behind an aloe hedge made the rascals fly. In a gap chopped out for the rails of the harbour branch line Nostromo appeared, mounted on his silver-grey mare. He shouted, sent after them one shot from his revolver, and galloped up to the café window. He had an idea that old Giorgio would choose that part of the house for a refuge.

His voice had penetrated to them, sounding breathlessly hurried : " Hola ! Vecchio ! Oh, Vecchio ! Is it all well with you in there ? "

" You see——" murmured old Viola to his wife.

Signora Teresa was silent now. Outside Nostromo laughed.

" I can hear the padrona is not dead."

" You have done your best to kill me with fear," cried Signora Teresa. She wanted to say something more, but her voice failed her.

Linda raised her eyes to her face for a moment, but old Giorgio shouted apologetically :

" She is a little upset."

Outside Nostromo shouted back with another laugh:

" She cannot upset me."

Signora Teresa found her voice.

" It is what I say. You have no heart—and you have no conscience, Gian' Battista——"

They heard him wheel his horse away from the shutters. The party he led were babbling excitedly in Italian and Spanish, inciting each other to the pursuit. He put himself at their head, crying, " Avanti ! "

" He has not stopped very long with us. There is no praise from strangers to be got here," Signora Teresa said tragically. " Avanti ! Yes ! That is all he cares for. To be first somewhere—somehow—to be first with these English. They will be showing him to everybody. ' This is our Nostromo ! ' " She laughed ominously. " What a name ! What is that ? Nostromo ? He would take a name that is properly no word from them."

Meantime Giorgio, with tranquil movements, had been unfastening the door ; the flood of light fell on Signora Teresa, with her two girls gathered to her side, a picturesque woman in a pose of maternal exaltation. Behind her the wall was dazzlingly white, and the crude colours of the Garibaldi lithograph paled in the sunshine.

Old Viola, at the door, moved his arm upward as if referring all his quick, fleeting thoughts to the picture of his old chief on the wall. Even when he was cooking for the " Signori Inglesi "—the engineers (he was a famous cook, though the kitchen was a dark place)—he was, as it were, under the eye of the great man who had led him in a glorious struggle where, under the walls of Gaeta, tyranny would have expired for ever had it not been for that accursed Piedmontese race of kings and ministers. When sometimes a frying-pan caught fire during a delicate operation with some shredded onions, and the old man

was seen backing out of the doorway, swearing and
coughing violently in an acrid cloud of smoke, the name
of Cavour—the arch intriguer sold to kings and tyrants
—could be heard involved in imprecations against the
China girls, cooking in general, and the brute of a country
where he was reduced to live for the love of liberty that
traitor had strangled.

Then Signora Teresa, all in black, issuing from
another door, advanced, portly and anxious, inclining
her fine black-browed head, opening her arms and crying
in a profound tone:

"Giorgio! thou passionate man! Misericordia
Divina! In the sun like this! He will make himself
ill."

At her feet the hens made off in all directions, with
immense strides; if there were any engineers from up
the line staying in Sulaco, a young English face or two
would appear at the billiard-room occupying one end of
the house; but at the other end, in the café, Luis, the
mulatto, took good care not to show himself. The Indian
girls, with hair like flowing black manes, and dressed only
in a shift and short petticoat, stared dully from under the
square-cut fringes on their foreheads; the noisy frizzling
of fat had stopped, the fumes floated upwards in sunshine, a strong smell of burnt onions hung in the drowsy
heat, enveloping the house; and the eye lost itself in a vast
flat expanse of grass to the west, as if the plain between
the sierra overtopping Sulaco and the coast range away
there towards Esmeralda had been as big as half the
world.

Signora Teresa, after an impressive pause, remonstrated:

"Eh, Giorgio! Leave Cavour alone and take care of
yourself now we are lost in this country all alone with two
children, because you cannot live under a king."

And while she looked at him she would sometimes
put her hand hastily to her side with a short twitch of her

fine lips and a knitting of her black, straight eyebrows like a flicker of pain or an angry thought on her handsome, regular features.

It was pain ; she suppressed the twinge. It had come to her first a few years after they had left Italy to emigrate to America and settle at last in Sulaco after wandering from town to town, trying shopkeeping in a small way here and there ; and once an organised enterprise of fishing—in Maldonado ; for Giorgio, like the great Garibaldi, had been a sailor in his time.

Sometimes she had no patience with pain. For years its gnawing had been part of the landscape embracing the glitter of the harbour under the wooded spurs of the range ; and the sunshine itself was heavy and dull— heavy with pain—not like the sunshine of her girlhood, in which middle-aged Giorgio had wooed her gravely and passionately on the shores of the Gulf of Spezzia.

" You go in at once, Giorgio," she directed. " One would think you do not wish to have any pity on me— with four Signori Inglesi staying in the house."

" Va bene, va bene," Giorgio would mutter.

He obeyed. The Signori Inglesi would require their midday meal presently. He had been one of the immortal and invincible band of liberators who had made the mercenaries of tyranny fly like chaff before a hurricane, " un uragano terribile." But that was before he was married and had children ; and before tyranny had reared its head again amongst the traitors who had imprisoned Garibaldi, his hero.

There were three doors in the front of the house, and each afternoon the Garibaldino could be seen at one or another of them with his big bush of white hair, his arms folded, his legs crossed, leaning back his leonine head against the side, and looking up the wooded slopes of the foothills at the snowy dome of Higuerota. The front of his house threw off a black long rectangle of shade, broadening slowly over the soft ox-cart track. Through

the gaps, chopped out in the oleander hedges, the harbour
branch railway, laid out temporarily on the level of the
plain, curved away its shining parallel ribbons in a belt
of scorched and withered grass within sixty yards of the
end of the house. In the evening the empty material
trains of flat cars circled round the dark green grove of
Sulaco, and ran, undulating slightly with white jets of
steam, over the plain towards the Casa Viola, on their way
to the railway yards by the harbour. The Italian drivers
saluted him from the foot-plate with raised hand, while
the negro brakesmen sat carelessly on the brakes, looking
straight forward, with the rims of their big hats flapping in
the wind. In return Giorgio would give a slight sideways
jerk of the head, without unfolding his arms.

On this memorable day of the riot his arms were not
folded on his chest. His hand grasped the barrel of the
gun grounded on the threshold ; he did not look up once
at the white dome of Higuerota, whose cool purity seemed
to hold itself aloof from a hot earth. His eyes examined
the plain curiously. Tall trails of dust subsided here
and there. In a speckless sky the sun hung clear and
blinding. Knots of men ran headlong ; others made a
stand ; and the irregular rattle of firearms came rippling
to his ears in the fiery, still air. Single figures on foot
raced desperately. Horsemen galloped towards each
other, wheeled round together, separated at speed.
Giorgio saw one fall, rider and horse disappearing as if
they had galloped into a chasm, and the movements of the
animated scene were like the passages of a violent game
played upon the plain by dwarfs mounted and on foot,
yelling with tiny throats, under the mountain that seemed
a colossal embodiment of silence. Never before had
Giorgio seen this bit of plain so full of active life ; his
gaze could not take in all its details at once ; he shaded
his eyes with his hand, till suddenly the thundering of
many hoofs near by startled him.

A troop of horses had broken out of the fenced

paddock of the Railway Company. They came on like a whirlwind, and dashed over the line snorting, kicking, squealing in a compact piebald tossing mob of bay, brown, grey backs, eyes staring, necks extended, nostrils red, long tails streaming. As soon as they had leaped upon the road the thick dust flew upwards from under their hoofs, and within six yards of Giorgio only a brown cloud with vague forms of necks and cruppers rolled by, making the soil tremble on its passage.

Viola coughed, turning his face away from the dust, and shaking his head slightly.

" There will be some horse-catching to be done before to-night," he muttered.

In the square of sunlight falling through the door Signora Teresa, kneeling before the chair, had bowed her head, heavy with a twisted mass of ebony hair streaked with silver, into the palm of her hands. The black lace shawl she used to drape about her face had dropped to the ground by her side. The two girls had got up, hand in hand, in short skirts, their loose hair falling in disorder. The younger had thrown her arm across her eyes, as if afraid to face the light. Linda, with her hand on the other's shoulder, stared fearlessly. Viola looked at his children.

The sun brought out the deep lines on his face, and, energetic in expression, it had the immobility of a carving. It was impossible to discover what he thought. Bushy grey eyebrows shaded his dark glance.

" Well ! And do you not pray like your mother ? "

Linda pouted, advancing her red lips, which were almost too red ; but she had admirable eyes, brown, with a sparkle of gold in the irises, full of intelligence and meaning, and so clear that they seemed to throw a glow upon her thin, colourless face. There were bronze glints in the sombre clusters of her hair, and the eyelashes, long and coal black, made her complexion appear still more pale.

" Mother is going to offer up a lot of candles in the church. She always does when Nostromo has been away fighting. I shall have some to carry up to the Chapel of the Madonna in the cathedral."

She said all this quickly, with great assurance, in an animated, penetrating voice. Then, giving her sister's shoulder a slight shake, she added :

" And she will be made to carry one too ! "

" Why made ? " inquired Giorgio gravely. " Does she not want to ? "

" She is timid," said Linda, with a little burst of laughter. " People notice her fair hair as she goes along with us. They call out after her, ' Look at the Rubia ! Look at the Rubiacita ! ' They call out in the streets. She is timid."

" And you ? You are not timid—eh ? " the father pronounced slowly.

She tossed back all her dark hair.

" Nobody calls out after me."

Old Giorgio contemplated his children thoughtfully. There was two years difference between them. They had been born to him late, years after the boy had died. Had he lived he would have been nearly as old as Gian' Battista —he whom the English called Nostromo ; but as to his daughters, the severity of his temper, his advancing age, his absorption in his memories, had prevented his taking much notice of them. He loved his children, but girls belong to the mother more, and much of his affection had been expended in the worship and service of liberty.

When quite a youth he had deserted from a ship trading to La Plata, to enlist in the navy of Montevideo, then under the command of Garibaldi. Afterwards, in the Italian legion of the Republic struggling against the encroaching tyranny of Rosas, he had taken part, on great plains, on the banks of immense rivers, in the fiercest fighting perhaps the world had ever known. He had lived amongst men who had declaimed about liberty, suffered for liberty, died for liberty, with a desperate exaltation, and with their eyes turned towards an oppressed Italy. His own enthusiasm had been fed on scenes of carnage, on the examples of lofty devotion, on the din of armed struggle, on the inflamed language of proclamations. He had never parted from the chief of his choice—the fiery apostle of independence—keeping by his side in America and in Italy till after the fatal day of Aspromonte, when the treachery of kings, emperors, and ministers had been revealed to the world in the wounding and imprisonment of his hero—a catastrophe that had instilled into him a gloomy doubt of ever being able to understand the ways of Divine justice.

He did not deny it, however. It required patience, he would say. Though he disliked priests, and would not put his foot inside a church for anything, he believed in God. Were not the proclamations against tyrants addressed to the peoples in the name of God and liberty ? " God for men—religions for women," he muttered sometimes. In Sicily, an Englishman who had turned up in Palermo after its evacuation by the army of the king, had given him a Bible in Italian—the publication of the British and Foreign Bible Society, bound in a dark leather cover. In periods of political adversity, in the pauses of silence when the revolutionists issued no proclamations, Giorgio earned his living with the first work that came to hand—as sailor, as dock labourer on the quays of Genoa, once as a hand on a farm in the hills above Spezzia—and in his spare time he studied the thick volume. He carried it with him into battles. Now it was his only reading, and in order not to be deprived of it (the print was small) he had consented to accept the present of a pair of silver-mounted spectacles from Señora Emilia Gould, the wife of the Englishman who managed the silver mine in the mountains three leagues from the town. She was the only Englishwoman in Sulaco.

Giorgio Viola had a great consideration for the English. This feeling, born on the battlefields of Uruguay, was forty years old at the very least. Several of them had poured their blood for the cause of freedom in America, and the first he had ever known he remembered by the name of Samuel; he commanded a negro company under Garibaldi, during the famous siege of Montevideo, and died heroically with his negroes at the fording of the Boyana. He, Giorgio, had reached the rank of ensign— *alferez*—and cooked for the general. Later, in Italy, he, with the rank of lieutenant, rode with the staff and still cooked for the general. He had cooked for him in Lombardy through the whole campaign; on the march to Rome he had lassoed his beef in the Campagna after the American manner; he had been wounded in the defence of the Roman Republic; he was one of the four fugitives who, with the general, carried out of the woods the inanimate body of the general's wife into the farmhouse where she died, exhausted by the hardships of that terrible retreat. He had survived that disastrous time to attend his general in Palermo when the Neapolitan shells from the castle crashed upon the town. He had cooked for him on the field of Volturno after fighting all day. And everywhere he had seen Englishmen in the front rank of the army of freedom. He respected their nation because they loved Garibaldi. Their very countesses and princesses had kissed the general's hands in London, it was said. He could well believe it; for the nation was noble, and the man was a saint. It was enough to look once at his face to see the divine force of faith in him and his great pity for all that was poor, suffering, and oppressed in this world.

The spirit of self-forgetfulness, the simple devotion to a vast humanitarian idea which inspired the thought and stress of that revolutionary time, had left its mark upon Giorgio in a sort of austere contempt for all personal advantage. This man, whom the lowest class in Sulaco suspected of having a buried hoard in his kitchen, had all his life despised money. The leaders of his youth had lived poor, had died poor. It had been a habit of his mind to disregard to-morrow. It was engendered partly by an existence of excitement, adventure, and wild warfare. But mostly it was a matter of principle. It did not resemble the carelessness of a condottiere; it was a puritanism of conduct, born of stern enthusiasm like the puritanism of religion.

This stern devotion to a cause had cast a gloom upon Giorgio's old age. It cast a gloom because the cause seemed lost. Too many kings and emperors flourished yet in the world which God had meant for the people. He was sad because of his simplicity. Though always ready to help his countrymen, and greatly respected by the Italian emigrants wherever he lived (in his exile he called it), he could not conceal from himself that they cared nothing for the wrongs of downtrodden nations. They listened to his tales of war readily, but seemed to ask themselves what he had got out of it after all. There was nothing that they could see. " We wanted nothing, we suffered for the love of all humanity ! " he cried out furiously sometimes ; and the powerful voice, the blazing eyes, the shaking of the white mane, the brown, sinewy hand pointing upwards as if to call heaven to witness, impressed his hearers. After the old man had broken off abruptly with a jerk of the head and a movement of the arm, meaning clearly, " But what's the good of talking to you ? " they nudged each other. There was in old Giorgio an energy of feeling, a personal quality of conviction, something they called " terribilità "—" an old lion," they used to say of him. Some slight incident, a chance word, would set him off talking on the beach to the Italian fishermen of Maldonado, in the little shop he kept afterwards (in Valparaiso) to his countrymen customers ; of an evening, suddenly, in the café at one end of the Casa Viola (the other was reserved for the

English engineers) to the select clientele of engine-drivers
and foremen of the railway shops.

With their handsome, bronzed, lean faces, shiny
black ringlets, glistening eyes, broad-chested, bearded,
sometimes a tiny gold ring in the lobe of the ear, the
aristocracy of the railway works listened to him, turning
away from their cards or dominoes.   Here and there a
fair-haired Basque studied his hand meantime, waiting
without protest.   No native of Costaguana intruded there.
This was the Italian stronghold.   Even the Sulaco
policemen on a night patrol let their horses pace softly
by, bending low in the saddle to glance through the
window at the heads in a fog of smoke ; and the drone
of old Giorgio's declamatory narrative seemed to sink
behind them into the plain.   Only now and then the
assistant of the chief of police, some broad-faced, brown
little gentleman, with a great deal of Indian in him, would
put in an appearance.   Leaving his man outside with the
horses, he advanced with a confident, sly smile and without
a word up to the long trestle table.   He pointed to one
of the bottles on the shelf ; Giorgio, thrusting his pipe
into his mouth abruptly, served him in person.   Nothing
would be heard but the slight jingle of the spurs.   His
glass emptied, he would take a leisurely, scrutinising
look all round the room, go out, and ride away slowly,
circling towards the town.

CHAPTER FIVE

IN this way only was the power of the local authorities vindicated amongst the great body of strong-limbed foreigners who dug the earth, blasted the rocks, drove the engines for the " progressive and patriotic undertaking." In these very words eighteen months before, the Excellentissimo Señor don Vincente Ribiera, the Dictator of Costaguana, had described the National Central Railway in his great speech at the turning of the first sod.

He had come on purpose to Sulaco, and there was a one o'clock dinner-party, a *convité* offered by the O.S.N. Company on board the *Juno* after the function on shore. Captain Mitchell had himself steered the cargo lighter, all draped with flags, which, in tow of the *Juno's* steam-launch, took the Excellentissimo from the jetty to the ship. Everybody of note in Sulaco had been invited— the one or two foreign merchants, all the representatives of the old Spanish families then in town, the great owners of estates on the plain, grave, courteous, simple men, caballeros of pure descent, with small hands and feet, conservative, hospitable, and kind. The Occidental Province was their stronghold ; their Blanco party had triumphed now ; it was their President-Dictator, a Blanco of the Blancos, who sat smiling urbanely between the representatives of two friendly foreign powers. They had come with him from Sta. Marta to countenance by their presence the enterprise in which the capital of their countries was engaged.

3

The only lady of that company was Mrs. Gould, the wife of Don Carlos, the Administrador of the San Tomé silver mine. The ladies of Sulaco were not advanced enough to take part in the public life to that extent. They had come out strongly at the great ball at the Intendencia the evening before, but Mrs. Gould alone had appeared, a bright spot in the group of black coats behind the President-Dictator, on the crimson cloth-covered stage erected under a shady tree on the shore of the harbour, where the ceremony of turning the first sod had taken place. She had come off in the cargo lighter, full of notabilities, sitting under the flutter of gay flags, in the place of honour by the side of Captain Mitchell, who steered, and her clear dress gave the only truly festive note to the sombre gathering in the long, gorgeous saloon of the *Juno*.

The head of the chairman of the railway board (from London), handsome and pale in a silvery mist of white hair and clipped beard, hovered near her shoulder attentive, smiling, and fatigued. The journey from London to Sta. Marta in mail-boats and the special carriages of the Sta. Marta coast-line (the only railway so far) had been tolerable—even pleasant—quite tolerable. But the trip over the mountains to Sulaco was another sort of experience, in an old diligencia over impassable roads skirting awful precipices.

" We have been upset twice in one day on the brink of very deep ravines," he was telling Mrs. Gould in an undertone. " And when we arrived here at last I don't know what we should have done without your hospitality. What an out-of-the-way place Sulaco is !—and for a harbour, too ! Astonishing ! "

" Ah, but we are very proud of it. It used to be historically important. The highest ecclesiastical court, for two viceroyalties, sat here in the olden time," she instructed him with animation.

" I am impressed. I didn't mean to be disparaging. You seem very patriotic."

" The place is lovable, if only by its situation. Perhaps you don't know what an old resident I am ! "

" How old, I wonder," he murmured, looking at her with a slight smile. Mrs. Gould's appearance was made youthful by the mobile intelligence of her face. " We can't give you your ecclesiastical court back again ; but you shall have more steamers, a railway, a telegraph-cable—a future in the great world which is worth infinitely more than any amount of ecclesiastical past. You shall be brought in touch with something greater than two viceroyalties. But I had no notion that a place on a sea-coast could remain so isolated from the world. If it had been a thousand miles inland now—most remarkable ! Has anything ever happened here for a hundred years before to-day ? "

While he talked in a slow, humorous tone, she kept her little smile. Abounding ironically in his sense, she assured him that certainly not—nothing ever happened in Sulaco. Even the revolutions, of which there had been two in her time, had respected the repose of the place. Their course ran in the more populous southern parts of the Republic, and in the great Valley of Sta. Marta, which was like one great battlefield of the parties, with the possession of the capital for a prize and an outlet to another ocean. They were more advanced over there. Here in Sulaco they heard only the echoes of these great questions, and, of course, their official world changed each time, coming to them over their rampart of mountains which he himself had traversed in an old diligencia, with such a risk to life and limb.

The chairman of the railway had been enjoying her hospitality for several days, and he was really grateful for it. It was only since he had left Sta. Marta that he had utterly lost touch with the feeling of European life on the background of his exotic surroundings. In the capital

he had been the guest of the Legation, and had been kept
busy negotiating with the members of Don Vincente's
Government — cultured men, men to whom the conditions of civilised business were not unknown.

What concerned him most at the time was the
acquisition of land for the railway.   In the Sta. Marta
Valley, where there was already one line in existence, the
people were tractable, and it was only a matter of price.
A commission had been nominated to fix the values, and
the difficulty resolved itself into the judicious influencing
of the Commissioners.   But in Sulaco—the Occidental
Province for whose very development the railway was
intended—there had been trouble.   It had been lying
for ages ensconced behind its natural barriers, repelling
modern enterprise by the precipices of its mountain
range, by its shallow harbour opening into the everlasting
calms of a gulf full of clouds, by the benighted state
of mind of the owners of its fertile territory—all these
aristocratic old Spanish families, all those Don Am-
brosios this and Don Fernandos that, who seemed actually to dislike and distrust the coming of the railway
over their lands.   It had happened that some of the
surveying parties scattered all over the province had been
warned off with threats of violence.   In other cases
outrageous pretensions as to price had been raised.   But
the man of railways prided himself on being equal to
every emergency.   Since he was met by the inimical
sentiment of blind conservatism in Sulaco he would meet
it by sentiment too before taking his stand on his right
alone.   The Government was bound to carry out its
part of the contract with the board of the new Railway
Company, even if it had to use force for the purpose.
But he desired nothing less than an armed disturbance in
the smooth working of his plans.   They were much too
vast and far-reaching, and too promising to leave a stone
unturned ; and so he imagined to get the President-
Dictator over there on a tour of ceremonies and speeches,

culminating in a great function at the turning of the first
sod by the harbour shore. After all, he was their own
creature—that Don Vincente. He was the embodied
triumph of the best elements in the State. These were
facts, and, unless facts meant nothing, Sir John argued to
himself, such a man's influence must be real, and his
personal action would produce the conciliatory effect he
required. He had succeeded in arranging the trip with
the help of a very clever advocate, who was known in Sta.
Marta as the agent of the Gould silver mine, the biggest
thing in Sulaco, and even in the whole Republic. It was
indeed a fabulously rich mine. Its so-called agent,
evidently a man of culture and ability, seemed, without
official position, to possess an extraordinary influence in
the highest Government spheres. He was able to assure
Sir John that the President-Dictator would make the
journey. He regretted, however, in the course of the
same conversation, that General Montero insisted upon
going too.

General Montero, whom the beginning of the struggle
had found an obscure army captain employed on the wild
eastern frontier of the State, had thrown in his lot with
the Ribiera party at a moment when special circumstances had given that small adhesion a fortuitous
importance. The fortunes of war served him marvellously, and the victory of Rio Seco (after a day of desperate fighting) put a seal to his success. At the end he
emerged General, Minister of War, and the military head
of the Blanco party, although there was nothing aristocratic in his descent. Indeed, it was said that he and
his brother, orphans, had been brought up by the munificence of a famous European traveller, in whose service
their father had lost his life. Another story was that
their father had been nothing but a charcoal burner in
the woods, and their mother a baptized Indian woman
from the far interior.

However that might be, the Costaguana Press was

in the habit of styling Montero's forest march from his commandancia to join the Blanco forces at the beginning of the troubles, the "most heroic military exploit of modern times." About the same time, too, his brother had turned up from Europe, where he had gone apparently as secretary to a consul. Having, however, collected a small band of outlaws, he showed some talent as guerrilla chief, and had been rewarded at the pacification by the post of Military Commandant of the capital.

The Minister of War, then, accompanied the Dictator. The board of the O.S.N. Company, working hand in hand with the railway people for the good of the Republic, had on this important occasion instructed Captain Mitchell to put the mail-boat *Juno* at the disposal of the distinguished party. Don Vincente, journeying south from Sta. Marta, had embarked at Cayta, the principal port of Costaguana, and came to Sulaco by sea. But the chairman of the Railway Company had courageously crossed the mountains in a ramshackle diligencia, mainly for the purpose of meeting his engineer-in-chief engaged in the final survey of the road.

For all the indifference of a man of affairs to nature, whose hostility can always be overcome by the resources of finance, he could not help being impressed by his surroundings during his halt at the surveying camp established at the highest point his railway was to reach. He spent the night there, arriving just too late to see the last dying glow of sunlight upon the snowy flank of Higuerota. Pillared masses of black basalt framed like an open portal a portion of the white field lying aslant against the west. In the transparent air of the high altitudes everything seemed very near, steeped in a clear stillness as in an imponderable liquid ; and with his ear ready to catch the first sound of the expected diligencia, the engineer-in-chief, at the door of a hut of rough stones, had contemplated the changing hues on the enormous

side of the mountain, thinking that in this sight, as in a
piece of inspired music, there could be found together the
utmost delicacy of shaded expression and a stupendous
magnificence of effect.

Sir John arrived too late to hear the magnificent and
inaudible strain sung by the sunset amongst the high
peaks of the sierra. It had sung itself out into the breathless pause of deep dusk before, climbing down the fore
wheel of the diligencia with stiff limbs, he shook hands
with the engineer.

They gave him his dinner in a stone hut like a cubical
boulder, with no door or windows in its two openings ; a
bright fire of sticks (brought on muleback from the first
valley below) burning outside sent in a wavering glare ;
and two candles in tin candlesticks—lighted, it was
explained to him, in his honour—stood on a sort of rough
camp table, at which he sat on the right hand of the chief.
He knew how to be amiable ; and the young men of the
engineering staff, for whom the surveying of the railway
track had the glamour of the first steps on the path of
life, sat there too, listening modestly, with their smooth
faces tanned by the weather, and very pleased to witness
so much affability in so great a man.

Afterwards, late at night, pacing to and fro outside,
he had a long talk with his chief engineer. He knew him
well of old. This was not the first undertaking in which
their gifts, as elementally different as fire and water, had
worked in conjunction. From the contact of these two
personalities, who had not the same vision of the world,
there was generated a power for the world's service—a
subtle force that could set in motion mighty machines,
men's muscles, and awaken also in human breasts an
unbounded devotion to the task. Of the young fellows
at the table, to whom the survey of the track was like the
tracing of the path of life, more than one would be called
to meet death before the work was done. But the work
would be done : the force would be almost as strong as

a faith. Not quite, however. In the silence of the
sleeping camp upon the moonlit plateau forming the top
of the pass like the floor of a vast arena surrounded by the
basalt walls of precipices, two strolling figures in thick
ulsters stood still, and the voice of the engineer pronounced distinctly the words :

" We can't move mountains ! "

Sir John, raising his head to follow the pointing
gesture, felt the full force of the words. The white
Higuerota soared out of the shadows of rock and earth like
a frozen bubble under the moon. All was still, till near
by, behind the wall of a corral for the camp animals,
built roughly of loose stones in the form of a circle,
a pack-mule stamped his forefoot and blew heavily
twice.

The engineer-in-chief had used the phrase in answer
to the chairman's tentative suggestion that the tracing
of the line could, perhaps, be altered in deference to the
prejudices of the Sulaco landowners. The chief engineer
believed that the obstinacy of men was the lesser obstacle.
Moreover, to combat that they had the great influence of
Charles Gould, whereas tunnelling under Higuerota would
have been a colossal undertaking.

" Ah, yes ! Gould. What sort of a man is he ? "

Sir John had heard much of Charles Gould in Sta.
Marta, and wanted to know more. The engineer-in-
chief assured him that the Administrador of the San Tomé
silver mine had an immense influence over all these
Spanish Dons. He had also one of the best houses
in Sulaco, and the Gould hospitality was beyond all
praise.

" They receive me as if they had known me for years,"
he said. " The little lady is kindness personified. I
stayed with them for a month. He helped me to organise
the surveying parties. His practical ownership of the
San Tomé silver mine gives him a special position. He
seems to have the ear of every provincial authority

apparently, and, as I said, he can wind all the hidalgos of the province round his little finger. If you follow his advice the difficulties will fall away, because he wants the railway. Of course, you must be careful in what you say. He's English, and, besides, he must be immensely wealthy. The Holroyd house is in with him in that mine, so you may imagine——"

He interrupted himself as, from before one of the little fires burning outside the low wall of the corral, arose the figure of a man wrapped in a poncho up to the neck. The saddle which he had been using for a pillow made a dark patch on the ground against the red glow of embers.

" I shall see Holroyd himself on my way back through the States," said Sir John. " I've ascertained that he too wants the railway."

The man who, perhaps disturbed by the proximity of the voices, had arisen from the ground, struck a match to light a cigarette. The flame showed a bronzed, black-whiskered face, a pair of eyes gazing straight ; then, rearranging his wrappings, he sank full length and laid his head again on the saddle.

" That's our camp-master, whom I must send back to Sulaco now we are going to carry our survey into the Sta. Marta Valley," said the engineer. " A most useful fellow, lent me by Captain Mitchell of the O.S.N. Company. It was very good of Mitchell. Charles Gould told me I couldn't do better than take advantage of the offer. He seems to know how to rule all these mule-teers and peons. We had not the slightest trouble with our people. He shall escort your diligencia right into Sulaco with some of our railway peons. The road is bad. To have him at hand may save you an upset or two. He promised me to take care of your person all the way down as if you were his father."

This camp-master was the Italian sailor whom all the Europeans in Sulaco, following Captain Mitchell's mispronunciation, were in the habit of calling Nostromo. And indeed, taciturn and ready, he did take excellent care of his charge at the bad parts of the road, as Sir John himself acknowledged to Mrs. Gould afterwards.

CHAPTER SIX

A T that time Nostromo had been already long
enough in the country to raise to the highest pitch
Captain Mitchell's opinion of the extraordinary
value of his discovery. Clearly he was one of those invaluable subordinates whom to possess is a legitimate
cause of boasting. Captain Mitchell plumed himself
upon his eye for men ; but he was not selfish, and in the
innocence of his pride was already developing that mania
for " lending you my Capataz de Cargadores " which was
to bring Nostromo into personal contact, sooner or later,
with every European in Sulaco, as a sort of universal
factotum—a prodigy of efficiency in his own sphere of
life.

" The fellow is devoted to me, body and soul ! "
Captain Mitchell was given to affirm ; and though
nobody, perhaps, could have explained why it should be
so, it was impossible on a survey of their relation to throw
doubt on that statement, unless, indeed, one were a bitter,
eccentric character like Dr. Monygham, for instance,
whose short, hopeless laugh expressed somehow an
immense mistrust of mankind. Not that Dr. Monygham
was a prodigal either of laughter or of words. He was
bitterly taciturn when at his best. At his worst people
feared the open scornfulness of his tongue. Only Mrs.
Gould could keep his unbelief in men's motives within
due bounds ; but even to her (on an occasion not connected with Nostromo, and in a tone which for him was
gentle), even to her, he had said once, " Really, it is most

unreasonable to demand that a man should think of other
people so much better than he is able to think of himself."

And Mrs. Gould had hastened to drop the subject.
There were strange rumours of the English doctor.
Years ago, in the time of Guzman Bento, he had been
mixed up, it was whispered, in a conspiracy which was
betrayed and, as people expressed it, drowned in blood.
His hair had turned grey, his hairless, seamed face was of a
brick-dust colour ; the large check pattern of his flannel
shirt and his old, stained Panama hat were an established
defiance to the conventionalities of Sulaco. Had it not
been for the immaculate cleanliness of his apparel he
might have been taken for one of those shiftless Europeans
that are a moral eyesore to the respectability of a foreign
colony in almost every exotic part of the world. The
young ladies of Sulaco, adorning with clusters of pretty
faces the balconies along the Street of the Constitution,
when they saw him pass, with his limping gait and bowed
head, a short linen jacket drawn on carelessly over the
flannel check shirt, would remark to each other, " Here
is the Señor doctor going to call on Doña Emilia. He
has got his little coat on." The inference was true. Its
deeper meaning was hidden from their simple intelligence.
Moreover, they expended no store of thought on the
doctor. He was old, ugly, learned—and a little " loco "
—mad, if not a bit of a sorcerer, as the common people
suspected him of being. The little white jacket was in
reality a concession to Mrs. Gould's humanising influence.
The doctor, with his habit of sceptical, bitter speech, had
no other means of showing his profound respect for the
character of the woman who was known in the country
as the English Señora. He presented this tribute very
seriously indeed ; it was no trifle for a man of his habits.
Mrs. Gould felt that, too, perfectly. She would never
have thought of imposing upon him this marked show of
deference.

She kept her old Spanish house (one of the finest

specimens in Sulaco) open for the dispensation of the
small graces of existence. She dispensed them with
simplicity and charm because she was guided by an alert
perception of values. She was highly gifted in the art of
human intercourse, which consists in delicate shades of
self-forgetfulness and in the suggestion of universal comprehension. Charles Gould (the Gould family, established in Costaguana for three generations, always went
to England for their education and for their wives)
imagined that he had fallen in love with a girl's sound
common sense like any other man ; but these were not
exactly the reasons why, for instance, the whole surveying
camp, from the youngest of the young men to their
mature chief, should have found occasion to allude to
Mrs. Gould's house so frequently amongst the high peaks
of the sierra. She would have protested that she had
done nothing for them, with a low laugh and a surprised
widening of her grey eyes, had anybody told her how
convincingly she was remembered on the edge of the
snowline above Sulaco. But directly, with a little
capable air of setting her wits to work, she would have
found an explanation. " Of course, it was such a surprise for these boys to find any sort of welcome here. And
I suppose they are home-sick. I suppose everybody must
be always just a little home-sick."
    She was always sorry for home-sick people.
    Born in the country, as his father before him, spare
and tall, with a flaming moustache, a neat chin, clear blue
eyes, auburn hair, and a thin, fresh, red face, Charles
Gould looked like a new arrival from over the sea. His
grandfather had fought in the cause of independence
under Bolivar, in that famous English legion which on
the battlefield of Carabobo had been saluted by the
great Liberator as Saviours of his country. One of
Charles Gould's uncles had been the elected President
of that very province of Sulaco (then called a State) in
the days of Federation, and afterwards had been put up

against the wall of a church and shot by the order of the
barbarous Unionist general, Guzman Bento. It was the
same Guzman Bento who, becoming later Perpetual
President, famed for his ruthless and cruel tyranny,
reached his apotheosis in the popular legend of a sanguinary land-haunting spectre whose body had been
carried off by the devil in person from the brick mauso-
leum in the nave of the Church of Assumption in Sta.
Marta. Thus, at least, the priests explained its disappearance to the barefooted multitude that streamed in,
awestruck, to gaze at the hole in the side of the ugly box
of bricks before the great altar.

Guzman Bento of cruel memory had put to death
great numbers of people besides Charles Gould's uncle ;
but with a relative martyred in the cause of aristocracy,
the Sulaco Oligarchs (this was the phraseology of Guzman
Bento's time ; now they were called Blancos, and had
given up the federal idea), which meant the families
of pure Spanish descent, considered Charles as one of
themselves. With such a family record, no one could be
more of a Costaguanero than Don Carlos Gould ; but
his aspect was so characteristic that in the talk of common
people he was just the Inglez—the Englishman of
Sulaco. He looked more English than a casual tourist,
a sort of heretic pilgrim, however, quite unknown in
Sulaco. He looked more English than the last arrived
batch of young railway engineers, than anybody out of
the hunting-field pictures in the numbers of *Punch*
reaching his wife's drawing-room two months or so after
date. It astonished you to hear him talk Spanish
(Castillan, as the natives say) or the Indian dialect of the
country-people so naturally. His accent had never been
English ; but there was something so indelible in all
these ancestral Goulds — liberators, explorers, coffee-
planters, merchants, revolutionists—of Costaguana, that
he, the only representative of the third generation in a
continent possessing its own style of horsemanship, went

on looking thoroughly English even on horseback. This is not said of him in the mocking spirit of the llaneros —men of the great plains—who think that no one in the world knows how to sit a horse but themselves. Charles Gould, to use the suitably lofty phrase, rode like a centaur. Riding for him was not a special form of exercise ; it was a natural faculty, as walking straight is to all men sound of mind and limb ; but, all the same, when cantering beside the rutty ox-cart track to the mine, he looked in his English clothes and with his imported saddlery as though he had come this moment to Costaguana at his easy swift *pasotrote*, straight out of some green meadow at the other side of the world.

His way would lie along the old Spanish road—the *camino real* of popular speech — the only remaining vestige of a fact and name left by that royalty old Giorgio Viola hated, and whose very shadow had departed from the land ; for the big equestrian statue of Charles IV. at the entrance of the Alameda, towering white against the trees, was only known to the folk from the country and to the beggars of the town that slept on the steps around the pedestal, as the Horse of Stone. The other Carlos, turning off to the left with a rapid clatter of hoofs on the disjointed pavement—Don Carlos Gould in his English clothes, looked as incongruous, but much more at home than the kingly cavalier reining in his steed on the pedestal above the sleeping leperos, with his marble arm raised towards the marble rim of a plumed hat.

The weather-stained effigy of the mounted king, with its vague suggestion of a saluting gesture, seemed to present an inscrutable breast to the political· changes which had robbed it of its very name ; but neither did the other horseman, well known to the people, keen and alive on his well-shaped, slate-coloured beast with a white eye, wear his heart on the sleeve of his English coat. His mind preserved its steady poise as if sheltered in the passionless stability of private and public decencies at home in Europe. He accepted with a like calm the shocking manner in which the Sulaco ladies smothered their faces with pearl powder till they looked like white plaster casts with beautiful living eyes, the peculiar gossip of the town, and the continuous political changes, the constant " saving of the country," which to his wife seemed a puerile and bloodthirsty game of murder and rapine played with terrible earnestness by depraved children. In the early days of her Costaguana life, the little lady used to clench her hands with exasperation at not being able to take the public affairs of the country as seriously as the incidental atrocity of methods deserved. She saw in them a comedy of naïve pretences, but hardly anything genuine, except her own appalled indignation. Charles, very quiet and twisting his long moustache, would decline to discuss them at all. Once, however, he observed to her gently :

" My dear, you seem to forget that I was born here."

These few words made her pause as if they had been a sudden revelation. Perhaps the mere fact of being born in the country did make a difference. She had a great confidence in her husband ; it had always been very great. He had struck her imagination from the first by his unsentimentalism, by that very quietude of mind which she had erected in her thought for a sign of perfect competency in the business of living. Don José Avellanos, their neighbour across the street, a statesman, a poet, a man of culture, who had represented his country at several European Courts (and had suffered untold indignities as a State prisoner in the time of the tyrant Guzman Bento), used to declare in Doña Emilia's drawing-room that Carlos had all the English qualities of character with a truly patriotic heart.

Mrs. Gould, raising her eyes to her husband's thin, red and tan face, could not detect the slightest quiver of a feature at what he must have heard said of his patriotism. Perhaps he had just dismounted on his return from the mine ; he was English enough to disregard the hottest hours of the day. Basilio, in a livery of white linen and a red sash, had squatted for a moment behind his heels to unstrap the heavy, blunt spurs in the patio ; and then the Señor Administrador would go up the staircase into the gallery. Rows of plants in pots, ranged on the balustrade between the pilasters of the arches, screened the *corrédor* with their leaves and flowers from the quadrangle below, whose paved space is the true hearthstone of a South American house, where the quiet hours of domestic life are marked by the shifting of light and shadow on the flagstones.

Señor Avellanos was in the habit of crossing the patio at five o'clock almost every day. Don José chose to come over at tea-time because the English rite at Doña Emilia's house reminded him of the time when he lived in London as Minister Plenipotentiary to the Court of St. James. He did not like tea ; and, usually, rocking his American chair, his neat little shiny boots crossed on the foot-rest, he would talk on and on with a sort of complacent virtuosity wonderful in a man of his age, while he held the cup in his hands for a long time. His close-cropped head was perfectly white ; his eyes coal-black.

On seeing Charles Gould step into the sala he would nod provisionally and go on to the end of the oratorial period. Only then he would say :

" Carlos, my friend, you have ridden from San Tomé in the heat of the day. Always the true English activity. No ? What ? "

He drank up all the tea at once in one draught. This performance was invariably followed by a slight shudder and a low involuntary " br-r-r-r," which was not covered by the hasty exclamation, " Excellent ! "

Then giving up the empty cup into his young friend's hand, extended with a smile, he continued to expatiate upon the patriotic nature of the San Tomé mine for the simple pleasure of talking fluently, it seemed, while his reclining

body jerked backwards and forwards in a rocking-chair
of the sort exported from the United States. The ceiling
of the largest drawing-room of the Casa Gould extended
its white level far above his head. The loftiness dwarfed
the mixture of heavy, straight-backed Spanish chairs of
brown wood with leathern seats, and European furniture,
low, and cushioned all over, like squat little monsters
gorged to bursting with steel springs and horsehair.
There were knick-knacks on little tables, mirrors let into
the wall above marble consoles, square spaces of carpet
under the two groups of arm-chairs, each presided over
by a deep sofa ; smaller rugs scattered all over the floor
of red tiles ; three windows from the ceiling down to the
ground, opening on a balcony, and flanked by the perpendicular folds of the dark hangings. The stateliness
of ancient days lingered between the four high, smooth
walls, tinted a delicate primrose colour ; and Mrs.
Gould, with her little head and shining coils of hair,
sitting in a cloud of muslin and lace before a slender
mahogany table, resembled a fairy posed lightly before
dainty philtres dispensed out of vessels of silver and
porcelain.

Mrs. Gould knew the history of the San Tomé mine.
Worked in the early days mostly by means of lashes on
the backs of slaves, its yield had been paid for in its own
weight of human bones. Whole tribes of Indians had
perished in the exploitation ; and then the mine was
abandoned, since with this primitive method it had ceased
to make a profitable return, no matter how many corpses
were thrown into its maw. Then it became forgotten.
It was rediscovered after the War of Independence. An
English company obtained the right to work it, and found
so rich a vein that neither the exactions of successive
governments, nor the periodical raids of recruiting
officers upon the population of paid miners they had
created, could discourage their perseverance. But in
the end, during the long turmoil of pronunciamientos

that followed the death of the famous Guzman Bento, the native miners, incited to revolt by the emissaries sent out from the capital, had risen upon their English chiefs and murdered them to a man. The decree of confiscation which appeared immediately afterwards in the *Diario Official*, published in Sta. Marta, began with the words : " Justly incensed at the grinding oppression of foreigners, actuated by sordid motives of gain rather than by love for a country where they come impoverished to seek their fortunes, the mining population of San Tomé, etc. . . ." and ended with the declaration : " The chief of the State has resolved to exercise to the full his power of clemency. The mine, which by every law, international, human, and divine, reverts now to the Government as national property, shall remain closed till the sword drawn for the sacred defence of liberal principles has accomplished its mission of securing the happiness of our beloved country."

And for many years this was the last of the San Tomé mine. What advantage that Government had expected from the spoliation, it is impossible to tell now. Costaguana was made with difficulty to pay a beggarly money compensation to the families of the victims, and then the matter dropped out of diplomatic dispatches. But afterwards another Government bethought itself of that valuable asset. It was an ordinary Costaguana Government—the fourth in six years—but it judged of its opportunities sanely. It remembered the San Tomé mine with a secret conviction of its worthlessness in their own hands, but with an ingenious insight into the various uses a silver mine can be put to, apart from the sordid process of extracting the metal from under the ground. The father of Charles Gould, for a long time one of the most wealthy merchants of Costaguana, had already lost a considerable part of his fortune in forced loans to the successive Governments. He was a man of calm judgment, who never dreamed of pressing his claims ; and

when, suddenly, the perpetual concession of the San
Tomé mine was offered to him in full settlement, his
alarm became extreme.   He was versed in the ways of
Governments.   Indeed, the intention of this affair,
though no doubt deeply meditated in the closet, lay open
on the surface of the document presented urgently for his
signature.   The third and most important clause stipu-
lated that the concession-holder should pay at once to
the Government five years' royalties on the estimated
output of the mine.

Mr. Gould, senior, defended himself from this fatal
favour with many arguments and entreaties, but without
success.   He knew nothing of mining ; he had no means
to put his concession on the European market ; the mine
as a working concern did not exist.   The buildings had
been burnt down, the mining plant had been destroyed,
the mining population had disappeared from the neighbourhood years and years ago ; the very road had
vanished under a flood of tropical vegetation as effectually
as if swallowed by the sea ; and the main gallery had
fallen in within a hundred yards from the entrance.   It
was no longer an abandoned mine ; it was a wild, inaccessible and rocky gorge of the sierra, where vestiges
of charred timber, some heaps of smashed bricks, and a
few shapeless pieces of rusty iron could have been found
under the matted mass of thorny creepers covering the
ground.   Mr. Gould, senior, did not desire the perpetual
possession of that desolate locality ; in fact, the mere
vision of it arising before his mind in the still watches of
the night had the power to exasperate him into hours of
hot and agitated insomnia.

It so happened, however, that the Finance Minister
of the time was a man to whom, in years gone by, Mr.
Gould had, unfortunately, declined to grant some small
pecuniary assistance, basing his refusal on the ground
that the applicant was a notorious gambler and cheat,
besides being more than half suspected of a robbery

with violence on a wealthy ranchero in a remote country district, where he was actually exercising the function of a judge. Now, after reaching his exalted position, that politician had proclaimed his intention to repay evil with good to Señor Gould—the poor man. He affirmed and reaffirmed this resolution in the drawing-rooms of Sta. Marta, in a soft and implacable voice, and with such malicious glances that Mr. Gould's best friends advised him earnestly to attempt no bribery to get the matter dropped. It would have been useless. Indeed, it would not have been a very safe proceeding. Such was also the opinion of a stout, loud-voiced lady of French extraction, the daughter, she said, of an officer of high rank (*officier supérieur de l'armée*), who was accommodated with lodgings within the walls of a secularised convent next door to the Ministry of Finance. That florid person, when approached on behalf of Mr. Gould in a proper manner, and with a suitable present, shook her head despondently. She was good-natured, and her despondency was genuine. She imagined she could not take money in consideration of something she could not accomplish. The friend of Mr. Gould charged with the delicate mission used to say afterwards that she was the only honest person closely or remotely connected with the Government he had ever met. "No go," she had said with a cavalier, husky intonation which was natural to her, and using turns of expression more suitable to a child of parents unknown than to the orphaned daughter of a general officer. "No; it's no go. *Pas moyen, mon garçon. C'est dommage, tout de même. Ah! zut! Je ne vole pas mon monde. Je ne suis pas ministre—moi! Vous pouvez emporter votre petit sac.*"

For a moment, biting her carmine lip, she deplored inwardly the tyranny of the rigid principles governing the sale of her influence in high places. Then, significantly, and with a touch of impatience, "*Allez,*" she

added, "*et dites bien à votre bonhomme—entendez-vous?
qu'il faut avaler la pilule.*"

After such a warning there was nothing for it but to
sign and pay. Mr. Gould had swallowed the pill, and it
was as though it had been compounded of some subtle
poison that acted directly on his brain. He became at
once mine-ridden, and as he was well read in light
literature, it took to his mind the form of the Old Man
of the Sea fastened upon his shoulders. He also began
to dream of vampires. Mr. Gould exaggerated to himself
the disadvantages of his new position, because he viewed
it emotionally. His position in Costaguana was no worse
than before. But man is a desperately conservative
creature, and the extravagant novelty of this outrage upon
his purse distressed his sensibilities. Everybody around
him was being robbed by the grotesque and murderous
bands that played their game of governments and revolutions after the death of Guzman Bento. His experience
had taught him that, however short the plunder might
fall of their legitimate expectations, no gang in possession
of the Presidential Palace would be so incompetent as to
suffer itself to be baffled by the want of a pretext. The first
casual colonel of the barefooted army of scarecrows that
came along was able to expose with force and precision
to any mere civilian his titles to a sum of ten thousand
dollars ; the while his hope would be immutably fixed
upon a gratuity, at any rate, of no less than a thousand.
Mr. Gould knew that very well, and, armed with resigna-
tion, had waited for better times. But to be robbed
under the forms of legality and business was intolerable
to his imagination. Mr. Gould, the father, had one fault
in his sagacious and honourable character : he attached
too much importance to form. It is a failing common to
mankind, whose views are tinged by prejudices. There
was for him in that affair a malignancy of perverted
justice which, by means of a moral shock, attacked his
vigorous physique. "It will end by killing me," he used

to affirm many times a day. And, in fact, since that time he began to suffer from fever, from liver pains, and mostly from a worrying inability to think of anything else. The Finance Minister could have formed no conception of the profound subtlety of his revenge. Even Mr. Gould's letters to his fourteen-year-old boy Charles, then away in England for his education, came at last to talk of practically nothing but the mine. He groaned over the injustice, the persecution, the outrage of that mine ; he occupied whole pages in the exposition of the fatal consequences attaching to the possession of that mine from every point of view, with every dismal inference, with words of horror at the apparently eternal character of that curse. For the concession had been granted to him and his descendants for ever. He implored his son never to return to Costaguana, never to claim any part of his inheritance there, because it was tainted by the infamous concession ; never to touch it, never to approach it, to forget that America existed, and pursue a mercantile career in Europe. And each letter ended with bitter self-reproaches for having stayed too long in that cavern of thieves, intriguers, and brigands.

To be told repeatedly that one's future is blighted because of the possession of a silver mine is not, at the age of fourteen, a matter of prime importance as to its main statement ; but in its form it is calculated to excite a certain amount of wonder and attention. In course of time the boy, at first only puzzled by the angry jeremiads, but rather sorry for his dad, began to turn the matter over in his mind in such moments as he could spare from play and study. In about a year he had evolved from the lecture of the letters a definite conviction that there was a silver mine in the Sulaco province of the Republic of Costaguana, where poor Uncle Harry had been shot by soldiers a great many years before. There was also connected closely with that mine a thing called the "iniquitous Gould Concession," apparently written on a paper which his father desired ardently to "tear and fling into the faces" of presidents, members of judicature, and ministers of State.   And this desire persisted, though the names of these people, he noticed, seldom remained the same for a whole year together. This desire (since the thing was iniquitous) seemed quite natural to the boy, though why the affair was iniquitous he did not know.   Afterwards, with advancing wisdom, he managed to clear the plain truth of the business from the fantastic intrusions of the Old Man of the Sea, vampires, and ghouls, which had lent to his father's correspondence the flavour of a gruesome *Arabian Nights* tale.   In the end, the growing youth attained to as close an intimacy with the San Tomé mine as the old man who wrote these plaintive and enraged letters on the other side of the sea.   He had been made several times already to pay heavy fines for neglecting to work the mine, he reported, besides other sums extracted from him on account of future royalties, on the ground that a man with such a valuable concession in his pocket could not refuse his financial assistance to the Government of the Republic. The last of his fortune was passing away from him against worthless receipts, he wrote, in a rage, whilst he was being pointed out as an individual who had known how to secure enormous advantages from the necessities of his country. And the young man in Europe grew more and more interested in that thing which could provoke such a tumult of words and passion.

He thought of it every day ; but he thought of it without bitterness.   It might have been an unfortunate affair for his poor dad, and the whole story threw a queer light upon the social and political life of Costaguana. The view he took of it was sympathetic to his father, yet calm and reflective.   His personal feelings had not been outraged, and it is difficult to resent with proper and durable indignation the physical or mental anguish of another organism, even if that other organism is one's own father. By the time he was twenty Charles Gould had, in his turn, fallen under the spell of the San Tomé mine. But it was another form of enchantment, more suitable to his youth, into whose magic formula there entered hope, vigour, and self-confidence, instead of weary indignation and despair. Left after he was twenty to his own guidance (except for the severe injunction not to return to Costaguana), he had pursued his studies in Belgium and France with the idea of qualifying for a mining engineer. But this scientific aspect of his labours remained vague and imperfect in his mind. Mines had acquired for him a dramatic interest. He studied their peculiarities from a personal point of view, too, as one would study the varied characters of men. He visited them as one goes with curiosity to call upon remarkable persons. He visited mines in Germany, in Spain, in Cornwall. Abandoned workings had for him strong fascination. Their desolation appealed to him like the sight of human misery, whose causes are varied and profound. They might have been worthless, but also they might have been misunderstood. His future wife was the first and perhaps the only person to detect this secret mood which governed the profoundly sensible, almost voiceless attitude of this man towards the world of material things. And at once her delight in him, lingering with half-open wings like those birds that cannot rise easily from a flat level, found a pinnacle from which to soar up into the skies.

They had become acquainted in Italy, where the future Mrs. Gould was staying with an old and pale aunt who, years before, had married a middle-aged, impoverished Italian marquis. She now mourned that man, who had known how to give up his life to the independence and unity of his country, who had known how to be as enthusiastic in his generosity as the youngest of those who fell for that very cause of which old Giorgio Viola was a drifting relic, as a broken spar is suffered to float away disregarded after a naval victory. The marchesa led a still, whispering existence, nun-like in her black robes and a white band over the forehead, in a corner of the first floor of an ancient and ruinous palace, whose big, empty halls downstairs sheltered under their painted ceilings the harvests, the fowls, and even the cattle, together with the whole family of the tenant farmer.

The two young people had met in Lucca. After that meeting Charles Gould visited no mines, though they went together in a carriage, once, to see some marble quarries, where the work resembled mining in so far that it also was the tearing of the raw material of treasure from the earth. Charles Gould did not open his heart to her in any set speeches. He simply went on acting and thinking in her sight. This is the true method of sincerity. One of his frequent remarks was, " I think sometimes that poor father takes a wrong view of that San Tomé business." And they discussed that opinion long and earnestly, as if they could influence a mind across half the globe ; but in reality they discussed it because the sentiment of love can enter into any subject and live ardently in remote phrases. For this natural reason these discussions were precious to Mrs. Gould in her engaged state. Charles feared that Mr. Gould, senior, was wasting his strength and making himself ill by his efforts to get rid of the concession. " I fancy that this is not the kind of handling it requires," he mused aloud, as if to himself. And when she wondered frankly that a man of character should devote his energies to plotting and intrigues, Charles would remark, with a gentle concern that understood her wonder, " You must not forget that he was born there."

She would set her quick mind to work upon that, and then make the inconsequent retort, which he accepted as perfectly sagacious, because, in fact, it was so :

" Well, and you ?   You were born there too."

He knew his answer.

" That's different. I've been away ten years. Dad never had such a long spell ; and it was more than thirty years ago."

She was the first person to whom he opened his lips after receiving the news of his father's death.

" It has killed him ! " he said.

He had walked straight out of town with the news, straight out before him in the noonday sun on the white road, and his feet had brought him face to face with her in the hall of the ruined palazzo, a room magnificent and naked, with here and there a long strip of damask, black with damp and age, drooping straight down on a bare panel of the wall. It was furnished with exactly one gilt arm-chair, with a broken back, and an octagon columnar stand bearing a heavy marble vase ornamented with sculptured masks and garlands of flowers, and cracked from top to bottom. Charles Gould was dusty with the white dust of the road lying on his boots, on his shoulders, on his cap with two peaks. Water dripped from under it all over his face, and he grasped a thick oaken cudgel in his bare right hand.

She went very pale under the roses of her big straw hat, gloved, swinging a clear sunshade, caught just as she was going out to meet him at the bottom of the hill, where three poplars stand near the wall of a vineyard.

" It has killed him ! " he repeated. " He ought to have had many years yet. We are a long-lived family."

She was too startled to say anything ; he was contemplating with a penetrating and motionless stare the cracked marble urn as though he had resolved to fix its shape for ever in his memory. It was only when, turning suddenly to her, he blurted out twice, " I've come to you—— I've come straight to you—— " without being able to finish his phrase, that the great pitifulness of that lonely and tormented death in Costaguana came to her with the full force of its misery. He caught hold of her hand, raised it to his lips, and at that she dropped her parasol to pat him on the cheek, murmured " Poor boy," and began to dry her eyes under the downward curve of her hat-brim, very small in her simple, white frock, almost like a lost child crying in the degraded grandeur of the noble hall, while he stood by her, again perfectly motionless in the contemplation of the marble urn.

Afterwards they went out for a long walk, which was silent till he exclaimed suddenly :

" Yes. But if he had only grappled with it in a proper way ! "

And then they stopped. Everywhere there were long shadows lying on the hills, on the roads, on the enclosed fields of olive trees ; the shadows of poplars, of wide chestnuts, of farm buildings, of stone walls ; and in mid-air the sound of a bell, thin and alert, was like the throbbing pulse of the sunset glow. Her lips were slightly parted as though in surprise that he should not be looking at her with his usual expression. His usual expression was unconditionally approving and attentive. He was in his talks with her the most anxious and deferential of dictators, an attitude that pleased her immensely. It affirmed her power without detracting from his dignity. That slight girl, with her little feet, little hands, little face attractively overweighted by great coils of hair ; with a rather large mouth, whose mere parting seemed to breathe upon you the fragrance of frankness and generosity, had the fastidious soul of an experienced woman. She was, before all things and all flatteries, careful of her pride in the object of her choice. But now he was actually not looking at her at all ; and his expression was tense and irrational, as is natural in a man who elects to stare at nothing past a young girl's head.

" Well, yes. It was iniquitous. They corrupted him thoroughly, the poor old boy. Oh ! why wouldn't

he let me go back to him ? But now I shall know how
to grapple with this."

After pronouncing these words with immense assurance, he glanced down at her, and at once fell a prey to
distress, incertitude, and fear.

The only thing he wanted to know now, he said, was
whether she did love him enough—whether she would
have the courage to go with him so far away ? He put
these questions to her in a voice that trembled with
anxiety—for he was a determined man.

She did. She would. And immediately the future
hostess of all the Europeans in Sulaco had the physical
experience of the earth falling away from under her.
It vanished completely, even to the very sound of the
bell. When her feet touched the ground again, the
bell was still ringing in the valley ; she put her hands
up to her hair, breathing quickly, and glanced up and
down the stony lane. It was reassuringly empty.
Meantime, Charles, stepping with one foot into a dry
and dusty ditch, picked up the open parasol, which had
bounded away from them with a martial sound of drum
taps. He handed it to her soberly, a little crestfallen.

They turned back, and after she had slipped her
hand on his arm, the first words he pronounced were :

" It's lucky that we shall be able to settle in a coast
town. You've heard its name. It is Sulaco. I am so
glad poor father did get that house. He bought a big
house there years ago, in order that there should always
be a Casa Gould in the principal town of what used to
be called the Occidental Province. I lived there once,
as a small boy, with my dear mother, for a whole year,
while poor father was away in the United States on
business. You shall be the new mistress of the Casa
Gould."

And later, in the inhabited corner of the palazzo
above the vineyards, the marble hills, the pines and olives
of Lucca, he also said :

"The name of Gould has been always highly
respected in Sulaco. My Uncle Harry was chief of the
State for some time, and has left a great name amongst the
first families. By this I mean the pure Creole families,
who take no part in the miserable farce of governments.
Uncle Harry was no adventurer. In Costaguana we
Goulds are no adventurers. He was of the country, and
he loved it, but he remained essentially an Englishman
in his ideas. He made use of the political cry of his
time. It was Federation. But he was no politician.
He simply stood up for social order out of pure love for
rational liberty and from his hate of oppression. There
was no nonsense about him. He went to work in his
own way because it seemed right, just as I feel I must lay
hold of that mine."

In such words he talked to her because his memory
was very full of the country of his childhood, his heart
of his life with that girl, and his mind of the San Tomé
Concession. He added that he would have to leave her
for a few days to find an American, a man from San
Francisco, who was still somewhere in Europe. A few
months before he had made his acquaintance in an old
historic German town, situated in a mining district. The
American had his womankind with him, but seemed
lonely while they were sketching all day long the old doorways and the turreted corners of the mediæval houses.
Charles Gould had with him the inseparable com-
panionship of the mine. The other man was interested
in mining enterprises, knew something of Costaguana,
and was no stranger to the name of Gould. They had
talked together with some intimacy, which was made
possible by the difference of their ages. Charles wanted
now to find that capitalist of shrewd mind and accessible
character. His father's fortune in Costaguana, which he
had supposed to be still considerable, seemed to have
melted in the rascally crucible of revolutions. Apart
from some ten thousand pounds deposited in England,

there appeared to be nothing left except the house in Sulaco, a vague right of forest exploitation in a remote and savage district, and the San Tomé Concession, which had attended his poor father to the very brink of the grave.

He explained those things. It was late when they parted. She had never before given him such a fascinating vision of herself. All the eagerness of youth for a strange life, for great distances, for a future in which there was an air of adventure, of combat—a subtle thought of redress and conquest, had filled her with an intense excitement, which she returned to the giver with a more open and exquisite display of tenderness.

He left her to walk down the hill, and directly he found himself alone he became sober. That irreparable change a death makes in the course of our daily thoughts can be felt in a vague and poignant discomfort of mind. It hurt Charles Gould to feel that never more, by no effort of will, would he be able to think of his father in the same way he used to think of him when the poor man was alive. His breathing image was no longer in his power. This consideration, closely affecting his own identity, filled his breast with a mournful and angry desire for action. In this his instinct was unerring. Action is consolatory. It is the enemy of thought and the friend of flattering illusions. Only in the conduct of our action can we find the sense of mastery over the Fates. For his action, the mine was obviously the only field. It was imperative sometimes to know how to disobey the solemn wishes of the dead. He resolved firmly to make his disobedience as thorough (by way of atonement) as it well could be. The mine had been the cause of an absurd moral disaster ; its working must be made a serious and moral success. He owed it to the dead man's memory. Such were the—properly speaking—emotions of Charles Gould. His thoughts ran upon the means of raising a large amount of capital in San Francisco or elsewhere ; and incidentally there occurred to him also the general reflection that the counsel of the departed must be an unsound guide. Not one of them could be aware beforehand what enormous changes the death of any given individual may produce in the very aspect of the world.

The latest phase in the history of the mine Mrs. Gould knew from personal experience. It was in essence the history of her married life. The mantle of the Goulds' hereditary position in Sulaco had descended amply upon her little person; but she would not allow the peculiarities of the strange garment to weigh down the vivacity of her character, which was the sign of no mere mechanical sprightliness, but of an eager intelligence. It must not be supposed that Mrs. Gould's mind was masculine. A woman with a masculine mind is not a being of superior efficiency; she is simply a phenomenon of imperfect differentiation—interestingly barren and without importance. Doña Emilia's intelligence being feminine led her to achieve the conquest of Sulaco, simply by lighting the way for her unselfishness and sympathy. She could converse charmingly, but she was not talkative. The wisdom of the heart having no concern with the erection or demolition of theories any more than with the defence of prejudices, has no random words at its command. The words it pronounces have the value of acts of integrity, tolerance, and compassion. A woman's true tenderness, like the true virility of man, is expressed in action of a conquering kind. The ladies of Sulaco adored Mrs. Gould. " They still look upon me as something of a monster," Mrs. Gould had said pleasantly to one of the three gentlemen from San Francisco she had to entertain in her new Sulaco house just about a year after her marriage.

They were her first visitors from abroad, and they had come to look at the San Tomé mine. She jested most agreeably, they thought; and Charles Gould, besides knowing thoroughly what he was about, had shown himself a real hustler. These facts caused them to be well disposed towards his wife. An unmistakable enthusiasm, pointed by a slight flavour of irony, made her talk of the mine absolutely fascinating to her visitors, and provoked them to grave and indulgent smiles in which there was a good deal of deference. Perhaps had they known how much she was inspired by an idealistic view of success, they would have been amazed at the state of her mind as the Spanish-American ladies had been amazed at the tireless activity of her body. She would—in her own words—have been for them " something of a monster." However, the Goulds were in essentials a reticent couple, and their guests departed without the suspicion of any other purpose but simple profit in the working of a silver mine. Mrs. Gould had out her own carriage, with two white mules, to drive them down to the harbour, whence the *Ceres* was to carry them off into the Olympus of plutocrats. Captain Mitchell had snatched at the occasion of leave-taking to remark to Mrs. Gould, in a low, confidential mutter, " This marks an epoch."

Mrs. Gould loved the patio of her Spanish house. A broad flight of stone steps was overlooked silently from a niche in the wall by a Madonna in blue robes with the crowned Child sitting on her arm. Subdued voices ascended in the early mornings from the paved well of the quadrangle, with the stamping of horses and mules led out in pairs to drink at the cistern. A tangle of slender bamboo stems drooped its narrow blade-like leaves over the square pool of water, and the fat coachman sat muffled up on the edge, holding lazily the ends of halters in his hand. Barefooted servants passed to and fro, issuing from dark, low doorways below, two laundry girls with baskets of washed linen, the baker with the tray of bread made for the day, Leonarda— her own camerista—bearing high up, swung from her hand raised above her raven black head, a bunch of starched underskirts dazzlingly white in the slant of sunshine. Then the old porter would hobble in, sweep-

5

ing the flagstones, and the house was ready for the day.
All the lofty rooms on three sides of the quadrangle
opened into each other and into the *corrédor*, with its
wrought-iron railings and a border of flowers, whence,
like the lady of the mediæval castle, she could witness
from above all the departures and arrivals of the Casa,
to which the sonorous arched gateway lent an air of
stately importance.

She had watched her carriage roll away with the
three guests from the North. She smiled. Their three
arms went up simultaneously to their three hats.
Captain Mitchell, the fourth, in attendance, had already
begun a pompous discourse. Then she lingered. She
lingered, approaching her face to the clusters of flowers
here and there as if to give time to her thoughts to catch
up with her slow footsteps along the straight vista of
the *corrédor*.

A fringed Indian hammock from Aroa, gay with
coloured featherwork, had been swung judiciously in
a corner that caught the early sun ; for the mornings
are cool in Sulaco. The clusters of *flor de noche buena*
blazed in great masses before the open glass doors of
the reception-rooms. A big green parrot, brilliant like
an emerald in a cage that flashed like gold, screamed out
ferociously, " Viva Costaguana ! " then called twice
mellifluously, " Leonarda ! Leonarda ! " in imitation
of Mrs. Gould's voice, and suddenly took refuge in
immobility and silence. Mrs. Gould reached the end
of the gallery and put her head through the door of her
husband's room.

Charles Gould, with one foot on a low wooden stool,
was already strapping his spurs. He wanted to hurry
back to the mine. Mrs. Gould, without coming in,
glanced about the room. One tall, broad bookcase,
with glass doors, was full of books ; but in the other,
without shelves, and lined with red baize, were arranged
firearms : Winchester carbines, revolvers, a couple of

shot-guns, and even two pairs of double-barrelled holster pistols. Between them, by itself, upon a strip of scarlet velvet, hung an old cavalry sabre, once the property of Don Enrique Gould, the hero of the Occidental Province, presented by Don José Avellanos, the hereditary friend of the family.

Otherwise, the plastered white walls were completely bare, except for a water-colour sketch of the San Tomé mountain—the work of Doña Emilia herself. In the middle of the red-tiled floor stood two long tables littered with plans and papers, a few chairs, and a glass show-case containing specimens of ore from the mine. Mrs. Gould, looking at all these things in turn, wondered aloud why the talk of these wealthy and enterprising men discussing the prospects, the working, and the safety of the mine rendered her so impatient and uneasy, whereas she could talk of the mine by the hour with her husband with unwearied interest and satisfaction.

And dropping her eyelids, expressively she added :

" What do *you* feel about it, Charley ? "

Then, surprised at her husband's silence, she raised her eyes, opened wide, as pretty as pale flowers. He had done with the spurs, and, twisting his moustache with both hands, horizontally, he contemplated her from the height of his long legs with a visible appreciation of her appearance. The consciousness of being thus contemplated pleased Mrs. Gould.

" They are considerable men," he said.

" I know. But have you listened to their conversation ? They don't seem to have understood anything they have seen here."

" They have seen the mine. They have understood that to some purpose," Charles Gould interjected, in defence of the visitors ; and then his wife mentioned the name of the most considerable of the three. He was considerable in finance and in industry. His name was familiar to many millions of people. He was so con-

siderable that he would never have travelled so far away
from the centre of his activity if the doctors had not
insisted, with veiled menaces, on his taking a long
holiday.

" Mr. Holroyd's sense of religion," Mrs. Gould
pursued, " was shocked and disgusted at the tawdriness
of the dressed-up saints in the cathedral—the worship,
he called it, of wood and tinsel. But it seemed to me
that he looked upon his own God as a sort of influential
partner, who gets his share of profits in the endowment
of churches. That's a sort of idolatry. He told me he
endowed churches every year, Charley."

" No end of them," said Mr. Gould, marvelling
inwardly at the mobility of her physiognomy. " All
over the country. He's famous for that sort of munificence."

" Oh, he didn't boast ! " Mrs. Gould declared scrupu-
lously. " I believe he's really a good man, but so
stupid ! A poor Chulo who offers a little silver arm or
leg to thank his god for a cure is as rational and more
touching."

" He's at the head of immense silver and iron
interests," Charles Gould observed.

" Ah, yes ! The religion of silver and iron. He's a
very civil man, though he looked awfully solemn when
he first saw the Madonna on the staircase, who's only
wood and paint ; but he said nothing to me. My dear
Charley, I heard those men talk among themselves.
Can it be that they really wish to become, for an immense
consideration, drawers of water and hewers of wood to all
the countries and nations of the earth ? "

" A man must work to some end," Charles Gould said
vaguely.

Mrs. Gould, frowning, surveyed him from head to
foot. With his riding breeches, leather leggings (an
article of apparel never before seen in Costaguana), a
Norfolk coat of grey flannel, and those great flaming

moustaches, he suggested an officer of cavalry turned gentleman farmer. This combination was gratifying to Mrs. Gould's tastes. " How thin the poor boy is ! " she thought. " He overworks himself." But there was no denying that his fine-drawn, keen red face, and his whole, long-limbed, lank person, had an air of breeding and distinction. And Mrs. Gould relented.

" I only wondered what you felt," she murmured gently.

During the last few days, as it happened, Charles Gould had been kept too busy thinking twice before he spoke to have paid much attention to the state of his feelings. But theirs was a successful match, and he had no difficulty in finding his answer.

" The best of my feelings are in your keeping, my dear," he said lightly ; and there was so much truth in that obscure phrase that he experienced towards her at the moment a great increase of gratitude and tenderness.

Mrs. Gould, however, did not seem to find this answer in the least obscure. She brightened up delicately ; already he had changed his tone.

" But there are facts. The worth of the mine—as a mine—is beyond doubt. It shall make us very wealthy. The mere working of it is a matter of technical knowledge, which I have—which ten thousand other men in the world have. But its safety, its continued existence as an enterprise, giving a return to men—to strangers, comparative strangers—who invest money in it, is left altogether in my hands. I have inspired confidence in a man of wealth and position. You seem to think this perfectly natural—do you ? Well, I don't know. I don't know why I have ; but it is a fact. This fact makes everything possible, because without it I would never have thought of disregarding my father's wishes. I would never have disposed of the concession as a speculator disposes of a valuable right to a company—for cash and shares, to grow rich eventually if possible, but at any rate

to put some money at once in his pocket. No. Even if
it had been feasible—which I doubt—I would not have
done so. Poor father did not understand. He was
afraid I would hang on to the ruinous thing, waiting for
just some such chance, and waste my life miserably.
That was the true sense of his prohibition, which we have
deliberately set aside."

They were walking up and down the *corrédor*. Her
head just reached to his shoulder. His arm, extended
downwards, was about her waist. His spurs jingled
slightly.

"He had not seen me for ten years. He did not
know me. He parted from me for my sake, and he would
never let me come back. He was always talking in his
letters of leaving Costaguana, of abandoning everything
and making his escape. But he was too valuable a prey.
They would have thrown him into one of their prisons at
the first suspicion."

His spurred feet clinked slowly. He was bending
over his wife as they walked. The big parrot, turning
its head askew, followed their pacing figures with a round
unblinking eye.

"He was a lonely man. Ever since I was ten years
old he used to talk to me as if I had been grown up.
When I was in Europe he wrote to me every month.
Ten, twelve pages every month of my life for ten years.
And, after all, he did not know me ! Just think of it—
ten whole years away ; the years I was growing up into a
man ! He could not know me. Do you think he could ? "

Mrs. Gould shook her head negatively ; which was
just what her husband had expected from the strength
of the argument. But she shook her head negatively only
because she thought that no one could know her Charles
—really know him for what he was, but herself. The
thing was obvious. It could be felt. It required no
argument. And poor Mr. Gould, senior, who had died
too soon to ever hear of their engagement, remained too

shadowy a figure for her to be credited with knowledge of
any sort whatever.

" No, he did not understand. In my view this mine
could never have been a thing to sell. Never ! After
all his misery I simply could not have touched it for
money alone," Charles Gould pursued ; and she pressed
her head to his shoulder approvingly.

These two young people remembered the life which
had ended wretchedly just when their own lives had come
together in that splendour of hopeful love, which to the
most sensible minds appears like a triumph of good over
all the evils of the earth. A vague idea of rehabilitation
had entered the plan of their life. That it was so vague
as to elude the support of argument made it only the
stronger. It had presented itself to them at the instant
when the woman's instinct of devotion and the man's
instinct of activity receive from the strongest of illusions
their most powerful impulse. The very prohibition
imposed the necessity of success. It was as if they had
been morally bound to make good their vigorous view of
life against the unnatural error of weariness and despair.
If the idea of wealth was present to them, it was only in so
far as it was bound with that other success. Mrs. Gould,
an orphan from early childhood and without fortune,
brought up in an atmosphere of intellectual interests,
had never considered the aspects of great wealth. They
were too remote, and she had not learned that they were
desirable. On the other hand, she had not known anything of absolute want. Even the very poverty of her
aunt, the marchesa, had nothing intolerable to a refined
mind ; it seemed in accord with a great grief ; it had the
austerity of a sacrifice offered to a noble ideal. Thus even
the most legitimate touch of materialism was wanting
in Mrs. Gould's character. The dead man of whom she
thought with tenderness (because he was Charley's father),
and with some impatience (because he had been weak),
must be put completely in the wrong. Nothing else

would do to keep their prosperity without a stain on its
only real, on its immaterial side !

Charles Gould, on his part, had been obliged to keep
the idea of wealth well to the fore ; but he brought it
forward as a means, not as an end. Unless the mine
was good business it could not be touched. He had to
insist on that aspect of the enterprise. It was his lever
to move men who had capital. And Charles Gould
believed in the mine. He knew everything that could be
known of it. His faith in the mine was contagious,
though it was not served by a great eloquence ; but
business men are frequently as sanguine and imaginative
as lovers. They are affected by a personality much
oftener than people would suppose ; and Charles Gould,
in his unshaken assurance, was absolutely convincing.
Besides, it was a matter of common knowledge to the men
to whom he addressed himself that mining in Costaguana
was a game that could be made considerably more than
worth the candle. The men of affairs knew that very well.
The real difficulty in touching it was elsewhere. Against
that there was an implication of calm and implacable
resolution in Charles Gould's very voice. Men of
affairs venture sometimes on acts that the common judgment of the world would pronounce absurd ; they make
their decisions on apparently impulsive and human
grounds. " Very well," had said the considerable personage to whom Charles Gould on his way out through
San Francisco had lucidly exposed his point of view.
" Let us suppose that the mining affairs of Sulaco are
taken in hand. There would then be in it : first, the house
of Holroyd, which is all right ; then, Mr. Charles Gould,
a citizen of Costaguana, who is also all right ; and, lastly,
the Government of the Republic. So far this resembles
the first start of the Atacama nitrate fields, where there
was a financing house, a gentleman of the name of
Edwards, and—a Government ; or, rather, two Governments—two South American Governments. And you

know what came of it. War came of it ; devastating and prolonged war came of it, Mr. Gould. However, here we possess the advantage of having only one South American Government hanging around for plunder out of the deal. It is an advantage ; but then there are degrees of badness, and that Government is the Costaguana Government."

Thus spoke the considerable personage, the millionaire endower of churches on a scale befitting the greatness of his native land—the same to whom the doctors used the language of horrid and veiled menaces. He was a big-limbed, deliberate man, whose quiet burliness lent to an ample silk-faced frock-coat a superfine dignity. His hair was iron-grey, his eyebrows were still black, and his massive profile was the profile of a Cæsar's head on an old Roman coin. But his parentage was German and Scotch and English, with remote strains of Danish and French blood, giving him the temperament of a Puritan and an insatiable imagination of conquest. He was completely unbending to his visitor, because of the warm introduction the visitor had brought from Europe, and because of an irrational liking for earnestness and determination wherever met, to whatever end directed.

" The Costaguana Government shall play its hand for all it's worth—and don't you forget it, Mr. Gould. Now, what is Costaguana ? It is the bottomless pit of 10 per cent. loans and other fool investments. European capital has been flung into it with both hands for years. Not ours, though. We in this country know just about enough to keep indoors when it rains. We can sit and watch. Of course, some day we shall step in. We are bound to. But there's no hurry. Time itself has got to wait on the greatest country in the whole of God's universe. We shall be giving the word for everything : industry, trade, law, journalism, art, politics, and religion, from Cape Horn clear over to Smith's Sound, and beyond too, if anything worth taking hold of turns up at

the North Pole.   And then we shall have the leisure to
take in hand the outlying islands and continents of the
earth.   We shall run the world's business whether the
world likes it or not.   The world can't help it—and
neither can we, I guess."

By this he meant to express his faith in destiny in
words suitable to his intelligence, which was unskilled
in the presentation of general ideas.   His intelligence was
nourished on facts ; and Charles Gould, whose imagination had been permanently affected by the one great fact
of a silver mine, had no objection to this theory of the
world's future.   If it had seemed distasteful for a moment,
it was because the sudden statement of such vast eventual-
ities dwarfed almost to nothingness the actual matter in
hand.   He and his plans and all the mineral wealth of the
Occidental Province appeared suddenly robbed of every
vestige of magnitude.   The sensation was disagreeable ;
but Charles Gould was not dull.   Already he felt that he
was producing a favourable impression ; the consciousness
of that flattering fact helped him to a vague smile, which
his big interlocutor took for a smile of discreet and
admiring assent.   He smiled quietly too ; and immediately Charles Gould, with that mental agility mankind will display in defence of a cherished hope, reflected
that the very apparent insignificance of his aim would
help him to success.   His personality and his mine would
be taken up because it was a matter of no great consequence, one way or another, to a man who referred
his action to such a prodigious destiny.   And Charles
Gould was not humiliated by this consideration, because
the thing remained as big as ever for him.   Nobody else's
vast conceptions of destiny could diminish the aspect of
his desire for the redemption of the San Tomé mine.   In
comparison with the correctness of his aim, definite in space
and absolutely attainable within a limited time, the other
man appeared for an instant as a dreamy idealist of no
importance.

The great man, massive and benignant, had been looking at him thoughtfully ; when he broke the short silence it was to remark that concessions flew about thick in the air of Costaguana. Any simple soul that just yearned to be taken in could bring down a concession at the first shot.

" Our consuls get their mouths stopped with them," he continued, with a twinkle of genial scorn in his eyes. But in a moment he became grave. " A conscientious, upright man, that cares nothing for boodle, and keeps clear of their intrigues, conspiracies, and factions, soon gets his passports. See that, Mr. Gould ? *Persona non grâta.* That's the reason our Government is never properly informed. On the other hand, Europe must be kept out of this continent, and for proper interference on our part the time is not yet ripe, I dare say. But we here—we are not this country's Government, neither are we simple souls. Your affair is all right. The main question for us is whether the second partner, and that's you, is the right sort to hold his own against the third and unwelcome partner, which is one or another of the high and mighty robber gangs that run the Costaguana Government. What do you think, Mr. Gould, eh ? "

He bent forward to look steadily into the unflinching eyes of Charles Gould, who, remembering the large box full of his father's letters, put the accumulated scorn and bitterness of many years into the tone of his answer :

" As far as the knowledge of these men and their methods and their politics is concerned, I can answer for myself. I have been fed on that sort of knowledge since I was a boy. I am not likely to fall into mistakes from excess of optimism."

" Not likely, eh ? That's all right. Tact and a stiff upper lip is what you'll want ; and you could bluff a little on the strength of your backing. Not too much, though. We will go with you as long as the thing runs straight. But we won't be drawn into any large trouble.

This is the experiment which I am willing to make. There is some risk, and we will take it ; but if you can't keep up your end, we will stand our loss, of course, and then—we'll let the thing go.   This mine can wait ; it has been shut up before, as you know.   You must understand that under no circumstances will we consent to throw good money after bad.''

Thus the great personage had spoken then, in his own private office, in a great city where other men (very considerable in the eyes of a vain populace) waited with alacrity upon a wave of his hand.   And rather more than a year later, during his unexpected appearance in Sulaco, he had emphasised his uncompromising attitude with a freedom of sincerity permitted to his wealth and influence.   He did this with the less reserve, perhaps, because the inspection of what had been done, and more still the way in which successive steps had been taken, had impressed him with the conviction that Charles Gould was perfectly capable of keeping up his end.

" This young fellow," he thought to himself, " may yet become a power in the land."

This thought flattered him, for hitherto the only account of this young man he could give to his intimates was :

" My brother-in-law met him in one of these one-horse old German towns, near some mines, and sent him on to me with a letter.   He's one of the Costaguana Goulds, pure-bred Englishmen, but all born in the country.   His uncle went into politics, was the last Provincial President of Sulaco, and got shot after a battle.   His father was a prominent business man in Sta. Marta, tried to keep clear of their politics, and died ruined after a lot of revolutions.   And that's your Costaguana in a nutshell."

Of course, he was too great a man to be questioned as to his motives, even by his intimates.   The outside world was at liberty to wonder respectfully at the hidden meaning of his actions. He was so great a man that his lavish patronage of the " purer forms of Christianity " (which in its naïve form of church-building amused Mrs. Gould) was looked upon by his fellow-citizens as the manifestation of a pious and humble spirit. But in his own circles of the financial world the taking up of such a thing as the San Tomé mine was regarded with respect, indeed, but rather as a subject for discreet jocularity. It was a great man's caprice. In the great Holroyd building (an enormous pile of iron, glass, and blocks of stone at the corner of two streets, cobwebbed aloft by the radiation of telegraph wires) the heads of principal departments exchanged humorous glances, which meant that they were not let into the secrets of the San Tomé business. The Costaguana mail (it was never large— one fairly heavy envelope) was taken unopened straight into the great man's room, and no instructions dealing with it had ever been issued thence. The office whispered that he answered personally—and not by dictation either, but actually writing in his own hand, with pen and ink, and, it was to be supposed, taking a copy in his own private press copy-book, inaccessible to profane eyes. Some scornful young men, insignificant pieces of minor machinery in that eleven-story-high workshop of great affairs, expressed frankly their private opinion that the great chief had done at last something silly, and was ashamed of his folly ; others, elderly and insignificant, but full of romantic reverence for the business that had devoured their best years, used to mutter darkly and knowingly that this was a portentous sign ; that the Holroyd connection meant by and by to get hold of the whole Republic of Costaguana, lock, stock, and barrel. But, in fact, the hobby theory was the right one. It interested the great man to attend personally to the San Tomé mine ; it interested him so much that he allowed this hobby to give a direction to the first complete

holiday he had taken for quite a startling number of
years. He was not running a great enterprise there ;
no mere railway board or industrial corporation. He
was running a man ! A success would have pleased
him very much on refreshingly novel grounds ; but,
on the other side of the same feeling, it was incumbent
upon him to cast it off utterly at the first sign of failure.
A man may be thrown off. The papers had, unfortunately, trumpeted all over the land his journey to Costaguana. If he was pleased at the way Charles Gould
was going on, he infused an added grimness into his
assurances of support. Even at the very last interview, half an hour or so before he rolled out of the patio,
hat in hand, behind Mrs. Gould's white mules, he had
said in Charles's room :

"You go ahead in your own way, and I shall know
how to help you as long as you hold your own. But you
may rest assured that in a given case we shall know
how to drop you in time."

To this Charles Gould's only answer had been :
"You may begin sending out the machinery as soon as
you like."

And the great man had liked this imperturbable
assurance. The secret of it was that to Charles Gould's
mind these uncompromising terms were agreeable.
Like this the mine preserved its identity, with which he
had endowed it as a boy ; and it remained dependent on
himself alone. It was a serious affair, and he, too, took
it grimly.

"Of course," he said to his wife, alluding to this
last conversation with the departed guest, while they
walked slowly up and down the *corrédor*, followed by
the irritated eye of the parrot—" of course, a man of
that sort can take up a thing or drop it when he likes. He
will suffer from no sense of defeat. He may have to
give in, or he may have to die to-morrow, but the great
silver and iron interests will survive, and some day

will get hold of Costaguana along with the rest of the world."

They had stopped near the cage. The parrot, catching the sound of a word belonging to his vocabulary, was moved to interfere. Parrots are very human.

" Viva Costaguana ! " he shrieked, with intense self-assertion, and, instantly ruffling up his feathers, assumed an air of puffed-up somnolence behind the glittering wires.

" And do you believe that, Charley ? " Mrs. Gould asked. " This seems to me most awful materialism, and——"

" My dear, it's nothing to me," interrupted her husband in a reasonable tone. " I make use of what I see. What's it to me whether his talk is the voice of destiny or simply a bit of clap-trap eloquence ? There's a good deal of eloquence of one sort or another produced in both Americas. The air of the New World seems favourable to the art of declamation. Have you forgotten how dear Avellanos can hold forth for hours here——"

" Oh, but that's different," protested Mrs. Gould, almost shocked. The allusion was not to the point. Don José was a dear good man, who talked very well, and was enthusiastic about the greatness of the San Tomé mine. " How can you compare them, Charles ? " she exclaimed reproachfully. " He has suffered—and yet he hopes."

The working competence of men—which she never questioned—was very surprising to Mrs. Gould, because upon so many obvious issues they showed themselves strangely muddle-headed.

Charles Gould, with a careworn calmness which secured for him at once his wife's anxious sympathy, assured her that he was not comparing. He was an American himself, after all, and perhaps he could under-stand both kinds of eloquence—" if it were worth while to try," he added grimly. But he had breathed the air of England longer than any of his people had done for three generations, and really he begged to be excused. His poor father could be eloquent, too. And he asked his wife whether she remembered a passage in one of his father's last letters where Mr. Gould had expressed the conviction that " God looked wrathfully at these countries, or else He would let some ray of hope fall through a rift in the appalling darkness of intrigue, bloodshed, and crime that hung over the Queen of Continents."

Mrs. Gould had not forgotten. " You read it to me, Charley," she murmured. " It was a striking pronouncement. How deeply your father must have felt its terrible sadness ! "

" He did not like to be robbed. It exasperated him," said Charles Gould. " But the image will serve well enough. What is wanted here is law, good faith, order, security. Any one can declaim about these things, but I pin my faith to material interests. Only let the material interests once get a firm footing, and they are bound to impose the conditions on which alone they can continue to exist. That's how your money-making is justified here in the face of lawlessness and disorder. It is justified because the security which it demands must be shared with an oppressed people. A better justice will come afterwards. That's your ray of hope." His arm pressed her slight form closer to his side for a moment. " And who knows whether in that sense even the San Tomé mine may not become that little rift in the darkness which poor father despaired- of ever seeing ? "

She glanced up at him with admiration. He was competent ; he had given a vast shape to the vagueness of her unselfish ambitions.

" Charley," she said, " you are splendidly disobedient."

He left her suddenly in the *corrédor* to go and get his

hat, a soft, grey sombrero, an article of national costume which combined unexpectedly well with his English get-up. He came back, a riding-whip under his arm, buttoning up a dogskin glove ; his face reflected the resolute nature of his thoughts. His wife had waited for him at the head of the stairs, and before he gave her the parting kiss he finished the conversation :

" What should be perfectly clear to us," he said, " is the fact that there is no going back. Where could we begin life afresh ? We are in now for all that there is in us."

He bent over her upturned face very tenderly and a little remorsefully. Charles Gould was competent because he had no illusions. The Gould Concession had to fight for life with such weapons as could be found at once in the mire of a corruption that was so universal as almost to lose its significance. He was prepared to stoop for his weapons. For a moment he felt as if the silver mine, which had killed his father, had decoyed him further than he meant to go ; and with the round-about logic of emotions, he felt that the worthiness of his life was bound up with success. There was no going back.

CHAPTER SEVEN

MRS. GOULD was too intelligently sympathetic not to share that feeling. It made life exciting, and she was too much of a woman not to like excitement. But it frightened her, too, a little ; and when Don José Avellanos, rocking in the American chair, would go so far as to say, " Even, my dear Carlos, if you had failed ; even if some untoward event were yet to destroy your work—which God forbid !—you would have deserved well of your country," Mrs. Gould would look up from the tea-table profoundly at her unmoved husband stirring the spoon in the cup as though he had not heard a word.

Not that Don José anticipated anything of the sort. He could not praise enough dear Carlos's tact and courage. His English, rock-like quality of character was his best safeguard, Don José affirmed ; and, turning to Mrs. Gould, " As to you, Emilia, my soul "—he would address her with the familiarity of his age and old friendship—" you are as true a patriot as though you had been born in our midst."

This might have been less or more than the truth. Mrs. Gould, accompanying her husband all over the province in the search for labour, had seen the land with a deeper glance than a true-born Costaguanera could have done. In her travel-worn riding-habit, her face powdered white like a plaster cast, with a further protection of a small silk mask during the heat of the day, she rode on a well-shaped, light-footed pony in the centre of a little cavalcade. Two *mozos de campo*, picturesque in great hats, with spurred bare heels, in white embroidered calzoneras, leather jackets, and striped ponchos, rode ahead with carbines across their shoulders, swaying in unison to the pace of the horses. A tropilla of pack-mules brought up the rear in charge of a thin brown muleteer, sitting his long-eared beast very near the tail, legs thrust far forward, the wide brim of his hat set far back, making a sort of halo for his head. An old Costaguana officer, a retired senior major of humble origin, but patronised by the first families on account of his Blanco opinions, had been recommended by Don José for commissary and organiser of that expedition. The points of his grey moustache hung far below his chin, and, riding on Mrs. Gould's left hand, he looked about with kindly eyes, pointing out the features of the country, telling the names of the little pueblos and of the estates, of the smooth-walled haciendas like long fortresses crowning the knolls above the level of the Sulaco Valley. It unrolled itself, with green young crops, plains, woodland, and gleams of water, park-like, from the blue vapour of the distant sierra to an immense quivering horizon of grass and sky, where big white clouds seemed to fall slowly into the darkness of their own shadows.

Men ploughed with wooden ploughs and yoked oxen, small on a boundless expanse, as if attacking immensity itself. The mounted figures of vaqueros galloped in the distance, and the great herds fed with all their horned heads one way, in one single wavering line as far as eye could reach across the broad *potreros*. A spreading cotton-wool tree shaded a thatched ranch by the road ; the trudging files of burdened Indians taking off their hats, would lift sad, mute eyes to the cavalcade raising the dust of the crumbling *camino real* made by the hands of their enslaved forefathers. And Mrs. Gould, with each day's journey, seemed to come nearer to the soul

of the land in the tremendous disclosure of this interior
unaffected by the slight European veneer of the coast
towns, a great land of plain and mountain and people,
suffering and mute, waiting for the future in a pathetic
immobility of patience.

She knew its sights and its hospitality, dispensed with
a sort of slumbrous dignity in those great houses presenting long, blind walls and heavy portals to the wind-
swept pastures. She was given the head of the tables,
where masters and dependants sat in a simple and
patriarchal state. The ladies of the house would talk
softly in the moonlight under the orange trees of the
courtyards, impressing upon her the sweetness of their
voices and the something mysterious in the quietude of
their lives. , In the morning the gentlemen, well mounted
in braided sombreros and embroidered riding-suits, with
much silver on the trappings of their horses, would ride
forth to escort the departing guests before committing
them, with grave good-byes, to the care of God at the
boundary pillars of their estates. In all these households
she could hear stories of political outrage ; friends,
relatives, ruined, imprisoned, killed in the battles of
senseless civil wars, barbarously executed in ferocious
proscriptions, as though the government of the country
had been a struggle of lust between bands of absurd
devils let loose upon the land with sabres and uniforms
and grandiloquent phrases. And on all the lips she
found a weary desire for peace, the dread of officialdom
with its nightmarish parody of administration without
law, without security, and without justice.

She bore a whole two months of wandering very well ;
she had that power of resistance to fatigue which one
discovers here and there in some quite frail-looking
women with surprise—like a state of possession by a
remarkably stubborn spirit. Don Pépé—the old Costaguana major—after much display of solicitude for the
delicate lady, had ended by conferring upon her the name

of the " Never-tired Señora." Mrs. Gould was indeed
becoming a Costaguanera. Having acquired in Southern
Europe a knowledge of true peasantry, she was able to
appreciate the great worth of the people. She saw the
man under the silent, sad-eyed beast of burden. She
saw them on the road carrying loads, lonely figures upon
the plain, toiling under great straw hats, with their white
clothing flapping about their limbs in the wind ; she
remembered the villages by some group of Indian women
at the fountain impressed upon her memory, by the face
of some young Indian girl with a melancholy and sensual
profile, raising an earthenware vessel of cool water at the
door of a dark hut with a wooden porch cumbered with
great brown jars. The solid wooden wheels of an ox-cart,
halted with its shafts in the dust, showed the strokes of
the axe ; and a party of charcoal carriers, with each man's
load resting above his head on the top of the low mud wall,
slept stretched in a row within the strip of shade.

The heavy stonework of bridges and churches left
by the conquerors proclaimed the disregard of human
labour, the tribute-labour of vanished nations. The
power of King and Church was gone, but at the sight of
some heavy ruinous pile overtopping from a knoll the
low mud walls of a village, Don Pépé would interrupt
the tale of his campaigns to exclaim :

" Poor Costaguana ! Before, it was everything for the
padres, nothing for the people ; and now, it is everything
for those great politicos in Sta. Marta, for negroes and
thieves."

Charles talked with the alcaldes, with the fiscales,
with the principal people in towns, and with the caballeros on the estates. The commandantes of the districts
offered him escorts—for he could show an authorisation
from the Sulaco political chief of the day. How much the
document had cost him in gold twenty-dollar pieces was a
secret between himself, a great man in the United States
(who condescended to answer the Sulaco mail with his

own hand), and a great man of another sort, with a dark olive complexion and shifty eyes, inhabiting then the Palace of the Intendencia in Sulaco, and who piqued himself on his culture and Europeanism generally in a rather French style because he had lived in Europe for some years—in exile, he said. However, it was pretty well known that just before this exile he had incautiously gambled away all the cash in the Custom House of a small port where a friend in power had procured for him the post of sub-collector. That youthful indiscretion had, amongst other inconveniences, obliged him to earn his living for a time as a café waiter in Madrid; but his talents must have been great, after all, since they had enabled him to retrieve his political fortunes so splendidly. Charles Gould, exposing his business with an imperturbable steadiness, called him Excellency.

The provincial Excellency assumed a weary superiority, tilting his chair far back near an open window in the true Costaguana manner. The military band happened to be braying operatic selections on the plaza just then, and twice he raised his hand imperatively for silence in order to listen to a favourite passage.

" Exquisite, delicious ! " he murmured; while Charles Gould waited, standing by with inscrutable patience. " *Lucia, Lucia di Lammermoor!* I am passionate for music. It transports me. Ha ! the divine —ha !—Mozart. Si ! divine . . . What is it you were saying ? "

Of course, rumours had reached him already of the newcomer's intentions. Besides, he had received an official warning from Sta. Marta. His manner was intended simply to conceal his curiosity and impress his visitor. But after he had locked up something valuable in the drawer of a large writing-desk in a distant part of the room, he became very affable, and walked back to his chair smartly.

" If you intend to build villages and assemble a

population near the mine, you shall require a decree of the Minister of the Interior for that," he suggested in a business-like manner.

"I have already sent a memorial," said Charles Gould steadily, "and I reckon now confidently upon your Excellency's favourable conclusions."

The Excellency was a man of many moods. With the receipt of the money a great mellowness had descended upon his simple soul. Unexpectedly he fetched a deep sigh.

"Ah, Don Carlos! What we want is advanced men like you in the province. The lethargy—the lethargy of these aristocrats! The want of public spirit! The absence of all enterprise! I, with my profound studies in Europe, you understand——"

With one hand thrust into his swelling bosom, he rose and fell on his toes, and for ten minutes, almost without drawing breath, went on hurling himself intellectually to the assault of Charles Gould's polite silence ; and when, stopping abruptly, he fell back into his chair, it was as though he had been beaten off from a fortress. To save his dignity he hastened to dismiss this silent man with a solemn inclination of the head and the words, pronounced with moody, fatigued condescension:

"You may depend upon my enlightened goodwill as long as your conduct as a good citizen deserves it."

He took up a paper fan and began to cool himself with a consequential air, while Charles Gould bowed and withdrew. Then he dropped the fan at once, and stared with an appearance of wonder and perplexity at the closed door for quite a long time. At last he shrugged his shoulders as if to assure himself of his disdain. Cold, dull. No intellectuality. Red hair. A true Englishman. He despised him.

His face darkened. What meant this unimpressed and frigid behaviour ? He was the first of the successive politicians sent out from the capital to rule the Occi-

dental Province whom the manner of Charles Gould
in official intercourse was to strike as offensively independent.

Charles Gould assumed that if the appearance of
listening to deplorable balderdash must form part of
the price he had to pay for being left unmolested, the
obligation of uttering balderdash personally was by no
means included in the bargain. He drew the line there.
To these provincial autocrats, before whom the peaceable
population of all classes had been accustomed to tremble,
the reserve of that English-looking engineer caused an
uneasiness which swung to and fro between cringing and
truculence. Gradually all of them discovered that, no
matter what party was in power, that man remained in
most effective touch with the higher authorities in Sta.
Marta.

This was a fact, and it accounted perfectly for the
Goulds being by no means so wealthy as the engineer-
in-chief on the new railway could legitimately suppose.
Following the advice of Don José Avellanos, who was a
man of good counsel (though rendered timid by his
horrible experiences of Guzman Bento's time), Charles
Gould had kept clear of the capital ; but in the current
gossip of the foreign residents there he was known (with a
good deal of seriousness underlying the irony) by the nickname of " King of Sulaco."   An advocate of the Costaguana Bar, a man of reputed ability and good character,
member of the distinguished Moraga family possessing
extensive estates in the Sulaco Valley, was pointed out to
strangers, with a shade of mystery and respect, as the
agent of the San Tomé mine—" political, you know."
He was tall, black-whiskered, and discreet. It was
known that he had easy access to ministers, and that the
numerous Costaguana generals were always anxious to
dine at his house. Presidents granted him audience with
facility. He corresponded actively with his maternal
uncle, Don José Avellanos ; but his letters—unless those

expressing formally his dutiful affection—were seldom
entrusted to the Costaguana Post Office. There the
envelopes are opened, indiscriminately, with the frankness of a brazen and childish impudence characteristic of
some Spanish-American Governments. But it must be
noted that at about the time of the reopening of the San
Tomé mine the muleteer who had been employed by
Charles Gould in his preliminary travels on the Campo
added his small train of animals to the thin stream of
traffic carried over the mountain passes between the Sta.
Marta upland and the Valley of Sulaco. There are no
travellers by that arduous and unsafe route unless under
very exceptional circumstances, and the state of inland
trade did not visibly require additional transport facilities ;
but the man seemed to find his account in it. A few
packages were always found for him whenever he took
the road. Very brown and wooden, in goatskin breeches
with the hair outside, he sat near the tail of his own
smart mule, his great hat turned against the sun, an expression of blissful vacancy on his long face, humming
day after day a love-song in a plaintive key, or, without
a change of expression, letting out a yell at his small
tropilla in front. A round little guitar hung high up
on his back ; and there was a place scooped out artistic-
ally in the wood of one of his pack-saddles where a
tightly rolled piece of paper could be slipped in, the
wooden plug replaced, and the coarse canvas nailed on
again. When in Sulaco it was his practice to smoke and
doze all day long (as though he had no care in the world)
on a stone bench outside the doorway of the Casa Gould
and facing the windows of the Avellanos house. Years
and years ago his mother had been chief laundry-woman
in that family—very accomplished in the matter of clear-
starching. He himself had been born on one of their
haciendas. His name was Bonifacio, and Don José,
crossing the street about five o'clock to call on Doña
Emilia, always acknowledged his humble salute by some

movement of hand or head. The porters of both houses
conversed lazily with him in tones of grave intimacy.
His evenings he devoted to gambling and to calls in a
spirit of generous festivity upon the *peyne d'oro* girls in
the more remote side-streets of the town. But he, too,
was a discreet man.

CHAPTER EIGHT

THOSE of us whom business or curiosity took to Sulaco in these years before the first advent of the railway can remember the steadying effect of the San Tomé mine upon the life of that remote province. The outward appearances had not changed then as they have changed since, as I am told, with cable cars running along the streets of the Constitution, and carriage roads far into the country, to Rincon and other villages, where the foreign merchants and the Ricos generally have their modern villas, and a vast railway goods yard by the harbour, which has a quayside, a long range of ware-houses, and quite serious, organised labour troubles of its own.

Nobody had ever heard of labour troubles then. The cargadores of the port formed, indeed, an unruly brother-hood of all sorts of scum, with a patron saint of their own. They went on strike regularly (every bull-fight day), a form of trouble that even Nostromo at the height of his prestige could never cope with efficiently ; but the morning after each fiesta, before the Indian market-women had opened their mat parasols on the plaza, when the snows of Higuerota gleamed pale over the town on a yet black sky, the appearance of a phantom-like horseman mounted on a silver-grey mare solved the problem of labour without fail. His steed paced the lanes of the slums and the weed-grown enclosures within the old ramparts, between the black, lightless cluster of huts, like cow-byres, like dog-kennels. The horseman hammered with the butt

of a heavy revolver at the doors of low pulperias, of
obscene lean-to sheds sloping against the tumble-down
piece of a noble wall, at the wooden sides of dwellings so
flimsy that the sound of snores and sleepy mutters within
could be heard in the pauses of the thundering clatter of
his blows. He called out men's names menacingly from
the saddle, once, twice. The drowsy answers—grumpy,
conciliating, savage, jocular, or deprecating—came out
into the silent darkness in which the horseman sat still,
and presently a dark figure would flit out coughing in the
still air. Sometimes a low-toned woman cried through
the window-hole softly, " He's coming directly, Señor,"
and the horseman waited silent on a motionless horse.
But if perchance he had to dismount, then, after a while,
from the door of that hovel or of that pulperia, with a
ferocious scuffle and stifled imprecations, a cargador
would fly out head first and hands abroad, to sprawl
under the forelegs of the silver-grey mare, who only
pricked forward her sharp little ears. She was used
to that work ; and the man, picking himself up, would
walk away hastily from Nostromo's revolver, reeling a
little along the street and snarling low curses. At sunrise Captain Mitchell, coming out anxiously in his night-
attire on to the wooden balcony running the whole length
of the O.S.N. Company's lonely building by the shore,
would see the lighters already under way, figures moving
busily about the cargo cranes, perhaps hear the invaluable
Nostromo, now dismounted and in the checked shirt and
red sash of a Mediterranean sailor, bawling orders from
the end of the jetty in a stentorian voice. A fellow in a
thousand !

The material apparatus of perfected civilisation
which obliterates the individuality of old towns under
the stereotyped conveniences of modern life had not
intruded as yet ; but over the worn-out antiquity of
Sulaco, so characteristic with its stuccoed houses and
barred windows, with the great yellowy-white walls of

abandoned convents behind the rows of sombre green cypresses, that fact—very modern in its spirit—the San Tomé mine had already thrown its subtle influence. It had altered, too, the outward character of the crowds on feast days on the plaza before the open portal of the cathedral, by the number of white ponchos with a green stripe affected as holiday wear by the San Tomé miners. They had also adopted white hats with green cord and braid—articles of good quality, which could be obtained in the storehouse of the administration for very little money. A peaceable Cholo wearing these colours (unusual in Costaguana) was somehow very seldom beaten to within an inch of his life on a charge of disrespect to the town police ; neither ran he much risk of being suddenly lassoed on the road by a recruiting party of lanceros—a method of voluntary enlistment looked upon as almost legal in the Republic. Whole villages were known to have volunteered for the army in that way ; but, as Don Pépé would say with a hopeless shrug to Mrs. Gould, " What would you ! Poor people ! Pobrecitos ! Pobrecitos ! But the State must have its soldiers."

Thus professionally spoke Don Pépé, the fighter, with pendent moustaches, a nut-brown, lean face, and a clean run of a cast-iron jaw, suggesting the type of a cattle-herd horseman from the great llanos of the South. " If you will listen to an old officer of Paez, Señores," was the exordium of all his speeches in the Aristocratic Club of Sulaco, where he was admitted on account of his past services to the extinct cause of Federation. The club, dating from the days of the proclamation of Costaguana's independence, boasted many names of liberators amongst its first founders. Suppressed arbitrarily innumerable times by various Governments, with memories of proscriptions and of at least one wholesale massacre of its members, sadly assembled for a banquet by the order of a zealous military com-

mandante (their bodies were afterwards stripped naked
and flung into the plaza out of the windows by the
lowest scum of the populace), it was again flourishing,
at that period, peacefully. It extended to strangers
the large hospitality of the cool, big rooms of its historic
quarters in the front part of a house, once the residence
of a high official of the Holy Office. The two wings,
shut up, crumbled behind the nailed doors, and what
may be described as a grove of young orange trees grown
in the unpaved patio, concealed the utter ruin of the
back part, facing the gate. You turned in from the
street, as if entering a secluded orchard, where you
came upon the foot of a disjointed staircase, guarded by a
moss-stained effigy of some saintly bishop, mitred and
staffed, and bearing the indignity of a broken nose
meekly, with his fine stone hands crossed on his breast.
The chocolate-coloured faces of servants with mops of
black hair peeped at you from above; the click of billiard
balls came to your ears; and ascending the steps, you
would perhaps see in the first sala, very stiff upon a
straight-backed chair, in a good light, Don Pépé moving
his long moustaches as he spelt his way, at arm's length,
through an old Sta. Marta newspaper. His horse—a
stony-hearted but persevering black brute with a hammer
head—you would have seen in the street dozing motionless under an immense saddle, with its nose almost
touching the curbstone of the sidewalk.

Don Pépé, when " down from the mountain," as the
phrase, often heard in Sulaco, went, could also be seen
in the drawing-room of the Casa Gould. He sat with
modest assurance at some distance from the tea-table.
With his knees close together, and a kindly twinkle of
drollery in his deep-set eyes, he would throw his small
and ironic pleasantries into the current of conversation.
There was in that man a sort of sane, humorous shrewd-
ness, and a vein of genuine humanity so often found in
simple old soldiers of proved courage who have seen

much desperate service. Of course he knew nothing whatever of mining, but his employment was of a special kind. He was in charge of the whole population in the territory of the mine, which extended from the head of the gorge to where the cart track from the foot of the mountain enters the plain, crossing a stream over a little wooden bridge painted green—green, the colour of hope, being also the colour of the mine.

It was reported in Sulaco that up there " at the mountain " Don Pépé walked about precipitous paths, girt with a great sword and in a shabby uniform with tarnished bullion epaulettes of a senior major. Most miners being Indians, with big wild eyes, addressed him as Taita (father), as these barefooted people of Costaguana will address anybody who wears shoes ; but it was Basilio, Mr. Gould's own mozo and the head servant of the Casa, who, in all good faith and from a sense of propriety, announced him once in the solemn words, " El Señor Gobernador has arrived."

Don José Avellanos, then in the drawing-room, was delighted beyond measure at the aptness of the title, with which he greeted the old major banteringly as soon as the latter's soldierly figure appeared in the doorway. Don Pépé only smiled in his long moustaches, as much as to say, " You might have found a worse name for an old soldier."

And El Señor Gobernador he had remained, with his small jokes upon his function and upon his domain, where he affirmed with humorous exaggeration to Mrs. Gould :

" No two stones could come together anywhere without the Gobernador hearing the click, Señora."

And he would tap his ear with the tip of his forefinger knowingly. Even when the number of the miners alone rose to over six hundred he seemed to know each of them individually, all the innumerable Josés, Manuels, Ignacios, from the villages primero — segundo—or tercero (there were three mining villages) under his government. He could distinguish them not only by their flat, joyless faces, which to Mrs. Gould looked all alike, as if run into the same ancestral mould of suffering and patience, but apparently also by the infinitely graduated shades of reddish-brown, of blackish-brown, of coppery-brown backs, as the two shifts, stripped to linen drawers and leather skull-caps, mingled together with a confusion of naked limbs, of shouldered picks, swinging lamps, in a great shuffle of sandalled feet on the open plateau before the entrance of the main tunnel. It was a time of pause. The Indian boys leaned idly against the long line of little cradle wagons standing empty; the screeners and ore-breakers squatted on their heels smoking long cigars; the great wooden shoots slanting over the edge of the tunnel plateau were silent; and only the ceaseless, violent rush of water in the open flumes could be heard, murmuring fiercely, with the splash and rumble of revolving turbine-wheels, and the thudding march of the stamps pounding to powder the treasure rock on the plateau below. The heads of gangs, distinguished by brass medals hanging on their bare breasts, marshalled their squads; and at last the mountain would swallow one-half of the silent crowd, while the other half would move off in long files down the zigzag paths leading to the bottom of the gorge. It was deep; and, far below, a thread of vegetation winding between the blazing rock-faces resembled a slender green cord, in which three lumpy knots of banana patches, palm-leaf roots, and shady trees marked the Village One, Village Two, Village Three, housing the miners of the Gould Concession.

Whole families had been moving from the first towards the spot in the Higuerota range, whence the rumour of work and safety had spread over the pastoral Campo, forcing its way also, even as the waters of a high flood, into the nooks and crannies of the distant blue walls of the sierras. Father first, in a pointed straw hat, then the mother with the bigger children, generally also a diminutive donkey, all under burdens, except the leader himself, or perhaps some grown girl, the pride of the family, stepping barefooted and straight as an arrow, with braids of raven hair, a thick, haughty profile, and no load to carry but the small guitar of the country and a pair of soft leather sandals tied together on her back. At the sight of such parties strung out on the cross trails between the pastures, or camped by the side of the royal road, travellers on horseback would remark to each other:

" More people going to the San Tomé mine. We shall see others to-morrow."

And spurring on in the dusk they would discuss the great news of the province, the news of the San Tomé mine. A rich Englishman was going to work it—and perhaps not an Englishman, *Quien sabe?* A foreigner with much money. Oh yes, it had begun. A party of men who had been to Sulaco with a herd of black bulls for the next corrida had reported that from the porch of the posada in Rincon, only a short league from the town, the lights on the mountain were visible, twinkling above the trees. And there was a woman seen riding a horse sideways, not in the chair seat, but upon a sort of saddle, and a man's hat on her head. She walked about, too, on foot up the mountain paths. A woman engineer, it seemed she was.

" What an absurdity ! Impossible, Señor ! "

" Si ! Si ! Una Americana del Norte."

" Ah, well ! if your worship is informed. Una Americana ; it need be something of that sort."

And they would laugh a little with astonishment and scorn, keeping a wary eye on the shadows of the road, for one is liable to meet bad men when travelling late on the Campo.

And it was not only the men that Don Pépé knew so well, but he seemed able, with one attentive, thoughtful

7

glance, to classify each woman, girl, or growing youth of his domain. It was only the small fry that puzzled him sometimes. He and the padre could be seen frequently side by side, meditative and gazing across the street of a village at a lot of sedate brown children, trying to sort them out, as it were, in low, consulting tones, or else they would together put searching questions as to the parentage of some small, staid urchin met wandering, naked and grave, along the road with a cigar in his baby mouth, and perhaps his mother's rosary, purloined for purposes of ornamentation, hanging in a loop of beads low down on his rotund little stomach. The spiritual and temporal pastors of the mine flock were very good friends. With Dr. Monygham, the medical pastor, who had accepted the charge from Mrs. Gould, and lived in the hospital building, they were on not so intimate terms. But no one could be on intimate terms with El Señor Doctor, who, with his twisted shoulders, drooping head, sardonic mouth, and sidelong bitter glance, was mysterious and uncanny. The other two authorities worked in harmony. Father Romàn, dried-up, small, alert, wrinkled, with big round eyes, a sharp chin, and a great snuff-taker, was an old campaigner too ; he had shriven many simple souls on the battle-fields of the Republic, kneeling by the dying on hill-sides, in the long grass, in the gloom of the forests, to hear the last confession with the smell of gunpowder smoke in his nostrils, the rattle of muskets, the hum and spatter of bullets in his ears. And where was the harm if, at the Presbytery, they had a game with a pack of greasy cards in the early evening, before Don Pépé went his last rounds to see that all the watchmen of the mine— a body organised by himself—were at their posts ? For that last duty before he slept Don Pépé did actually gird his old sword on the verandah of an unmistakable American white frame house, which Father Romàn called the Presbytery. Near by, a long, low, dark building, steeple-roofed, like a vast barn with a wooden cross over the gable, was the miners' chapel. There Father Romàn said Mass every day before a sombre altarpiece representing the Resurrection, the grey slab of the tombstone balanced on one corner, a figure soaring upwards, long-limbed and livid, in an oval of pallid light, and a helmeted brown legionary smitten down, right across the bituminous foreground. " This picture, my children, *muy linda e maravillosa*," Father Romàn would say to some of his flock, " which you behold here through the munificence of the wife of our Señor Administrador, has been painted in Europe, a country of saints and miracles, and much greater than our Costaguana." And he would take a pinch of snuff with unction. But when once an inquisitive spirit desired to know in what direction this Europe was situated, whether up or down the coast, Father Romàn, to conceal his perplexity, became very reserved and severe. " No doubt it is extremely far away. But ignorant sinners like you of the San Tomé mine should think earnestly of everlasting punishment instead of inquiring into the magnitude of the earth, with its countries and populations altogether beyond your understanding."

With a " Good-night, Padre," " Good-night, Don Pépé," the Gobernador would go off, holding up his sabre against his side, his body bent forward, with a long, plodding stride, in the dark. The jocularity proper to an innocent card game for a few cigars or a bundle of yerba was replaced at once by the stern duty mood of an officer setting out to visit the outposts of an encamped army. One loud blast of the whistle that hung from his neck provoked instantly a great shrilling of responding whistles, mingled with the barking of dogs, that would calm down slowly at last, away up at the head of the gorge ; and in the stillness two serenos, on guard by the bridge, would appear walking noiselessly towards him. On one side of the road a long frame building—the

store—would be closed and barricaded from end to
end ; facing it another white frame house, still longer,
and with a verandah—the hospital—would have lights
in the two windows of Dr. Monygham's quarters. Even
the delicate foliage of a clump of pepper trees did not
stir, so breathless would be the darkness warmed by
the radiation of the overheated rocks. Don Pépé
would stand still for a moment with the two motionless
serenos before him, and, abruptly, high up on the sheer
face of the mountain, dotted with single torches, like
drops of fire fallen from the two great blazing clusters
of lights above, the ore shoots would begin to rattle.
The great clattering, shuffling noise, gathering speed
and weight, would be caught up by the walls of the gorge,
and sent upon the plain in a growl of thunder. The
posadero in Rincon swore that on calm nights, by listening intently, he could catch the sound in his doorway
as of a storm in the mountains.

To Charles Gould's fancy it seemed that the sound
must reach the uttermost limits of the province. Riding
at night towards the mine, it would meet him at the edge
of a little wood just beyond Rincon. There was no mistaking the growling mutter of the mountain pouring its
stream of treasure under the stamps ; and it came to his
heart with the peculiar force of a proclamation thundered
forth over the land and the marvellousness of an accomplished fact fulfilling an audacious desire. He had heard
this very sound in his imagination on that far-off evening
when his wife and himself, after a tortuous ride through a
strip of forest, had reined in their horses near the stream,
and had gazed for the first time upon the jungle-grown
solitude of the gorge. The head of a palm rose here and
there. In a high ravine round the corner of the San
Tomé mountain (which is square like a blockhouse), the
thread of a slender waterfall flashed bright and glassy
through the dark green of the heavy fronds of tree-ferns.
Don Pépé, in attendance, rode up, and, stretching his

arm up the gorge, had declared with mock solemnity, " Behold the very paradise of snakes, Señora."

And then they had wheeled their horses and ridden back to sleep that night at Rincon. The alcalde—an old, skinny Moreno, a sergeant of Guzman Bento's time— had cleared respectfully out of his house with his three pretty daughters, to make room for the foreign Señora and their worships the caballeros. All he asked Charles Gould (whom he took for a mysterious and official person) to do for him was to remind the supreme Government— El Gobierno supremo—of a pension (amounting to about a dollar a month) to which he believed himself entitled. It had been promised to him, he affirmed, straightening his bent back martially, " many years ago, for my valour in the wars with the wild Indios when a young man, Señor."

The waterfall existed no longer. The tree-ferns that had luxuriated in its spray had died around the dried-up pool, and the high ravine was only a big trench half filled up with the refuse of excavations and tailings. The torrent, dammed up above, sent its water rushing along the open flumes of scooped tree trunks striding on trestle- legs to the turbines working the stamps on the lower plateau—the *mesa grande* of the San Tomé mountain. Only the memory of the waterfall, with its amazing fernery, like a hanging garden above the rocks of the gorge, was preserved in Mrs. Gould's water-colour sketch ; she had made it hastily one day from a cleared patch in the bushes, sitting in the shade of a roof of straw erected for her on three rough poles under Don Pépé's direction.

Mrs. Gould had seen it all from the beginning : the clearing of the wilderness, the making of the road, the cutting of new paths up the cliff face of San Tomé. For weeks together she had lived on the spot with her husband ; and she was so little in Sulaco during that year that the appearance of the Gould carriage on the Alameda would cause a social excitement. From the heavy family coaches full of stately señoras and black-eyed señoritas rolling solemnly in the shaded alley white hands were waved towards her with animation in a flutter of greetings. Doña Emilia was " down from the mountain."

But not for long. Doña Emilia would be gone " up to the mountain " in a day or two, and her sleek carriage mules would have an easy time of it for another long spell. She had watched the erection of the first frame-house put up on the lower mesa for an office and Don Pépé's quarters ; she heard with a thrill of thankful emotion the first wagon-load of ore rattle down the then only shoot ; she had stood by her husband's side perfectly silent, and gone cold all over with excitement at the instant when the first battery of only fifteen stamps was put in motion for the first time. On the occasion when the fires under the first set of retorts in their shed had glowed far into the night, she did not retire to rest on the rough cadre set up for her in the as yet bare frame-house till she had seen the first spongy lump of silver yielded to the hazards of the world by the dark depths of the Gould Concession ; she had laid her unmercenary hands, with an eagerness that made them tremble, upon the first silver ingot turned out still warm from the mould ; and by her imaginative estimate of its power she endowed that lump of metal with a justificative conception, as though it were not a mere fact, but something far-reaching and impalpable, like the true expression of an emotion or the emergence of a principle.

Don Pépé, extremely interested too, looked over her shoulder with a smile that, making longitudinal folds on his face, caused it to resemble a leathern mask with a benignantly diabolic expression.

" Would not the muchachos of Hernandez like to get hold of this insignificant object, that looks, *por Dios*, very much like a piece of tin ? " he remarked jocularly.

Hernandez, the robber, had been an inoffensive, small ranchero, kidnapped with circumstances of peculiar atrocity from his home during one of the civil wars, and forced to serve in the army. There his conduct as soldier was exemplary, till, watching his chance, he killed his colonel, and managed to get clear away. With a band of deserters, who chose him for their chief, he had taken refuge beyond the wild and waterless Bolson de Tonoro. The haciendas paid him blackmail in cattle and horses ; extraordinary stories were told of his powers and of his wonderful escapes from capture. He used to ride, single-handed, into the villages and the little towns on the Campo, driving a pack-mule before him, with two revolvers in his belt, go straight to the shop or store, select what he wanted, and ride away unopposed because of the terror his exploits and his audacity inspired. Poor country people he usually left alone ; the upper class were often stopped on the roads and robbed ; but any unlucky official that fell into his hands was sure to get a severe flogging. The army officers did not like his name to be mentioned in their presence. His followers, mounted on stolen horses, laughed at the pursuit of the regular cavalry sent to hunt them down, and whom they took pleasure in ambushing most scientifically in the broken ground of their own fastness. Expeditions had been fitted out ; a price had been put upon his head ; even attempts had been made, treacherously of course, to open negotiations with him, without in the slightest way affecting the even tenor of his career. At last, in true Costaguana fashion, the Fiscal of Tonoro, who was ambitious of the glory of having reduced the famous Hernandez, offered him a sum of money and a safe-conduct out of the country for the betrayal of his band. But Hernandez evidently was not of the stuff of which the distinguished military politicians and conspirators of Costaguana are made. This clever but common device (which frequently works like a charm in putting down revolutions) failed with the chief of vulgar salteadores. It promised well for the Fiscal at first, but ended very badly for the squadron of lanceros posted (by the Fiscal's directions) in a fold of the ground into which Hernandez had promised to lead his unsuspecting followers. They came, indeed, at the appointed time, but creeping on their hands and knees through the bush, and only let their presence be known by a general discharge of fire-arms, which emptied many saddles. The troopers who escaped came riding very hard into Tonoro. It is said that their commanding officer (who, being better mounted, rode far ahead of the rest) afterwards got into a state of despairing intoxication and beat the ambitious Fiscal severely with the flat of his sabre in the presence of his wife and daughters, for bringing this disgrace upon the National Army. The highest civil official of Tonoro, falling to the ground in a swoon, was further kicked all over the body and rowelled with sharp spurs about the neck and face because of the great sensitiveness of his military colleague. This gossip of the inland Campo, so characteristic of the rulers of the country with its story of oppression, inefficiency, fatuous methods, treachery, and savage brutality, was perfectly known to Mrs. Gould. That it should be accepted with no indignant comment by people of intelligence, refinement, and character as something inherent in the nature of things, was one of the symptoms of degradation that had the power to exasperate her almost to the verge of despair. Still, looking at the ingot of silver, she shook her head at Don Pépé's remark :

" If it had not been for the lawless tyranny of your Government, Don Pépé, many an outlaw now with Hernandez would be living peaceably and happy by the honest work of his hands."

" Señora," cried Don Pépé, with enthusiasm, " it is true ! It is as if God had given you the power to look into the very breasts of people. You have seen them working round you, Doña Emilia—meek as lambs, patient like their own burros, brave like lions. I have led them to the very muzzles of guns—I, who stand here before you, Señora—in the time of Paez, who was full of generosity, and in courage only approached by the uncle of Don Carlos here, as far as I know.   No wonder there are bandits in the Campo when there are none but thieves, swindlers, and sanguinary macaques to rule us in Sta. Marta !   However, all the same, a bandit is a bandit, and we shall have a dozen good straight Winchesters to ride with the silver down to Sulaco."

Mrs. Gould's ride with the first silver escort to Sulaco was the closing episode of what she called " my camp life " before she had settled in her town house permanently, as was proper and even necessary for the wife of the administrator of such an important institution as the San Tomé mine.   For the San Tomé mine was to become an institution, a rallying-point for everything in the province that needed order and stability to live.   Security seemed to flow upon this land from the mountain gorge.   The authorities of Sulaco had learned that the San Tomé mine could make it worth their while to leave things and people alone.   This was the nearest approach to the rule of common sense and justice Charles Gould felt it possible to secure at first. In fact, the mine, with its organisation, its population growing fiercely attached to their position of privileged safety, with its armoury, with its Don Pépé, with its armed body of serenos (where, it was said, many an outlaw and deserter — and even some members of Hernandez's band—had found a place), the mine was a power in the land.   As a certain prominent man in Sta. Marta had exclaimed with a hollow laugh, once, when discussing the line of action taken by the Sulaco authorities at a time of political crisis :

" You call these men Government officials ?   They ? Never !   They are officials of the mine—officials of the Concession—I tell you."

The prominent man (who was then a person in power,

with a lemon-coloured face and a very short and curly, not to say woolly, head of hair) went so far in his temporary discontent as to shake his yellow fist under the nose of his interlocutor, and shriek :

" Yes ! All ! Silence ! All ! I tell you ! The political Jefé, the chief of the police, the chief of the customs, the general, all, all, are the officials of that Gould."

Thereupon an intrepid but low and argumentative murmur would flow on for a space in the ministerial cabinet, and the prominent man's passion would end in a cynical shrug of the shoulders. After all, he seemed to say, what did it matter as long as the minister himself was not forgotten during his brief day of authority? But all the same, the unofficial agent of the San Tomé mine, working for a good cause, had his moments of anxiety, which were reflected in his letters to Don José Avellanos, his maternal uncle.

" No sanguinary macaque from Sta. Marta shall set foot on that part of Costaguana which lies beyond the San Tomé bridge," Don Pépé used to assure Mrs. Gould. " Except, of course, as an honoured guest—for our Señor Administrador is a deep politico." But to Charles Gould, in his own room, the old Major would remark with a grim and soldierly cheeriness, " We are all playing our heads at this game."

Don José Avellanos would mutter " Imperium in imperio, Emilia, my soul," with an air of profound self-satisfaction which, somehow, in a curious way, seemed to contain a queer admixture of bodily discomfort. But that, perhaps, could only be visible to the initiated.

And for the initiated it was a wonderful place, this drawing-room of the Casa Gould, with its momentary glimpses of the master—El Señor Administrador—older, harder, mysteriously silent, with the lines deepened on his English, ruddy, out-of-doors complexion ; flitting on his thin cavalryman's legs across the doorways, either just " back from the mountain " or, with jingling spurs and riding-whip under his arm, on the point of starting " for the mountain." Then Don Pépé, modestly martial in his chair, the llanero who seemed somehow to have found his martial jocularity, his knowledge of the world, and his manner perfect for his station, in the midst of savage armed contests with his kind ; Avellanos, polished and familiar, the diplomatist with his loquacity covering much caution and wisdom in delicate advice, with his manuscript of an historical work on Costaguana, entitled *Fifty Years of Misrule*, which, at present, he thought it was not prudent (even if it were possible) " to give to the world " ; these three, and also Doña Emilia amongst them, gracious, small, and fairy-like, before the glittering tea-set, with one common master-thought in their heads, with one common feeling of a tense situation, with one ever-present aim to preserve the inviolable character of the mine at every cost. And there was also to be seen Captain Mitchell, a little apart, near one of the long windows, with an air of old-fashioned, neat old bachelorhood about him, slightly pompous, in a white waistcoat, a little disregarded and unconscious of it ; utterly in the dark, and imagining himself to be in the thick of things. The good man, having spent a clear thirty years of his life on the high seas before getting what he called a " shore billet," was astonished at the importance of transactions (other than relating to shipping) which take place on dry land. Almost every event out of the usual daily course " marked an epoch " for him or else was " history " ; unless with his pomposity struggling with a discomfited droop of his rubicund, rather handsome face, set off by snow-white close hair and short whiskers, he would mutter :

" Ah, that ! That, sir, was a mistake."

The reception of the first consignment of San Tomé silver for shipment to San Francisco in one of the O.S.N. Company's mail-boats had, of course, " marked an epoch " for Captain Mitchell. The ingots packed in boxes of stiff ox-hide with plaited handles, small enough to be carried easily by two men, were brought down by the serenos of the mine walking in careful couples along the half-mile or so of steep, zigzag paths to the foot of the mountain. There they would be loaded into a string of two-wheeled carts, resembling roomy coffers with a door at the back, and harnessed tandem with two mules each, waiting under the guard of armed and mounted serenos. Don Pépé padlocked each door in succession, and at the signal of his whistle the string of carts would move off, closely surrounded by the clank of spur and carbine, with jolts and cracking of whips, with a sudden deep rumble over the boundary bridge (" into the land of thieves and sanguinary macaques," Don Pépé defined that crossing); hats bobbing in the first light of the dawn, on the heads of cloaked figures; Winchesters on hip; bridle hands protruding lean and brown from under the falling folds of the ponchos. The convoy skirting a little wood, along the mine trail, between the mud huts and low walls of Rincon, increased its pace on the *camino real*, mules urged to speed, escort galloping, Don Carlos riding alone ahead of a dust-storm, affording a vague vision of long ears of mules, of fluttering little green and white flags stuck upon each cart; of raised arms in a mob of sombreros with the white gleam of ranging eyes; and Don Pépé, hardly visible in the rear of that rattling dust trail, with a stiff seat and impassive face, rising and falling rhythmically on a ewe-necked silver-bitted black brute with a hammer head.

The sleepy people in the little clusters of huts, in the small ranchos near the road, recognised by the headlong sound the charge of the San Tomé silver escort towards the crumbling wall of the city on the Campo side. They came to the doors to see it dash by over ruts and stones, with a clatter and clank and cracking of whips, with the

reckless rush and precise driving of a field battery hurrying into action, and the solitary English figure of the
Señor Administrador riding far ahead in the lead.

In the fenced roadside paddocks loose horses galloped
wildly for a while ; the heavy cattle stood up breast-deep
in the grass, lowing mutteringly at the flying noise ; a
meek Indian villager would glance back once and hasten
to shove his loaded little donkey bodily against a wall, out
of the way of the San Tomé silver escort going to the sea ;
a small knot of chilly leperos under the Stone Horse of the
Alameda would mutter " Caramba ! " on seeing it take
a wide curve at a gallop and dart into the empty Street of
the Constitution ; for it was considered the correct thing,
the only proper style, by the mule-drivers of the San Tomé
mine, to go through the waking town from end to end
without a check in the speed, as if chased by a devil.

The early sunshine glowed on the delicate primrose,
pale pink, pale blue fronts of the big houses with all their
gates shut yet, and no face behind the iron bars of the
windows. In the whole sunlit range of empty balconies
along the street only one white figure would be visible
high up above the clear pavement—the wife of the Señor
Administrador—leaning over to see the escort go by to
the harbour, a mass of heavy fair hair twisted up negligently on her little head, and a lot of lace about the neck
of her muslin wrapper. With a smile to her husband's
single, quick, upward glance, she would watch the whole
thing stream past below her feet with an orderly uproar,
till she answered by a friendly sign the salute of the
galloping Don Pépé, the stiff, deferential inclination with
a sweep of the hat below the knee.

The string of padlocked carts lengthened, the size of
the escort grew bigger as the years went on. Every three
months an increasing stream of treasure swept through
the streets of Sulaco on its way to the strong-room in the
O.S.N. Company's building by the harbour, there to await
shipment for the North. Increasing in volume, and of

immense value also ; for, as Charles Gould told his wife once with some exultation, there had never been seen anything in the world to approach the vein of the Gould Concession. For them both, each passing of the escort under the balconies of the Casa Gould was like another victory gained in the conquest of peace for Sulaco.

No doubt the initial action of Charles Gould had been helped at the beginning by a period of comparative peace which occurred just about that time ; and also by the general softening of manners as compared with the epoch of civil wars whence had emerged the iron tyranny of Guzman Bento of fearful memory. In the contests that broke out at the end of his rule (which had kept peace in the country for a whole fifteen years) there was more fatuous imbecility, plenty of cruelty and suffering still, but much less of the old-time fierce and blind ferocious political fanaticism. It was all more vile, more base, more contemptible, and infinitely more manageable in the very outspoken cynicism of motives. It was more clearly a brazen-faced scramble for a constantly diminishing quantity of booty ; since all enterprise had been stupidly killed in the land. Thus it came to pass that the province of Sulaco, once the field of cruel party vengeances, had become in a way one of the considerable prizes of political career. The great of the earth (in Sta. Marta) reserved the posts in the old Occidental State to those nearest and dearest to them : nephews, brothers, husbands of favourite sisters, bosom friends, trusty supporters—or prominent supporters of whom perhaps they were afraid. It was the blessed province of great opportunities and of largest salaries ; for the San Tomé mine had its own unofficial pay list, whose items and amounts, fixed in consultation by Charles Gould and Señor Avellanos, were known to a prominent business man in the United States, who for twenty minutes or so in every month gave his undivided attention to Sulaco affairs. At the same time the material interests of all sorts, backed up by the influence of the San Tomé mine, were quietly gathering substance in that part of the Republic. If, for instance, the Sulaco collectorship was generally understood, in the political world of the capital, to open the way to the Ministry of Finance, and so on for every official post, then, on the other hand, the despondent business circles of the Republic had come to consider the Occidental Province as the promised land of safety, especially if a man managed to get on good terms with the administration of the mine. " Charles Gould ; excellent fellow ! Absolutely necessary to make sure of him before taking a single step. Get an introduction to him from Moraga if you can—the agent of the King of Sulaco, don't you know."

No wonder, then, that Sir John, coming from Europe to smooth the path for his railway, had been meeting the name (and even the nickname) of Charles Gould at every turn in Costaguana. The agent of the San Tomé Administration in Sta. Marta (a polished, well-informed gentleman, Sir John thought him) had certainly helped so greatly in bringing about the presidential tour that he began to think that there was something in the faint whispers hinting at the immense occult influence of the Gould Concession. What was currently whispered was this—that the San Tomé Administration had, in part at least, financed the last revolution, which had brought into a five-year dictatorship Don Vincente Ribiera, a man of culture and of unblemished character, invested with a mandate of reform by the best elements of the State. Serious, well-informed men seemed to believe the fact, to hope for better things, for the establishment of legality, of good faith and order in public life. So much the better, then, thought Sir John. He worked always on a great scale ; there was a loan to the State, and a project for systematic colonisation of the Occidental Province, involved in one vast scheme with the construction of the National Central Railway. Good faith, order, honesty,

peace, were badly wanted for this great development of
material interests.   Anybody on the side of these things,
and especially if able to help, had an importance in Sir
John's eyes.   He had not been disappointed in the " King
of Sulaco."   The local difficulties had fallen away, as the
engineer-in-chief had foretold they would, before Charles
Gould's mediation.   Sir John had been extremely fêted
in Sulaco, next to the President-Dictator, a fact which
might have accounted for the evident ill-humour General
Montero displayed at lunch given on board the *Juno* just
before she was to sail, taking away from Sulaco the
President-Dictator and the distinguished foreign guests in
his train.

The Excellentissimo ("the hope of honest men," as
Don José had addressed him in a public speech delivered
in the name of the Provincial Assembly of Sulaco) sat
at the head of the long table ; Captain Mitchell, positively stony-eyed and purple in the face with the solemnity
of this " historical event," occupied the foot as the
representative of the O.S.N. Company in Sulaco, the
hosts of that informal function, with the captain of the
ship and some minor officials from the shore around
him.   Those cheery, swarthy little gentlemen cast
jovial side-glances at the bottles of champagne beginning
to pop behind the guests' backs in the hands of the ship's
stewards.   The amber wine creamed up to the rims of
the glasses.

Charles Gould had his place next to a foreign envoy,
who, in a listless undertone, had been talking to him
fitfully of hunting and shooting.   The well-nourished,
pale face, with an eyeglass and drooping yellow moustache,
made the Señor Administrador appear by contrast
twice as sunbaked, more flaming red, a hundred times
more intensely and silently alive.   Don José Avellanos
touched elbows with the other foreign diplomat, a dark
man with a quiet, watchful, self-confident demeanour,
and a touch of reserve.   All etiquette being laid aside

on the occasion, General Montero was the only one there in full uniform, so stiff with embroideries in front that his broad chest seemed protected by a cuirass of gold. Sir John at the beginning had got away from high places for the sake of sitting near Mrs. Gould.

The great financier was trying to express to her his grateful sense of her hospitality and of his obligation to her husband's " enormous influence in this part of the country," when she interrupted him by a low " Hush ! " The President was going to make an informal pronouncement.

The Excellentissimo was on his legs. He said only a few words, evidently deeply felt, and meant perhaps mostly for Avellanos—his old friend—as to the necessity of unremitting effort to secure the lasting welfare of the country emerging after this last struggle, he hoped, into a period of peace and material prosperity.

Mrs. Gould, listening to the mellow, slightly mournful voice, looking at this rotund, dark, spectacled face, at the short body, obese to the point of infirmity, thought that this man of delicate and melancholy mind, physically almost a cripple, coming out of his retirement into a dangerous strife at the call of his fellows, had the right to speak with the authority of his self-sacrifice. And yet she was made uneasy. He was more pathetic than promising, this first civilian Chief of the State Costaguana had ever known, pronouncing, glass in hand, his simple watchwords of honesty, peace, respect for law, political good faith abroad and at home—the safeguards of national honour.

He sat down. During the respectful, appreciative buzz of voices that followed the speech, General Montero raised a pair of heavy, drooping eyelids and rolled his eyes with a sort of uneasy dullness from face to face. The military backwoods hero of the party, though secretly impressed by the sudden novelties and splendours of his position (he had never been on board a ship before,

8

and had hardly ever seen the sea except from a distance),
understood by a sort of instinct the advantage his surly,
unpolished attitude of a savage fighter gave him amongst
all these refined Blanco aristocrats. But why was it
that nobody was looking at him ? he wondered to himself
angrily. He was able to spell out the print of newspapers,
and knew that he had performed the " greatest military
exploit of modern times."

" My husband wanted the railway," Mrs. Gould
said to Sir John in the general murmur of resumed
conversations. " All this brings nearer the sort of future
we desire for the country, which has waited for it in
sorrow long enough, God knows. But I will confess
that the other day, during my afternoon drive, when I
suddenly saw an Indian boy ride out of a wood with the
red flag of a surveying party in his hand, I felt something
of a shock. The future means change—an utter change.
And yet even here there are simple and picturesque
things that one would like to preserve."

Sir John listened, smiling. But it was his turn now
to hush Mrs. Gould.

" General Montero is going to speak," he whispered ;
and almost immediately added, in comic alarm, " Heavens !
he's going to propose my own health, I believe."

General Montero had risen with a jingle of steel
scabbard and a ripple of glitter on his gold-embroidered
breast ; a heavy sword-hilt appeared at his side above
the edge of the table. In this gorgeous uniform, with
his bull neck, his hooked nose flattened on the tip upon
a blue-back, dyed moustache, he looked like a disguised
and sinister vaquero. The drone of his voice had a
strangely rasping, soulless ring. He floundered, lowering, through a few vague sentences ; then suddenly
raising his big head and his voice together, burst out
harshly :

" The honour of the country is in the hands of the
army. I assure you I shall be faithful to it." He hesi-

tated till his roaming eyes met Sir John's face, upon which he fixed a lurid, sleepy glance ; and the figure of the lately negotiated loan came into his mind. He lifted his glass. " I drink to the health of the man who brings us a million and a half of pounds."

He tossed off his champagne, and sat down heavily with a half-surprised, half-bullying look all round the faces in the profound, as if appalled, silence which succeeded the felicitous toast. Sir John did not move.

" I don't think I am called upon to rise," he murmured to Mrs. Gould. " That sort of thing speaks for itself." But Don José Avellanos came to the rescue with a short oration, in which he alluded pointedly to England's goodwill towards Costaguana—" a goodwill," he continued significantly, " of which I, having been in my time accredited to the Court of St. James, am able to speak with some knowledge."

Only then Sir John thought fit to respond, which he did gracefully in bad French, punctuated by bursts of applause and the " Hear, hears ! " of Captain Mitchell, who was able to understand a word now and then. Directly he had done, the financier of railways turned to Mrs. Gould :

" You were good enough to say that you intended to ask me for something," he reminded her gallantly. " What is it ? Be assured that any request from you would be considered in the light of a favour to myself."

She thanked him by a gracious smile. Everybody was rising from the table.

" Let us go on deck," she proposed, " where I'll be able to point out to you the very object of my request."

An enormous national flag of Costaguana, diagonal red and yellow, with two green palm trees in the middle, floated lazily at the mainmast head of the *Juno*. A multitude of fireworks being let off in their thousands at the water's edge in honour of the President kept up a mysterious crepitating noise half round the harbour.

Now and then a lot of rockets, swishing upwards invisibly, detonated overhead with only a puff of smoke in the bright sky. Crowds of people could be seen between the town gate and the harbour, under the bunches of multicoloured flags fluttering on tall poles. Faint bursts of military music would be heard suddenly, and the remote sound of shouting. A knot of ragged negroes at the end of the wharf kept on loading and firing a small iron cannon time after time. A greyish haze of dust hung thin and motionless against the sun.

Don Vincente Ribiera made a few steps under the deck-awning, leaning on the arm of Señor Avellanos ; a wide circle was formed round him, where the mirthless smile of his dark lips and the sightless glitter of his spectacles could be seen turning amiably from side to side. The informal function arranged on purpose on board the *Juno* to give the President-Dictator an opportunity to meet intimately some of his most notable adherents in Sulaco, was drawing to an end. On one side, General Montero, his bald head covered now by a plumed cocked hat, remained motionless on a skylight seat, a pair of big gauntleted hands folded on the hilt of the sabre standing upright between his legs. The white plume, the coppery tint of his broad face, the blue-black of the moustaches under the curved beak, the mass of gold on sleeves and breast, the high shining boots with enormous spurs, the working nostrils, the imbecile and domineering stare of the glorious victor of Rio Seco had in them something ominous and incredible ; the exaggeration of a cruel caricature, the fatuity of solemn masquerading, the atrocious grotesqueness of some military idol of Aztec conception and European bedecking, awaiting the homage of worshippers. Don José approached diplomatically this weird and inscrutable portent, and Mrs. Gould turned her fascinated eyes away at last.

Charles, coming up to take leave of Sir John, heard

him say, as he bent over his wife's hand, " Certainly. Of
course, my dear Mrs. Gould, for a *protégé* of yours !
Not the slightest difficulty. Consider it done."

Going ashore in the same boat with the Goulds, Don
José Avellanos was very silent. Even in the Gould
carriage he did not open his lips for a long time. The
mules trotted slowly away from the wharf between the
extended hands of the beggars, who for that day seemed
to have abandoned in a body the portals of churches.
Charles Gould sat on the back seat and looked away
upon the plain. A multitude of booths made of green
boughs, of rushes, of odd pieces of plank eked out with
bits of canvas, had been erected all over it for the sale
of cana, of dulces, of fruit, of cigars. Over little heaps
of glowing charcoal Indian women, squatting on mats,
cooked food in black earthen pots, and boiled the water
for the maté gourds, which they offered in soft, caressing
voices to the country people. A racecourse had been
staked out for the vaqueros ; and away to the left, from
where the crowd was massed thickly about a huge
temporary erection, like a circus tent of wood with a
conical grass roof, came the resonant twanging of harp
strings, the sharp ping of guitars, with the grave drumming throb of an Indian gombo pulsating steadily
through the shrill choruses of the dancers.

Charles Gould said presently :
" All this piece of land belongs now to the Railway
Company. There will be no more popular feasts held
here."

Mrs. Gould was rather sorry to think so. She took
this opportunity to mention how she had just obtained
from Sir John the promise that the house occupied
by Giorgio Viola should not be interfered with. She
declared she could never understand why the survey
engineers ever talked of demolishing that old building.
It was not in the way of the projected harbour branch
of the line in the least.

She stopped the carriage before the door to reassure
at once the old Genoese, who came out bareheaded and
stood by the carriage step. She talked to him in Italian,
of course, and he thanked her with calm dignity. An old
Garibaldino was grateful to her from the bottom of his
heart for keeping the roof over the heads of his wife and
children. He was too old to wander any more.

" And is it for ever, Signora ? " he asked.

" For as long as you like."

" Bene. Then the place must be named. It was
not worth while before."

He smiled ruggedly, with a running together of
wrinkles at the corners of his eyes. " I shall set about
the painting of the name to-morrow."

" And what is it going to be, Giorgio ? "

" Albergo d'Italia Una," said the old Garibaldino,
looking away for a moment. " More in memory of
those who have died," he added, " than for the country
stolen from us soldiers of liberty by the craft of that
accursed Piedmontese race of kings and ministers."

Mrs. Gould smiled slightly, and, bending over a little,
began to inquire about his wife and children. He had
sent them into town on that day. The padrona was
better in health ; many thanks to the Signora for inquiring.

People were passing in twos and threes, in whole
parties of men and women attended by trotting children.
A horseman mounted on a silver-grey mare drew rein
quietly in the shade of the house after taking off his hat
to the party in the carriage, who returned smiles and
familiar nods. Old Viola, evidently very pleased with
the news he had just heard, interrupted himself for a
moment to tell him rapidly that the house was secured,
by the kindness of the English Signora, for as long as he
liked to keep it. The other listened attentively, but
made no response.

When the carriage moved on he took off his hat again,

a grey sombrero with a silver cord and tassels. The bright colours of a Mexican serape twisted on the cantle, the enormous silver buttons on the embroidered leather jacket, the row of tiny silver buttons down the seam of the trousers, the snowy linen, a silk sash with embroidered ends, the silver plates on headstall and saddle, proclaimed the unapproachable style of the famous Capataz de Cargadores—a Mediterranean sailor—got up with more finished splendour than any well-to-do young ranchero of the Campo had ever displayed on a high holiday.

" It is a great thing for me," murmured old Giorgio, still thinking of the house, for now he had grown weary of change. " The Signora just said a word to the English-man."

" The old Englishman who has enough money to pay for a railway ? He is going off in an hour," remarked Nostromo carelessly. " Buon viaggio, then. I've guarded his bones all the way from the Entrada Pass down to the plain and into Sulaco, as though he had been my own father."

Old Giorgio only moved his head sideways absently. Nostromo pointed after the Goulds' carriage, nearing the grass-grown gate in the old town wall that was like a wall of matted jungle.

" And I have sat alone at night with my revolver in the Company's warehouse time and again by the side of that other Englishman's heap of silver, guarding it as though it had been my own."

Viola seemed lost in thought. " It is a great thing for me," he repeated again, as if to himself.

" It is," agreed the magnificent Capataz de Carga-dores calmly. " Listen, Vecchio—go in and bring me out a cigar, but don't look for it in my room. There's nothing there."

Viola stepped into the café and came out directly, still absorbed in his idea, and tendered him a cigar, mumbling thoughtfully in his moustache, " Children

growing up—and girls, too! Girls!" He sighed and
fell silent.

"What, only one?" remarked Nostromo, looking
down with a sort of comic inquisitiveness at the unconscious old man. "No matter," he added, with lofty
negligence; "one is enough till another is wanted."

He lit it, and let the match drop from his passive fingers.
Giorgio Viola looked up, and said abruptly:

"My son would have been just such a fine young man
as you, Gian' Battista, if he had lived."

"What? Your son? But you are right, padrone.
If he had been like me he would have been a man."

He turned his horse slowly, and paced on between the
booths, checking the mare almost to a standstill now and
then for children, for the groups of people from the distant
Campo, who stared after him with admiration. The
Company's lightermen saluted him from afar; and the
greatly envied Capataz de Cargadores advanced, amongst
murmurs of recognition and obsequious greetings, towards
the huge circus-like erection. The throng thickened;
the guitars tinkled louder; other horsemen sat motionless,
smoking calmly above the heads of the crowd; it eddied
and pushed before the doors of the high-roofed building,
whence issued a shuffle and thumping of feet in time to
the dance music vibrating and shrieking with a racking
rhythm, overhung by the tremendous, sustained, hollow
roar of the gombo. The barbarous and imposing noise
of the big drum, that can madden a crowd, and that even
Europeans cannot hear without a strange emotion, seemed
to draw Nostromo on to its source; while a man, wrapped
up in a faded, torn poncho, walked by his stirrup, and,
buffeted right and left, begged "his worship" insistently
for employment on the wharf. He whined, offering the
Señor Capataz half his daily pay for the privilege of being
admitted to the swaggering fraternity of cargadores; the
other half would be enough for him, he protested. But
Captain Mitchell's right-hand man—"invaluable for our

work—a perfectly incorruptible fellow "—after looking down critically at the ragged mozo, shook his head without a word in the uproar going on around.

The man fell back ; and a little farther on Nostromo had to pull up. From the doors of the dance-hall men and women emerged tottering, streaming with sweat, trembling in every limb, to lean, panting, with staring eyes and parted lips, against the wall of the structure, where the harps and guitars played on with mad speed in an incessant roll of thunder. Hundreds of hands clapped in there ; voices shrieked, and then all at once would sink low, chanting in unison the refrain of a love song, with a dying fall. A red flower, flung with a good aim from somewhere in the crowd, struck the resplendent Capataz on the cheek.

He caught it as it fell, neatly, but for some time did not turn his head. When at last he condescended to look round, the throng near him had parted to make way for a pretty Morenita, her hair held up by a small golden comb, who was walking towards him in the open space.

Her arms and neck emerged plump and bare from a snowy chemisette ; the blue woollen skirt, with all the fullness gathered in front, scanty on the hips and tight across the back, disclosed the provoking action of her walk. She came straight on and laid her hand on the mare's neck with a timid, coquettish look upwards out of the corner of her eyes.

" Querido," she murmured caressingly, " why do you pretend not to see me when I pass ? "

" Because I don't love thee any more," said Nostromo deliberately, after a moment of reflective silence.

The hand on the mare's neck trembled suddenly. She dropped her head before all the eyes in the wide circle formed round the generous, the terrible, the inconstant Capataz de Cargadores and his Morenita.

Nostromo, looking down, saw tears beginning to fall down her face.

"Has it come, then, ever beloved of my heart?"
she whispered. "Is it true?"

"No," said Nostromo, looking away carelessly. "It
was a lie. I love thee as much as ever."

"Is that true?" she cooed joyously, her cheeks still
wet with her tears.

"It is true."

"True on the life?"

"As true as that ; but thou must not ask me to swear
it on the Madonna that stands in thy room." And the
Capataz laughed a little in response to the grins of the
crowd.

She pouted—very pretty—a little uneasy.

"No, I will not ask for that. I can see love in your
eyes." She laid her hand on his knee. "Why are you
trembling like this? From love?" she continued, while
the cavernous thundering of the gombo went on without a
pause. "But if you love her as much as that, you must
give your Paquita a gold-mounted rosary of beads for the
neck of her Madonna."

"No," said Nostromo, looking into her uplifted,
begging eyes, which suddenly turned stony with surprise.

"No? Then what else will your worship give me on
the day of the fiesta?" she asked angrily ; "so as not to
shame me before all these people."

"There is no shame for thee in getting nothing from
thy lover for once."

"True! The shame is your worship's—my poor
lover's," she flared up sarcastically.

Laughs were heard at her anger, at her retort. What
an audacious spitfire she was! The people aware of this
scene were calling out urgently to others in the crowd.
The circle round the silver-grey mare narrowed slowly.

The girl went off a pace or two, confronting the mocking curiosity of the eyes, then flung back to the stirrup,
tiptoeing, her enraged face turned up to Nostromo with
a pair of blazing eyes. He bent low to her in the saddle.

" Juan," she hissed, " I could stab thee to the heart ! "

The dreaded Capataz de Cargadores, magnificent and carelessly public in his amours, flung his arm round her neck and kissed her spluttering lips. A murmur went round.

" A knife ! " he demanded at large, holding her firmly by the shoulder.

Twenty blades flashed out together in the circle. A young man in holiday attire, bounding in, thrust one in Nostromo's hand and bounded back into the ranks, very proud of himself. Nostromo had not even looked at him.

" Stand on my foot," he commanded the girl, who, suddenly subdued, rose lightly, and when he had her up, encircling her waist, her face near to his, he pressed the knife into her little hand.

" No, Morenita ! You shall not put me to shame," he said. " You shall have your present ; and so that every one should know who is your lover to-day, you may cut all the silver buttons off my coat."

There were shouts of laughter and applause at this witty freak, while the girl passed the keen blade, and the impassive rider jingled in his palm the increasing hoard of silver buttons. He eased her to the ground with both her hands full. After whispering for a while with a very strenuous face, she walked away, staring haughtily, and vanished into the crowd.

The circle had broken up, and the lordly Capataz de Cargadores, the indispensable man, the tried and trusty Nostromo, the Mediterranean sailor come ashore casually to try his luck in Costaguana, rode slowly towards the harbour. The *Juno* was just then swinging round ; and even as Nostromo reined up again to look on, a flag ran up on the improvised flagstaff erected in an ancient and dismantled little fort at the harbour entrance. Half a battery of field-guns had been hurried over there from the Sulaco barracks for the purpose of firing the regulation salutes for the President-Dictator and the War Minister. As the mail-boat headed through the pass, the badly timed reports announced the end of Don Vincente Ribiera's first official visit to Sulaco, and for Captain Mitchell the end of another " historic occasion." Next time when the " Hope of honest men " was to come that way, a year and a half later, it was unofficially, over the mountain tracks, fleeing after a defeat on a lame mule, to be only just saved by Nostromo from an ignominious death at the hands of a mob. It was a very different event, of which Captain Mitchell used to say :

" It was history—history, sir ! And that fellow of mine, Nostromo, you know, was right in it. Absolutely making history, sir."

But this event, creditable to Nostromo, was to lead immediately to another, which could not be classed either as " history " or as " a mistake " in Captain Mitchell's phraseology. He had another word for it.

" Sir," he used to say afterwards, " that was no mistake. It was a fatality. A misfortune, pure and simple, sir. And that poor fellow of mine was right in it—right in the middle of it ! A fatality, if ever there was one—and to my mind he has never been the same man since."

PART II
THE ISABELS

CHAPTER ONE

THROUGH good and evil report in the varying fortune of that struggle which Don José had characterised in the phrase, " The fate of national honesty trembles in the balance," the Gould Concession, " Imperium in imperio," had gone on working ; the square mountain had gone on pouring its treasure down the wooden shoots to the unresting batteries of stamps ; the lights of San Tomé had twinkled night after night upon the great, limitless shadow of the Campo ; every three months the silver escort had gone down to the sea as if neither the war nor its consequences could ever affect the ancient Occidental State secluded beyond its high barrier of the Cordillera. All the fighting took place on the other side of that mighty wall of serrated peaks lorded over by the white dome of Higuerota and as yet unbreached by the railway, of which only the first part, the easy Campo part from Sulaco to the Ivie Valley at the foot of the pass, had been laid. Neither did the telegraph line cross the mountains yet ; its poles, like slender beacons on the plain, penetrated into the forest fringe of the foot-hills cut by the deep avenue of the track ; and its wire ended abruptly in the Construction Camp at a white deal table supporting a Morse apparatus, in a long hut of planks with a corrugated iron roof over-shadowed by gigantic cedar trees—the quarters of the engineer in charge of the advance section.

The harbour was busy, too, with the traffic in railway material, and with the movements of troops along the

coast. The O.S.N. Company found much occupation
for its fleet. Costaguana had no navy, and, apart from
a few coastguard cutters, there were no national ships
except a couple of old merchant steamers used as transports.

Captain Mitchell, feeling more and more in the thick
of history, found time for an hour or so during an afternoon in the drawing-room of the Casa Gould, where, with
a strange ignorance of the real forces at work around
him, he professed himself delighted to get away from the
strain of affairs. He did not know what he would have
done without his invaluable Nostromo, he declared.
Those confounded Costaguana politics gave him more
work—he confided to Mrs. Gould—than he had bar-
gained for.

Don José Avellanos had displayed in the service
of the endangered Ribiera Government an organising
activity and an eloquence of which the echoes reached
even Europe. For, after the new loan to the Ribiera
Government, Europe had become interested in Costaguana. The Sala of the Provincial Assembly (in the
Municipal Buildings of Sulaco), with its portraits of
the Liberators on the walls and an old flag of Cortez
preserved in a glass case above the President's chair,
had heard all these speeches—the early one containing
the impassioned declaration " Militarism is the enemy,"
the famous one of the " trembling balance " delivered
on the occasion of the vote for the raising of a second
Sulaco regiment in the defence of the reforming Government ; and when the provinces again displayed their
old flags (proscribed in Guzman Bento's time) there
was another of those great orations, when Don José
greeted these old emblems of the war of Independence,
brought out again in the name of new Ideals. The old
idea of Federalism had disappeared. For his part he
did not wish to revive old political doctrines. They were
perishable. They died. But the doctrine of political

rectitude was immortal. The second Sulaco regiment, to whom he was presenting this flag, was going to show its valour in a contest for order, peace, progress ; for the establishment of national self-respect, without which, he declared with energy, " we are a reproach and a byword amongst the powers of the world."

Don José Avellanos loved his country. He had served it lavishly with his fortune during his diplomatic career, and the later story of his captivity and barbarous ill-usage under Guzman Bento was well known to his listeners. It was a wonder that he had not been a victim of the ferocious and summary executions which marked the course of that tyranny ; for Guzman had ruled the country with the sombre imbecility of political fanaticism. The power of Supreme Government had become in his dull mind an object of strange worship, as if it were some sort of cruel deity. It was incarnated in himself, and his adversaries, the Federalists, were the supreme sinners, objects of hate, abhorrence, and fear, as heretics would be to a convinced Inquisitor. For years he had carried about at the tail of the Army of Pacification, all over the country, a captive band of such atrocious criminals, who considered themselves most unfortunate at not having been summarily executed. It was a diminishing company of nearly naked skeletons, loaded with irons, covered with dirt, with vermin, with raw wounds, all men of position, of education, of wealth, who had learned to fight amongst themselves for scraps of rotten beef thrown to them by soldiers, or to beg a negro cook for a drink of muddy water in pitiful accents. Don José Avellanos, clanking his chains amongst the others, seemed only to exist in order to prove how much hunger, pain, degradation, and cruel torture a human body can stand without parting with the last spark of life. Sometimes interrogatories, backed by some primitive method of torture, were administered to them by a commission of officers hastily assembled in a hut of

9

sticks and branches, and made pitiless by the fear for
their own lives. A lucky one or two of that spectral
company of prisoners would perhaps be led tottering
behind a bush to be shot by a file of soldiers. Always
an army chaplain—some unshaven, dirty man, girt with
a sword and with a tiny cross embroidered in white
cotton on the left breast of a lieutenant's uniform—
would follow, cigarette in the corner of the mouth,
wooden stool in hand, to hear the confession and give
absolution ; for the Citizen Saviour of the Country
(Guzman Bento was called thus officially, in petitions)
was not averse from the exercise of rational clemency.
The irregular report of the firing squad would be heard,
followed sometimes by a single finishing shot ; a little
bluish cloud of smoke would float up above the green
bushes, and the Army of Pacification would move on
over the savannas, through the forests, crossing rivers,
invading rural pueblos, devastating the haciendas of the
horrid aristocrats, occupying the inland towns in the
fulfilment of its patriotic mission, and leaving behind
a united land wherein the evil taint of Federalism could
no longer be detected in the smoke of burning houses
and the smell of spilt blood.

Don José Avellanos had survived that time.

Perhaps, when contemptuously signifying to him his
release, the Citizen Saviour of the Country might have
thought this benighted aristocrat too broken in health
and spirit and fortune to be any longer dangerous. Or,
perhaps, it may have been a simple caprice. Guzman
Bento, usually full of fanciful fears and brooding suspicions, had sudden accesses of unreasonable self-
confidence when he perceived himself elevated on a
pinnacle of power and safety beyond the reach of mere
mortal plotters. At such times he would impulsively
command the celebration of a solemn Mass of thanks-
giving, which would be sung in great pomp in the
cathedral of Sta. Marta by the trembling subservient

Archbishop of his creation. He heard it sitting in a
gilt arm-chair placed before the high altar, surrounded
by the civil and military heads of his Government. The
unofficial world of Sta. Marta would crowd into the
cathedral ; for it was not quite safe for anybody of mark
to stay away from these manifestations of presidential
piety. Having thus acknowledged the only power he was
at all disposed to recognise as above himself, he would
scatter acts of political grace in a sardonic wanton-
ness of clemency. There was no other way left now to
enjoy his power but by seeing his crushed adversaries
crawl impotently into the light of day out of the dark,
noisome cells of the Collegio. Their harmlessness fed
his insatiable vanity, and they could always be got hold
of again. It was the rule for all the women of their
families to present thanks afterwards in a special
audience. The incarnation of that strange god, El
Gobierno Supremo, received them standing, cocked
hat on head, and exhorted them in a menacing mutter to
show their gratitude by bringing up their children in
fidelity to the democratic form of government, " which
I have established for the happiness of our country."
His front teeth having been knocked out in some accident
of his former herdsman's life, his utterance was spluttering and indistinct. He had been working for Costaguana alone in the midst of treachery and opposition.
Let it cease now lest he should become weary of forgiving !

    Don José Avellanos had known this forgiveness.

    He was broken in health and fortune deplorably
enough to present a truly gratifying spectacle to the
supreme chief of democratic institutions. He retired
to Sulaco. His wife had an estate in that province, and
she nursed him back to life out of the house of death and
captivity. When she died, their daughter, an only child,
was old enough to devote herself to " poor papa."

    Miss Avellanos, born in Europe, and educated partly

in England, was a tall, grave girl, with a self-possessed
manner, a wide, white forehead, a wealth of rich brown
hair, and blue eyes.

The other young ladies of Sulaco stood in awe of her
character and accomplishments. She was reputed to be
terribly learned and serious. As to pride, it was well
known that all the Corbelàns were proud, and her mother
was a Corbelàn. Don José Avellanos depended very
much upon the devotion of his beloved Antonia. He
accepted it in the benighted way of men, who, though
made in God's image, are like stone idols without sense
before the smoke of certain burnt-offerings. He was
ruined in every way, but a man possessed of passion is
not a bankrupt in life. Don José Avellanos desired
passionately for his country peace, prosperity, and (as
the end of the preface to *Fifty Years of Misrule* has it)
" an honourable place in the comity of civilised nations."
In this last phrase the Minister Plenipotentiary, cruelly
humiliated by the bad faith of his Government towards
the foreign bondholders, stands disclosed in the patriot.

The fatuous turmoil of greedy factions succeeding the
tyranny of Guzman Bento seemed to bring his desire to
the very door of opportunity. He was too old to descend
personally into the centre of the arena at Sta. Marta.
But the men who acted there sought his advice at every
step. He himself thought that he could be most useful
at a distance in Sulaco. His name, his connections, his
former position, his experience commanded the respect
of his class. The discovery that this man, living in
dignified poverty in the Corbelàn town residence
(opposite the Casa Gould), could dispose of material
means towards the support of the cause increased his
influence. It was his open letter of appeal that decided
the candidature of Don Vincente Ribiera for the Presidency. Another of these informal State papers drawn up
by Don José (this time in the shape of an address from
the Province) induced that scrupulous constitutionalist

to accept the extraordinary powers conferred upon him for five years by an overwhelming vote of congress in Sta. Marta. It was a specific mandate to establish the prosperity of the people on the basis of firm peace at home, and to redeem the national credit by the satisfaction of all just claims abroad.

On the afternoon the news of that vote had reached Sulaco by the usual roundabout postal way through Cayta, and up the coast by steamer. Don José, who had been waiting for the mail in the Goulds' drawing-room, got out of the rocking-chair, letting his hat fall off his knees. He rubbed his silvery, short hair with both hands, speechless with the excess of joy.

" Emilia, my soul," he had burst out, " let me embrace you ! Let me——"

Captain Mitchell, had he been there, would no doubt have made an apt remark about the dawn of a new era ; but if Don José thought something of the kind, his eloquence failed him on this occasion. The inspirer of that revival of the Blanco party tottered where he stood. Mrs. Gould moved forward quickly, and, as she offered her cheek with a smile to her old friend, managed very cleverly to give him the support of her arm he really needed.

Don José had recovered himself at once, but for a time he could do no more than murmur, " Oh, you two patriots ! Oh, you two patriots ! "—looking from one to the other. Vague plans of another historical work, wherein all the devotions to the regeneration of the country he loved would be enshrined for the reverent worship of posterity, flitted through his mind. The historian who had enough elevation of soul to write of Guzman Bento : " Yet this monster, imbrued in the blood of his countrymen, must not be held unreservedly to the execration of future years. It appears to be true that he, too, loved his country. He had given it twelve years of peace ; and, absolute master of lives and fortunes

as he was, he died poor. His worst fault, perhaps, was
not his ferocity, but his ignorance "; the man who could
write thus of a cruel persecutor (the passage occurs in his
History of Misrule) felt at the foreshadowing of success an
almost boundless affection for his two helpers, for these
two young people from over the sea.

Just as years ago, calmly, from the conviction of
practical necessity, stronger than any abstract political
doctrine, Henry Gould had drawn the sword, so now,
the times being changed, Charles Gould had flung the
silver of the San Tomé into the fray. The Inglez of
Sulaco, the " Costaguana Englishman " of the third
generation, was as far from being a political intriguer as
his uncle from a revolutionary swashbuckler. Springing
from the instinctive uprightness of their natures, their
action was reasoned. They saw an opportunity and used
the weapon to hand.

Charles Gould's position—a commanding position in
the background of that attempt to retrieve the peace and
the credit of the Republic—was very clear. At the
beginning he had had to accommodate himself to existing
circumstances of corruption so naïvely brazen as to disarm
the hate of a man courageous enough not to be afraid of
its irresponsible potency to ruin everything it touched.
It seemed to him too contemptible for hot anger even.
He made use of it with a cold, fearless scorn, manifested
rather than concealed by the forms of stony courtesy
which did away with much of the ignominy of the
situation. At bottom, perhaps, he suffered from it, for
he was not a man of cowardly illusions, but he refused to
discuss the ethical view with his wife. He trusted that,
though a little disenchanted, she would be intelligent
enough to understand that his character safeguarded the
enterprise of their lives as much or more than his policy.
The extraordinary development of the mine had put a
great power into his hands. To feel that prosperity
always at the mercy of unintelligent greed had grown

irksome to him.   To Mrs. Gould it was humiliating.   At any rate, it was dangerous.   In the confidential communications passing between Charles Gould, the King of Sulaco, and the head of the silver and steel interests far away in California, the conviction was growing that any attempt made by men of education and integrity ought to be discreetly supported.   " You may tell your friend Avellanos that I think so."   Mr. Holroyd had written at the proper moment from his inviolable sanctuary within the eleven-story-high factory of great affairs.   And shortly afterwards, with a credit opened by the Third Southern Bank (located next door but one to the Holroyd Building), the Ribierist party in Costaguana took a practical shape under the eye of the Administrador of the San Tomé mine.   And Don José, the hereditary friend of the Gould family, could say, " Perhaps, my dear Carlos, I shall not have believed in vain."

CHAPTER TWO

AFTER another armed struggle, decided by Montero's victory of Rio Seco, had been added to the tale of civil wars, the "honest men," as Don José called them, could breathe freely for the first time in half a century. The Five-Year-Mandate law became the basis of that regeneration, the passionate desire and hope for which had been like the elixir of everlasting youth for Don José Avellanos.

And when it was suddenly—and not quite unexpectedly—endangered by that "brute Montero," it was a passionate indignation that gave him a new lease of life, as it were. Already, at the time of the President-Dictator's visit to Sulaco, Moraga had sounded a note of warning from Sta. Marta about the War Minister. Montero and his brother made the subject of an earnest talk between the Dictator-President and the Nestor-inspirer of the party. But Don Vincente, a doctor of philosophy from the Cordova University, seemed to have an exaggerated respect for military ability, whose mysteriousness—since it appeared to be altogether independent of intellect—imposed upon his imagination. The victor of Rio Seco was a popular hero. His services were so recent that the President-Dictator quailed before the obvious charge of political ingratitude. Great regenerating transactions were being initiated—the fresh loan, a new railway line, a vast colonisation scheme. Anything that could unsettle the public opinion in the capital was to be avoided. Don José bowed to these arguments and tried to dismiss from his mind the gold-laced portent in boots, and with a sabre, made meaningless now at last, he hoped, in the new order of things.

Less than six months after the President-Dictator's visit, Sulaco learned with stupefaction of the military revolt in the name of national honour. The Minister of War, in a barrack-square allocution to the officers of the artillery regiment he had been inspecting, had declared the national honour sold to foreigners. The Dictator, by his weak compliance with the demands of the European powers—for the settlement of long outstanding money claims—had showed himself unfit to rule. A letter from Moraga explained afterwards that the initiative, and even the very text, of the incendiary allocution came, in reality, from the other Montero, the ex-guerrillero, the Commandante de Plaza. The energetic treatment of Dr. Monygham, sent for in haste "to the mountain," who came galloping three leagues in the dark, saved Don José from a dangerous attack of jaundice.

After getting over the shock, Don José refused to let himself be prostrated. Indeed, better news succeeded at first. The revolt in the capital had been suppressed after a night of fighting in the streets. Unfortunately, both the Monteros had been able to make their escape south, to their native province of Entre-Montes. The hero of the forest march, the victor of Rio Seco, had been received with frenzied acclamations in Nicoya, the provincial capital. The troops in garrison there had gone to him in a body. The brothers were organising an army, gathering malcontents, sending emissaries primed with patriotic lies to the people, and with promises of plunder to the wild llaneros. Even a Monterist press had come into existence, speaking oracularly of the secret promises of support given by "our great sister Republic of the North" against the sinister land-grabbing designs of European powers, cursing in every issue the " miserable Ribiera," who had plotted to deliver his country, bound hand and foot, for a prey to foreign speculators.

Sulaco, pastoral and sleepy, with its opulent Campo and the rich silver mine, heard the din of arms fitfully in its fortunate isolation. It was nevertheless in the very forefront of the defence with men and money ; but the very rumours reached it circuitously—from abroad even, so much was it cut off from the rest of the Republic, not only by natural obstacles, but also by the vicissitudes of the war. The Monteristos were besieging Cayta, an important postal link. The overland couriers ceased to come across the mountains, and no muleteer would consent to risk the journey at last ; even Boni-facio on one occasion failed to return from Sta. Marta, either not daring to start, or perhaps captured by the parties of the enemy raiding the country between the Cordillera and the capital. Monterist publications, however, found their way into the province, mysteri-ously enough, and also Monterist emissaries preaching death to aristocrats in the villages and towns of the Campo. Very early, at the beginning of the trouble, Hernandez, the bandit, had proposed (through the agency of an old priest of a village in the wilds) to deliver two of them to the Ribierist authorities in Tonoro. They had come to offer him a free pardon and the rank of colonel from General Montero in consideration of joining the rebel army with his mounted band. No notice was taken at the time of the proposal. It was joined, as an evidence of good faith, to a petition praying the Sulaco Assembly for permission to enlist, with all his followers, in the forces being then raised in Sulaco for the defence of the Five Year Mandate of regenera-tion. The petition, like everything else, had found its way into Don José's hands. He had shown to Mrs. Gould these pages of dirty-greyish rough paper (perhaps looted in some village store), covered with the crabbed, illiterate handwriting of the old padre, carried off from his hut by the side of a mud-walled church to be the secretary of the dreaded salteador. They had both bent in the lamplight of the Gould drawing-room over the document containing the fierce and yet humble appeal of the man against the blind and stupid barbarity turning an honest ranchero into a bandit. A postscript of the priest stated that, but for being deprived of his liberty for ten days, he had been treated with humanity and the respect due to his sacred calling. He had been, it appears, confessing and absolving the chief and most of the band, and he guaranteed the sincerity of their good disposition. He had distributed heavy penances, no doubt in the way of litanies and fasts; but he argued shrewdly that it would be difficult for them to make their peace with God durably till they had made peace with men.

Never before, perhaps, had Hernandez's head been in less jeopardy than when he petitioned humbly for permission to buy a pardon for himself and his gang of deserters by armed service. He could range afar from the waste lands protecting his fastness, unchecked, because there were no troops left in the whole province. The usual garrison of Sulaco had gone south to the war, with its brass band playing the Bolivar march on the bridge of one of the O.S.N. Company's steamers. The great family coaches drawn up along the shore of the harbour were made to rock on the high leathern springs by the enthusiasm of the señoras and the señoritas standing up to wave their lace handkerchiefs, as lighter after lighter packed full of troops left the end of the jetty.

Nostromo directed the embarkation, under the super-intendence of Captain Mitchell, red-faced in the sun, conspicuous in a white waistcoat, representing the allied and anxious goodwill of all the material interests of civilisation. General Barrios, who commanded the troops, assured Don José on parting that in three weeks he would have Montero in a wooden cage drawn by three pair of oxen ready for a tour through all the towns of the Republic.

" And then, Señora," he continued, baring his curly iron-grey head to Mrs. Gould in her landau—" and then, Señora, we shall convert our swords into plough-shares and grow rich. Even I, myself, as soon as this little business is settled, shall open a fundacion on some land I have on the llanos and try to make a little money in peace and quietness. Señora, you know, all Costa-guana knows—what do I say ?—this whole South American continent knows, that Pablo Barrios has had his fill of military glory."

Charles Gould was not present at the anxious and patriotic send-off. It was not his part to see the soldiers embark. It was neither his part, nor his inclination, nor his policy. His part, his inclination, and his policy were united in one endeavour to keep unchecked the flow of treasure he had started single-handed from the reopened scar in the flank of the mountain. As the mine had developed he had trained for himself some native help. There were foremen, artificers, and clerks, with Don Pépé for the gobernador of the mining population. For the rest, his shoulders alone sustained the whole weight of the " Imperium in imperio," the great Gould Con-cession whose mere shadow had been enough to crush the life out of his father.

Mrs. Gould had no silver mine to look after. In the general life of the Gould Concession she was repre-sented by her two lieutenants, the doctor and the priest ; but she fed her woman's love of excitement on events whose significance was purified to her by the fire of her imaginative purpose. On that day she had brought the Avellanos, father and daughter, down to the harbour with her.

Amongst his other activities of that stirring time, Don José had become the chairman of a Patriotic Committee which had armed a great proportion of troops in the Sulaco command with an improved model of a military rifle. It had been just discarded for something still more deadly by one of the great European powers. How much of the market-price for second-hand weapons was covered by the voluntary contributions of the principal families, and how much came from those funds Don José was understood to command abroad, remained a secret which he alone could have disclosed ; but the Ricos, as the populace called them, had contributed under the pressure of their Nestor's eloquence. Some of the more enthusiastic ladies had been moved to bring offerings of jewels into the hands of the man who was the life and soul of the party.

There were moments when both his life and his soul seemed overtaxed by so many years of undiscouraged belief in regeneration. He appeared almost inanimate, sitting rigidly by the side of Mrs. Gould in the landau, with his fine, old, clean-shaven face of a uniform tint as if modelled in yellow wax, shaded by a soft felt hat, and the dark eyes looking out fixedly Antonia, the beautiful Antonia, as Miss Avellanos was called in Sulaco, leaned back, facing them ; and her full figure, the grave oval of her face with full red lips, made her look more mature than Mrs. Gould, with her mobile expression and small erect person under a slightly swaying sunshade.

Whenever possible Antonia attended her father ; her recognised devotion weakened the shocking effect of her scorn for the rigid conventions regulating the life of Spanish-American girlhood. And, in truth, she was no longer girlish. It was said that she often wrote State papers from her father's dictation, and was allowed to read all the books in his library. At the receptions— where the situation was saved by the presence of a very decrepit old lady (a relation of the Corbelàns), quite deaf

and motionless in an arm-chair—Antonia could hold her
own in a discussion with two or three men at a time.
Obviously she was not the girl to be content with peeping
through a barred window at a cloaked figure of a lover
ensconced in a doorway opposite—which is the correct
form of Costaguana courtship. It was generally believed
that with her foreign upbringing and foreign ideas the
learned and proud Antonia would never marry—unless,
indeed, she married a foreigner from Europe or North
America, now that Sulaco seemed on the point of being
invaded by all the world.

CHAPTER THREE

WHEN General Barrios stopped to address Mrs.
Gould, Antonia raised negligently her hand
holding an open fan, as if to shade from the
sun her head, wrapped in a light lace shawl. The clear
gleam of her blue eyes gliding behind the black fringe
of eyelashes paused for a moment upon her father, then
travelled further to a figure of a young man of thirty
at most, of medium height, rather thick-set, wearing a
light overcoat. Bearing down with the open palm of
his hand upon the knob of a flexible cane, he had been
looking on from a distance ; but directly he saw himself noticed, he approached quietly and put his elbow
over the door of the landau.

The shirt collar, cut low in the neck, the big bow
of his cravat, the style of his clothing, from the round
hat to the varnished shoes, suggested an idea of French
elegance ; but otherwise he was the very type of a fair
Spanish creole. The fluffy moustache and the short,
curly, golden beard did not conceal his lips, rosy, fresh,
almost pouting in expression. His full round face was
of that warm, healthy creole white which is never tanned
by its native sunshine. Martin Decoud was seldom
exposed to the Costaguana sun under which he was born.
His people had been long settled in Paris, where he had
studied law, had dabbled in literature, had hoped now
and then in moments of exaltation to become a poet
like that other foreigner of Spanish blood, José Maria
Herédia. In other moments he had, to pass the time,

condescended to write articles on European affairs for
the *Semenario*, the principal newspaper in Sta. Marta,
which printed them under the heading "From our
special correspondent," though the authorship was an
open secret. Everybody in Costaguana, where the tale
of compatriots in Europe is jealously kept, knew that
it was "the son Decoud," a talented young man, supposed
to be moving in the higher spheres of Society. As a
matter of fact, he was an idle boulevardier, in touch with
some smart journalists, made free of a few newspaper
offices, and welcomed in the pleasure-haunts of pressmen.
This life, whose dreary superficiality is covered by the
glitter of universal *blague*, like the stupid clowning of a
harlequin by the spangles of a motley costume, induced
in him a Frenchified—but most un-French—cosmo-
politanism, in reality a mere barren indifferentism posing
as intellectual superiority. Of his own country he used
to say to his French associates : " Imagine an atmosphere
of opera-bouffe in which all the comic business of stage
statesmen, brigands, etc. etc., all their farcical stealing,
intriguing, and stabbing, is done in dead earnest. It is
screamingly funny ; the blood flows all the time, and the
actors believe themselves to be influencing the fate of the
universe. Of course, government in general, any government anywhere, is a thing of exquisite comicality to a dis-
cerning mind ; but really we Spanish-Americans do over-
step the bounds. No man of ordinary intelligence can
take part in the intrigues of *une farce macabre*. However,
these Ribierists, of whom we hear so much just now, are
really trying in their own comical way to make the country habitable, and even to pay some of its debts. My
friends, you had better write up Señor Ribiera all you
can in kindness to your own bondholders. Really, if
what I am told in my letters is true, there is some chance
for them at last."

And he would explain with railing verve what Don
Vincente Ribiera stood for—a mournful little man op-

pressed by his own good intentions ; the significance of
battles won, who Montero was (*un grotesque vaniteux et
féroce*), and the manner of the new loan connected with
railway development, and the colonisation of vast tracts
of land in one great financial scheme.

And his French friends would remark that evidently
this little fellow Decoud *connaissait la question à fond*.
An important Parisian review asked him for an article on
the situation. It was composed in a serious tone and
in a spirit of levity. Afterwards he asked one of his
intimates :

" Have you read my thing about the regeneration of
Costaguana—*une bonne blague, hein* ? "

He imagined himself Parisian to the tips of his fingers.
But far from being that, he was in danger of remaining a
sort of nondescript dilettante all his life. He had pushed
the habit of universal raillery to a point where it blinded
him to the genuine impulses of his own nature. To be
suddenly selected for the executive member of the patriotic small-arms committee of Sulaco seemed to him the
height of the unexpected, one of those fantastic moves
of which only his " dear countrymen " were capable.

" It's like a tile falling on my head. I—I—executive
member ! It's the first I hear of it ! What do I know
of military rifles ? *C'est funambulesque !* " he had exclaimed to his favourite sister ; for the Decoud family—
except the old father and mother—used the French
language amongst themselves. " And you should see the
explanatory and confidential letter ! Eight pages of it—
no less ! "

This letter, in Antonia's handwriting, was signed by
Don José, who appealed to the " young and gifted Costaguanero " on public grounds, and privately opened his
heart to his talented godson, a man of wealth and
leisure, with wide relations, and by his parentage and
bringing-up worthy of all confidence.

" Which means," Martin commented cynically to

his sister, " that I am not likely to misappropriate the
funds, or go blabbing to our Chargé d'Affaires here."

The whole thing was being carried out behind the
back of the War Minister, Montero, a mistrusted member
of the Ribiera Government, but difficult to get rid of at
once. He was not to know anything of it till the troops
under Barrios's command had the new rifle in their hands.
The President-Dictator, whose position was very difficult,
was alone in the secret.

" How funny ! " commented Martin's sister and con-
fidante ; to which the brother, with an air of best Parisian
blague, had retorted :

" It's immense ! The idea of that Chief of the State
engaged, with the help of private citizens, in digging
a mine under his own indispensable War Minister.
No ! We are unapproachable ! " And he laughed
immoderately.

Afterwards, his sister was surprised at the earnestness
and ability he displayed in carrying out his mission,
which circumstances made delicate and his want of
special knowledge rendered difficult. She had never
seen Martin take so much trouble about anything in
his whole life.

" It amuses me," he had explained briefly. " I am
beset by a lot of swindlers trying to sell all sorts of gas-
pipe weapons. They are charming ; they invite me to
expensive luncheons ; I keep up their hopes ; it's
extremely entertaining. Meanwhile, the real affair is
being carried through in quite another quarter."

When the business was concluded he declared
suddenly his intention of seeing the precious consignment delivered safely in Sulaco. The whole burlesque
business, he thought, was worth following up to the end.
He mumbled his excuses, tugging at his golden beard,
before the acute young lady, who (after the first wide stare
of astonishment) looked at him with narrowed eyes, and
pronounced slowly :

" I believe you want to see Antonia."

" What Antonia ? " asked the Costaguana boulevardier, in a vexed and disdainful tone. He shrugged
his shoulders, and spun round on his heel. His sister
called out after him joyously :

" The Antonia you used to know when she wore her
hair in two plaits down her back."

He had known her some eight years since, shortly
before the Avellanos had left Europe for good, as a tall
girl of sixteen, youthfully austere, and of a character
already so formed that she ventured to treat slightingly
his pose of disabused wisdom. On one occasion, as
though she had lost all patience, she flew out at him about
the aimlessness of his life and the levity of his opinions.
He was twenty then, an only son, spoiled by his adoring
family. This attack disconcerted him so greatly that he
had faltered in his affectation of amused superiority before
that insignificant chit of a schoolgirl. But the impression left was so strong that ever since all the girl
friends of his sisters recalled to him Antonia Avellanos by
some faint resemblance, or by the great force of contrast.
It was, he told himself, like a ridiculous fatality. And,
of course, in the news the Decouds received regularly
from Costaguana, the name of their friends, the Avellanos, cropped up frequently—the arrest and the abominable treatment of the ex-Minister, the dangers and hardships endured by the family, its withdrawal in poverty to
Sulaco, the death of the mother.

The Monterist pronunciamiento had taken place before
Martin Decoud reached Costaguana. He came out in a
roundabout way, through Magellan's Straits by the main
line and the West Coast Service of the O.S.N. Company.
His precious consignment arrived just in time to convert
the first feelings of consternation into a mood of hope and
resolution. Publicly he was made much of by the
familias principales. Privately Don José, still shaken and
weak, embraced him with tears in his eyes.

"You have come out yourself! No less could be expected from a Decoud. Alas! our worst fears have been realised," he moaned affectionately. And again he hugged his godson. This was indeed the time for men of intellect and conscience to rally round the endangered cause.

It was then that Martin Decoud, the adopted child of Western Europe, felt the absolute change of atmosphere. He submitted to being embraced and talked to without a word. He was moved in spite of himself by that note of passion and sorrow unknown on the more refined stage of European politics. But when the tall Antonia, advancing with her light step in the dimness of the big, bare sala of the Avellanos house, offered him her hand (in her emancipated way), and murmured, "I am glad to see you here, Don Martin," he felt how impossible it would be to tell these two people that he had intended to go away by the next month's packet. Don José, meantime, continued his praises. Every accession added to public confidence ; and, besides, what an example to the young men at home from the brilliant defender of the country's regeneration, the worthy expounder of the party's political faith before the world ! Everybody had read the magnificent article in the famous Parisian review. The world was now informed : and the author's appearance at this moment was like a public act of faith. Young Decoud felt overcome by a feeling of impatient confusion. His plan had been to return by way of the United States through California, visit the Yellowstone Park, see Chicago, Niagara, have a look at Canada, perhaps make a short stay in New York, a longer one in Newport, use his letters of introduction. The pressure of Antonia's hand was so frank, the tone of her voice was so unexpectedly unchanged in its approving warmth, that all he found to say after his low bow was :

"I am inexpressibly grateful for your welcome ; but why need a man be thanked for returning to his

native country? I am sure Doña Antonia does not
think so."

"Certainly not, Señor," she said, with that perfectly
calm openness of manner which characterised all her
utterances. "But when he returns, as you return, one
may be glad—for the sake of both."

Martin Decoud said nothing of his plans. He not
only never breathed a word of them to any one, but only a
fortnight later asked the mistress of Casa Gould (where
he had of course obtained admission at once), leaning
forward in his chair with an air of well-bred familiarity,
whether she could not detect in him that day a marked
change—an air, he explained, of more excellent gravity.
At this Mrs. Gould turned her face full towards him with
the silent inquiry of slightly widened eyes and the merest
ghost of a smile, an habitual movement with her, which
was very fascinating to men by something subtly devoted,
finely self-forgetful in its lively readiness of attention.
Because, Decoud continued imperturbably, he felt no
longer an idle cumberer of the earth. She was, he assured
her, actually beholding at that moment the Journalist of
Sulaco. At once Mrs. Gould glanced towards Antonia,
posed upright in the corner of a high, straight-backed
Spanish sofa, a large black fan waving slowly against the
curves of her fine figure, the tips of crossed feet peeping
from under the hem of the black skirt. Decoud's eyes
also remained fixed there, while in an undertone he added
that Miss Avellanos was quite aware of his new and unexpected vocation, which in Costaguana was generally the
speciality of half-educated negroes and wholly penniless
lawyers. Then, confronting with a sort of urbane
effrontery Mrs. Gould's gaze, now turned sympathetically
upon himself, he breathed out the words, " Pro patria ! "

What had happened was that he had all at once yielded
to Don José's pressing entreaties to take the direction of
a newspaper that would " voice the aspirations of the
province." It had been Don José's old and cherished

idea. The necessary plant (on a modest scale) and a large consignment of paper had been received from America some time before ; the right man alone was wanted. Even Señor Moraga in Sta. Marta had not been able to find one, and the matter was now becoming pressing ; some organ was absolutely needed to counteract the effect of the lies disseminated by the Monterist press : the atrocious calumnies, the appeals to the people calling upon them to rise with their knives in their hands and put an end once for all to the Blancos, to these Gothic remnants, to these sinister mummies, these impotent paraliticos, who plotted with foreigners for the surrender of the lands and the slavery of the people.

The clamour of this *Negro Liberalism* frightened Señor Avellanos. A newspaper was the only remedy. And now that the right man had been found in Decoud, great black letters appeared painted between the windows above the arcaded ground floor of a house on the plaza. It was next to Anzani's great emporium of boots, silks, ironware, muslins, wooden toys, tiny silver arms, legs, heads, hearts (for ex-voto offerings), rosaries, champagne, women's hats, patent medicines, even a few dusty books in paper covers and mostly in the French language. The big black letters formed the words : " Offices of the *Porvenir*." From these offices a single folded sheet of Martin's journalism issued three times a week ; and the sleek yellow Anzani, prowling in a suit of ample black and carpet slippers before the many doors of his establishment, greeted by a deep, sidelong inclination of his body the Journalist of Sulaco going to and fro on the business of his august calling.

CHAPTER FOUR

PERHAPS it was in the exercise of his calling that he had come to see the troops depart. The *Porvenir* of the day after next would no doubt relate the event, but its editor, leaning his side against the landau, seemed to look at nothing. The front rank of the company of infantry drawn up three deep across the shore end of the jetty when pressed too closely would bring their bayonets to the charge ferociously, with an awful rattle; and then the crowd of spectators swayed back bodily, even under the noses of the big white mules. Notwithstanding the great multitude there was only a low, muttering noise; the dust hung in a brown haze, in which the horsemen, wedged in the throng here and there, towered from the hips upwards, gazing all one way over the heads. Almost every one of them had mounted a friend, who steadied himself with both hands grasping his shoulders from behind; and the rims of their hats touching, made like one disc sustaining the cones of two pointed crowns with a double face underneath. A hoarse mozo would bawl out something to an acquaintance in the ranks, or a woman would shriek suddenly the word *Adios!* followed by the Christian name of a man.

General Barrios, in a shabby blue tunic and white peg-top trousers falling upon strange red boots, kept his head uncovered and stooped slightly, propping himself up with a thick stick. No! He had earned enough military glory to satiate any man, he insisted to Mrs.

Gould, trying at the same time to put an air of gallantry
into his attitude.   A few jetty hairs hung sparsely
from his upper lip, he had a salient nose, a thin, long
jaw, and a black silk patch over one eye.   His other
eye, small and deep-set, twinkled erratically in all directions, aimlessly affable.   The few European spectators,
all men, who had naturally drifted into the neighbourhood of the Gould carriage, betrayed by the solemnity
of their faces their impression that the general must
have had too much punch (Swedish punch, imported
in bottles by Anzani) at the Amarilla Club before he
had started with his Staff on a furious ride to the harbour.
But Mrs. Gould bent forward, self-possessed, and declared her conviction that still more glory awaited the
general in the near future.

" Señora ! " he remonstrated, with great feeling, " in
the name of God, reflect !   How can there be any glory
for a man like me in overcoming that bald-headed
embustero with the dyed moustaches ? "

Pablo Ignacio Barrios, son of a village alcade, general
of division, commanding in chief the Occidental Military
District, did not frequent the higher society of the town.
He preferred the unceremonious gatherings of men where
he could tell jaguar-hunt stories, boast of his powers with
the lasso, with which he could perform extremely difficult
feats of the sort " no married man should attempt," as
the saying goes amongst the llaneros, relate tales of
extraordinary night rides, encounters with wild bulls,
struggles with crocodiles, adventures in the great forests,
crossings of swollen rivers.   And it was not mere boast-
fulness that prompted the general's reminiscences, but a
genuine love of that wild life which he had led in his
young days before he turned his back for ever on the
thatched roof of the parental tolderia in the woods.
Wandering away as far as Mexico he had fought against
the French by the side (as he said) of Juarez, and was
the only military man of Costaguana who had ever

encountered European troops in the field.   That fact shed
a great lustre upon his name till it became eclipsed by
the rising star of Montero.   All his life he had been
an inveterate gambler.   He alluded himself quite openly
to the current story how once, during some campaign
(when in command of a brigade), he had gambled away
his horses, pistols, and accoutrements, to the very
epaulettes, playing *monte* with his colonels the night
before the battle.   Finally, he had sent under escort
his sword (a presentation sword, with a gold hilt) to the
town in the rear of his position to be immediately pledged
for five hundred pesetas with a sleepy and frightened
shopkeeper.   By daybreak he had lost the last of that
money too, when his only remark, as he rose calmly,
was, " Now let us go and fight to the death."   From
that time he had become aware that a general could
lead his troops into battle very well with a simple stick
in his hand.   " It has been my custom ever since," he
would say.

He was always overwhelmed with debts ; even during
the periods of splendour in his varied fortunes of a
Costaguana general, when he held high military com-
mands, his gold-laced uniforms were almost always in
pawn with some tradesman.   And at last, to avoid the
incessant difficulties of costume caused by the anxious
lenders, he had assumed a disdain of military trappings,
an eccentric fashion of shabby old tunics, which had
become like a second nature.   But the faction Barrios
joined needed to fear no political betrayal.   He was too
much of a real soldier for the ignoble traffic of buying
and selling victories.   A member of the foreign diplomatic body in Sta. Marta had once passed a judgment
upon him : " Barrios is a man of perfect honesty and
even of some talent for war, *mais il manque de tenue.*"
After the triumph of the Ribierists he had obtained the
reputedly lucrative Occidental command, mainly through
the exertions of his creditors (the Sta. Marta shopkeepers,

all great politicians), who moved heaven and earth in his interest publicly, and privately besieged Señor Moraga, the influential agent of the San Tomé mine, with the exaggerated lamentations that if the general were passed over, " We shall all be ruined." An incidental but favourable mention of his name in Mr. Gould senior's long correspondence with his son had something to do with his appointment, too ; but most of all undoubtedly his established political honesty. No one questioned the personal bravery of the Tiger-killer, as the populace called him. He was, however, said to be unlucky in the field—but this was to be the beginning of an era of peace. The soldiers liked him for his humane temper, which was like a strange and precious flower unexpectedly blooming on the hotbed of corrupt revolutions ; and when he rode slowly through the streets during some military display, the contemptuous good humour of his solitary eye roaming over the crowds extorted the acclamations of the populace. The women of that class especially seemed positively fascinated by the long dropping nose, the peaked chin, the heavy lower lip, the black silk eye-patch and band slanting rakishly over the forehead. His high rank always procured an audience of caballeros for his sporting stories, which he detailed very well with a simple, grave enjoyment. As to the society of ladies, it was irksome by the restraints it imposed without any equivalent, as far as he could see. He had not, perhaps, spoken three times on the whole to Mrs. Gould since he had taken up his high command, but he had observed her frequently riding with the Señor Administrador, and had pronounced that there was more sense in her little bridle-hand than in all the female heads of Sulaco. His impulse had been to be very civil on parting to a woman who did not wobble in the saddle, and happened to be the wife of a personality very important to a man always short of money. He even pushed his attentions so far as to desire the aide-de-camp at his side (a thick-set, short captain with a Tartar physiognomy) to bring along a corporal with a file of men in front of the carriage, lest the crowd in its backward surges should " incommode the mules of the Señora." Then, turning to the small knot of silent Europeans looking on within earshot, he raised his voice protectingly :

" Señores, have no apprehension. Go on quietly making your Ferro Carril—your railways, your telegraphs. Your—— There's enough wealth in Costaguana to pay for everything—or else you would not be here. Ha! ha! Don't mind this little *picardia* of my friend Montero. In a little while you shall behold his dyed moustaches through the bars of a strong wooden cage. Si, Señores! Fear nothing, develop the country, work, work ! "

The little group of engineers received this exhortation without a word, and after waving his hand at them loftily, he addressed himself again to Mrs. Gould :

" That is what Don José says we must do. Be enterprising ! Work ! Grow rich ! To put Montero in a cage is my work ; and when that insignificant piece of business is done, then, as Don José wishes us, we shall grow rich, one and all, like so many Englishmen, because it is money that saves a country, and——"

But a young officer in a very new uniform, hurrying up from the direction of the jetty, interrupted his interpretation of Señor Avellanos's ideals. The general made a movement of impatience ; the other went on talking to him insistently, with an air of respect. The horses of the Staff had been embarked, the steamer's gig was awaiting the general at the boat steps, and Barrios, after a fierce stare of his one eye, began to take leave. Don José roused himself for an appropriate phrase pronounced mechanically. The terrible strain of hope and fear was telling on him, and he seemed to husband the last sparks of his fire for those oratorical efforts of

which even the distant Europe was to hear. Antonia,
her red lips firmly closed, averted her head behind the
raised fan ; and young Decoud, though he felt the
girl's eyes upon him, gazed away persistently, hooked
on his elbow, with a scornful and complete detachment.
Mrs. Gould heroically concealed her dismay at the appearance of men and events so remote from her racial
conventions, dismay too deep to be uttered in words
even to her husband. She understood his voiceless
reserve better now. Their confidential intercourse fell,
not in moments of privacy, but precisely in public, when
the quick meeting of their glances would comment upon
some fresh turn of events. She had gone to his school of
uncompromising silence, the only one possible, since so
much that seemed shocking, weird, and grotesque in
the working out of their purposes had to be accepted as
normal in this country. Decidedly, the stately Antonia
looked more mature and infinitely calm ; but she would
never have known how to reconcile the sudden sinkings
of her heart with an amiable mobility of expression.

    Mrs. Gould smiled a good-bye at Barrios, nodded
round to the Europeans (who raised their hats simultaneously) with an engaging invitation, " I hope to see
you all presently, at home," then said nervously to
Decoud, " Get in, Don Martin," and heard him mutter
to himself in French, as he opened the carriage door,
" *Le sort en est jeté.*" She heard him with a sort of
exasperation. Nobody ought to have known better
than himself that the first cast of dice had been already
thrown long ago in a most desperate game. Distant
acclamations, words of command yelled out, and a roll
of drums on the jetty greeted the departing general.
Something like a slight faintness came over her, and she
looked blankly at Antonia's still face, wondering what
would happen to Charley if that absurd man failed.
" *A la casa, Ignacio,*" she cried at the motionless broad
back of the coachman, who gathered the reins without

haste, mumbling to himself under his breath, " *Si, la casa. Si, si, nina.*"

The carriage rolled noiselessly on the soft track, the shadows fell long on the dusty little plain interspersed with dark bushes, mounds of turned-up earth, low wooden buildings with iron roofs of the Railway Company ; the sparse row of telegraph poles strode obliquely clear of the town, bearing a single, almost invisible wire far into the great Campo—like a slender vibrating feeler of that progress waiting outside for a moment of peace to enter and twine itself about the weary heart of the land.

The café window of the Albergo d'Italia Una was full of sunburnt, whiskered faces of railwaymen. But at the other end of the house, the end of the Signori Inglesi, old Giorgio, at the door with one of his girls on each side, bared his bushy head, as white as the snows of Higuerota. Mrs. Gould stopped the carriage. She seldom failed to speak to her *protégé* ; moreover, the excitement, the heat, and the dust had made her thirsty. She asked for a glass of water. Giorgio sent the children indoors for it, and approached with pleasure expressed in his whole rugged countenance. It was not often that he had occasion to see his benefactress, who was also an English-woman—another title to his regard. He offered some excuses for his wife. It was a bad day with her ; her oppressions—he tapped his own broad chest. She could not move from her chair that day.

Decoud, ensconced in the corner of his seat, observed gloomily Mrs. Gould's old revolutionist ; then, off-hand :

" Well, and what do you think of it all, Garibaldino ? "

Old Giorgio, looking at him with some curiosity, said civilly that the troops had marched very well. One-eyed Barrios and his officers had done wonders with the recruits in a short time. Those Indios, only caught the other day, had gone swinging past in double-quick time, like bersaglieri ; they looked well fed, too, and had whole uniforms. " Uniforms ! " he repeated with a half-smile of pity. A look of grim restrospect stole over his piercing, steady eyes. It had been otherwise in his time when men fought against tyranny, in the forests of Brazil, or on the plains of Uruguay, starving on half-raw beef without salt, half naked, with often only a knife tied to a stick for a weapon. " And yet we used to prevail against the oppressor," he concluded proudly.

His animation fell ; the slight gesture of his hand expressed discouragement ; but he added that he had asked one of the sergeants to show him the new rifle. There was no such weapon in his fighting days ; and if Barrios could not——

" Yes, yes," broke in Don José, almost trembling with eagerness. " We are safe. The good Señor Viola is a man of experience. Extremely deadly—is it not so ? You have accomplished your mission admirably, my dear Martin."

Decoud, lolling back moodily, contemplated old Viola.

" Ah, yes ! A man of experience. But who are you for, really, in your heart ? "

Mrs. Gould leaned over to the children. Linda had brought out a glass of water on a tray, with extreme care ; Giselle presented her with a bunch of flowers gathered hastily.

" For the people," declared old Viola sternly.

" We are all for the people—in the end."

" Yes," muttered old Viola savagely. " And mean-time they fight for you. Blind. Esclavos ! "

At that moment young Scarfe of the railway staff emerged from the door of the part reserved for the Signori Inglesi. He had come down to headquarters from somewhere up the line on a light engine, and had had just time to get a bath and change his clothes. He was a nice boy, and Mrs. Gould welcomed him.

" It's a delightful surprise to see you, Mrs. Gould.

I've just come down. Usual luck. Missed everything, of course. This show is just over, and I hear there has been a great dance at Don Juste Lopez's last night. Is it true ? "

" The young patricians," Decoud began suddenly in his precise English, " have indeed been dancing before they started off to the war with the Great Pompey."

Young Scarfe stared, astounded. " You haven't met before," Mrs. Gould intervened. " Mr. Decoud—Mr. Scarfe."

" Ah ! But we are not going to Pharsalia," protested Don José, with nervous haste, also in English. " You should not jest like this, Martin."

Antonia's breast rose and fell with a deeper breath. The young engineer was utterly in the dark. " Great what ? " he muttered vaguely.

" Luckily, Montero is not a Cæsar," Decoud continued. " Not the two Monteros put together would make a decent parody of a Cæsar." He crossed his arms on his breast, looking at Señor Avellanos, who had returned to his immobility. " It is only you, Don José, who are a genuine old Roman—*vir Romanus*—eloquent and inflexible."

Since he had heard the name of Montero pronounced, young Scarfe had been eager to express his simple feelings. In a loud and youthful tone he hoped that this Montero was going to be licked once for all and done with. There was no saying what would happen to the railway if the revolution got the upper hand. Perhaps it would have to be abandoned. It would not be the first railway gone to pot in Costaguana. " You know, it's one of their so-called national things," he ran on, wrinkling up his nose as if the word had a suspicious flavour to his profound experience of South American affairs. And, of course, he chatted with animation, it had been such an immense piece of luck for him at his age to get appointed on the staff " of a big thing like that—don't

you know." It would give him the pull over a lot of
chaps all through life, he asserted. "Therefore—down
with Montero! Mrs. Gould." His artless grin disappeared slowly before the unanimous gravity of the
faces turned upon him from the carriage; only that " old
chap," Don José, presenting a motionless, waxy profile,
stared straight on as if deaf. Scarfe did not know
the Avellanos very well. They did not give balls, and
Antonia never appeared at a ground-floor window, as
some other young ladies used to do attended by elder
women, to chat with the caballeros on horseback in the
calle. The stares of these creoles did not matter much ;
but what on earth had come to Mrs. Gould ? She said,
" Go on, Ignacio," and gave him a slow inclination of
the head. He heard a short laugh from that round-
faced, Frenchified fellow. He coloured up to the eyes,
and stared at Giorgio Viola, who had fallen back with the
children, hat in hand.

" I shall want a horse presently," he said with some
asperity to the old man.

" Si, Señor. There are plenty of horses," murmured
the Garibaldino, smoothing absently with his brown
hands the two heads, one dark with bronze glints, the
other fair with a coppery ripple, of the two girls by his
side. The returning stream of sightseers raised a great
dust on the road. Horsemen noticed the group. " Go
to your mother," he said. " They are growing up as I
am growing older, and there is nobody——"

He looked at the young engineer and stopped, as if
awakened from a dream ; then, folding his arms on his
breast, took up his usual position, leaning back in the
doorway with an upward glance fastened on the white
shoulder of Higuerota far away.

In the carriage Martin Decoud, shifting his position as
though he could not make himself comfortable, muttered
as he swayed towards Antonia, " I suppose you hate me."
Then in a loud voice he began to congratulate Don José

upon all the engineers being convinced Ribierists. The interest of all those foreigners was gratifying. " You have heard this one. He is an enlightened well-wisher. It is pleasant to think that the prosperity of Costaguana is of some use to the world."

" He is very young," Mrs. Gould remarked quietly.

" And so very wise for his age," retorted Decoud. " But here we have the naked truth from the mouth of that child. You are right, Don José. The natural treasures of Costaguana are of importance to the progressive Europe represented by this youth, just as three hundred years ago the wealth of our Spanish fathers was a serious object to the rest of Europe—-as represented by the bold buccaneers. There is a curse of futility upon our character : Don Quixote and Sancho Panza, chivalry and materialism, high-sounding sentiments and a supine morality, violent efforts for an idea and a sullen acquiescence in every form of corruption. We convulsed a continent for our independence only to become the passive prey of a democratic parody, the helpless victims of scoundrels and cutthroats, our institutions a mockery, our laws a farce—-a Guzman Bento our master ! And we have sunk so low that when a man like you has awakened our conscience, a stupid barbarian of a Montero—great heavens ! a Montero !—becomes a deadly danger, and an ignorant, boastful Indio, like Barrios, is our defender."

But Don José, disregarding the general indictment as though he had not heard a word of it, took up the defence of Barrios. The man was competent enough for his special task in the plan of campaign. It consisted in an offensive movement, with Cayta as base, upon the flank of the Revolutionist forces advancing from the south against Sta. Marta, which was covered by another army with the President-Dictator in its midst. Don José became quite animated with a great flow of speech, bending forward anxiously under the steady eyes of his daughter. Decoud, as if silenced by so much ardour, did not make a

II

sound. The bells of the city were striking the hour of
Oracion when the carriage rolled under the old gateway
facing the harbour like a shapeless monument of leaves
and stones. The rumble of wheels under the sonorous
arch was traversed by a strange, piercing shriek, and
Decoud, from his back seat, had a view of the people
behind the carriage trudging along the road outside, all
turning their heads, in sombreros and rebozos, to look
at a locomotive which rolled quickly out of sight behind
Giorgio Viola's house, under a white trail of steam that
seemed to vanish in the breathless, hysterically prolonged scream of warlike triumph. And it was all like a
fleeting vision, the shrieking ghost of a railway engine
fleeing across the frame of the archway, behind the
startled movement of the people streaming back from a
military spectacle with silent footsteps on the dust of the
road. It was a material train returning from the Campo
to the palisaded yards. The empty cars rolled lightly on
the single track ; there was no rumble of wheels, no
tremor of the ground. The engine-driver, running past
the Casa Viola with the salute of an uplifted arm, checked
his speed smartly before entering the yard ; and when the
ear-splitting screech of the steam-whistle for the brakes
had stopped, a series of hard, battering shocks, mingled
with the clanking of chain-couplings, made a tumult of
blows and shaken fetters under the vault of the gate.

CHAPTER FIVE

THE Gould carriage was the first to return from the harbour to the empty town. On the ancient pavement, laid out in patterns, sunk into ruts and holes, the portly Ignacio, mindful of the springs of the Parisian-built landau, had pulled up to a walk, and Decoud in his corner contemplated moodily the inner aspect of the gate. The squat turreted sides held up between them a mass of masonry with bunches of grass growing at the top, and a grey, heavily scrolled armorial shield of stone above the apex of the arch with the arms of Spain nearly smoothed out as if in readiness for some new device typical of the impending progress.

The explosive noise of the railway trucks seemed to augment Decoud's irritation. He muttered something to himself, then began to talk aloud in curt, angry phrases thrown at the silence of the two women. They did not look at him at all ; while Don José, with his semi-translucent, waxy complexion, overshadowed by the soft grey hat, swayed a little to the jolts of the carriage by the side of Mrs. Gould.

" This sound puts a new edge on a very old truth."

Decoud spoke in French, perhaps because of Ignacio on the box above him ; the old coachman, with his broad back filling a short silver-braided jacket, had a big pair of ears, whose thick rims stood well away from his cropped head.

" Yes, the noise outside the city wall is new, but the principle is old."

He ruminated his discontent for a while, then began afresh with a sidelong glance at Antonia :

" No, but just imagine our forefathers in morions and corselets drawn up outside this gate, and a band of adventurers just landed from their ships in the harbour there. Thieves, of course. Speculators, too. Their expeditions, each one, were the speculations of grave and reverend persons in England. That is history, as that absurd sailor Mitchell is always saying."

" Mitchell's arrangements for the embarkation of the troops were excellent ! " exclaimed Don José.

" That !—that ! oh, that's really the work of that Genoese seaman ! But to return to my noises ; there used to be in the old days the sound of trumpets outside that gate. War trumpets ! I'm sure they were trumpets. I have read somewhere that Drake, who was the greatest of these men, used to dine alone in his cabin on board ship to the sound of trumpets. In those days this town was full of wealth. Those men came to take it. Now the whole land is like a treasure-house, and all these people are breaking into it, whilst we are cutting each other's throats. The only thing that keeps them out is mutual jealousy. But they'll come to an agreement some day—and by the time we've settled our quarrels and become decent and honourable, there'll be nothing left for us. It has always been the same. We are a wonderful people, but it has always been our fate to be "—he did not say " robbed," but added, after a pause—" exploited ! "

Mrs. Gould said, " Oh, this is unjust ! " And Antonia interjected, " Don't answer him, Emilia. He is attacking me."

" You surely do not think I was attacking Don Carlos ! " Decoud answered.

And then the carriage stopped before the door of the Casa Gould. The young man offered his hand to the ladies. They went in first together ; Don José walked by the side of Decoud, and the gouty old porter tottered after them with some light wraps on his arm.

Don José slipped his hand under the arm of the Journalist of Sulaco.

" The *Porvenir* must have a long and confident article upon Barrios and the irresistibleness of his army of Cayta ! The moral effect should be kept up in the country. We must cable encouraging extracts to Europe and the United States to maintain a favourable impression abroad."

Decoud muttered, " Oh yes, we must comfort our friends, the speculators."

The long open gallery was in shadow, with its screen of plants in vases along the balustrade, holding out motionless blossoms, and all the glass doors of the reception-rooms thrown open. A jingle of spurs died out at the farther end.

Basilio, standing aside against the wall, said in a soft tone to the passing ladies, " The Señor Administrador is just back from the mountain."

In the great sala, with its groups of ancient Spanish and modern European furniture making as if different centres under the high white spread of the ceiling, the silver and porcelain of the tea-service gleamed among a cluster of dwarf chairs, like a bit of a lady's boudoir, putting in a note of feminine and intimate delicacy.

Don José in his rocking-chair placed his hat on his lap, and Decoud walked up and down the whole length of the room, passing between tables loaded with knick-knacks and almost disappearing behind the high backs of leathern sofas. He was thinking of the angry face of Antonia ; he was confident that he would make his peace with her. He had not stayed in Sulaco to quarrel with Antonia.

Martin Decoud was angry with himself. All he saw and heard going on around him exasperated the pre conceived views of his European civilisation. To contemplate revolutions from the distance of the Parisian boulevards was quite another matter. Here on the spot it was not possible to dismiss their tragic comedy with the expression, " *Quelle farce !* "

The reality of the political action, such as it was, seemed closer, and acquired poignancy by Antonia's belief in the cause. Its crudeness hurt his feelings. He was surprised at his own sensitiveness.

" I suppose I am more of a Costaguanero than I would have believed possible," he thought to himself.

His disdain grew like a reaction of his scepticism against the action into which he was forced by his infatuation for Antonia. He soothed himself by saying he was not a patriot, but a lover.

The ladies came in bareheaded, and Mrs. Gould sank low before the little tea-table. Antonia took up her usual place at the reception-hour—the corner of a leathern couch—with a rigid grace in her pose and a fan in her hand. Decoud, swerving from the straight line of his march, came to lean over the high back of her seat.

For a long time he talked into her ear from behind, softly, with a half smile and an air of apologetic familiarity. Her fan lay half grasped on her knees. She never looked at him. His rapid utterance grew more and more insistent and caressing. At last he ventured a slight laugh.

" No, really. You must forgive me. One must be serious sometimes." He paused. She turned her head a little ; her blue eyes glided slowly towards him, slightly upwards, mollified and questioning.

" You can't think I am serious when I call Montero a *gran' bestia* every second day in the *Porvenir* ? That is not a serious occupation. No occupation is serious, not even when a bullet through the heart is the penalty of failure ! "

Her hand closed firmly on her fan.

" Some reason, you understand, I mean some sense,

may creep into thinking ; some glimpse of truth. I mean some effective truth, for which there is no room in politics or journalism. I happen to have said what I thought. And you are angry ! If you do me the kindness to think a little you will see that I spoke like a patriot."

She opened her red lips for the first time, not unkindly.

" Yes, but you never see the aim. Men must be used as they are. I suppose nobody is really disinterested, unless, perhaps, you, Don Martin."

" God forbid ! It's the last thing I should like you to believe of me." He spoke lightly, and paused.

She began to fan herself with a slow movement without raising her hand. After a time he whispered passionately :

" Antonia ! "

She smiled, and extended her hand after the English manner towards Charles Gould, who was bowing before her ; while Decoud, with his elbows spread on the back of the sofa, dropped his eyes and murmured, " *Bonjour*."

The Señor Administrador of the San Tomé mine bent over his wife for a moment. They exchanged a few words, of which only the phrase, " The greatest enthusiasm," pronounced by Mrs. Gould, could be heard.

" Yes," Decoud began in a murmur. " Even he ! "

" This is sheer calumny," said Antonia, not very severely.

" You just ask him to throw his mine into the melting-pot for the great cause," Decoud whispered.

Don José had raised his voice. He rubbed his hands cheerily. The excellent aspect of the troops and the great quantity of new deadly rifles on the shoulders of those brave men seemed to fill him with an ecstatic confidence.

Charles Gould, very tall and thin before his chair,

listened, but nothing could be discovered in his face except a kind and deferential attention.

Meantime, Antonia had risen, and, crossing the room, stood looking out of one of the three long windows giving on the street. Decoud followed her. The window was thrown open, and he leaned against the thickness of the wall. The long folds of the damask curtain, falling straight from the broad brass cornice, hid him partly from the room. He folded his arms on his breast, and looked steadily at Antonia's profile.   `

The people returning from the harbour filled the pavements ; the shuffle of sandals and a low murmur of voices ascended to the window. Now and then a coach rolled slowly along the disjointed roadway of the Calle de la Constitucion. There were not many private carriages in Sulaco ; at the most crowded hour on the Alameda they could be counted with one glance of the eye. The great family arks swayed on high leathern springs, full of pretty, powdered faces in which the eyes looked intensely alive and black. And first Don Juste Lopez, the President of the Provincial Assembly, passed with his three lovely daughters, solemn in a black frock-coat and stiff white tie, as when directing a debate from a high tribune. Though they all raised their eyes, Antonia did not make the usual greeting gesture of a fluttered hand, and they affected not to see the two young people, Costaguaneros with European manners, whose eccentricities were dis· cussed behind the barred windows of the first families in Sulaco. And then the widowed Señora Gavilaso de Valdes rolled by, handsome and dignified, in a great machine in which she used to travel to and from her country house, surrounded by an armed retinue in leather suits and big sombreros, with carbines at the bows of their saddles. She was a woman of most distinguished family, proud, rich, and kind-hearted. Her second son, Jaime, had just gone off on the Staff of Barrios. The eldest, a worthless fellow of a moody disposition, filled

Sulaco with the noise of his dissipations, and gambled heavily at the club. The two youngest boys, with yellow Ribierist cockades in their caps, sat on the front seat. She, too, affected not to see the Señor Decoud talking publicly with Antonia in defiance of every convention. And he not even her *novio* as far as the world knew! Though, even in that case, it would have been scandal enough. But the dignified old lady, respected and admired by the first families, would have been still more shocked if she could have heard the words they were exchanging.

"Did you say I lost sight of the aim? I have only one aim in the world."

She made an almost imperceptible negative movement of her head, still staring across the street at the Avellanos's house, grey, marked with decay, and with iron bars like a prison.

"And it would be so easy of attainment," he continued, "this aim which, whether knowingly or not, I have always had in my heart—ever since the day when you snubbed me so horribly once in Paris, you remember."

A slight smile seemed to move the corner of the lip that was on his side.

"You know you were a very terrible person, a sort of Charlotte Corday in a schoolgirl's dress; a ferocious patriot. I suppose you would have stuck a knife into Guzman Bento?"

She interrupted him. "You do me too much honour."

"At any rate," he said, changing suddenly to a tone of bitter levity, "you would have sent me to stab him without compunction."

"Ah, *par exemple*!" she murmured in a shocked tone.

"Well," he argued mockingly, "you do keep me here writing deadly nonsense. Deadly to me! It has

already killed my self-respect. And you may imagine,"
he continued, his tone passing into light banter, " that
Montero, should he be successful, would get even with
me in the only way such a brute can get even with a man
of intelligence who condescends to call him a *gran' bestia*
three times a week. It's a sort of intellectual death ;
but there is the other one in the background for a
journalist of my ability."

" If he is successful ! " said Antonia thoughtfully.

" You seem satisfied to see my life hang on a thread,"
Decoud replied, with a broad smile. " And the other
Montero, the ' my trusted brother ' of the proclamations,
the guerrillero—haven't I written that he was taking the
guests' overcoats and changing plates in Paris at our
Legation in the intervals of spying on our refugees there,
in the time of Rojas ? He will wash out that sacred
truth in blood. In my blood ! Why do you look
annoyed ? This is simply a bit of the biography of one
of our great men. What do you think he will do to me ?
There is a certain convent wall round the corner of the
plaza, opposite the door of the Bull Ring. You know ?
Opposite the door with the inscription, ' Intrada de la
Sombra.' Appropriate, perhaps ! That's where the
uncle of our host gave up his Anglo-South-American
soul. And, note, he might have run away. A man who
has fought with weapons may run away. You might
have let me go with Barrios if you had cared for me. I
would have carried one of those rifles, in which Don
José believes, with the greatest satisfaction, in the ranks
of poor peons and Indios, that know nothing either of
reason or politics. The most forlorn hope in the most
forlorn army on earth would have been safer than that
for which you made me stay here. When you make
war you may retreat, but not when you spend your time
in inciting poor ignorant fools to kill and to die."

His tone remained light, and as if unaware of his
presence she stood motionless, her hands clasped lightly,

the fan hanging down from her interlaced fingers. He
waited for a while, and then :

"I shall go to the wall," he said, with a sort of
jocular desperation.

Even that declaration did not make her look at him.
Her head remained still, her eyes fixed upon the house of
the Avellanos, whose chipped pilasters, broken cornices,
the whole degradation of dignity, was hidden now by the
gathering dusk of the street. In her whole figure her lips
alone moved, forming the words :

"Martin, you will make me cry."

He remained silent for a minute, startled, as if overwhelmed by a sort of awed happiness, with the lines of
the mocking smile still stiffened about his mouth, and
incredulous surprise in his eyes. The value of a sentence
is in the personality which utters it, for nothing new can
be said by man or woman ; and those were the last words,
it seemed to him, that could ever have been spoken by
Antonia. He had never made it up with her so completely in all their intercourse of small encounters ; but
even before she had time to turn towards him, which she
did slowly with a rigid grace, he had begun to plead :

"My sister is only waiting to embrace you. My
father is transported with joy. I won't say anything of
my mother. Our mothers were like sisters. There is
the mail-boat for the south next week—let us go. That
Moraga is a fool ! A man like Montero is bribed. It's
the practice of the country. It's tradition—it's politics.
Read *Fifty Years of Misrule*."

"Leave poor papa alone, Don Martin. He believes——"

"I have the greatest tenderness for your father," he
began hurriedly. "But I love you, Antonia ! And
Moraga has miserably mismanaged this business. Perhaps your father did, too ; I don't know. Montero was
bribable. Why, I suppose he only wanted his share
of this famous loan for national development. Why

didn't the stupid Sta. Marta people give him a mission
to Europe, or something ? He would have taken five
years' salary in advance, and gone on loafing in Paris,
this stupid, ferocious Indio ! "

" The man," she said thoughtfully, and very calm
before this outburst, " was intoxicated with vanity. We
had all the information, not from Moraga only ; from
others too. There was his brother intriguing too."

" Oh yes ! " he said. " Of course you know. You
know everything. You read all the correspondence, you
write all the papers—all those State papers that are
inspired here, in this room, in blind deference to a
theory of political purity. Hadn't you Charles Gould
before your eyes ? Rey de Sulaco ! He and his mine
are the practical demonstration of what could have been
done. Do you think he succeeded by his fidelity to a
theory of virtue ? And all those railway people, with
their honest work ! Of course, their work is honest !
But what if you cannot work honestly till the thieves
are satisfied ? Could he not, a gentleman, have told
this Sir John What's-his-name that Montero had to be
bought off—he and all his Negro Liberals hanging on to
his gold-laced sleeve ? He ought to have been bought
off with his own stupid weight of gold—his weight of
gold, I tell you, boots, sabre, spurs, cocked hat and all."

She shook her head slightly. " It was impossible,"
she murmured.

" He wanted the whole lot ?   What ? "

She was facing him now in the deep recess of the
window, very close and motionless. Her lips moved
rapidly. Decoud, leaning his back against the wall,
listened with crossed arms and lowered eyelids. He
drank the tones of her even voice, and watched the
agitated life of her throat, as if waves of emotion had
run from her heart to pass out into the air in her reasonable words. He also had his aspirations ; he aspired
to carry her away out of these deadly futilities of

pronunciamientos and reforms. All this was wrong—
utterly wrong; but she fascinated him, and sometimes
the sheer sagacity of a phrase would break the charm,
replace the fascination by a sudden unwilling thrill of
interest. Some women hovered, as it were, on the
threshold of genius, he reflected. They did not want
to know, or think, or understand. Passion stood for all
that, and he was ready to believe that some startlingly
profound remark, some appreciation of character, or a
judgment upon an event, bordered on the miraculous.
In the mature Antonia he could see with an extraordinary
vividness the austere schoolgirl of the earlier days. She
seduced his attention ; sometimes he could not restrain
a murmur of assent ; now and then he advanced an
objection quite seriously. Gradually they began to
argue ; the curtain half hid them from the people in
the sala.

Outside it had grown dark. From the deep trench
of shadow between the houses, lit up vaguely by the
glimmer of street lamps, ascended the evening silence
of Sulaco : the silence of a town with few carriages, of
unshod horses, and a softly sandalled population. The
windows of the Casa Gould flung their shining parallelograms upon the house of the Avellanos. Now and then
a shuffle of feet passed below with the pulsating red glow
of a cigarette at the foot of the walls ; and the night air,
as if cooled by the snows of Higuerota, refreshed their
faces.

" We Occidentals," said Martin Decoud, using the
usual term the provincials of Sulaco applied to themselves,
" have been always distinct and separated. As long as
we hold Cayta nothing can reach us. In all our troubles
no army has marched over these mountains. A revolution in the central provinces isolates us at once. Look
how complete it is now ! The news of Barrios's movement will be cabled to the United States, and only
in that way will it reach Sta. Marta by the cable from

the other seaboard. We have the greatest riches, the greatest fertility, the purest blood in our great families, the most laborious population. The Occidental Province should stand alone. The early Federalism was not bad for us. Then came this union which Don Henrique Gould resisted. It opened the road to tyranny; and, ever since, the rest of Costaguana hangs like a millstone round our necks. The Occidental territory is large enough to make any man's country. Look at the mountains! Nature itself seems to cry to us, ' Separate ! ' "

She made an energetic gesture of negation. A silence fell.

" Oh yes, I know it's contrary to the doctrine laid down in the *History of Fifty Years' Misrule*. I am only trying to be sensible. But my sense seems always to give you cause for offence. Have I startled you very much with this perfectly reasonable aspiration ? "

She shook her head. No, she was not startled, but the idea shocked her early convictions. Her patriotism was larger. She had never considered that possibility.

" It may yet be the means of saving some of your convictions," he said prophetically.

She did not answer. She seemed tired. They leaned side by side on the rail of the little balcony, very friendly, having exhausted politics, giving themselves up to the silent feeling of their nearness, in one of those profound pauses that fall upon the rhythm of passion. Towards the plaza end of the street the glowing coals in the brazeros of the market-women cooking their evening meal gleamed red along the edge of the pavement. A man appeared without a sound in the light of a street lamp, showing the coloured inverted triangle of his bordered poncho, square on his shoulders, hanging to a point below his knees. From the harbour end of the calle a horseman walked his soft-stepping mount, gleaming silver-grey abreast each lamp under the dark shape of the rider.

"Behold the illustrious Capataz de Cargadores," said Decoud gently, "coming in all his splendour after his work is done. The next great man of Sulaco after Don Carlos Gould. But he is good-natured, and let me make friends with him."

"Ah, indeed!" said Antonia. "How did you make friends?"

"A journalist ought to have his finger on the popular pulse—and this man is one of the leaders of the populace. A journalist ought to know remarkable men—and this man is remarkable in his way."

"Ah, yes!" said Antonia thoughtfully. "It is known that this Italian has a great influence."

The horseman had passed below them, with a gleam of dim light on the shining broad quarters of the grey mare, on a bright, heavy stirrup, on a long silver spur; but the short flick of yellowish flame in the dusk was powerless against the muffled-up mysteriousness of the dark figure with an invisible face concealed by a great sombrero.

Decoud and Antonia remained leaning over the balcony, side by side, touching elbows, with their heads overhanging the darkness of the street, and the brilliantly lighted sala at their backs. This was a *tête-à-tête* of extreme impropriety; something of which in the whole extent of the Republic only the extraordinary Antonia could be capable—the poor, motherless girl, never accompanied, with a careless father, who had thought only of making her learned. Even Decoud himself seemed to feel that this was as much as he could expect of having her to himself till—till the revolution was over and he could carry her off to Europe, away from the endlessness of civil strife, whose folly seemed even harder to bear than its ignominy. After one Montero there would be another, the lawlessness of a populace of all colours and races, barbarism, irremediable tyranny. As the great Liberator Bolivar had said in the bitterness of his spirit, "America is ungovernable. Those who worked for her independence have ploughed the sea." He did not care, he declared boldly; he seized every opportunity to tell her that though she had managed to make a Blanco journalist of him, he was no patriot. First of all, the word had no sense for cultured minds, to whom the narrowness of every belief is odious; and secondly, in connection with the everlasting troubles of this unhappy country it was hopelessly besmirched; it had been the cry of dark barbarism, the cloak of lawlessness, of crimes, of rapacity, of simple thieving.

He was surprised at the warmth of his own utterance. He had no need to drop his voice; it had been low all the time, a mere murmur in the silence of dark houses with their shutters closed early against the night air, as is the custom of Sulaco. Only the sala of the Casa Gould flung out defiantly the blaze of its four windows, the bright appeal of light in the whole dumb obscurity of the street. And the murmur on the little balcony went on after a short pause.

"But we are labouring to change all that," Antonia protested. "It is exactly what we desire. It is our object. It is the great cause. And the word you despise has stood also for sacrifice, for courage, for constancy, for suffering. Papa, who——"

"Ploughing the sea," interrupted Decoud, looking down.

There was below the sound of hasty and ponderous footsteps.

"Your uncle, the Grand Vicar of the cathedral, has just turned under the gate," observed Decoud. "He said Mass for the troops in the plaza this morning. They had built for him an altar of drums, you know. And they brought outside all the painted blocks to take the air. All the wooden saints stood militarily in a row at the top of the great flight of steps. They looked like a gorgeous escort attending the Vicar-General. I saw the great function from the windows of the *Porvenir*. He is amazing, your uncle, the last of the Corbelàns. He glittered exceedingly in his vestments with a great crimson velvet cross down his back. And all the time our saviour Barrios sat in the Amarilla Club drinking punch at an open window. *Esprit fort*—our Barrios. I expected every moment your uncle to launch an excommunication there and then at the black eye-patch in the window across the plaza. But not at all. Ultimately the troops marched off. Later, Barrios came down with some of the officers, and stood with his uniform all unbuttoned, discoursing at the edge of the pavement. Suddenly your uncle appeared, no longer glittering, but all black, at the cathedral door with that threatening aspect he has—you know, like a sort of avenging spirit. He gives one look, strides over straight to the group of uniforms, and leads away the general by the elbow. He walked him for a quarter of an hour in the shade of a wall. Never let go his elbow for a moment, talking all the time with exaltation, and gesticulating with a long black arm. It was a curious scene. The officers seemed struck with astonishment. Remarkable man, your missionary uncle. He hates an infidel much less than a heretic, and prefers a heathen many times to an infidel. He condescends graciously to call me a heathen, sometimes, you know."

Antonia listened with her hands over the balustrade, opening and shutting the fan gently ; and Decoud talked a little nervously, as if afraid that she would leave him at the first pause. Their comparative isolation, the precious sense of intimacy, the slight contact of their arms, affected him softly ; for now and then a tender inflection crept into the flow of his ironic murmurs.

" Any slight sign of favour from a relative of yours is welcome, Antonia. And perhaps he understands me,

I 2

after all ! But I know him, too, our Padre Corbelàn.
The idea of political honour, justice, and honesty for
him consists in the restitution of the confiscated Church
property. Nothing else could have drawn that fierce
converter of savage Indians out of the wilds to work for
the Ribierist cause ! Nothing else but that wild hope !
He would make a pronunciamiento himself for such an
object against any Government if he could only get
followers ! What does Don Carlos Gould think of
that ? But, of course, with his English impenetrability,
nobody can tell what he thinks. Probably he thinks of
nothing apart from his mine, of his ' Imperium in
imperio.' As to Mrs. Gould, she thinks of her schools,
of her hospitals, of the mothers with the young babies,
of every sick old man in the three villages. If you were
to turn your head now you would see her extracting a
report from that sinister doctor in a check shirt—what's
his name ? Monygham—or else catechising Don Pépé,
or perhaps listening to Padre Romàn. They are all
down here to-day—all her ministers of state. Well, she
is a sensible woman, and perhaps Don Carlos is a
sensible man. It's a part of solid English sense not to
think too much ; to see only what may be of practical
use at the moment. These people are not like ourselves.
We have no political reason ; we have political passions—
sometimes. What is a conviction ? A particular view
of our personal advantage either practical or emotional.
No one is a patriot for nothing. The word serves us
well. But I am clear-sighted, and I shall not use that
word to you, Antonia ! I have no patriotic illusions. I
have only the supreme illusion of a lover."

He paused, then muttered almost inaudibly, " That
can lead one very far, though."   .

Behind their backs the political tide that once in every
twenty-four hours set with a strong flood through the
Gould drawing-room could be heard, rising higher in a
hum of voices. Men had been dropping in singly, or

in twos and threes ; the higher officials of the province,
engineers of the railway, sunburnt and in tweeds, with the
frosted head of their chief smiling with slow, humorous
indulgence amongst the young, eager faces. Scarfe, the
lover of fandangos, had already slipped out in search of
some dance, no matter where, on the outskirts of the
town. Don Juste Lopez, after taking his daughters
home, had entered solemnly, in a black creased coat
buttoned up under his spreading brown beard. The
few members of the Provincial Assembly present
clustered at once around their President to discuss the
news of the war and the last proclamation of the rebel
Montero, the miserable Montero, calling in the name
of " a justly incensed democracy " upon all the Provincial Assemblies of the Republic to suspend their
sittings till his sword had made peace and the will of
the people could be consulted. It was practically an
invitation to dissolve : an unheard-of audacity of that
evil madman.

   The indignation ran high in the knot of deputies
behind José Avellanos. Don José, lifting up his voice,
cried out to them over the high back of his chair, " Sulaco
has answered by sending to-day an army upon his flank.
If all the other provinces show only half as much patriotism
as we, Occidentals——"

   A great outburst of acclamations covered the vibrating treble of the life and soul of the party. Yes !
Yes ! This was true ! A great truth ! Sulaco was in
the forefront, as ever ! It was a boastful tumult, the
hopefulness inspired by the event of the day breaking out
amongst those caballeros of the Campo thinking of their
herds, of their lands, of the safety of their families.
Everything was at stake. . . . No ! It was impossible
that Montero should succeed ! This criminal, this
shameless Indio ! The clamour continued for some
time, everybody else in the room looking towards the
group where Don Juste had put on his air of impartial

solemnity as if presiding at a sitting of the Provincial
Assembly. Decoud had turned round at the noise, and,
leaning his back on the balustrade, shouted into the room
with all the strength of his lungs, " *Gran' bestia !* "

This unexpected cry had the effect of stilling the
noise. All the eyes were directed to the window with an
approving expectation; but Decoud had already turned
his back upon the room, and was again leaning out over
the quiet street.

" This is the quintessence of my journalism; that is
the supreme argument," he said to Antonia. " I have
invented this definition, this last word on a great question.
But I am no patriot. I am no more of a patriot than the
Capataz of the Sulaco Cargadores, this Genoese who has
done such great things for this harbour—this active
usher-in of the material implements for our progress.
You have heard Captain Mitchell confess over and over
again that till he got this man he could never tell how long
it would take to unload a ship. That is bad for progress.
You have seen him pass by after his labours on his famous
horse to dazzle the girls in some ballroom with an earthen
floor. He is a fortunate fellow! His work is an exercise
of personal powers; his leisure is spent in receiving the
marks of extraordinary adulation. And he likes it, too.
Can anybody be more fortunate? To be feared and
admired is——"

" And are these your highest aspirations, Don
Martin ? " interrupted Antonia.

" I was speaking of a man of that sort," said Decoud
curtly. " The heroes of the world have been feared and
admired. What more could he want ? "

Decoud had often felt his familiar habit of ironic
thought fall shattered against Antonia's gravity. She
irritated him as if she, too, had suffered from that inexplicable feminine obtuseness which stands so often
between a man and a woman of the more ordinary sort.
But he overcame his vexation at once. He was very far

from thinking Antonia ordinary, whatever verdict his scepticism might have pronounced upon himself. With a touch of penetrating tenderness in his voice he assured her that his only aspiration was to a felicity so high that it seemed almost unrealisable on this earth.

She coloured invisibly, with a warmth against which the breeze from the sierra seemed to have lost its cooling power in the sudden melting of the snows. His whisper could not have carried so far, though there was enough ardour in his tone to melt a heart of ice. Antonia turned away abruptly, as if to carry his whispered assurance into the room behind, full of light, noisy with voices.

The tide of political speculation was beating high within the four walls of the great sala, as if driven beyond the marks by a great gust of hope. Don Juste's fan-shaped beard was still the centre of loud and animated discussions. There was a self-confident ring in all the voices. Even the few Europeans around Charles Gould —a Dane, a couple of Frenchmen, a discreet fat German, smiling, with downcast eyes, the representatives of those material interests that had got a footing in Sulaco under the protecting might of the San Tomé mine—had infused a lot of good humour into their deference. Charles Gould, to whom they were paying their court, was the visible sign of the stability that could be achieved in the shifting ground of revolutions. They felt hopeful about their various undertakings. One of the two Frenchmen, small, black, with glittering eyes lost in an immense growth of bushy beard, waved his tiny brown hands and delicate wrists. He had been travelling in the interior of the province for a syndicate of European capitalists. His forcible "*Monsieur l'Administrateur*," returning every minute, shrilled above the steady hum of conversations. He was relating his discoveries. He was ecstatic. Charles Gould glanced down at him courteously.

At a given moment of these necessary receptions it was

Mrs. Gould's habit to withdraw quietly into a little drawing-room, especially her own, next to the great sala. She
had risen, and, waiting for Antonia, listened with a
slightly worried graciousness to the engineer-in-chief of
the railway, who stooped over her, relating slowly, without the slightest gesture, something apparently amusing,
for his eyes had a humorous twinkle. Antonia, before
she advanced into the room to join Mrs. Gould, turned
her head over her shoulder towards Decoud, only for a
moment.

"Why should any one of us think his aspirations
unrealisable ? " she said rapidly.

"I am going to cling to mine to the end, Antonia,"
he answered, through clenched teeth, then bowed very
low, a little distantly.

The engineer-in-chief had not finished telling his
amusing story. The humours of railway building in
South America appealed to his keen appreciation of the
absurd, and he told his instances of ignorant prejudice
and as ignorant cunning very well. Now, Mrs. Gould
gave him all her attention as he walked by her side escorting the ladies out of the room. Finally all three passed
unnoticed through the glass doors in the gallery. Only
a tall priest stalking silently in the noise of the sala
checked himself to look after them. Father Corbelàn,
whom Decoud had seen from the balcony turning into
the gateway of the Casa Gould, had addressed no one
since coming in. The long, skimpy soutane accentuated
the tallness of his stature ; he carried his powerful torso
thrown forward ; and the straight, black bar of his joined
eyebrows, the pugnacious outline of the bony face, the
white spot of a scar on the bluish shaven cheeks (a testi-
monial to his apostolic zeal from a party of unconverted
Indians), suggested something unlawful behind his priest-
hood, the idea of a chaplain of bandits.

He separated his bony, knotted hands clasped behind
his back, to shake his finger at Martin.

Decoud had stepped into the room after Antonia. But he did not go far. He had remained just within, against the curtain, with an expression of not quite genuine gravity, like a grown-up person taking part in a game of children. He gazed quietly at the threatening finger.

" I have watched your reverence converting General Barrios by a special sermon on the plaza," he said, without making the slightest movement.

" What miserable nonsense ! " Father Corbelàn's deep voice resounded all over the room, making all the heads turn on the shoulders. " The man is a drunkard. Señores, the god of your general is a bottle ! "

His contemptuous arbitrary voice caused an uneasy suspension of every sound, as if the self-confidence of the gathering had been staggered by a blow. But nobody took up Father Corbelàn's declaration.

It was known that Father Corbelàn had come out of the wilds to advocate the sacred rights of the Church with the same fanatical fearlessness with which he had gone preaching to bloodthirsty savages, devoid of human compassion or worship of any kind. Rumours of legendary proportions told of his successes as a missionary beyond the eye of Christian men. He had baptized whole nations of Indians, living with them like a savage himself. It was related that the padre used to ride with his Indians for days, half naked, carrying a bullock-hide shield, and, no doubt, a long lance, too—who knows ? That he had wandered clothed in skins, seeking for proselytes somewhere near the snowline of the Cordillera. Of these exploits Padre Corbelàn himself was never known to talk. But he made no secret of his opinion that the politicians of Sta. Marta had harder hearts and more corrupt minds than the heathen to whom he had carried the word of God. His injudicious zeal for the temporal welfare of the Church was damaging the Ribierist cause. It was common knowledge that he had refused to be made titular bishop

of the Occidental diocese till justice was done to a de-
spoiled Church. The political Géfé of Sulaco (the same
dignitary whom Captain Mitchell saved from the mob
afterwards) hinted with naïve cynicism that doubtless their
Excellencies the Ministers sent the padre over the mountains to Sulaco in the worst season of the year in the hope
that he would be frozen to death by the icy blasts of the
high paramos. Every year a few hardy muleteers—men
inured to exposure—were known to perish in that way.
But what would you have ? Their Excellencies possibly
had not realised what a tough priest he was. Meantime
the ignorant were beginning to murmur that the Ribierist
reforms meant simply the taking away of the land from
the people. Some of it was to be given to foreigners who
made the railway ; the greater part was to go to the
padres.

These were the results of the Grand Vicar's zeal.
Even from the short allocution to the troops on the plaza
(which only the first ranks could have heard) he had not
been able to keep out his fixed idea of an outraged Church
waiting for reparation from a penitent country. The
political Géfé had been exasperated. But he could not
very well throw the brother-in-law of Don José into the
prison of the Cabildo. The chief magistrate, an easy-
going and popular official, visited the Casa Gould, walking over after sunset from the Intendencia, unattended,
acknowledging with dignified courtesy the salutations of
high and low alike. That evening he had walked up
straight to Charles Gould and had hissed out to him that
he would have liked to deport the Grand Vicar out of
Sulaco, anywhere, to some desert island, to the Isabels,
for instance. " The one without water preferably—
eh, Don Carlos ? " he had added in a tone between
jest and earnest. This uncontrollable priest, who had
rejected his offer of the episcopal palace for a residence
and preferred to hang his shabby hammock amongst
the rubble and spiders of the sequestrated Dominican

Convent, had taken into his head to advocate an uncon-
ditional pardon for Hernandez the Robber ! And this
was not enough ; he seemed to have entered into communication with the most audacious criminal the country
had known for years. The Sulaco police knew, of course,
what was going on. Padre Corbelàn had got hold of
that reckless Italian, the Capataz de Cargadores, the only
man fit for such an errand, and had sent a message through
him. Father Corbelàn had studied in Rome, and could
speak Italian. The Capataz was known to visit the old
Dominican Convent at night. An old woman who served
the Grand Vicar had heard the name of Hernandez pronounced ; and only last Saturday afternoon the Capataz
had been observed galloping out of town. He did not
return for two days. The police would have laid the
Italian by the heels if it had not been for fear of the
cargadores, a turbulent body of men, quite apt to raise a
tumult. Nowadays it was not so easy to govern Sulaco.
Bad characters flocked into it, attracted by the money in
the pockets of the railway workmen. The populace was
made restless by Father Corbelàn's discourses. And
the first magistrate explained to Charles Gould that now
the province was stripped of troops, any outbreak of lawlessness would find the authorities with their boots off, as
it were.

      Then he went away moodily to sit in an arm-chair,
smoking a long, thin cigar, not very far from Don José,
with whom, bending over sideways, he exchanged
a few words from time to time. He ignored the
entrance of the priest, and whenever Father Corbelàn's
voice was raised behind him, he shrugged his shoulders
impatiently.

      Father Corbelàn had remained quite motionless for
a time with that something vengeful in his immobility
which seemed to characterise all his attitudes. A lurid
glow of strong convictions gave its peculiar aspect to the
black figure. But its fierceness became softened as the

padre, fixing his eyes upon Decoud, raised his long, black arm slowly, impressively :

" And you—you are a perfect heathen," he said in a subdued, deep voice.

He made a step nearer, pointing a forefinger at the young man's breast. Decoud, very calm, felt the wall behind the curtain with the back of his head. Then, with his chin tilted well up, he smiled.

" Very well," he agreed, with the slightly weary nonchalance of a man well used to these passages. " But is it perhaps that you have not discovered yet what is the god of my worship ? It was an easier task with our Barrios."

The priest suppressed a gesture of discouragement. " You believe neither in stick nor stone," he said.

" Nor bottle," added Decoud, without stirring. " Neither does the other of your reverence's confidants. I mean the Capataz of the Cargadores. He does not drink. Your reading of my character does honour to your perspicacity. But why call me a heathen ? "

" True," retorted the priest. " You are ten times worse. A miracle could not convert you."

" I certainly do not believe in miracles," said Decoud quietly. Father Corbelàn shrugged his high, broad shoulders doubtfully.

" A sort of Frenchman—godless—a materialist," he pronounced slowly, as if weighing the terms of a careful analysis. " Neither the son of his own country nor of any other," he continued thoughtfully.

" Scarcely human, in fact," Decoud commented under his breath, his head at rest against the wall, his eyes gazing up at the ceiling.

" The victim of this faithless age," Father Corbelàn resumed in a deep but subdued voice.

" But of some use as a journalist." Decoud changed his pose and spoke in a more animated tone. " Has your worship neglected to read the last number of the

Porvenir ?   I assure you it is just like the others.   On
the general policy it continues to call Montero a *gran'*
bestia, and stigmatise his brother, the guerrillero, for a
combination of lackey and spy.   What could be more
effective ?   In local affairs it urges the Provincial Government to enlist bodily into the national army the band of
Hernandez the Robber—who is apparently the *protégé*
of the Church—or at least of the Grand Vicar.   Nothing
could be more sound."

The priest nodded, and turned on the heels of his
square-toed shoes with big steel buckles.   Again, with
his hands clasped behind his back, he paced to and fro,
planting his feet firmly.   When he swung about, the
skirt of his soutane was inflated slightly by the brusqueness of his movements.

The great sala had been emptying itself slowly.
When the Géfé Politico rose to go, most of those still
remaining stood up suddenly in sign of respect, and Don
José Avellanos stopped the rocking of his chair.   But the
good-natured First Official made a deprecatory gesture,
waved his hand to Charles Gould, and went out discreetly.

In the comparative peace of the room the screaming
" *Monsieur l'Administrateur* " of the frail, hairy Frenchman seemed to acquire a preternatural shrillness.   The
explorer of the Capitalist syndicate was still enthusiastic.
" Ten million dollars' worth of copper practically in
sight, *Monsieur l'Administrateur*.   Ten millions in sight !
And a railway coming—a railway !   They will never
believe my report.   *C'est trop beau*."   He fell a prey
to a screaming ecstasy, in the midst of sagely nodding
heads, before Charles Gould's imperturbable calm.

And only the priest continued his pacing, flinging
round the skirt of his soutane at each end of his beat.
Decoud murmured to him ironically, " Those gentlemen talk about their gods."

Father Corbelàn stopped short, looked at the

Journalist of Sulaco fixedly for a moment, shrugged his
shoulders slightly, and resumed his plodding walk of an
obstinate traveller.

And now the Europeans were dropping off from the
group around Charles Gould till the Administrador of
the Great Silver Mine could be seen in his whole lank
length, from head to foot, left stranded by the ebbing tide
of his guests on the great square of carpet, as it were a
multicoloured shoal of flowers and arabesques under his
brown boots. Father Corbelàn approached the rocking-
chair of Don José Avellanos.

" Come, brother," he said, with kindly brusqueness
and a touch of relieved impatience a man may feel at the
end of a perfectly useless ceremony. "*A la Casa! A
la Casa!* This has been all talk. Let us now go and
think and pray for guidance from Heaven."

He rolled his black eyes upwards. By the side of
the frail diplomatist—the life and soul of the party—he
seemed gigantic, with a gleam of fanaticism in the glance.
But the voice of the party, or, rather, its mouthpiece, the
" son Decoud " from Paris, turned journalist for the
sake of Antonia's eyes, knew very well that it was not so,
that he was only a strenuous priest with one idea, feared
by the women and execrated by the men of the people.
Martin Decoud, the dilettante in life, imagined himself
to derive an artistic pleasure from watching the picturesque extreme of wrong-headedness into which an
honest, almost sacred, conviction may drive a man.
" It is like madness. It must be—because it's self-
destructive," Decoud had said to himself often. It
seemed to him that every conviction, as soon as it became
effective, turned into that form of dementia the gods
send upon those they wish to destroy. But he enjoyed
the bitter flavour of that example with the zest of a
connoisseur in the art of his choice. Those two men
got on well together, as if each had felt respectively
that a masterful conviction, as well as utter scepticism,

may lead a man very far on the bypaths of political action.

Don José obeyed the touch of the big, hairy hand. Decoud followed out the brothers-in-law. And there remained only one visitor in the vast, empty sala, bluishly hazy with tobacco smoke, a heavy-eyed, round-cheeked man, with a drooping moustache, a hide merchant from Esmeralda, who had come overland to Sulaco, riding with a few peons across the coast range. He was very full of his journey, undertaken mostly for the purpose of seeing the Señor Administrador of San Tomé in relation to some assistance he required in his hide-exporting business. He hoped to enlarge it greatly now that the country was going to be settled. It was going to be settled, he repeated several times, degrading by a strange, anxious whine the sonority of the Spanish language, which he pattered rapidly, like some sort of cringing jargon. A plain man could carry on his little business now in the country, and even think of enlarging it—with safety. Was it not so ? He seemed to beg Charles Gould for a confirmatory word, a grunt of assent, a simple nod even.

He could get nothing. His alarm increased, and in the pauses he would dart his eyes here and there ; then, loth to give up, he would branch off into feeling allusion to the dangers of his journey. The audacious Hernandez, leaving his usual haunts, had crossed the Campo of Sulaco, and was known to be lurking in the ravines of the coast range. Yesterday, when distant only a few hours from Sulaco, the hide merchant and his servants had seen three men on the road arrested suspiciously, with their horses' heads together. Two of these rode off at once and disappeared in a shallow quebrada to the left. " We stopped," continued the man from Esmeralda, " and I tried to hide behind a small bush. But none of my mozos would go forward to find out what it meant, and the third horseman seemed to be waiting for us to come up. It was no use. We had been seen. So we rode slowly on, trembling. He let us pass—a man on a grey horse with his hat down on his eyes—without a word of greeting; but by and by we heard him galloping after us. We faced about, but that did not seem to intimidate him. He rode up at speed, and touching my foot with the toe of his boot, asked me for a cigar, with a blood-curdling laugh. He did not seem armed, but when he put his hand back to reach for the matches I saw an enormous revolver strapped to his waist. I shuddered. He had very fierce whiskers, Don Carlos, and as he did not offer to go on we dared not move. At last, blowing the smoke of my cigar into the air through his nostrils, he said, ' Señor, it would be perhaps better for you if I rode behind your party. You are not very far from Sulaco now. Go you with God.' What would you ? We went on. There was no resisting him. He might have been Hernandez himself; though my servant, who has been many times to Sulaco by sea, assured me that he had recognised him very well for the Capataz of the Steamship Company's Cargadores. Later, that same evening, I saw that very man at the corner of the plaza talking to a girl, a Morenita, who stood by the stirrup with her hand on the grey horse's mane."

" I assure you, Señor Hirsch," murmured Charles Gould, " that you ran no risk on this occasion."

" That may be, Señor, though I tremble yet. A most fierce man—to look at. And what does it mean ? A person employed by the Steamship Company talking with salteadores—no less, Señor ; the other horsemen were salteadores—in a lonely place, and behaving like a robber himself ! A cigar is nothing, but what was there to prevent him asking me for my purse ? "

" No, no, Señor Hirsch," Charles Gould murmured, letting his glance stray away a little vacantly from the round face, with its hooked beak upturned towards him in an almost childlike appeal. " If it was the Capataz de Cargadores you met—and there is no doubt, is there ? —you were perfectly safe."

" Thank you. You are very good. A very fierce-looking man, Don Carlos. He asked me for a cigar in a most familiar manner. What would have happened if I had not had a cigar ? I shudder yet. What business had he to be talking with robbers in a lonely place ? "

But Charles Gould, openly preoccupied now, gave not a sign, made no sound. The impenetrability of the embodied Gould Concession had its surface shades. To be dumb is merely a fatal affliction ; but the King of Sulaco had words enough to give him all the mysterious weight of a taciturn force. His silences, backed by the power of speech, had as many shades of significance as uttered words in the way of assent, of doubt, of negation —even of simple comment. Some seemed to say plainly, " Think it over "; others meant clearly, " Go ahead "; a simple, low " I see," with an affirmative nod, at the end of a patient listening half-hour was the equivalent of a verbal contract, which men had learned to trust implicitly, since behind it all there was the great San Tomé mine, the head and front of the material interests, so strong that it depended on no man's good-will in the whole length and breadth of the Occidental Province—that is, on no goodwill which it could not buy ten times over. But to the little hook-nosed man from Esmeralda, anxious about the export of hides, the silence of Charles Gould portended a failure. Evidently this was no time for extending a modest man's business. He enveloped in a swift mental malediction the whole country, with all its inhabitants, partisans of Ribiera and Montero alike ; and there were incipient tears in his mute anger at the thought of the innumerable ox-hides going to waste upon the dreamy expanse of the Campo, with its single palms rising like ships at sea within the perfect circle of the horizon, its clumps of heavy timber motionless like solid islands of leaves above the running waves of grass. There were hides there, rotting, with no profit to anybody—rotting where they had been dropped by men called away to attend the urgent necessities of political revolutions. The practical, mercantile soul of Señor Hirsch rebelled against all that foolishness, while he was taking a respectful but disconcerted leave of the might and majesty of the San Tomé mine in the person of Charles Gould. He could not restrain a heart-broken murmur, wrung out of his very aching heart, as it were.

" It is a great, great foolishness, Don Carlos, all this. The price of hides in Hamburg is gone up—up. Of course the Ribierist Government will do away with all that—when it gets established firmly. Meantime——"

He sighed.

"Yes, meantime," repeated Charles Gould inscrutably.

The other shrugged his shoulders. But he was not ready to go yet. There was a little matter he would like to mention very much if permitted. It appeared he had some good friends in Hamburg (he murmured the name of the firm) who were very anxious to do business in dynamite, he explained. A contract for dynamite with the San Tomé mine, and then, perhaps, later on, other mines, which were sure to—— The little man from Esmeralda was ready to enlarge, but Charles interrupted him. It seemed as though the patience of the Señor Administrador was giving way at last.

" Señor Hirsch," he said, " I have enough dynamite stored up at the mountain to send it down crashing into the valley "—his voice rose a little—" to send half Sulaco into the air if I liked."

Charles Gould smiled at the round, startled eyes of the dealer in hides, who was murmuring hastily, " Just so. Just so." And now he was going. It was impossible to do business in explosives with an Administrador so

well provided and so discouraging. He had suffered
agonies in the saddle and had exposed himself to the
atrocities of the bandit Hernandez for nothing at all.
Neither hides nor dynamite—and the very shoulders of
the enterprising Israelite expressed dejection. At the
door he bowed low to the engineer-in-chief. But at the
bottom of the stairs in the patio he stopped short, with
his podgy hand over his lips in an attitude of meditative
astonishment.

"What does he want to keep so much dynamite for?"
he muttered. "And why does he talk like this to me?"

The engineer-in-chief, looking in at the door of the
empty sala, whence the political tide had ebbed out to the
last insignificant drop, nodded familiarly to the master of
the house, standing motionless like a tall beacon amongst
the deserted shoals of furniture.

"Good-night; I am going. Got my bike downstairs.
The railway will know where to go for dynamite should
we get short at any time. We have done cutting and
chopping for a while now. We shall begin soon to blast
our way through."

"Don't come to me," said Charles Gould, with
perfect serenity. "I shan't have an ounce to spare for
anybody. Not an ounce. Not for my own brother, if I
had a brother, and he were the engineer-in-chief of the
most promising railway in the world."

"What's that?" asked the engineer-in-chief, with
equanimity. "Unkindness?"

"No," said Charles Gould stolidly. "Policy."

"Radical, I should think," the engineer-in-chief
observed from the doorway.

"Is that the right name?" Charles Gould said, from
the middle of the room.

"I mean, going to the roots, you know," the engineer
explained, with an air of enjoyment.

"Why, yes," Charles pronounced slowly. "The
Gould Concession has struck such deep roots in this

13

country, in this province, in that gorge of the mountains, that nothing but dynamite shall be allowed to dislodge it from there. It's my choice. It's my last card to play."

The engineer-in-chief whistled low. "A pretty game," he said, with a shade of discretion. "And have you told Holroyd of that extraordinary trump card you hold in your hand?"

"Card only when it's played; when it falls at the end of the game. Till then you may call it a—a——"

"Weapon," suggested the railway man.

"No. You may call it rather an argument," corrected Charles Gould gently. "And that's how I've presented it to Mr. Holroyd."

"And what did he say to it?" asked the engineer, with undisguised interest.

"He"—Charles Gould spoke after a slight pause—"he said something about holding on like grim death and putting our trust in God. I should imagine he must have been rather startled. But then," pursued the Administrador of the San Tomé mine—"but then, he is very far away, you know, and, as they say in this country, God is very high above."

The engineer's appreciative laugh died away down the stairs, where the Madonna with the Child on her arm seemed to look after his shaking broad back from her shallow niche.

CHAPTER SIX

A PROFOUND stillness reigned in the Casa Gould. The master of the house, walking along the *corrédor*, opened the door of his room, and saw his wife sitting in a big arm-chair—his own smoking arm-chair—thoughtful, contemplating her little shoes. And she did not raise her eyes when he walked in.

" Tired ? " asked Charles Gould.

" A little," said Mrs. Gould. Still without looking up, she added with feeling, " There is an awful sense of unreality about all this."

Charles Gould, before the long table strewn with papers, on which lay a hunting-crop and a pair of spurs, stood looking at his wife. " The heat and dust must have been awful this afternoon by the waterside," he murmured sympathetically. " The glare on the water must have been simply terrible."

" One could close one's eyes to the glare," said Mrs. Gould. " But, my dear Charley, it is impossible for me to close my eyes to our position ; to this awful . . ."

She raised her eyes and looked at her husband's face, from which all sign of sympathy or any other feeling had disappeared. " Why don't you tell me something ? " she almost wailed.

" I thought you had understood me perfectly from the first," Charles Gould said slowly. " I thought we had said all there was to say a long time ago. There is nothing to say now. There were things to be done. We have done them ; we have gone on doing them. There

is no going back now. I don't suppose that, even from
the first, there was really any possible way back. And,
what's more, we can't even afford to stand still."

"Ah, if one only knew how far you mean to go!" said
his wife, inwardly trembling, but in an almost playful
tone.

"Any distance, any length, of course," was the
answer, in a matter-of-fact tone, which caused Mrs.
Gould to make another effort to repress a shudder.

She stood up, smiling graciously, and her little figure
seemed to be diminished still more by the heavy mass of
her hair and the long train of her gown.

"But always to success," she said persuasively.

Charles Gould, enveloping her in the steely blue
glance of his attentive eyes, answered without hesitation:
"Oh, there is no alternative."

He put an immense assurance into his tone. As to the
words, this was all that his conscience would allow him to
say.

Mrs. Gould's smile remained a shade too long upon
her lips. She murmured:

"I will leave you; I've a slight headache. The heat,
the dust, were indeed—— I suppose you are going back
to the mine before the morning?"

"At midnight," said Charles Gould. "We are
bringing down the silver to-morrow. Then I shall take
three whole days off in town with you."

"Ah, you are going to meet the escort! I shall be
on the balcony at five o'clock to see you pass. Till then,
good-bye."

Charles Gould walked rapidly round the table, and,
seizing her hands, bent down, pressing them both to his
lips. Before he straightened himself up again to his full
height she had disengaged one to smooth his cheek with
a light touch, as if he were a little boy.

"Try to get some rest for a couple of hours," she murmured, with a glance at a hammock stretched in a distant

part of the room.   Her long train swished softly after her
on the red tiles.   At the door she looked back.

Two big lamps with unpolished glass globes bathed in
a soft and abundant light the four white walls of the room,
with a glass case of arms, the brass hilt of Henry Gould's
cavalry sabre on its square of velvet, and the water-colour
sketch of the San Tomé gorge.   And Mrs. Gould, gazing
at the last in its black wooden frame, sighed out :

" Ah, if we had left it alone, Charley ! "

" No," Charles Gould said moodily ; " it was impossible to leave it alone."

" Perhaps it was impossible," Mrs. Gould admitted
slowly.   Her lips quivered a little, but she smiled with an
air of dainty bravado.   " We have disturbed a good many
snakes in that paradise, Charley, haven't we ? "

" Yes ; I remember," said Charles Gould, " it was
Don Pépé who called the gorge the paradise of snakes.
No doubt we have disturbed a great many.   But remember, my dear, that it is not now as it was when you
made that sketch."   He waved his hand towards the
small water-colour hanging alone upon the great bare
wall.   " It is no longer a paradise of snakes.   We have
brought mankind into it, and we cannot turn our backs
upon them to go and begin a new life elsewhere."

He confronted his wife with a firm concentrated gaze,
which Mrs. Gould returned with a brave assumption of
fearlessness before she went out, closing the door gently
after her.

In contrast with the white glaring room the dimly-lit
corrédor had a restful mysteriousness of a forest glade,
suggested by the stems and the leaves of the plants
ranged along the balustrade of the open side.   In the
streaks of light falling through the open doors of the
reception-rooms, the blossoms, white and red and pale
lilac, came out vivid with the brilliance of flowers in a
stream of sunshine ; and Mrs. Gould, passing on, had the
vividness of a figure seen in the clear patches of sun that

chequer the gloom of open glades in the woods. The stones in the rings upon her hand pressed to her forehead glittered in the lamplight abreast of the door of the sala.

" Who's there ? " she asked in a startled voice. " Is that you, Basilio ? " She looked in, and saw Martin Decoud walking about, with an air of having lost something, amongst the chairs and tables.

" Antonia has forgotten her fan in here," said Decoud, with a strange air of distraction ; " so I entered to see."

But, even as he said this, he had obviously given up his search, and walked straight towards Mrs. Gould, who looked at him with doubtful surprise.

" Señora," he began in a low voice.

" What is it, Don Martin ? " asked Mrs. Gould. And then she added, with a slight laugh, " I am so nervous to-day," as if to explain the eagerness of the question.

" Nothing immediately dangerous," said Decoud, who now could not conceal his agitation. " Pray don't distress yourself. No, really, you must not distress yourself."

Mrs. Gould, with her candid eyes very wide open, her lips composed into a smile, was steadying herself with a little bejewelled hand against the side of the door.

" Perhaps you don't know how alarming you are, appearing like this unexpectedly——"

" I ! Alarming ! " he protested, sincerely vexed and surprised. " I assure you that I am not in the least alarmed myself. A fan is lost ; well, it will be found again. But I don't think it is here. It is a fan I am looking for. I cannot understand how Antonia could—— Well ! Have you found it, amigo ? "

" No, Señor," said behind Mrs. Gould the soft voice of Basilio, the head servant of the Casa. " I don't think the Señorita could have left it in this house at all."

" Go and look for it in the patio again. Go now, my friend ; look for it on the steps, under the gate ; examine

every flagstone ; search for it till I come down again. . . .
That fellow "—he addressed himself in English to Mrs.
Gould—" is always stealing up behind one's back on his
bare feet. I set him to look for that fan directly I came
in to justify my reappearance, my sudden return."

He paused, and Mrs. Gould said amiably, " You are
always welcome."   She paused for a second too.   " But
I am waiting to learn the cause of your return."

Decoud affected suddenly the utmost nonchalance.

" I can't bear to be spied upon. Oh, the cause ?
Yes, there is a cause ; there is something else that is lost
besides Antonia's favourite fan. As I was walking home
after seeing Don José and Antonia to their house, the
Capataz de Cargadores, riding down the street, spoke to
me."

" Has anything happened to the Violas ? " inquired
Mrs. Gould.

" The Violas ? You mean the old Garibaldino who
keeps the hotel where the engineers live ? Nothing
happened there. The Capataz said nothing of them ;
he only told me that the telegraphist of the Cable
Company was walking on the plaza, bareheaded, looking out for me. There is news from the interior, Mrs.
Gould. I should rather say rumours of news."

" Good news ? " said Mrs. Gould in a low voice.

" Worthless, I should think. But if I must define
them, I would say bad. They are to the effect that a
two days' battle had been fought near Sta. Marta, and
that the Ribierists are defeated. It must have happened
a few days ago—perhaps a week. The rumour has just
reached Cayta, and the man in charge of the cable
station there has telegraphed the news to his colleague
here. We might just as well have kept Barrios in
Sulaco."

" What's to be done now ? " murmured Mrs. Gould.

" Nothing. He's at sea with the troops. He will get
to Cayta in a couple of days' time and learn the news

there. What he will do then, who can say? Hold
Cayta? Offer his submission to Montero? Disband
his army?—this last most likely, and go himself in one
of the O.S.N. Company's steamers, north or south—to
Valparaiso or to San Francisco, no matter where. Our
Barrios has a great practice in exiles and repatriations,
which mark the points in the political game."

Decoud, exchanging a steady stare with Mrs. Gould,
added, tentatively as it were, " And yet, if we had
Barrios with his two thousand improved rifles here,
something could have been done."

" Montero victorious, completely victorious ! " Mrs.
Gould breathed out in a tone of unbelief.

" A canard, probably. That sort of bird is hatched
in great numbers in such times as these. And even if
it were true ? Well, let us put things at their worst, let
us say it is true."

" Then everything is lost," said Mrs. Gould, with the
calmness of despair.

Suddenly she seemed to divine, she seemed to see
Decoud's tremendous excitement under its cloak of
studied carelessness. It was, indeed, becoming visible
in his audacious and watchful stare, in the curve, half
reckless, half contemptuous, of his lips. And a French
phrase came upon them as if, for this Costaguanero
of the Boulevard, that had been the only forcible
language :

" *Non, Madame. Rien n'est perdu.*"

It electrified Mrs. Gould out of her benumbed
attitude, and she said vivaciously :

" What would you think of doing ? "

But already there was something of mockery in
Decoud's suppressed excitement.

" What would you expect a true Costaguanero to
do ? Another revolution, of course. On my word of
honour, Mrs. Gould, I believe I am a true *hijo del pays*,
a true son of the country, whatever Father Corbelàn

may say. And I'm not so much of an unbeliever as not
to have faith in my own ideas, in my own remedies, in
my own desires."

"Yes," said Mrs. Gould doubtfully.

"You don't seem convinced," Decoud went on again
in French. "Say, then, in my passions."

Mrs. Gould received this addition unflinchingly. To
understand it thoroughly she did not require to hear his
muttered assurance:

"There is nothing I would not do for the sake of
Antonia. There is nothing I am not prepared to under-
take. There is no risk I am not ready to run."

Decoud seemed to find a fresh audacity in this
voicing of his thoughts. "You would not believe me
if I were to say that it is the love of the country
which——"

She made a sort of discouraged protest with her arm,
as if to express that she had given up expecting that
motive from any one.

"A Sulaco revolution," Decoud pursued in a forcible
undertone. "The Great Cause may be served here, on
the very spot of its inception, in the place of its birth,
Mrs. Gould."

Frowning, and biting her lower lip thoughtfully, she
made a step away from the door.

"You are not going to speak to your husband?"
Decoud arrested her anxiously.

"But you will need his help?"

"No doubt," Decoud admitted without hesitation.
"Everything turns upon the San Tomé mine; but I
would rather he didn't know anything as yet of my—
my hopes."

A puzzled look came upon Mrs. Gould's face, and
Decoud, approaching, explained confidentially:

"Don't you see, he's such an idealist."

Mrs. Gould flushed pink, and her eyes grew darker
at the same time.

" Charley an idealist ! " she said, as if to herself, wonderingly. " What on earth do you mean ? "

" Yes," conceded Decoud ; " it's a wonderful thing to say with the sight of the San Tomé mine, the greatest fact in the whole of South America, perhaps, before our very eyes. But look even at that ; he has idealised this fact to a point——" He paused. " Mrs. Gould, are you aware to what point he has idealised the existence, the worth, the meaning of the San Tomé mine ? Are you aware of it ? "

He must have known what he was talking about. The effect he expected was produced. Mrs. Gould, ready to take fire, gave it up suddenly with a low little sound that resembled a moan.

" What do you know ? " she asked in a feeble voice.

" Nothing," answered Decoud firmly. " But, then, don't you see, he's an Englishman ! "

" Well, what of that ? " asked Mrs. Gould.

" Simply that he cannot act or exist without idealising every simple feeling, desire, or achievement. He could not believe his own motives if he did not make them first a part of some fairy tale. The earth is not quite good enough for him, I fear. Do you excuse my frankness ? Besides, whether you excuse it or not, it is part of the truth of things which hurts the—what do you call them ? —the Anglo-Saxon's susceptibilities, and at the present moment I don't feel as if I could treat seriously either his conception of things or—if you allow me to say so— or yet yours."

Mrs. Gould gave no sign of being offended. " I suppose Antonia understands you thoroughly ? "

" Understands ? Well, yes. But I am not sure that she approves. That, however, makes no difference. I am honest enough to tell you that, Mrs. Gould."

" Your idea, of course, is separation," she said.

" Separation, of course," declared Martin. " Yes ; separation of the whole Occidental Province from the rest of the unquiet body. But my true idea, the only one I care for, is not to be separated from Antonia."

" And that is all ? " asked Mrs. Gould, without severity.

" Absolutely. I am not deceiving myself about my motives. She won't leave Sulaco for my sake, therefore Sulaco must leave the rest of the Republic to its fate. Nothing could be clearer than that. I like a clearly defined situation. I cannot part with Antonia, therefore the one and indivisible Republic of Costaguana must be made to part with its western province. Fortunately it happens to be also a sound policy. The richest, the most fertile part of this land may be saved from anarchy. Personally, I care little, very little ; but it's a fact that the establishment of Montero in power would mean death to me. In all the proclamations of general pardon which I have seen, my name, with a few others, is specially excepted. The brothers hate me, as you know very well, Mrs. Gould ; and behold, here is the rumour of them having won a battle. You say that, supposing it is true, I have plenty of time to run away."

The slight protesting murmur on the part of Mrs. Gould made him pause for a moment, while he looked at her with a sombre and resolute glance.

" Ah, but I would, Mrs. Gould ! I would run away if it served that which at present is my only desire. I am courageous enough to say that, and to do it, too. But women, even our women, are idealists. It is Antonia that won't run away. A novel sort of vanity."

" You call it vanity ! " said Mrs. Gould in a shocked voice.

" Say pride, then, which, Father Corbelàn would tell you, is a mortal sin. But I am not proud. I am simply too much in love to run away. At the same time I want to live. There is no love for a dead man. Therefore it is necessary that Sulaco should not recognise the victorious Montero."

"And you think my husband will give you his support?"

"I think he can be drawn into it, like all idealists, when he once sees a sentimental basis for his action. But I wouldn't talk to him. Mere clear facts won't appeal to his sentiment. It is much better for him to convince himself in his own way. And, frankly, I could not, perhaps, just now pay sufficient respect to either his motives or even, perhaps, to yours, Mrs. Gould."

It was evident that Mrs. Gould was very determined not to be offended. She smiled vaguely, while she seemed to think the matter over. As far as she could judge from the girl's half-confidences, Antonia understood that young man. Obviously there was promise of safety in his plan, or rather in his idea. Moreover, right or wrong, the idea could do no harm. And it was quite possible, also, that the rumour was false.

"You have some sort of plan?" she said.

"Simplicity itself. Barrios has started, let him go on then; he will hold Cayta, which is the door of the sea route to Sulaco. They cannot send a sufficient force over the mountains. No; not even to cope with the band of Hernandez. Meantime we shall organise our resistance here. And for that, this very Hernandez will be useful. He has defeated troops as a bandit; he will no doubt accomplish the same thing if he is made a colonel or even a general. You know the country well enough not to be shocked by what I say, Mrs. Gould. I have heard you assert that this poor bandit was the living, breathing example of cruelty, injustice, stupidity, and oppression, that ruin men's souls as well as their fortunes in this country. Well, there would be some poetical retribution in that man arising to crush the evils which had driven an honest ranchero into a life of crime. A fine idea of retribution in that, isn't there?"

Decoud had dropped easily into English, which he

spoke with precision, very correctly, but with too many
z sounds.

" Think also of your hospitals, of your schools, of
your ailing mothers and feeble old men, of all that
population which you and your husband have brought
into the rocky gorge of San Tomé. Are you not responsible to your conscience for all these people ? Is
it not worth while to make another effort, which is not
at all so desperate as it looks, rather than——"

Decoud finished his thought with an upward toss
of the arm, suggesting annihilation ; and Mrs. Gould
turned away her head with a look of horror.

" Why don't you say all this to my husband ? " she
asked, without looking at Decoud, who stood watching
the effect of his words.

" Ah ! But Don Carlos is so English," he began.
Mrs. Gould interrupted :

" Leave that alone, Don Martin. He's as much a
Costaguanero—no, he's more of a Costaguanero than
yourself."

" Sentimentalist, sentimentalist," Decoud almost
cooed, in a tone of gentle and soothing deference.
" Sentimentalist, after the amazing manner of your
people. I have been watching El Rey de Sulaco since
I came here on a fool's errand, and perhaps impelled
by some treason of fate lurking behind the unaccountable
turns of a man's life. But I don't matter, I am not a
sentimentalist, I cannot endow my personal desires with
a shining robe of silk and jewels. Life is not for me a
moral romance derived from the tradition of a pretty
fairy tale. No, Mrs. Gould ; I am practical. I am not
afraid of my motives. But, pardon me, I have been
rather carried away. What I wish to say is that I have
been observing. I won't tell you what I have discovered——"

" No. That is unnecessary," whispered Mrs. Gould,
once more averting her head.

"It is. Except one little fact, that your husband does not like me. It's a small matter, which, in the circumstances, seems to acquire a perfectly ridiculous importance. Ridiculous and immense; for, clearly, money is required for my plan," he reflected; then added meaningly, " And we have two sentimentalists to deal with."

" I don't know that I understand you, Don Martin," said Mrs. Gould coldly, preserving the low key of their conversation. " But, speaking as if I did, who is the other ? "

" The great Holroyd in San Francisco, of course," Decoud whispered lightly. " I think you understand me very well. Women are idealists; but then they are so perspicacious."

But whatever was the reason of that remark, disparaging and complimentary at the same time, Mrs. Gould seemed not to pay attention to it. The name of Holroyd had given a new tone to her anxiety.

" The silver escort is coming down to the harbour to-morrow; a whole six months' working, Don Martin ! " she cried in dismay.

" Let it come down, then," breathed out Decoud earnestly, almost into her ear.

" But if the rumour should get about, and especially if it turned out true, troubles might break out in the town," objected Mrs. Gould.

Decoud admitted that it was possible. He knew well the town children of the Sulaco Campo : sullen, thievish, vindictive, and bloodthirsty, whatever great qualities their brothers of the plain might have had. But then there was that other sentimentalist, who attached a strangely idealistic meaning to concrete facts. This stream of silver must be kept flowing north to return in the form of financial backing from the great house of Holroyd. Up at the mountain in the strong-room of the mine the silver bars were worth less for his purpose than so much lead,

from which at least bullets may be run.   Let it come
down to the harbour, ready for shipment.

The next north-going steamer would carry it off for
the very salvation of the San Tomé mine, which had produced so much treasure.   And, moreover, the rumour
was probably false, he remarked, with much conviction
in his hurried tone.

" Besides, Señora," concluded Decoud, " we may
suppress it for many days.   I have been talking with
the telegraphist in the middle of the Plaza Mayor ; thus
I am certain that we could not have been overheard.
There was not even a bird in the air near us.   And also
let me tell you something more.   I have been making
friends with this man called Nostromo, the Capataz.   We
had a conversation this very evening, I walking by the side
of his horse as he rode slowly out of the town just now.
He promised me that if a riot took place for any reason—
even for the most political of reasons, you understand—
his cargadores, an important part of the populace, you will
admit, should be found on the side of the Europeans."

" He has promised you that ? " Mrs. Gould inquired,
with interest.   " What made him make that promise to
you ? "

" Upon my word, I don't know," declared Decoud
in a slightly surprised tone.   " He certainly promised
me that, but now you ask me why, I could not tell
you his reasons.   He talked with his usual carelessness,
which, if he had been anything else but a common sailor,
I would call a pose or an affectation."

Decoud, interrupting himself, looked at Mrs. Gould
curiously.

" Upon the whole," he continued, " I suppose he
expects something to his advantage from it.   You
mustn't forget that he does not exercise his extraordinary
power over the lower classes without a certain amount of
personal risk and without a great profusion in spending
his money.   One must pay in some way or other for such

a solid thing as individual prestige. He told me after we made friends at a dance, in a posada kept by a Mexican just outside the walls, that he had come here to make his fortune. I suppose he looks upon his prestige as a sort of investment."

" Perhaps he prizes it for its own sake," Mrs. Gould said, in a tone as if she were repelling an undeserved aspersion. " Viola, the Garibaldino, with whom he has lived for some years, calls him the Incorruptible."

" Ah! he belongs to the group of your *protégés* out there towards the harbour, Mrs. Gould. *Muy bien*. And Captain Mitchell calls him wonderful. I have heard no end of tales of his strength, his audacity, his fidelity. No end of fine things. H'm! incorruptible! It is indeed a name of honour for the Capataz of the Cargadores of Sulaco. Incorruptible! Fine, but vague. However, I suppose he's sensible, too. And I talked to him upon that sane and practical assumption."

" I prefer to think him disinterested, and therefore trustworthy," Mrs. Gould said, with the nearest approach to curtness it was in her nature to assume.

" Well, if so, then the silver will be still more safe. Let it come down, Señora. Let it come down, so that it may go north and return to us in the shape of credit."

Mrs. Gould glanced along the *corrédor* towards the door of her husband's room. Decoud, watching her as if she had his fate in her hands, detected an almost imperceptible nod of assent. He bowed with a smile, and, putting his hand into the breast pocket of his coat, pulled out a fan of light feathers set upon painted leaves of sandal-wood. " I had it in my pocket," he murmured triumphantly, " for a plausible pretext." He bowed again. " Good-night, Señora."

Mrs. Gould continued along the *corrédor* away from her husband's room. The fate of the San Tomé mine was lying heavy upon her heart. It was a long time now since she had begun to fear it. It had been an idea. She had watched it with misgivings turning into a fetish, and now the fetish had grown into a monstrous and crushing weight. It was as if the inspiration of their early years had left her heart to turn into a wall of silver bricks, erected by the silent work of evil spirits, between her and her husband. He seemed to dwell alone within a circumvallation of precious metal, leaving her outside with her school, her hospital, the sick mothers and the feeble old men, mere insignificant vestiges of the initial inspiration. " Those poor people ! " she murmured to herself.

Below she heard the voice of Martin Decoud in the patio speaking loudly.

" I have found Doña Antonia's fan, Basilio. Look, here it is ! "

CHAPTER SEVEN

IT was part of what Decoud would have called his sane materialism that he did not believe in the possibility of friendship between man and woman.

The one exception he allowed confirmed, he maintained, that absolute rule. Friendship was possible between brother and sister, meaning by friendship the frank unreserve, as before another human being, of thoughts and sensations ; all the objectless and necessary sincerity of one's innermost life trying to react upon the profound sympathies of another existence.

His favourite sister, the handsome, slightly arbitrary and resolute angel, ruling the father and mother Decoud in the first-floor apartments of a very fine Parisian house, was the recipient of Martin Decoud's confidences as to his thoughts, actions, purposes, doubts, and even failures. . . .

" Prepare our little circle in Paris for the birth of another South American Republic. One more or less, what does it matter ? They may come into the world like evil flowers on a hotbed of rotten institutions ; but the seed of this one has germinated in your brother's brain, and that will be enough for your devoted assent. I am writing this to you by the light of a single candle, in a sort of inn, near the harbour, kept by an Italian called Viola, a *protégé* of Mrs. Gould. The whole building, which, for all I know, may have been contrived by a Conquistador farmer of the pearl fishery three hundred years ago, is perfectly silent. So is the plain between the town and the harbour ; silent, but not so dark as the house, because the pickets of Italian workmen guarding the railway have lighted little fires all along the line. It was not so quiet around here yesterday. We had an awful riot—a sudden outbreak of the populace, which was not suppressed till late to-day. Its object, no doubt, was loot, and that was defeated, as you may have learned already from the cablegram sent via San Francisco and New York last night, when the cables were still open. You have read already there that the energetic action of the Europeans of the railway has saved the town from destruction, and you may believe that. I wrote out the cable myself. We have no Reuter's agency man here. I have also fired at the mob from the windows of the club, in company with some other young men of position. Our object was to keep the Calle de la Constitucion clear for the exodus of the ladies and children, who have taken refuge on board a couple of cargo ships now in the harbour here. That was yesterday. You should also have learned from the cable that the missing President, Ribiera, who had disappeared after the battle of Sta. Marta, has turned up here in Sulaco by one of those strange coincidences that are almost incredible, riding on a lame mule into the very midst of the street fighting. It appears that he had fled, in company of a muleteer called Bonifacio, across the mountains from the threats of Montero into the arms of an enraged mob.

"The Capataz of Cargadores, that Italian sailor of whom I have written to you before, has saved him from an ignoble death. That man seems to have a particular talent for being on the spot whenever there is something picturesque to be done.

"He was with me at four o'clock in the morning at the offices of the *Porvenir*, where he had turned up so early in order to warn me of the coming trouble, and

also to assure me that he would keep his cargadores on
the side of order.   When the full daylight came we were
looking together at the crowd on foot and on horseback,
demonstrating on the plaza and shying stones at the
windows of the Intendencia. Nostromo (that is the
name they call him by here) was pointing out to me his
cargadores interspersed in the mob.

"The sun shines late upon Sulaco, for it has first
to climb above the mountains. In that clear morning
light, brighter than twilight, Nostromo saw right across
the vast plaza, at the end of the street beyond the
cathedral, a mounted man apparently in difficulties
with a yelling knot of leperos. At once he said to me,
'That's a stranger. What is it they are doing to him?'
Then he took out the silver whistle he is in the habit of
using on the wharf (this man seems to disdain the use
of any metal less precious than silver) and blew into it
twice, evidently a preconcerted signal for his cargadores.
He ran out immediately, and they rallied round him.
I ran out, too, but was too late to follow them and help
in the rescue of the stranger, whose animal had fallen.
I was set upon at once as a hated aristocrat, and was
only too glad to get into the club, where Don Jaime
Berges (you may remember him visiting at our house in
Paris some three years ago) thrust a sporting gun into
my hands.   They were already firing from the windows.
There were little heaps of cartridges lying about on the
open card-tables.   I remember a couple of overturned
chairs, some bottles rolling on the floor amongst the
packs of cards scattered suddenly as the caballeros rose
from their game to open fire upon the mob.   Most of
the young men had spent the night at the club in the
expectation of some such disturbance.   In two of the
candelabra, on the consoles, the candles were burning
down in their sockets.   A large iron nut, probably
stolen from the railway workshops, flew in from the
street as I entered, and broke one of the large mirrors

set in the wall. I noticed also one of the club servants
tied up hand and foot with the cords of the curtain
and flung in a corner. I have a vague recollection of
Don Jaime assuring me hastily that the fellow had been
detected putting poison into the dishes at supper. But
I remember distinctly he was shrieking for mercy,
without stopping at all, continuously, and so absolutely
disregarded that nobody even took the trouble to gag
him. The noise he made was so disagreeable that I
had half a mind to do it myself. But there was no time
to waste on such trifles. I took my place at one of the
windows and began firing.

" I didn't learn till later in the afternoon whom it was
that Nostromo, with his cargadores and some Italian
workmen as well, had managed to save from those drunken
rascals. That man has a peculiar talent when anything
striking to the imagination has to be done. I made
that remark to him afterwards when we met after some
sort of order had been restored in the town, and the
answer he made rather surprised me. He said quite
moodily, ' And how much do I get for that, Señor ? '
Then it dawned upon me that perhaps this man's vanity
has been satiated by the adulation of the common people
and the confidence of his superiors ! "

Decoud paused to light a cigarette, then, with his
head still over his writing, he blew a cloud of smoke, which
seemed to rebound from the paper. He took up the
pencil again.

" That was yesterday evening on the plaza, while he
sat on the steps of the cathedral, his hands between his
knees, holding the bridle of his famous silver-grey mare.
He had led his body of cargadores splendidly all day long.
He looked fatigued. I don't know how I looked. Very
dirty, I suppose. But I suppose I also looked pleased.
From the time the fugitive President had been got off to
the s.s. *Minerva*, the tide of success had turned against the
mob. They had been driven off the harbour, and out

of the better streets of the town, into their own maze of
ruins and tolderias. You must understand that this riot,
whose primary object was undoubtedly the getting hold of
the San Tomé silver stored in the lower rooms of the
Custom House (besides the general looting of the Ricos),
had acquired a political colouring from the fact of two
deputies to the Provincial Assembly, Señores Gamacho
and Fuentes, both from Bolson, putting themselves at the
head of it—late in the afternoon, it is true, when the
mob, disappointed in their hopes of loot, made a stand
in the narrow streets to the cries of ' Viva la Libertad !
Down with Feudalism ! ' (I wonder what they imagine
feudalism to be ?) ' Down with the Goths and Paralytics.'
I suppose the Señores Gamacho and Fuentes knew what
they were doing. They are prudent gentlemen. In the
Assembly they called themselves Moderates, and opposed
every energetic measure with philanthropic pensiveness.
At the first rumours of Montero's victory they showed
a subtle change of pensive temper, and began to defy
poor Don Juste Lopez in his Presidential tribune
with an effrontery to which the poor man could only
respond by a dazed smoothing of his beard and the
ringing of the Presidential bell. Then, when the downfall of the Ribierist cause became confirmed beyond the
shadow of a doubt, they have blossomed into convinced
Liberals, acting together as if they were Siamese twins,
and ultimately taking charge, as it were, of the riot in the
name of Monterist principles.

"Their last move at eight o'clock last night was to
organise themselves into a Monterist Committee which
sits, as far as I know, in a posada kept by a retired
Mexican bull-fighter, a great politician, too, whose name
I have forgotten. Thence they have issued a communication to us, the Goths and Paralytics of the Amarilla
Club (who have our own committee), inviting us to come
to some provisional understanding for a truce, in order,
they have the impudence to say, that the noble cause of

Liberty ' should not be stained by the criminal excesses
of Conservative selfishness ' ! As I came out to sit with
Nostromo on the cathedral steps, the club was busy con-
sidering a proper reply in the principal room, littered
with exploded cartridges, with a lot of broken glass, blood
smears, candlesticks, and all sorts of wreckage on the floor.
But all this is nonsense. Nobody in the town has any
real power except the railway engineers, whose men
occupy the dismantled houses acquired by the Company
for their town station on one side of the plaza, and Nostromo, whose cargadores were sleeping under the Arcades
along the front of Anzani's shops. A fire of broken
furniture out of the Intendencia saloons, mostly gilt, was
burning on the plaza, in a high flame swaying right upon
the statue of Charles IV. The dead body of a man was
lying on the steps of the pedestal, his arms thrown wide
open, and his sombrero covering his face—the attention
of some friend, perhaps. The light of the flames touched
the foliage of the first trees on the Alameda, and played
on the end of a side street near by, blocked up by a
jumble of ox-carts and dead bullocks. Sitting on one of
the carcasses, a lepero, muffled up, smoked a cigarette.
It was a truce, you understand. The only other living
being on the plaza besides ourselves was a cargador,
walking to and fro, with a long, bare knife in his hand,
like a sentry before the Arcades, where his friends were
sleeping. And the only other spot of light in the dark
town were the lighted windows of the club, at the corner
of the calle."

After having written so far, Don Martin Decoud, the
exotic dandy of the Parisian boulevard, got up and walked
across the sanded floor of the café at one end of the
Albergo of United Italy, kept by Giorgio Viola, the old
companion of Garibaldi. The highly coloured lithograph
of the " Faithful Hero " seemed to look dimly, in the
light of one candle, at the man with no faith in anything
except the truth of his own sensations. Looking out of

the window, Decoud was met by a darkness so impenetrable that he could see neither the mountains nor the
town, nor yet the buildings near the harbour ; and there
was not a sound, as if the tremendous obscurity of the
Placid Gulf, spreading from the waters over the land, had
made it dumb as well as blind. Presently Decoud felt a
light tremor of the floor and a distant clank of iron. A
bright white light appeared, deep in the darkness, growing bigger with a thundering noise. The rolling stock
usually kept on the sidings in Rincon was being run back
to the yards for safe keeping. Like a mysterious stirring
of the darkness behind the headlight of the engine, the
train passed in a gust of hollow uproar, by the end of
the house, which seemed to vibrate all over in response.
And nothing was clearly visible but, on the end of the last
flat car, a negro, in white trousers and naked to the waist,
swinging a blazing torch basket incessantly with a circular
movement of his bare arm. Decoud did not stir.

Behind him, on the back of the chair from which he
had risen, hung his elegant Parisian overcoat, with a
pearl-grey silk lining. But when he turned back to come
to the table the candlelight fell upon a face that was
grimy and scratched. His rosy lips were blackened with
heat, the smoke of gunpowder. Dirt and rust tarnished
the lustre of his short beard. His shirt collar and cuffs
were crumpled, the blue silken tie hung down his breast
like a rag ; a greasy smudge crossed his white brow. He
had not taken off his clothing nor used water, except to
snatch a hasty drink greedily, for some forty hours. An
awful restlessness had made him its own, had marked him
with all the signs of desperate strife, and put a dry, sleepless stare into his eyes. He murmured to himself in a
hoarse voice, " I wonder if there's any bread here ? "
looked vaguely about him, then dropped into the chair
and took the pencil up again. He became aware he had
not eaten anything for many hours.

It occurred to him that no one could understand him

so well as his sister. In the most sceptical heart there lurks at such moments, when the chances of existence are involved, a desire to leave a correct impression of the feelings, like a light by which the action may be seen when personality is gone—gone where no light of investigation can ever reach the truth which every death takes out of the world. Therefore, instead of looking for something to eat, or trying to snatch an hour or so of sleep, Decoud was filling the pages of a large pocket-book with a letter to his sister.

In the intimacy of that intercourse he could not keep out his weariness, his great fatigue, the close touch of his bodily sensations. He began again as if he were talking to her. With almost an illusion of her presence, he wrote the phrase, " I am very hungry."

" I have the feeling of a great solitude around me," he continued. " Is it, perhaps, because I am the only man with a definite idea in his head, in the complete collapse of every resolve, intention, and hope about me ? But the solitude is also very real. All the engineers are out, and have been for two days, looking after the property of the National Central Railway, of that great Costaguana undertaking which is to put money into the pockets of Englishmen, Frenchmen, Americans, Germans, and God knows who else. The silence about me is ominous. There is above the middle part of this house a sort of first floor, with narrow openings like loop-holes for windows, probably used in old times for the better defence against the savages, when the persistent barbarism of our native continent did not wear the black coats of politicians, but went about yelling, half naked, with bows and arrows in its hands. The woman of the house is dying up there, I believe, all alone with her old husband. There is a narrow staircase, the sort of staircase one man could easily defend against a mob, leading up there, and I have just heard, though the thickness of the wall, the old fellow going down into their kitchen for

something or other.   It was a sort of noise a mouse might
make behind the plaster of a wall.   All the servants they
had ran away yesterday and have not returned yet, if
ever they do.   For the rest, there are only two children
here, two girls.   The father has sent them downstairs,
and they have crept into this café, perhaps because I am
here.   They huddle together in a corner, in each other's
arms ; I just noticed them a few minutes ago, and I feel
more lonely than ever."

Decoud turned half round in his chair, and asked, " Is
there any bread here ? "

Linda's dark head was shaken negatively in response,
above the fair head of her sister nestling on her breast.

" You couldn't get me some bread ? " insisted Decoud.
The child did not move ; he saw her large eyes stare
at him very dark from the corner.   " You're not afraid
of me ? " he said.

" No," said Linda, " we are not afraid of you.   You
came here with Gian' Battista."

" You mean Nostromo ? " said Decoud.

" The English call him so, but that is no name either
for man or beast," said the girl, passing her hand gently
over her sister's hair.

" But he lets people call him so," remarked Decoud.

" Not in this house," retorted the child.

" Ah, well, I shall call him the Capataz, then."

Decoud gave up the point, and after writing steadily
for a while turned round again.

" When do you expect him back ? " he asked.

" After he brought you here he rode off to fetch the
Señor Doctor from the town for mother.   He will be
back soon."

" He stands a good chance of getting shot somewhere
on the road," Decoud murmured to himself audibly ;
and Linda declared in her high-pitched voice :

" Nobody would dare to fire a shot at Gian' Battista."

" You believe that," asked Decoud, " do you ? "

" I know it," said the child, with conviction. " There is no one in this place brave enough to attack Gian' Battista."

" It doesn't require much bravery to pull a trigger behind a bush," muttered Decoud to himself. " Fortunately, the night is dark, or there would be but little chance of saving the silver of the mine."

He turned again to his pocket-book, glanced back through the pages, and again started his pencil.

" That was the position yesterday, after the *Minerva* with the fugitive President had gone out of harbour, and the rioters had been driven back into the side lanes of the town. I sat on the steps of the cathedral with Nostromo, after sending out the cable message for the information of a more or less attentive world. Strangely enough, though the offices of the Cable Company are in the same building as the *Porvenir*, the mob, which has thrown my presses out of the window and scattered the type all over the plaza, has been kept from interfering with the instruments on the other side of the courtyard. As I sat talking with Nostromo, Bernhardt, the telegraphist, came out from under the Arcades with a piece of paper in his hand. The little man had tied himself up to an enormous sword and was hung all over with revolvers. He is ridiculous, but the bravest German of his size that ever tapped the key of a Morse transmitter. He had received the message from Cayta reporting the transports with Barrios's army just entering the port, and ending with the words, ' The greatest enthusiasm prevails.' I walked off to drink some water at the fountain, and I was shot at from the Alameda by somebody hiding behind a tree. But I drank, and didn't care ; with Barrios in Cayta and the great Cordillera between us and Montero's victorious army I seemed, notwithstanding Messrs. Gamacho and Fuentes, to hold my new State in the hollow of my hand. I was ready to sleep, but when I got as far as the Casa Gould I found the patio full of wounded laid out on

straw. Lights were burning, and in that enclosed courtyard on that hot night a faint odour of chloroform and
blood hung about. At one end Dr. Monygham, the
doctor of the mine, was dressing the wounds ; at the other,
near the stairs, Father Corbelàn, kneeling, listened to the
confession of a dying cargador. Mrs. Gould was walking about through these shambles with a large bottle in
one hand and a lot of cotton-wool in the other. She
just looked at me and never even winked. Her camerista
was following her, also holding a bottle, and sobbing
gently to herself.

" I busied myself for some time in fetching water from
the cistern for the wounded. Afterwards I wandered
upstairs, meeting some of the first ladies of Sulaco,
paler than I had ever seen them before, with bandages
over their arms. Not all of them had fled to the ships.
A good many had taken refuge for the day in the Casa
Gould. On the landing a girl, with her hair half down,
was kneeling against the wall under the niche where
stands a Madonna in blue robes and a gilt crown on her
head. I think it was the eldest Miss Lopez ; I couldn't
see her face, but I remember looking at the high French
heel of her little shoe. She did not make a sound, she
did not stir, she was not sobbing ; she remained there,
perfectly still, all black against the white wall, a silent
figure of passionate piety. I am sure she was no more
frightened than the other white-faced ladies I met
carrying bandages. One was sitting on the top step
tearing a piece of linen hastily into strips—the young
wife of an elderly man of fortune here. She interrupted herself to wave her hand to my bow, as though
she were in her carriage on the Alameda. The women
of our country are worth looking at during a revolution.
The rouge and pearl powder fall off, together with that
passive attitude towards the outer world which education,
tradition, custom impose upon them from the earliest
infancy. I thought of your face, which from your

infancy had the stamp of intelligence instead of that patient and resigned cast which appears when some political commotion tears down the veil of cosmetics and usage.

" In the great sala upstairs a sort of Junta of Notables was sitting, the remnant of the vanished Provincial Assembly. Don Juste Lopez had had half his beard singed off at the muzzle of a trabuco loaded with slugs, of which every one missed him, providentially. And as he turned his head from side to side it was exactly as if there had been two men inside his frock-coat, one nobly whiskered and solemn, the other untidy and scared.

" ' They raised a cry of ' Decoud ! Don Martin ! ' at my entrance. I asked them, ' What are you deliberating upon, gentlemen ? ' There did not seem to be any president, though Don José Avellanos sat at the head of the table. They all answered together, ' On the pre- servation of life and property.' ' Till the new officials arrive,' Don Juste explained to me, with the solemn side of his face offered to my view. It was as if a stream of water had been poured upon my glowing idea of a new State. There was a hissing sound in my ears, and the room grew dim, as if suddenly filled with vapour.

" I walked up to the table blindly, as though I had been drunk. ' You are deliberating upon surrender,' I said. They all sat still, with their noses over the sheet of paper each had before him, God only knows why. Only Don José hid his face in his hands, muttering, ' Never, never ! ' But as I looked at him, it seemed to me that I could have blown him away with my breath, he looked so frail, so weak, so worn out. Whatever happens, he will not survive. The deception is too great for a man of his age ; and hasn't he seen the sheets of *Fifty Years of Misrule*, which we have begun printing on the presses of the *Porvenir*, littering the plaza, floating in the gutters, fired out as wads for trabucos loaded with handfuls of type, blown in the wind, trampled in the mud ? I have seen pages floating upon the very waters of the harbour. It would be unreasonable to expect him to survive. It would be cruel.

" ' Do you know,' I cried, ' what surrender means to you, to your women, to your children, to your property ? '

" I declaimed for five minutes without drawing breath, it seems to me, harping on our best chances, on the ferocity of Montero, whom I made out to be as great a beast as I have no doubt he would like to be if he had intelligence enough to conceive a systematic reign of terror. And then for another five minutes or more I poured out an impassioned appeal to their courage and manliness, with all the passion of my love for Antonia. For if ever man spoke well, it would be from a personal feeling, denouncing an enemy, defending himself, or pleading for what really may be dearer than life. My dear girl, I absolutely thundered at them. It seemed as if my voice would burst the walls asunder, and when I stopped I saw all their scared eyes looking at me dubiously. And that was all the effect I had produced ! Only Don José's head had sunk lower and lower on his breast. I bent my ear to his withered lips, and made out his whisper, something like, ' In God's name, then, Martin, my son ! ' I don't know exactly. There was the name of God in it, I am certain. It seems to me I have caught his last breath—the breath of his departing soul on his lips.

" He lives yet, it is true. I have seen him since ; but it was only a senile body, lying on its back, covered to the chin, with open eyes, and so still that you might have said it was breathing no longer. I left him thus, with Antonia kneeling by the side of the bed, just before I came to this Italian's posada, where the ubiquitous death is also waiting. But I know that Don José has really died there, in the Casa Gould, with that whisper urging me to attempt what no doubt his soul, wrapped up in the sanctity of diplomatic treaties and solemn declarations, must have abhorred. I had exclaimed very loud, ' There is never any God in a country where men will not help themselves.'

" Meanwhile Don Juste had begun a pondered oration, whose solemn effect was spoiled by the ridiculous disaster to his beard. I did not wait to make it out. He seemed to argue that Montero's (he called him the general) intentions were probably not evil, though, he went on, ' that distinguished man ' (only a week ago he used to call him a *gran' bestia*) ' was perhaps mistaken as to the true means.' As you may imagine, I didn't stay to hear the rest. I know the intentions of Montero's brother, Pedrito, the guerrillero, whom I exposed in Paris, some years ago, in a café frequented by South American students, where he tried to pass himself off for a Secretary of Legation. He used to come in and talk for hours, twisting his felt hat in his hairy paws, and his ambition seemed to become a sort of Duc de Morny to a sort of Napoleon. Already, then, he used to talk of his brother in inflated terms. He seemed fairly safe from being found out, because the students, all of the Blanco families, did not, as you may imagine, frequent the Legation. It was only Decoud, a man without faith and principles, as they used to say, that went in there sometimes for the sake of the fun, as it were to an assembly of trained monkeys. I know his intentions. I have seen him change the plates at table. Whoever is allowed to live on in terror, I must die the death.

" No, I didn't stay to the end to hear Don Juste Lopez trying to persuade himself in a grave oration of the clemency and justice and honesty and purity of the brothers Montero. I went out abruptly to seek Antonia. I saw her in the gallery. As I opened the door, she extended to me her clasped hands.

" ' What are they doing in there ? ' she asked.

" ' Talking,' I said, with my eyes looking into hers.

" ' Yes, yes, but——'

" ' Empty speeches,' I interrupted her. ' Hiding their fears behind imbecile hopes. They are all great Parliamentarians there—on the English model, as you know.' I was so furious that I could hardly speak. She made a gesture of despair.

" Through the door I held a little ajar behind me, we heard Don Juste's measured mouthing monotone go on from phrase to phrase, like a sort of awful and solemn madness.

" ' After all, the Democratic aspirations have, perhaps, their legitimacy. The ways of human progress are inscrutable, and if the fate of the country is in the hand of Montero, we ought——'

" I crashed the door to on that ; it was enough ; it was too much. There was never a beautiful face expressing more horror and despair than the face of Antonia. I couldn't bear it ; I seized her wrists.

" ' Have they killed my father in there ? ' she asked.

" Her eyes blazed with indignation, but as I looked on, fascinated, the light in them went out.

" ' It is a surrender,' I said. And I remember I was shaking her wrists I held apart in my hands. ' But it's more than talk. Your father told me to go on in God's name.'

" My dear girl, there is that in Antonia which would make me believe in the feasibility of anything. One look at her face is enough to set my brain on fire. And yet I love her as any other man would—with the heart, and with that alone. She is more to me than his Church to Father Corbelàn (the Grand Vicar disappeared last night from the town ; perhaps gone to join the band of Hernandez). She is more to me than his precious mine to that sentimental Englishman. I won't speak of his wife. She may have been sentimental once. The San

Tomé mine stands now between those two people.
'Your father himself, Antonia,' I repeated; 'your
father—do you understand?—has told me to go on.'

"She averted her face, and in a pained voice:

"'He has?' she cried. 'Then, indeed, I fear he
will never speak again.'

"She freed her wrists from my clutch and began to
cry in her handkerchief. I disregarded her sorrow; I
would rather see her miserable than not see her at all,
never any more; for whether I escaped or stayed to die,
there was for us no coming together, no future. And
that being so, I had no pity to waste upon the passing
moments of her sorrow. I sent her off in tears to fetch
Doña Emilia and Don Carlos, too. Their sentiment was
necessary to the very life of my plan; the sentimentalism
of the people that will never do anything for the sake of
their passionate desire, unless it comes to them clothed
in the fair robes of an idea.

"Late at night we formed a small junta of four—the
two women, Don Carlos, and myself—in Mrs. Gould's
blue and white boudoir.

"El Rey de Sulaco thinks himself, no doubt, a very
honest man. And so he is, if one could look behind
his taciturnity. Perhaps he thinks that this alone makes
his honesty unstained. Those Englishmen live on illusions which somehow or other help them to get a firm
hold of the substance. When he speaks it is by a
rare 'yes' or 'no' that seems as impersonal as the words
of an oracle. But he could not impose on me by his
dumb reserve. I knew what he had in his head: he
has his mine in his head; and his wife has nothing in
her head but his precious person, which he has bound
up with the Gould Concession and tied up to that little
woman's neck. No matter. The thing was to make
him present the affair to Holroyd (the Steel and Silver
King) in such a manner as to secure his financial support.
At that time last night, just twenty-four hours ago, we

15

thought the silver of the mine safe in the Custom House
vaults till the north-bound steamer came to take it away.
And as long as the treasure flowed north, without a
break, that utter sentimentalist, Holroyd, would not
drop his idea of introducing not only justice, industry,
peace to the benighted continents, but also that pet
dream of his of a purer form of Christianity. Later on,
the principal European really in Sulaco, the engineer-
in-chief of the railway, came riding up the calle, from
the harbour, and was admitted to our conclave. Meantime, the Junta of the Notables in the great sala was still
deliberating ; only, one of them had run out into the
corrédor to ask the servant whether something to eat
couldn't be sent in. The first words the engineer-in-
chief said as he came into the boudoir were : ' What is
your house, dear Mrs. Gould ? A war hospital below,
and apparently a restaurant above. I saw them carrying
trays full of good things into the sala.'

" ' And here, in this boudoir,' I said, ' you behold the
inner cabinet of the Occidental Republic that is to be.'

" He was so preoccupied that he didn't smile at
that ; he didn't even look surprised.

" He told us that he was attending to the general
dispositions for the defence of the railway property at
the railway yards when he was sent for to go into the
railway telegraph office. The engineer at the railhead, at
the foot of the mountains, wanted to talk to him from
his end of the wire. There was nobody in the office
but himself and the operator of the railway telegraph,
who read off the clicks aloud as the tape coiled its length
upon the floor. And the purport of that talk, clicked
nervously from a wooden shed in the depths of the forest,
had informed the chief that President Ribiera had been,
or was being, pursued. This was news, indeed, to all
of us in Sulaco. Ribiera himself, when rescued, revived,
and soothed by us, had been inclined to think that he
had not been pursued.

" Ribiera had yielded to the urgent solicitations of his friends, and had left the headquarters of his discomfited army alone, under the guidance of Bonifacio, the muleteer, who had been willing to take the responsibility with the risk. He had departed at daybreak of the third day. His remaining forces had melted away during the night. Bonifacio and he rode hard on horses towards the Cordillera ; then they obtained mules, entered the passes, and crossed the Paramo of Ivie just before a freezing blast swept over that stony plateau, burying in a drift of snow the little shelter-hut of stones in which they had spent the night. Afterwards poor Ribiera had many adventures, got separated from his guide, lost his mount, struggled down to the Campo on foot, and if he had not thrown himself on the mercy of a ranchero would have perished a long way from Sulaco. That man, who, as a matter of fact, recognised him at once, let him have a fresh mule, which the fugitive, heavy and unskilful, had ridden to death. And it was true he had been pursued by a party commanded by no less a person than Pedro Montero, the brother of the general. The cold wind of the paramo luckily caught the pursuers on the top of the pass. Some few men, and all the animals, perished in the icy blast. The stragglers died, but the main body kept on. They found poor Bonifacio lying half dead at the foot of a snow-slope, and bayoneted him promptly in the true Civil War style. They would have had Ribiera too, if they had not, for some reason or other, turned off the track of the old *camino real*, only to lose their way in the forests at the foot of the lower slopes. And there they were at last, having stumbled in unexpectedly upon the Construction Camp. The engineer at the railhead told his chief by wire that he had Pedro Montero absolutely there, in the very office, listening to the clicks. He was going to take possession of Sulaco in the name of the Democracy. He was very overbearing. His men slaughtered some of the Railway Company's cattle without asking leave, and went to work broiling the meat on the embers. Pedrito made many pointed inquiries as to the silver mine, and what had become of the product of the last six months' working. He had said peremptorily : ' Ask your chief up there by wire, he ought to know ; tell him that Don Pedro Montero, Chief of the Campo and Minister of the Interior of the new Government, desires to be correctly informed.'

" He had his feet wrapped up in bloodstained rags, a lean, haggard face, ragged beard and hair, and had walked in limping, with a crooked branch of a tree for a staff. His followers were perhaps in a worse plight, but apparently they had not thrown away their arms, and, at any rate, not all their ammunition. Their lean faces filled the door and the windows of the telegraph hut. As it was at the same time the bedroom of the engineer-in-charge there, Montero had thrown himself on his clean blankets and lay there shivering and dictating requisitions to be transmitted by wire to Sulaco. He demanded a train of cars to be sent down at once to transport his men up.

" ' To this I answered from my end,' the engineer-in-chief related to us, ' that I dared not risk the rolling-stock in the interior, as there had been attempts to wreck trains all along the line several times. I did that for your sake, Gould,' said the chief engineer. ' The answer to this was, in the words of my subordinate, " The filthy brute on my bed said, ' Suppose I were to have you shot ? ' " To which my subordinate, who, it appears, was himself operating, remarked that it would not bring the cars up. Upon that, the other, yawning, said, " Never mind, there is no lack of horses on the Campo." And, turning over, went to sleep on Harris's bed.'

" This is why, my dear girl, I am a fugitive to-night. The last wire from railhead says that Pedro Montero and his men left at daybreak, after feeding on asado beef all night. They took all the horses ; they will find more on the road ; they'll be here in less than thirty hours, and thus Sulaco is no place either for me or the great store of silver belonging to the Gould Concession.

" But that is not the worst. The garrison of Esmeralda has gone over to the victorious party. We have heard this by means of the telegraphist of the Cable Company, who came to the Casa Gould in the early morning with the news. In fact, it was so early that the day had not yet quite broken over Sulaco. His colleague in Esmeralda had called him up to say that the garrison, after shooting some of their officers, had taken possession of a Government steamer laid up in the harbour. It is really a heavy blow for me. I thought I could depend on every man in this province. It was a mistake. It was a Monterist Revolution in Esmeralda, just such as was attempted in Sulaco, only that *that* one came off. The telegraphist was signalling to Bernhardt all the time, and his last transmitted words were : ' They are bursting in the door, and taking possession of the cable office. You are cut off. Can do no more.'

" But, as a matter of fact, he managed somehow to escape the vigilance of his captors, who had tried to stop the communication with the outer world. He did manage it. How it was done I don't know, but a few hours afterwards he called up Sulaco again, and what he said was : ' The insurgent army has taken possession of the Government transport in the bay and are filling her with troops, with the intention of going round the coast to Sulaco. Therefore look out for yourselves. They will be ready to start in a few hours, and may be upon you before daybreak.'

" This is all he could say. They drove him away from his instrument this time for good, because Bernhardt has been calling up Esmeralda ever since without getting an answer."

After setting these words down in the pocket-book which he was filling up for the benefit of his sister, Decoud lifted his head to listen. But there were no sounds, neither in the room nor in the house, except the drip of the water from the filter into the vast earthenware jar under the wooden stand. And outside the house there was a great silence. Decoud lowered his head again over the pocket-book.

" I am not running away, you understand," he wrote on. " I am simply going away with that great treasure of silver which must be saved at all costs. Pedro Montero from the Campo and the revolted garrison of Esmeralda from the sea are converging upon it. That it is there lying ready for them is only an accident. The real objective is the San Tomé mine itself, as you may well imagine ; otherwise the Occidental Province would have been, no doubt, left alone for many weeks, to be gathered at leisure into the arms of the victorious party. Don Carlos Gould will have enough to do to save his mine, with its organisation and its people ; this ' Imperium in imperio,' this wealth-producing thing, to which his sentimentalism attaches a strange idea of justice. He holds to it as some men hold to the idea of love or revenge. Unless I am much mistaken in the man, it must remain inviolate or perish by an act of his will alone. A passion has crept into his cold and idealistic life ; a passion which I can only comprehend intellectually ; a passion that is not like the passion we know, we men of another blood. But it is as dangerous as any of ours.

" His wife has understood it too. That is why she is such a good ally of mine. She seizes upon all my suggestions with a sure instinct that in the end they make for the safety of the Gould Concession. And he defers to her because he trusts her perhaps, but I fancy rather as if he wished to make up for some subtle wrong, for that sentimental unfaithfulness which surrenders her happiness, her life, to the seduction of an idea. The little woman has discovered that he lives for the mine rather than for her. But let them be. To each his fate,

shaped by passion or sentiment. The principal thing is
that she has backed up my advice to get the silver out of
the town, out of the country, at once, at any cost, at any
risk. Don Carlos's mission is to preserve unstained the
fair name of his mine ; Mrs. Gould's mission is to save
him from the effects of that cold and overmastering passion, which she dreads more than if it were an infatuation
for another woman. Nostromo's mission is to save the
silver. The plan is to load it into the largest of the Company's lighters, and send it across the gulf to a small port
out of Costaguana territory just on the other side of the
Azuera, where the first north-bound steamer will get
orders to pick it up. The waters here are calm ; we shall
slip away into the darkness of the gulf before the Esmeralda rebels arrive ; and by the time the day breaks over the
ocean we shall be out of sight, invisible, hidden by Azuera,
which itself looks from the Sulaco shore like a faint blue
cloud on the horizon.

" The incorruptible Capataz de Cargadores is the man
for that work ; and I, the man with a passion, but without
a mission, I go with him to return—to play my part in
the farce to the end, and, if successful, to receive my
reward, which no one but Antonia can give me.

" I shall not see her again now before I depart. I
left her, as I have said, by Don José's bedside. The
street was dark, the houses shut up, and I walked out of
the town in the night. Not a single street-lamp had been
lit for two days, and the archway of the gate was only a
mass of darkness in the vague form of a tower, in which
I heard low, dismal groans, that seemed to answer the
murmurs of a man's voice.

" I recognised something impassive and careless in
its tone, characteristic of that Genoese sailor who, like
me, has come casually here to be drawn into the events
for which his scepticism as well as mine seems to entertain a sort of passive contempt. The only thing he seems
to care for, as far as I have been able to discover, is to be

well spoken of.   An ambition fit for noble souls, but also
a profitable one for an exceptionally intelligent scoundrel.
Yes.   His very words, ' To be well spoken of.   Si,
Señor.'   He does not seem to make any difference
between speaking and thinking.   Is it sheer naïveness
or the practical point of view, I wonder ?   Exceptional
individualities always interest me, because they are true
to the general formula expressing the moral state of
humanity.

   " He joined me on the harbour road after I had passed
them under the dark archway without stopping.   It was
a woman in trouble he had been talking to.   Through
discretion I kept silent while he walked by my side.
After a time he began to talk himself.   It was not what I
expected.   It was only an old woman, an old lace-maker,
in search of her son, one of the street-sweepers employed
by the municipality.   Friends had come the day before
at daybreak to the door of their hovel calling him out.
He had gone with them, and she had not seen him since ;
so she had left the food she had been preparing half
cooked on the extinct embers, and had crawled out as far
as the harbour, where she had heard that some town
mozos had been killed on the morning of the riot.   One
of the cargadores guarding the Custom House had
brought out a lantern, and had helped her to look at the
few dead left lying about there.   Now she was creeping
back, having failed in her search.   So she sat down on
the stone seat under the arch, moaning, because she was
very tired.   The Capataz had questioned her, and after
hearing her broken and groaning tale had advised her to
go and look amongst the wounded in the patio of the Casa
Gould.   He had also given her a quarter dollar, he mentioned carelessly.

   " ' Why did you do that ? ' I asked.   ' Do you know
her ? '

   " ' No, Señor.   I don't suppose I have ever seen
her before.   How should I ?   She has not probably been

out in the streets for years. She is one of those old women that you find in this country at the back of huts, crouching over fireplaces, with a stick on the ground by their side, and almost too feeble to drive away the stray dogs from their cooking-pots. Caramba ! I could tell by her voice that Death had forgotten her. But, old or young, they like money, and will speak well of the man who gives it to them.' He laughed a little. ' Señor, you should have felt the clutch of her paw as I put the piece in her palm.' He paused. ' My last, too,' he added.

" I made no comment. He's known for his liberality and his bad luck at the game of *monte*, which keeps him as poor as when he first came here.

" ' I suppose, Don Martin,' he began in a thoughtful, speculative tone, ' that the Señor Administrador of San Tomé will reward me some day if I save his silver ? '

" I said that it could not be otherwise, surely. He walked on, muttering to himself. ' Si, si, without doubt, without doubt ; and, look you, Señor Martin, what it is to be well spoken of ! There is not another man that could have been even thought of for such a thing. I shall get something great for it some day. And let it come soon,' he mumbled. ' Time passes in this country as quick as anywhere else.'

" This, *sœur chérie*, is my companion in the great escape for the sake of the Great Cause. He is more naïve than shrewd, more masterful than crafty, more generous with his personality than the people who make use of him are with their money. At least, that is what he thinks himself with more pride than sentiment. I am glad I have made friends with him. As a companion he acquires more importance than he ever had as a sort of minor genius in his way—as an original Italian sailor whom I allowed to come in in the small hours and talk familiarly to the editor of the *Porvenir* while the paper was going through the press. And it is curious to have met a man for whom the value of life seems to consist in personal prestige.

" I am waiting for him here now. On arriving at the posada kept by Viola we found the children alone down below, and the old Genoese shouted to his countryman to go and fetch the doctor. Otherwise we would have gone on to the wharf, where it appears Captain Mitchell with some volunteer Europeans and a few picked cargadores are loading the lighter with the silver that must be saved from Montero's clutches in order to be used for Montero's defeat. Nostromo galloped furiously back towards the town. He has been long gone already. This delay gives me time to talk to you. By the time this pocket-book reaches your hands much will have happened. But now it is a pause under the hovering wing of Death in that silent house buried in the black night, with this dying woman, the two children crouching without a sound, and that old man whom I can hear through the thickness of the wall passing up and down with a light rubbing noise no louder than a mouse. And I, the only other with them, don't really know whether to count myself with the living or with the dead. ' *Quien sabe?* ' as the people here are prone to say in answer to every question. But no! feeling for you is certainly not dead ; and the whole thing, the house, the dark night, the silent children in this dim room, my very presence here—all this is life, must be life, since it is so much like a dream."

With the writing of the last line there came upon Decoud a moment of sudden and complete oblivion. He swayed over the table as if struck by a bullet. The next moment he sat up, confused, with the idea that he had heard his pencil roll on the floor. The low door of the café, wide open, was filled with the glare of a torch in which was visible half of a horse, switching its tail against the leg of a rider with a long iron spur strapped to the naked heel. The two girls were gone, and

Nostromo, standing in the middle of the room, looked at him from under the round brim of the sombrero low down over his brow.

" I have brought that sour-faced English doctor in Señora Gould's carriage," said Nostromo. " I doubt if, with all his wisdom, he can save the padrona this time. They have sent for the children. A bad sign that."

He sat down on the end of a bench. " She wants to give them her blessing, I suppose."

Dazedly Decoud observed that he must have fallen sound asleep, and Nostromo said, with a vague smile, that he had looked in at the window and had seen him lying still across the table with his head on his arms. The English Señora had also come in the carriage, and went upstairs at once with the doctor. She had told him not to wake up Don Martin yet ; but when they sent for the children he had come into the café.

The half of the horse with its half of the rider swung round outside the door ; the torch of tow and resin in the iron basket which was carried on a stick at the saddle-bow flared right into the room for a moment, and Mrs. Gould entered hastily with a very white, tired face. The hood of her dark blue cloak had fallen back. Both men rose.

" Teresa wants to see you, Nostromo," she said.

The Capataz did not move. Decoud, with his back to the table, began to button up his coat.

" The silver, Mrs. Gould, the silver," he murmured in English. " Don't forget that the Esmeralda garrison have got a steamer. They may appear at any moment at the harbour entrance."

" The doctor says there is no hope," Mrs. Gould spoke rapidly, also in English. " I shall take you down to the wharf in my carriage and then come back to fetch away the girls." She changed swiftly into Spanish to address Nostromo. " Why are you wasting time ? Old Giorgio's wife wishes to see you."

"I am going to her, Señora," muttered the Capataz.

Dr. Monygham now showed himself, bringing back the children. To Mrs. Gould's inquiring glance he only shook his head and went outside at once, followed by Nostromo.

The horse of the torch-bearer, motionless, hung his head low, and the rider had dropped the reins to light a cigarette. The glare of the torch played on the front of the house crossed by the big black letters of its inscription, in which only the word ITALIA was lighted fully. The patch of wavering glare reached as far as Mrs. Gould's carriage waiting on the road, with the yellow-faced, portly Ignacio apparently dozing on the box. By his side Basilio, dark and skinny, held a Winchester carbine in front of him, with both hands, and peered fearfully into the darkness. Nostromo touched lightly the doctor's shoulder.

"Is she really dying, Señor Doctor?"

"Yes," said the doctor, with a strange twitch of his scarred cheek. "And why she wants to see you I cannot imagine."

"She has been like that before," suggested Nostromo, looking away.

"Well, Capataz, I can assure you she will never be like that again," snarled Dr. Monygham. "You may go to her or stay away. There is very little to be got from talking to the dying. But she told Doña Emilia in my hearing that she has been like a mother to you ever since you first set foot ashore here."

"Si! And she never had a good word to say for me to anybody. It is more as if she could not forgive me for being alive; and such a man, too, as she would have liked her son to be."

"Maybe!" exclaimed a mournful deep voice near them. "Women have their own ways of tormenting themselves." Giorgio Viola had come out of the house. He threw a heavy black shadow in the torchlight, and the glare fell on his big face, on the great bushy head of white hair. He motioned the Capataz indoors with his extended arm.

Dr. Monygham, after busying himself with a little medicament box of polished wood on the seat of the landau, turned to old Giorgio and thrust into his big, trembling hand one of the glass-stoppered bottles out of the case.

" Give her a spoonful of this now and then, in water," he said. " It will make her easier."

" And there is nothing more for her ? " asked the old man patiently.

" No. Not on earth," said the doctor, with his back to him, clicking the lock of the medicine-case.

Nostromo slowly crossed the large kitchen, all dark but for the glow of a heap of charcoal under the heavy mantel of the cooking-range, where water was boiling in an iron pot with a loud bubbling sound. Between the two walls of a narrow staircase a bright light streamed from the sick-room above ; and the magnificent Capataz de Cargadores, stepping noiselessly in soft leather sandals, bushy whiskered, his muscular neck and bronzed chest bare in the open check shirt, resembled a Mediterranean sailor just come ashore from some wine or fruit laden felucca. At the top he paused, broad shouldered, narrow hipped, and supple, looking at the large bed, like a white couch of state, with a profusion of snowy linen, amongst which the padrona sat unpropped and bowed, her handsome, black-browed face bent over her chest. A mass of raven hair with only a few white threads in it covered her shoulders ; one thick strand fallen forward half veiled her cheek. Perfectly motion-less in that pose, expressing physical anxiety and unrest, she turned her eyes alone towards Nostromo.

The Capataz had a red sash wound many times round his waist, and a heavy silver ring on the forefinger of the hand he raised to give a twist to his moustache.

"Their revolutions, their revolutions," gasped
Señora Teresa. "Look, Gian' Battista, it has killed
me at last!"

Nostromo said nothing, and the sick woman with an
upward glance insisted. "Look, this one has killed me,
while you were away fighting for what did not concern
you, foolish man."

"Why talk like this?" mumbled the Capataz between
his teeth. "Will you never believe in my good sense?
It concerns me to keep on being what I am : every day
alike."

"You never change, indeed," she said bitterly.
"Always thinking of yourself, and taking your pay out
in fine words from those who care nothing for you."

There was between them an intimacy of antagonism
as close in its way as the intimacy of accord and affection.
He had not walked along the way of Teresa's expectations. It was she who had encouraged him to leave his
ship, in the hope of securing a friend and defender for
the girls. The wife of old Giorgio was aware of her
precarious health, and was haunted by the fear of her
aged husband's loneliness and the unprotected state of
the children. She had wanted to annex that apparently
quiet and steady young man, affectionate and pliable,
an orphan from his tenderest age, as he had told her,
with no ties in Italy except an uncle, owner and master
of a felucca, from whose ill-usage he had run away before
he was fourteen. He had seemed to her courageous, a
hard worker, determined to make his way in the world.
From gratitude and the ties of habit he would become
like a son to herself and Giorgio ; and then, who knows,
when Linda had grown up. . . . Ten years' difference
between husband and wife was not so much. Her own
great man was nearly twenty years older than herself.
Gian' Battista was an attractive young fellow, besides ;
attractive to men, women, and children, just by that
profound quietness of personality which, like a serene

twilight, rendered more seductive the promise of his vigorous form and the resolution of his conduct.

Old Giorgio, in profound ignorance of his wife's views and hopes, had a great regard for his young countryman. " A man ought not to be tame," he used to tell her, quoting the Spanish proverb in defence of the splendid Capataz. She was growing jealous of his success. He was escaping from her, she feared. She was practical, and he seemed to her to be an absurd spendthrift of these qualities which made him so valuable. He got too little for them. He scattered them with both hands amongst too many people, she thought. He laid no money by. She railed at his poverty, his exploits, his adventures, his loves, and his reputation ; but in her heart she had never given him up, as though, indeed, he had been her son.

Even now, ill as she was, ill enough to feel the chill, black breath of the approaching end, she had wished to see him. It was like putting out her benumbed hand to regain her hold. But she had presumed too much on her strength. She could not command her thoughts ; they had become dim, like her vision. The words faltered on her lips, and only the paramount anxiety and desire of her life seemed to be too strong for death.

The Capataz said, " I have heard these things many times. You are unjust, but it does not hurt me. Only now you do not seem to have much strength to talk, and I have but little time to listen. I am engaged in a work of very great moment."

She made an effort to ask him whether it was true that he had found time to go and fetch a doctor for her. Nostromo nodded affirmatively.

She was pleased ; it relieved her sufferings to know that the man had condescended to do so much for those who really wanted his help. It was a proof of his friendship. Her voice became stronger.

" I want a priest more than a doctor," she said

pathetically. She did not move her head; only her eyes ran into the corners to watch the Capataz standing by the side of her bed. "Would you go to fetch a priest for me now? Think! A dying woman asks you!"

Nostromo shook his head resolutely. He did not believe in priests in their sacerdotal character. A doctor was an efficacious person; but a priest, as priest, was nothing, incapable of doing either good or harm. Nostromo did not even dislike the sight of them as old Giorgio did. The utter uselessness of the errand was what struck him most.

"Padrona," he said, "you have been like this before, and got better after a few days. I have given you already the very last moments I can spare. Ask Señora Gould to send you one."

He was feeling uneasy at the impiety of this refusal. The padrona believed in priests, and confessed herself to them. But all women did that. It could not be of much consequence. And yet his heart felt oppressed for a moment—at the thought what absolution would mean to her if she believed in it only ever so little. No matter. It was quite true that he had given her already the very last moment he could spare.

"You refuse to go?" she gasped. "Ah, you are always yourself, indeed!"

"Listen to reason, padrona," he said. "I am needed to save the silver of the mine. Do you hear? A greater treasure than the one which they say is guarded by ghosts and devils on Azuera. It is true. I am resolved to make this the most desperate affair I was ever engaged on in my whole life."

She felt a despairing indignation. The supreme test had failed. Standing above her, Nostromo did not see the distorted features of her face, distorted by a paroxysm of pain and anger. Only she began to tremble all over. Her bowed head shook. The broad shoulders quivered.

" Then God, perhaps, will have mercy upon me! But do you look to it, man, that you get something for yourself out of it, besides the remorse that shall overtake you some day."

She laughed feebly. " Get riches at least for once, you indispensable, admired Gian' Battista, to whom the peace of a dying woman is less than the praise of people who have given you a silly name—and nothing besides— in exchange for your soul and body."

The Capataz de Cargadores swore to himself under his breath.

" Leave my soul alone, padrona, and I shall know how to take care of my body. Where is the harm of people having need of me? What are you envying me that I have robbed you and the children of? Those very people you are throwing in my teeth have done more for old Giorgio than they ever thought of doing for me."

He struck his breast with his open palm; his voice had remained low though he had spoken in a forcible tone. He twisted his moustaches one after another, and his eyes wandered a little about the room.

" Is it my fault that I am the only man for their purposes? What angry nonsense are you talking, mother? Would you rather have me timid and foolish, selling water-melons on the market-place or rowing a boat for passengers along the harbour, like a soft Neapolitan without courage or reputation? Would you have a young man live like a monk? I do not believe it. Would you want a monk for your eldest girl? Let her grow. What are you afraid of? You have been angry with me for everything I did for years; ever since you first spoke to me, in secret from old Giorgio, about your Linda. Husband to one and brother to the other, did you say? Well, why not? I like the little ones, and a man must marry some time. But ever since that time you have been making little of me to every one. Why? Did you think you could put a collar and chain on me as if I were one of the

16

watch-dogs they keep over there in the railway yards ?
Look here, padrona, I am the same man who came ashore
one evening and sat down in the thatched ranch you
lived in at that time on the other side of the town and told
you all about himself. You were not unjust to me then.
What has happened since ? I am no longer an insignificant youth. A good name, Giorgio says, is a treasure,
padrona."

" They have turned your head with their praises,"
gasped the sick woman. " They have been paying you
with words. Your folly shall betray you into poverty,
misery, starvation. The very leperos shall laugh at you
—the great Capataz."

Nostromo stood for a time as if struck dumb. She
never looked at him. A self-confident, mirthless smile
passed quickly from his lips, and then he backed away.
His disregarded figure sank down beyond the doorway.
He descended the stairs backwards, with the usual sense
of having been somehow baffled by this woman's dis-
paragement of this reputation he had obtained and
desired to keep.

Downstairs in the big kitchen a candle was burning,
surrounded by the shadows of the walls, of the ceiling,
but no ruddy glare filled the open square of the outer
door. The carriage with Mrs. Gould and Don Martin,
preceded by the horseman bearing the torch, had gone
on to the jetty. Dr. Monygham, who had remained,
sat on the corner of a hardwood table near the candlestick, his seamed, shaven face inclined sideways, his arms
crossed on his breast, his lips pursed up, and his prominent eyes glaring stonily upon the floor of black earth.
Near the overhanging mantel of the fireplace, where the
pot of water was still boiling violently, old Giorgio held
his chin in his hand, one foot advanced, as if arrested by
a sudden thought.

" *Adios, viejo*," said Nostromo, feeling the handle of
his revolver in the belt and loosening his knife in its

sheath. He picked up a blue poncho lined with red from the table, and put it over his head. " *Adios*, look after the things in my sleeping-room, and if you hear from me no more, give up the box to Paquita. There is not much of value there, except my new serape from Mexico, and a few silver buttons on my best jacket. No matter ! The things will look well enough on the next lover she gets, and the man need not be afraid I shall linger on earth after I am dead, like those gringos that haunt the Azuera."

Dr. Monygham twisted his lips into a bitter smile. After old Giorgio, with an almost imperceptible nod and without a word, had gone up the narrow stairs, he said :

" Why, Capataz ! I thought you could never fail in anything."

Nostromo, glancing contemptuously at the doctor, lingered in the doorway rolling a cigarette, then struck a match, and, after lighting it, held the burning piece of wood above his head till the flame nearly touched his fingers.

" No wind ! " he muttered to himself. " Look here, Señor—do you know the nature of my undertaking ? "

Dr. Monygham nodded sourly.

" It is as if I were taking up a curse upon me, Señor Doctor. A man with a treasure on this coast will have every knife raised against him in every place upon the shore. You see that, Señor Doctor ? I shall float along with a spell upon my life till I meet somewhere the north-bound steamer of the Company, and then indeed they will talk about the Capataz of the Sulaco Cargadores from one end of America to another."

Dr. Monygham laughed his short, throaty laugh. Nostromo turned round in the doorway.

" But if your worship can find any other man ready and fit for such business I will stand back. I am not exactly tired of my life, though I am so poor that I can carry all I have with myself on my horse's back."

" You gamble too much, and never say ' no ' to a pretty face, Capataz," said Dr. Monygham, with sly simplicity. " That's not the way to make a fortune. But nobody that I know ever suspected you of being poor. I hope you have made a good bargain in case you come back safe from this adventure."

" What bargain would your worship have made ? " asked Nostromo, blowing the smoke out of his lips through the doorway.

Dr. Monygham listened up the staircase for a moment before he answered, with another of his short, abrupt laughs :

" Illustrious Capataz, for taking the curse of death upon my back, as you call it, nothing else but the whole treasure would do."

Nostromo vanished out of the doorway with a grunt of discontent at this jeering answer. Dr. Monygham heard him gallop away. Nostromo rode furiously in the dark. There were lights in the buildings of the O.S.N. Company near the wharf, but before he got there he met the Gould carriage. The horseman preceded it with the torch, whose light showed the white mules trotting, the portly Ignacio driving, and Basilio with the carbine on the box. From the dark body of the landau Mrs. Gould's voice cried, " They are waiting for you, Capataz ! " She was returning, chilly and excited, with Decoud's pocket-book still held in her hand. He had confided it to her to send to his sister. " Perhaps my last words to her," he had said, pressing Mrs. Gould's hand.

The Capataz never checked his speed. At the head of the wharf vague figures with rifles leapt to the head of his horse ; others closed upon him—cargadores of the Company posted by Captain Mitchell on the watch. At a word from him they fell back with subservient murmurs, recognising his voice. At the other end of the jetty, near a cargo crane, in a dark group with glowing cigars, his name was pronounced in a tone of relief. Most of the Europeans in Sulaco were there, rallied round Charles Gould, as if the silver of the mine had been the emblem of a common cause, the symbol of the supreme importance of material interests. They had loaded it into the lighter with their own hands. Nostromo recognised Don Carlos Gould, a thin, tall shape, standing a little apart and silent, to whom another tall shape, the engineer-in-chief, said aloud, " If it must be lost, it is a million times better that it should go to the bottom of the sea."

Martin Decoud called out from the lighter, " Au revoir, messieurs, till we clasp hands again over the new-born Occidental Republic."   Only a subdued murmur responded to his clear, ringing tones ; and then it seemed to him that the wharf was floating away into the night ; but it was Nostromo, who was already pushing against a pile with one of the heavy sweeps. Decoud did not move ; the effect was that of being launched into space. After a splash or two there was not a sound but the thud of Nostromo's feet leaping about the boat. He hoisted the big sail ; a breath of wind fanned Decoud's cheek. Everything had vanished but the light of the lantern Captain Mitchell had hoisted upon the post at the end of the jetty to guide Nostromo out of the harbour.

The two men, unable to see each other, kept silent till the lighter, slipping before the fitful breeze, passed out between almost invisible headlands into the still deeper darkness of the gulf.   For a time the lantern on the jetty shone after them. The wind failed, then fanned up again, but so faintly that the big, half-decked boat slipped along with no more noise than if she had been suspended in the air.

" We are out in the gulf now," said the calm voice of Nostromo. A moment after he added : " Señor Mitchell has lowered the light."

" Yes," said Decoud ; " nobody can find us now."

A great recrudescence of obscurity embraced the boat. The sea in the gulf was as black as the clouds above.

Nostromo, after striking a couple of matches to get a glimpse of the boat compass he had with him in the lighter, steered by the feel of the wind on his cheek.

It was a new experience for Decoud, this mysteriousness of the great waters spread out strangely smooth, as if their restlessness had been crushed by the weight of that dense night. The Placido was sleeping profoundly under its black poncho.

The main thing now for success was to get away from the coast and gain the middle of the gulf before day broke. The Isabels were somewhere at hand. " On your left as you look forward, Señor," said Nostromo suddenly. When his voice ceased, the enormous stillness, without light or sound, seemed to affect Decoud's senses like a powerful drug. He didn't even know at times whether he were asleep or awake. Like a man lost in slumber, he heard nothing, he saw nothing. Even his hand held before his face did not exist for his eyes. The change from the agitation, the passions, and the dangers, from the sights and sounds of the shore, was so complete that it would have resembled death had it not been for the survival of his thoughts. In this foretaste of eternal peace they floated vivid and light, like unearthly clear dreams of earthly things that may haunt the souls freed by death from the misty atmosphere of regrets and hopes. Decoud shook himself, shuddered a bit, though the air that drifted past him was warm. He had the strangest sensation of his soul having just returned into his body from the circumambient darkness in which land, sea, sky, the mountains, and the rocks were as if they had not been.

Nostromo's voice was speaking, though he, at the tiller, was also as if he were not. " Have you been asleep, Don Martin ? Caramba ! If it were possible I would think that I, too, have dozed off. I have a strange notion somehow of having dreamt that there was a sound of blubbering, a sound a sorrowing man could

make, somewhere near this boat.   Something between a
sigh and a sob."

" Strange ! " muttered Decoud, stretched upon the
pile of treasure boxes covered by many tarpaulins.
" Could it be that there is another boat near us in the
gulf ?   We could not see it, you know."

Nostromo laughed a little at the absurdity of the idea.
They dismissed it from their minds.   The solitude could
almost be felt.   And when the breeze ceased, the blackness seemed to weigh upon Decoud like a stone.

" This is overpowering," he muttered.   " Do we
move at all, Capataz ? "

" Not so fast as a crawling beetle tangled in the
grass," answered Nostromo, and his voice seemed
deadened by the thick veil of obscurity that felt warm
and hopeless all about them.   There were long periods
when he made no sound, invisible and inaudible as if
he had mysteriously stepped out of the lighter.

In the featureless night Nostromo was not even
certain which way the lighter headed after the wind had
completely died out.   He peered for the islands.   There
was not a hint of them to be seen, as if they had sunk to
the bottom of the gulf.   He threw himself down by the
side of Decoud at last, and whispered into his ear that
if daylight caught them near the Sulaco shore through
want of wind, it would be possible to sweep the lighter
behind the cliff at the high end of the Great Isabel,
where she would lie concealed.   Decoud was surprised
at the grimness of his anxiety.   To him the removal
of the treasure was a political move.   It was necessary
for several reasons that it should not fall into the hands
of Montero ; but here was a man who took another
view of this enterprise.   The caballeros over there did
not seem to have the slightest idea of what they had
given him to do.   Nostromo, as if affected by the
gloom around, seemed nervously resentful.   Decoud was
surprised.   The Capataz, indifferent to those dangers

that seemed obvious to his companion, allowed himself to become scornfully exasperated by the deadly nature of the trust put, as a matter of course, into his hands. It was more dangerous, Nostromo said, with a laugh and a curse, than sending a man to get the treasure that people said was guarded by devils and ghosts in the deep ravines of Azuera. "Señor," he said, "we must catch the steamer at sea. We must keep out in the open looking for her till we have eaten and drunk all that has been put on board here. And if we miss her by some mischance, we must keep away from the land till we grow weak, and perhaps mad, and die, and drift dead, until one or another of the steamers of the Compañia comes upon the boat with the two dead men who have saved the treasure. That, Señor, is the only way to save it ; for, don't you see ? for us to come to the land anywhere in a hundred miles along this coast with this silver in our possession is to run the naked breast against the point of a knife. This thing has been given to me like a deadly disease. If men discover it I am dead, and you, too, Señor, since you would come with me. There is enough silver to make a whole province rich, let alone a seaboard pueblo inhabited by thieves and vagabonds. Señor, they would think that Heaven itself sent these riches into their hands, and would cut our throats without hesitation. I would trust no fair words from the best man around the shores of this wild gulf. Reflect that, even by giving up the treasure at the first demand, we would not be able to save our lives. Do you understand this, or must I explain ? "

"No, you needn't explain," said Decoud a little listlessly. "I can see it well enough myself, that the possession of this treasure is very much like a deadly disease for men situated as we are. But it had to be removed from Sulaco, and you were the man for the task."

"I was ; but I cannot believe," said Nostromo, "that its loss would have impoverished Don Carlos Gould very much. There is more wealth in the mountain. I have heard it rolling down the shoots on quiet nights when I used to ride to Rincon to see a certain girl, after my work at the harbour was done. For years the rich rocks have been pouring down with a noise like thunder, and the miners say that there is enough at the heart of the mountain to thunder on for years and years to come. And yet, the day before yesterday, we have been fighting to save it from the mob, and to-night I am sent out with it into this darkness, where there is no wind to get away with ; as if it were the last lot of silver on earth to get bread for the hungry with. Ha ! ha ! Well, I am going to make it the most famous and desperate affair of my life—wind or no wind. It shall be talked about when the little children are grown up and the grown men are old. Aha ! the Monterists must not get hold of it, I am told, whatever happens to Nostromo the Capataz ; and they shall not have it, I tell you, since it has been tied for safety round Nostromo's neck."

"I see it," murmured Decoud. He saw, indeed, that his companion had his own peculiar view of this enterprise.

Nostromo interrupted his reflections upon the way men's qualities are made use of, without any fundamental knowledge of their nature, by the proposal that they should slip the long oars out and sweep the lighter in the direction of the Isabels. It wouldn't do for daylight to reveal the treasure floating within a mile or so of the harbour entrance. The denser the darkness generally, the smarter were the puffs of wind on which he had reckoned to make his way ; but to-night the gulf, under its poncho of clouds, remained breathless, as if dead rather than asleep.

Don Martin's soft hands suffered cruelly, tugging

at the thick handle of the enormous oar. He stuck to it manfully, setting his teeth. He, too, was in the toils of an imaginative existence, and that strange work of pulling a lighter seemed to belong naturally to the inception of a new State, acquired an ideal meaning from his love for Antonia. For all their efforts, the heavily laden lighter hardly moved. Nostromo could be heard swearing to himself between the regular splashes of the sweeps. " We are making a crooked path," he muttered to himself. " I wish I could see the islands."

In his unskilfulness Don Martin overexerted himself. Now and then a sort of muscular faintness would run from the tips of his aching fingers through every fibre of his body, and pass off in a flush of heat. He had fought, talked, suffered mentally and physically, exerting his mind and body for the last forty-eight hours without intermission. He had had no rest, very little food, no pause in the stress of his thoughts and his feelings. Even his love for Antonia, whence he drew his strength and his inspiration, had reached the point of tragic tension during their hurried interview by Don José's bedside. And now, suddenly, he was thrown out of all this into a dark gulf, whose very gloom, silence, and breathless peace added a torment to the necessity for physical exertion. He imagined the lighter sinking to the bottom with an extraordinary shudder of delight. " I am on the verge of delirium," he thought. He mastered the trembling of all his limbs, of his breast, the inward trembling of all his body exhausted of its nervous force.

" Shall we rest, Capataz ? " he proposed in a careless tone. " There are many hours of night yet before us."

" True. It is but a mile or so, I suppose. Rest your arms, Señor, if that is what you mean. You will find no other sort of rest, I can promise you, since you let yourself be bound to this treasure whose loss would make no poor man poorer. No, Señor ; there is no rest till we find a north-bound steamer, or else some ship finds us drifting about stretched out dead upon the Englishman's silver. Or rather—no; *por Dios!* I shall cut down the gunwale with the axe right to the water's edge before thirst and hunger rob me of my strength. By all the saints and devils I shall let the sea have the treasure rather than give it up to any stranger. Since it was the good pleasure of the caballeros to send me off on such an errand, they shall learn I am just the man they take me for."

Decoud lay on the silver boxes panting. All his active sensations and feelings from as far back as he could remember seemed to him the maddest of dreams. Even his passionate devotion to Antonia into which he had worked himself up out of the depths of his scepticism had lost all appearance of reality. For a moment he was the prey of an extremely languid but not unpleasant indifference.

" I am sure they didn't mean you to take such a desperate view of this affair," he said.

" What was it, then ?   A joke ? " snarled the man who, on the pay-sheets of the O.S.N. Company's establishment in Sulaco, was described as " Foreman of the wharf " against the figure of his wages. " Was it for a joke they woke me up from my sleep after two days of street fighting to make me stake my life upon a bad card ? Everybody knows, too, that I am not a lucky gambler."

" Yes, everybody knows of your good luck with women, Capataz," Decoud propitiated his companion in a weary drawl.

" Look here, Señor," Nostromo went on.   " I never even remonstrated about this affair. Directly I heard what was wanted I saw what a desperate affair it must be, and I made up my mind to see it out. Every minute was of importance. I had to wait for you first. Then, when we arrived at the Italia Una, old Giorgio shouted

to me to go for the English doctor. Later on, that poor
dying woman wanted to see me, as you know. Señor, I
was reluctant to go. I felt already this cursed silver
growing heavy upon my back, and I was afraid that,
knowing herself to be dying, she would ask me to ride
off again for a priest. Father Corbelàn, who is fearless,
would have come at a word ; but Father Corbelàn
is far away, safe with the band of Hernandez, and the
populace, that would have liked to tear him to pieces,
are much incensed against the priests. Not a single fat
padre would have consented to put his head out of his
hiding-place to-night to save a Christian soul, except,
perhaps, under my protection. That was in her mind.
I pretended I did not believe she was going to die. Señor,
I refused to fetch a priest for a dying woman. . . ."

Decoud was heard to stir.

" You did, Capataz ! " he exclaimed. His tone
changed. " Well, you know—it was rather fine."

" You do not believe in priests, Don Martin ?
Neither do I. What was the use of wasting time ? But
she—she believes in them. The thing sticks in my
throat. She may be dead already, and here we are
floating helpless with no wind at all. Curse on all
superstition. She died thinking I deprived her of
paradise, I suppose. It shall be the most desperate
affair of my life."

Decoud remained lost in reflection. He tried to
analyse the sensations awakened by what he had been
told. The voice of the Capataz was heard again.

" Now, Don Martin, let us take up the sweeps and
try to find the Isabels. It is either that, or sinking the
lighter if the day overtakes us. We must not forget
that the steamer from Esmeralda with the soldiers may
be coming along. We will pull straight on now. I
have discovered a bit of a candle here, and we must
take the risk of a small light to make a course by the
boat compass. There is not enough wind to blow it

out—may the curse of Heaven fall upon this blind gulf ! "

A small flame appeared burning quite straight. It showed fragmentally the stout ribs and planking in the hollow, empty part of the lighter. Decoud could see Nostromo standing up to pull. He saw him as high as the red sash on his waist, with a gleam of a white-handled revolver and the wooden haft of a long knife protruding on his left side. Decoud nerved himself for the effort of rowing. Certainly there was not enough wind to blow the candle out, but its flame swayed a little to the slow movement of the heavy boat. It was so big that with their utmost efforts they could not move it quicker than about a mile an hour. This was sufficient, however, to sweep them amongst the Isabels long before daylight came. There was a good six hours of darkness before them, and the distance from the harbour to the Great Isabel did not exceed two miles. Decoud put this heavy toil to the account of the Capataz's impatience. Sometimes they paused, and then strained their ears to hear the boat from Esmeralda. In this perfect quietness a steamer moving would have been heard from far off. As to seeing anything it was out of the question. They could not see each other. Even the lighter's sail, which remained set, was invisible. Very often they rested.

" Caramba ! " said Nostromo suddenly, during one of those intervals when they lolled idly against the heavy handles of the sweeps. " What is it ? Are you distressed, Don Martin ? "

Decoud assured him that he was not distressed in the least. Nostromo for a time kept perfectly still, and then in a whisper invited Martin to come aft.

With his lips touching Decoud's ear he declared his belief that there was somebody else besides themselves upon the lighter. Twice now he had heard the sound of stifled sobbing.

"Señor," he whispered with awed wonder, "I am certain that there is somebody weeping in this lighter."

Decoud had heard nothing. He expressed his incredulity. However, it was easy to ascertain the truth of the matter.

"It is most amazing," muttered Nostromo. "Could anybody have concealed himself on board while the lighter was lying alongside the wharf?"

"And you say it was like sobbing?" asked Decoud, lowering his voice too. "If he is weeping, whoever he is he cannot be very dangerous."

Clambering over the precious pile in the middle, they crouched low on the foreside of the mast and groped under the half-deck. Right forward, in the narrowest part, their hands came upon the limbs of a man, who remained as silent as death. Too startled themselves to make a sound, they dragged him aft by one arm and the collar of his coat. He was limp—lifeless.

The light of the bit of candle fell upon a round, hook-nosed face with black moustaches and little side-whiskers. He was extremely dirty. A greasy growth of beard was sprouting on the shaven parts of the cheeks. The thick lips were slightly parted, but the eyes remained closed. Decoud, to his immense astonishment, recognised Señor Hirsch, the hide merchant from Esmeralda. Nostromo, too, had recognised him. And they gazed at each other across that body, lying with its naked feet higher than its head, in an absurd pretence of sleep, faintness, or death.

CHAPTER EIGHT

FOR a moment, before this extraordinary find, they forgot their own concerns and sensations. Señor Hirsch's sensations as he lay there must have been those of extreme terror. For a long time he refused to give a sign of life, till at last Decoud's objurgations, and, perhaps more, Nostromo's impatient suggestion that he should be thrown overboard, as he seemed to be dead, induced him to raise one eyelid first, and then the other.

It appeared that he had never found a safe opportunity to leave Sulaco. He lodged with Anzani, the universal storekeeper, on the Plaza Mayor. But when the riot broke out he had made his escape from his host's house before daylight, and in such a hurry that he had forgotten to put on his shoes. He had run out impulsively in his socks, and with his hat in his hand, into the garden of Anzani's house. Fear gave him the necessary agility to climb over several low walls, and afterwards he blundered into the overgrown cloisters of the ruined Franciscan Convent in one of the by-streets. He forced himself into the midst of matted bushes with the recklessness of desperation, and this accounted for his scratched body and his torn clothing. He lay hidden there all day, his tongue cleaving to the roof of his mouth with all the intensity of thirst engendered by heat and fear. Three times different bands invaded the place with shouts and imprecations, looking for Father Corbelàn ; but towards the evening, still lying on his face in the bushes, he thought he would die from the fear of silence. He was not very clear as to

what had induced him to leave the place, but evidently
he had got out and slunk successfully out of town along
the deserted back lanes. He wandered in the darkness
near the railway, so maddened by apprehension that he
dared not even approach the fires of the pickets of
Italian workmen guarding the line. He had a vague idea
evidently of finding refuge in the railway yards, but the
dogs rushed upon him, barking ; men began to shout ; a
shot was fired at random. He fled away from the gates.
By the merest accident, as it happened, he took the
direction of the O.S.N. Company's offices. Twice he
stumbled upon the bodies of men killed during the day.
But everything living frightened him much more. He
crouched, crept, crawled, made dashes, guided by a sort
of animal instinct, keeping away from every light and
from every sound of voices. His idea was to throw himself at the feet of Captain Mitchell and beg for shelter
in the Company's offices. It was all dark there as he
approached on his hands and knees, but suddenly some
one on guard challenged loudly, " *Quien vive ?* " There
were more dead men lying about, and he flattened himself
down at once by the side of a cold corpse. He heard a
voice saying, " Here is one of those wounded rascals
crawling about. Shall I go and finish him ? " And
another voice objected that it was not safe to go out without a lantern upon such an errand ; perhaps it was only
some negro Liberal looking for a chance to stick a knife
into the stomach of an honest man. Hirsch didn't stay
to hear any more, but crawling away to the end of the
wharf, hid himself amongst a lot of empty casks. After
a while some people came along, talking, and with glowing cigarettes. He did not stop to ask himself whether
they would be likely to do him any harm, but bolted
incontinently along the jetty, saw a lighter lying moored
at the end, and threw himself into it. In his desire to
find cover he crept right forward under the half-deck, and
he had remained there more dead than alive, suffering

agonies of hunger and thirst, and almost fainting with terror, when he heard numerous footsteps and the voices of the Europeans who came in a body escorting the wagon-load of treasure, pushed along the rails by a squad of cargadores. He understood perfectly what was being done from the talk, but did not disclose his presence from the fear that he would not be allowed to remain. His only idea at the time, overpowering and masterful, was to get away from this terrible Sulaco. And now he regretted it very much. He had heard Nostromo talk to Decoud, and wished himself back on shore. He did not desire to be involved in any desperate affair—in a situation where one could not run away. The involuntary groans of his anguished spirit had betrayed him to the sharp ears of the Capataz.

They had propped him up in a sitting posture against the side of the lighter, and he went on with the moaning account of his adventures till his voice broke, his head fell forward. "Water," he whispered with difficulty. Decoud held one of the cans to his lips. He revived after an extraordinarily short time, and scrambled up to his feet wildly. Nostromo, in an angry and threatening voice, ordered him forward. Hirsch was one of those men whom fear lashes like a whip, and he must have had an appalling idea of the Capataz's ferocity. He displayed an extraordinary agility in disappearing forward into the darkness. They heard him getting over the tarpaulin; then there was the sound of a heavy fall, followed by a weary sigh. Afterwards all was still in the forepart of the lighter, as though he had killed himself in his headlong tumble. Nostromo shouted in a menacing voice:

"Lie still there! Do not move a limb! If I hear as much as a loud breath from you I shall come over there and put a bullet through your head!"

The mere presence of a coward, however passive, brings an element of treachery into a dangerous situation.

17

Nostromo's nervous impatience passed into gloomy thoughtfulness. Decoud, in an undertone, as if speaking to himself, remarked that, after all, this bizarre event made no great difference. He could not conceive what harm the man could do. At most he would be in the way, like an inanimate and useless object—like a block of wood, for instance.

" I would think twice before getting rid of a piece of wood," said Nostromo calmly. " Something may happen unexpectedly where you could make use of it. But in an affair like ours a man like this ought to be thrown overboard. Even if he were as brave as a lion we would not want him here. We are not running away for our lives. Señor, there is no harm in a brave man trying to save himself with ingenuity and courage ; but you have heard his tale, Don Martin. His being here is a miracle of fear——" Nostromo paused. " There is no room for fear in this lighter," he added through his teeth.

Decoud had no answer to make. It was not a position for argument, for a display of scruples or feelings. There were a thousand ways in which a panic-stricken man could make himself dangerous. It was evident that Hirsch could not be spoken to, reasoned with, or persuaded into a rational line of conduct. The story of his own escape demonstrated that clearly enough. Decoud thought that it was a thousand pities the wretch had not died of fright. Nature, who had made him what he was, seemed to have calculated cruelly how much he could bear in the way of atrocious anguish without actually expiring. Some compassion was due to so much terror. Decoud, though imaginative enough for sympathy, resolved not to interfere with any action that Nostromo would take. But Nostromo did nothing. And the fate of Señor Hirsch remained suspended in the darkness of the gulf at the mercy of events which could not be foreseen.

The Capataz, extending his hand, put out the candle

suddenly. It was to Decoud as if his companion had destroyed, by a single touch, the world of affairs, of loves, of revolution, where his complacent superiority analysed fearlessly all motives and all passions, including his own.

He gasped a little. Decoud was affected by the novelty of his position. Intellectually self-confident, he suffered from being deprived of the only weapon he could use with effect. No intelligence could penetrate the darkness of the Placid Gulf. There remained only one thing he was certain of, and that was the overweening vanity of his companion. It was direct, uncomplicated, naïve, and effectual. Decoud, who had been making use of him, had tried to understand his man thoroughly. He had discovered a complete singleness of motive behind the varied manifestations of a consistent character. This was why the man remained so astonishingly simple in the jealous greatness of his conceit. And now there was a complication. It was evident that he resented having been given a chance in which there were so many chances of failure. " I wonder," thought Decoud, " how he would behave if I were not here ? "

He heard Nostromo mutter again, " No ! there is no room for fear on this lighter. Courage itself does not seem good enough. I have a good eye and a steady hand ; no man can say he ever saw me tired or uncertain what to do ; but, *por Dios*, Don Martin, I have been sent out into this black calm on a business where neither a good eye, nor a steady hand, nor judgment is any use. . . ." He swore a string of oaths in Spanish and Italian under his breath. " Nothing but sheer desperation will do for this affair."

These words were in strange contrast to the prevailing peace—to this almost solid stillness of the gulf. A shower fell with an abrupt whispering sound all round the boat, and Decoud took off his hat, and, letting his head get wet, felt greatly refreshed. Presently a steady little draught of air caressed his cheek. The lighter began to move, but the shower distanced it. The drops ceased to fall upon his head and hands, the whispering died out in the distance. Nostromo emitted a grunt of satisfaction, and, grasping the tiller, chirruped softly, as sailors do, to encourage the wind. Never for the last three days had Decoud felt less the need for what the Capataz would call desperation.

" I fancy I hear another shower on the water," he observed in a tone of quiet content. " I hope it will catch us up."

Nostromo ceased chirruping at once. " You hear another shower ? " he said doubtfully. A sort of thinning of the darkness seemed to have taken place, and Decoud could see now the outline of his companion's figure, and even the sail came out of the night like a square block of dense snow.

The sound which Decoud had detected came along the water harshly. Nostromo recognised that noise partaking of a hiss and a rustle which spreads out on all sides of a steamer making her way through a smooth water on a quiet night. It could be nothing else but the captured transport with troops from Esmeralda. She carried no lights. The noise of her steaming, growing louder every minute, would stop at times altogether, and then begin again abruptly, and sound startlingly nearer, as if that invisible vessel, whose position could not be precisely guessed, were making straight for the lighter. Meantime that last kept on sailing slowly and noiselessly before a breeze so faint that it was only by leaning over the side and feeling the water slip through his fingers that Decoud convinced himself they were moving at all. His drowsy feeling had departed. He was glad to know that the lighter was moving. After so much stillness the noise of the steamer seemed uproarious and distracting. There was a weirdness in not being able to see her. Suddenly all was still. She had stopped, but so close to them that the steam, blowing off, sent its rumbling vibration right over their heads.

" They are trying to make out where they are," said Decoud in a whisper. Again he leaned over and put his fingers into the water. " We are moving quite smartly," he informed Nostromo.

" We seem to be crossing her bows," said the Capataz in a cautious tone. " But this is a blind game with Death. Moving on is of no use. We mustn't be seen or heard."

His whisper was hoarse with excitement. Of all his face there was nothing visible but a gleam of white eyeballs. His fingers gripped Decoud's shoulder. " That is the only way to save this treasure from this steamer full of soldiers. Any other would have carried lights. But you observe there is not a gleam to show us where she is."

Decoud stood as if paralysed ; only his thoughts were wildly active. In the space of a second he remembered the desolate glance of Antonia as he left her at the bedside of her father in the gloomy house of Avellanos, with shuttered windows, but all the doors standing open, and deserted by all the servants except an old negro at the gate. He remembered the Casa Gould on his last visit, the arguments, the tones of his voice, the impenetrable attitude of Charles, Mrs. Gould's face so blanched with anxiety and fatigue that her eyes seemed to have changed colour, appearing nearly black by contrast. Even whole sentences of the proclamation which he meant to make Barrios issue from his headquarters at Cayta as soon as he got there passed through his mind ; the very germ of the new State, the Separationist proclamation which he had tried before he left to read hurriedly to Don José, stretched out on his bed under the fixed gaze of his daughter. God knows whether the old statesman had understood it ; he was unable to speak, but he had certainly lifted his arm off

the coverlet ; his hand had moved as if to make the
sign of the cross in the air, a gesture of blessing, of
consent. Decoud had that very draft in his pocket,
written in pencil on several loose sheets of paper, with
the heavily-printed heading, " Administration of the
San Tomé Silver Mine.   Sulaco.   Republic of Costaguana."   He had written it furiously, snatching page
after page on Charles Gould's table.   Mrs. Gould had
looked several times over his shoulder as he wrote ;
but the Señor Administrador, standing straddle-legged,
would not even glance at it when it was finished.   He
had waved it away firmly.   It must have been scorn,
and not caution, since he never made a remark about
the use of the Administration's paper for such a compromising document.   And that showed his disdain,
the true English disdain of common prudence, as if
everything outside the range of their own thoughts and
feelings were unworthy of serious recognition.   Decoud
had the time in a second or two to become furiously
angry with Charles Gould, and even resentful against
Mrs. Gould, in whose care, tacitly it is true, he had left
the safety of Antonia.   Better perish a thousand times
than owe your preservation to such people, he exclaimed mentally.   The grip of Nostromo's fingers never
removed from his shoulder, tightening fiercely, recalled
him to himself.

  " The darkness is our friend," the Capataz murmured into his ear.   " I am going to lower the sail,
and trust our escape to this black gulf.   No eyes could
make us out lying silent with a naked mast.   I will do it
now, before this steamer closes still more upon us.   The
faint creak of a block would betray us and the San Tomé
treasure into the hands of those thieves."

  He moved about as warily as a cat.   Decoud heard
no sound ; and it was only by the disappearance of the
square blotch of darkness that he knew the yard had come
down, lowered as carefully as if it had been made of

glass. Next moment he heard Nostromo's quiet breathing by his side.

"You had better not move at all from where you
are, Don Martin," advised the Capataz earnestly.
"You might stumble or displace something which
would make a noise. The sweeps and the punting
poles are lying about. Move not for your life. *Por
Dios*, Don Martin," he went on in a keen but friendly
whisper, "I am so desperate that if I didn't know your
worship to be a man of courage, capable of standing
stock-still whatever happens, I would drive my knife
into your heart."

A deathlike stillness surrounded the lighter. It was
difficult to believe that there was near a steamer full of
men with many pairs of eyes peering from her bridge
for some hint of land in the night. Her steam had ceased
blowing off, and she remained stopped too far off apparently for any other sound to reach the lighter.

"Perhaps you would, Capataz," Decoud began in a
whisper. "However, you need not trouble. There are
other things than the fear of your knife to keep my
heart steady. It shall not betray you. Only, have you
forgotten——"

"I spoke to you openly as to a man as desperate as
myself," explained the Capataz. "The silver must be
saved from the Monterists. I told Captain Mitchell
three times that I preferred to go alone. I told Don
Carlos Gould too. It was in the Casa Gould. They
had sent for me. The ladies were there ; and when I
tried to explain why I did not wish to have you with me,
they promised me, both of them, great rewards for your
safety. A strange way to talk to a man you are sending out to an almost certain death. Those gentlefolk do
not seem to have sense enough to understand what they
are giving one to do. I told them I could do nothing
for you. You would have been safer with the bandit
Hernandez. It would have been possible to ride out of

the town with no greater risk than a chance shot sent after you in the dark. But it was as if they had been deaf. I had to promise I would wait for you under the harbour gate. I did wait. And now because you are a brave man you are as safe as the silver. Neither more nor less."

At that moment, as if by way of comment upon Nostromo's words, the invisible steamer went ahead at half speed only, as could be judged by the leisurely beat of her propeller. The sound shifted its place markedly, but without coming nearer. It even grew a little more distant right abeam of the lighter, and then ceased again.

" They are trying for a sight of the Isabels," muttered Nostromo, " in order to make for the harbour in a straight line and seize the Custom House with the treasure in it. Have you ever seen the Commandant of Esmeralda—Sotillo ? A handsome fellow, with a soft voice. When I first came here I used to see him in the calle talking to the Señoritas at the windows of the houses, and showing his white teeth all the time. But one of my cargadores, who had been a soldier, told me that he had once ordered a man to be flayed alive in the remote Campo, where he was sent recruiting amongst the people of the estancias. It has never entered his head that the Compañia had a man capable of baffling his game."

The murmuring loquacity of the Capataz disturbed Decoud like a hint of weakness. And yet, talkative resolution may be as genuine as grim silence.

" Sotillo is not baffled so far," he said. " Have you forgotten that crazy man forward ? "

Nostromo had not forgotten Señor Hirsch. He reproached himself bitterly for not having visited the lighter carefully before leaving the wharf. He reproached himself for not having stabbed and flung Hirsch overboard at the very moment of discovery without even looking at his face. That would have been consistent with the desperate character of the affair. Whatever happened,

Sotillo *was* already baffled. Even if that wretch, now as silent as death, did anything to betray the nearness of the lighter, Sotillo—if Sotillo it was in command of the troops on board—would be still baffled of his plunder.

" I have an axe in my hand," Nostromo whispered wrathfully, " that in three strokes would cut through the side to the water's edge. Moreover, each lighter has a plug in the stern, and I know exactly where it is. I feel it under the sole of my foot."

Decoud recognised the ring of genuine determination in the nervous murmurs, the vindictive excitement of the famous Capataz. Before the steamer, guided by a shriek or two (for there could be no more than that, Nostromo said, gnashing his teeth audibly), could find the lighter, there would be plenty of time to sink this treasure tied up round his neck.

The last words he hissed into Decoud's ear. Decoud said nothing. He was perfectly convinced. The usual characteristic quietness of the man was gone. It was not equal to the situation as he conceived it. Something deeper, something unsuspected by every one, had come to the surface. Decoud, with careful movements, slipped off his overcoat and divested himself of his boots ; he did not consider himself bound in honour to sink with the treasure. His object was to get down to Barrios, in Cayta, as the Capataz knew very well ; and he, too, meant, in his own way, to put into that attempt all the desperation of which he was capable. Nostromo muttered, " True, true ! You are a politician, Señor. Rejoin the army, and start another revolution." He pointed out, however, that there was a little boat belonging to every lighter fit to carry two men, if not more. Theirs was towing behind.

Of that Decoud had not been aware. Of course, it was too dark to see, and it was only when Nostromo put his hand upon its painter fastened to a cleat in the stern that he experienced a full measure of relief. The pros-

pect of finding himself in the water and swimming, overwhelmed by ignorance and darkness, probably in a circle,
till he sank from exhaustion, was revolting. The barren
and cruel futility of such an end intimidated his affectation of careless pessimism. In comparison to it, the
chance of being left floating in a boat, exposed to thirst,
hunger, discovery, imprisonment, execution, presented
itself with an aspect of amenity worth securing even at
the cost of some self-contempt. He did not accept
Nostromo's proposal that he should get into the boat at
once. " Something sudden may overwhelm us, Señor,"
the Capataz remarked, promising faithfully, at the same
time, to let go the painter at the moment when the
necessity became manifest.

But Decoud assured him lightly that he did not mean
to take to the boat till the very last moment, and that then
he meant the Capataz to come along too. The darkness
of the gulf was no longer for him the end of all things.
It was part of a living world since, pervading it, failure
and death could be felt at your elbow. And at the same
time it was a shelter. He exulted in its impenetrable
obscurity. " Like a wall, like a wall," he muttered to
himself.

The only thing which checked his confidence was the
thought of Señor Hirsch. Not to have bound and gagged
him seemed to Decoud now the height of improvident
folly. As long as the miserable creature had the power
to raise a yell he was a constant danger. His abject
terror was mute now, but there was no saying from what
cause it might suddenly find vent in shrieks.

This very madness of fear which both Decoud and
Nostromo had seen in the wild and irrational glances, and
in the continuous twitchings of his mouth, protected
Señor Hirsch from the cruel necessities of this desperate
affair. The moment of silencing him for ever had passed.
As Nostromo remarked, in answer to Decoud's regrets,
it was too late. It could not be done without noise,

especially in the ignorance of the man's exact position. Wherever he had elected to crouch and tremble, it was too hazardous to go near him. He would begin probably to yell for mercy. It was much better to leave him quite alone since he was keeping so still. But to trust to his silence became every moment a greater strain upon Decoud's composure.

" I wish, Capataz, you had not let the right moment pass," he murmured.

" What! To silence him for ever? I thought it good to hear first how he came to be here. It was too strange. Who could imagine that it was all an accident? Afterwards, Señor, when I saw you giving him water to drink, I could not do it. Not after I had seen you holding up the can to his lips as though he were your brother. Señor, that sort of necessity must not be thought of too long. And yet it would have been no cruelty to take away from him his wretched life. It is nothing but fear. Your compassion saved him then, Don Martin, and now it is too late. It couldn't be done without noise."

In the steamer they were keeping a perfect silence, and the stillness was so profound that Decoud felt as if the slightest sound conceivable must travel unchecked and audible to the end of the world. What if Hirsch coughed or sneezed? To feel himself at the mercy of such an idiotic contingency was too exasperating to be looked upon with irony. Nostromo, too, seemed to be getting restless. Was it possible, he asked himself, that the steamer, finding the night too dark altogether, intended to remain stopped where she was till daylight? He began to think that this, after all, was the real danger. He was afraid that the darkness, which was his protection, would, in the end, cause his undoing.

Sotillo, as Nostromo had surmised, was in command on board the transport. The events of the last forty-eight hours in Sulaco were not known to him; neither

was he aware that the telegraphist in Esmeralda had
managed to warn his colleague in Sulaco. Like a good
many officers of the troops garrisoning the province,
Sotillo had been influenced in his adoption of the Ribierist
cause by the belief that it had the enormous wealth
of the Gould Concession on its side. He had been
one of the frequenters of the Casa Gould, where he
had aired his Blanco convictions and his ardour for
reform before Don José Avellanos, casting frank, honest
glances towards Mrs. Gould and Antonia the while.
He was known to belong to a good family persecuted
and impoverished during the tyranny of Guzman Bento.
The opinions he expressed appeared eminently natural
and proper in a man of his parentage and antecedents.
And he was not a deceiver ; it was perfectly natural for
him to express elevated sentiments while his whole
faculties were taken up with what seemed then a solid
and practical notion—the notion that the husband of
Antonia Avellanos would be, naturally, the intimate
friend of the Gould Concession. He even pointed this
out to Anzani once, when negotiating the sixth or seventh
small loan in the gloomy, damp apartment with enormous
iron bars, behind the principal shop in the whole row
under the Arcades. He hinted to the universal shopkeeper at the excellent terms he was on with the emancipated Señorita, who was like a sister to the Englishwoman.
He would advance one leg and put his arms akimbo,
posing for Anzani's inspection, and fixing him with a
haughty stare.

" Look, miserable shopkeeper !   How can a man like
me fail with any woman, let alone an emancipated girl
living in scandalous freedom ? " he seemed to say.

His manner in the Casa Gould was, of course, very
different—devoid of all truculence, and even slightly
mournful. Like most of his countrymen, he was
carried away by the sound of fine words, especially if
uttered by himself. He had no convictions of any sort

upon anything except as to the irresistible power of his personal advantages. But that was so firm that even Decoud's appearance in Sulaco, and his intimacy with the Goulds and the Avellanos, did not disquiet him. On the contrary, he tried to make friends with that rich Costaguanero from Europe in the hope of borrowing a large sum by and by. The only guiding motive of his life was to get money for the satisfaction of his expensive tastes, which he indulged recklessly, having no self-control. He imagined himself a master of intrigue, but his corruption was as simple as an animal instinct. At times, in solitude, he had his moments of ferocity, and also on such occasions as, for instance, when alone in a room with Anzani trying to get a loan.

He had talked himself into the command of the Esmeralda garrison. That small seaport had its importance as the station of the main submarine cable connecting the Occidental Provinces with the outer world, and the junction with it of the Sulaco branch. Don José Avellanos proposed him, and Barrios, with a rude and jeering guffaw, had said, " Oh, let Sotillo go. He is a very good man to keep guard over the cable, and the ladies of Esmeralda ought to have their turn." Barrios, an indubitably brave man, had no great opinion of Sotillo.

It was through the Esmeralda cable alone that the San Tomé mine could be kept in constant touch with the great financier, whose tacit approval made the strength of the Ribierist movement. This movement had its adversaries even there. Sotillo governed Esmeralda with repressive severity till the adverse course of events upon the distant theatre of civil war forced upon him the reflection that, after all, the great silver mine was fated to become the spoil of the victors. But caution was necessary. He began by assuming a dark and mysterious attitude towards the faithful Ribierist municipality of Esmeralda. Later on, the information that

the commandant was holding assemblies of officers in
the dead of night (which had leaked out somehow)
caused those gentlemen to neglect their civil duties
altogether, and remain shut up in their houses. Suddenly
one day all the letters from Sulaco by the overland
courier were carried off by a file of soldiers from the
post office to the Commandancia, without disguise, concealment, or apology. Sotillo had heard through Cayta
of the final defeat of Ribiera.

This was the first open sign of the change in his
convictions. Presently notorious democrats, who had
been living till then in constant fear of arrest, leg irons,
and even floggings, could be observed going in and out
at the great door of the Commandancia, where the horses
of the orderlies doze under their heavy saddles, while
the men, in ragged uniforms and pointed straw hats,
lounge on a bench, with their naked feet stuck out beyond
the strip of shade ; and a sentry, in a red baize coat with
holes at the elbows, stands at the top of the steps glaring
haughtily at the common people, who uncover their heads
to him as they pass.

Sotillo's ideas did not soar above the care for his
personal safety and the chance of plundering the town in
his charge, but he feared that such a late adhesion would
earn but scant gratitude from the victors. He had believed just a little too long in the power of the San Tomé
mine. The seized correspondence had confirmed his
previous information of a large amount of silver ingots
lying in the Sulaco Custom House. To gain possession
of it would be a clear Monterist move ; a sort of service
that would have to be rewarded. With the silver in his
hands he could make terms for himself and his soldiers.
He was aware neither of the riots, nor of the President's
escape to Sulaco and the close pursuit led by Montero's
brother, the guerrillero. The game seemed in his own
hands. The initial moves were the seizure of the cable
telegraph office and the securing of the Government

steamer lying in the narrow creek which is the harbour
of Esmeralda. The last was effected without difficulty
by a company of soldiers swarming with a rush over the
gangways as she lay alongside the quay; but the lieutenant charged with the duty of arresting the telegraphist
halted on the way before the only café in Esmeralda, where
he distributed some brandy to his men, and refreshed
himself at the expense of the owner, a known Ribierist.
The whole party became intoxicated, and proceeded on
their mission up the street yelling and firing random
shots at the windows. This little festivity, which might
have turned out dangerous to the telegraphist's life,
enabled him in the end to send his warning to Sulaco.
The lieutenant, staggering upstairs with a drawn sabre, was
before long kissing him on both cheeks in one of those
swift changes of mood peculiar to a state of drunkenness.
He clasped the telegraphist close round the neck, assuring
him that all the officers of the Esmeralda garrison were
going to be made colonels, while tears of happiness
streamed down his sodden face. Thus it came about
that the town major, coming along later, found the whole
party sleeping on the stairs and in passages, and the
telegraphist (who scorned this chance of escape) very
busy clicking the key of the transmitter. The major led
him away bareheaded, with his hands tied behind his back,
but concealed the truth from Sotillo, who remained in
ignorance of the warning dispatched to Sulaco. ·

The colonel was not the man to let any sort of darkness stand in the way of the planned surprise. It appeared
to him a dead certainty; his heart was set upon his object
with an ungovernable, childlike impatience. Ever since
the steamer had rounded Punta Mala to enter the deeper
shadow of the gulf, he had remained on the bridge in a
group of officers as excited as himself. Distracted between the coaxings and menaces of Sotillo and his staff,
the miserable commander of the steamer kept her moving
with as much prudence as they would let him exercise.

Some of them had been drinking heavily, no doubt; but the prospect of laying hands on so much wealth made them absurdly foolhardy, and, at the same time, extremely anxious. The old major of the battalion, a stupid, suspicious man, who had never been afloat in his life, distinguished himself by putting out suddenly the binnacle light, the only one allowed on board for the necessities of navigation. He could not understand of what use it could be for finding the way. To the vehement protestations of the ship's captain, he stamped his foot and tapped the handle of his sword. " Aha! I have unmasked you! " he cried triumphantly. " You are tearing your hair from despair at my acuteness. Am I a child to believe that a light in that brass box can show you where the harbour is ? I am an old soldier, I am. I can smell a traitor a league off. You wanted that gleam to betray our approach to your friend the Englishman. A thing like that show you the way ! What a miserable lie ! *Que picardia!* You Sulaco people are all in the pay of those foreigners. You deserve to be run through the body with my sword." Other officers, crowding round, tried to calm his indignation, repeating persuasively, " No, no! This is an appliance of the mariners, major. This is no treachery." The captain of the transport flung himself face downwards on the bridge, and refused to rise. " Put an end to me at once," he repeated in a stifled voice. Sotillo had to interfere.

The uproar and confusion on the bridge became so great that the helmsman fled from the wheel. He took refuge in the engine-room, and alarmed the engineers, who, disregarding the threats of the soldiers set on guard over them, stopped the engines, protesting that they would rather be shot than run the risk of being drowned down below.

This was the first time Nostromo and Decoud heard the steamer stop. After order had been restored, and the binnacle lamp relighted, she went ahead again, passing wide of the lighter in her search for the Isabels. The group could not be made out, and, at the pitiful entreaties of the captain, Sotillo allowed the engines to be stopped again to wait for one of those periodical lightenings of darkness caused by the shifting of the cloud canopy spread above the waters of the gulf.

Sotillo, on the bridge, muttered from time to time angrily to the captain. The other, in an apologetic and cringing tone, begged *su merced* the colonel to take into consideration the limitations put upon human faculties by the darkness of the night. Sotillo swelled with rage and impatience. It was the chance of a lifetime.

" If your eyes are of no more use to you than this, I shall have them put out," he yelled.

The captain of the steamer made no answer, for just then the mass of the Great Isabel loomed up darkly after a passing shower, then vanished, as if swept away by a wave of greater obscurity preceding another downpour.

This was enough for him. In the voice of a man come back to life again, he informed Sotillo that in an hour he would be alongside the Sulaco wharf. The ship was then put full speed on the course, and a great bustle of preparation for landing arose among the soldiers on her deck.

It was heard distinctly by Decoud and Nostromo. The Capataz understood its meaning. They had made out the Isabels, and were going on now in a straight line for Sulaco. He judged that they would pass close ; but believed that lying still like this, with the sail lowered, the lighter could not be seen. " No, not even if they rubbed sides with us," he muttered.

The rain began to fall again ; first like a wet mist, then with a heavier touch, thickening into a smart perpendicular downpour ; and the hiss and thump of the approaching steamer was coming extremely near. Decoud, with his eyes full of water, and lowered head, asked himself how long it would be before she drew past,

18

when unexpectedly he felt a lurch. An inrush of foam broke swishing over the stern, simultaneously with a crack of timbers and a staggering shock. He had the impression of an angry hand laying hold of the lighter and dragging it along to destruction. The shock, of course, had knocked him down, and he found himself rolling in a lot of water at the bottom of the lighter. A violent churning went on alongside ; a strange and amazed voice cried out something above him in the night. He heard a piercing shriek for help from Señor Hirsch. He kept his teeth hard set all the time. It was a collision !

The steamer had struck the lighter obliquely, heeling her over till she was half swamped, starting some of her timbers, and swinging her head parallel to her own course with the force of the blow. The shock of it on board of her was hardly perceptible. All the violence of that collision was, as usual, felt only on board the smaller craft. Even Nostromo himself thought that this was perhaps the end of his desperate adventure. He, too, had been flung away from the long tiller, which took charge in the lurch. Next moment the steamer would have passed on, leaving the lighter to sink or swim after having shouldered her thus out of her way, and without even getting a glimpse of her form, had it not been that, being deeply laden with stores and the great number of people on board, her anchor was low enough to hook itself into one of the wire shrouds of the lighter's mast. For the space of two or three gasping breaths that new rope held against the sudden strain. It was this that gave Decoud the sensation of the snatching pull, dragging the lighter away to destruction. The cause of it, of course, was inexplicable to him. The whole thing was so sudden that he had no time to think. But all his sensations were perfectly clear ; he had kept complete possession of himself ; in fact, he was even pleasantly aware of that calmness at the very moment of being pitched head first over the transom, to struggle on his back in a lot of water. Señor Hirsch's shriek he had heard and recognised while he was regaining his feet, always with that mysterious sensation of being dragged headlong through the darkness. Not a word, not a cry escaped him; he had no time to see anything; and following upon the despairing screams for help, the dragging motion ceased so suddenly that he staggered forward with open arms and fell against the pile of the treasure boxes. He clung to them instinctively, in the vague apprehension of being flung about again; and immediately he heard another lot of shrieks for help, prolonged and despairing, not near him at all, but unaccountably in the distance, away from the lighter altogether, as if some spirit in the night were mocking at Señor Hirsch's terror and despair.

Then all was still—as still as when you wake up in your bed in a dark room from a bizarre and agitated dream. The lighter rocked slightly; the rain was still falling. Two groping hands took hold of his bruised sides from behind, and the Capataz's voice whispered in his ear, "Silence, for your life! Silence! The steamer has stopped."

Decoud listened. The gulf was dumb. He felt the water nearly up to his knees. "Are we sinking?" he asked in a faint breath.

"I don't know," Nostromo breathed back to him. "Señor, make not the slightest sound."

Hirsch, when ordered forward by Nostromo, had not returned into his first hiding-place. He had fallen near the mast, and had no strength to rise; moreover, he feared to move. He had given himself up for dead, but not on any rational grounds. It was simply a cruel and terrifying feeling. Whenever he tried to think what would become of him his teeth would start chattering violently. He was too absorbed in the utter misery of his fear to take notice of anything.

Though he was stifling under the lighter's sail, which

Nostromo had unwittingly lowered on top of him, he did not even dare to put out his head till the very moment of the steamer striking.   Then, indeed, he leaped right out, spurred on to new miracles of bodily vigour by this new shape of danger.   The inrush of water when the lighter heeled over unsealed his lips.   His shriek, " Save me ! " was the first distinct warning of the collision for the people on board the steamer.   Next moment the wire shroud parted, and the released anchor swept over the lighter's forecastle.   It came against the breast of Señor Hirsch, who simply seized hold of it, without in the least knowing what it was, but curling his arms and legs upon the part above the fluke with an invincible, unreasonable tenacity.   The lighter yawed off wide, and the steamer, moving on, carried him away, clinging hard, and shouting for help.   It was some time, however, after the steamer had stopped that his position was discovered.   His sustained yelping for help seemed to come from somebody swimming in the water.   At last a couple of men went over the bows and hauled him on board.   He was carried straight off to Sotillo on the bridge.   His examination confirmed the impression that some craft had been run over and sunk ; but it was impracticable on such a dark night to look for the positive proof of floating wreckage. Sotillo was more anxious than ever now to enter the harbour without loss of time ; the idea that he had destroyed the principal object of his expedition was too intolerable to be accepted.   This feeling made the story he had heard appear the more incredible.   Señor Hirsch, after being beaten a little for telling lies, was thrust into the chart-room.   But he was beaten only a little.   His tale had taken the heart out of Sotillo's staff, though they all repeated round their chief, " Impossible ! Impossible ! " with the exception of the old major, who triumphed gloomily.

   " I told you ; I told you," he mumbled.   " I could smell some treachery, some *diableria*, a league off."

Meantime the steamer had kept on her way towards Sulaco, where only the truth of that matter could be ascertained. Decoud and Nostromo heard the loud churning of her propeller diminish and die out ; and then, with no useless words, busied themselves in making for the Isabels. The last shower had brought with it a gentle but steady breeze. The danger was not over yet, and there was no time for talk. The lighter was leaking like a sieve. They splashed in the water at every step. The Capataz put into Decoud's hands the handle of the pump which was fitted at the side aft, and at once, without question or remark, Decoud began to pump in utter forgetfulness of every desire but that of keeping the treasure afloat. Nostromo hoisted the sail, flew back to the tiller, pulled at the sheet like mad. The short flare of a match (they had been kept dry in a tight tin box, though the man himself was completely wet) disclosed to the toiling Decoud the eagerness of his face, bent low over the box of the compass, and the attentive stare of his eyes. He knew now where he was, and he hoped to run the sinking lighter ashore in the shallow cove where the high, cliff-like end of the Great Isabel is divided in two equal parts by a deep and overgrown ravine.

Decoud pumped without intermission. Nostromo steered without relaxing for a second the intense peering effort of his stare. Each of them was as if utterly alone with his task. It did not occur to them to speak. There was nothing in common between them but the knowledge that the damaged lighter must be slowly but surely sinking. In that knowledge, which was like the crucial test of their desires, they seemed to have become completely estranged, as if they had discovered in the very shock of the collision that the loss of the lighter would not mean the same thing to them both. This common danger brought their differences in aim, in view, in character, and in position into absolute prominence in

the private vision of each. There was no bond of
conviction, of common idea ; they were merely two
adventurers pursuing each his own adventure, involved
in the same imminence of deadly peril. Therefore
they had nothing to say to each other. But this peril,
this only incontrovertible truth in which they shared,
seemed to act as an inspiration to their mental and
bodily powers.

There was certainly something almost miraculous in
the way the Capataz made the cove with nothing but the
shadowy hint of the island's shape and the vague gleam
of a small, sandy strip for a guide. Where the ravine
opens between the cliffs, and a slender, shallow rivulet
meanders out of the bushes to lose itself in the sea, the
lighter was run ashore ; and the two men, with a taciturn,
undaunted energy, began to discharge her precious
freight, carrying each ox-hide box up the bed of the
rivulet beyond the bushes to a hollow place which the
caving in of the soil had made below the roots of a large
tree. Its big, smooth trunk leaned like a falling column
far over the trickle of water running amongst the loose
stones.

A couple of years before, Nostromo had spent a whole
Sunday, all alone, exploring the island. He explained
this to Decoud after their task was done, and they sat,
weary in every limb, with their legs hanging down the
low bank, and their backs against the tree, like a pair of
blind men aware of each other and their surroundings
by some indefinable sixth sense.

" Yes," Nostromo repeated, " I never forget a place
I have carefully looked at once." He spoke slowly,
almost lazily, as if there had been a whole leisurely life
before him, instead of the scanty two hours before daylight. The existence of the treasure, barely concealed
in this improbable spot, laid a burden of secrecy upon
every contemplated step, upon every intention and plan
of future conduct. He felt the partial failure of this

desperate affair entrusted to the great reputation he had
known how to make for himself.   However, it was also
a partial success.   His vanity was half appeased.   His
nervous irritation had subsided.

"You never know what may be of use," he pursued,
with his usual quietness of tone and manner.   "I
spent a whole miserable Sunday in exploring this crumb
of land."

"A misanthropic sort of occupation," muttered
Decoud viciously.   "You had no money, I suppose,
to gamble with, and to fling about amongst the girls
in your usual haunts, Capataz."

"È vero!" exclaimed the Capataz, surprised into
the use of his native tongue by so much perspicacity.
"I had not!   Therefore I did not want to go amongst
those beggarly people accustomed to my generosity.
It is looked for from the Capataz of the Cargadores,
who are the rich men, and, as it were, the caballeros
amongst the common people.   I don't care for cards but
as a pastime; and as to those girls that boast of having
opened their doors to my knock, you know I wouldn't
look at any one of them twice except for what the people
would say.   They are queer, the good people of Sulaco,
and I have got much useful information simply by
listening patiently to the talk of the women that everybody believed I was in love with.   Poor Teresa could
never understand that.   On that particular Sunday,
Señor, she scolded so that I went out of the house swearing that I would never darken their door again unless
to fetch away my hammock and my chest of clothes.
Señor, there is nothing more exasperating than to hear
a woman you respect rail against your good reputation
when you have not a single brass coin in your pocket.
I untied one of the small boats and pulled myself out
of the harbour with nothing but three cigars in my pocket
to help me spend the day on this island.   But the water
of this rivulet you hear under your feet is cool and sweet

and good, Señor, both before and after a smoke."
He was silent for a while, then added reflectively:
"That was the first Sunday after I brought the white-
whiskered English *rico* all the way down the mountains
from the paramo on the top of the Entrada Pass—and
in the coach, too! No coach had gone up or down that
mountain road within the memory of man, Señor, till I
brought this one down in charge of fifty peons working
like one man with ropes, pickaxes, and poles under my
direction. That was the rich Englishman who, as
people say, pays for the making of this railway. He
was very pleased with me. But my wages were not due
till the end of the month."

He slid down the bank suddenly. Decoud heard
the splash of his feet in the brook and followed his
footsteps down the ravine. His form was lost among the
bushes till he had reached the strip of sand under the
cliff. As often happens in the gulf when the showers
during the first part of the night have been frequent and
heavy, the darkness had thinned considerably towards the
morning, though there were no signs of daylight as yet.

The cargo-lighter, relieved of its precious burden,
rocked feebly, half afloat, with her forefoot on the sand.
A long rope stretched away like a black cotton thread
across the strip of white beach to the grapnel Nostromo
had carried ashore and hooked to the stem of a tree-like
shrub in the very opening of the ravine.

There was nothing for Decoud but to remain on the
island. He received from Nostromo's hands whatever
food the foresight of Captain Mitchell had put on board
the lighter, and deposited it temporarily in the little
dinghy which, on their arrival, they had hauled up out
of sight amongst the bushes. It was to be left with him.
The island was to be a hiding-place, not a prison; he
could pull out to a passing ship. The O.S.N. Company's
mail-boats passed close to the islands when going into
Sulaco from the north. But the *Minerva*, carrying off

the ex-President, had taken the news up north of the disturbances in Sulaco. It was possible that the next steamer down would get instructions to miss the port altogether, since the town, as far as the *Minerva's* officers knew, was for the time being in the hands of the rabble. This would mean that there would be no steamer for a month, as far as the mail service went ; but Decoud had to take his chance of that. The island was his only shelter from the proscription hanging over his head. The Capataz was, of course, going back. The unloaded lighter leaked much less, and he thought that she would keep afloat as far as the harbour.

He passed to Decoud, standing knee-deep alongside, one of the two spades which belonged to the equipment of each lighter for use when ballasting ships. By working with it carefully as soon as there was daylight enough to see, Decoud could loosen a mass of earth and stones overhanging the cavity in which they had deposited the treasure, so that it would look as if it had fallen naturally. It would cover up not only the cavity, but even all traces of their work—the footsteps, the displaced stones, and even the broken bushes.

" Besides, who would think of looking either for you or the treasure here ? " Nostromo continued, as if he could not tear himself away from the spot. " Nobody is ever likely to come here. What could any man want with this piece of earth as long as there is room for his feet on the mainland ? The people in this country are not curious. There are even no fishermen here to intrude upon your worship. All the fishing that is done in the gulf goes on near Zapiga, over there. Señor, if you are forced to leave this island before anything can be arranged for you, do not try to make for Zapiga. It is a settlement of thieves and matreros, where they would cut your throat promptly for the sake of your gold watch and chain. And, Señor, think twice before confiding in any one whatever ; even in the officers of

the Company's steamers, if you ever get on board one.
Honesty alone is not enough for security. You must
look to discretion and prudence in a man. And always
remember, Señor, before you open your lips for a confidence, that this treasure may be left safely here for
hundreds of years. Time is on its side, Señor. And
silver is an incorruptible metal that can be trusted to keep
its value for ever. . . . An incorruptible metal," he repeated, as if the idea had given him a profound pleasure.

" As some men are said to be," Decoud pronounced
inscrutably, while the Capataz, who busied himself in
baling out the lighter with a wooden bucket, went on
throwing the water over the side with a regular splash.
Decoud, incorrigible in his scepticism, reflected, not
cynically, but with general satisfaction, that this man
was made incorruptible by his enormous vanity, that
finest form of egoism which can take on the aspect of
every virtue.

Nostromo ceased baling, and, as if struck with a
sudden thought, dropped the bucket with a clatter into
the lighter.

" Have you any message ? " he asked in a lowered
voice. " Remember, I shall be asked questions."

" You must find the hopeful words that ought to
be spoken to the people in town. I trust for that your
intelligence and your experience, Capataz. You understand ? "

" Si, Señor. . . . For the ladies."

" Yes, yes," said Decoud hastily. " Your wonderful
reputation will make them attach great value to your
words ; therefore be careful what you say. I am looking
forward," he continued, feeling the fatal touch of contempt for himself to which his complex nature was
subject—" I am looking forward to a glorious and successful ending to my mission. Do you hear, Capataz ?
Use the words glorious and successful when you speak
to the Señorita. Your own mission is accomplished

gloriously and successfully. You have indubitably saved the silver of the mine. Not only this silver, but probably all the silver that shall ever come out of it."

Nostromo detected the ironic tone. " I dare say, Señor Don Martin," he said moodily. " There are very few things that I am not equal to. Ask the foreign Signori. I, a man of the people, who cannot always understand what you mean. But as to this lot which I must leave here, let me tell you that I would believe it in greater safety if you had not been with me at all."

An exclamation escaped Decoud, and a short pause followed. " Shall I go back with you to Sulaco ? " he asked in an angry tone.

" Shall I strike you dead with my knife where you stand ? " retorted Nostromo contemptuously. " It would be the same thing as taking you to Sulaco. Come, Señor. Your reputation is in your politics, and mine is bound up with the fate of this silver. Do you wonder I wish there had been no other man to share my knowledge ? I wanted no one with me, Señor."

" You could not have kept the lighter afloat without me," Decoud almost shouted. " You would have gone to the bottom with her."

" Yes," uttered Nostromo slowly ; " alone."

Here was a man, Decoud reflected, that seemed as though he would have preferred to die rather than deface the perfect form of his egoism. Such a man was safe. In silence he helped the Capataz to get the grapnel on board. Nostromo cleared the shelving shore with one push of the heavy oar, and Decoud found himself solitary on the beach like a man in a dream. A sudden desire to hear a human voice once more seized upon his heart. The lighter was hardly distinguishable from the black water upon which she floated.

" What do you think has become of Hirsch ? " he shouted.

" Knocked overboard and drowned," cried Nostromo's voice confidently out of the black wastes of sky and sea around the islet. " Keep close in the ravine, Señor. I shall try to come out to you in a night or two."

A slight swishing rustle showed that Nostromo was setting the sail. It filled all at once with a sound as of a single loud drum-tap. Decoud went back to the ravine. Nostromo, at the tiller, looked back from time to time at the vanishing mass of the Great Isabel, which, little by little, merged into the uniform texture of the night. At last, when he turned his head again, he saw nothing but a smooth darkness, like a solid wall.

Then he, too, experienced that feeling of solitude which had weighed heavily on Decoud after the lighter had slipped off the shore. But while the man on the island was oppressed by a bizarre sense of unreality affecting the very ground upon which he walked, the mind of the Capataz of the Cargadores turned alertly to the problem of future conduct. Nostromo's faculties, working on parallel lines, enabled him to steer straight, to keep a look out for Hermosa, near which he had to pass, and to try to imagine what would happen to-morrow in Sulaco. To-morrow, or, as a matter of fact, to-day, since the dawn was not very far, Sotillo would find out in what way the treasure had gone. A gang of cargadores had been employed in loading it into a railway truck from the Custom House storerooms, and running the truck on to the wharf. There would be arrests made, and certainly before noon Sotillo would know in what manner the silver had left Sulaco, and who it was that took it out.

Nostromo's intention had been to sail right into the harbour ; but at this thought by a sudden touch of the tiller he threw the lighter into the wind and checked her rapid way. His reappearance with the very boat would raise suspicions, would cause surmises, would absolutely put Sotillo on the track. He himself would be arrested ;

and once in the calabozo there was no saying what they would do to him to make him speak. He trusted himself, but he stood up to look round. Near by, Hermosa showed low its white surface as flat as a table, with the slight run of the sea raised by the breeze washing over its edges noisily. The lighter must be sunk at once.

He allowed her to drift with her sail aback. There was already a good deal of water in her. He allowed her to drift towards the harbour entrance, and, letting the tiller swing about, squatted down and busied himself in loosening the plug. With that out she would fill very quickly, and every lighter carried a little iron ballast—enough to make her go down when full of water. When he stood up again the noisy wash about the Hermosa sounded far away, almost inaudible; and already he could make out the shape of land about the harbour entrance. This was a desperate affair, and he was a good swimmer. A mile was nothing to him, and he knew of an easy place for landing just below the earthworks of the old abandoned fort. It occurred to him with a peculiar fascination that this fort was a good place in which to sleep the day through after so many sleepless nights.

With one blow of the tiller he unshipped for the purpose, he knocked the plug out, but did not take the trouble to lower the sail. He felt the water welling up heavily about his legs before he leaped on to the taffrail. There, upright and motionless, in his shirt and trousers only, he stood waiting. When he had felt her settle he sprang far away with a mighty splash.

At once he turned his head. The gloomy, clouded dawn from behind the mountains showed him on the smooth waters the upper corner of the sail, a dark, wet triangle of canvas waving slightly to and fro. He saw it vanish, as if jerked under, and then struck out for the shore.

PART III

THE LIGHTHOUSE

CHAPTER ONE

D IRECTLY the cargo boat had slipped away
from the wharf and got lost in the darkness
of the harbour the Europeans of Sulaco separated, to prepare for the coming of the Monterist régime,
which was approaching Sulaco from the mountains as
well as from the sea.

This bit of manual work in loading the silver was
their last concerted action. It ended the three days of
danger, during which, according to the newspaper press
of Europe, their energy had preserved the town from the
calamities of popular disorder. At the shore end of the
jetty Captain Mitchell said good-night and turned back.
His intention was to walk the planks of the wharf till the
steamer from Esmeralda turned up. The engineers of
the railway staff, collecting their Basque and Italian
workmen, marched them away to the railway yards,
leaving the Custom House, so well defended on the
first day of the riot, standing open to the four winds of
heaven. Their men had conducted themselves bravely
and faithfully during the famous " three days " of Sulaco.
In a great part this faithfulness and that courage had been
exercised in self-defence rather than in the cause of
those material interests to which Charles Gould had
pinned his faith. Amongst the cries of the mob not
the least loud had been the cry of death to foreigners.
It was, indeed, a lucky circumstance for Sulaco that the
relations of those imported workmen with the people of
the country had been uniformly bad from the first.

19

Dr. Monygham, going to the door of Viola's kitchen, observed this retreat marking the end of the foreign interference, this withdrawal of the army of material progress from the field of Costaguana revolutions.

Algarrobe torches carried on the outskirts of the moving body sent their penetrating aroma into his nostrils. Their light, sweeping along the front of the house, made the letters of the inscription, " Albergo d'Italia Una," leap out black from end to end of the long wall. His eyes blinked in the clear blaze. Several young men, mostly fair and tall, shepherding this mob of dark bronzed heads, surmounted by the glint of slanting rifle barrels, nodded to him familiarly as they went by. The doctor was a well-known character. Some of them wondered what he was doing there. Then on the flank of their workmen they tramped on, following the line of rails.

" Withdrawing your people from the harbour ? " said the doctor, addressing himself to the chief engineer of the railway, who had accompanied Charles Gould so far on his way to the town, walking by the side of the horse, with his hand on the saddle-bow. They had stopped just outside the open door to let the workmen cross the road.

" As quick as I can. We are not a political faction," answered the engineer meaningly. " And we are not going to give our new rulers a handle against the railway. You approve me, Gould ? "

" Absolutely," said Charles Gould's impassive voice, high up and outside the dim parallelogram of light falling on the road through the open door.

With Sotillo expected from one side, and Pedro Montero from the other, the engineer-in-chief's only anxiety now was to avoid a collision with either. Sulaco, for him, was a railway station, a terminus, workshops, a great accumulation of stores. As against the mob the railway defended its property, but politically the railway was neutral. He was a brave man ; and in that spirit of neutrality he had carried proposals of truce to the self-appointed chiefs of the popular party, the deputies Fuentes and Gamacho. Bullets were still flying about when he had crossed the plaza on that mission, waving above his head a white napkin belonging to the table-linen of the Amarilla Club.

He was rather proud of this exploit; and reflecting that the doctor, busy all day with the wounded in the patio of the Casa Gould, had not had time to hear the news, he began a succinct narrative. He had communicated to them the intelligence from the Construction Camp as to Pedro Montero. The brother of the victorious general, he had assured them, could be expected at Sulaco at any time now. This news (as he anticipated), when shouted out of the window by Señor Gamacho, induced a rush of the mob along the Campo Road towards Rincon. The two deputies also, after shaking hands with him effusively, mounted and galloped off to meet the great man. " I have misled them a little as to the time," the chief engineer confessed. " However hard he rides, he can scarcely get here before the morning. But my object is attained. I've secured several hours' peace for the losing party. But I did not tell them anything about Sotillo, for fear they would take it into their heads to try to get hold of the harbour again, either to oppose him or welcome him—there's no saying which. There was Gould's silver, on which rests the remnants of our hopes. Decoud's retreat had to be thought of too. I think the railway has done pretty well by its friends without compromising itself hopelessly. Now the parties must be left to themselves."

" Costaguana for the Costaguaneros," interjected the doctor sardonically. " It is a fine country, and they have raised a fine crop of hates, vengeance, murder, and rapine—those sons of the country."

" Well, I am one of them," Charles Gould's voice sounded calmly, " and I must be going on to see to

my own crop of trouble. My wife has driven straight
on, doctor ? ”

" Yes. All was quiet on this side. Mrs. Gould has
taken the two girls with her."

Charles Gould rode on, and the engineer-in-chief
followed the doctor indoors.

" That man is calmness personified," he said appre-
ciatively, dropping on a bench, and stretching his well-
shaped legs in cycling stockings nearly across the doorway. " He must be extremely sure of himself."

" If that's all he is sure of, then he is sure of nothing,"
said the doctor. He had perched himself again on the
end of the table. He nursed his cheek in the palm of one
hand, while the other sustained the elbow. " It is the
last thing a man ought to be sure of." The candle, half
consumed and burning dimly with a long wick, lighted
up from below his inclined face, whose expression,
affected by the drawn-in cicatrices in the cheeks, had
something vaguely unnatural, an exaggerated remorseful
bitterness. As he sat there he had the air of meditating
upon sinister things. The engineer-in-chief gazed at him
for a time before he protested.

" I really don't see that. For me there seems to be
nothing else. However——”

He was a wise man, but he could not quite conceal
his contempt for that sort of paradox ; in fact, Dr. Monygham was not liked by the Europeans of Sulaco. His
outward aspect of an outcast, which he preserved even
in Mrs. Gould's drawing-room, provoked unfavourable
criticism. There could be no doubt of his intelligence ;
and as he had lived for over twenty years in the country,
the pessimism of his outlook could not be altogether
ignored. But instinctively, in self-defence of their activities and hopes, his hearers put it to the account of
some hidden imperfection in the man's character. It was
known that many years before, when quite young, he had
been made by Guzman Bento chief medical officer of the

army. Not one of the Europeans then in the service of
Costaguana had been so much liked and trusted by the
fierce old Dictator.

Afterwards his story was not so clear. It lost itself
amongst the innumerable tales of conspiracies and plots
against the tyrant as a stream is lost in an arid belt of
sandy country before it emerges, diminished and troubled,
perhaps, on the other side. The doctor made no secret
of it that he had lived for years in the wildest parts of the
Republic, wandering with almost unknown Indian tribes
in the great forests of the far interior where the great
rivers have their sources. But it was mere aimless
wandering ; he had written nothing, collected nothing,
brought nothing for science out of the twilight of the
forests, which seemed to cling to his battered personality
limping about Sulaco, where it had drifted in casually, only
to get stranded on the shores of the sea.

It was also known that he had lived in a state of
destitution till the arrival of the Goulds from Europe.
Don Carlos and Doña Emilia had taken up the mad
English doctor, when it became apparent that for all his
savage independence he could be tamed by kindness.
Perhaps it was only hunger that had tamed him. In
years gone by he had certainly been acquainted with
Charles Gould's father in Sta. Marta ; and now, no
matter what were the dark passages of his history, as the
medical officer of the San Tomé mine he became a
recognised personality. He was recognised, but not
unreservedly accepted. So much defiant eccentricity
and such an outspoken scorn for mankind seemed to
point to mere recklessness of judgment, the bravado of
guilt. Besides, since he had become again of some
account, vague whispers had been heard that years ago,
when fallen into disgrace and thrown into prison by
Guzman Bento at the time of the so-called Great Conspiracy, he had betrayed some of his best friends amongst
the conspirators. Nobody pretended to believe that

whisper ; the whole story of the Great Conspiracy was hopelessly involved and obscure ; it is admitted in Costaguana that there never had been a conspiracy except in the diseased imagination of the Tyrant ; and, therefore, nothing and no one to betray ; though the most distinguished Costaguaneros had been imprisoned and executed upon that accusation. The procedure had dragged on for years, decimating the better class like a pestilence. The mere expression of sorrow for the fate of executed kinsmen had been punished with death. Don José Avellanos was perhaps the only one living who knew the whole story of those unspeakable cruelties. He had suffered from them himself, and he, with a shrug of the shoulders and a nervous, jerky gesture of the arm, was wont to put away from him, as it were, every allusion to it. But whatever the reason, Dr. Monygham, a personage in the administration of the Gould Concession, treated with reverent awe by the miners, and indulged in his peculiarities by Mrs. Gould, remained somehow outside the pale.

It was not from any liking for the doctor that the engineer-in-chief had lingered in the inn upon the plain. He liked old Viola much better. He had come to look upon the Albergo d'Italia Una as a dependence of the railway. Many of his subordinates had their quarters there. Mrs. Gould's interest in the family conferred upon it a sort of distinction. The engineer-in-chief, with an army of workers under his orders, appreciated the moral influence of the old Garibaldino upon his countrymen. His austere, old-world Republicanism had a severe, soldier-like standard of faithfulness and duty, as if the world were a battlefield where men had to fight for the sake of universal love and brotherhood, instead of a more or less large share of booty.

" Poor old chap ! " he said, after he had heard the doctor's account of Teresa. " He'll never be able to keep the place going by himself. I shall be sorry."

" He's quite alone up there," grunted Dr. Mony-gham, with a toss of his heavy head towards the narrow staircase. " Every living soul has cleared out, and Mrs. Gould took the girls away just now. It might not be oversafe for them out here before very long. Of course, as a doctor I can do nothing more here ; but she has asked me to stay with old Viola, and as I have no horse to get back to the mine, where I ought to be, I made no diffi-culty to stay. They can do without me in the town."

" I have a good mind to remain with you, doctor, till we see whether anything happens to-night at the har-bour," declared the engineer-in-chief. " He must not be molested by Sotillo's soldiery, who may push on as far as this at once. Sotillo used to be very cordial to me at the Goulds' and at the club. How that man 'll ever dare to look any of his friends here in the face I can't imagine."

" He'll no doubt begin by shooting some of them to get over the first awkwardness," said the doctor. " Nothing in this country serves better your military man who has changed sides than a few summary executions." He spoke with a gloomy positiveness that left no room for protest. The engineer-in-chief did not attempt any. He simply nodded several times regretfully, then said :

" I think we shall be able to mount you in the morning, doctor. Our peons have recovered some of our stam-peded horses. By riding hard and taking a wide circuit by Los Hatos and along the edge of the forest, clear of Rincon altogether, you may hope to reach the San Tomé bridge without being interfered with. The mine is just now, to my mind, the safest place for anybody at all com-promised. I only wish the railway was as difficult to touch."

" Am I compromised ? " Dr. Monygham brought out slowly after a short silence.

" The whole Gould Concession is compromised. It could not have remained for ever outside the political

life of the country—if those convulsions may be called
life. The thing is—Can it be touched ? The moment
was bound to come when neutrality would become
impossible, and Charles Gould understood this well. I
believe he is prepared for every extremity. A man of
his sort has never contemplated remaining indefinitely
at the mercy of ignorance and corruption. It was like
being a prisoner in a cavern of banditti with the price of
your ransom in your pocket, and buying your life from
day to day. Your mere safety, not your liberty, mind,
doctor. I know what I am talking about. The image
at which you shrug your shoulders is perfectly correct,
especially if you conceive such a prisoner endowed with
the power of replenishing his pocket by means as remote
from the faculties of his captors as if they were magic.
You must have understood that as well as I do, doctor.
He was in the position of the goose with the golden eggs.
I broached this matter to him as far back as Sir John's
visit here. The prisoner of stupid and greedy banditti
is always at the mercy of the first imbecile ruffian, who
may blow out his brains in a fit of temper or for some
prospect of an immediate big haul. The tale of killing
the goose with the golden eggs has not been evolved for
nothing out of the wisdom of mankind. It is a story that
will never grow old. That is why Charles Gould in his
deep, dumb way has countenanced the Ribierist Mandate,
the first public act that promised him safety on other
than venal grounds. Ribierism has failed, as everything
merely rational fails in this country. But Gould remains
logical in wishing to save this big lot of silver. Decoud's
plan of a counter-revolution may be practicable or not, it
may have a chance, or it may not have a chance. With
all my experience of this revolutionary continent, I can
hardly yet look at their methods seriously. Decoud has
been reading to us his draft of a proclamation, and talking
very well for two hours about his plan of action. He had
arguments which should have appeared solid enough if

we, members of old, stable political and national organisa-
tions, were not startled by the mere idea of a new State
evolved like this out of the head of a scoffing young man
fleeing for his life, with a proclamation in his pocket, to a
rough, jeering, half-bred swashbuckler, who in this part
of the world is called a general. It sounds like a comic
fairy tale—and behold, it may come off; because it is
true to the very spirit of the country."

" Is the silver gone off, then ? " asked the doctor
moodily.

The chief engineer pulled out his watch. " By
Captain Mitchell's reckoning—and he ought to know—
it has been gone long enough now to be some three or
four miles outside the harbour ; and, as Mitchell says,
Nostromo is the sort of seaman to make the best of his
opportunities."   Here the doctor grunted so heavily that
the other changed his tone.

" You have a poor opinion of that move, doctor ?
But why ?   Charles Gould has got to play his game out,
though he is not the man to formulate his conduct even
to himself, perhaps, let alone to others. It may be
that the game has been partly suggested to him by
Holroyd ; but it accords with his character, too ; and
that is why it has been so successful. Haven't they
come to calling him ' El Rey de Sulaco ' in Sta. Marta ?
A nickname may be the best record of a success. That's
what I call putting the face of a joke upon the body of a
truth. My dear sir, when I first arrived in Sta. Marta
I was struck by the way all those journalists, dema-
gogues, members of Congress, and all those generals
and judges cringed before a sleepy-eyed advocate without practice simply because he was the plenipotentiary
of the Gould Concession. Sir John when he came out
was impressed, too."

" A new State, with that plump dandy, Decoud, for
the first President ! " mused Dr. Monygham, nursing his
cheek and swinging his legs all the time.

" Upon my word, and why not ? " the chief engineer retorted in an unexpectedly earnest and confidential voice. It was as if something subtle in the air of Costaguana had inoculated him with the local faith in pronunciamientos. All at once he began to talk, like an expert revolutionist, of the instrument ready to hand in the intact army at Cayta, which could be brought back in a few days to Sulaco if only Decoud managed to make his way at once down the coast. For the military chief there was Barrios, who had nothing but a bullet to expect from Montero, his former professional rival and bitter enemy. Barrios's concurrence was assured. As to his army, it had nothing to expect from Montero either ; not even a month's pay. From that point of view the existence of the treasure was of enormous importance. The mere knowledge that it had been saved from the Monterists would be a strong inducement for the Cayta troops to embrace the cause of the new State.

The doctor turned round and contemplated his companion for some time.

" This Decoud, I see, is a persuasive young beggar," he remarked at last. " And pray is it for this, then, that Charles Gould has let the whole lot of ingots go out to sea in charge of that Nostromo ? "

" Charles Gould," said the engineer-in-chief, " has said no more about his motive than usual. You know, he doesn't talk. But we all here know his motive, and he has only one—the safety of the San Tomé mine with the preservation of the Gould Concession in the spirit of his compact with Holroyd. Holroyd is another uncommon man. They understand each other's imaginative side. One is thirty, the other nearly sixty, and they have been made for each other. To be a millionaire, and such a millionaire as Holroyd, is like being eternally young. The audacity of youth reckons upon what it fancies an unlimited time at its disposal ; but a millionaire has unlimited means in his hand—which is better. One's time on earth is an uncertain quantity, but about the long reach of millions there is no doubt. The introduction of a pure form of Christianity into this continent is a dream for a youthful enthusiast, and I have been trying to explain to you why Holroyd at fifty-eight is like a man on the threshold of life, and better, too. He's not a missionary, but the San Tomé mine holds just that for him. I assure you, in sober truth, that he could not manage to keep this out of a strictly business conference upon the finances of Costaguana he had with Sir John a couple of years ago. Sir John mentioned it with amazement in a letter he wrote to me here, from San Francisco, when on his way home. Upon my word, doctor, things seem to be worth nothing by what they are in themselves. I begin to believe that the only solid thing about them is the spiritual value which every one discovers in his own form of activity——"

" Bah ! " interrupted the doctor, without stopping for an instant the idle swinging movement of his legs. " Self-flattery. Food for that vanity which makes the world go round. Meantime, what do you think is going to happen to the treasure floating about the gulf with the great Capataz and the great politician ? "

" Why are you uneasy about it, doctor ? "

" I uneasy ? And what the devil is it to me ? I put no spiritual value into my desires, or my opinions, or my actions. They have not enough vastness to give me room for self-flattery. Look, for instance, I should certainly have liked to ease the last moments of that poor woman. And I can't. It's impossible. Have you met the impossible face to face—or have you, the Napoleon of railways, no such word in your dictionary ? "

" Is she bound to have a very bad time of it ? " asked the chief engineer, with humane concern.

Slow, heavy footsteps moved across the planks above the heavy hardwood beams of the kitchen. Then down

the narrow opening of the staircase made in the thickness
of the wall, and narrow enough to be defended by one
man against twenty enemies, came the murmur of two
voices, one faint and broken, the other deep and gentle
answering it, and in its graver tone covering the weaker
sound.

The two men remained still and silent till the murmurs ceased, then the doctor shrugged his shoulders and
muttered :

" Yes, she's bound to. And I could do nothing if I
went up now."

A long period of silence above and below ensued.

" I fancy," began the engineer in a subdued voice,
" that you mistrust Captain Mitchell's Capataz."

" Mistrust him ? " muttered the doctor through his
teeth. " I believe him capable of anything—even of
the most absurd fidelity. I am the last person he spoke
to before he left the wharf, you know. The poor woman
up there wanted to see him, and I let him go up to her.
The dying must not be contradicted, you know. She
seemed then fairly calm and resigned, but the scoundrel
in those ten minutes or so has done or said something
which seems to have driven her into despair. You
know," went on the doctor hesitatingly, " women are so
very unaccountable in every position, and at all times of
life, that I thought sometimes she was in a way, don't
you see ? in love with him—the Capataz. The rascal
has his own charm indubitably, or he would not have
made the conquest of all the populace of the town. No,
no, I am not absurd. I may have given a wrong name
to some strong sentiment for him on her part, to an unreasonable and simple attitude a woman is apt to take
up emotionally towards a man. She used to abuse him
to me frequently, which, of course, is not inconsistent
with my idea. Not at all. It looked to me as if she were
always thinking of him. He was something important
in her life. You know, I have seen a lot of those people.

Whenever I came down from the mine Mrs. Gould used to ask me to keep my eye on them. She likes Italians ; she has lived a long time in Italy, I believe, and she took a special fancy to that old Garibaldino. A remarkable chap enough. A rugged and dreamy character, living in the republicanism of his young days as if in a cloud. He has encouraged much of the Capataz's confounded nonsense—the high-strung, exalted old beggar ! "

" What sort of nonsense ? " wondered the chief engineer. " I found the Capataz always a very shrewd and sensible fellow, absolutely fearless, and remarkably useful. A perfect handy man. Sir John was greatly impressed by his resourcefulness and attention when he made that overland journey from Sta. Marta. Later on, as you might have heard, he rendered us a service by disclosing to the then chief of police the presence in the town of some professional thieves, who came from a distance to wreck and rob our monthly pay train. He has certainly organised the lighterage service of the harbour for the O.S.N. Company with great ability. He knows how to make himself obeyed, foreigner though he is. It is true that the cargadores are strangers here too, for the most part—immigrants, isleños."

" His prestige is his fortune," muttered the doctor sourly.

" The man has proved his trustworthiness up to the hilt on innumerable occasions and in all sorts of ways," argued the engineer. " When this question of the silver arose, Captain Mitchell naturally was very warmly of the opinion that his Capataz was the only man fit for the trust. As a sailor, of course, I suppose so. But as a man, don't you know, Gould, Decoud, and myself judged that it didn't matter in the least who went. Any boatman would have done just as well. Pray, what could a thief do with such a lot of ingots ? If he ran off with them, he would have in the end to land somewhere ; and how could he conceal his cargo from the knowledge

of the people ashore ?   We dismissed that consideration from our minds. Moreover, Decoud was going.
There have been occasions when the Capataz has been
more implicitly trusted."

" He took a slightly different view," the doctor said.
" I heard him declare in this very room that it would be
the most desperate affair of his life. He made a sort of
verbal will here in my hearing, appointing old Viola his
executor ; and, by Jove ! do you know, he—he's not
grown rich by his fidelity to you good people of the railway and the harbour. I suppose he obtains some—how
do you say that ?—some spiritual value for his labours,
or else I don't know why the devil he should be faithful
to you, Gould, Mitchell, or anybody else. He knows this
country well. He knows, for instance, that Gamacho,
the deputy from Javira, has been nothing else but a
tramposo of the commonest sort, a petty pedlar of the
Campo, till he managed to get enough goods on credit
from Anzani to open a little store in the wilds, and got
himself elected by the drunken mozos that hang about
the estancias and the poorest sort of rancheros who were
in his debt. And Gamacho, who to-morrow will be
probably one of our high officials, is a stranger too—an
isleño. He might have been a cargador on the O.S.N.
wharf had he not (the posadero of Rincon is ready to
swear it) murdered a pedlar in the woods and stolen his
pack to begin life on. And do you think that Gamacho,
then, would have ever become a hero with the democracy of this place, like our Capataz ? Of course not.
He isn't half the man. No ; decidedly, I think that
Nostromo is a fool."

The doctor's talk was distasteful to the builder of
railways. " It is impossible to argue that point," he said
philosophically. " Each man has his gifts. You should
have heard Gamacho haranguing his friends in the
street. He has a howling voice, and he shouted like
mad, lifting his clenched fist right above his head, and

throwing his body half out of the window. At every pause the rabble below yelled, ' Down with the Oligarchs ! Viva la Libertad ! ' Fuentes inside looked extremely miserable. You know, he is the brother of Jorge Fuentes, who has been Minister of the Interior for six months or so, some few years back. Of course, he has no conscience ; but he is a man of birth and education— at one time the director of the Customs of Cayta. That idiot-brute Gamacho fastened himself upon him with his following of the lowest rabble. His sickly fear of that ruffian was the most rejoicing sight imaginable."

He got up and went to the door to look out towards the harbour. " All quiet," he said ; " I wonder if Sotillo really means to turn up here ? "

CHAPTER TWO

CAPTAIN MITCHELL, pacing the wharf, was asking himself the same question. There was always the doubt whether the warning of the Esmeralda telegraphist—a fragmentary and interrupted message—had been properly understood. However, the good man had made up his mind not to go to bed till daylight, if even then. He imagined himself to have rendered an enormous service to Charles Gould. When he thought of the saved silver he rubbed his hands together with satisfaction. In his simple way he was proud at being a party to this extremely clever expedient. It was he who had given it a practical shape by suggesting the possibility of intercepting at sea the north-bound steamer. And it was advantageous to his Company too, which would have lost a valuable freight if the treasure had been left ashore to be confiscated. The pleasure of disappointing the Monterists was also very great. Authoritative by temperament and the long habit of command, Captain Mitchell was no democrat. He even went so far as to profess a contempt for parliamentarism itself. " His Excellency Don Vincente Ribiera," he used to say, " whom I and that fellow of mine, Nostromo, had the honour, sir, and the pleasure of saving from a cruel death, deferred too much to his Congress. It was a mistake—a distinct mistake, sir."

The guileless old seaman superintending the O.S.N. service imagined that the last three days had exhausted every startling surprise the political life of Costaguana could offer. He used to confess afterwards that the events which followed surpassed his imagination. To begin with, Sulaco (because of the seizure of the cables and the disorganisation of the steam service) remained for a whole fortnight cut off from the rest of the world like a besieged city.

" One would not have believed it possible ; but so it was, sir. A full fortnight."

The account of the extraordinary things that happened during that time, and the powerful emotions he experienced, acquired a comic impressiveness from the pompous manner of his personal narrative. He opened it always by assuring his hearer that he was " in the thick of things from first to last." Then he would begin by describing the getting away of the silver, and his natural anxiety lest " his fellow " in charge of the lighter should make some mistake. Apart from the loss of so much precious metal, the life of Señor Martin Decoud, an agreeable, wealthy, and well-informed young gentleman, would have been jeopardised through his falling into the hands of his political enemies. Captain Mitchell also admitted that in his solitary vigil on the wharf he had felt a certain measure of concern for the future of the whole country.

" A feeling, sir," he explained, " perfectly comprehensible in a man properly grateful for the many kindnesses received from the best families of merchants and other native gentlemen of independent means, who, barely saved by us from the excesses of the mob, seemed, to my mind's eye, destined to become the prey in person and fortune of the native soldiery, which, as is well known, behave with regrettable barbarity to the inhabitants during their civil commotions. And then, sir, there were the Goulds, for both of whom, man and wife, I could not but entertain the warmest feelings deserved by their hospitality and kindness. I felt, too, the dangers of the gentlemen of the Amarilla Club, who had made me honorary member, and had treated me with uniform

20

regard and civility, both in my capacity of Consular Agent
and as Superintendent of an important Steam Service.
Miss Antonia Avellanos, the most beautiful and accomplished young lady whom it has ever been my privilege
to speak to, was not a little in my mind, I confess. How
the interests of my Company would be affected by the
impending change of officials claimed a large share of
my attention too. In short, sir, I was extremely anxious
and very tired, as you may suppose, by the exciting and
memorable events in which I had taken my little part.
The Company's building containing my residence was
within five minutes' walk, with the attraction of some
supper and of my hammock (I always take my nightly
rest in a hammock, as the most suitable to the climate);
but somehow, sir, though evidently I could do nothing
for any one by remaining about, I could not tear myself
away from that wharf, where the fatigue made me stumble
painfully at times. The night was excessively dark—the
darkest I remember in my life ; so that I began to think
that the arrival of the transport from Esmeralda could not
possibly take place before daylight, owing to the difficulty
of navigating the gulf. The mosquitoes bit like fury.
We have been infested here with mosquitoes before the
late improvements ; a peculiar harbour brand, sir, renowned for its ferocity. They were like a cloud about
my head, and I shouldn't wonder that but for their attacks
I would have dozed off as I walked up and down, and got
a heavy fall. I kept on smoking cigar after cigar, more to
protect myself from being eaten up alive than from any
real relish for the weed. Then, sir, when perhaps for
the twentieth time I was approaching my watch to the
lighted end in order to see the time, and observing with
surprise that it wanted yet ten minutes to midnight, I
heard the splash of a ship's propeller—an unmistakable
sound to a sailor's ear on such a calm night. It was
faint indeed, because they were advancing with precaution and dead slow, both on account of the darkness

and from their desire of not revealing too soon their presence : a very unnecessary care, because, I verily believe, in all the enormous extent of this harbour I was the only living soul about. Even the usual staff of work-men and others had been absent from their posts for several nights owing to the disturbances. I stood stock-still, after dropping and stamping out my cigar—a circum-stance highly agreeable, I should think, to the mosquitoes, if I may judge from the state of my face next morning. But that was a trifling inconvenience in comparison with the brutal proceedings I became victim of on the part of Sotillo—something utterly inconceivable, sir; more like the proceedings of a maniac than the action of a sane man, however lost to all sense of honour and decency. But Sotillo was furious at the failure of his thievish scheme."

In this Captain Mitchell was right. Sotillo was indeed infuriated. Captain Mitchell, however, had not been arrested at once ; a vivid curiosity induced him to remain on the wharf (which is nearly four hundred feet long) to see, or rather hear, the whole process of dis-embarkation. Concealed by the railway truck used for the silver, which had been run back afterwards to the shore end of the jetty, Captain Mitchell saw the small detach-ment thrown forward, pass by, taking different directions upon the plain. Meantime the troops were being landed and formed into a column, whose head crept up gradually so close to him that he made it out, barring nearly the whole width of the wharf, only a very few yards from him. Then the low, shuffling, murmuring, clinking sounds ceased, and the whole mass remained for about an hour motionless and silent, awaiting the return of the scouts. On land nothing was to be heard except the deep baying of the mastiffs at the railway yards, answered by the faint barking of the curs infesting the outer limits of the town. A detached knot of dark shapes stood in front of the head of the column.

Presently the picket at the end of the wharf began to

challenge in undertones single figures approaching from the plain. Those messengers sent back from the scouting parties flung to their comrades brief sentences and passed on rapidly, becoming lost in the great motionless mass, to make their report to the Staff. It occurred to Captain Mitchell that his position could become disagreeable and perhaps dangerous, when suddenly, at the head of the jetty, there was a shout of command, a bugle call, followed by a stir and a rattling of arms, and a murmuring noise that ran right up the column. Near by a loud voice directed hurriedly, " Push that railway car out of the way ! " At the rush of bare feet to execute the order Captain Mitchell skipped back a pace or two ; the car, suddenly impelled by many hands, flew away from him along the rails, and before he knew what had happened he found himself surrounded and seized by his arms and the collar of his coat.

" We have caught a man hiding here, *mi Teniente* ! " cried one of his captors.

" Hold him on one side till the rearguard comes along," answered the voice. The whole column streamed past Captain Mitchell at a run, the thundering noise of their feet dying away suddenly on the shore. His captors held him tightly, disregarding his declaration that he was an Englishman and his loud demands to be taken at once before their commanding officer. Finally he lapsed into dignified silence. With a hollow rumble of wheels on the planks a couple of field-guns, dragged by hand, rolled by. Then, after a small body of men had marched past escorting four or five figures which walked in advance, with a jingle of steel scabbards, he felt a tug at his arms, and was ordered to come along. During the passage from the wharf to the Custom House it is to be feared that Captain Mitchell was subjected to certain indignities at the hands of the soldiers—such as jerks, thumps on the neck, forcible application of the butt of a rifle to the small of his back. Their ideas of speed were not in accord with his notion of his dignity. He became flustered, flushed, and helpless. It was as if the world were coming to an end. The long building was surrounded by troops, which were already piling arms by companies and preparing to pass the night lying on the ground in their ponchos with their sacks under their heads. Corporals moved with swinging lanterns posting sentries all round the walls wherever there was a door or an opening. Sotillo was taking his measures to protect his conquest as if it had indeed contained the treasure. His desire to make his fortune at one audacious stroke of genius had over-mastered his reasoning faculties. He would not believe in the possibility of failure ; the mere hint of such a thing made his brain reel with rage. Every circum-stance pointing to it appeared incredible. The state-ment of Hirsch, which was so absolutely fatal to his hopes, could by no means be admitted. It is true, too, that Hirsch's story had been told so incoherently, with such excessive signs of distraction, that it really looked improbable. It was extremely difficult, as the saying is, to make head or tail of it. On the bridge of the steamer, directly after his rescue, Sotillo and his officers, in their impatience and excitement, would not give the wretched man time to collect such few wits as remained to him. He ought to have been quieted, soothed, and reassured, whereas he had been roughly handled, cuffed, shaken, and addressed in menacing tones. His struggles, his wriggles, his attempts to get down on his knees, followed by the most violent efforts to break away, as if he meant incontinently to jump overboard, his shrieks and shrink-ings and cowering wild glances, had filled them first with amazement, then with a doubt of his genuineness, as men are wont to suspect the sincerity of every great passion. His Spanish, too, became so mixed up with German that the better half of his statements remained incompre-hensible. He tried to propitiate them by calling them *hochwohlgeboren herren*, which in itself sounded suspicious.

When admonished sternly not to trifle, he repeated his
entreaties and protestations of loyalty and innocence again
in German, obstinately, because he was not aware in what
language he was speaking. His identity, of course, was
perfectly known as an inhabitant of Esmeralda ; but this
made the matter nȯ clearer. As he kept on forgetting
Decoud's name, mixing him up with several other people
he had seen in the Casa Gould, it looked as if they all had
been in the lighter together ; and for a moment Sotillo
thought that he had drowned every prominent Ribierist
of Sulaco. The improbability of such a thing threw a
doubt upon the whole statement. Hirsch was either mad
or playing a part—pretending fear and distraction on the
spur of the moment to cover the truth. Sotillo's rapacity,
excited to the highest pitch by the prospect of an immense
booty, could believe in nothing adverse. This Jew might
have been very much frightened by the accident, but he
knew where the silver was concealed, and had invented
this story, with his Jewish cunning, to put him entirely
off the track as to what had been done.

Sotillo had taken up his quarters on the upper floor
in a vast apartment with heavy black beams. But there
was no ceiling, and the eye lost itself in the darkness under
the high pitch of the roof. The thick shutters stood open.
On a long table could be seen a large inkstand, some
stumpy, inky quill pens, and two square wooden boxes,
each holding half a hundredweight of sand. Sheets of
grey coarse official paper bestrewed the floor. It must
have been a room occupied by some higher official of the
Customs, because a large leathern arm-chair stood behind
the table, with other high-backed chairs scattered about.
A net hammock was swung under one of the beams—
for the official's afternoon siesta, no doubt. A couple
of candles stuck into tall iron candlesticks gave a dim
reddish light. The colonel's hat, sword, and revolver lay
between them, and a couple of his more trusty officers
lounged gloomily against the table. The colonel threw

himself into the arm-chair, and a big negro with a sergeant's stripes on his ragged sleeve, kneeling down, pulled off his boots. Sotillo's ebony moustache contrasted violently with the livid colouring of his cheeks. His eyes were sombre and as if sunk very far into his head. He seemed exhausted by his perplexities, languid with disappointment ; but when the sentry on the landing thrust his head in to announce the arrival of a prisoner, he revived at once.

" Let him be brought in," he shouted fiercely.

The door flew open, and Captain Mitchell, bareheaded, his waistcoat open, the bow of his tie under his ear, was hustled into the room.

Sotillo recognised him at once. He could not have hoped for a more precious capture ; here was a man who could tell him, if he chose, everything he wished to know—and directly the problem of how best to make him talk to the point presented itself to his mind. The resentment of a foreign nation had no terrors for Sotillo. The might of the whole armed Europe would not have protected Captain Mitchell from insults and ill-usage so well as the quick reflection of Sotillo that this was an Englishman who would most likely turn obstinate under bad treatment, and become quite unmanageable. At all events, the colonel smoothed the scowl on his brow.

" What ! The excellent Señor Mitchell ! " he cried in affected dismay. The pretended anger of his swift advance and of his shout, " Release the caballero at once," was so effective that the astounded soldiers positively sprang away from their prisoner. Thus suddenly deprived of forcible support, Captain Mitchell reeled as though about to fall. Sotillo took him familiarly under the arm, led him to a chair, waved his hand at the room. " Go out, all of you," he commanded.

When they had been left alone he stood looking down, irresolute and silent, watching till Captain Mitchell had recovered his power of speech.

Here in his very grasp was one of the men concerned in the removal of the silver. Sotillo's temperament was of that sort that he experienced an ardent desire to beat him; just as formerly when negotiating with difficulty a loan from the cautious Anzani, his fingers always itched to take the shopkeeper by the throat. As to Captain Mitchell, the suddenness, unexpectedness, and general inconceivableness of this experience had confused his thoughts. Moreover, he was physically out of breath.

"I've been knocked down three times between this and the wharf," he gasped out at last. "Somebody shall be made to pay for this." He had certainly stumbled more than once, and had been dragged along for some distance before he could regain his stride. With his recovered breath his indignation seemed to madden him. He jumped up, crimson, all his white hair bristling, his eyes glaring vengefully, and shook violently the flaps of his ruined waistcoat before the disconcerted Sotillo. "Look! Those uniformed thieves of yours downstairs have robbed me of my watch."

The old sailor's aspect was very threatening. Sotillo saw himself cut off from the table on which his sabre and revolver were lying.

"I demand restitution and apologies," Mitchell thundered at him, quite beside himself. "From you! Yes, from you!"

For the space of a second or so the colonel stood with a perfectly stony expression of face; then, as Captain Mitchell flung out an arm towards the table as if to snatch up the revolver, Sotillo, with a yell of alarm, bounded to the door and was gone in a flash, slamming it after him. Surprise calmed Captain Mitchell's fury. Behind the closed door Sotillo shouted on the landing, and there was a great tumult of feet on the wooden staircase.

"Disarm him! Bind him!" the colonel could be heard vociferating.

Captain Mitchell had just the time to glance once

at the windows, with three perpendicular bars of iron each and some twenty feet from the ground, as he well knew, before the door flew open and the rush upon him took place. In an incredibly short time he found himself bound with many turns of a hide rope to a high-backed chair, so that his head alone remained free. Not till then did Sotillo, who had been leaning in the doorway trembling visibly, venture again within. The soldiers, picking up from the floor the rifles they had dropped to grapple with the prisoner, filed out of the room. The officers remained leaning on their swords and looking on.

" The watch ! the watch ! " raved the colonel, pacing to and fro like a tiger in a cage. " Give me that man's watch ! "

It was true that, when searched for arms in the hall downstairs, before being taken into Sotillo's presence, Captain Mitchell had been relieved of his watch and chain ; but at the colonel's clamour it was produced quickly enough, a corporal bringing it up, carried carefully in the palms of his joined hands. Sotillo snatched it, and pushed the clenched fist from which it dangled close to Captain Mitchell's face.

" Now then, you arrogant Englishman ! You dare to call the soldiers of the army thieves ! Behold your watch ! "

He flourished his fist as if aiming blows at the prisoner's nose. Captain Mitchell, helpless as a swathed infant, looked anxiously at the sixty-guinea gold half-chronometer, presented to him years ago by a Committee of Underwriters for saving a ship from total loss by fire. Sotillo, too, seemed to perceive its valuable appearance. He became silent suddenly, stepped aside to the table, and began a careful examination in the light of the candles. He had never seen anything so fine. His officers closed in and craned their necks behind his back.

He became so interested that for an instant he for‐

got his precious prisoner. There is always something
childish in the rapacity of the passionate, clear-minded,
Southern races, wanting in the misty idealism of the
Northerners, who at the smallest encouragement dream
of nothing less than the conquest of the earth. Sotillo
was fond of jewels, gold trinkets, of personal adornment.
After a moment he turned about, and with a commanding
gesture made all his officers fall back. He laid down the
watch on the table, then, negligently, pushed his hat
over it.

"Ha !" he began, going up very close to the chair.
"You dare call my valiant soldiers of the Esmeralda
regiment thieves ! You dare ! What impudence ! You
foreigners come here to rob our country of its wealth.
You never have enough. Your audacity knows no
bounds."

He looked towards the officers, amongst whom there
was an approving murmur. The old major was moved
to declare :

"Si, mi Colonel. They are all traitors."

"I shall say nothing," continued Sotillo, fixing the
motionless and powerless Mitchell with an angry but
uneasy stare—"I shall say nothing of your treacherous
attempt to get possession of my revolver to shoot me
while I was trying to treat you with a consideration you
did not deserve. You have forfeited your life. Your only
hope is in my clemency."

He watched for the effect of his words, but there was
no obvious sign of fear on Captain Mitchell's face. His
white hair was full of dust, which covered also the rest
of his helpless person. As if he had heard nothing, he
twitched an eyebrow to get rid of a bit of straw which
hung amongst the hairs.

Sotillo advanced one leg and put his arms akimbo.
"It is you, Mitchell," he said emphatically, "who are
the thief, not my soldiers !" He pointed at his prisoner
a forefinger with a long, almond-shaped nail. "Where

is the silver of the San Tomé mine ? I ask you, Mitchell, where is the silver that was deposited in this Custom House ? Answer me that ! You stole it. You were a party to stealing it. It is stolen from the Government. Aha ! you think I do not know what I say ; but I am up to your foreign tricks. It is gone, the silver ! No ? Gone in one of your lanchas, you miserable man ! How dared you ? ''

This time he produced his effect. " How on earth could Sotillo know that ? '' thought Mitchell. His head, the only part of his body that could move, betrayed his surprise by a sudden jerk.

" Ha ! you tremble ! " Sotillo shouted suddenly. " It is a conspiracy. It is a crime against the State. Did you not know that the silver belongs to the Republic till the Government claims are satisfied ? Where is it ? Where have you hidden it, you miserable thief ? ''

At this question Captain Mitchell's sinking spirits revived. In whatever incomprehensible manner Sotillo had already got his information about the lighter, he had not captured it. That was clear. In his outraged heart, Captain Mitchell had resolved that nothing would induce him to say a word while he remained so disgracefully bound ; but his desire to help the escape of the silver made him depart from this resolution. His wits were very much at work. He detected in Sotillo a certain air of doubt, of irresolution.

" That man," he said to himself, " is not certain of what he advances." For all his pomposity in social intercourse, Captain Mitchell could meet the realities of life in a resolute and ready spirit. Now he had got over the first shock of the abominable treatment he was cool and collected enough. The immense contempt he felt for Sotillo steadied him, and he said oracularly, " No doubt it is well concealed by this time."

Sotillo, too, had time to cool down. " *Muy bien*,

Mitchell," he said in a cold and threatening manner. " But can you produce the Government receipt for the royalty and the Custom House permit of embarkation, hey ? Can you ? No. Then the silver has been removed illegally, and the guilty shall be made to suffer, unless it is produced within five days from this." He gave orders for the prisoner to be unbound and locked up in one of the smaller rooms downstairs. He walked about the room, moody and silent, till Captain Mitchell, with each of his arms held by a couple of men, stood up, shook himself, and stamped his feet.

" How did you like to be tied up, Mitchell ? " he asked derisively.

" It is the most incredible, abominable use of power ! " Captain Mitchell declared in a loud voice. " And whatever your purpose, you shall gain nothing from it, I can promise you."

The tall colonel, livid, with his coal-black ringlets and moustache, crouched, as it were, to look into the eyes of the short, thick-set, red-faced prisoner with rumpled white hair.

" That we shall see. You shall know my power a little better when I tie you up to a *potalon* outside in the sun for a whole day." He drew himself up haughtily, and made a sign for Captain Mitchell to be led away.

" What about my watch ? " cried Captain Mitchell, hanging back from the efforts of the men pulling him towards the door.

Sotillo turned to his officers. " No ! But only listen to this picaro, caballeros," he pronounced with affected scorn, and was answered by a chorus of derisive laughter. " He demands his watch ! " . . . He ran up again to Captain Mitchell, for the desire to relieve his feelings by inflicting blows and pain upon this Englishman was very strong within him. " Your watch ! You are a prisoner in war-time, Mitchell ! In war-time ! You have no rights and no property ! Caramba ! The very breath in your body belongs to me. Remember that."

" Bosh ! " said Captain Mitchell, concealing a disagreeable impression.

Down below, in a great hall, with the earthen floor and with a tall mound thrown up by white ants in a corner, the soldiers had kindled a small fire with broken chairs and tables near the arched gateway, through which the faint murmur of the harbour waters on the beach could be heard. While Captain Mitchell was being led down the staircase, an officer passed him, running up to report to Sotillo the capture of more prisoners. A lot of smoke hung about in the vast, gloomy place, the fire crackled, and, as if through a haze, Captain Mitchell made out, surrounded by short soldiers with fixed bayonets, the heads of three tall prisoners—the doctor, the engineer-in-chief, and the white leonine mane of old Viola, who stood half turned away from the others with his chin on his breast and his arms crossed. Mitchell's astonishment knew no bounds. He cried out ; the other two exclaimed also. But he was hurried on, diagonally, across the big, cavern-like hall. Lots of thoughts, surmises, hints of caution, and so on, crowded his head to distraction.

" Is he actually keeping you ? " shouted the chief engineer, whose single eyeglass glittered in the firelight.

An officer from the top of the stairs was shouting urgently, " Bring them all up—all three."

In the clamour of voices and the rattle of arms, Captain Mitchell made himself heard imperfectly. " By heavens, the fellow has stolen my watch ! "

The engineer-in-chief on the staircase resisted the pressure long enough to shout, " What ? What did you say ? "

" My chronometer ! " Captain Mitchell yelled violently at the very moment of being thrust head fore-most through a small door into a sort of cell, perfectly black, and so narrow that he fetched up against the opposite wall. The door had been instantly slammed. He knew where they had put him. This was the strong-room of the Custom House, whence the silver had been removed only a few hours earlier. It was almost as narrow as a corridor, with a small square aperture, barred by a heavy grating, at the distant end. Captain Mitchell staggered for a few steps, then sat down on the earthen floor with his back to the wall. Nothing, not even a gleam of light from anywhere, interfered with Captain Mitchell's meditation. He did some hard but not very extensive thinking. It was not of a gloomy cast. The old sailor, with all his small weaknesses and absurdities, was constitutionally incapable of enter-taining for any length of time a fear of his personal safety. It was not so much firmness of soul as the lack of a certain kind of imagination—the kind whose undue development caused intense suffering to Señor Hirsch ; that sort of imagination which adds the blind terror of bodily suffering and of death, envisaged as an accident to the body alone, strictly—to all the other appre-hensions on which the sense of one's existence is based. Unfortunately, Captain Mitchell had not much pene-tration of any kind ; characteristic, illuminating trifles of expression, action, or movement escaped him com-pletely. He was too pompously and innocently aware of his own existence to observe that of others. For in-stance, he could not believe that Sotillo had been really afraid of him, and this simply because it would never have entered into his head to shoot any one except in the most pressing case of self-defence. Anybody could see he was not a murdering kind of man, he reflected quite gravely. Then why this preposterous and insulting charge ? he asked himself. But his thoughts mainly clung around the astounding and unanswerable question, how the devil the fellow got to know that the silver had gone off in the lighter. It was obvious that he had not captured it.

And, obviously, he could not have captured it ! In this last conclusion Captain Mitchell was misled by the assumption drawn from his observation of the weather during his long vigil on the wharf. He thought that there had been much more wind than usual that night in the gulf ; whereas, as a matter of fact, the reverse was the case.

" How in the name of all that's marvellous has that confounded fellow got wind of the affair ? " was the first question he asked directly after the bang, clatter, and flash of the open door (which was closed again almost before he could lift his dropped head) informed him that he had a companion in captivity. Dr. Monygham's voice stopped muttering curses in English and Spanish.

" Is that you, Mitchell ? " he made answer surlily. " I struck my forehead against this confounded wall with enough force to fell an ox. Where are you ? "

Captain Mitchell, accustomed to the darkness, could make out the doctor stretching out his hands blindly.

" I am sitting here on the floor. Don't fall over my legs," Captain Mitchell's voice announced with great dignity of tone. The doctor, entreated not to walk about in the dark, sank down to the ground too. The two prisoners of Sotillo, with their heads nearly touching, began to exchange confidences.

" Yes," the doctor related in a low tone to Captain Mitchell's vehement curiosity, " we have been nabbed in old Viola's place. It seems that one of their pickets, commanded by an officer, pushed as far as the town gate. They had orders not to enter, but to bring along every soul they could find on the plain. We had been talking in there with the door open, and no doubt they saw the glimmer of our light. They must have been making their approaches for some time. The engineer laid himself on a bench in a recess by the fireplace, and I went upstairs to have a look. I hadn't heard any sound from there for a long time. Old Viola, as soon as he saw me come up,

lifted his arm for silence. I stole in on tiptoe. By
Jove, his wife was lying down and had gone to sleep.
The woman had actually dropped off to sleep ! ' Señor
Doctor,' Viola whispers to me, ' it looks as if her oppression was going to get better.' ' Yes,' I said, very much
surprised ; ' your wife is a wonderful woman, Giorgio.'
Just then a shot was fired in the kitchen, which made us
jump and cower as if at a thunder-clap. It seems that the
party of soldiers had stolen quite close up, and one of
them had crept up to the door. He looked in, thought
there was no one there, and, holding his rifle ready, entered
quietly. The chief told me that he had just closed his
eyes for a moment. When he opened them, he saw the
man already in the middle of the room peering into the
dark corners. The chief was so startled that, without
thinking, he made one leap from the recess right out in front
of the fireplace. The soldier, no less startled, up with
his rifle and pulls the trigger, deafening and singeing the
engineer, but in his flurry missing him completely. But,
look what happens ! At the noise of the report the sleeping woman sat up, as if moved by a spring, with a shriek,
' The children, Gian' Battista ! Save the children ! '
I have it in my ears now. It was the truest cry of distress
I ever heard. I stood as if paralysed, but the old husband
ran across to the bedside, stretching out his hands. She
clung to them ! I could see her eyes go glazed ; the old
fellow lowered her down on the pillows and then looked
round at me. She was dead ! All this took less than five
minutes, and then I ran down to see what was the matter.
It was no use thinking of any resistance. Nothing we two
could say availed with the officer, so I volunteered to go
up with a couple of soldiers and fetch down old Viola.
He was sitting at the foot of the bed, looking at his wife's
face, and did not seem to hear what I said ; but after I had
pulled the sheet over her head, he got up and followed us
downstairs quietly, in a sort of thoughtful way. They
marched us off along the road, leaving the door open

and the candle burning. The chief engineer strode on without a word, but I looked back once or twice at the feeble gleam. After we had gone some considerable distance, the Garibaldino, who was walking by my side, suddenly said, ' I have buried many men on battlefields on this continent. The priests talk of consecrated ground ! Bah ! All the earth made by God is holy ; but the sea, which knows nothing of kings and priests and tyrants, is the holiest of all. Doctor, I should like to bury her in the sea. No mummeries, candles, incense, no holy water mumbled over by priests. The spirit of liberty is upon the waters.' . . . Amazing old man. He was saying all this in an undertone as if talking to himself."

" Yes, yes," interrupted Captain Mitchell impatiently. " Poor old chap ! But have you any idea how that ruffian Sotillo obtained his information ? He did not get hold of any of our cargadores who helped with the truck, did he ? But no, it is impossible ! These were picked men we've had in our boats for these five years, and I paid them myself specially for the job, with instructions to keep out of the way for twenty-four hours at least. I saw them with my own eyes march on with the Italians to the railway yards. The chief promised to give them rations as long as they wanted to remain there."

" Well," said the doctor slowly, " I can tell you that you may say good-bye for ever to your best lighter, and to the Capataz of Cargadores."

At this, Captain Mitchell scrambled up to his feet in the excess of his excitement. The doctor, without giving him time to exclaim, stated briefly the part played by Hirsch during the night.

Captain Mitchell was overcome. " Drowned ! " he muttered, in a bewildered and appalled whisper. " Drowned ! " Afterwards he kept still, apparently listening, but too absorbed in the news of the catastrophe to follow the doctor's narrative with attention.

21

The doctor had taken up an attitude of perfect ignorance, till at last Sotillo was induced to have Hirsch
brought in to repeat the whole story, which was got out
of him again with the greatest difficulty, because every
moment he would break out into lamentations. At last,
Hirsch was led away, looking more dead than alive, and
shut up in one of the upstairs rooms to be close at hand.
Then the doctor, keeping up his character of a man not
admitted to the inner councils of the San Tomé Administration, remarked that the story sounded incredible. Of
course, he said, he couldn't tell what had been the action
of the Europeans, as he had been exclusively occupied
with his own work in looking after the wounded, and also
in attending Don José Avellanos. He had succeeded in
assuming so well a tone of impartial indifference, that
Sotillo seemed to be completely deceived. Till then a
show of regular inquiry had been kept up : one of the
officers sitting at the table wrote down the questions and
the answers; the others, lounging about the room, listened
attentively, puffing at their long cigars and keeping their
eyes on the doctor. But at that point Sotillo ordered
everybody out.

CHAPTER THREE

DIRECTLY they were alone, the colonel's severe official manner changed. He rose and approached the doctor. His eyes shone with rapacity and hope ; he became confidential. " The silver might have indeed been put on board the lighter, but it was not conceivable that it should have been taken out to sea." The doctor, watching every word, nodded slightly, smoking with apparent relish the cigar which Sotillo had offered him as a sign of his friendly intentions. The doctor's manner of cold detachment from the rest of the Europeans led Sotillo on, till, from conjecture to conjecture, he arrived at hinting that in his opinion this was a put-up job on the part of Charles Gould, in order to get hold of that immense treasure all to himself. The doctor, observant and self-possessed, muttered, " He is very capable of that."

Here Captain Mitchell exclaimed with amazement and indignation, " You said that of Charles Gould ? " Disgust, and even some suspicion, crept into his tone ; for to him too, as to other Europeans, there appeared to be something dubious about the doctor's personality.

" What on earth made you say that to this watch-stealing scoundrel ? " he asked. " What's the object of an infernal lie of that sort ? That confounded pickpocket was quite capable of believing you."

He snorted. For a time the doctor remained silent in the dark.

" Yes, that is exactly what I did say," he uttered at last, in a tone which would have made it clear enough to a third party that the pause was not of a reluctant but of a reflective character. Captain Mitchell thought that he had never heard anything so brazenly impudent in his life.

" Well, well ! " he muttered to himself ; but he had not the heart to voice his thoughts. They were swept away by others full of astonishment and regret. A heavy sense of discomfiture crushed him : the loss of the silver, the death of Nostromo, which was really quite a blow to his sensibilities, because he had become attached to his Capataz as people get attached to their inferiors from love of ease and almost unconscious gratitude. And when he thought of Decoud being drowned too, his sensibility was almost overcome by this miserable end. What a heavy blow for that poor young woman ! Captain Mitchell did not belong to the species of crabbed old bachelors ; on the contrary, he liked to see young men paying attentions to young women. It seemed to him a natural and proper thing. Proper especially. As to sailors, it was different ; it was not their place to marry, he maintained, but it was on moral grounds, as a matter of self-denial ; for, he explained, life on board ship is not fit for a woman even at best, and if you leave her on shore, first of all it is not fair, and next she either suffers from it or doesn't care a bit, which, in both cases, is bad. He couldn't have told what upset him most—Charles Gould's immense material loss ; the death of Nostromo, which was a heavy loss to himself ; or the idea of that beautiful and accomplished young woman being plunged into mourning.

" Yes," the doctor, who had been apparently reflecting, began again, " he believed me right enough. I thought he would have hugged me. ' Si, si,' he said, ' he will write to that partner of his, the rich Americano in San Francisco, that it is all lost. Why not ? There is enough to share with many people.' "

" But this is perfectly imbecile ! " cried Captain Mitchell.

The doctor remarked that Sotillo *was* imbecile, and that his imbecility was ingenious enough to lead him completely astray. He had helped him only but a little way.

" I mentioned," the doctor said, " in a sort of casual way, that treasure is generally buried in the earth rather than being set afloat upon the sea. At this my Sotillo slapped his forehead. ' *Por Dios*, yes,' he said ; ' they must have buried it on the shores of this harbour somewhere before they sailed out.' "

" Heavens and earth ! " muttered Captain Mitchell. " I should not have believed that anybody could be ass enough——" He paused, then went on mournfully : " But what's the good of all this ? It would have been a clever enough lie if the lighter had been still afloat. It would have kept that inconceivable idiot perhaps from sending out the steamer to cruise in the gulf. That was the danger that worried me no end." Captain Mitchell sighed profoundly.

" I had an object," the doctor pronounced slowly.

" Had you ? " muttered Captain Mitchell. " Well, that's lucky, or else I would have thought that you went on fooling him for the fun of the thing. And perhaps that was your object. Well, I must say I personally wouldn't condescend to that sort of thing. It is not to my taste. No, no. Blackening a friend's character is not my idea of fun, if it were to fool the greatest blackguard on earth."

Had it not been for Captain Mitchell's depression, caused by the fatal news, his disgust of Dr. Monygham would have taken a more outspoken shape ; but he thought to himself that now it really did not matter what that man, whom he had never liked, would say and do.

" I wonder," he grumbled, " why they have shut us

up together, or why Sotillo should have shut you up at
all, since it seems to me you have been fairly chummy
up there?"

"Yes, I wonder," said the doctor grimly.

Captain Mitchell's heart was so heavy that he would
have preferred for the time being a complete solitude
to the best of company. But any company would have
been preferable to the doctor's, at whom he had always
looked askance as a sort of beach-comber of superior
intelligence partly reclaimed from his abased state.
That feeling led him to ask:

"What has that ruffian done with the other
two?"

"The chief engineer he would have let go in any
case," said the doctor. "He wouldn't like to have a
quarrel with the railway upon his hands. Not just yet,
at any rate. I don't think, Captain Mitchell, that you
understand exactly what Sotillo's position is——"

"I don't see why I should bother my head about it,"
snarled Captain Mitchell.

"No," assented the doctor, with the same grim
composure. "I don't see why you should. It wouldn't
help a single human being in the world if you thought
ever so hard upon any subject whatever."

"No," said Captain Mitchell simply, and with
evident depression. "A man locked up in a confounded
dark hole is not much use to anybody."

"As to old Viola," the doctor continued, as though
he had not heard, "Sotillo released him for the same
reason he is presently going to release you."

"Eh? What?" exclaimed Captain Mitchell, staring like an owl in the darkness. "What is there in
common between me and old Viola? More likely because the old chap has no watch and chain for the pickpocket to steal. And I tell you what, Dr. Monygham,"
he went on with rising choler, "he will find it more
difficult than he thinks to get rid of me. He will burn

his fingers over that job yet, I can tell you. To begin
with, I won't go without my watch, and as to the rest—
we shall see. I dare say it is no great matter for you to
be locked up. But Joe Mitchell is a different kind of
man, sir. I don't mean to submit tamely to insult and
robbery. I am a public character, sir."

And then Captain Mitchell became aware that the
bars of the opening had become visible, a black grating
upon a square of grey. The coming of the day silenced
Captain Mitchell as if by the reflection that now in all
the future days he would be deprived of the invaluable
services of his Capataz. He leaned against the wall with
his arms folded on his breast, and the doctor walked up
and down the whole length of the place with his peculiar
hobbling gait, as if slinking about on damaged feet. At
the end farthest from the grating he would be lost altogether in the darkness. Only the slight limping shuffle
could be heard. There was an air of moody detachment in that painful growl kept up without a pause.
When the door of the prison was suddenly flung open
and his name shouted out he showed no surprise. He
swerved sharply in his walk, and passed out at once, as
though much depended upon his speed; but Captain
Mitchell remained for some time with his shoulders
against the wall, quite undecided in the bitterness of his
spirit whether it wouldn't be better to refuse to stir a
limb in the way of protest. He had half a mind to get
himself carried out, but after the officer at the door had
shouted three or four times in tones of remonstrance and
surprise he condescended to walk out.

Sotillo's manner had changed. The colonel's off-
hand civility was slightly irresolute, as though he were in
doubt if civility were the proper course in this case. He
observed Captain Mitchell attentively before he spoke
from the big arm-chair behind the table in a condescending voice:

" I have concluded not to detain you, Señor Mitchell.

I am of a forgiving disposition.   I make allowances.
Let this be a lesson to you, however."

The peculiar dawn of Sulaco, which seems to break
far away to the westward and creep back into the shade
of the mountains, mingled with the reddish light of the
candles.   Captain Mitchell, in sign of contempt and indifference, let his eyes roam all over the room, and he
gave a hard stare at the doctor, perched already on the
casement of one of the windows, with his eyelids lowered,
careless and thoughtful—or perhaps ashamed.

Sotillo, ensconced in the vast arm-chair, remarked,
" I should have thought that the feelings of a caballero
would have dictated to you an appropriate reply."

He waited for it ; but Captain Mitchell remaining
mute, more from extreme resentment than from reasoned
intention, Sotillo hesitated, glanced towards the doctor,
who looked up and nodded, then went on with a slight
effort :

" Here, Señor Mitchell, is your watch.   Learn how
hasty and unjust has been your judgment of my patriotic
soldiers."

Lying back in his seat, he extended his arm over
the table and pushed the watch away slightly.   Captain
Mitchell walked up with undisguised eagerness, put it to
his ear, then slipped it into his pocket coolly.

Sotillo seemed to overcome an immense reluctance.
Again he looked aside at the doctor, who stared at him
unwinkingly.

But as Captain Mitchell was turning away, without as
much as a nod or a glance, he hastened to say :

" You may go and wait downstairs for the Señor
Doctor, whom I am going to liberate too.   You foreigners
are insignificant, to my mind."

He forced a slight discordant laugh out of himself,
while Captain Mitchell, for the first time, looked at him
with some interest.

" The law shall take note later on of your transgressions," Sotillo hurried on. "But as for me, you can live free, unguarded, unobserved. Do you hear, Señor Mitchell? You may depart to your affairs. You are beneath my notice. My attention is claimed by matters of the very highest importance."

Captain Mitchell was very nearly provoked to an answer. It displeased him to be liberated insultingly; but want of sleep, prolonged anxieties, a profound disappointment with the fatal ending of the silver-saving business, weighed upon his spirits. It was as much as he could do to conceal his uneasiness, not about himself perhaps, but about things in general. It occurred to him distinctly that something underhand was going on. As he went out he ignored the doctor pointedly.

"A brute!" said Sotillo, as the door shut.

Dr. Monygham slipped off the window-sill, and, thrusting his hands into the pockets of the long, grey dust-coat he was wearing, made a few steps into the room.

Sotillo got up too, and, putting himself in the way, examined him from head to foot.

"So your countrymen do not confide in you very much, Señor Doctor. They do not love you, eh? Why is that, I wonder?"

The doctor, lifting his head, answered by a long, lifeless stare and the words, "Perhaps because I have lived too long in Costaguana."

Sotillo had a gleam of white teeth under the black moustache.

"Aha! But you love yourself," he said encouragingly.

"If you leave them alone," the doctor said, looking with the same lifeless stare at Sotillo's handsome face, "they will betray themselves very soon. Meantime, I may try to make Don Carlos speak."

"Ah, Señor Doctor," said Sotillo, wagging his head, "you are a man of quick intelligence. We were made to understand each other." He turned away. He could bear no longer that expressionless and motionless stare, which seemed to have a sort of impenetrable emptiness like the black depth of an abyss.

Even in a man utterly devoid of moral sense there remains an appreciation of rascality which, being conventional, is perfectly clear. Sotillo thought that Dr. Monygham, so different from all Europeans, was ready to sell his countrymen and Charles Gould, his employer, for some share of the San Tomé silver. Sotillo did not despise him for that. The colonel's want of moral sense was of a profound and innocent character. It bordered upon stupidity, moral stupidity. Nothing that served his ends could appear to him really reprehensible. Nevertheless, he despised Dr. Monygham. He had for him an immense and satisfactory contempt. He despised him with all his heart because he did not mean to let the doctor have any reward at all. He despised him, not as a man without faith and honour, but as a fool. Dr. Monygham's insight into his character had deceived Sotillo completely. Therefore he thought the doctor a fool.

Since his arrival in Sulaco the colonel's ideas had undergone some modification.

He no longer wished for a political career in Montero's administration. He had always doubted the safety of that course. Since he had learned from the chief engineer that at daylight most likely he would be confronted by Pedro Montero, his misgivings on that point had considerably increased. The guerrillero brother of the general—the Pedrito of popular speech—had a reputation of his own. He wasn't safe to deal with. Sotillo had vaguely planned seizing not only the treasure but the town itself, and then negotiating at leisure. But in the face of facts learned from the chief engineer (who had frankly disclosed to him the whole situation) his audacity, never of a very dashing kind, had been replaced by a most cautious hesitation.

"An army—an army crossed the mountains under Pedrito already?" he had repeated, unable to hide his consternation. "If it had not been that I am given the news by a man of your position I would never have believed it. Astonishing!"

"An armed force," corrected the engineer suavely.

His aim was attained. It was to keep Sulaco clear of any armed occupation for a few hours longer, to let those whom fear impelled leave the town. In the general dismay there were families hopeful enough to fly upon the road towards Los Hatos, which was left open by the withdrawal of the armed rabble under Señores Fuentes and Gamacho, to Rincon, with their enthusiastic welcome for Pedro Montero. It was a hasty and risky exodus, and it was said that Hernandez, occupying with his band the woods about Los Hatos, was receiving the fugitives. That a good many people he knew were contemplating such a flight had been well known to the chief engineer.

Father Corbelàn's efforts in the cause of that most pious robber had not been altogether fruitless. The political chief of Sulaco had yielded at the last moment to the urgent entreaties of the priest, had signed a provisional nomination appointing Hernandez a general, and calling upon him officially in this new capacity to preserve order in the town. The fact is that the political chief, seeing the situation desperate, did not care what he signed. It was the last official document he signed before he left the palace of the Intendencia for the refuge of the O.S.N. Company's office. But even had he meant his act to be effective it was already too late. The riot which he feared and expected broke out in less than an hour after Father Corbelàn had left him. Indeed, Father Corbelàn, who had appointed a meeting with Nostromo in the Dominican Convent, where he had his residence in one of the cells, never managed to reach the place. From the Intendencia he had gone straight on to the Avellanos's house to tell his brother-in-law, and

though he stayed there no more than half an hour he had
found himself cut off from his ascetic abode. Nostromo,
after waiting there for some time, watching uneasily the
increasing uproar in the street, had made his way to
the offices of the *Porvenir*, and stayed there till daylight, as Decoud had mentioned in the letter to his sister.
Thus the Capataz, instead of riding towards the Los
Hatos woods as bearer of Hernandez's nomination, had
remained in town to save the life of the President-Dictator,
to assist in repressing the outbreak of the mob, and at
last to sail out with the silver of the mine.

But Father Corbelàn, escaping to Hernandez, had the
document in his pocket, a piece of official writing turning
a bandit into a general in a memorable last official act
of the Ribierist party, whose watchwords were honesty,
peace, and progress. Probably neither the priest nor the
bandit saw the irony of it. Father Corbelàn must have
found messengers to send into the town, for early on
the second day of the disturbances there were rumours
of Hernandez being on the road to Los Hatos ready
to receive those who would put themselves under his
protection. A strange-looking horseman, elderly and
audacious, had appeared in the town, riding slowly while
his eyes examined the fronts of the houses, as though
he had never seen high buildings before. At the
cathedral he had dismounted, and, kneeling in the middle
of the plaza, his bridle over his arm and his hat lying in
front of him on the ground, had bowed his head, crossing
himself and beating his breast for some little time. Re-
mounting his horse, with a fearless but not unfriendly
look round the little gathering formed about his public
devotions, he had asked for the Casa Avellanos. A score
of hands were extended in answer, with fingers pointing
up the Calle de la Constitucion.

The horseman had gone on with only a glance of
casual curiosity upwards to the windows of the Amarilla
Club at the corner. His stentorian voice shouted period-

ically in the empty street, " Which is the Casa Avellanos ? " till an answer came from the scared porter,
and he disappeared under the gate. The letter he was
bringing, written by Father Corbelàn with a pencil by the
camp-fire of Hernandez, was addressed to Don José, of
whose critical state the priest was not aware. Antonia
read it, and, after consulting Charles Gould, sent it on for
the information of the gentlemen garrisoning the Amarilla
Club. For herself, her mind was made up : she would
rejoin her uncle ; she would entrust the last day—the last
hours perhaps—of her father's life to the keeping of the
bandit, whose existence was a protest against the irresponsible tyranny of all parties alike, against the moral darkness of the land. The gloom of Los Hatos woods was
preferable ; a life of hardships in the train of a robber
band less debasing. Antonia embraced with all her soul
her uncle's obstinate defiance of misfortune.   It was
grounded in the belief in the man whom she loved.

    In his message the Vicar-General answered upon his
head for Hernandez's fidelity. As to his power, he
pointed out that he had remained unsubdued for so many
years. In that letter Decoud's idea of the new Occidental State (whose flourishing and stable condition is a
matter of common knowledge now) was for the first time
made public and used as an argument. Hernandez, ex-
bandit and the last general of Ribierist creation, was
confident of being able to hold the tract of country
between the woods of Los Hatos and the coast range till
that devoted patriot, Don Martin Decoud, could bring
General Barrios back to Sulaco for the reconquest of the
town.

    " Heaven itself wills it.   Providence is on our side,"
wrote Father Corbelàn.   There was no time to reflect
upon or to controvert his statement ; and if the discussion started upon the reading of that letter in the
Amarilla Club was violent, it was also shortlived.   In the
general bewilderment of the collapse some jumped at

the idea with joyful astonishment as upon the amazing
discovery of a new hope. Others became fascinated by
the prospect of immediate personal safety for their
women and children. The majority caught at it as a
drowning man catches at a straw. Father Corbelàn was
unexpectedly offering them a refuge from Pedrito
Montero with his llaneros allied to Señores Fuentes and
Gamacho with their armed rabble.

All the latter part of the afternoon an animated discussion went on in the big rooms of the Amarilla Club.
Even those members posted at the windows with rifles
and carbines to guard the end of the street in case of an
offensive return of the populace shouted their opinions
and arguments over their shoulders. As dusk fell Don
Juste Lopez, inviting those caballeros who were of his
way of thinking to follow him, withdrew into the *corrédor*,
where at a little table in the light of two candles he busied
himself in composing an address, or rather a solemn
declaration to be presented to Pedrito Montero by a
deputation of such members of Assembly as had elected
to remain in town. His idea was to propitiate him in
order to save the form at least of parliamentary institutions.
Seated before a blank sheet of paper, a goose-quill pen in
his hand, and surged upon from all sides, he turned to the
right and to the left, repeating with solemn insistence :

" Caballeros, a moment of silence ! A moment of
silence ! We ought to make it clear that we bow in all
good faith to the accomplished facts."

The utterance of that phrase seemed to give him a
melancholy satisfaction. The hubbub of voices round
him was growing strained and hoarse. In the sudden
pauses the excited grimacing of the faces would sink all
at once into the stillness of profound dejection.

Meantime the exodus had begun. Carretas full of
ladies and children rolled swaying across the plaza, with
men walking or riding by their side ; mounted parties
followed on mules and horses ; the poorest were setting

out on foot, men and women carrying bundles, clasping babies in their arms, leading old people, dragging along the bigger children. When Charles Gould, after leaving the doctor and the engineer at the Casa Viola, entered the town by the harbour gate, all those that had meant to go were gone, and the others had barricaded themselves in their houses. In the whole dark street there was only one spot of flickering lights and moving figures, where the Señor Administrador recognised his wife's carriage waiting at the door of the Avellanos's house. He rode up, almost unnoticed, and looked on without a word while some of his own servants came out of the gate carrying Don José Avellanos, who, with closed eyes and motionless features, appeared perfectly lifeless. His wife and Antonia walked on each side of the improvised stretcher, which was put at once into the carriage. The two women embraced ; while from the other side of the landau Father Corbelàn's emissary, with his ragged beard all streaked with grey, and high, bronzed cheek-bones, stared, sitting upright in the saddle. Then Antonia, dry-eyed, got in by the side of the stretcher, and, after making the sign of the cross rapidly, lowered a thick veil upon her face. The servants and the three or four neighbours who had come to assist, stood back, uncovering their heads. On the box, Ignacio, resigned now to driving all night (and to having perhaps his throat cut before daylight), looked back surlily over his shoulder.

" Drive carefully," cried Mrs. Gould in a tremulous voice.

" Si, carefully ; si, nina," he mumbled, chewing his lips, his round, leathery cheeks quivering. And the landau rolled slowly out of the light.

" I will see them as far as the ford," said Charles Gould to his wife. She stood on the edge of the sidewalk with her hands clasped lightly, and nodded to him as he followed after the carriage. And now the windows of the Amarilla Club were dark. The last spark of

resistance had died out. Turning his head at the corner,
Charles Gould saw his wife crossing over to their own
gate in the lighted patch of the street. One of their
neighbours, a well-known merchant and landowner of
the province, followed at her elbow, talking with great
gestures. As she passed in all the lights went out in the
street, which remained dark and empty from end to end.

The houses of the vast plaza were lost in the night.
High up, like a star, there was a small gleam in one of
the towers of the cathedral ; and the equestrian statue
gleamed pale against the black trees of the Alameda, like
a ghost of royalty haunting the scenes of revolution. The
rare prowlers they met ranged themselves against the
wall. Beyond the last houses the carriage rolled noiselessly on the soft cushion of dust, and with a greater
obscurity a feeling of freshness seemed to fall from the
foliage of the trees bordering the country road. The
emissary from Hernandez's camp pushed his horse close
to Charles Gould.

" Caballero," he said in an interested voice, " you are
he whom they call the King of Sulaco, the master of the
mine ? Is it not so ? "

" Yes, I am the master of the mine," answered
Charles Gould.

The man cantered for a time in silence, then said, " I
have a brother, a sereno in your service in the San Tomé
valley. You have proved yourself a just man. There
has been no wrong done to any one since you called upon
the people to work in the mountains. My brother says
that no official of the Government, no oppressor of the
Campo, had been seen on your side of the stream. Your
own officials do not oppress the people in the gorge.
Doubtless they are afraid of your severity. You are a
just man and a powerful one," he added.

He spoke in an abrupt, independent tone, but evidently he was communicative with a purpose. He told
Charles Gould that he had been a ranchero in one of the

lower valleys, far south, a neighbour of Hernandez in the old days, and godfather to his eldest boy ; one of those who joined him in his resistance to the recruiting raid which was the beginning of all their misfortunes. It was he that, when his compadre had been carried off, had buried his wife and children, murdered by the soldiers.

" Si, Señor," he muttered hoarsely, " I and two or three others, the lucky ones left at liberty, buried them all in one grave near the ashes of their ranch, under the tree that had shaded its roof."

It was to him, too, that Hernandez came after he had deserted, three years afterwards. He had still his uniform on with the sergeant's stripes on the sleeve, and the blood of his colonel upon his hands and breast. Three troopers followed him, of those who had started in pursuit but had ridden on for liberty. And he told Charles Gould how he and a few friends, seeing those soldiers, lay in ambush behind some rocks ready to pull the trigger on them, when he recognised his compadre and jumped up from cover, shouting his name, because he knew that Hernandez could not have been coming back on an errand of injustice and oppression. Those three soldiers, together with the party who lay behind the rocks, had formed the nucleus of the famous band ; and he, the narrator, had been the favourite lieutenant of Hernandez for many, many years. He mentioned proudly that the officials had put a price upon his head too ; but it did not prevent it getting sprinkled with grey upon his shoulders. And now he had lived long enough to see his compadre made a general.

He had a burst of muffled laughter. " And now from robbers we have become soldiers. But look, caballero, at those who made us soldiers and him a general ! Look at these people ! "

Ignacio shouted. The light of the carriage lamps, running along the nopal hedges that crowned the bank on each side, flashed upon the scared faces of people

22

standing aside in the road, sunk deep, like an English
country lane, into the soft soil of the Campo. They
cowered ; their eyes glistened very big for a second ;
and then the light, running on, fell upon the half-
denuded roots of a big tree, on another stretch of nopal
hedge, caught up another bunch of faces glaring back
apprehensively. Three women—of whom one was carrying a child—and a couple of men in civilian dress—one
armed with a sabre and another with a gun—were grouped
about a donkey carrying two bundles tied up in blankets.
Farther on Ignacio shouted again to pass a carreta, a
long, wooden box on two high wheels, with the door at
the back swinging open. Some ladies in it must have
recognised the white mules, because they screamed out,
" Is it you, Doña Emilia ? "
    At the turn of the road the glare of a big fire filled the
short stretch vaulted over by the branches meeting overhead. Near the ford of a shallow stream a roadside
rancho of woven rushes and a roof of grass had been set
on fire by accident, and the flames, roaring viciously, lit
up an open space blocked with horses, mules, and a distracted shouting crowd of people. When Ignacio pulled
up, several ladies on foot assailed the carriage, begging
Antonia for a seat. To their clamour she answered by
pointing silently to her father.
    " I must leave you here," said Charles Gould in the
uproar. The flames leaped up sky-high, and in the
recoil from the scorching heat across the road the stream
of fugitives pressed against the carriage. A middle-aged
lady dressed in black silk, but with a coarse manta over
her head and a rough branch for a stick in her hand,
staggered against the front wheel. Two young girls,
frightened and silent, were clinging to her arms. Charles
Gould knew her very well.
    " Misericordia ! We are getting terribly bruised in
this crowd ! " she exclaimed, smiling up courageously to
him. " We have started on foot. All our servants ran

away yesterday to join the democrats. We are going to put ourselves under the protection of Father Corbelàn, of your sainted uncle, Antonia. He has wrought a miracle in the heart of a most merciless robber. A miracle ! "

She raised her voice gradually up to a scream as she was borne along by the pressure of people getting out of the way of some carts coming up out of the ford at a gallop, with loud yells and cracking of whips. Great masses of sparks mingled with black smoke flew over the road ; the bamboos of the walls detonated in the fire with the sound of an irregular fusillade. And then the bright blaze sank suddenly, leaving only a red dusk crowded with aimless dark shadows drifting in contrary directions ; the noise of voices seemed to die away with the flame ; and the tumult of heads, arms, quarrelling, and imprecations passed on fleeing into the darkness.

" I must leave you now," repeated Charles Gould to Antonia. She turned her head slowly and uncovered her face. The emissary and compadre of Hernandez spurred his horse close up.

" Has not the master of the mine any message to send to Hernandez, the master of the Campo ? "

The truth of the comparison struck Charles Gould heavily. In his determined purpose he held the mine, and the indomitable bandit held the Campo by the same precarious tenure. They were equals before the lawlessness of the land. It was impossible to disentangle one's activity from its debasing contacts. A close-meshed net of crime and corruption lay upon the whole country. An immense and weary discouragement sealed his lips for a time.

" You are a just man," urged the emissary of Hernandez. " Look at those people who made my compadre a general and have turned us all into soldiers ! Look at those oligarchs fleeing for life, with only the clothes on their backs ! My compadre does not think of that, but our followers may be wondering greatly,

and I would speak for them to you. Listen, Señor!
For many months now the Campo has been our own.
We need ask no man for anything; but soldiers must
have their pay to live honestly when the wars are over.
It is believed that your soul is so just that a prayer from
you would cure the sickness of every beast, like the
orison of the upright judge. Let me have some words
from your lips that would act like a charm upon the
doubts of our *partida*, where all are men."

"Do you hear what he says?" Charles Gould said
in English to Antonia.

"Forgive us our misery!" she exclaimed hurriedly.
"It is your character that is the inexhaustible treasure
which may save us all yet; your character, Carlos, not
your wealth. I entreat you to give this man your word
that you will accept any arrangement my uncle may make
with their chief. One word. He will want no more."

On the site of the roadside hut there remained nothing
but an enormous heap of embers, throwing afar a darken-
ing red glow, in which Antonia's face appeared deeply
flushed with excitement. Charles Gould, with only a
short hesitation, pronounced the required pledge. He
was like a man who had ventured on a precipitous path
with no room to turn, where the only chance of safety
is to press forward. At that moment he understood it
thoroughly as he looked down at Don José stretched
out, hardly breathing, by the side of the erect Antonia,
vanquished in a lifelong struggle with the powers of
moral darkness, whose stagnant depths breed monstrous
crimes and monstrous illusions. In a few words the
emissary from Hernandez expressed his complete satisfaction. Stoically Antonia lowered her veil, resisting the
longing to inquire about Decoud's escape. But Ignacio
leered morosely over his shoulder.

"Take a good look at the mules, *mi amo*," he grumbled.
"You shall never see them again!"

CHAPTER FOUR

CHARLES GOULD turned towards the town.
Before him the jagged peaks of the sierra
came out all black in the clear dawn. Here
and there a muffled lepero whisked round the corner
of a grass-grown street before the ringing hoofs of his
horse. Dogs barked behind the walls of the gardens ; and
with the colourless light the chill of the snows seemed
to fall from the mountains upon the disjointed pavements and the shuttered houses with broken cornices
and the plaster peeling in patches between the flat
pilasters of the fronts. The daybreak struggled with the
gloom under the Arcades on the plaza, with no signs
of country people disposing their goods for the day's
market—piles of fruit, bundles of vegetables ornamented
with flowers—on low benches under enormous mat
umbrellas ; with no cheery early morning bustle of
villagers, women, children, and loaded donkeys. Only a
few scattered knots of revolutionists stood in the vast
space, all looking one way from under their slouched
hats for some sign of news from Rincon. The largest
of those groups turned about like one man as Charles
Gould passed, and shouted, " Viva la Libertad ! " after
him in a menacing tone.

Charles Gould rode on, and turned into the archway of his house. In the patio littered with straw, a
practicante, one of Dr. Monygham's native assistants,
sat on the ground with his back against the rim of the
fountain, fingering a guitar discreetly, while two girls of

the lower class, standing up before him, shuffled their
feet a little and waved their arms, humming a popular
dance tune. Most of the wounded during the two days
of rioting had been taken away already by their friends
and relations, but several figures could be seen sitting
up balancing their bandaged heads in time to the music.
Charles Gould dismounted. A sleepy mozo coming
out of the bakery door took hold of the horse's bridle;
the practicante endeavoured to conceal his guitar hastily;
the girls, unabashed, stepped back smiling; and Charles
Gould, on his way to the staircase, glanced into a dark
corner of the patio at another group, a mortally wounded
cargador with a woman kneeling by his side; she
mumbled prayers rapidly, trying at the same time to
force a piece of orange between the stiffening lips of
the dying man.

The cruel futility of things stood unveiled in the
levity and sufferings of that incorrigible people; the
cruel futility of lives and of deaths thrown away in
the vain endeavour to attain an enduring solution of the
problem. Unlike Decoud, Charles Gould could not play
lightly a part in a tragic farce. It was tragic enough
for him in all conscience, but he could see no farcical
element. He suffered too much under a conviction of
irremediable folly. He was too severely practical and
too idealistic to look upon its terrible humours with
amusement, as Martin Decoud, the imaginative materialist, was able to do in the dry light of his scepticism.
To him, as to all of us, the compromises with his conscience appeared uglier than ever in the light of failure.
His taciturnity, assumed with a purpose, had prevented
him from tampering openly with his thoughts; but
the Gould Concession had insidiously corrupted his
judgment. He might have known, he said to himself,
leaning over the balustrade of the *corrédor*, that Ribierism
could never come to anything. The mine had corrupted
his judgment by making him sick of bribing and in-

triguing merely to have his work left alone from day to day. Like his father, he did not like to be robbed. It exasperated him. He had persuaded himself that, apart from higher considerations, the backing up Don José's hopes of reform was good business. He had gone forth into the senseless fray as his poor uncle, whose sword hung on the wall of his study, had gone forth— in the defence of the commonest decencies of organised society. Only his weapon was the wealth of the mine, more far-reaching and subtle than an honest blade of steel fitted into a simple brass guard.

More dangerous to the wielder, too, this weapon of wealth, double-edged with the cupidity and misery of mankind, steeped in all the vices of self-indulgence as in a concoction of poisonous roots, tainting the very cause for which it is drawn, always ready to turn awkwardly in the hand. There was nothing for it now but to go on using it. But he promised himself to see it shattered into small bits before he let it be wrenched from his grasp.

After all, with his English parentage and English upbringing, he perceived that he was an adventurer in Costaguana, the descendant of adventurers enlisted in a foreign legion, of men who had sought fortune in a revolutionary war, who had planned revolutions, who had believed in revolutions. For all the uprightness of his character, he had something of an adventurer's easy morality which takes count of personal risk in the ethical appraising of his action. He was prepared, if need be, to blow up the whole San Tomé mountain sky-high out of the territory of the Republic. This resolution expressed the tenacity of his character, the remorse of that subtle conjugal infidelity through which his wife was no longer the sole mistress of his thoughts, something of his father's imaginative weakness, and something, too, of the spirit of a buccaneer throwing a lighted match into the magazine rather than surrender his ship.

Down below in the patio the wounded cargador had breathed his last. The woman cried out once, and her cry, unexpected and shrill, made all the wounded sit up. The practicante scrambled to his feet, and, guitar in hand, gazed steadily in her direction with elevated eyebrows. The two girls—sitting now one on each side of their wounded relative, with their knees drawn up and long cigars between their lips—nodded at each other significantly.

Charles Gould, looking down over the balustrade, saw three men dressed ceremoniously in black frockcoats with white shirts, and wearing European round hats, enter the patio from the street. One of them, head and shoulders taller than the two others, advanced with marked gravity, leading the way. This was Don Juste Lopez, accompanied by two of his friends, members of Assembly, coming to call upon the Administrador of the San Tomé mine at this early hour. They saw him too, waved their hands to him urgently, walking up the stairs as if in procession.

Don Juste, astonishingly changed by having shaved off altogether his damaged beard, had lost with it nine-tenths of his outward dignity. Even at that time of serious preoccupation Charles Gould could not help noting the revealed ineptitude in the aspect of the man. His companions looked crestfallen and sleepy. One kept on passing the tip of his tongue over his parched lips ; the other's eyes strayed dully over the tiled floor of the *corrédor* ; while Don Juste, standing a little in advance, harangued the Señor Administrador of the San Tomé mine. It was his firm opinion that forms had to be observed. A new governor is always visited by deputations from the Cabildo, which is the Municipal Council, from the Consulado, the Commercial Board, and it was proper that the Provincial Assembly should send a deputation too, if only to assert the existence of parliamentary institutions. Don Juste proposed that

Don Carlos Gould, as the most prominent citizen of the province, should join the Assembly's deputation. His position was exceptional, his personality known through the length and breadth of the whole Republic. Official courtesies must not be neglected, if they are gone through with a bleeding heart. The acceptance of accomplished facts may save yet the precious vestiges of parliamentary institutions. Don Juste's eyes glowed dully ; he believed in parliamentary institutions—and the convinced drone of his voice lost itself in the stillness of the house like the deep buzzing of some ponderous insect.

Charles Gould had turned round to listen patiently, leaning his elbow on the balustrade. He shook his head a little, refusing, almost touched by the anxious gaze of the President of the Provincial Assembly. It was not Charles Gould's policy to make the San Tomé mine a party to any formal proceedings.

" My advice, Señores, is that you should wait for your fate in your houses. There is no necessity for you to give yourselves up formally into Montero's hands. Submission to the inevitable, as Don Juste calls it, is all very well, but when the inevitable is called Pedrito Montero there is no need to exhibit pointedly the whole extent of your surrender. The fault of this country is the want of measure in political life. Flat acquiescence in illegality, followed by sanguinary reaction—that, Señores, is not the way to a stable and prosperous future."

Charles Gould stopped before the sad bewilderment of the faces, the wondering, anxious glances of the eyes. The feeling of pity for those men, putting all their trust into words of some sort, while murder and rapine stalked over the land, had betrayed him into what seemed empty loquacity. Don Juste murmured :

" You are abandoning us, Don Carlos. . . . And yet, parliamentary institutions——"

He could not finish from grief. For a moment he put his hand over his eyes. Charles Gould, in his fear

of empty loquacity, made no answer to the charge. He
returned in silence their ceremonious bows. His taciturnity was his refuge. He understood that what they
sought was to get the influence of the San Tomé mine
on their side. They wanted to go on a conciliating
errand to the victor under the wing of the Gould Concession. Other public bodies—the Cabildo, the Consulado—would be coming too presently, seeking the
support of the most stable, the most effective force
they had ever known to exist in their province.

The doctor, arriving with his sharp, jerky walk, found
that the master had retired into his own room with orders
not to be disturbed on any account. But Dr. Monygham
was not anxious to see Charles Gould at once. He spent
some time in a rapid examination of his wounded. He
gazed down upon each in turn, rubbing his chin between his thumb and forefinger ; his steady stare met
without expression their silently inquisitive look. All
these cases were doing well ; but when he came to the
dead cargador he stopped a little longer, surveying not
the man who had ceased to suffer, but the woman
kneeling in silent contemplation of the rigid face, with
its pinched nostrils and a white gleam in the imperfectly
closed eyes. She lifted her head slowly, and said in a
dull voice :

" It is not long since he had become a cargador—
only a few weeks. His worship the Capataz had accepted
him after many entreaties."

" I am not responsible for the great Capataz,"
muttered the doctor, moving off.

Directing his course upstairs towards the door of
Charles Gould's room, the doctor at the last moment
hesitated ; then, turning away from the handle with a
shrug of his uneven shoulders, slunk off hastily along the
corrédor in search of Mrs. Gould's camerista.

Leonarda told him that the Señora had not risen yet.
The Señora had given into her charge the girls belonging

to that Italian posadero. She, Leonarda, had put them to bed in her own room. The fair girl had cried herself to sleep, but the dark one—the biggest—had not closed her eyes yet. She sat up in bed clutching the sheets right under her chin and staring before her like a little witch. Leonarda did not approve of the Viola children being admitted to the house. She made this feeling clear by the indifferent tone in which she inquired whether their mother was dead yet. As to the Señora, she must be asleep. Ever since she had gone into her room after seeing the departure of Doña Antonia with her dying father, there had been no sound behind her door.

The doctor, rousing himself out of profound reflection, told her abruptly to call her mistress at once. He hobbled off to wait for Mrs. Gould in the sala. He was very tired, but too excited to sit down. In this great drawing-room, now empty, in which his withered soul had been refreshed after many arid years and his outcast spirit had accepted silently the toleration of many side-glances, he wandered haphazard amongst the chairs and tables till Mrs. Gould, enveloped in a morning wrapper, came in rapidly.

" You know that I never approved of the silver being sent away," the doctor began at once, as a preliminary to the narrative of his night's adventures in association with Captain Mitchell, the engineer-in-chief, and old Viola, at Sotillo's headquarters. To the doctor, with his special conception of this political crisis, the removal of the silver had seemed an irrational and ill-omened measure. It was as if a general were sending the best part of his troops away on the eve of battle upon some recondite pretext. The whole lot of ingots might have been concealed somewhere where they could have been got at for the purpose of staving off the dangers which were menacing the security of the Gould Concession. The Administrador had acted as if the immense and

powerful prosperity of the mine had been founded on
methods of probity, on the sense of usefulness. And it
was nothing of the kind. The method followed had
been the only one possible. The Gould Concession had
ransomed its way through all those years. It was a
nauseous process. He quite understood that Charles
Gould had got sick of it and had left the old path to back
up that hopeless attempt at reform. The doctor did not
believe in the reform of Costaguana. And now the mine
was back again in its old path, with the disadvantage that
henceforth it had to deal not only with the greed provoked by its wealth, but with the resentment awakened
by the attempt to free itself from its bondage to moral
corruption. That was the penalty of failure. What made
him uneasy was that Charles Gould seemed to him to
have weakened at the decisive moment when a frank
return to the old methods was the only chance. Listening to Decoud's wild scheme had been a weakness.

The doctor flung up his arms, exclaiming, " Decoud !
Decoud ! " He hobbled about the room with slight,
angry laughs. Many years ago both his ankles had been
seriously damaged in the course of a certain investigation
conducted in the castle of Sta. Marta by a commission
composed of military men. Their nomination had been
signified to them unexpectedly at the dead of night, with
scowling brow, flashing eyes, and in a tempestuous voice,
by Guzman Bento. The old tyrant, maddened by one of
his sudden accesses of suspicion, mingled spluttering
appeals to their fidelity with imprecations and horrible
menaces. The cells and casements of the castle on the
hill had been already filled with prisoners. The commission was charged now with the task of discovering
the iniquitous conspiracy against the Citizen-Saviour of
his country.

Their dread of the raving tyrant translated itself
into a hasty ferocity of procedure. The Citizen-Saviour
was not accustomed to wait. A conspiracy had to be

discovered. The courtyards of the castle resounded with the clanking of leg-irons, sounds of blows, yells of pain ; and the commission of high officers laboured feverishly, concealing their distress and apprehensions from each other, and especially from their secretary, Father Beron, an army chaplain, at that time very much in the confidence of the Citizen-Saviour. That priest was a big, round-shouldered man, with an unclean-looking, overgrown tonsure on the top of his flat head, of a dingy, yellow complexion, softly fat, with greasy stains all down the front of his lieutenant's uniform, and a small cross embroidered in white cotton on his left breast. He had a heavy nose and a pendent lip. Dr. Monygham remembered him still. He remembered him against all the force of his will striving its utmost to forget. Father Beron had been adjoined to the commission by Guzman Bento expressly for the purpose that his enlightened zeal should assist them in their labours. Dr. Monygham could by no manner of means forget the zeal of Father Beron, or his face, or the pitiless, monotonous voice in which he pronounced the words, " Will you confess now ? "

This memory did not make him shudder, but it had made of him what he was in the eyes of respectable people —a man careless of common decencies, something between a clever vagabond and a disreputable doctor. But not all respectable people would have had the necessary delicacy of sentiment to understand with what trouble of mind and accuracy of vision Dr. Monygham, medical officer of the San Tomé mine, remembered Father Beron, army chaplain, and once a secretary of a military commission. After all these years Dr. Monygham, in his rooms at the end of the hospital building in the San Tomé gorge, remembered Father Beron as distinctly as ever. He remembered that priest at night, sometimes, in his sleep. On such nights the doctor waited for daylight with a candle lighted, and walking the whole length of his room to and fro, staring down at his bare feet, his arms hugging his sides tightly.   He would dream of Father Beron sitting at the end of a long black table, behind which, in a row, appeared the heads, shoulders, and epaulettes of the military members, nibbling the feather of a quill pen, and listening with weary and impatient scorn to the protestations of some prisoner calling Heaven to witness of his innocence, till he burst out, "What's the use of wasting time over that miserable nonsense?   Let me take him outside for a while."   And Father Beron would go outside after the clanking prisoner, led away between two soldiers.   Such interludes happened on many days, many times, with many prisoners.   When the prisoner returned he was ready to make a full confession, Father Beron would declare, leaning forward with that dull, surfeited look which can be seen in the eyes of gluttonous persons after a heavy meal.

The priest's inquisitorial instincts suffered but little from the want of classical apparatus of the Inquisition. At no time of the world's history have men been at a loss how to inflict mental and bodily anguish upon their fellow-creatures.   This aptitude came to them in the growing complexity of their passions and the early refinement of their ingenuity.   But it may safely be said that primeval man did not go to the trouble of inventing tortures.   He was indolent and pure of heart.   He brained his neighbour ferociously with a stone axe from necessity and without malice.   The stupidest mind may invent a rankling phrase or brand the innocent with a cruel aspersion.   A piece of string and a ramrod; a few muskets in combination with a length of hide rope; or even a simple mallet of heavy hardwood applied with a swing to human fingers or to the joints of a human body, is enough for the infliction of the most exquisite torture.   The doctor had been a very stubborn prisoner, and, as a natural consequence of that "bad disposition" (so Father Beron called it), his subjugation had been very crushing and very complete.

That is why the limp in his walk, the twist of his shoulders, the scars on his cheeks, were so pronounced. His confessions, when they came at last, were very complete too. Sometimes on the nights when he walked the floor, he wondered, grinding his teeth with shame and rage, at the fertility of his imagination when stimulated by a sort of pain which makes truth, honour, self-respect, and life itself matters of little moment.

And he could not forget Father Beron with his monotonous phrase, " Will you confess now ? " reaching him in an awful iteration and lucidity of meaning through the delirious incoherence of unbearable pain. He could not forget. But that was not the worst. Had he met Father Beron in the street after all these years, Dr. Monygham was sure he would have quailed before him. This contingency was not to be feared now. Father Beron was dead ; but the sickening certitude prevented Dr. Monygham from looking anybody in the face.

Dr. Monygham had become, in a manner, the slave of a ghost. It was obviously impossible to take his knowledge of Father Beron home to Europe. When making his extorted confessions to the Military Board, Dr. Monygham was not seeking to avoid death. He longed for it. Sitting half naked for hours on the wet earth of his prison, and so motionless that the spiders, his companions, attached their webs to his matted hair, he consoled the misery of his soul with acute reasonings that he had confessed to crimes enough for a sentence of death—that they had gone too far with him to let him live to tell the tale.

But, as if by a refinement of cruelty, Dr. Monygham was left for months to decay slowly in the darkness of his grave-like prison. It was no doubt hoped that it would finish him off without the trouble of an execution ; but Dr. Monygham had an iron constitution. It was Guzman Bento who died, not by the knife-thrust of a conspirator, but from a stroke of apoplexy, and Dr. Monygham was liberated hastily. His fetters were struck off by the light of a candle, which, after months of gloom, hurt his eyes so much that he had to cover his face with his hands. He was raised up. His heart was beating violently with the fear of this liberty. When he tried to walk, the extra-ordinary lightness of his feet made him giddy, and he fell down. Two sticks were thrust into his hands, and he was pushed out of the passage. It was dusk ; candles glimmered already in the windows of the officers' quarters round the courtyard ; but the twilight sky dazed him by its enormous and overwhelming brilliance. A thin poncho hung over his naked, bony shoulders ; the rags of his trousers came down no lower than his knees ; an eighteen months' growth of hair fell in dirty grey locks on each side of his sharp cheek-bones. As he dragged himself past the guardroom door, one of the soldiers, lolling outside, moved by some obscure impulse, leaped forward with a strange laugh and rammed a broken old straw hat on his head. And Dr. Monygham, after having tottered, continued on his way. He advanced one stick, then one maimed foot, then the other stick ; the other foot followed only a very short distance along the ground, toilfully, as though it were almost too heavy to be moved at all ; and yet his legs under the hanging angles of the poncho appeared no thicker than the two sticks in his hands. A ceaseless trembling agitated his bent body, all his wasted limbs, his bony head, the conical, ragged crown of the sombrero, whose ample flat rim rested on his shoulders.

In such conditions of manner and attire did Dr. Mony-gham go forth to take possession of his liberty. And these conditions seemed to bind him indissolubly to the land of Costaguana like an awful procedure of naturalisation, in-volving him deep in the national life, far deeper than any amount of success and honour could have done. They did away with his Europeanism ; for Dr. Monygham had made himself an ideal conception of his disgrace.

It was a conception eminently fit and proper for an officer and a gentleman.   Dr. Monygham, before he went out to Costaguana, had been surgeon in one of Her Majesty's regiments of foot.   It was a conception which took no account of physiological facts or reasonable arguments ; but it was not stupid for all that.   It was simple.   A rule of conduct resting mainly on severe rejections is necessarily simple.   Dr. Monygham's view of what it behoved him to do was severe ; it was an ideal view, in so much that it was the imaginative exaggeration of a correct feeling.   It was also, in its force, influence, and persistency, the view of an eminently loyal nature.

There was a great fund of loyalty in Dr. Monygham's nature.   He had settled it all on Mrs. Gould's head.   He believed her worthy of every devotion.   At the bottom of his heart he felt an angry uneasiness before the prosperity of the San Tomé mine, because its growth was robbing her of all peace of mind.   Costaguana was no place for a woman of that kind.   What could Charles Gould have been thinking of when he brought her out there ?   It was outrageous !   And the doctor had watched the course of events with a grim and distant reserve which, he imagined, his lamentable history imposed upon him.

Loyalty to Mrs. Gould could not, however, leave out of account the safety of her husband.   The doctor had contrived to be in town at the critical time because he mistrusted Charles Gould.   He considered him hopelessly infected with the madness of revolutions.   That is why he hobbled in distress in the drawing-room of the Casa Gould on that morning, exclaiming, " Decoud ! Decoud ! " in a tone of mournful irritation.

Mrs. Gould, her colour heightened, and with glistening eyes, looked straight before her at the sudden enormity of that disaster.   The finger-tips of one hand rested lightly on a low little table by her side, and the arm trembled right up to the shoulder.   The sun, which looks late upon Sulaco, issuing in all the fullness of its power high up on the sky from behind the dazzling snow-edge of Higuerota, had precipitated the delicate, smooth, pearly greyness of light, in which the town lies steeped during the early hours, into sharp-cut masses of black shade and spaces of hot, blinding glare. Three long rectangles of sunshine fell through the windows of the sala ; while just across the street the front of the Avellanos's house appeared very sombre in its own shadow seen through the flood of light.

A voice said at the door, " What of Decoud ? "

It was Charles Gould. They had not heard him coming along the *corrédor*. His glance just glided over his wife and struck full at the doctor.

" You have brought some news, doctor ? "

Dr. Monygham blurted it all out at once, in the rough. For some time after he had done, the Administrador of the San Tomé mine remained looking at him without a word. Mrs. Gould sank into a low chair with her hands lying on her lap. A silence reigned between those three motionless persons. Then Charles Gould spoke :

" You must want some breakfast."

He stood aside to let his wife pass first. She caught up her husband's hand and pressed it as she went out, raising her handkerchief to her eyes. The sight of her husband had brought Antonia's position to her mind, and she could not contain her tears at the thought of the poor girl. When she rejoined the two men in the dining-room after having bathed her face, Charles Gould was saying to the doctor across the table :

" No, there does not seem any room for doubt."

And the doctor assented.

" No, I don't see myself how we could question that wretched Hirsch's tale. It's only too true, I fear."

She sat down desolately at the head of the table and looked from one to the other. The two men, without absolutely turning their heads away, tried to avoid her glance. The doctor even made a show of being hungry ; he seized his knife and fork, and began to eat with emphasis, as if on the stage. Charles Gould made no pretence of the sort ; with his elbows raised squarely, he twisted both ends of his flaming moustaches—they were so long that his hands were quite away from his face.

" I am not surprised," he muttered, abandoning his moustaches and throwing one arm over the back of his chair. His face was calm with that immobility of expression which betrays the intensity of a mental struggle. He felt that this accident had brought to a point all the consequences involved in his line of conduct, with its conscious and subconscious intentions. There must be an end now of this silent reserve, of that air of impenetrability behind which he had been safeguarding his dignity. It was the least ignoble form of dissembling forced upon him by that parody of civilised institutions which offended his intelligence, his uprightness, and his sense of right. He was like his father. He had no ironic eye. He was not amused at the absurdities that prevail in this world. They hurt him in his innate gravity. He felt that the miserable death of that poor Decoud took from him his inaccessible position of a force in the background. It committed him openly, unless he wished to throw up the game—and that was impossible. The material interests required from him the sacrifice of his aloofness—perhaps his own safety too. And he reflected that Decoud's separationist plan had not gone to the bottom with the lost silver.

The only thing that was not changed was his position towards Mr. Holroyd. The head of silver and steel interests had entered into Costaguana affairs with a sort of passion. Costaguana had become necessary to his existence ; in the San Tomé mine he had found the imaginative satisfaction which other minds would get from drama, from art, or from a risky and fascinating

sport. It was a special form of the great man's extravagance, sanctioned by a moral intention, big enough to
flatter his vanity. Even in this aberration of his genius
he served the progress of the world. Charles Gould
felt sure of being understood with precision and judged
with the indulgence of their common passion. Nothing
now could surprise or startle this great man. And
Charles Gould imagined himself writing a letter to San
Francisco in some such words : " . . . The men at the
head of the movement are dead or have fled ; the civil
organisation of the province is at an end for the present ;
the Blanco party in Sulaco has collapsed inexcusably,
but in the characteristic manner of this country. But
Barrios, untouched in Cayta, remains still available. I
am forced to take up openly the plan of a provincial
revolution as the only way of placing the enormous
material interests involved in the prosperity and peace
of Sulaco in a position of permanent safety. . . ." That
was clear. He saw these words as if written in letters of
fire upon the wall at which he was gazing abstractedly.

Mrs. Gould watched his abstraction with dread. It
was a domestic and frightful phenomenon that darkened
and chilled the house for her like a thunder-cloud passing over the sun. Charles Gould's fits of abstraction
depicted the energetic concentration of a will haunted by
a fixed idea. A man haunted by a fixed idea is insane.
He is dangerous even if that idea is an idea of justice ;
for may he not bring the heaven down pitilessly upon
a loved head ? The eyes of Mrs. Gould, watching her
husband's profile, filled with tears again. And again she
seemed to see the despair of the unfortunate Antonia.

" What would I have done if Charley had been
drowned while we were engaged ? " she exclaimed
mentally, with horror. Her heart turned to ice, while
her cheeks flamed up as if scorched by the blaze of a
funeral pyre consuming all her earthly affections. The
tears burst out of her eyes.

" Antonia will kill herself ! " she cried out.

This cry fell into the silence of the room with strangely little effect. Only the doctor, crumbling up a piece of bread, with his head inclined on one side, raised his face, and the few long hairs sticking out of his shaggy eyebrows stirred in a slight frown. Dr. Monygham thought quite sincerely that Decoud was a singularly unworthy object for any woman's affection. Then he lowered his head again, with a curl of his lip and his heart full of tender admiration for Mrs. Gould.

" She thinks of that girl," he said to himself ; " she thinks of the Viola children ; she thinks of me ; of the wounded ; of the miners ; she always thinks of everybody who is poor and miserable ! But what will she do if Charles gets the worst of it in this infernal scrimmage those confounded Avellanos have drawn him into ? No one seems to be thinking of her."

Charles Gould, staring at the wall, pursued his reflections subtly.

" I shall write to Holroyd that the San Tomé mine is big enough to take in hand the making of a new State. It'll please him. It'll reconcile him to the risk."

But was Barrios really available ? Perhaps. But he was inaccessible. To send off a boat to Cayta was no longer possible, since Sotillo was master of the harbour, and had a steamer at his disposal. And now, with all the democrats in the province up, and every Campo township in a state of disturbance, where could he find a man who would make his way successfully overland to Cayta with a message, a ten days' ride at least—a man of courage and resolution, who would avoid arrest or murder, and if arrested would faithfully eat the paper ? The Capataz de Cargadores would have been just such a man. But the Capataz of the Cargadores was no more.

And Charles Gould, withdrawing his eyes from the wall, said gently, " That Hirsch ! What an extraordinary thing ! Saved himself by clinging to the anchor, did he ?

I had no idea that he was still in Sulaco. I thought
he had gone back overland to Esmeralda more than a
week ago. He came here once to talk to me about his
hide business and some other things. I made it clear
to him that nothing could be done."

"He was afraid to start back on account of Hernandez
being about," remarked the doctor.

"And but for him we might not have known anything of what has happened," marvelled Charles
Gould.

Mrs. Gould cried out :

"Antonia must not know ! She must not be told.
Not now."

"Nobody's likely to carry the news," remarked the
doctor. "It's no one's interest. Moreover, the people
here are afraid of Hernandez as if he were the devil."
He turned to Charles Gould. "It's even awkward, because if you wanted to communicate with the refugees
you could find no messenger. When Hernandez was
ranging hundreds of miles away from here, the Sulaco
populace used to shudder at the tales of him roasting
his prisoners alive."

"Yes," murmured Charles Gould ; "Captain Mitchell's Capataz was the only man in the town who
had seen Hernandez eye to eye. Father Corbelàn
employed him. He opened the communications first.
It is a pity that——"

His voice was covered by the booming of the great
bell of the cathedral. Three single strokes, one after
another, burst out explosively, dying away in deep and
mellow vibrations. And then all the bells in the tower
of every church, convent, or chapel in town, even those
that had remained shut up for years, pealed out together
with a crash. In this furious flood of metallic uproar
there was a power of suggesting images of strife and
violence which blanched Mrs. Gould's cheek. Basilio,
who had been waiting at table, shrinking within himself,

clung to the sideboard with chattering teeth. It was impossible to hear yourself speak.

" Shut these windows ! " Charles Gould yelled at him angrily. All the other servants, terrified at what they took for the signal of a general massacre, had rushed upstairs, tumbling over each other, men and women, the obscure and generally invisible population of the ground floor on the four sides of the patio. The women, screaming " Misericordia ! " ran right into the room, and, falling on their knees against the walls, began to cross themselves convulsively. The staring heads of men blocked the doorway in an instant—mozos from the stable, gardeners, nondescript helpers living on the crumbs of the munificent house—and Charles Gould beheld all the extent of his domestic establishment, even to the gatekeeper. This was a half-paralysed old man, whose long white locks fell down to his shoulders : an heirloom taken up by Charles Gould's familial piety. He could remember Henry Gould, an Englishman and a Costaguanero of the second generation, chief of the Sulaco province ; he had been his personal mozo years and years ago in peace and war ; had been allowed to attend his master in prison ; had, on the fatal morning, followed the firing squad ; and, peeping from behind one of the cypresses growing along the wall of the Franciscan Convent, had seen, with his eyes starting out of his head, Don Enrique throw up his hands and fall with his face in the dust. Charles Gould noted particularly the big patriarchal head of that witness in the rear of the other servants. But he was surprised to see a shrivelled old hag or two, of whose existence within the walls of his house he had not been aware. They must have been the mothers, or even the grandmothers, of some of his people. There were a few children, too, more or less naked, crying and clinging to the legs of their elders. He had never before noticed any sign of a child in his patio. Even Leonarda, the camerista, came in a fright, pushing through, with her spoiled, pouting face of a favourite maid, leading the Viola girls by the hand. The crockery rattled on table and sideboard, and the whole house seemed to sway in the deafening wave of sound.

CHAPTER FIVE

DURING the night the expectant populace had taken possession of all the belfries in the town in order to welcome Pedrito Montero, who was making his entry after having slept the night in Rincon. And first came straggling in through the land gate the armed mob of all colours, complexions, types, and states of raggedness, calling themselves the Sulaco National Guard, and commanded by Señor Gamacho. Through the middle of the street streamed, like a torrent of rubbish, a mass of straw hats, ponchos, gun-barrels, with an enormous green-and-yellow flag flapping in their midst, in a cloud of dust, to the furious beating of drums. The spectators recoiled against the walls of the houses shouting their *vivas*. Behind the rabble could be seen the lances of the cavalry, the " army " of Pedrito Montero. He advanced between Señores Fuentes and Gamacho at the head of his llaneros, who had accomplished the feat of crossing the paramos of the Higuerota in a snowstorm. They rode four abreast, mounted on confiscated Campo horses, clad in the heterogeneous stock of roadside stores they had looted hurriedly in their rapid ride through the northern part of the province ; for Pedrito Montero had been in a great hurry to occupy Sulaco. The handkerchiefs knotted loosely around their bare throats were glaringly new, and all the right sleeves of their cotton shirts had been cut off close to the shoulder for greater freedom in throwing the lazo. Emaciated greybeards rode by the side of lean, dark

youths, marked by all the hardships of campaigning,
with strips of raw beef twined round the crowns of their
hats, and huge iron spurs fastened to their naked heels.
Those that in the passes of the mountain had lost their
lances had provided themselves with the goads used by
the Campo cattlemen : slender shafts of palm fully ten
feet long, with a lot of loose rings jingling under the
ironshod point. They were armed with knives and
revolvers. A haggard fearlessness characterised the expression of all these sun-blacked countenances ; they
glared down haughtily with their scorched eyes at the
crowd, or, blinking upwards insolently, pointed out to
each other some particular head amongst the women
at the windows. When they had ridden into the plaza
and caught sight of the equestrian statue of the King
dazzlingly white in the sunshine, towering enormous and
motionless above the surges of the crowd, with its eternal
gesture of saluting, a murmur of surprise ran through
their ranks. " What is that saint in the big hat ? " they
asked each other.

     They were a good sample of the cavalry of the
plains with which Pedrito Montero had helped so much
the victorious career of his brother the general. The
influence which that man, brought up in coast towns,
acquired in a short time over the plainsmen of the
Republic can be ascribed only to a genius for treachery
of so effective a kind that it must have appeared to those
violent men but little removed from a state of utter
savagery, as the perfection of sagacity and virtue. The
popular lore of all nations testifies that duplicity and cunning, together with bodily strength, were looked upon,
even more than courage, as heroic virtues by primitive
mankind. To overcome your adversary was the great
affair of life. Courage was taken for granted. But the
use of intelligence awakened wonder and respect. Strata-
gems, providing they did not fail, were honourable ;
the easy massacre of an unsuspecting enemy evoked

no feelings but those of gladness, pride, and admiration. Not perhaps that primitive men were more faithless than their descendants of to-day, but that they went straighter to their aim, and were more artless in their recognition of success as the only standard of morality.

We have changed since. The use of intelligence awakens little wonder and less respect. But the ignorant and barbarous plainsmen engaging in civil strife followed willingly a leader who often managed to deliver their enemies bound, as it were, into their hands. Pedrito Montero had a talent for lulling his adversaries into a sense of security. And as men learn wisdom with extreme slowness, and are always ready to believe promises that flatter their secret hopes, Pedrito Montero was successful time after time. Whether only a servant or some inferior official in the Costaguana Legation in Paris, he had rushed back to his country directly he heard that his brother had emerged from the obscurity of his frontier commandancia. He had managed to deceive by his gift of plausibility the chiefs of the Ribierist movement in the capital, and even the acute agent of the San Tomé mine had failed to understand him thoroughly. At once he had obtained an enormous influence over his brother. They were very much alike in appearance, both bald, with bunches of crisp hair above their ears, arguing the presence of some negro blood. Only Pedrito was smaller than the general, more delicate altogether, with an ape-like faculty for imitating all the outward signs of refinement and distinction, and with a parrot-like talent for languages. Both brothers had received some elementary instruction by the munificence of a great European traveller, to whom their father had been a body-servant during his journeys in the interior of the country. In General Montero's case it enabled him to rise from the ranks. Pedrito, the younger, incorrigibly lazy and slovenly, had drifted aimlessly from one coast town to another, hanging about counting-houses, attaching himself to strangers as a sort of *valet de place*, picking up an easy and disreputable living. His ability to read did nothing for him¡but fill his head with absurd visions. His actions were usually determined by motives so improbable in themselves as to escape the penetration of a rational person.

Thus at first sight the agent of the Gould Concession in Sta. Marta had credited him with the possession of sane views, and even with a restraining power over the general's everlastingly discontented vanity. It could never have entered his head that Pedrito Montero, lackey or inferior scribe, lodged in the garrets of the various Parisian hotels where the Costaguana Legation used to shelter its diplomatic dignity, had been devouring the lighter sort of historical works in the French language, such, for instance, as the books of Imbert de Saint Amand upon the Second Empire. But Pedrito had been struck by the splendour of a brilliant court, and had conceived the idea of an existence for himself where, like the Duc de Morny, he would associate the command of every pleasure with the conduct of political affairs and enjoy power supremely in every way. Nobody could have guessed that. And yet this was one of the immediate causes of the Monterist Revolution. This will appear less incredible by the reflection that the fundamental causes were the same as ever, rooted in the political immaturity of the people, in the indolence of the upper classes and the mental darkness of the lower.

Pedrito Montero saw in the elevation of his brother the road wide open to his wildest imaginings. This was what made the Monterist pronunciamiento so unpreventable. The general himself probably could have been bought off, pacified with flatteries, dispatched on a diplomatic mission to Europe. It was his brother who had egged him on from first to last. He wanted to become the most brilliant statesman of South America. He did not desire supreme power. He would have been

afraid of its labour and risk, in fact. Before all, Pedrito
Montero, taught by his European experience, meant to
acquire a serious fortune for himself. With this object in
view he obtained from his brother, on the very morrow of
the successful battle, the permission to push on over the
mountains and take possession of Sulaco. Sulaco was the
land of future prosperity, the chosen land of material
progress, the only province in the Republic of interest
to European capitalists. Pedrito Montero, following the
example of the Duc de Morny, meant to have his share of
this prosperity. This is what he meant literally. Now
his brother was master of the country, whether as President, Dictator, or even as Emperor—why not as an
Emperor ?—he meant to demand a share in every enterprise—in railways, in mines, in sugar estates, in cotton
mills, in land companies, in each and every undertaking—
as the price of his protection. The desire to be on the
spot early was the real cause of the celebrated ride over
the mountains with some two hundred llaneros, an enterprise of which the dangers had not appeared at first
clearly to his impatience. Coming from a series of victories, it seemed to him that a Montero had only to appear
to be master of the situation. This illusion had betrayed
him into a rashness of which he was becoming aware.
As he rode at the head of his llaneros, he regretted that
there were so few of them. The enthusiasm of the populace reassured him. They yelled, " Viva Montero ! Viva
Pedrito ! " In order to make them still more enthusiastic,
and from the natural pleasure he had in dissembling, he
dropped the reins on his horse's neck, and with a tremendous effect of familiarity and confidence slipped his
hands under the arms of Señores Fuentes and Gamacho.
In that posture, with a ragged town mozo holding his
horse by the bridle, he rode triumphantly across the
plaza to the door of the Intendencia. Its old, gloomy
walls seemed to shake in the acclamations that rent the
air and covered the crashing peals of the cathedral bells.

Pedrito Montero, the brother of the general, dismounted into a shouting and perspiring throng of enthusiasts, whom the ragged Nationals were pushing back fiercely. Ascending a few steps, he surveyed the large crowd gaping at him, and the bullet-speckled walls of the houses opposite lightly veiled by a sunny haze of dust. The word *PORVENIR* in immense black capitals, alternating with broken windows, stared at him across the vast space; and he thought with delight of the hour of vengeance, because he was very sure of laying his hands upon Decoud. On his left hand, Gamacho, big and hot, wiping his hairy wet face, uncovered a set of yellow fangs in a grin of stupid hilarity. On his right Señor Fuentes, small and lean, looked on with compressed lips. The crowd stared literally open-mouthed, lost in eager stillness, as though they had expected the great guerrillero, the famous Pedrito, to begin scattering at once some sort of visible largesse. What he began was a speech. He began it with the shouted word " Citizens ! " which reached even those in the middle of the plaza. Afterwards the greater part of the citizens remained fascinated by the orator's action alone—his tiptoeing, the arms flung above his head with the fists clenched, a hand laid flat upon the heart, the silver gleam of rolling eyes, the sweeping, pointing, embracing gestures, a hand laid familiarly on Gamacho's shoulder; a hand waved formally towards the little, black-coated person of Señor Fuentes, advocate and politician and a true friend of the people. The *vivas* of those nearest to the orator bursting out suddenly propagated themselves irregularly to the confines of the crowd, like flames running over dry grass, and expired in the opening of the streets. In the intervals, over the swarming plaza brooded a heavy silence, in which the mouth of the orator went on opening and shutting, and detached phrases—" The happiness of the people," " Sons of the country," " The entire world, *el mundo entiero* "—reached even the packed steps of the cathedral with a feeble, clear ring, thin as the buzzing of a mosquito. But the orator struck his breast ; he seemed to prance between his two supporters. It was a supreme effort of his peroration. Then the two smaller figures disappeared from the public gaze, and the enormous Gamacho, left alone, advanced, raising his hat high above his head. Then he covered himself proudly, and yelled out, " Ciudadanos ! " A dull roar greeted Señor Gamacho, ex-pedlar of the Campo, Commandante of the National Guards.

Upstairs Pedrito Montero walked about rapidly from one wrecked room of the Intendencia to another, snarling incessantly :

" What stupidity ! What destruction ! "

Señor Fuentes, following, would relax his taciturn disposition to murmur :

" It is all the work of Gamacho and his Nationals " ; and then, inclining his head on his left shoulder, would press together his lips so firmly that a little hollow would appear at each corner. He had his nomination for Political Chief of the town in his pocket, and was all impatience to enter upon his functions.

In the long audience-room, with its tall mirrors all starred by stones, the hangings torn down and the canopy over the platform at the upper end pulled to pieces, the vast, deep muttering of the crowd and the howling voice of Gamacho speaking just below reached them through the shutters as they stood idly in dimness and desolation.

" The brute ! " observed His Excellency Don Pedrito Montero through clenched teeth. " We must contrive as quickly as possible to send him and his Nationals out there to fight Hernandez."

The new Géfé Politico only jerked his head sideways, and took a puff at his cigarette in sign of his agreement with this method of ridding the town of Gamacho and his inconvenient rabble.

Pedrito Montero looked with disgust at the abso-

lutely bare floor, and at the belt of heavy gilt picture-
frames running round the room, out of which the
remnants of torn and slashed canvases fluttered like
dingy rags.

" We are not barbarians," he said.

This was what said His Excellency, the popular Pedrito,
the guerrillero skilled in the art of laying ambushes,
charged by his brother at his own demand with the
organisation of Sulaco on democratic principles. The
night before, during the consultation with his partisans,
who had come out to meet him in Rincon, he had opened
his intentions to Señor Fuentes :

" We shall organise a popular vote, by yes or no, confiding the destinies of our beloved country to the wisdom
and valiance of my heroic brother, the invincible general.
A plebiscite. Do you understand ? "

And Señor Fuentes, puffing out his leathery cheeks,
had inclined his head slightly to the left, letting a thin,
bluish jet of smoke escape through his pursed lips. He
had understood.

His Excellency was exasperated at the devastation.
Not a single chair, table, sofa, *étagère*, or console had been
left in the state-rooms of the Intendencia. His Excellency, though twitching all over with rage, was restrained
from bursting into violence by a sense of his remoteness
and isolation. His heroic brother was very far away.
Meantime, how was he going to take his siesta ? He had
expected to find comfort and luxury in the Intendencia
after a year of hard camp life, ending with the hardships
and privations of the daring dash upon Sulaco—upon the
province which was worth more in wealth and influence
than all the rest of the Republic's territory. He would
get even with Gamacho by and by. And Señor Gamacho's oration, delectable to popular ears, went on in the
heat and glare of the plaza like the uncouth howlings of an
inferior sort of devil cast into a white-hot furnace. Every
moment he had to wipe his streaming face with his bare

forearm ; he had flung off his coat, and had turned up the sleeves of his shirt high above the elbows ; but he kept on his head the large cocked hat with white plumes. His ingenuousness cherished this sign of his rank as Commandante of the National Guards. Approving and grave murmurs greeted his periods. His opinion was that war should be declared at once against France, England, Germany, and the United States, who, by introducing railways, mining enterprises, colonisation, and under such other shallow pretences, aimed at robbing poor people of their lands, and, with the help of these Goths and paralytics, the aristocrats would convert them into toiling and miserable slaves. And the leperos, flinging about the corners of their dirty white mantas, yelled their approbation. General Montero, Gamacho howled with conviction, was the only man equal to the patriotic task. They assented to that too.

The morning was wearing on ; there were already signs of disruption, currents, and eddies in the crowd. Some were seeking the shade of the walls and under the trees of the Alameda. Horsemen spurred through shouting ; groups of sombreros set level on heads against the vertical sun were drifting away into the streets, where the open doors of pulperias revealed an enticing gloom resounding with the gentle tinkling of guitars. The National Guards were thinking of siesta, and the eloquence of Gamacho, their chief, was exhausted. Later on, when, in the cooler hours of the afternoon, they tried to assemble again for further consideration of public affairs, detachments of Montero's cavalry camped on the Alameda charged them without parley, at speed, with long lances levelled at their flying backs as far as the ends of the streets. The National Guards of Sulaco were surprised by this proceeding. But they were not indignant. No Costaguanero had ever learned to question the eccentricities of a military force. They were part of the natural order of things. This

24

must be, they concluded, some kind of administrative measure, no doubt. But the motive of it escaped their unaided intelligence, and their chief and orator, Gamacho, Commandante of the National Guard, was lying drunk and asleep in the bosom of his family. His bare feet were upturned in the shadows repulsively, in the manner of a corpse. His eloquent mouth had dropped open. His youngest daughter, scratching her head with one hand, with the other waved a green bough over his scorched and peeling face.

CHAPTER SIX

THE declining sun had shifted the shadows from west to east amongst the houses of the town. It had shifted them upon the whole extent of the immense Campo, with the white walls of its haciendas on the knolls dominating the green distances; with its grass-thatched ranchos crouching in the folds of ground by the banks of streams; with the dark islands of clustered trees on a clear sea of grass, and the precipitous range of the Cordillera, immense and motionless, emerging from the billows of the lower forests like the barren coast of a land of giants. The sunset rays striking the snow-slope of Higuerota from afar gave it an air of rosy youth, while the serrated mass of distant peaks remained black, as if calcined in the fiery radiance. The undulating surface of the forests seemed powdered with pale gold dust; and away there, beyond Rincon, hidden from the town by two wooded spurs, the rocks of the San Tomé gorge, with the flat wall of the mountain itself crowned by gigantic ferns, took on warm tones of brown and yellow, with red rusty streaks, and the dark green clumps of bushes rooted in crevices. From the plain the stamp sheds and the houses of the mine appeared dark and small, high up, like the nests of birds clustered on the ledges of a cliff. The zigzag paths resembled faint tracings scratched on the wall of a cyclopean block-house. To the two serenos of the mine on patrol duty, strolling, carbine in hand and watchful eyes, in the shade of the trees lining the stream near the

bridge, Don Pépé, descending the path from the upper
plateau, appeared no bigger than a large beetle.

With his air of aimless, insect-like going to and fro
upon the face of the rock, Don Pépé's figure kept on
descending steadily, and, when near the bottom, sank
at last behind the roofs of storehouses, forges, and
workshops. For a time the pair of serenos strolled
back and forth before the bridge, on which they had
stopped a horseman holding a large white envelope in his
hand. Then Don Pépé, emerging in the village street
from amongst the houses, not a stone's-throw from
the frontier bridge, approached, striding in wide, dark
trousers tucked into boots, a white linen jacket, sabre
at his side, and revolver at his belt. In this disturbed
time nothing could find the Señor Gobernador with his
boots off, as the saying is.

At a slight nod from one of the serenos, the man, a
messenger from the town, dismounted, and crossed the
bridge, leading his horse by the bridle.

Don Pépé received the letter from his other hand,
slapped his left side and his hips in succession, feeling
for his spectacle case. After settling the heavy silver-
mounted affair astride his nose, and adjusting it carefully
behind his ears, he opened the envelope, holding it up
at about a foot in front of his eyes. The paper he pulled
out contained some three lines of writing. He looked
at them for a long time. His grey moustache moved
slightly up and down, and the wrinkles, radiating at the
corners of his eyes, ran together. He nodded serenely.
" Bueno ! " he said. " There is no answer."

Then, in his quiet, kindly way, he engaged a cautious
conversation with the man, who was willing to talk
cheerily, as if something lucky had happened to him
recently. He had seen from a distance Sotillo's infantry
camped along the shore of the harbour on each side of
the Custom House. They had done no damage to the
buildings. The foreigners of the railway remained shut

up within the yards. They were no longer anxious
to shoot poor people. He cursed the foreigners ; then
he reported Montero's entry and the rumours of the
town. The poor were going to be made rich now. That
was very good. More he did not know, and, breaking
into propitiatory smiles, he intimated that he was hungry
and thirsty. The old major directed him to go to the
alcalde of the first village. The man rode off, and Don
Pépé, striding slowly in the direction of a little wooden
belfry, looked over a hedge into a little garden, and saw
Father Romàn sitting in a white hammock slung between
two orange trees in front of the Presbytery.

An enormous tamarind shaded with its dark foliage
the whole white frame-house. A young Indian girl
with long hair, big eyes, and small hands and feet
carried out a wooden chair, while a thin old woman,
crabbed and vigilant, watched her all the time from the
verandah. Don Pépé sat down in the chair and lighted
a cigar ; the priest drew in an immense quantity of
snuff out of the hollow of his palm. On his reddish-
brown face, worn, hollowed as if crumbled, the eyes,
fresh and candid, sparkled like two black diamonds.

Don Pépé, in a mild and humorous voice, informed
Father Romàn that Pedrito Montero, by the hand of
Señor Fuentes, had asked him on what terms he would
surrender the mine in proper working order to a legally
constituted commission of patriotic citizens, escorted by
a small military force. The priest cast his eyes up to
heaven. However, Don Pépé continued, the mozo who
brought the letter said that Don Carlos Gould was alive,
and so far unmolested.

Father Romàn expressed in a few words his thankfulness at hearing of the Señor Administrador's safety.

The hour of oration had gone by in the silvery
ringing of a bell in the little belfry. The belt of forest
closing the entrance of the valley stood like a screen
between the low sun and the street of the village. At the

other end of the rocky gorge, between the walls of basalt
and granite, a forest-clad mountain, hiding all the range
from the San Tomé dwellers, rose steeply, lighted up
and leafy to the very top. Three small rosy clouds
hung motionless overhead in the great depth of blue.
Knots of people sat in the street between the wattled
huts. Before the casa of the alcalde, the foremen of the
night-shift, already assembled to lead their men, squatted
on the ground in a circle of leather skull-caps, and,
bowing their bronze backs, were passing round the
gourd of maté. The mozo from the town, having
fastened his horse to a wooden post before the door,
was telling them the news of Sulaco as the blackened
gourd of the decoction passed from hand to hand.
The grave alcalde himself, in a white waistcloth and a
flowered chintz gown with sleeves, open wide upon his
naked stout person with an effect of a gaudy bathing
robe, stood by, wearing a rough beaver hat at the back
of his head, and grasping a tall staff with a silver knob
in his hand. These insignia of his dignity had been
conferred upon him by the Administration of the mine,
the fountain of honour, of prosperity, and peace. He
had been one of the first immigrants into this valley;
his sons and sons-in-law worked within the mountain,
which seemed with its treasures to pour down the thundering ore shoots of the upper mesa the gifts of well-being,
security, and justice upon the toilers. He listened to the
news from the town with curiosity and indifference, as
if concerning another world than his own. And it was
true that they appeared to him so. In a very few years
the sense of belonging to a powerful organisation had
been developed in these harassed, half-wild Indians.
They were proud of, and attached to, the mine. It had
secured their confidence and belief. They invested it
with a protecting and invincible virtue as though it were
a fetish made by their own hands, for they were ignorant,
and in other respects did not differ appreciably from the

rest of mankind which puts infinite trust in its own creations. It never entered the alcalde's head that the mine could fail in its protection and force. Politics were good enough for the people of the town and the Campo. His yellow, round face, with wide nostrils, and motionless in expression, resembled a fierce full moon. He listened to the excited vapourings of the mozo without misgivings, without surprise, without any active sentiment whatever.

Padre Romàn sat dejectedly balancing himself, his feet just touching the ground, his hands gripping the edge of the hammock. With less confidence, but as ignorant as his flock, he asked the major what did he think was going to happen now.

Don Pépé, bolt upright in the chair, folded his hands peacefully on the hilt of his sword, standing perpendicular between his thighs, and answered that he did not know. The mine could be defended against any force likely to be sent to take possession. On the other hand, from the arid character of the valley, when the regular supplies from the Campo had been cut off, the population of the three villages could be starved into submission. Don Pépé exposed these contingencies with serenity to Father Romàn, who, as an old campaigner, was able to understand the reasoning of a military man. They talked with simplicity and directness. Father Romàn was saddened at the idea of his flock being scattered or else enslaved. He had no illusions as to their fate, not from penetration, but from long experience of political atrocities, which seemed to him fatal and un-avoidable in the life of a State. The working of the usual public institutions presented itself to him most distinctly as a series of calamities overtaking private in-dividuals and flowing logically from each other through hate, revenge, folly, and rapacity, as though they had been part of a divine dispensation. Father Romàn's clear-sightedness was served by an uninformed intelligence ; but his heart, preserving its tenderness amongst scenes of carnage, spoliation, and violence, abhorred these calamities the more as his association with the victims was closer. He entertained towards the Indians of the valley feelings of paternal scorn. He had been marrying, baptizing, confessing, absolving, and burying the workers of the San Tomé mine with dignity and unction for five years or more ; and he believed in the sacredness of these ministrations, which made them his own in a spiritual sense. They were dear to his sacerdotal supremacy. Mrs. Gould's earnest interest in the concerns of these people enhanced their import-ance in the priest's eyes, because it really augmented his own. When talking over with her the innumer-able Marias and Brigidas of the villages, he felt his own humanity expand. Padre Romàn was incapable of fanaticism to an almost reprehensible degree. The English Señora was evidently a heretic ; but at the same time she seemed to him wonderful and angelic. When-ever that confused state of his feelings occurred to him,—while strolling, for instance, his breviary under his arm, in the wide shade of the tamarind,—he would stop short to inhale with a strong snuffling noise a large quantity of snuff, and shake his head profoundly. At the thought of what might befall the illustrious Señora presently, he became gradually overcome with dismay. He voiced it in an agitated murmur. Even Don Pépé lost his serenity for a moment. He leaned forward stiffly.

" Listen, Padre. The very fact that those thieving macaques in Sulaco are trying to find out the price of my honour proves that Señor Don Carlos and all in the Casa Gould are safe. As to my honour, that also is safe, as every man, woman, and child knows. But the negro Liberals who have snatched the town by surprise do not know that. Bueno ! Let them sit and wait. While they wait they can do no harm."

And he regained his composure. He regained it

easily, because whatever happened his honour of an old officer of Paez was safe. He had promised Charles Gould that at the approach of an armed force he would defend the gorge just long enough to give himself time to destroy scientifically the whole plant, buildings, and workshops of the mine with heavy charges of dynamite ; block with ruins the main tunnel, break down the pathways, blow up the dam of the water-power, shatter the famous Gould Concession into fragments, flying sky-high out of a horrified world. The mine had got hold of Charles Gould with a grip as deadly as ever it had laid upon his father. But this extreme resolution had seemed to Don Pépé the most natural thing in the world. His measures had been taken with judgment. Everything was prepared with a careful completeness. And Don Pépé folded his hands pacifically on his sword hilt, and nodded at the priest. In his excitement, Father Romàn had flung snuff in handfuls at his face, and, all besmeared with tobacco, round-eyed, and beside himself, had got out of the hammock to walk about, uttering exclamations.

Don Pépé stroked his grey and pendent moustache, whose fine ends hung far below the clean-cut line of his jaw, and spoke with a conscious pride in his reputation.

" So, Padre, I don't know what will happen. But I know that as long as I am here Don Carlos can speak to that macaque, Pedrito Montero, and threaten the destruction of the mine with perfect assurance that he will be taken seriously. For people know me."

He began to turn the cigar in his lips a little nervously, and went on :

" But that is talk—good for the politicos. I am a military man. I do not know what may happen. But I know what ought to be done—the mine should march upon the town with guns, axes, knives tied up to sticks— *por Dios*. That is what should be done. Only——"

His folded hands twitched on the hilt. The cigar turned faster in the corner of his lips.

" And who should lead but I ? Unfortunately—observe—I have given my word of honour to Don Carlos not to let the mine fall into the hands of these thieves. In war—you know this, Padre—the fate of battles is uncertain, and whom could I leave here to act for me in case of defeat ? The explosives are ready. But it would require a man of high honour, of intelligence, of judgment, of courage, to carry out the prepared destruction. Somebody I can trust with my honour as I can trust myself. Another old officer of Paez, for instance. Or—or—perhaps one of Paez's old chaplains would do."

He got up, long, lank, upright, hard, with his martial moustache and the bony structure of his face, from which the glance of the sunken eyes seemed to transfix the priest, who stood still, an empty wooden snuff-box held upside down in his hand, and glared back, speechlessly, at the governor of the mine.

CHAPTER SEVEN

AT about that time, in the Intendencia of Sulaco, Charles Gould was assuring Pedrito Montero, who had sent a request for his presence there, that he would never let the mine pass out of his hands for the profit of a Government who had robbed him of it. The Gould Concession could not be resumed. His father had not desired it. The son would never surrender it. He would never surrender it alive. And once dead, where was the power capable of resuscitating such an enterprise in all its vigour and wealth out of the ashes and ruin of destruction? There was no such power in the country. And where was the skill and capital abroad that would condescend to touch such an ill-omened corpse? Charles Gould talked in the impassive tone which had for many years served to conceal his anger and contempt. He suffered. He was disgusted with what he had to say. It was too much like heroics. In him the strictly practical instinct was in profound discord with the almost mystic view he took of his right. The Gould Concession was symbolic of abstract justice. Let the heavens fall. But since the San Tomé mine had developed into world-wide fame, his threat had enough force and effectiveness to reach the rudimentary intelligence of Pedrito Montero, wrapped up as it was in the futilities of historical anecdotes. The Gould Concession was a serious asset in the country's finance, and, what was more, in the private budgets of many officials as well. It was traditional. It was known. It was said. It was credible. Every

379

Minister of Interior drew a salary from the San Tomé
mine. It was natural. And Pedrito intended to be
Minister of the Interior and President of the Council
in his brother's Government. The Duc de Morny had
occupied those high posts during the Second French
Empire with conspicuous advantage to himself.

A table, a chair, a wooden bedstead had been
procured for His Excellency, who, after a short siesta,
rendered absolutely necessary by the labours and the
pomps of his entry into Sulaco, had been getting hold
of the administrative machine by making appointments,
giving orders, and signing proclamations. Alone with
Charles Gould in the audience-room, His Excellency
managed with his well-known skill to conceal his annoy-
ance and consternation. He had begun at first to talk
loftily of confiscation, but the want of all proper feeling
and mobility in the Señor Administrador's features ended
by affecting adversely his power of masterful expression.
Charles Gould had repeated : " The Government can
certainly bring about the destruction of the San Tomé
mine if it likes ; but without me it can do nothing else."
It was an alarming pronouncement, and well calculated to
hurt the sensibilities of a politician whose mind is bent
upon the spoils of victory. And Charles Gould said
also that the destruction of the San Tomé mine would
cause the ruin of other undertakings, the withdrawal of
European capital, the withholding, most probably, of the
last instalment of the foreign loan. That stony fiend of
a man said all these things (which were accessible to
His Excellency's intelligence) in a cold-blooded manner
which made one shudder.

A long course of reading historical works, light and
gossipy in tone, carried out in garrets of Parisian hotels,
sprawling on an untidy bed, to the neglect of his duties
menial or otherwise, had affected the manners of Pedrito
Montero. Had he seen around him the splendour of the
old Intendencia, the magnificent hangings, the gilt furni-

ture ranged along the walls ; had he stood upon a dais
on a noble square of red carpet, he probably would have
been very dangerous from a sense of success and elevation.
But in this sacked and devastated residence, with the three
pieces of common furniture huddled up in the middle of
the vast apartment, Pedrito's imagination was subdued
by a feeling of insecurity and impermanence.   That feeling, and the firm attitude of Charles Gould, who had
not once, so far, pronounced the word " Excellency,"
diminished him in his own eyes.   He assumed the tone
of an enlightened man of the world, and begged Charles
Gould to dismiss from his mind every cause for alarm.
He was now conversing, he reminded him, with the
brother of the master of the country, charged with a
reorganising mission.   The trusted brother of the master
of the country, he repeated.   Nothing was further from
the thoughts of that wise and patriotic hero than ideas
of destruction.   " I entreat you, Don Carlos, not to give
way to your anti-democratic prejudices," he cried, in a
burst of condescending effusion.

Pedrito Montero surprised one at first sight by the
vast development of his bald forehead, a shiny, yellow
expanse between the crinkly coal-black tufts of hair
without any lustre, the engaging form of his mouth,
and an unexpectedly cultivated voice.   But his eyes, very
glistening as if freshly painted on each side of his hooked
nose, had a round, hopeless, birdlike stare when opened
fully.   Now, however, he narrowed them agreeably,
throwing his square chin up and speaking with closed
teeth slightly through the nose, with what he imagined
to be the manner of a grand seigneur.

In that attitude, he declared suddenly that the highest
expression of democracy was Cæsarism : the imperial
rule based upon the direct popular vote.   Cæsarism was
conservative.   It was strong.   It recognised the legitimate needs of democracy which requires orders, titles,
and   distinctions.   They   would   be   showered   upon

deserving men. Cæsarism was peace. It was progressive. It secured the prosperity of a country. Pedrito
Montero was carried away. Look at what the Second
Empire had done for France. It was a regime which
delighted to honour men of Don Carlos's stamp. The
Second Empire fell, but that was because its chief was
devoid of that military genius which had raised General
Montero to the pinnacle of fame and glory. Pedrito
elevated his hand jerkily to help the idea of pinnacle
of fame. "We shall have many talks yet. We shall
understand each other thoroughly, Don Carlos!" he
cried in a tone of fellowship. Republicanism had done
its work. Imperial democracy was the power of the
future. Pedrito, the guerrillero, showing his hand,
lowered his voice forcibly. A man singled out by his
fellow-citizens for the honourable nickname of El Rey de
Sulaco could not but receive a full recognition from an
imperial democracy as a great captain of industry and a
person of weighty counsel, whose popular designation
would be soon replaced by a more solid title. "Eh, Don
Carlos? No! What do you say? Conde de Sulaco—
eh?—or marquis . . ."

He ceased. The air was cool on the plaza, where a
patrol of cavalry rode round and round without penetrating into the streets, which resounded with shouts and
the strumming of guitars issuing from the open doors of
pulperias. The orders were not to interfere with the
enjoyments of the people. And above the roofs, next
to the perpendicular lines of the cathedral towers, the
snowy curve of Higuerota blocked a large space of dark-
ening blue sky before the windows of the Intendencia.
After a time Pedrito Montero, thrusting his hand in the
bosom of his coat, bowed his head with slow dignity.
The audience was over.

Charles Gould on going out passed his hand over his
forehead as if to disperse the mists of an oppressive dream,
whose grotesque extravagance leaves behind a subtle

sense of bodily danger and intellectual decay. In the passages and on the staircases of the old palace Montero's troopers lounged about insolently, smoking, and making way for no one ; the clanking of sabres and spurs resounded all over the building. Three silent groups of civilians in severe black awaited in the main gallery, formal and helpless, a little huddled up, each keeping apart from the others, as if in the exercise of a public duty they had been overcome by a desire to shun the notice of every eye. These were the deputations waiting for their audience. The one from the Provincial Assembly, more restless and uneasy in its corporate expression, was overtopped by the big face of Don Juste Lopez, soft and white, with prominent eyelids and wreathed in impenetrable solemnity as if in a dense cloud. The President of the Provincial Assembly, coming bravely to save the last shred of parliamentary institutions (on the English model), averted his eyes from the Administrador of the San Tomé mine as a dignified rebuke of his little faith in that only saving principle.

The mournful severity of that reproof did not affect Charles Gould, but he was sensible of the glances of the others directed upon him without reproach, as if only to read their own fate upon his face. All of them had talked, shouted, and declaimed in the great sala of the Casa Gould. The feeling of compassion for those men, struck with a strange impotence in the toils of moral degradation, did not induce him to make a sign. He suffered from his fellowship in evil with them too much. He crossed the plaza unmolested. The Amarilla Club was full of festive ragamuffins. Their frowzy heads protruded from every window, and from within came drunken shouts, the thumping of feet, and the twanging of harps. Broken bottles strewed the pavement below. Charles Gould found the doctor still in his house.

Dr. Monygham came away from the crack in the shutter through which he had been watching the street.

" Ah ! You are back at last ! " he said in a tone of relief. " I have been telling Mrs. Gould that you were perfectly safe, but I was not by any means certain that the fellow would have let you go."

" Neither was I," confessed Charles Gould, laying his hat on the table.

" You will have to take action."

The silence of Charles Gould seemed to admit that this was the only course. This was as far as Charles Gould was accustomed to go towards expressing his intentions.

" I hope you did not warn Montero of what you mean to do ? " the doctor said anxiously.

" I tried to make him see that the existence of the mine was bound up with my personal safety," continued Charles Gould, looking away from the doctor, and fixing his eyes upon the water-colour sketch upon the wall.

" He believed you ? " the doctor asked eagerly.

" God knows ! " said Charles Gould. " I owed it to my wife to say that much. He is well enough informed. He knows that I have Don Pépé there. Fuentes must have told him. They know that the old major is perfectly capable of blowing up the San Tomé mine without hesitation or compunction. Had it not been for that I don't think I'd have left the Intendencia a free man. He would blow everything up from loyalty and from hate —from hate of these Liberals, as they call themselves. Liberals ! The words one knows so well have a nightmarish meaning in this country. Liberty, democracy, patriotism, government—all of them have a flavour of folly and murder. Haven't they, doctor ? . . . I alone can restrain Don Pépé. If they were to—to do away with me, nothing could prevent him."

" They will try to tamper with him ? " the doctor suggested thoughtfully.

" It is very possible," Charles Gould said very low, as if speaking to himself, and still gazing at the sketch of the San Tomé gorge upon the wall. " Yes, I expect they will try that." Charles Gould looked for the first time at the doctor. " It would give me time," he added.

" Exactly," said Dr. Monygham, suppressing his excitement. " Especially if Don Pépé behaves diplomatically. Why shouldn't he give them some hope of success ? Eh ? Otherwise you wouldn't gain so much time. Couldn't he be instructed to——"

Charles Gould, looking at the doctor steadily, shook his head, but the doctor continued with a certain amount of fire :

" Yes, to enter into negotiations for the surrender of the mine. It is a good notion. You would mature your plan. Of course, I don't ask what it is. I don't want to know. I would refuse to listen to you if you tried to tell me. I am not fit for confidences."

" What nonsense ! " muttered Charles Gould, with displeasure.

He disapproved of the doctor's sensitiveness about that far-off episode of his life. So much memory shocked Charles Gould. It was like morbidness. And again he shook his head. He refused to tamper with the open rectitude of Don Pépé's conduct, both from taste and from policy. Instructions would have to be either verbal or in writing. In either case they ran the risk of being intercepted. It was by no means certain that a messenger could reach the mine ; and, besides, there was no one to send. It was on the tip of Charles's tongue to say that only the late Capataz de Cargadores could have been employed with some chance of success and the certitude of discretion. But he did not say that. He pointed out to the doctor that it would have been bad policy. Directly Don Pépé let it be supposed that he could be bought over, the Administrador's personal safety and the safety of his friends would become endangered. For there would be then no reason for moderation. The incorruptibility of Don Pépé was the essential and restraining

25

fact. The doctor hung his head and admitted that in a way it was so.

He couldn't deny to himself that the reasoning was sound enough. Don Pépé's usefulness consisted in his unstained character. As to his own usefulness, he reflected bitterly it was also in his own character. He declared to Charles Gould that he had the means of keeping Sotillo from joining his forces with Montero, at least for the present.

"If you had had all this silver here," the doctor said, "or even if it had been known to be at the mine, you could have bribed Sotillo to throw off his recent Monterism. You could have induced him either to go away in his steamer or even to join you."

"Certainly not that last," Charles Gould declared firmly. "What could one do with a man like that afterwards—tell me, doctor? The silver is gone, and I am glad of it. It would have been an immediate and strong temptation. The scramble for that visible plunder would have precipitated a disastrous ending. I would have had to defend it, too. I am glad we've removed it—even if it is lost. It would have been a danger and a curse."

"Perhaps he is right," the doctor, an hour later, said hurriedly to Mrs. Gould, whom he met in the *corrédor*. "The thing is done, and the shadow of the treasure may do just as well as the substance. Let me try to serve you to the whole extent of my evil reputation. I am off now to play my game of betrayal with Sotillo, and keep him off the town."

She put out both her hands impulsively. "Dr. Monygham, you are running a terrible risk," she whispered, averting from his face her eyes, full of tears, for a short glance at the door of her husband's room. She pressed both his hands, and the doctor stood as if rooted to the spot, looking down at her, and trying to twist his lips into a smile.

" Oh, I know you will defend my memory," he uttered at last, and ran tottering down the stairs across the patio, and out of the house. In the street he kept up a great pace with his smart, hobbling walk, a case of instruments under his arm. He was known for being *loco*. Nobody interfered with him. From under the seaward gate, across the dusty, arid plain, interspersed with low bushes, he saw, more than a mile away, the ugly enormity of the Custom House, and the two or three other buildings which at that time constituted the seaport of Sulaco. Far away to the south groves of palm trees edged the curve of the harbour shore. The distant peaks of the Cordillera had lost their identity of clear-cut shapes in the steadily deepening blue of the eastern sky. The doctor walked briskly. A darkling shadow seemed to fall upon him from the zenith. The sun had set. For a time the snows of Higuerota continued to glow with the reflected glory of the west. The doctor, holding a straight course for the Custom House, appeared lonely, hopping amongst the dark bushes like a tall bird with a broken wing.

Tints of purple, gold, and crimson were mirrored in the clear water of the harbour. A long tongue of land, straight as a wall, with the grass-grown ruins of the fort making a sort of rounded green mound, plainly visible from the inner shore, closed its circuit ; while beyond the Placid Gulf repeated those splendours of colouring on a greater scale and with a more sombre magnificence. The great mass of cloud filling the head of the gulf had long red smears amongst its convoluted folds of grey and black, as of a floating mantle stained with blood. The Three Isabels, overshadowed and clear cut in a great smoothness confounding the sea and sky, appeared suspended, purple-black, in the air. The little wave-lets seemed to be tossing tiny red sparks upon the sandy beaches. The glassy bands of water along the horizon gave out a fiery red glow, as if fire and

water had been mingled together in the vast bed of
the ocean.

At last the conflagration of sea and sky, lying embraced and still in a flaming contact upon the edge of the
world, went out. The red sparks in the water vanished
together with the stains of blood in the black mantle
draping the sombre head of the Placid Gulf ; a sudden
breeze sprang up and died out after rustling heavily the
growth of bushes on the ruined earthwork of the fort.
Nostromo woke up from a fourteen hours' sleep, and
arose full length from his lair in the long grass. He stood
knee-deep amongst the whispering undulations of the
green blades with the lost air of a man just born into
the world. Handsome, robust, and supple, he threw back
his head, flung his arms open, and stretched himself
with a slow twist of the waist and a leisurely growling
yawn of white teeth, as natural and free from evil in
the moment of waking as a magnificent and unconscious
wild beast. Then, in the suddenly steadied glance fixed
upon nothing from under a thoughtful frown, appeared
the man.

CHAPTER EIGHT

AFTER landing from his swim Nostromo had scrambled up, all dripping, into the main quadrangle of the old fort ; and there, amongst ruined bits of walls and rotting remnants of roofs and sheds, he had slept the day through. He had slept in the shadow of the mountains, in the white blaze of noon, in the stillness and solitude of that overgrown piece of land between the oval of the harbour and the spacious semicircle of the gulf. He lay as if dead. A rey-zamuro, appearing like a tiny black speck in the blue, stooped, circling prudently with a stealthiness of flight startling in a bird of that great size. The shadow of his pearly-white body, of his black-tipped wings, fell on the grass no more silently than he alighted himself on a hillock of rubbish within three yards of that man, lying as still as a corpse. The bird stretched his bare neck, craned his bald head, loathsome in the brilliance of varied colouring, with an air of voracious anxiety towards the promising stillness of that prostrate body. Then, sinking his head deeply into his soft plumage, he settled himself to wait. The first thing upon which Nostromo's eyes fell on waking was this patient watcher for the signs of death and corruption. When the man got up the vulture hopped away in great, sidelong, fluttering jumps. He lingered for a while, morose and reluctant, before he rose, circling noiselessly with a sinister droop of beak and claws.

Long after he had vanished, Nostromo, lifting

his eyes up to the sky, muttered, "I am not dead yet."

The Capataz of the Sulaco Cargadores had lived in splendour and publicity up to the very moment, as it were, when he took charge of the lighter containing the treasure of silver ingots.

The last act he had performed in Sulaco was in complete harmony with his vanity, and as such perfectly genuine. He had given his last dollar to an old woman moaning with the grief and fatigue of a dismal search under the arch of the ancient gate. Performed in obscurity and without witnesses, it had still the characteristics of splendour and publicity, and was in strict keeping with his reputation. But this awakening in solitude, except for the watchful vulture, amongst the ruins of the fort, had no such characteristics. His first confused feeling was exactly this—that it was not in keeping. It was more like the end of things. The necessity of living concealed somehow, for God knows how long, which assailed him on his return to consciousness, made everything that had gone before for years appear vain and foolish, like a flattering dream come suddenly to an end.

He climbed the crumbling slope of the rampart, and, putting aside the bushes, looked upon the harbour. He saw a couple of ships at anchor upon the sheet of water reflecting the last gleams of light, and Sotillo's steamer moored to the jetty. And behind the pale, long front of the Custom House, there appeared the extent of the town like a grove of thick timber on the plain with a gateway in front, and the cupolas, towers, and miradors rising above the trees, all dark, as if surrendered already to the night. The thought that it was no longer open to him to ride through the streets, recognised by every one, great and little, as he used to do every evening on his way to play *monte* in the posada of the Mexican Domingo ; or to sit in the place of honour, listening to songs and looking at dances, made it appear to him as a town that had no existence.

For a long time he gazed on, then let the parted bushes spring back, and, crossing over to the other side of the fort, surveyed the vaster emptiness of the great gulf. The Isabels stood out heavily upon the narrowing long band of red in the west, which gleamed low between their black shapes, and the Capataz thought of Decoud alone there with the treasure. That man was the only one who cared whether he fell into the hands of the Monterists or not, the Capataz reflected bitterly. And that merely would be an anxiety for his own sake. As to the rest, they neither knew nor cared. What he had heard Giorgio Viola say once was very true. Kings, ministers, aristocrats, the rich in general, kept the people in poverty and subjection; they kept them as they kept dogs, to fight and hunt for their service.

The darkness of the sky had descended to the line of the horizon, enveloping the whole gulf, the islets, and the lover of Antonia alone with the treasure on the Great Isabel. The Capataz, turning his back on these things invisible and existing, sat down and took his face between his fists. He felt the pinch of poverty for the first time in his life. To find himself without money after a run of bad luck at *monte* in the low, smoky room of Domingo's posada, where the fraternity of cargadores gambled, sang, and danced of an evening; to remain with empty pockets after a burst of public generosity to some *peyne d'oro* girl or other (for whom he did not care), had none of the humiliation of destitution. He remained rich in glory and reputation. But since it was no longer possible for him to parade the streets of the town, and be hailed with respect in the usual haunts of his leisure, this sailor felt himself destitute indeed.

His mouth was dry. It was dry with heavy sleep and extremely anxious thinking, as it had never been dry

before. It may be said that Nostromo tasted the dust
and ashes of the fruit of life into which he had bitten
deeply in his hunger for praise. Without removing his
head from between his fists, he tried to spit before him—
" Tfui "—and muttered a curse upon the selfishness of
all the rich people.

Since everything seemed lost in Sulaco (and that was
the feeling of his waking), the idea of leaving the country
altogether had presented itself to Nostromo. At that
thought he had seen, like the beginning of another dream,
a vision of steep and tideless shores, with dark pines on
the heights and white houses low down near a very
blue sea. He saw the quays of a big port, where the
coasting feluccas, with their lateen sails outspread like
motionless wings, enter gliding silently between the end
of long moles of squared blocks that project angularly
towards each other, hugging a cluster of shipping to the
superb bosom of a hill covered with palaces. He remembered these sights not without some filial emotion,
though he had been habitually and severely beaten as a
boy on one of these feluccas by a short-necked, shaven
Genoese, with a deliberate and distrustful manner, who
(he firmly believed) had cheated him out of his orphan's
inheritance. But it is mercifully decreed that the evils
of the past should appear but faintly in retrospect.
Under the sense of loneliness, abandonment, and failure,
the idea of return to these things appeared tolerable.
But, what ? Return ? With bare feet and head, with
one check shirt and a pair of cotton calzoneras for all
worldly possessions ?

The renowned Capataz, his elbows on his knees and
a fist dug into each cheek, laughed with self-derision, as
he had spat with disgust, straight out before him into
the night. The confused and intimate impressions of
universal dissolution which beset a subjective nature at
any strong check to its ruling passion had a bitterness
approaching that of death itself. He was simple. He

was as ready to become the prey of any belief, super-stition, or desire as a child.

The facts of his situation he could appreciate like a man with a distinct experience of the country. He saw them clearly. He was as if sobered after a long bout of intoxication. His fidelity had been taken advantage of. He had persuaded the body of cargadores to side with the Blancos against the rest of the people ; he had had inter-views with Don José ; he had been made use of by Father Corbelàn for negotiating with Hernandez ; it was known that Don Martin Decoud had admitted him to a sort of intimacy, so that he had been free of the offices of the *Porvenir*. All these things had flattered him in the usual way. What did he care about their politics ? Nothing at all. And at the end of it all—Nostromo here and Nostromo there—where is Nostromo ? Nostromo can do this and that—work all day and ride all night —behold ! he found himself a marked Ribierist for any sort of vengeance Gamacho, for instance, would choose to take, now the Montero party had, after all, mastered the town. The Europeans had given up ; the caballeros had given up. Don Martin had indeed explained it was only temporary—that he was going to bring Barrios to the rescue. Where was that now—with Don Martin (whose ironic manner of talk had always made the Capataz feel vaguely uneasy) stranded on the Great Isabel ? Everybody had given up. Even Don Carlos had given up. The hurried removal of the treasure out to sea meant nothing else than that. The Capataz de Cargadores, in a revulsion of subjectiveness, exasperated almost to in-sanity, beheld all his world without faith and courage. He had been betrayed !

With the boundless shadows of the sea behind him, out of his silence and immobility, facing the lofty shapes of the lower peaks crowded around the white, misty sheen of Higuerota, Nostromo laughed aloud again, sprang abruptly to his feet, and stood still. He must go. But where ?

" There is no mistake. They keep us and encourage us as if we were dogs born to fight and hunt for them. The vecchio is right," he said slowly and scathingly. He remembered old Giorgio taking his pipe out of his mouth to throw these words over his shoulder at the café, full of engine-drivers and fitters from the railway workshops. This image fixed his wavering purpose. He would try to find old Giorgio if he could. God knows what might have happened to him! He made a few steps, then stopped again and shook his head. To the left and right, in front and behind him, the scrubby bush rustled mysteriously in the darkness.

" Teresa was right, too," he added in a low tone touched with awe. He wondered whether she was dead in her anger with him or still alive. As if in answer to this thought, half of remorse and half of hope, with a soft flutter and oblique flight, a big owl, whose appalling cry, " Ya-acabo!   Ya-acabo!—it is finished ; it is finished ! " announces calamity and death in the popular belief, drifted vaguely like a large, dark ball across his path. In the downfall of all the realities that made his force, he was affected by the superstition, and shuddered slightly. Signora Teresa must have died, then. It could mean nothing else. The cry of the ill-omened bird, the first sound he was to hear on his return, was a fitting welcome for his betrayed individuality. The unseen powers which he had offended by refusing to bring a priest to a dying woman, were lifting up their voice against him. She was dead. With admirable and human consistency he referred everything to himself. She had been a woman of good counsel always. And the bereaved old Giorgio remained stunned by his loss just as he was likely to require the advice of his sagacity. The blow would render the dreamy old man quite stupid for a time.

As to Captain Mitchell, Nostromo, after the manner of trusted subordinates, considered him as a person fitted by education perhaps to sign papers in an office and to give orders, but otherwise of no use whatever, and something of a fool. The necessity of winding round his little finger, almost daily, the pompous and testy self-importance of the old seaman had grown irksome with use to Nostromo. At first it had given him an inward satisfaction. But the necessity of overcoming small obstacles becomes wearisome to a self-confident personality as much by the certitude of success as by the monotony of effort. He mistrusted his superior's proneness to fussy action. That old Englishman had no judgment, he said to himself. It was useless to suppose that, acquainted with the true state of the case, he would keep it to himself. He would talk of doing impracticable things. Nostromo feared him as one would fear saddling oneself with some persistent worry. He had no discretion. He would betray the treasure. And Nostromo had made up his mind that the treasure should not be betrayed.

The word had fixed itself tenaciously in his intelligence. His imagination had seized upon the clear and simple notion of betrayal to account for the dazed feeling of enlightenment as to being done for, of having inadvertently gone out of his existence on an issue in which his personality had not been taken into account. A man betrayed is a man destroyed. Signora Teresa (may God have her soul!) had been right. He had never been taken into account. Destroyed! Her white form sitting up bowed in bed, the falling black hair, the wide-browed suffering face raised to him, the anger of her denunciations, appeared to him now majestic with the awfulness of inspiration and of death. For it was not for nothing that the evil bird had uttered its lamentable shriek over his head. She was dead—may God have her soul!

Sharing in the anti-priestly freethought of the masses, his mind used the pious formula from the superficial force of habit, but with a deep-seated sincerity. The popular mind is incapable of scepticism ; and that incapacity delivers their helpless strength to the wiles of swindlers and to the pitiless enthusiasms of leaders inspired by visions of a high destiny. She was dead. But would God consent to receive her soul ? She had died without confession or absolution, because he had not been willing to spare her another moment of his time. His scorn of priests as priests remained ; but, after all, it was impossible to know whether what they affirmed was not true. Power, punishment, pardon are simple and credible notions. The magnificent Capataz de Cargadores, deprived of certain simple realities, such as the admiration of women, the adulation of men, the admired publicity of his life, was ready to feel the burden of sacrilegious guilt descend upon his shoulders.

Bareheaded, in a thin shirt and drawers, he felt the lingering warmth of the fine sand under the soles of his feet. The narrow strand gleamed far ahead in a long curve, defining the outline of this wild side of the harbour. He flitted along the shore like a pursued shadow between the sombre palm-groves and the sheet of water lying as still as death on his right hand. He strode with headlong haste in the silence and solitude, as though he had forgotten all prudence and caution. But he knew that on this side of the water he ran no risk of discovery. The only inhabitant was a lonely, silent, apathetic Indian in charge of the palmarias, who brought sometimes a load of cocoanuts to the town for sale. He lived without a woman in an open shed, with a perpetual fire of dry sticks smouldering near an old canoe lying bottom up on the beach. He could be easily avoided.

The barking of the dogs about that man's rancho was the first thing that checked his speed. He had forgotten the dogs. He swerved sharply, and plunged into the palm-grove as into a wilderness of columns in an immense hall, whose dense obscurity seemed to whisper and rustle faintly high above his head. He traversed it, entered a ravine, and climbed to the top of a steep ridge free of trees and bushes.

From there, open and vague in the starlight, he saw the plain between the town and the harbour. In the woods above some night-bird made a strange, drumming noise. Below, beyond the palmaria on the beach, the Indian's dogs continued to bark uproariously. He wondered what had upset them so much, and, peering down from this elevation, was surprised to detect unaccountable movements of the ground below, as if several oblong pieces of the plain had been in motion. Those dark, shifting patches, alternately catching and eluding the eye, altered their place always away from the harbour, with a suggestion of consecutive order and purpose. A light dawned upon him. It was a column of infantry on a night march towards the higher broken country at the foot of the hills. But he was too much in the dark about everything for wonder and speculation.

The plain had resumed its shadowy immobility. He descended the ridge and found himself in the open solitude, between the harbour and the town. Its spaciousness, extended indefinitely by an effect of obscurity, rendered more sensible his profound isolation. His pace became slower. No one waited for him ; no one thought of him ; no one expected or wished his return. " Betrayed ! Betrayed ! " he muttered to himself. No one cared. He might have been drowned by this time. No one would have cared—unless, perhaps, the children, he thought to himself. But they were with the English Signora, and not thinking of him at all.

He wavered in his purpose of making straight for the Casa Viola. To what end ? What could he expect there ? His life seemed to fail him in all its details, even to the scornful reproaches of Teresa. He was aware painfully of his reluctance. Was it that remorse which she had prophesied with what, he saw now, was her last breath ?

Meantime he had deviated from the straight course, inclining by a sort of instinct to the right, towards the jetty and the harbour, the scene of his daily labours. The great length of the Custom House loomed up all at once like the wall of a factory. Not a soul challenged his approach, and his curiosity became excited as he passed cautiously towards the front by the unexpected sight of two lighted windows.

They had the fascination of a lonely vigil kept by some mysterious watcher up there, those two windows shining dimly upon the harbour in the whole vast extent of the abandoned building. The solitude could almost be felt. A strong smell of wood smoke hung about in a thin haze, which was faintly perceptible to his raised eyes against the glitter of the stars. As he advanced in the profound silence, the shrilling of innumerable cicalas in the dry grass seemed positively deafening to his strained ears. Slowly, step by step, he found himself in the great hall, sombre and full of acrid smoke.

A fire built against the staircase had burnt down impotently to a low heap of embers. The hardwood had failed to catch ; only a few steps at the bottom smouldered, with a creeping glow of sparks defining their charred edges. At the top he saw a streak of light from an open door. It fell upon the vast landing, all foggy with a slow drift of smoke. That was the room. He climbed the stairs, then checked himself, because he had seen within the shadow of a man cast upon one of the walls. It was a shapeless, high-shouldered shadow of somebody standing still, with a lowered head, out of his line of sight. The Capataz, remembering that he was totally unarmed, stepped aside, and, effacing himself upright in a dark corner, waited with his eyes fixed on the door.

The whole enormous ruined barrack of a place, unfinished, without ceilings under its lofty roof, was pervaded by the smoke swaying to and fro in the faint cross-draughts playing in the obscurity of many lofty rooms and barn-like passages. Once one of the swinging shutters came against the wall with a single sharp crack, as if pushed by an impatient hand. A piece of paper scurried out from somewhere, rustling along the landing. The man, whoever he was, did not darken the lighted doorway. Twice the Capataz, advancing a couple of steps out of his corner, craned his neck in the hope of catching sight of what he would be at, so quietly, in there. But every time he saw only the distorted shadow of broad shoulders and bowed head. He was doing apparently nothing, and stirred not from the spot, as though he were meditating—or, perhaps, reading a paper. And not a sound issued from the room.

Once more the Capataz stepped back. He wondered who it was—some Monterist? But he dreaded to show himself. To discover his presence on shore, unless after many days, would, he believed, endanger the treasure. With his own knowledge possessing his whole soul, it seemed impossible that anybody in Sulaco should fail to jump at the right surmise. After a couple of weeks or so it would be different. Who could tell ɪe had not returned overland from some port beyond the limits of the Republic? The existence of the treasure confused his thoughts with a peculiar sort of anxiety, as though his life had become bound up with it. It rendered him timorous for a moment before that enigmatic, lighted door. Devil take the fellow! He did not want to see him. There would be nothing to learn from his face, known or unknown. He was a fool to waste his time there in waiting.

Less than five minutes after entering the place the Capataz began his retreat. He got away down the stairs with perfect success, gave one upward look over his shoulder at the light on the landing, and ran stealthily across the hall. But at the very moment he was turning out of the great door, with his mind fixed upon escaping the notice of the man upstairs, somebody he had not

heard coming briskly along the front ran full into him.
Both muttered a stifled exclamation of surprise, and
leaped back and stood still, each indistinct to the other.
Nostromo was silent. The other man spoke first, in an
amazed and deadened tone.

" Who are you ? "

Already Nostromo had seemed to recognise Dr.
Monygham. He had no doubt now. He hesitated the
space of a second. The idea of bolting without a word
presented itself to his mind. No use ! An inexplicable
repugnance to pronounce the name by which he was
known kept him silent a little longer. At last he said
in a low voice :

" A cargador."

He walked up to the other. Dr. Monygham had
received a shock. He flung his arms up and cried out
his wonder aloud, forgetting himself before the marvel
of this meeting. Nostromo ' angrily warned him to
moderate his voice. The Custom House was not so
deserted as it looked. There was somebody in the
lighted room above.

There is no more evanescent quality in an accomplished fact than its wonderfulness. Solicited incessantly by the considerations affecting its fears and desires,
the human mind turns naturally away from the marvellous side of events. And it was in the most natural
way possible that the doctor asked this man, whom only
two minutes before he believed to have been drowned in
the gulf :

" You have seen somebody up there ?   Have you ? "

" No, I have not seen him."

" Then how do you know ? "

" I was running away from his shadow when we
met."

" His shadow ? "

" Yes. His shadow in the lighted room," said
Nostromo in a contemptuous tone. Leaning back with

folded arms at the foot of the immense building, he dropped his head, biting his lips slightly and not looking at the doctor. " Now," he thought to himself, " he will begin asking me about the treasure."

But the doctor's thoughts were concerned with an event not as marvellous as Nostromo's appearance, but in itself much less clear. Why had Sotillo taken himself off with his whole command with this suddenness and secrecy ? What did this move portend ? However, it dawned upon the doctor that the man upstairs was one of the officers left behind by the disappointed colonel to communicate with him.

" I believe he is waiting for me," he said.

" It is possible."

" I must see. Do not go away yet, Capataz."

" Go away where ? " muttered Nostromo.

Already the doctor had left him. He remained leaning against the wall, staring at the dark water of the harbour ; the shrilling of cicalas filled his ears. An invincible vagueness coming over his thoughts took from them all power to determine his will.

" Capataz ! Capataz ! " the doctor's voice called urgently from above.

The sense of betrayal and ruin floated upon his sombre indifference as upon a sluggish sea of pitch. But he stepped out from under the wall, and, looking up, saw Dr. Monygham leaning out of a lighted window.

" Come up and see what Sotillo has done. You need not fear the man up here."

He answered by a slight, bitter laugh. Fear a man ! The Capataz of the Sulaco Cargadores fear a man ! It angered him that anybody should suggest such a thing. It angered him to be disarmed and skulking and in danger because of the accursed treasure, which was of so little account to the people who had tied it round his neck. He could not shake off the worry of it. To Nostromo the doctor represented all these people. . . . And he

26

had never even asked after it. Not a word of inquiry
about the most desperate undertaking of his life.

Thinking these thoughts, Nostromo passed again
through the cavernous hall, where the smoke was considerably thinned, and went up the stairs, not so warm to
his feet now, towards the streak of light at the top. The
doctor appeared in it for a moment, agitated and impatient.

" Come up ! Come up ! "

At the moment of crossing the doorway the Capataz
experienced a shock of surprise. The man had not
moved. He saw his shadow in the same place. He
started, then stepped in with a feeling of being about
to solve a mystery.

It was very simple. For an infinitesimal fraction of a
second, against the light of two flaring and guttering
candles, through a blue, pungent, thin haze which made
his eyes smart, he saw the man standing, as he had
imagined him, with his back to the door, casting an
enormous and distorted shadow upon the wall. Swifter
than a flash of lightning followed the impression of his
constrained, toppling attitude—the shoulders projecting
forward, the head sunk low upon the breast. Then he
distinguished the arms behind his back, and wrenched so
terribly that the two clenched fists, lashed together, had
been forced up higher than the shoulder-blades. From
there his eyes traced in one instantaneous glance the hide
rope going upwards from the tied wrists over a heavy
beam and down to a staple in the wall. He did not want
to look at the rigid legs, at the feet hanging down nerve-
lessly, with their bare toes some six inches above the floor,
to know that the man had been given the estrapade till he
had swooned. His first impulse was to dash forward and
sever the rope at one blow. He felt for his knife. He
had no knife—not even a knife. He stood quivering,
and the doctor, perched on the edge of the table, facing
thoughtfully the cruel and lamentable sight, his chin in
his hand, uttered, without stirring :

" Tortured—and shot dead through the breast—getting cold."

This information calmed the Capataz. One of the candles flickering in the socket went out. " Who did this ? " he asked.

" Sotillo, I tell you. Who else ? Tortured—of course. But why shot ? " The doctor looked fixedly at Nostromo, who shrugged his shoulders slightly. " And mark, shot suddenly, on impulse. It is evident. I wish I had his secret."

Nostromo had advanced, and stooped slightly to look. " I seem to have seen that face somewhere," he muttered. " Who is he ? "

The doctor turned his eyes upon him again. " I may yet come to envying his fate. What do you think of that, Capataz, eh ? "

But Nostromo did not even hear these words. Seizing the remaining light, he thrust it under the drooping head. The doctor sat oblivious, with a lost gaze. Then the heavy iron candlestick, as if struck out of Nostromo's hand, clattered on the floor.

" Hullo ! " exclaimed the doctor, looking up with a start. He could hear the Capataz stagger against the table and gasp. In the sudden extinction of the light within, the dead blackness sealing the window-frames became alive with stars to his sight.

" Of course, of course," the doctor muttered to himself in English. " Enough to make him jump out of his skin."

Nostromo's heart seemed to force itself into his throat. His head swam. Hirsch ! The man was Hirsch ! He held on tight to the edge of the table.

" But he was hiding in the lighter," he almost shouted. His voice fell. " In the lighter, and—and——"

" And Sotillo brought him in," said the doctor. " He is no more startling to you than you were to me. What I want to know is how he induced some compassionate soul to shoot him."

"So Sotillo knows——" began Nostromo in a more equable voice.

"Everything!" interrupted the doctor.

The Capataz was heard striking the table with his fist. "Everything? What are you saying, there? Everything? Know everything? It is impossible! Everything?"

"Of course. What do you mean by impossible? I tell you I have heard this Hirsch questioned last night, here, in this very room. He knew your name, Decoud's name, and all about the loading of the silver. . . . The lighter was cut in two. He was grovelling in abject terror before Sotillo, but he remembered that much. What do you want more? He knew least about himself. They found him clinging to their anchor. He must have caught at it just as the lighter went to the bottom."

"Went to the bottom?" repeated Nostromo slowly. "Sotillo believes that? Bueno!"

The doctor, a little impatiently, was unable to imagine what else anybody could believe. Yes, Sotillo believed that the lighter was sunk, and the Capataz de Cargadores, together with Martin Decoud and perhaps one or two other political fugitives, had been drowned.

"I told you well, Señor Doctor," remarked Nostromo at that point, "that Sotillo did not know everything."

"Eh? What do you mean?"

"He did not know I was not dead."

"Neither did we."

"And you did not care—none of you caballeros on the wharf—once you got off a man of flesh and blood like yourselves on a fool's business that could not end well."

"You forget, Capataz, I was not on the wharf. And I did not think well of the business. So you need not taunt me. I tell you what, man, we had but little leisure to think of the dead. Death stands near behind us all. You were gone."

" I went, indeed ! " broke in Nostromo. " And for the sake of what—tell me ? "

" Ah ! that is your own affair," the doctor said roughly. " Do not ask me."

Their flowing murmurs paused in the dark. Perched on the edge of the table with slightly averted faces, they felt their shoulders touch, and their eyes remained directed towards an upright shape nearly lost in the obscurity of the inner part of the room, that with projecting head and shoulders, in ghastly immobility, seemed intent on catching every word.

" *Muy bien !* " Nostromo muttered at last. " So be it. Teresa was right. It is my own affair."

" Teresa is dead," remarked the doctor absently, while his mind followed a new line of thought suggested by what might have been called Nostromo's return to life. " She died, the poor woman."

" Without a priest ? " the Capataz asked anxiously.

" What a question ! Who could have got a priest for her last night ? "

" May God keep her soul ! " ejaculated Nostromo, with a gloomy and hopeless fervour which had no time to surprise Dr. Monygham, before, reverting to their previous conversation, he continued in a sinister tone : " Si, Señor Doctor. As you were saying, it is my own affair. A very desperate affair."

" There are no two men in this part of the world that could have saved themselves by swimming as you have done," the doctor said admiringly.

And again there was silence between those two men. They were both reflecting, and the diversity of their natures made their thoughts born from their meeting swing afar from each other. The doctor, impelled to risky action by his loyalty to the Goulds, wondered with thankfulness at the chain of accident which had brought that man back where he would be of the greatest use in the work of saving the San Tomé mine. The doctor

was loyal to the mine. It presented itself to his fifty-
year-old eyes in the shape of a little woman in a soft
dress with a long train, with a head attractively overweighted by a great mass of fair hair, and the delicate
preciousness of her inner worth, partaking of a gem and
a flower, revealed in every attitude of her person. As
the dangers thickened round the San Tomé mine this
illusion acquired force, permanency, and authority. It
claimed him at last ! This claim, exalted by a spiritual
detachment from the usual sanctions of hope and reward,
made Dr. Monygham's thinking, acting, individuality
extremely dangerous to himself and to others, all his
scruples vanishing in the proud feeling that his devotion
was the only thing that stood between an admirable
woman and a frightful disaster.

It was a sort of intoxication which made him utterly
indifferent to Decoud's fate, but left his wits perfectly
clear for the appreciation of Decoud's political idea. It
was a good idea—and Barrios was the only instrument
of its realisation. The doctor's soul, withered and shrunk
by the shame of a moral disgrace, became implacable in
the expansion of its tenderness. Nostromo's return was
providential. He did not think of him humanely, as of
a fellow-creature just escaped from the jaws of death.
The Capataz for him was the only possible messenger
to Cayta. The very man. The doctor's misanthropic
mistrust of mankind (the bitterer because based on
personal failure) did not lift him sufficiently above
common weaknesses. He was under the spell of an
established reputation. Trumpeted by Captain Mitchell,
grown in repetition, and fixed in general assent, Nostromo's faithfulness had never been questioned by Dr.
Monygham as a fact. It was not likely to be questioned
now he stood in desperate need of it himself. Dr.
Monygham was human ; he accepted the popular
conception of the Capataz's incorruptibility simply
because no word or fact had ever contradicted a mere

affirmation. It seemed to be a part of the man, like his whiskers or his teeth. It was impossible to conceive him otherwise. The question was whether he would consent to go on such a dangerous and desperate errand. The doctor was observant enough to have become aware from the first of something peculiar in the man's temper. He was no doubt sore about the loss of the silver.

" It will be necessary to take him into my fullest confidence," he said to himself, with a certain acuteness of insight into the nature he had to deal with.

On Nostromo's side the silence had been full of black irresolution, anger, and mistrust. He was the first to break it, however.

" The swimming was no great matter," he said. " It is what went before, and what comes after, that——"

He did not quite finish what he meant to say, breaking off short, as though his thought had butted against a solid obstacle. The doctor's mind pursued its own schemes with Machiavellian subtlety. He said as sympathetically as he was able :

" It is unfortunate, Capataz. But no one would think of blaming you. Very unfortunate. To begin with, the treasure ought never to have left the mountain. But it was Decoud who—— However, he is dead. There is no need to talk of him."

" No," assented Nostromo, as the doctor paused, " there is no need to talk of dead men. But I am not dead yet."

" You are all right. Only a man of your intrepidity could have saved himself."

In this Dr. Monygham was sincere. He esteemed highly the intrepidity of that man, whom he valued but little, being disillusioned as to mankind in general, because of the particular instance in which his own manhood had failed. Having had to encounter single-handed during his period of eclipse many physical dangers, he was well aware of the most dangerous element common to them all : of the crushing paralysing sense of human littleness, which is what really defeats a man struggling with natural forces, alone, far from the eyes of his fellows. He was eminently fit to appreciate the mental image he made for himself of the Capataz, after hours of tension and anxiety, precipitated suddenly into an abyss of waters and darkness, without earth or sky, and confronting it not only with an undismayed mind, but with sensible success. Of course, the man was an incomparable swimmer, that was known, but the doctor judged that this instance testified to a still greater intrepidity of spirit. It was pleasing to him ; he augured well from it for the success of the arduous mission with which he meant to entrust the Capataz so marvellously restored to usefulness. And in a tone vaguely gratified, he observed :

" It must have been terribly dark ! "

" It was the worst darkness of the Golfo," the Capataz assented briefly. He was mollified by what seemed a sign of some faint interest in such things as had befallen him, and dropped a few descriptive phrases with an affected and curt nonchalance. At that moment he felt communicative. He expected the continuance of that interest which, whether accepted or rejected, would have restored to him his personality—the only thing lost in that desperate affair. But the doctor, engrossed by a desperate adventure of his own, was terrible in the pursuit of his idea. He let an exclamation of regret escape him.

" I could almost wish you had shouted and shown a light."

This unexpected utterance astounded the Capataz by its character of cold-blooded atrocity. It was as much as to say, " I wish you had shown yourself a coward ; I wish you had had your throat cut for your pains." Naturally he referred it to himself, whereas it related only to the silver, being uttered simply and with many mental reservations. Surprise and rage rendered him speechless, and the doctor pursued, practically unheard by Nostromo, whose stirred blood was beating violently in his ears.

" For I am convinced Sotillo in possession of the silver would have turned short round and made for some small port abroad. Economically it would have been wasteful, but still less wasteful than having it sunk. It was the next best thing to having it at hand in some safe place and using part of it to buy up Sotillo. But I doubt whether Don Carlos would have ever made up his mind to it. He is not fit for Costaguana, and that is a fact, Capataz."

The Capataz had mastered the fury that was like a tempest in his ears in time to hear the name of Don Carlos. He seemed to have come out of it a changed man—a man who spoke thoughtfully in a soft and even voice.

" And would Don Carlos have been content if I had surrendered this treasure ? "

" I should not wonder if they were all of that way of thinking now," the doctor said grimly. " I was never consulted. Decoud had it his own way. Their eyes are opened by this time, I should think. I for one know that if that silver turned up this moment miraculously ashore I would give it to Sotillo. And, as things stand, I would be approved."

" Turned up miraculously ? " repeated the Capataz very low ; then raised his voice : " That, Señor, would be a greater miracle than any saint could perform."

" I believe you, Capataz," said the doctor dryly.

He went on to develop his view of Sotillo's dangerous influence upon the situation. And the Capataz, listening as if in a dream, felt himself of as little account as the indistinct, motionless shape of the dead man whom he saw upright under the beam, with his air of listening also, disregarded, forgotten, like a terrible example of neglect.

" Was it for an unconsidered and foolish whim that they came to me, then ? " he interrupted suddenly. " Had I not done enough for them to be of some account, *por*

Dios ?   Is it that the *hombres finos*—the gentlemen—need
not think as long as there is a man of the people ready to
risk his body and soul ?   Or, perhaps, we have no souls
—like dogs ? "

" There was Decoud, too, with his plan," the doctor
reminded him again.

" Si !   And the rich man in San Francisco who had
something to do with that treasure, too—what do I
know ?   No !   I have heard too many things.   It seems
to me that everything is permitted to the rich."

" I understand, Capataz——" the doctor began.

" What Capataz ? " broke in Nostromo in a forcible
but even voice.   " The Capataz is undone, destroyed.
There is no Capataz.   Oh no !   You will find the
Capataz no more."

" Come, this is childish ! " remonstrated the doctor ;
and the other calmed down suddenly.

" I have been indeed like a little child," he muttered.

And as his eyes met again the shape of the murdered
man suspended in his awful immobility, which seemed the
uncomplaining immobility of attention, he asked, wondering gently :

" Why did Sotillo give the estrapade to this pitiful
wretch ?   Do you know ?   No torture could have been
worse than his fear.   Killing I can understand.   His
anguish was intolerable to behold.   But why should he
torment him like this ?   He could tell no more."

" No ;   he could tell nothing more.   Any sane man
would have seen that.   He had told him everything.   But
I tell you what it is, Capataz.   Sotillo would not believe
what he was told.   Not everything."

" What is it he would not believe ?   I cannot understand."

" I can, because I have seen the man.   He refuses to
believe that the treasure is lost."

" What ? " the Capataz cried out in a discomposed
tone.

" That startles you—eh ? "

" Am I to understand, Señor," Nostromo went on in a deliberate and, as it were, watchful tone, " that Sotillo thinks the treasure has been saved by some means ? "

" No ! no ! That would be impossible," said the doctor, with conviction ; and Nostromo emitted a grunt in the dark. " That would be impossible. He thinks that the silver was no longer in the lighter when she was sunk. He has convinced himself that the whole show of getting it away to sea is a mere sham got up to deceive Gamacho and his Nationals, Pedrito Montero, Señor Fuentes, our new Géfé Politico, and himself too. Only, he says, he is no such fool."

" But he is devoid of sense. He is the greatest imbecile that ever called himself a colonel in this country of evil," growled Nostromo.

" He is no more unreasonable than many sensible men," said the doctor. " He has convinced himself that the treasure can be found because he desires passion- ately to possess himself of it. And he is also afraid of his officers turning upon him and going over to Pedrito, whom he has not the courage either to fight or trust. Do you see that, Capataz ? He need fear no desertion as long as some hope remains of that enormous plunder turning up. I have made it my business to keep this very hope up."

" You have ? " the Capataz de Cargadores repeated cautiously. " Well, that is wonderful. And how long do you think you are going to keep it up ? "

" As long as I can."

" What does that mean ? "

" I can tell you exactly. As long as I live," the doctor retorted in a stubborn voice. Then, in a few words, he described the story of his arrest and the circumstances of his release. " I was going back to that silly scoundrel when we met," he concluded.

Nostromo had listened with profound attention.

" You have made up your mind, then, to a speedy death,"
he muttered through his clenched teeth.

" Perhaps, my illustrious Capataz," the doctor said
testily. " You are not the only one here who can look
an ugly death in the face."

" No doubt," mumbled Nostromo, loud enough to be
overheard. " There may be even more than two fools in
this place. Who knows ? "

" And that is my affair," said the doctor curtly.

" As taking out the accursed silver to sea was my
affair," retorted Nostromo. " I see. Bueno ! Each of us
has his reasons. But you were the last man I conversed
with before I started, and you talked to me as if I were a
fool."

Nostromo had a great distaste for the doctor's
sardonic treatment of his great reputation. Decoud's
faintly ironic recognition used to make him uneasy ; but
the familiarity of a man like Don Martin was flattering,
whereas the doctor was a nobody. He could remember
him a penniless outcast, slinking about the streets of
Sulaco, without a single friend or acquaintance, till Don
Carlos Gould took him into the service of the mine.

" You may be very wise," he went on thoughtfully,
staring into the obscurity of the room, pervaded by the
gruesome enigma of the tortured and murdered Hirsch ;
" but I am not such a fool as when I started. I have
learned one thing since, and that is that you are a
dangerous man."

Dr. Monygham was too startled to do more than
exclaim :

" What is it you say ? "

" If he could speak he would say the same thing,"
pursued Nostromo, with a nod of his shadowy head
silhouetted against the starlit window.

" I do not understand you," said Dr. Monygham
faintly.

" No ? Perhaps, if you had not confirmed Sotillo in

his madness, he would have been in no haste to give the estrapade to that miserable Hirsch."

The doctor started at the suggestion. But his devotion, absorbing all his sensibilities, had left his heart steeled against remorse and pity. Still, for complete relief, he felt the necessity of repelling it loudly and contemptuously.

" Bah ! You dare to tell me that, with a man like Sotillo ! I confess I did not give a thought to Hirsch. If I had it would have been useless. Anybody can see that the luckless wretch was doomed from the moment he caught hold of the anchor. He was doomed, I tell you ! Just as I myself am doomed—most probably."

This is what Dr. Monygham said in answer to Nostromo's remark, which was plausible enough to prick his conscience. He was not a callous man. But the necessity, the magnitude, the importance of the task he had taken upon himself dwarfed all merely humane considerations. He had undertaken it in a fanatical spirit. He did not like it. To lie, to deceive, to circumvent even the basest of mankind was odious to him. It was odious to him by training, instinct, and tradition. To do these things in the character of a traitor was abhorrent to his nature and terrible to his feelings. He had made that sacrifice in a spirit of abasement. He had said to himself bitterly, " I am the only one fit for that dirty work." And he believed this. He was not subtle. His simplicity was such that, though he had no sort of heroic idea of seeking death, the risk, deadly enough, to which he exposed himself had a sustaining and comforting effect. To that spiritual state the fate of Hirsch presented itself as part of the general atrocity of things. He considered that episode practically. What did it mean ? Was´ it a sign of some dangerous change in Sotillo's delusion ? That the man should have been killed like this was what the doctor could not understand.

" Yes. But why shot ? " he murmured to himself.

Nostromo kept very still.

CHAPTER NINE

DISTRACTED between doubts and hopes, dismayed by the sound of bells pealing out the arrival of Pedrito Montero, Sotillo had spent the morning in battling with his thoughts ; a contest to which he was unequal, from the vacuity of his mind and the violence of his passions. Disappointment, greed, anger, and fear made a tumult in the colonel's breast louder than the din of bells in the town. Nothing he had planned had come to pass. Neither Sulaco nor the silver of the mine had fallen into his hands. He had performed no military exploit to secure his position, and had obtained no enormous booty to make off with. Pedrito Montero, either as friend or foe, filled him with dread. The sound of bells maddened him.

Imagining at first that he might be attacked at once, he had made his battalion stand to arms on the shore. He walked to and fro all the length of the room, stopping sometimes to gnaw the finger-tips of his right hand with a lurid sideways glare fixed on the floor ; then, with a sullen repelling glance all round, he would resume his tramping in savage aloofness. His hat, horsewhip, sword, and revolver were lying on the table. His officers, crowding the window giving the view of the town gate, disputed amongst themselves the use of his field-glass bought last year on long credit from Anzani. It passed from hand to hand, and the possessor for the time being was besieged by anxious inquiries.

"There is nothing; there is nothing to see!" he would repeat impatiently.

There was nothing. And when the picket in the bushes near the Casa Viola had been ordered to fall back upon the main body, no stir of life appeared on the stretch of dusty and arid land between the town and the waters of the port. But late in the afternoon a horseman issuing from the gate was made out riding up fearlessly. It was an emissary from Señor Fuentes. Being all alone, he was allowed to come on. Dismounting at the great door, he greeted the silent bystanders with cheery impudence, and begged to be taken up at once to the *muy valiente* colonel.

Señor Fuentes, on entering upon his functions of Géfé Politico, had turned his diplomatic abilities to getting hold of the harbour as well as of the mine. The man he pitched upon to negotiate with Sotillo was a Notary Public, whom the revolution had found languishing in the common jail on a charge of forging documents. Liberated by the mob along with the other "victims of Blanco tyranny," he had hastened to offer his services to the new Government.

He set out determined to display much zeal and eloquence in trying to induce Sotillo to come into town alone for a conference with Pedrito Montero. Nothing was further from the colonel's intentions. The mere fleeting idea of trusting himself into the famous Pedrito's hands had made him feel unwell several times. It was out of the question—it was madness. And to put himself in open hostility was madness too. It would render impossible a systematic search for that treasure, for that wealth of silver which he seemed to feel somewhere about, to scent somewhere near. But where? Where? Heavens! Where? Oh, why had he allowed that doctor to go! Imbecile that he was. But no! It was the only right course, he reflected distractedly, while the messenger waited downstairs chat-

ting agreeably to the officers.   It was in that scoundrelly
doctor's true interest to return with positive information.   But what if anything stopped him ?   A general
prohibition to leave the town, for instance ?   There
would be patrols !

The colonel, seizing his head in his hands, turned in
his tracks as if struck with vertigo.   A flash of craven
inspiration suggested to him an expedient not unknown
to European statesmen when they wish to delay a difficult
negotiation.   Booted and spurred, he scrambled into the
hammock with undignified haste.   His handsome face
had turned yellow with the strain of weighty cares.   The
ridge of his shapely nose had grown sharp ; the audacious
nostrils appeared mean and pinched.   The velvety,
caressing glance of his fine eyes seemed dead, and even
decomposed ; for these almond-shaped, languishing orbs
had become inappropriately bloodshot with much sinister
sleeplessness.   He addressed the surprised envoy of
Señor Fuentes in a deadened, exhausted voice.   It came
pathetically feeble from under a pile of ponchos, which
buried his elegant person right up to the black moustaches,
uncurled, pendent, in sign of bodily prostration and
mental incapacity.   Fever, fever—a heavy fever had
overtaken the *muy valiente* colonel.   A wavering wild-
ness of expression, caused by the passing spasms of a
slight colic which had declared itself suddenly, and the
rattling teeth of repressed panic, had a genuineness which
impressed the envoy.   It was a cold fit.   The colonel
explained that he was unable to think, to listen, to speak.
With an appearance of superhuman effort the colonel
gasped out that he was not in a state to return a suitable
reply or to execute any of His Excellency's orders.   But
to-morrow ! To-morrow ! Ah, to-morrow ! Let His
Excellency Don Pedro be without uneasiness.   The
brave Esmeralda regiment held the harbour, held——
And closing his eyes, he rolled his aching head like a
half-delirious invalid under the inquisitive stare of the

envoy, who was obliged to bend down over the hammock in order to catch the painful and broken accents. Meantime Colonel Sotillo trusted that His Excellency's humanity would permit the doctor, the English doctor, to come out of town with his case of foreign remedies to attend upon him. He begged anxiously his worship the caballero now present for the grace of looking in as he passed the Casa Gould, and informing the English doctor, who was probably there, that his services were immediately required by Colonel Sotillo, lying ill of fever in the Custom House. Immediately. Most urgently required. Awaited with extreme impatience. A thousand thanks. He closed his eyes wearily and would not open them again, lying perfectly still, deaf, dumb, insensible, overcome, vanquished, crushed, annihilated by the fell disease.

But as soon as the other had shut after him the door of the landing, the colonel leaped out with a fling of both feet in an avalanche of woollen coverings. His spurs having become entangled in a perfect welter of ponchos, he nearly pitched on his head, and did not recover his balance till the middle of the room. Concealed behind the half-closed jalousies he listened to what went on below.

The envoy had already mounted, and, turning to the morose officers occupying the great doorway, took off his hat formally.

" Caballeros," he said in a very loud tone, " allow me to recommend you to take great care of your colonel. It has done me much honour and gratification to have seen you all, a fine body of men exercising the soldierly virtue of patience in this exposed situation, where there is much sun and no water to speak of, while a town full of wine and feminine charms is ready to embrace you for the brave men you are. Caballeros, I have the honour to salute you. There will be much dancing to-night in Sulaco. Good-bye ! "

But he reined in his horse and inclined his head sideways on seeing the old major step out, very tall and meagre, in a straight, narrow coat coming down to his ankles, as it were the casing of the regimental colours rolled round their staff.

The intelligent old warrior, after enunciating in a dogmatic tone the general proposition that the " world was full of traitors," went on pronouncing deliberately a panegyric upon Sotillo. He ascribed to him with leisurely emphasis every virtue under heaven, summing it all up in an absurd colloquialism current amongst the lower class of Occidentals (especially about Esmeralda). " And," he concluded, with a sudden rise in the voice, " a man of many teeth—*hombre de muchos dientes*. Si, Señor. As to us," he pursued, portentous and impressive, " your worship is beholding the finest body of officers in the Republic, men unequalled for valour and sagacity, *y hombres de muchos dientes*."

" What ? All of them ? " inquired the disreputable envoy of Señor Fuentes, with a faint, derisive smile.

" Todos. Si, Señor," the major affirmed gravely, with conviction. " Men of many teeth."

The other wheeled his horse to face the portal resembling the high gate of a dismal barn. He raised himself in his stirrups, extended one arm. He was a facetious scoundrel, entertaining for these stupid Occidentals a feeling of great scorn natural in a native from the central provinces. The folly of Esmeraldians especially aroused his amused contempt. He began an oration upon Pedrito Montero, keeping a solemn countenance. He flourished his hand as if introducing him to their notice. And when he saw every face set, all the eyes fixed upon his lips, he began to shout a sort of catalogue of perfections : " Generous, valorous, affable, profound "—he snatched off his hat enthusiastically—" a statesman, an invincible chief of partisans " — he

dropped his voice startlingly to a deep hollow note—
" and a dentist."

He was off instantly at a smart walk ; the rigid
straddle of his legs, the turned-out feet, the stiff back,
the rakish slant of the sombrero above the square,
motionless set of the shoulders expressing an infinite,
awe-inspiring impudence.

Upstairs, behind the jalousies, Sotillo did not move
for a long time. The audacity of the fellow appalled
him. What were his officers saying below ? They
were saying nothing. Complete silence. He quaked.
It was not thus that he had imagined himself at that
stage of the expedition. He had seen himself triumphant,
unquestioned, appeased, the idol of the soldiers, weighing in secret complacency the agreeable alternatives of
power and wealth open to his choice. Alas, how
different ! Distracted, restless, supine, burning with
fury or frozen with terror, he felt a dread as fathomless
as the sea creep upon him from every side. That rogue
of a doctor had to come out with his information. That
was clear. It would be of no use to him—alone. He
could do nothing with it. Malediction ! The doctor
would never come out. He was probably under arrest
already, shut up together with Don Carlos. He laughed
aloud insanely. Ha ! ha ! ha ! ha ! It was Pedrito
Montero who would get the information. Ha ! ha !
ha ! ha !—and the silver. Ha !

All at once, in the midst of the laugh, he became
motionless and silent as if turned into stone. He, too,
had a prisoner. A prisoner who must, must know the
real truth. He would have to be made to speak. And
Sotillo, who all that time had not quite forgotten Hirsch,
felt an inexplicable reluctance at the notion of proceeding
to extremities.

He felt a reluctance—part of that unfathomable
dread that crept on all sides upon him. He remembered reluctantly, too, the dilated eyes of the hide

merchant, his contortions, his loud sobs and protestations. It was not compassion or even mere nervous
sensibility. The fact was that though Sotillo did never
for a moment believe his story—he could not believe it;
nobody could believe such nonsense—yet those accents
of despairing truth impressed him disagreeably. They
made him feel sick. And he suspected also that the
man might have gone mad with fear. A lunatic is a
hopeless subject. Bah! a pretence. Nothing but a
pretence. He would know how to deal with that.

He was working himself up to the right pitch of
ferocity. His fine eyes squinted slightly; he clapped
his hands; a barefooted orderly appeared noiselessly—
a corporal, with his bayonet hanging on his thigh and a
stick in his hand.

The colonel gave his orders, and presently the
miserable Hirsch, pushed in by several soldiers, found
him frowning awfully in a broad arm-chair, hat on head,
knees wide apart, arms akimbo, masterful, imposing, irresistible, haughty, sublime, terrible.

Hirsch, with his arms tied behind his back, had been
bundled violently into one of the smaller rooms. For
many hours he remained apparently forgotten, stretched
lifelessly on the floor. From that solitude, full of
despair and terror, he was torn out brutally, with kicks
and blows, passive, sunk in hebetude. He listened to
threats and admonitions, and afterwards made his usual
answers to questions, with his chin sunk on his breast,
his hands tied behind his back, swaying a little in front
of Sotillo, and never looking up. When he was forced to
hold up his head, by means of a bayonet-point prodding
him under the chin, his eyes had a vacant, trance-like
stare, and drops of perspiration as big as peas were
seen hailing down the dirt, bruises, and scratches of his
white face. Then they stopped suddenly.

Sotillo looked at him in silence. "Will you depart
from your obstinacy, you rogue?" he asked. Already a

rope, whose one end was fastened to Señor Hirsch's wrists, had been thrown over a beam, and three soldiers held the other end, waiting. He made no answer. His heavy lower lip hung stupidly. Sotillo made a sign. Hirsch was jerked up off his feet, and a yell of despair and agony burst out in the room, filled the passage of the great buildings, rent the air outside, caused every soldier of the camp along the shore to look up at the windows, started some of the officers in the hall babbling excitedly, with shining eyes ; others, setting their lips, looked gloomily at the floor.

Sotillo, followed by the soldiers, had left the room. The sentry on the landing presented arms. Hirsch went on screaming all alone behind the half-closed jalousies, while the sunshine, reflected from the water of the harbour, made an ever-running ripple of light high up on the wall. He screamed with uplifted eyebrows and a wide open mouth—incredibly wide, black, enormous, full of teeth—comical.

In the still burning air of the windless afternoon he made the waves of his agony travel as far as the O.S.N. Company's offices. Captain Mitchell on the balcony, try- ing to make out what went on generally, had heard him faintly but distinctly, and the feeble and appalling sound lingered in his ears after he had retreated indoors with blanched cheeks. He had been driven off the balcony several times during that afternoon.

Sotillo, irritable, moody, walked restlessly about, held consultations with his officers, gave contradictory orders in the shrill clamour pervading the whole empty edifice. Sometimes there would be long and awful silences. Several times he had entered the torture- chamber, where his sword, horsewhip, revolver, and field- glass were lying on the table, to ask with forced calmness, " Will you speak the truth now ? No ? I can wait." But he could not afford to wait much longer. That was just it. Every time he went in and came out with a slam of the door, the sentry on the landing presented arms, and got in return a black, venomous, unsteady glance, which, in reality, saw nothing at all, being merely the reflection of the soul within—a soul of gloomy hatred, irresolution, avarice, and fury.

The sun had set when he went in once more. A soldier carried in two lighted candles and slunk out, shutting the door without noise.

" Speak, thou Jewish child of the devil ! The silver ! The silver, I say ! Where is it ? Where have you foreign rogues hidden it ? Confess or——"

A slight quiver passed up the taut rope from the racked limbs, but the body of Señor Hirsch, enterprising business man from Esmeralda, hung under the heavy beam perpendicular and silent, facing the colonel awfully. The inflow of the night air, cooled by the snows of the sierra, spread gradually a delicious freshness through the close heat of the room.

" Speak—thief—scoundrel—picaro—or——"

Sotillo had seized the riding-whip, and stood with his arm lifted up. For a word, for one little word, he felt he would have knelt, cringed, grovelled on the floor before the drowsy, conscious stare of those fixed eyeballs starting out of the grimy, dishevelled head that drooped very still with its mouth closed askew. The colonel ground his teeth with rage and struck. The rope vibrated leisurely to the blow, like the long string of a pendulum starting from a rest. But no swinging motion was imparted to the body of Señor Hirsch, the well-known hide merchant on the coast. With a convulsive effort of the twisted arms it leaped up a few inches, curling upon itself like a fish on the end of a line. Señor Hirsch's head was flung back on his straining throat ; his chin trembled. For a moment the rattle of his chattering teeth pervaded the vast, shadowy room, where the candles made a patch of light round the two flames burning side by side. And as Sotillo, staying his raised hand, waited for him to speak,

with the sudden flash of a grin and a straining forward of
the wrenched shoulders, he spat violently into his face.

The uplifted whip fell, and the colonel sprang back
with a low cry of dismay, as if aspersed by a jet of deadly
venom.   Quick as thought he snatched up his revolver,
and fired twice.   The report and the concussion of the
shots seemed to throw him at once from ungovernable
rage into idiotic stupor.   He stood with drooping jaw
and stony eyes.   What had he done, *Sangre de Dios* ?
What had he done ?   He was basely appalled at his
impulsive act, sealing for ever these lips from which so
much was to be extorted.   What could he say ?   How
could he explain ?   Ideas of headlong flight somewhere,
anywhere, passed through his mind ; even the craven and
absurd notion of hiding under the table occurred to his
cowardice.   It was too late ; his officers had rushed in
tumultuously, in a great clatter of scabbards, clamouring
with astonishment and wonder.   But since they did not
immediately proceed to plunge their swords into his
breast, the brazen side of his character asserted itself.
Passing the sleeve of his uniform over his face he pulled
himself together.   His truculent glance, turned slowly
here and there, checked the noise where it fell ; and the
stiff body of the late Señor Hirsch, merchant, after swaying imperceptibly, made a half turn, and came to a rest
in the midst of awed murmurs and uneasy shuffling.

A voice remarked loudly, " Behold a man who will
never speak again."   And another, from the back row of
faces, timid and pressing, cried out :

" Why did you kill him, mi Coronel ? "

" Because he has confessed everything," answered
Sotillo, with the hardihood of desperation.   He felt
himself cornered.   He brazened it out on the strength
of his reputation with very fair success.   His hearers
thought him very capable of such an act.   They were disposed to believe his flattering tale.   There is no credulity so eager and blind as the credulity of covetousness,

which, in its universal extent, measures the moral misery
and the intellectual destitution of mankind. Ah, he
had confessed everything, this fractious Jew, this *bribon*!
Good! Then he was no longer wanted. A sudden
dense guffaw was heard from the senior captain—a big-
headed man, with little round eyes and monstrously fat
cheeks which never moved. The old major, tall and
fantastically ragged like a scarecrow, walked round the
body of the late Señor Hirsch, muttering to himself with
ineffable complacency that like this there was no need
to guard against any future treacheries of that scoundrel.
The others stared, shifting from foot to foot, and whispering short remarks to each other.

Sotillo buckled on his sword and gave curt, peremp-
tory orders to hasten the retirement decided upon in the
afternoon. Sinister, impressive, his sombrero pulled right
down upon his eyebrows, he marched first through the
door in such disorder of mind that he forgot utterly to
provide for Dr. Monygham's possible return. As the
officers trooped out after him, one or two looked back
hastily at the late Señor Hirsch, merchant from Esmeralda, left swinging rigidly at rest, alone with the two
burning candles. In the emptiness of the room the
burly shadow of head and shoulders on the wall had
an air of life.

Below, the troops fell in silently and moved off by
companies without drum or trumpet. The old scarecrow major commanded the rearguard; but the party he
left behind with orders to fire the Custom House (and
" burn the carcass of the treacherous Jew where it hung ")
failed somehow in their haste to set the staircase properly
alight. The body of the late Señor Hirsch dwelt alone
for a time in the dismal solitude of the unfinished building,
resounding weirdly with sudden slams and clicks of doors
and latches, with rustling scurries of torn papers, and the
tremulous sighs that at each gust of wind passed under
the high roof. The light of the two candles burning

before the perpendicular and breathless immobility of the late Señor Hirsch threw a gleam afar over land and water, like a signal in the night. He remained to startle Nostromo by his presence, and to puzzle Dr. Monygham by the mystery of his atrocious end.

"But why shot?" the doctor again asked himself audibly. This time he was answered by a dry laugh from Nostromo.

"You seem much concerned at a very natural thing, Señor Doctor. I wonder why? It is very likely that before long we shall all get shot one after another, if not by Sotillo, then by Pedrito, or Fuentes, or Gamacho. And we may even get the estrapade too, or worse—*quien sabe?*—with your pretty tale of the silver you put into Sotillo's head."

"It was in his head already," the doctor protested. "I only——"

"Yes. And you only nailed it there so that the devil himself——"

"That is precisely what I meant to do," caught up the doctor.

"That is what you meant to do? Bueno! It is as I say. You are a dangerous man."

Their voices, which without rising had been growing quarrelsome, ceased suddenly. The late Señor Hirsch, erect and shadowy against the stars, seemed to be waiting attentive, in impartial silence.

But Dr. Monygham had no mind to quarrel with Nostromo. At this supremely critical point of Sulaco's fortunes it was borne upon him at last that this man was really indispensable, more indispensable than ever the infatuation of Captain Mitchell, his proud discoverer, could conceive; far beyond what Decoud's best dry raillery about "my illustrious friend, the unique Capataz de Cargadores," had ever intended. The fellow was unique. He was not "one in a thousand." He was absolutely the only one. The doctor surrendered.

There was something in the genius of that Genoese seaman which dominated the destinies of great enterprises and of many people, the fortunes of Charles Gould, the fate of an admirable woman. At this last thought the doctor had to clear his throat before he could speak.

In a completely changed tone he pointed out to the Capataz that, to begin with, he personally ran no great risk. As far as everybody knew he was dead. It was an enormous advantage. He had only to keep out of sight in the Casa Viola, where the old Garibaldino was known to be alone—with his dead wife. The servants had all run away. No one would think of searching for him there, or anywhere else on earth, for that matter.

"That would be very true," Nostromo spoke up bitterly, "if I had not met you."

For a time the doctor kept silent. "Do you mean to say that you think I may give you away?" he asked in an unsteady voice. "Why? Why should I do that?"

"What do I know? Why not? To gain a day perhaps. It would take Sotillo a day to give me the estrapade, and try some other things perhaps, before he puts a bullet through my heart—as he did to that poor wretch here. Why not?"

The doctor swallowed with difficulty. His throat had gone dry in a moment. It was not from indignation. The doctor, pathetically enough, believed that he had forfeited the right to be indignant with any one—for anything. It was simple dread. Had the fellow heard his story by some chance? If so, there was an end of his usefulness in that direction. The indispensable man escaped his influence, because of that indelible blot which made him fit for dirty work. A feeling as of sickness came upon the doctor. He would have given anything to know, but he dared not clear up the point. The fanaticism of his devotion, fed on the sense of his abasement, hardened his heart in sadness and scorn.

"Why not, indeed?" he re-echoed sardonically.

" Then the safe thing for you is to kill me on the spot. I would defend myself. But you may just as well know I am going about unarmed."

" *Por Dios !* " said the Capataz passionately. " You fine people are all alike. All dangerous. All betrayers of the poor who are your dogs."

" You do not understand," began the doctor slowly.

" I understand you all ! " cried the other, with a violent movement, as shadowy to the doctor's eyes as the persistent immobility of the late Señor Hirsch. " A poor man amongst you has got to look after himself. I say that you do not care for those who serve you. Look at me ! After all these years, suddenly, here I find myself like one of these curs that bark outside the walls— without a kennel or a dry bone for my teeth. Caramba ! " But he relented with a contemptuous fairness. " Of course," he went on quietly, " I do not suppose that you would hasten to give me up to Sotillo, for example. It is not that. It is that I am nothing ! Suddenly——" He swung his arm downwards. " Nothing to any one," he repeated.

The doctor breathed freely. " Listen, Capataz," he said, stretching out his arm almost affectionately towards Nostromo's shoulder. " I am going to tell you a very simple thing. You are safe because you are needed. I would not give you away for any conceivable reason, because I want you."

In the dark Nostromo bit his lip. He had heard enough of that. He knew what that meant. No more of that for him. But he had to look after himself now, he thought. And he thought, too, that it would not be prudent to part in anger from his companion. The doctor, admitted to be a great healer, had, amongst the populace of Sulaco, the reputation of being an evil sort of man. It was based solidly on his personal appearance, which was strange, and on his rough, ironic manner —proofs visible, sensible, and incontrovertible of the doctor's malevolent disposition. And Nostromo was of the people. So he only grunted incredulously.

" You, to speak plainly, are the only man," the doctor pursued. " It is in your power to save this town and —everybody from the destructive rapacity of men who——"

" No, Señor," said Nostromo sullenly. " It is not in my power to get the treasure back for you to give up to Sotillo, or Pedrito, or Gamacho. What do I know ? "

" Nobody expects the impossible," was the answer.

" You have said it yourself—nobody," muttered Nostromo in a gloomy, threatening tone.

But Dr. Monygham, full of hope, disregarded the enigmatic words and the threatening tone. To their eyes, accustomed to obscurity, the late Señor Hirsch, growing more distinct, seemed to have come nearer. And the doctor lowered his voice in exposing his scheme as though afraid of being overheard.

He was taking the indispensable man into his fullest confidence. Its implied flattery and suggestion of great risks came with a familiar sound to the Capataz. His mind, floating in irresolution and discontent, recognised it with bitterness. He understood well that the doctor was anxious to save the San Tomé mine from annihilation. He would be nothing without it. It was his interest. Just as it had been the interest of Señor Decoud, of the Blancos, and of the Europeans to get his cargadores on their side. His thought became arrested upon Decoud. What would happen to him ?

Nostromo's prolonged silence made the doctor uneasy. He pointed out, quite unnecessarily, that though for the present he was safe, he could not live concealed for ever. The choice was between accepting the mission to Barrios, with all its dangers and difficulties, and leaving Sulaco by stealth, ingloriously, in poverty.

" None of your friends could reward you and protect you just now, Capataz. Not even Don Carlos himself."

" I would have none of your protection and none of
your rewards. I only wish I could trust your courage
and your sense. When I return in triumph, as you
say, with Barrios, I may find you all destroyed. You
have the knife at your throat now."

It was the doctor's turn to remain silent in the contemplation of horrible contingencies.

" Well, we would trust your courage and your sense.
And you, too, have a knife at your throat."

" Ah ! And whom am I to thank for that ? What
are your politics and your mines to me—your silver
and your constitutions—your Don Carlos this, and Don
José that——"

" I don't know," burst out the exasperated doctor.
" There are innocent people in danger whose little
finger is worth more than you or I and all the Ribierists
together. I don't know. You should have asked yourself before you allowed Decoud to lead you into all
this. It was your place to think like a man ; but if
you did not think then, try to act like a man now. Did
you imagine Decoud cared very much for what would
happen to you ? "

" No more than you care for what will happen to me,"
muttered the other.

" No ; I care for what will happen to you as little
as I care for what will happen to myself."

" And all this because you are such a devoted
Ribierist ? " Nostromo said in an incredulous tone.

" All this because I am such a devoted Ribierist,"
repeated Dr. Monygham grimly.

Again Nostromo, gazing abstractedly at the body of
the late Señor Hirsch, remained silent, thinking that the
doctor was a dangerous person in more than one sense.
It was impossible to trust him.

" Do you speak in the name of Don Carlos ? " he
asked at last.

" Yes, I do," the doctor said loudly, without hesitation. " He must come forward now. He must," he added in a mutter, which Nostromo did not catch.

" What did you say, Señor ? "

The doctor started. " I say that you must be true to yourself, Capataz. It would be worse than folly to fail now."

" True to myself ? " repeated Nostromo. " How do you know that I would not be true to myself if I told you to go to the devil with your propositions ? "

" I do not know. Maybe you would," the doctor said, with a roughness of tone intended to hide the sinking of his heart and the faltering of his voice. " All I know is, that you had better get away from here. Some of Sotillo's men may turn up here looking for me."

He slipped off the table, listening intently. The Capataz, too, stood up.

" Suppose I went to Cayta, what would you do mean-time ? " he asked.

" I would go to Sotillo directly you had left—in the way I am thinking of."

" A very good way—if only that engineer-in-chief consents. Remind him, Señor, that I looked after the old, rich Englishman who pays for the railway, and that I saved the lives of some of his people that time when a gang of thieves came from the south to wreck one of his pay-trains. It was I who discovered it all, at the risk of my life, by pretending to enter into their plans. Just as you are doing with Sotillo."

" Yes. Yes, of course. But I can offer him better arguments," the doctor said hastily. " Leave it to me."

" Ah, yes ! True. I am nothing."

" Not at all. You are everything."

They moved a few paces towards the door. Behind them the late Señor Hirsch preserved the immobility of a disregarded man.

" That will be all right. I know what to say to the

engineer," pursued the doctor in a low tone. " My difficulty will be with Sotillo."

And Dr. Monygham stopped short in the doorway as if intimidated by the difficulty. He had made the sacrifice of his life. He considered this a fitting opportunity. But he did not want to throw his life away too soon. In his quality of betrayer of Don Carlos's confidence, he would have ultimately to indicate the hiding-place of the treasure. That would be the end of his deception, and the end of himself as well, at the hands of the infuriated colonel. He wanted to delay him to the very last moment ; and he had been racking his brains to invent some place of concealment at once plausible and difficult of access.

He imparted his trouble to Nostromo, and concluded :

" Do you know what, Capataz ? I think that when the time comes and some information must be given, I shall indicate the Great Isabel. That is the best place I can think of. What is the matter ? "

A low exclamation had escaped Nostromo. The doctor waited, surprised, and after a moment of profound silence, heard a thick voice stammer out, " Utter folly," and stop with a gasp.

" Why folly ? "

" Ah ! You do not see it," began Nostromo scathingly, gathering scorn as he went on. " Three men in half an hour would see that no ground had been disturbed anywhere on that island. Do you think that such a treasure can be buried without leaving traces of the work—eh, Señor Doctor ? Why ! you would not gain half a day more before having your throat cut by Sotillo. The Isabel ! What stupidity ! What miserable invention ! Ah, you are all alike, you fine men of intelligence ! All you are fit for is to betray men of the people into undertaking deadly risks for objects that you are not even sure about. If it comes off you get the benefit. If not, then it does not matter. He is only a

dog. Ah ! *Madre de Dios*, I would——" He shook
his fists above his head.

The doctor was overwhelmed at first by this fierce,
hissing vehemence.

" Well ! It seems to me on your own showing that
the men of the people are no mean fools too," he said
sullenly. " No, but come. You are so clever. Have
you a better place ? "

Nostromo had calmed down as quickly as he had
flared up.

" I am clever enough for that," he said quietly,
almost with indifference. " You want to tell him of a
hiding-place big enough to take days in ransacking—a
place where a treasure of silver ingots can be buried
without leaving a sign on the surface ? "

" And close at hand," the doctor put in.

" Just so, Señor. Tell him it is sunk."

" This has the merit of being the truth," the doctor
said contemptuously. " He will not believe it."

" You tell him that it is sunk where he may hope to
lay his hands on it, and he will believe you quick enough.
Tell him it has been sunk in the harbour in order to be
recovered afterwards by divers. Tell him you found out
that I had orders from Don Carlos Gould to lower the
cases quietly overboard somewhere in a line between the
end of the jetty and the entrance. The depth is not too
great there. He has no divers, but he has a ship, boats,
ropes, chains, sailors—of a sort. Let him fish for the
silver. Let him set his fools to drag backwards and
forwards and crossways while he sits and watches till his
eyes drop out of his head."

" Really, this is an admirable idea," muttered the
doctor.

" Si. You tell him that, and see whether he will not
believe you ! He will spend days in rage and torment—
and still he will believe. He will have no thought for
anything else. He will not give up till he is driven off—

why, he may even forget to kill you. He will neither
eat nor sleep. He——"

"The very thing ! The very thing !" the doctor
repeated in an excited whisper. "Capataz, I begin to
believe that you are a great genius in your way."

Nostromo had paused ; then began again in a changed
tone, sombre, speaking to himself as though he had forgotten the doctor's existence.

"There is something in a treasure that fastens upon
a man's mind. He will pray and blaspheme and still
persevere, and will curse the day he ever heard of it, and
will let his last hour come upon him unawares, still
believing that he missed it only by a foot. He will see
it every time he closes his eyes. He will never forget it
till he is dead—and even then—— Doctor, did you
ever hear of the miserable gringos on Azuera, that
cannot die ? Ha ! ha ! Sailors like myself. There
is no getting away from a treasure that once fastens
upon your mind."

"You are a devil of a man, Capataz. It is the most
plausible thing."

Nostromo pressed his arm.

"It will be worse for him than thirst at sea or hunger
in a town full of people. Do you know what that is ?
He shall suffer greater torments than he inflicted upon
that terrified wretch who had no invention. None !
none ! Not like me. I could have told Sotillo a deadly
tale for very little pain."

He laughed wildly and turned in the doorway towards
the body of the late Señor Hirsch, an opaque, long blotch
in the semi-transparent obscurity of the room between the
two tall parallelograms of the windows full of stars.

"You man of fear !" he cried. "You shall be
avenged by me—Nostromo. Out of my way, doctor !
Stand aside, or, by the suffering soul of a woman dead
without confession, I will strangle you with my two
hands."

28

He bounded downwards into the black, smoky hall. With a grunt of astonishment, Dr. Monygham threw himself recklessly into the pursuit. At the bottom of the charred stairs he had a fall, pitching forward on his face with a force that would have stunned a spirit less intent upon a task of love and devotion. He was up in a moment, jarred, shaken, with a queer impression of the terrestrial globe having been flung at his head in the dark. But it wanted more than that to stop Dr. Monygham's body, possessed by the exaltation of self-sacrifice ; a reasonable exaltation, determined not to lose whatever advantage chance put into its way. He ran with head-long, tottering swiftness, his arms going like a windmill in his effort to keep his balance on his crippled feet. He lost his hat ; the tails of his open gaberdine flew behind him. He had no mind to lose sight of the indispensable man. But it was a long time, and a long way from the Custom House, before he managed to seize his arm from behind, roughly, out of breath.

" Stop ! Are you mad ? "

Already Nostromo was walking slowly, his head drooping, as if checked in his pace by the weariness of irresolution.

" What is that to you ? Ah ! I forgot you want me for something. Always. Siempre Nostromo."

" What do you mean by talking of strangling me ? " panted the doctor.

" What do I mean ? I mean that the king of the devils himself has sent you out of this town of cowards and talkers to meet me to-night of all the nights of my life."

Under the starry sky the Albergo d'Italia Una emerged, black and low, breaking the dark level of the plain. Nostromo stopped altogether.

" The priests say he is a tempter, do they not ? " he added, through his clenched teeth.

" My good man, you drivel. The devil has nothing to do with this. Neither has the town, which you may call by what name you please. But Don Carlos is neither a coward nor an empty talker. You will admit that ? " He waited. " Well ? "

" Could I see Don Carlos ? "

" Great heavens ! No ! Why ? What for ? " exclaimed the doctor in agitation. " I tell you it is madness. I will not let you go into the town for anything."

" I must."

" You must not ! " hissed the doctor fiercely, almost beside himself with the fear of the man doing away with his usefulness for an imbecile whim of some sort. " I tell you you shall not. I would rather——"

He stopped at loss for words, feeling fagged out, powerless, holding on to Nostromo's sleeve, absolutely for support after his run.

" I am betrayed ! " muttered the Capataz to himself ; and the doctor, who overheard the last word, made an effort to speak calmly.

" That is exactly what would happen to you. You would be betrayed."

He thought with a sickening dread that the man was so well known that he could not escape recognition. The house of the Señor Administrador was beset by spies, no doubt. And even the very servants of the Casa were not to be trusted. " Reflect, Capataz," he said impressively. . . . " What are you laughing at ? "

" I am laughing to think that if somebody that did not approve of my presence in town, for instance—you understand, Señor Doctor ?—if somebody were to give me up to Pedrito, it would not be beyond my power to make friends even with him. It is true. What do you think of that ? "

" You are a man of infinite resource, Capataz," said Dr. Monygham dismally. " I recognise that. But the town is full of talk about you ; and those few cargadores that are not in hiding with the railway people have been shouting ' Viva Montero ! ' on the plaza all day."

"My poor cargadores!" muttered Nostromo. "Betrayed! Betrayed!"

"I understand that on the wharf you were pretty free in laying about you with a stick amongst your poor cargadores," the doctor said in a grim tone, which showed that he was recovering from his exertions. "Make no mistake. Pedrito is furious at Señor Ribiera's rescue, and at having lost the pleasure of shooting Decoud. Already there are rumours in the town of the treasure having been spirited away. To have missed that does not please Pedrito either; but let me tell you that if you had all that silver in your hand for ransom it would not save you."

Turning swiftly, and catching the doctor by the shoulders, Nostromo thrust his face close to his.

"Maladetta! You follow me speaking of the treasure. You have sworn my ruin. You were the last man who looked upon me before I went out with it. And Sidoni the engine-driver says you have an evil eye."

"He ought to know. I saved his broken leg for him last year," the doctor said stoically. He felt on his shoulders the weight of these hands famed amongst the populace for snapping thick ropes and bending horseshoes. "And to you I offer the best means of saving yourself—let me go!—and of retrieving your great reputation. You boasted of making the Capataz de Cargadores famous from one end of America to the other about this wretched silver. But I bring you a better opportunity—let me go, *hombre*!"

Nostromo released him abruptly, and the doctor feared that the indispensable man would run off again. But he did not. He walked on slowly. The doctor hobbled by his side till, within a stone's-throw from the Casa Viola, Nostromo stopped again.

Silent in inhospitable darkness, the Casa Viola seemed to have changed its nature; his home appeared to repel him with an air of hopeless and inimical mystery. The doctor said :

" You will be safe there. Go in, Capataz."

" How can I go in ? " Nostromo seemed to ask himself in a low, inward tone. " She cannot unsay what she said, and I cannot undo what I have done."

" I tell you it is all right. Viola is all alone in there. I looked in as I came out of the town. You will be perfectly safe in that house till you leave it to make your name famous on the Campo. I am going now to arrange for your departure with the engineer-in-chief, and I shall bring you news here long before daybreak."

Dr. Monygham, disregarding, or perhaps fearing to penetrate the meaning of Nostromo's silence, clapped him lightly on the shoulder, and, starting off with his smart lame walk, vanished utterly at the third or fourth hop in the direction of the railway track. Arrested between the two wooden posts for people to fasten their horses to, Nostromo did not move, as if he too had been planted solidly in the ground. At the end of half an hour he lifted his head to the deep baying of the dogs at the railway yards, which had burst out suddenly, tumultuous and deadened as if coming from under the plain. That lame doctor with the evil eye had got there pretty fast.

Step by step Nostromo approached the Albergo d'Italia Una, which he had never known so lightless, so silent before. The door, all black in the pale wall, stood open as he had left it, twenty-four hours before, when he had nothing to hide from the world. He remained before it, irresolute, like a fugitive, like a man betrayed. Poverty, misery, starvation ! Where had he heard these words ? The anger of a dying woman had prophesied that fate for his folly. It looked as if it would come true very quickly. And the leperos would laugh, she had said. Yes, they would laugh if they knew that the Capataz de Cargadores was at the mercy of the mad doctor whom they could remember, only a few years ago, buying cooked food from a stall on the plaza for a copper coin—like one of themselves.

At that moment the notion of seeking Captain Mitchell passed through his mind. He glanced in the direction of the jetty, and saw a small gleam of light in the O.S.N. Company's building. The thought of lighted windows was not attractive. Two lighted windows had decoyed him into the empty Custom House, only to fall into the clutches of that doctor. No! He would not go near lighted windows again on that night. Captain Mitchell was there. And what could he be told? That doctor would worm it all out of him as if he were a child.

On the threshold he called out "Giorgio!" in an undertone. Nobody answered. He stepped in. "Olà! viejo! Are you there?" . . . In the impenetrable darkness his head swam with the illusion that the obscurity of the kitchen was as vast as the Placid Gulf, and that the floor dipped forward like a sinking lighter. "Olà! viejo!" he repeated falteringly, swaying where he stood. His hand, extended to steady himself, fell upon the table. Moving a step forward, he shifted it, and felt a box of matches under his fingers. He fancied he had heard a quiet sigh. He listened for a moment, holding his breath; then, with trembling hands, tried to strike a light.

The tiny piece of wood flamed up quite blindingly at the end of his fingers, raised above his blinking eyes. A concentrated glare fell upon the leonine white head of old Giorgio against the black fireplace—showed him leaning forward in a chair in staring immobility, surrounded, overhung, by great masses of shadow, his legs crossed, his cheek in his hand, an empty pipe in the corner of his mouth. It seemed hours before he attempted to turn his face; at the very moment the match went out, and he disappeared, overwhelmed by the shadows, as if the walls and roof of the desolate house had collapsed upon his white head in ghostly silence.

Nostromo heard him stir and utter dispassionately the words :

" It may have been a vision."

" No," he said softly ; " it is no vision, old man."

A strong chest voice asked in the dark :

" Is that you I hear, Giovann' Battista ? "

" Si, *viejo*. Steady. Not so loud."

After his release by Sotillo, Giorgio Viola, attended to the very door by the good-natured engineer-in-chief, had re-entered the house, which he had been made to leave almost at the very moment of his wife's death. All was still. The lamp above was burning. He nearly called out to her by name ; and the thought that no call from him would ever again evoke the answer of her voice, made him drop heavily into the chair with a loud groan, wrung out by the pain as of a keen blade piercing his breast.

The rest of the night he made no sound. The darkness turned to grey, and on the colourless, clear, glassy dawn the jagged sierra stood out flat and opaque, as if cut out of paper.

The enthusiastic and severe soul of Giorgio Viola, sailor, champion of oppressed humanity, enemy of kings, and, by the grace of Mrs. Gould, hotel-keeper of the Sulaco harbour, had descended into the open abyss of desolation amongst the shattered vestiges of his past. He remembered his wooing between two campaigns, a single short week in the season of gathering olives. Nothing approached the grave passion of that time but the deep, passionate sense of his bereavement. He discovered all the extent of his dependence upon the silenced voice of that woman. It was her voice that he missed. Abstracted, busy, lost in inward contemplation, he seldom looked at his wife in those later years. The thought of his girls was a matter of concern, not of consolation. It was her voice that he would miss. And he remembered the other child—the little boy who died at sea. Ah, a man would have been something to lean upon! And, alas! even Gian' Battista—he of whom, and of Linda, his wife had spoken to him so anxiously before she dropped off into her last sleep on earth, he on whom she had called aloud to save the children, just before she died—even he was dead!

And the old man, bent forward, his head in his hand, sat through the day in immobility and solitude. He never heard the brazen roar of the bells in town. When it ceased, the earthenware filter in the corner of the kitchen kept on its swift musical drip, drip into the great porous jar below.

Towards sunset he got up, and with slow movements disappeared up the narrow staircase. His bulk filled it; and the rubbing of his shoulders made a small noise as of a mouse running behind the plaster of a wall. While he remained up there the house was as dumb as a grave. Then, with the same faint rubbing noise, he descended. He had to catch at the chairs and tables to regain his seat. He seized his pipe off the high mantel of the fireplace—but made no attempt to reach the tobacco—thrust it empty into the corner of his mouth, and sat down again in the same staring pose. The sun of Pedrito's entry into Sulaco, the last sun of Señor Hirsch's life, the first of Decoud's solitude on the Great Isabel, passed over the Albergo d'Italia Una on its way to the west. The tinkling drip, drip of the filter had ceased, the lamp upstairs had burnt itself out, and the night beset Giorgio Viola and his dead wife with its obscurity and silence that seemed invincible till the Capataz de Cargadores, returning from the dead, put them to flight with the splutter and flare of a match.

" Si, *viejo*. It is me. Wait."

Nostromo, after barricading the door and closing the shutters carefully, groped upon a shelf for a candle, and lit it.

Old Viola had risen. He followed with his eyes in

the dark the sounds made by Nostromo. The light disclosed him standing without support, as if the mere presence of that man who was loyal, brave, incorruptible, who was all his son would have been, were enough for the support of his decaying strength.

He extended his hand, grasping the briar-wood pipe, whose bowl was charred on the edge, and knitted his bushy eyebrows heavily at the light.

"You have returned," he said, with shaky dignity. " Ah ! Very well ! I——"

He broke off. Nostromo, leaning back against the table, his arms folded on his breast, nodded at him slightly.

" You thought I was drowned ! No ! The best dog of the rich, of the aristocrats, of these fine men who can only talk and betray the people, is not dead yet."

The Garibaldino, motionless, seemed to drink in the sound of the well-known voice. His head moved slightly once as if in sign of approval ; but Nostromo saw clearly that the old man understood nothing of the words. There was no one to understand ; no one he could take into the confidence of Decoud's fate, of his own, into the secret of the silver. That doctor was an enemy of the people—a tempter. . . .

Old Giorgio's heavy frame shook from head to foot with the effort to overcome his emotion at the sight of that man, who had shared the intimacies of his domestic life as though he had been a grown-up son.

" She believed you would return," he said solemnly.

Nostromo raised his head.

" She was a wise woman. How could I fail to come back——"

He finished the thought mentally : " Since she has prophesied for me an end of poverty, misery, and starvation ? " These words of Teresa's anger, from the circumstances in which they had been uttered, like the cry of a soul prevented from making its peace with God, stirred

the obscure superstition of personal fortune from which
even the greatest genius amongst men of adventure and
action is seldom free. They reigned over Nostromo's
mind with the force of a potent malediction. And what
a curse it was, that which her words had laid upon him !
He had been orphaned so young that he could remember
no other woman whom he called mother. Henceforth
there would be no enterprise in which he would not fail.
The spell was working already. Death itself would elude
him now. . . . He said violently :

" Come, *viejo* ! Get me something to eat. I am
hungry ! *Sangre de Dios !* The emptiness of my belly
makes me light-headed."

With his chin dropped again upon his bare breast
above his folded arms, barefooted, watching from under
a gloomy brow the movements of old Viola foraging
amongst the cupboards, he seemed as if indeed fallen
under a curse—a ruined and sinister Capataz.

Old Viola walked out of a dark corner, and, without a
word, emptied upon the table out of his hollowed palms
a few dry crusts of bread and half a raw onion.

While the Capataz began to devour this beggar's fare,
taking up with stony-eyed voracity piece after piece lying
by his side, the Garibaldino went off, and, squatting
down in another corner, filled an earthenware mug with
red wine out of a wicker-covered demi-john. With a
familiar gesture, as when serving customers in the café,
he had thrust his pipe between his teeth to have his
hands free.

The Capataz drank greedily. A slight flush deepened
the bronze of his cheek. Before him, Viola, with a turn
of his white and massive head towards the staircase, took
his empty pipe out of his mouth, and pronounced slowly :

" After the shot was fired down here, which killed
her as surely as if the bullet had struck her oppressed
heart, she called upon you to save the children. Upon
you, Gian' Battista."

The Capataz looked up.

" Did she do that, padrone ?   To save the children !
They are with the English Señora, their rich benefactress.
Hey, old man of the people !   Thy benefactress . . ."

" I am old," muttered Giorgio Viola.   " An English-
woman was allowed to give a bed to Garibaldi lying
wounded in prison.   The greatest man that ever lived.
A man of the people, too—a sailor.   I may let another
keep a roof over my head.   Si . . . I am old.   I may
let her.   Life lasts too long sometimes."

" And she herself may not have a roof over her head
before many days are out, unless I . . . What do you
say ?   Am I to keep a roof over her head ?   Am I to
try—and save all the Blancos together with her ? "

" You shall do it," said old Viola in a strong voice.
" You shall do it as my son would have . . ."

" Thy son, *viejo* ! . . . There never has been a man
like thy son.   Ha, I must try ! . . . But what if it were
only a part of the curse to lure me on ? . . . And so she
called upon me to save—and then——? "

" She spoke no more."   The heroic follower of
Garibaldi, at the thought of the eternal stillness and
silence fallen upon the shrouded form stretched out on
the bed upstairs, averted his face and raised his hand to
his furrowed brow.   " She was dead before I could seize
her hands," he stammered out pitifully.

Before the wide eyes of the Capataz, staring at the
doorway of the dark staircase, floated the shape of the
Great Isabel, like a strange ship in distress, freighted
with enormous wealth and the solitary life of a man.   It
was impossible for him to do anything.   He could only
hold his tongue, since there was no one to trust.   The
treasure would be lost, probably—unless Decoud . . .
And his thought came abruptly to an end.   He perceived
that he could not imagine in the least what Decoud was
likely to do.

Old Viola had not stirred.   And the motionless

Capataz dropped his long, soft eyelashes, which gave to
the upper part of his fierce, black-whiskered face a
touch of feminine ingenuousness. The silence had lasted
for a long time.

" God rest her soul ! " he murmured gloomily.

CHAPTER TEN

THE next day was quiet in the morning, except for the faint sound of firing to the northward, in the direction of Los Hatos. Captain Mitchell had listened to it from his balcony anxiously. The phrase, " In my delicate position as the only consular agent then in the port, everything, sir, everything was a just cause for anxiety," had its place in the more or less stereotyped relation of the " historical events " which for the next few years was at the service of distinguished strangers visiting Sulaco. The mention of the dignity and neutrality of the flag, so difficult to preserve in his position, " right in the thick of these events between the lawlessness of that piratical villain Sotillo and the more regularly established but scarcely less atrocious tyranny of His Excellency Don Pedro Montero," came next in order. Captain Mitchell was not the man to enlarge upon mere dangers much. But he insisted that it was a memorable day. On that day, towards dusk, he had seen " that poor fellow of mine —Nostromo. The sailor whom I discovered, and, I may say, made, sir. The man of the famous ride to Cayta, sir. An historical event, sir ! "

Regarded by the O.S.N. Company as an old and faithful servant, Captain Mitchell was allowed to attain the term of his usefulness in ease and dignity at the head of the enormously extended service. The augmentation of the establishment, with its crowds of clerks, an office in town, the old office in the harbour, the division into

departments—passengers, cargo, lighterage, and so on—
secured a greater leisure for his last years in the regener-
ated Sulaco, the capital of the Occidental Republic.
Liked by the natives for his good nature and the formality
of his manner, self-important and simple, known for
years as a " friend of our country," he felt himself a
personality of mark in the town.   Getting up early for
a turn in the market-place while the gigantic shadow of
Higuerota was still lying upon the fruit and flower
stalls piled up with masses of gorgeous colouring,
attending easily to current affairs, welcomed in houses,
greeted by ladies on the Alameda, with his entry into
all the clubs and a footing in the Casa Gould, he led his
privileged old bachelor, man-about-town existence with
great comfort and solemnity.   But on mail-boat days
he was down at the Harbour Office at an early hour,
with his own gig, manned by a smart crew in white
and blue, ready to dash off and board the ship directly
she showed her bows between the harbour heads.

It would be into the Harbour Office that he would
lead some privileged passenger he had brought off in his
own boat, and invite him to take a seat for a moment
while he signed a few papers.   And Captain Mitchell,
seating himself at his desk, would keep on talking
hospitably :
" There isn't much time if you are to see everything
in a day.   We shall be off in a moment.   We'll have
lunch at the Amarilla Club—though I belong also to the
Anglo-American—mining engineers and business men,
don't you know—and to the Mirliflores as well, a new
club—English, French, Italians, all sorts—lively young
fellows mostly, who wanted to pay a compliment to an
old resident, sir.   But we'll lunch at the Amarilla.
Interest you, I fancy.   Real thing of the country.   Men
of the first families.   The President of the Occidental
Republic himself belongs to it, sir.   Fine old bishop
with a broken nose in the patio.   Remarkable piece of

statuary, I believe. Cavaliere Parrochetti—you know
Parrochetti, the famous Italian sculptor ?—was working
here for two years—thought very highly of our old
bishop. . . . There ! I am very much at your service
now."

Proud of his experience, penetrated by the sense of
historical importance of men, events, and buildings, he
talked pompously in jerky periods, with slight sweeps of
his short, thick arm, letting nothing " escape the attention " of his privileged captive.

" Lot of building going on, as you observe. Before
the Separation it was a plain of burnt grass smothered
in clouds of dust, with an ox-cart track to our jetty.
Nothing more. This is the Harbour Gate. Picturesque,
is it not ? Formerly the town stopped short there. We
enter now the Calle de la Constitucion. Observe the old
Spanish houses. Great dignity. Eh ? I suppose it's
just as it was in the time of the Viceroys, except for
the pavement. Wood blocks now. Sulaco National Bank
there, with the sentry-boxes each side of the gate. Casa
Avellanos this side, with all the ground-floor windows
shuttered. A wonderful woman lives there — Miss
Avellanos—the beautiful Antonia. A character, sir !
An historical woman ! Opposite—Casa Gould. Noble
gateway. Yes, *the* Goulds of the original Gould Concession, that all the world knows of now. I hold seventeen of the thousand-dollar shares in the Consolidated
San Tomé mines. All the poor savings of my lifetime,
sir, and it will be enough to keep me in comfort to the
end of my days at home when I retire. I got in on the
ground floor, you see. Don Carlos, great friend of mine.
Seventeen shares—quite a little fortune to leave behind
one, too. I have a niece—married a parson—most
worthy man, incumbent of a small parish in Sussex ;
no end of children. I was never married myself. A
sailor should exercise self-denial. Standing under that
very gateway, sir, with some young engineer fellows,

NOSTROMO

ready to defend that house where we had received so much kindness and hospitality, I saw the first and last charge of Pedrito's horsemen upon Barrios's troops, who had just taken the Harbour Gate. They could not stand the new rifles brought out by that poor Decoud. It was a murderous fire. In a moment the street became blocked with a mass of dead men and horses. They never came on again."

And all day Captain Mitchell would talk like this to his more or less willing victim :

" The plaza ! I call it magnificent ! Twice the area of Trafalgar Square."

From the very centre, in the blazing sunshine, he pointed out the buildings :

" The Intendencia, now President's Palace—Cabildo, where the Lower Chamber of Parliament sits. You notice the new houses on that side of the plaza ? Compañia Anzani, a great general store, like those co-operative things at home. Old Anzani was murdered by the National Guards in front of his safe. It was even for that specific crime that the deputy Gamacho, commanding the Nationals, a bloodthirsty and savage brute, was executed publicly by garrotte upon the sentence of a court-martial ordered by Barrios. Anzani's nephews converted the business into a company. All that side of the plaza had been burnt ; used to be colonnaded before. A terrible fire, by the light of which I saw the last of the fighting, the llaneros flying, the Nationals throwing their arms down, and the miners of San Tomé, all Indians from the sierra, rolling by like a torrent to the sound of pipes and cymbals, green flags flying, a wild mass of men in white ponchos and green hats, on foot, on mules, on donkeys. Such a sight, sir, will never be seen again. The miners had marched upon the town, Don Pépé leading on his black horse, and their very wives in the rear on burros, screaming encouragement, sir, and beating tambourines. I remember one of these women had a

green parrot seated on her shoulder, as calm as a bird of
stone. They had just saved their Señor Administrador ;
for Barrios, though he ordered the assault at once, at
night too, would have been too late. Pedrito Montero
had Don Carlos led out to be shot—like his uncle many
years ago—and then, as Barrios said afterwards, ' Sulaco
would not have been worth fighting for.' Sulaco without
the concession was nothing ; and there were tons and
tons of dynamite distributed all over the mountain with
detonators arranged, and an old priest, Father Romàn,
standing by to annihilate the San Tomé mine at the first
news of failure. Don Carlos had made up his mind not
to leave it behind, and he had the right men to see to it,
too."

Thus Captain Mitchell would talk in the middle of
the plaza, holding over his head a white umbrella with a
green lining ; but inside the cathedral, in the dim light,
with a faint scent of incense floating in the cool atmosphere, and here and there a kneeling female figure, black
or all white, with a veiled head, his lowered voice became
solemn and impressive.

" Here," he would say, pointing to a niche in the wall
of the dusky aisle, " you see the bust of Don José Avellanos, ' Patriot and Statesman,' as the inscription says,
' Minister to Courts of England and Spain, etc. etc., died
in the woods of Los Hatos worn out with his lifelong
struggle for Right and Justice at the dawn of the New
Era.' A fair likeness. Parrochetti's work from some
old photographs and a pencil sketch by Mrs. Gould. I
was well acquainted with that distinguished Spanish-
American of the old school, a true hidalgo, beloved by
everybody who knew him. The marble medallion in the
wall, in the antique style, representing a veiled woman
seated with her hands clasped loosely over her knees,
commemorates that unfortunate young gentleman who
sailed out with Nostromo on that fatal night, sir. See :
' To the memory of Martin Decoud, his betrothed

29

Antonia Avellanos.' Frank, simple, noble. There you
have that lady, sir, as she is. An exceptional woman.
Those who thought she would give way to despair were
mistaken, sir. She has been blamed in many quarters
for not having taken the veil. It was expected of her.
But Doña Antonia is not the stuff they make nuns of.
Bishop Corbelàn, her uncle, lives with her in the Corbelàn town house. He is a fierce sort of priest, everlastingly worrying the Government about the old Church
lands and convents. I believe they think a lot of him in
Rome. Now let us go to the Amarilla Club, just across
the plaza, to get some lunch."

Directly outside the cathedral on the very top of the
noble flight of steps, his voice rose pompously, his arm
found again its sweeping gesture.

" *Porvenir*, over there on that first floor, above those
French plate-glass shop-fronts ; our biggest daily. Conservative, or, rather, I should say, Parliamentary. We
have the Parliamentary party here of which the actual
Chief of the State, Don Juste Lopez, is the head ; a very
sagacious man, I think. A first-rate intellect, sir. The
Democratic party in opposition rests mostly, I am sorry
to say, on these socialistic Italians, sir, with their secret
societies, camorras, and such-like. There are lots of
Italians settled here on the railway lands, dismissed
navvies, mechanics, and so on, all along the trunk line.
There are whole villages of Italians on the Campo. And
the natives, too, are being drawn into these ways. . . .
American bar ? Yes. And over there you can see
another. New Yorkers mostly frequent that one. . . .
Here we are at the Amarilla. Observe the bishop at
the foot of the stairs to the right as we go in."

And the lunch would begin and terminate its lavish
and leisurely course at a little table in the gallery, Captain
Mitchell nodding, bowing, getting up to speak for a
moment to different officials in black clothes, merchants
in jackets, officers in uniform, middle-aged caballeros

from the Campo—sallow, little, nervous men, and fat, placid, swarthy men, and Europeans or North Americans of superior standing, whose faces looked very white amongst the majority of dark complexions and black, glistening eyes.

Captain Mitchell would lie back in the chair, casting around looks of satisfaction, and tender over the table a case full of thick cigars.

" Try a weed with your coffee. Local tobacco. The black coffee you get at the Amarilla, sir, you don't meet anywhere in the world. We get the bean from a famous *caféteria* in the foothills, whose owner sends three sacks every year as a present to his fellow-members in re-membrance of the fight against Gamacho's Nationals, carried on from these very windows by the caballeros. He was in town at the time, and took part, sir, to the bitter end. It arrives on three mules—not in the common way, by rail ; no fear !—right into the patio, escorted by mounted peons, in charge of the Mayoral of his estate, who walks upstairs, booted and spurred, and delivers it to our committee formally with the words : ' For the sake of those fallen on the third of May.' We call it *Très de Mayo* coffee. Taste it."

Captain Mitchell, with an expression as though mak-ing ready to hear a sermon in a church, would lift the tiny cup to his lips. And the nectar would be sipped to the bottom during a restful silence in a cloud of cigar smoke.

" Look at this man in black just going out," he would begin, leaning forward hastily. " This is the famous Hernandez, Minister of War. The *Times* special corre-spondent, who wrote that striking series of letters call-ing the Occidental Republic the ' Treasure House of the World,' gave a whole article to him and the force he has organised—the renowned Carabineers of the Campo."

Captain Mitchell's guest, staring curiously, would see a figure in a long-tailed black coat walking gravely, with downcast eyelids in a long, composed face, a brow furrowed horizontally, a pointed head, whose grey hair, thin at the top, combed down carefully on all sides and rolled at the ends, fell low on the neck and shoulders. This, then, was the famous bandit of whom Europe had heard with interest. He put on a high-crowned sombrero with a wide, flat brim ; a rosary of wooden beads was twisted about his right wrist. And Captain Mitchell would proceed :

"The protector of the Sulaco refugees from the rage of Pedrito. As general of cavalry with Barrios, he distinguished himself at the storming of Tonoro, where Señor Fuentes was killed with the last remnant of the Monterists. He is the friend and humble servant of Bishop Corbelàn. Hears three Masses every day. I bet you he will step into the cathedral to say a prayer or two on his way home to his siesta."

He took several puffs at his cigar in silence ; then, in his most important manner, pronounced :

"The Spanish race, sir, is prolific of remarkable characters in every rank of life. . . . I propose we go now into the billiard-room, which is cool, for a quiet chat. There's never anybody there till after five. I could tell you episodes of the Separationist revolution that would astonish you. When the great heat's over, we'll take a turn on the Alameda."

The programme went on relentless, like a law of Nature. The turn on the Alameda was taken with slow steps and stately remarks.

"All the great world of Sulaco here, sir." Captain Mitchell bowed right and left with no end of formality ; then with animation : "Doña Emilia, Mrs. Gould's carriage. Look ! Always white mules. The kindest, most gracious woman the sun ever shone upon. A great position, sir. A great position. First lady in Sulaco— far before the President's wife. And worthy of it." He took off his hat ; then, with a studied change of tone, added, negligently, that the man in black by her side,

with a high white collar and a scarred, snarly face, was Dr.
Monygham, Inspector of State Hospitals, Chief Medical
Officer of the Consolidated San Tomé Mines. "A
familiar of the house. Everlastingly there. No wonder.
The Goulds made him. Very clever man and all that,
but I never liked him. Nobody does. I can recollect
him limping about the streets in a check shirt and native
sandals with a water-melon under his arm—all he would
get to eat for the day. A big-wig now, sir, and as nasty
as ever. However . . . There's no doubt he played his
part fairly well at the time. He saved us all from the
deadly incubus of Sotillo, where a more particular man
might have failed——"

His arm went up.

"The equestrian statue that used to stand on the
pedestal over there has been removed. It was an
anachronism," Captain Mitchell commented obscurely.
"There is some talk of replacing it by a marble shaft
commemorative of Separation, with angels of peace at
the four corners, and bronze Justice holding an even
balance, all gilt, on the top. Cavaliere Parrochetti was
asked to make a design, which you can see framed under
glass in the Municipal Sala. Names are to be engraved
all round the base. Well! They could do no better
than begin with the name of Nostromo. He has done for
Separation as much as anybody else, and," added Captain
Mitchell, "has got less than many others by it—when it
comes to that." He dropped on to a stone seat under a
tree, and tapped invitingly at the place by his side. "He
carried to Barrios the letters from Sulaco which decided
the general to abandon Cayta for a time, and come back to
our help here by sea. The transports were still in harbour,
fortunately. Sir, I did not even know that my Capataz de
Cargadores was alive. I had no idea. It was Dr. Monygham who came upon him, by chance, in the Custom
House, evacuated an hour or two before by the wretched
Sotillo. I was never told; never given a hint, nothing

—as if I were unworthy of confidence. Monygham
arranged it all. He went to the railway yards, and got
admission to the engineer-in-chief, who, for the sake of
the Goulds as much as for anything else, consented to
let an engine make a dash down the line, one hundred and
eighty miles, with Nostromo aboard. It was the only way
to get him off. In the Construction Camp at the railhead he obtained a horse, arms, some clothing, and
started alone on that marvellous ride—four hundred
miles in six days, through a disturbed country, ending
by the feat of passing through the Monterist lines outside
Cayta. The history of that ride, sir, would make a most
exciting book. He carried all our lives in his pocket.
Devotion, courage, fidelity, intelligence were not enough.
Of course, he was perfectly fearless and incorruptible.
But a man was wanted who would know how to succeed.
He was that man, sir. On the fifth of May, being practically a prisoner in the Harbour Office of my Company,
I suddenly heard the whistle of an engine in the railway
yards, a quarter of a mile away. I could not believe my
ears. I made one jump on to the balcony, and beheld
a locomotive under a great head of steam run out of the
yard gates, screeching like mad, enveloped in a white
cloud, and then, just abreast of old Viola's inn, check
almost to a standstill. I made out, sir, a man—I couldn't
tell who—dash out of the Albergo d'Italia Una, climb into
the cab, and then, sir, that engine seemed positively to
leap clear of the house, and was gone in the twinkling of
an eye. As you blow a candle out, sir! There was a
first-rate driver on the footplate, sir, I can tell you.
They were fired heavily upon by the National Guards in
Rincon and one other place. Fortunately the line had
not been torn up. In four hours they reached the Construction Camp. Nostromo had his start. . . . The
rest you know. You've got only to look round you.
There are people on this Alameda that ride in their
carriages, or even are alive at all to-day, because years ago

I engaged a runaway Italian sailor for a foreman of our
wharf simply on the strength of his looks. And that's a
fact. You can't get over it, sir. On the seventeenth
of May, just twelve days after I saw the man from the
Casa Viola get on the engine, and wondered what it
meant, Barrios's transports were entering this harbour, and
the ' Treasure House of the World,' as the *Times* man
calls Sulaco in his book, was saved intact for civilisation
—for a great future, sir. Pedrito, with Hernandez on the
west, and the San Tomé miners pressing on the land gate,
was not able to oppose the landing. He had been sending messages to Sotillo for a week to join him. Had
Sotillo done so there would have been massacres and proscription that would have left no man or woman of position alive. But that's where Dr. Monygham comes in.
Sotillo, blind and deaf to everything, stuck on board his
steamer watching the dragging for silver, which he
believed to be sunk at the bottom of the harbour. They
say that for the last three days he was out of his mind,
raving and foaming with disappointment at getting
nothing, flying about the deck, and yelling curses at the
boats with the drags, ordering them in, and then suddenly
stamping his foot and crying out, ' And yet it is there !
I see it ! I feel it ! '

" He was preparing to hang Dr. Monygham (whom
he had on board) at the end of the after-derrick, when the
first of Barrios's transports, one of our own ships at that,
steamed right in, and ranging close alongside opened a
small-arm fire without as much preliminaries as a hail.
It was the completest surprise in the world, sir. They
were too astounded at first to bolt below. Men were
falling right and left like ninepins. It's a miracle that
Monygham, standing on the after-hatch with the rope
already round his neck, escaped being riddled through
and through like a sieve. He told me since that he had
given himself up for lost, and kept on yelling with all
the strength of his lungs, ' Hoist a white flag ! Hoist a

white flag ! ' Suddenly an old major of the Esmeralda regiment, standing by, unsheathed his sword with a shriek, ' Die, perjured traitor ! ' and ran Sotillo clean through the body, just before he fell himself shot through the head."

Captain Mitchell stopped for a while.

" Begad, sir, I could spin you a yarn for hours. But it's time we started off to Rincon. It would not do for you to pass through Sulaco and not see the lights of the San Tomé mine, a whole mountain ablaze like a lighted palace above the dark Campo. It's a fashionable drive. . . . But let me tell you one little anecdote, sir ; just to show you. A fortnight or more later, when Barrios, declared Generalissimo, was gone in pursuit of Pedrito away south, when the Provisional Junta, with Don Juste Lopez at its head, had promulgated the new Constitution, and our Don Carlos Gould was packing up his trunks bound on a mission to San Francisco and Washington (the United States, sir, were the first great power to recognise the Occidental Republic) —a fortnight later, I say, when we were beginning to feel that our heads were safe on our shoulders, if I may express myself so, a prominent man, a large shipper by our line, came to see me on business, and, says he, the first thing : ' I say, Captain Mitchell, is that fellow ' (meaning Nostromo) ' still the Capataz of your Cargadores or not ? ' ' What's the matter ? ' says I. ' Because, if he is, then I don't mind ; I send and receive a good lot of cargo by your ships ; but I have observed him several days loafing about the wharf, and just now he stopped me as cool as you please, with a request for a cigar. Now, you know, my cigars are rather special, and I can't get them so easily as all that.' ' I hope you stretched a point ? ' I said very gently. ' Why, yes. But it's a confounded nuisance. The fellow's everlastingly cadging for smokes.' Sir, I turned my eyes away, and then asked, ' Weren't you one of the prisoners in the

Cabildo ? ' ' You know very well I was, and in chains, too,' says he. ' And under a fine of fifteen thousand dollars ? ' He coloured, sir, because it got about that he fainted from fright when they came to arrest him, and then behaved before Fuentes in a manner to make the very *policianos*, who had dragged him there by the hair of his head, smile at his cringing. ' Yes,' he says in a sort of shy way. ' Why ? ' ' Oh, nothing. You stood to lose a tidy bit,' says I, ' even if you saved your life. . . . But what can I do for you ? ' He never even saw the point. Not he. And that's how the world wags, sir."

He rose a little stiffly, and the drive to Rincon would be taken with only one philosophical remark, uttered by the merciless cicerone, with his eyes fixed upon the lights of San Tomé, that seemed suspended in the dark night between earth and heaven.

" A great power, this, for good and evil, sir. A great power."

And the dinner at the Mirliflores would be eaten, excellent as to cooking, and leaving upon the traveller's mind an impression that there were in Sulaco many pleasant, able young men with salaries apparently too large for their discretion, and amongst them a few, mostly Anglo-Saxon, skilled in the art of, as the saying is, " taking a rise " out of his kind host.

With a rapid, jingling drive to the harbour in a two-wheeled machine (which Captain Mitchell called a curricle) behind a fleet and scraggy mule beaten all the time by an obviously Neapolitan driver, the cycle would be nearly closed before the lighted-up offices of the O.S.N. Company, remaining open so late because of the steamer. Nearly—but not quite.

" Ten o'clock. Your ship won't be ready to leave till half-past twelve, if by then. Come in for a brandy-and-soda and one more cigar."

And in the superintendent's private room the

privileged passenger by the *Ceres*, or *Juno*, or *Pallas*,
stunned and, as it were, annihilated mentally by a sudden
surfeit of sights, sounds, names, facts, and complicated
information imperfectly apprehended, would listen like a
tired child to a fairy tale ; would hear a voice, familiar
and surprising in its pompousness, tell him, as if from
another world, how there was " in this very harbour "
an international naval demonstration, which put an
end to the Costaguana-Sulaco War.   How the United
States cruiser, *Powhattan*, was the first to salute the
Occidental flag—white, with a wreath of green laurel in
the middle encircling a yellow amarilla flower.   Would
hear how General Montero, in less than a month after
proclaiming himself Emperor of Costaguana, was shot
dead (during a solemn and public distribution of orders
and crosses) by a young artillery officer, the brother of
his then mistress.

"The abominable Pedrito, sir, fled the country," the
voice would say.   And it would continue : " A captain
of one of our ships told me lately that he recognised
Pedrito the guerrillero, arrayed in purple slippers and
a velvet smoking-cap with a gold tassel, keeping a disorderly house in one of the southern ports."

"Abominable Pedrito !   Who the devil was he ? "
would wonder the distinguished bird of passage, hovering
on the confines of waking and sleep with resolutely open
eyes and a faint but amiable curl upon his lips, from
between which stuck out the eighteenth or twentieth
cigar of that memorable day.

"He appeared to me in this very room like a haunting ghost, sir "—Captain Mitchell was talking of his
Nostromo with true warmth of feeling and a touch of
wistful pride.   "You may imagine, sir, what an effect
it produced on me.   He had come round by sea with
Barrios, of course.   And the first thing he told me after
I became fit to hear him was that he had picked up the
lighter's boat floating in the gulf !   He seemed quite

overcome by the circumstance. And a remarkable enough circumstance it was, when you remember that it was then sixteen days since the sinking of the silver. At once I could see he was another man. He stared at the wall, sir, as if there had been a spider or something running about there. The loss of the silver preyed on his mind. The first thing he asked me about was whether Doña Antonia had heard yet of Decoud's death. His voice trembled. I had to tell him that Doña Antonia, as a matter of fact, was not back in town yet. Poor girl! And just as I was making ready to ask him a thousand questions, with a sudden, ' Pardon me, Señor,' he cleared out of the office altogether. I did not see him again for three days. I was terribly busy, you know. It seems that he wandered about in and out of the town, and on two nights turned up to sleep in the baracoons of the railway people. He seemed absolutely indifferent to what went on. I asked him on the wharf, ' When are you going to take hold again, Nostromo? There will be plenty of work for the cargadores presently.'

" ' Señor,' says he, looking at me in a slow, inquisitive manner, ' would it surprise you to hear that I am too tired to work just yet? And what work could I do now? How can I look my cargadores in the face after losing a lighter?'

" I begged him not to think any more about the silver, and he smiled—a smile that went to my heart, sir. ' It was no mistake,' I told him. ' It was a fatality. A thing that could not be helped.' ' Si, si!' he said, and turned away. I thought it best to leave him alone for a bit to get over it. Sir, it took him years really, to get over it. I was present at his interview with Don Carlos. I must say that Gould is rather a cold man. He had to keep a tight hand on his feelings, dealing with thieves and rascals, in constant danger of ruin for himself and wife for so many years, that it had become a second nature. They looked at each other for a long time. Don Carlos asked what he could do for him, in his quiet, reserved way.

" ' My name is known from one end of Sulaco to the other,' he said, as quiet as the other. ' What more can you do for me ? ' That was all that passed on that occasion. Later, however, there was a very fine coasting schooner for sale, and Mrs. Gould and I put our heads together to get her bought and presented to him. It was done, but he paid all the price back within the next three years. Business was booming all along this seaboard, sir. Moreover, that man always succeeded in everything except in saving the silver. Poor Doña Antonia, fresh from her terrible experiences in the woods of Los Hatos, had an interview with him too. Wanted to hear about Decoud : what they said, what they did, what they thought up to the last on that fatal night. Mrs. Gould told me his manner was perfect for quietness and sympathy. Miss Avellanos burst into tears only when he told her how Decoud had happened to say that his plan would be a glorious success. . . . And there's no doubt, sir, that it is. It is a success."

The cycle was about to close at last. And while the privileged passenger, shivering with the pleasant anticipations of his berth, forgot to ask himself what on earth Decoud's plan could be, Captain Mitchell was saying, " Sorry we must part so soon. Your intelligent interest made this a pleasant day to me. I shall see you now on board. You had a glimpse of the ' Treasure House of the World.' A very good name that." And the coxswain's voice at the door, announcing that the gig was ready, closed the cycle.

Nostromo had, indeed, found the lighter's boat, which he had left on the Great Isabel with Decoud, floating empty far out in the gulf. He was then on the bridge of the first of Barrios's transports, and within an hour's steaming from Sulaco. Barrios, always delighted with a feat of daring and a good judge of courage, had taken a great liking to the Capataz. During the passage round the coast the general kept Nostromo near his person, addressing him frequently in that abrupt and boisterous manner which was the sign of his high favour.

Nostromo's eyes were the first to catch, broad on the bow, the tiny, elusive dark speck, which, alone with the forms of the Three Isabels right ahead, appeared on the flat, shimmering emptiness of the gulf. There are times when no fact should be neglected as insignificant; a small boat so far from the land might have had some meaning worth finding out. At a nod of consent from Barrios the transport swept out of her course, passing near enough to ascertain that no one manned the little cockle-shell. It was merely a common small boat gone adrift with her oars in her. But Nostromo, to whose mind Decoud had been insistently present for days, had long before recognised with excitement the dinghy of the lighter.

There could be no question of stopping to pick up that thing. Every minute of time was momentous with the lives and futures of a whole town. The head of the leading ship, with the general on board, fell off to her course. Behind her, the fleet of transports, scattered haphazard over a mile or so in the offing, like the finish of an ocean race, pressed on, all black and smoking on the western sky.

" Mi General," Nostromo's voice rang out loud, but quiet, from behind a group of officers, " I should like to save that little boat. *Por Dios*, I know her. She belongs to my Company."

" And, *por Dios*," guffawed Barrios in a noisy, good-humoured voice, " you belong to me. I am going to make you a captain of cavalry directly we get within sight of a horse again."

" I can swim far better than I can ride, mi General,"

cried Nostromo, pushing through to the rail with a set
stare in his eyes. " Let me——"

" Let you ? What a conceited fellow that is ! "
bantered the general jovially, without even looking at
him. " Let him go ! Ha ! ha ! ha ! He wants me to
admit that we cannot take Sulaco without him ! Ha !
ha ! ha ! Would you like to swim off to her, my son ? "

A tremendous shout from one end of the ship to the
other stopped his guffaw. Nostromo had leaped overboard ; and his black head bobbed up far away already
from the ship. The general muttered an appalled
" *Cielo !* Sinner that I am ! " in a thunder-struck tone.
One anxious glance was enough to show him that
Nostromo was swimming with perfect ease ; and then
he thundered terribly, " No ! no ! We shall not stop
to pick up this impertinent fellow. Let him drown—
that mad Capataz."

Nothing short of main force would have kept Nostromo from leaping overboard. That empty boat, coming
out to meet him mysteriously, as if rowed by an invisible
spectre, exercised the fascination of some sign, of some
warning, seemed to answer in a startling and enigmatic
way the persistent thought of a treasure and of a man's
fate. He would have leaped if there had been death in
that half-mile of water. It was as smooth as a pond, and
for some reason sharks are unknown in the Placid Gulf,
though on the other side of the Punta Mala the coast-line
swarms with them.

The Capataz seized hold of the stern and blew with
force. A queer, faint feeling had come over him while he
swam. He had got rid of his boots and coat in the water.
He hung on for a time, regaining his breath. In the distance the transports, more in a bunch now, held on
straight for Sulaco with their air of friendly contest, of
nautical sport, of a regatta ; and the united smoke of
their funnels drove like a thin, sulphurous fog-bank right
over his head. It was his daring, his courage, his act

that had set these ships in motion upon the sea, hurrying on to save the lives and fortunes of the Blancos, the task-masters of the people ; to save the San Tomé mine ; to save the children.

With a vigorous and skilful effort he clambered over the stern. The very boat ! No doubt of it ; no doubt whatever. It was the dinghy of the lighter No. 3—the dinghy left with Martin Decoud on the Great Isabel so that he should have some means to help himself if nothing could be done for him from the shore. And here she had come out to meet him, empty and inexplicable. What had become of Decoud ? The Capataz made a minute examination. He looked for some scratch, for some mark, for some sign. All he discovered was a brown stain on the gunwale abreast of the thwart. He bent his face over it and rubbed hard with his finger. Then he sat down in the stern-sheets, passive, with his knees close together and legs aslant.

Streaming from head to foot, with his hair and whiskers hanging lank and dripping and a lustreless stare fixed upon the bottom boards, the Capataz of the Sulaco Carga-dores resembled a drowned corpse come up from the bottom to idle away the sunset hour in a small boat. The excitement of his adventurous ride, the excitement of the return in time, of achievement, of success, all this excite-ment centred round the associated ideas of the great trea-sure and of the only other man who knew of its existence, had departed from him. To the very last moment he had been cudgelling his brains as to how he could manage to visit the Great Isabel without loss of time and un-detected. For the idea of secrecy had come to be con-nected with the treasure so closely that even to Barrios himself he had refrained from mentioning the existence of Decoud and of the silver on the island. The letters he carried to the general, however, made brief mention of the loss of the lighter, as having its bearing upon the situation in Sulaco. In the circumstances, the one-eyed

Tiger-slayer, scenting battle from afar, had not wasted his time in making inquiries from the messenger. In fact, Barrios, talking with Nostromo, assumed that both Don Martin and the ingots of San Tomé were lost together, and Nostromo, not questioned directly, had kept silent, under the influence of some indefinable form of resentment and distrust. Let Don Martin speak of everything with his own lips, was what he told himself mentally.

And now, with the means of gaining the Great Isabel thrown thus in his way at the earliest possible moment, his excitement had departed, as when the soul takes flight leaving the body inert upon an earth it knows no more. Nostromo did not seem to know the gulf. For a long time even his eyelids did not flutter once upon the glazed emptiness of his stare. Then slowly, without a limb having stirred, without a twitch of muscle or quiver of an eyelash, an expression, a living expression came upon the still features, deep thought crept into the empty stare—as if an outcast soul, a quiet, brooding soul, finding that untenanted body in its way, had come in stealthily to take possession.

The Capataz frowned : and in the immense stillness of sea, islands, and coast, of cloud-forms on the sky and trails of light upon the water, the knitting of that brow had the emphasis of a powerful gesture. Nothing else budged for a long time ; then the Capataz shook his head and again surrendered himself to the universal repose of all visible things. Suddenly he seized the oars, and with one movement made the dinghy spin round, head-on to the Great Isabel. But before he began to pull he bent once more over the brown stain on the gunwale.

" I know that thing," he muttered to himself, with a sagacious jerk of the head. " That's blood."

His stroke was long, vigorous, and steady. Now and then he looked over his shoulder at the Great Isabel, presenting its low cliff to his anxious gaze like an impenetrable face. At last the stem touched the strand. He flung, rather than dragged, the boat up the little beach. At once, turning his back upon the sunset, he plunged with long strides into the ravine, making the water of the stream spurt and fly upwards at every step, as if spurning its shallow, clear, murmuring spirit with his feet. He wanted to save every moment of day-light.

A mass of earth, grass, and smashed bushes had fallen down very naturally from above upon the cavity under the leaning tree. Decoud had attended to the concealment of the silver as instructed, using the spade with some intelligence. But Nostromo's half-smile of approval changed into a scornful curl of the lip by the sight of the spade itself flung here in full view, as if in utter careless-ness or sudden panic, giving away the whole thing. Ah! They were all alike in their folly, these *hombres finos* that invented laws and governments and barren tasks for the people.

The Capataz picked up the spade, and with the feel of the handle in his palm the desire of having a look at the horse-hide boxes of treasure came upon him suddenly. In a very few strokes he uncovered the edges and corners of several ; then, clearing away more earth, became aware that one of them had been slashed with a knife.

He exclaimed at that discovery in a stifled voice, and dropped on his knees with a look of irrational appre-hension over one shoulder, then over the other. The stiff hide had closed, and he hesitated before he pushed his hand through the long slit and felt the ingots inside. There they were. One, two, three. Yes, four gone. Taken away. Four ingots. But who ? Decoud ? Nobody else. And why ? For what purpose ? For what cursed fancy ? Let him explain. Four ingots carried off in a boat, and—blood !

In the face of the open gulf, the sun, clear, unclouded, unaltered, plunged into the waters in a grave and un-troubled mystery of self-immolation consummated far

30

from all mortal eyes, with an infinite majesty of silence and peace.   Four ingots short !—and blood !

The Capataz got up slowly.

" He might simply have cut his hand," he muttered. " But, then——"

He sat down on the soft earth, unresisting, as if he had been chained to the treasure, his drawn-up legs clasped in his hands with an air of hopeless submission, like a slave set on guard.   Once only he lifted his head smartly : the rattle of hot musketry fire had reached his ears, like pouring from on high a stream of dry peas upon a drum.   After listening for a while, he said, half aloud :

" He will never come back to explain."

And he lowered his head again.

" Impossible ! " he muttered gloomily.

The sounds of firing died out.   The loom of a great conflagration in Sulaco flashed up red above the coast, played on the clouds at the head of the gulf, seemed to touch with a ruddy and sinister reflection the forms of the Three Isabels.   He never saw it, though he raised his head.

" But, then, I cannot know," he pronounced distinctly, and remained silent and staring for hours.

He could not know.   Nobody was to know.   As might have been supposed, the end of Don Martin Decoud never became a subject of speculation for any one except Nostromo.   Had the truth of the facts been known, there would always have remained the question, Why ?   Whereas the version of his death at the sinking of the lighter had no uncertainty of motive.   The young apostle of Separation had died striving for his idea by an ever-lamented accident.   But the truth was that he died from solitude, the enemy known but to few on this earth, and whom only the simplest of us are fit to withstand.   The brilliant Costaguanero of the boulevards had died from solitude and want of faith in himself and others.

For some good and valid reasons beyond mere human comprehension, the sea-birds of the gulf shun the Isabels. The rocky head of Azuera is their haunt, whose stony levels and chasms resound with their wild and tumultuous clamour as if they were for ever quarrelling over the legendary treasure.

At the end of his first day on the Great Isabel, Decoud, turning in his lair of coarse grass, under the shade of a tree, said to himself:

" I have not seen as much as one single bird all day."

And he had not heard a sound, either, all day but that one now of his own muttering voice. It had been a day of absolute silence—the first he had known in his life. And he had not slept a wink. Not for all these wakeful nights and the days of fighting, planning, talking; not for all that last night of danger and hard physical toil upon the gulf, had he been able to close his eyes for a moment. And yet from sunrise to sunset he had been lying prone on the ground, either on his back or on his face.

He stretched himself, and with slow steps descended into the gully to spend the night by the side of the silver. If Nostromo returned—as he may have done at any moment—it was there that he would look first; and night would, of course, be the proper time for an attempt to communicate. He remembered with profound indifference that he had not eaten anything yet since he had been left alone on the island.

He spent the night open-eyed, and when the day broke he ate something with the same indifference. The brilliant " Son Decoud," the spoiled darling of the family, the lover of Antonia and Journalist of Sulaco, was not fit to grapple with himself single-handed. Solitude from mere outward condition of existence becomes very swiftly a state of soul in which the affectations of irony and scepticism have no place. It takes possession of the mind, and drives forth the thought

into the exile of utter unbelief. After three days of
waiting for the sight of some human face, Decoud caught
himself entertaining a doubt of his own individuality.
It had merged into the world of cloud and water, of
natural forces and forms of nature. In our activity alone
do we find the sustaining illusion of an independent
existence as against the whole scheme of things of which
we form a helpless part. Decoud lost all belief in the
reality of his action past and to come. On the fifth day
an immense melancholy descended upon him palpably.
He resolved not to give himself up to these people
in Sulaco, who had beset him, unreal and terrible,
like jibbering and obscene spectres. He saw himself
struggling feebly in their midst, and Antonia, gigantic
and lovely like an allegorical statue, looking on with
scornful eyes at his weakness.

Not a living being, not a speck of distant sail, appeared
within the range of his vision ; and, as if to escape from
this solitude, he absorbed himself in his melancholy.
The vague consciousness of a misdirected life given up
to impulses whose memory left a bitter taste in his mouth,
was the first moral sentiment of his manhood. But at
the same time he felt no remorse. What should he
regret ? He had recognised no other virtue than intelligence, and had erected passions into duties. Both his
intelligence and his passion were swallowed up easily
in this great unbroken solitude of waiting without faith.
Sleeplessness had robbed his will of all energy, for he
had not slept seven hours in the seven days. His
sadness was the sadness of a sceptical mind. He beheld
the universe as a succession of incomprehensible images.
Nostromo was dead. Everything had failed ignomini-
ously. He no longer dared to think of Antonia. She
had not survived. But if she survived, he could not
face her. And all exertion seemed senseless.

On the tenth day, after a night spent without even
dozing off at once (it had occurred to him that Antonia

could not possibly have ever loved a being so impalpable as himself), the solitude appeared like a great void, and the silence of the gulf like a tense, thin cord to which he hung suspended by both hands, without fear, without surprise, without any sort of emotion whatever. Only towards the evening, in the comparative relief of coolness, he began to wish that this cord would snap. He imagined it snapping with a report as of a pistol—a sharp, full crack. And that would be the end of him. He contemplated that eventuality with pleasure, because he dreaded the sleepless nights in which the silence, remaining unbroken in the shape of a cord to which he hung with both hands, vibrated with senseless phrases, always the same but utterly incomprehensible, about Nostromo, Antonia, Barrios, and proclamations mingled into an ironical and senseless buzzing. In the daytime he could look at the silence like a still cord stretched to breaking-point, with his life, his vain life, suspended to it like a weight.

" I wonder whether I would hear it snap before I fell ? " he asked himself.

The sun was two hours above the horizon when he got up, gaunt, dirty, white-faced, and looked at it with his red-rimmed eyes. His limbs obeyed him slowly, as if full of lead, yet without tremor ; and the effect of that physical condition gave to his movements an unhesitating, deliberate dignity. He acted as if accomplishing some sort of rite. He descended into the gully ; for the fascination of all that silver, with its potential power, survived alone outside of himself. He picked up the belt with the revolver, that was lying there, and buckled it round his waist. The cord of silence could never snap on the island. It must let him fall and sink into the sea, he thought. And sink ! He was looking at the loose earth covering the treasure. In the sea ! His aspect was that of a somnambulist. He lowered himself down on his knees slowly and went on grubbing with his fingers with industrious patience till he uncovered one of the boxes. Without a pause, as if doing some work done many times before, he slit open and took four ingots, which he put in his pockets. He covered up the exposed box again, and step by step came out of the gully. The bushes closed after him with a swish.

It was on the third day of his solitude that he had dragged the dinghy near the water with an idea of rowing away somewhere, but had desisted partly at the whisper of lingering hope that Nostromo would return, partly from conviction of utter uselessness of all effort. Now she wanted only a slight shove to be set afloat. He had eaten a little every day after the first, and had some muscular strength left yet. Taking up the oars slowly, he pulled away from the cliff of the Great Isabel, that stood behind him warm with sunshine, as if with the heat of life, bathed in a rich light from head to foot as if in a radiance of hope and joy. He pulled straight towards the setting sun. When the gulf had grown dark, he ceased rowing and flung the sculls in. The hollow clatter they made in falling was the loudest noise he had ever heard in his life. It was a revelation. It seemed to recall him from far away. Actually the thought, " Perhaps I may sleep to-night," passed through his mind. But he did not believe it. He believed in nothing ; and he remained sitting on the thwart.

The dawn from behind the mountains put a gleam into his unwinking eyes. After a clear daybreak the sun appeared splendidly above the peaks of the range. The great gulf burst into a glitter all around the boat ; and in this glory of merciless solitude the silence appeared again before him, stretched taut like a dark, thin string.

His eyes looked at it while, without haste, he shifted his seat from the thwart to the gunwale. They looked at it fixedly, while his hand, feeling about his waist, un-buttoned the flap of the leather case, drew the revolver, cocked it, brought it forward pointing at his breast, pulled the trigger, and, with convulsive force, sent the still smoking weapon hurtling through the air. His eyes looked at it while he fell forward and hung with his breast on the gunwale and the fingers of his right hand hooked under the thwart. They looked——

"It is done," he stammered out in a sudden flow of blood. His last thought was : "I wonder how that Capataz died ?" The stiffness of the fingers relaxed, and the lover of Antonia Avellanos rolled overboard without having heard the cord of silence snap in the solitude of the Placid Gulf, whose glittering surface remained untroubled by the fall of his body.

A victim of the disillusioned weariness which is the retribution meted out to intellectual audacity, the brilliant Don Martin Decoud, weighted by the bars of San Tomé silver, disappeared without a trace, swallowed up in the immense indifference of things. His sleepless, crouching figure was gone from the side of the San Tomé silver ; and for a time the spirits of good and evil that hover near every concealed treasure of the earth might have thought that this one had been forgotten by all mankind. Then, after a few days, another form appeared striding away from the setting sun to sit motionless and awake in the narrow black gully all through the night, in nearly the same pose, in the same place in which had sat that other sleepless man who had gone away for ever so quietly in a small boat, about the time of sunset. And the spirits of good and evil that hover about a forbidden treasure understood well that the silver of San Tomé was provided now with a faithful and lifelong slave.

The magnificent Capataz de Cargadores, victim of the disenchanted vanity which is the reward of audacious action, sat in the weary pose of a hunted outcast through a night of sleeplessness as tormenting as any known to Decoud, his companion in the most desperate affair of his life. And he wondered how Decoud had died. But he knew the part he had played himself. First a woman, then a man, abandoned both in their last extremity, for the sake of this accursed treasure. It was paid for by a soul lost and by a vanished life. The blank stillness of awe was succeeded by a gust of immense pride. There was no one in the world but Gian' Battista Fidanza, Capataz de Cargadores, the incorruptible and faithful Nostromo, to pay such a price.

He had made up his mind that nothing should be allowed now to rob him of his bargain. Nothing. Decoud had died. But how? That he was dead he had not a shadow of a doubt. But four ingots? . . . What for? Did he mean to come for more—some other time?

The treasure was putting forth its latent power. It troubled the clear mind of the man who had paid the price. He was sure that Decoud was dead. The island seemed full of that whisper. Dead! Gone! And he caught himself listening for the swish of bushes and the splash of the footfalls in the bed of the brook. Dead! The talker, the *novio* of Doña Antonia!

"Ha!" he murmured, with his head on his knees, under the livid, clouded dawn breaking over the liberated Sulaco and upon the gulf as grey as ashes. "It is to her that he will fly! To her that he will fly!"

And four ingots! Did he take them in revenge, to cast a spell, like the angry woman who had prophesied remorse and failure, and yet had laid upon him the task of saving the children? Well, he had saved the children. He had defeated the spell of poverty and starvation. He had done it all alone—or perhaps helped by the devil. Who cared? He had done it, betrayed as he was, and saving by the same stroke the San Tomé mine, which appeared to him hateful and immense, lording it by its vast wealth over the valour, the toil, the fidelity of the poor, over war and peace, over the labours of the town, the sea, and the Campo.

The sun lit up the sky behind the peaks of the Cordillera. The Capataz looked down for a time upon the fall of loose earth, stones, and smashed bushes, concealing the hiding-place of the silver.

" I must grow rich very slowly," he meditated aloud.

CHAPTER ELEVEN

SULACO outstripped Nostromo's prudence, growing rich swiftly on the hidden treasures of the earth, hovered over by the anxious spirits of good and evil, torn out by the labouring hands of the people. It was like a second youth, like a new life, full of promise, of unrest, of toil, scattering lavishly its wealth to the four corners of an excited world. Material changes swept along in the train of material interests. And other changes more subtle, outwardly unmarked, affected the minds and hearts of the workers. Captain Mitchell had gone home to live on his savings invested in the San Tomé mine ; and Dr. Monygham had grown older, with his head steel-grey and the unchanged expression of his face, living on the inexhaustible treasure of his devotion drawn upon in the secret of his heart like a store of unlawful wealth.

The Inspector-General of State Hospitals (whose maintenance is a charge upon the Gould Concession), Official Adviser on Sanitation to the Municipality, Chief Medical Officer of the San Tomé Consolidated Mines (whose territory, containing gold, silver, copper, lead, cobalt, extends for miles along the foothills of the Cordillera), had felt poverty-stricken, miserable, and starved during the prolonged second visit the Goulds paid to Europe and the United States of America. Intimate of the Casa, proved friend, a bachelor without ties and without establishment (except of the professional sort), he had been asked to take up his quarters in the

Gould house. In the eleven months of their absence, the familiar rooms, recalling at every glance the woman to whom he had given all his loyalty, had grown intolerable. As the day approached for the arrival of the mail-boat *Hermes* (the latest addition to the O.S.N. Company's splendid fleet), the doctor hobbled about more vivaciously, snapped more sardonically at simple and gentle out of sheer nervousness.

He packed up his modest trunk with speed, with fury, with enthusiasm, and saw it carried out past the old porter at the gate of the Casa Gould with delight, with intoxication ; then, as the hour approached, sitting alone in the great landau behind the white mules, a little sideways, his drawn-in face positively venomous with the effort of self-control, and holding a pair of new gloves in his left hand, he drove to the harbour.

His heart dilated within him so, when he saw the Goulds on the deck of the *Hermes*, that his greetings were reduced to a casual mutter. Driving back to town all three were silent. And in the patio the doctor, in a more natural manner, said :

" I'll leave you now to yourselves. I'll call to-morrow, if I may ? "

" Come to lunch, dear Dr. Monygham, and come early," said Mrs. Gould, in her travelling dress and her veil down, turning to look at him at the foot of the stairs ; while at the top of the flight the Madonna, in blue robes and the Child on her arm, seemed to welcome her with an aspect of pitying tenderness.

" Don't expect to find me at home," Charles Gould warned him. " I'll be off early to the mine."

After lunch, Doña Emilia and the Señor Doctor came slowly through the inner gateway of the patio. The large gardens of the Casa Gould, surrounded by high walls, and the red-tile slopes of neighbouring roofs, lay open before them, with masses of shade under the trees and level surfaces of sunlight upon the lawns. A triple row of old orange trees surrounded the whole. Bare-footed brown gardeners, in snowy white shirts and wide calzoneras, dotted the grounds, squatting over flower-beds, passing between the trees, dragging slender india-rubber tubes across the gravel of the paths ; and the fine jets of water crossed each other in graceful curves, spark-ling in the sunshine with a slight pattering noise upon the bushes, and an effect of showered diamonds upon the grass.

Doña Emilia, holding up the train of a clear dress, walked by the side of Dr. Monygham, in a longish black coat and severe black bow on an immaculate shirt-front. Under a shady clump of trees, where stood scattered little tables and wicker easy-chairs, Mrs. Gould sat down in a low and ample seat.

" Don't go yet," she said to Dr. Monygham, who was unable to tear himself away from the spot. His chin nestling within the points of his collar, he devoured her stealthily with his eyes, which, luckily, were round and hard like clouded marbles, and incapable of disclosing his sentiments. His pitying emotion at the marks of time upon the face of that woman, the air of frailty and weary fatigue that had settled upon the eyes and temples of the " Never-tired Señora " (as Don Pépé years ago used to call her with admiration), touched him almost to tears. " Don't go yet. To-day is all my own," Mrs. Gould urged gently. " We are not back yet officially. No one will come. It's only to-morrow that the windows of the Casa Gould are to be lit up for a reception."

The doctor dropped into a chair.

" Giving a tertulia ? " he said, with a detached air.

" A simple greeting for all the kind friends who care to come."

" And only to-morrow ? "

" Yes. Charles would be tired out after a day at the mine, and so I—— It would be good to have him to myself for one evening on our return to this house I love. It has seen all my life."

" Ah, yes ! " snarled the doctor suddenly. " Women count time from the marriage feast. Didn't you live a little before ? "

" Yes ; but what is there to remember ? There were no cares."

Mrs. Gould sighed. And as two friends, after a long separation, will revert to the most agitated period of their lives, they began to talk of the Sulaco Revolution. It seemed strange to Mrs. Gould that people who had taken part in it seemed to forget its memory and its lesson.

" And yet," struck in the doctor, " we who played our part in it had our reward. Don Pépé, though super-annuated, still can sit a horse. Barrios is drinking himself to death in jovial company away somewhere on his *fundacion* beyond the Bolson de Tonoro. And the heroic Father Romàn—I imagine the old padre blowing up systematically the San Tomé mine, uttering a pious exclamation at every bang, and taking handfuls of snuff between the explosions—the heroic Padre Romàn says that he is not afraid of the harm Holroyd's missionaries can do to his flock, as long as *he* is alive."

Mrs. Gould shuddered a little at the allusion to the destruction that had come so near to the San Tomé mine.

" Ah, but you, dear friend ? "

" I did the work I was fit for."

" You faced the most cruel dangers of all. Something more than death."

" No, Mrs. Gould ! Only death—by hanging. And I am rewarded beyond my deserts."

Noticing Mrs. Gould's gaze fixed upon him, he dropped his eyes.

" I've made my career—as you see," said the In-spector-General of State Hospitals, taking up lightly the lapels of his superfine black coat. The doctor's self-

respect, marked inwardly by the almost complete disappearance from his dreams of Father Beron, appeared
visibly in what, by contrast with former carelessness,
seemed an immoderate cult of personal appearance.
Carried out within severe limits of form and colour, and
in perpetual freshness, this change of apparel gave to
Dr. Monygham an air at the same time professional and
festive ; while his gait and the unchanged crabbed
character of his face acquired from it a startling force
of incongruity.

" Yes," he went on. " We all had our rewards—the
engineer-in-chief, Captain Mitchell——"

" We saw him," interrupted Mrs. Gould in her
charming voice. " The poor dear man came up from
the country on purpose to call on us in our hotel in
London. He comported himself with great dignity, but
I fancy he regrets Sulaco. He rambled feebly about
' historical events ' till I felt I could have a cry."

" H'm !" grunted the doctor ; " getting old, I suppose. Even Nostromo is getting older—though he is not
changed. And, speaking of that fellow, I wanted to tell
you something——"

For some time the house had been full of murmurs, of
agitation. Suddenly the two gardeners, busy with rose
trees at the side of the garden arch, fell upon their knees
with bowed heads on the passage of Antonia Avellanos,
who appeared walking beside her uncle.

Invested with the red hat after a short visit to Rome,
where he had been invited by the Propaganda, Father
Corbelàn, missionary to the wild Indians, conspirator,
friend and patron of Hernandez the robber, advanced
with big, slow strides, gaunt and leaning forward, with
his powerful hands clasped behind his back. The first
Cardinal - Archbishop of Sulaco had preserved his
fanatical and morose air : the aspect of a chaplain of
bandits. It was believed that his unexpected elevation
to the purple was a counter-move to the Protestant

invasion of Sulaco organised by the Holroyd Missionary Fund. Antonia, the beauty of her face as if a little blurred, her figure slightly fuller, advanced with her light walk and her high serenity, smiling from a distance to Mrs. Gould. She had brought her uncle over to see dear Emilia, without ceremony, just for a moment before the siesta.

When all were seated again, Dr. Monygham, who had come to dislike heartily everybody who approached Mrs. Gould with any intimacy, kept aside, pretending to be lost in profound meditation. A louder phrase of Antonia's made him lift his head.

" How can we abandon, groaning under oppression, those who have been our countrymen only a few years ago, who *are* our countrymen now ? " Miss Avellanos was saying. " How can we remain blind, and deaf, and without pity to the cruel wrongs suffered by our brothers ? There is a remedy."

" Annex the rest of Costaguana to the order and prosperity of Sulaco," snapped the doctor. " There is no other remedy."

" I am convinced, Señor Doctor," Antonia said, with the earnest calm of invincible resolution, " that this was from the first poor Martin's intention."

" Yes ; but the material interests will not let you jeopardise their development for a mere idea of pity and justice," the doctor muttered grumpily. " And it is just as well, perhaps."

The Cardinal-Archbishop straightened up his gaunt, bony frame.

" We have worked for them, we have made them, these material interests of the foreigners," the last of the Corbelàns uttered in a deep, denunciatory tone.

" And without them you are nothing," cried the doctor from the distance. " They will not let you."

" Let them beware, then, lest the people, prevented from their aspirations, should rise and claim their share of the wealth and their share of the power," the popular Cardinal-Archbishop of Sulaco declared significantly, menacingly.

A silence ensued, during which His Eminence stared, frowning at the ground, and Antonia, graceful and rigid in her chair, breathed calmly in the strength of her convictions. Then the conversation took a social turn, touching on the visit of the Goulds to Europe. The Cardinal-Archbishop, when in Rome, had suffered from neuralgia in the head all the time. It was the climate—the bad air.

When uncle and niece had gone away, with the servants again falling on their knees, and the old porter, who had known Henry Gould, almost totally blind and impotent now, creeping up to kiss His Eminence's extended hand, Dr. Monygham, looking after them, pronounced the one word :

" Incorrigible ! "

Mrs. Gould, with a look upwards, dropped wearily on her lap her white hands flashing with the gold and stones of many rings.

" Conspiring. Yes ! " said the doctor. " The last of the Avellanos and the last of the Corbelàns are conspiring with the refugees from Sta. Marta that flock here after every revolution. The Café Lambroso at the corner of the plaza is full of them ; you can hear their chatter across the street like the noise of a parrot-house. They are conspiring for the invasion of Costaguana. And do you know where they go for strength, for the necessary force ? To the secret societies amongst immigrants and natives, where Nostromo—I should say Captain Fidanza—is the great man. What gives him that position ? Who can say ? Genius ? He has genius. He is greater with the populace than ever he was before. It is as if he had some secret power ; some mysterious means to keep up his influence. He holds conferences with the Archbishop, as in those old

days which you and I remember. Barrios is useless.
But for a military head they have the pious Hernandez.
And they may raise the country with the new cry of the
wealth for the people."

"Will there be never any peace? Will there be
no rest?" Mrs. Gould whispered. "I thought that
we——"

"No!" interrupted the doctor. "There is no
peace and no rest in the development of material interests.
They have their law and their justice. But it is founded
on expediency, and is inhuman; it is without rectitude,
without the continuity and the force that can be found
only in a moral principle. Mrs. Gould, the time approaches when all that the Gould Concession stands for
shall weigh as heavily upon the people as the barbarism,
cruelty, and misrule of a few years back."

"How can you say that, Dr. Monygham?" she cried
out, as if hurt in the most sensitive place of her soul.

"I can say what is true," the doctor insisted obstinately. "It'll weigh as heavily, and provoke resentment,
bloodshed, and vengeance, because the men have
grown different. Do you think that now the mine
would march upon the town to save their Señor
Administrador? Do you think that?"

She pressed the backs of her entwined hands on her
eyes and murmured hopelessly:

"Is it this we have worked for, then?"

The doctor lowered his head. He could follow her
silent thought. Was it for this that her life had been
robbed of all the intimate felicities of daily affection
which her tenderness needed as the human body needs
air to breathe? And the doctor, indignant with Charles
Gould's blindness, hastened to change the conversation.

"It is about Nostromo that I wanted to talk to you.
Ah! that fellow has some continuity and force. Nothing
will put an end to him. But never mind that. There's
something inexplicable going on—or perhaps only too

31

easy to explain. You know, Linda is practically the
lighthouse-keeper of the Great Isabel light. The Garibaldino is too old now. His part is to clean the lamps
and to cook in the house; but he can't get up the stairs
any longer. The black-eyed Linda sleeps all day and
watches the light all night. Not all day, though. She is
up towards five in the afternoon, when our Nostromo,
whenever he is in harbour with his schooner, comes out
on his courting visit, pulling in a small boat."

"Aren't they married yet?" Mrs. Gould asked.
" The mother wished it, as far as I can understand, while
Linda was yet quite a child. When I had the girls with
me for a year or so during the War of Separation, that
extraordinary Linda used to declare quite simply that she
was going to be Gian' Battista's wife."

" They are not married yet," said the doctor curtly.
" I have looked after them a little."

" Thank you, dear Dr. Monygham," said Mrs.
Gould; and under the shade of the big trees her little,
even teeth gleamed in a youthful smile of gentle malice.
" People don't know how really good you are. You will
not let them know, as if on purpose to annoy me, who
have put my faith in your good heart long ago."

The doctor, with a lifting up of his upper lip, as
though he were longing to bite, bowed stiffly in his chair.
With the utter absorption of a man to whom love comes
late, not as the most splendid of illusions, but like an
enlightening and priceless misfortune, the sight of that
woman (of whom he had been deprived for nearly a year)
suggested ideas of adoration, of kissing the hem of her
robe. And this excess of feeling translated itself naturally
into an augmented grimness of speech.

" I am afraid of being overwhelmed by too much
gratitude. However, these people interest me. I went
out several times to the Great Isabel light to look after
old Giorgio."

He did not tell Mrs. Gould that it was because he

found there, in her absence, the relief of an atmosphere
of congenial sentiment in old Giorgio's austere admiration
for the " English Signora—the benefactress "; in black-
eyed Linda's voluble, torrential, passionate affection for
" our Doña Emilia—that angel "; in the white-throated,
fair Giselle's adoring upward turn of the eyes, which
then glided towards him with a sidelong half-arch, half-
candid glance, which made the doctor exclaim to himself
mentally, " If I weren't what I am, old and ugly, I would
think the minx is making eyes at me. And perhaps she
is. I dare say she would make eyes at anybody." Dr.
Monygham said nothing of this to Mrs. Gould, the providence of the Viola family, but reverted to what he called
" our great Nostromo."

" What I wanted to tell you is this: our great
Nostromo did not take much notice of the old man and the
children for some years. It's true, too, that he was away
on his coasting voyages certainly ten months out of the
twelve. He was making his fortune, as he told Captain
Mitchell once. He seems to have done uncommonly
well. It was only to be expected. He is a man full
of resource, full of confidence in himself, ready to take
chances and risks of every sort. I remember being in
Mitchell's office one day, when he came in with that calm,
grave air he always carries everywhere. He had been
away trading in the Gulf of California, he said, looking
straight past us at the wall, as his manner is, and was
glad to see on his return that a lighthouse was being
built on the cliff of the Great Isabel. Very glad, he
repeated. Mitchell explained that it was the O.S.N.
Company who was building it, for the convenience of
the mail service, on his own advice. Captain Fidanza
was good enough to say that it was excellent advice. I
remember him twisting up his moustaches and looking
all round the cornice of the room before he proposed that
old Giorgio should be made the keeper of that light."

" I heard of this. I was consulted at the time," Mrs.

Gould said. " I doubted whether it would be good for
these girls to be shut up on that island as if in a prison."

" The proposal fell in with the old Garibaldino's
humour. As to Linda, any place was lovely and delightful
enough for her as long as it was Nostromo's suggestion.
She could wait for her Gian' Battista's good pleasure there
as well as anywhere else. My opinion is that she was
always in love with that incorruptible Capataz. Moreover, both father and sister were anxious to get Giselle
away from the attentions of a certain Ramirez."

" Ah ! " said Mrs. Gould, interested. " Ramirez ?
What sort of man is that ? "

" Just a mozo of the town. His father was a cargador. As a lanky boy he ran about the wharf in rags,
till Nostromo took him up and made a man of him.
When he got a little older he put him into a lighter, and
very soon gave him charge of the No. 3 boat—the boat
which took the silver away, Mrs. Gould. Nostromo
selected that lighter for the work because she was the best
sailing and the strongest boat of all the Company's fleet.
Young Ramirez was one of the five cargadores entrusted
with the removal of the treasure from the Custom House
on that famous night. As the boat he had charge of was
sunk, Nostromo, on leaving the Company's service,
recommended him to Captain Mitchell for his successor.
He had trained him in the routine of work perfectly, and
thus Mr. Ramirez, from a starving waif, becomes a man
and the Capataz of the Sulaco Cargadores."

" Thanks to Nostromo," said Mrs. Gould, with warm
approval.

" Thanks to Nostromo," repeated Dr. Monygham.
" Upon my word, the fellow's power frightens me when
I think of it. That our poor old Mitchell was only too
glad to appoint somebody trained to the work, who saved
him trouble, is not surprising. What is wonderful is the
fact that the Sulaco Cargadores accepted Ramirez for
their chief, simply because such was Nostromo's good

pleasure. Of course, he is not a second Nostromo, as he fondly imagined he would be ; but still, the position was brilliant enough. It emboldened him to make up to Giselle Viola, who, you know, is the recognised beauty of the town. The old Garibaldino, however, took a violent dislike to him. I don't know why. Perhaps because he was not a model of perfection like his Gian' Battista, the incarnation of the courage, the fidelity, the honour of 'the people.' Signor Viola does not think much of Sulaco natives. Both of them, the old Spartan and that white-faced Linda, with her red mouth and coal-black eyes, were looking rather fiercely after the fair one. Ramirez was warned off. Father Viola, I am told, threatened him with his gun once."

" But what of Giselle herself ? " asked Mrs. Gould.

" She's a bit of a flirt, I believe," said the doctor. " I don't think she cared much one way or another. Of course she likes men's attentions. Ramirez was not the only one, let me tell you, Mrs. Gould. There was one engineer, at least, on the railway staff who got warned off with a gun, too. Old Viola does not allow any trifling with his honour. He has grown uneasy and suspicious since his wife died. He was very pleased to remove his youngest girl away from the town. But look what happens, Mrs. Gould. Ramirez, the honest lovelorn swain, is forbidden the island. Very well. He respects the prohibition, but naturally turns his eyes frequently towards the Great Isabel. It seems as though he had been in the habit of gazing late at night upon the light. And during these sentimental vigils he discovers that Nostromo, Captain Fidanza that is, returns very late from his visits to the Violas. As late as midnight at times."

The doctor paused, and stared meaningly at Mrs. Gould.

" Yes. But I don't understand," she began, looking puzzled.

" Now comes the strange part," went on Dr. Monygham. " Viola, who is king on his island, will allow no
visitor on it after dark. Even Captain Fidanza has got
to leave after sunset, when Linda has gone up to tend the
light. And Nostromo goes away obediently. But what
happens afterwards ? What does he do in the gulf between half-past six and midnight ? He has been seen
more than once at that late hour pulling quietly into the
harbour. Ramirez is devoured by jealousy. He dared
not approach old Viola ; but he plucked up courage to
rail at Linda about it one Sunday morning as she came to
the mainland to hear Mass and visit her mother's grave.
There was a scene on the wharf, which, as a matter of fact,
I witnessed. It was early morning. He must have been
waiting for her on purpose. I was there by the merest
chance, having been called to an urgent consultation by
the doctor of the German gunboat in the harbour. She
poured wrath, scorn, and flame upon Ramirez, who
seemed out of his mind. It was a strange sight, Mrs.
Gould : the long jetty, with this raving cargador in his
crimson sash and the girl all in black, at the end ; the
early Sunday morning quiet of the harbour in the shade
of the mountains ; nothing but a canoe or two moving
between the ships at anchor, and the German gunboat's
gig coming to take me off. Linda passed me within a
foot. I noticed her wild eyes. I called out to her. She
never heard me. She never saw me. But I looked at
her face. It was awful in its anger and wretchedness."

Mrs. Gould sat up, opening her eyes very wide.

" What do you mean, Dr. Monygham ? Do you
mean to say that you suspect the younger sister ? "

" *Quien sabe !* Who can tell ? " said the doctor,
shrugging his shoulders like a born Costaguanero.
" Ramirez came up to me on the wharf. He reeled—he
looked insane. He took his head into his hands. He
had to talk to some one—simply had to. Of course, for
all his mad stare he recognised me. People know me

well here. I have lived too long amongst them to be anything else but the evil-eyed doctor, who can cure all the ills of the flesh, and bring bad luck by a glance. He came up to me. He tried to be calm. He tried to make it out that he wanted merely to warn me against Nostromo. It seems that Captain Fidanza at some secret meeting or other had mentioned me as the worst despiser of all the poor—of the people. It's very possible. He honours me with his undying dislike. And a word from the great Fidanza may be quite enough to send some fool's knife into my back. The Sanitary Commission I preside over is not in favour with the populace. 'Beware of him, Señor Doctor. Destroy him, Señor Doctor,' Ramirez hissed right into my face. And then he broke out. 'That man,' he spluttered, 'has cast a spell upon both these girls.' As to himself, he had said too much. He must run away now—run away and hide somewhere. He moaned tenderly about Giselle, and then called her names that cannot be repeated. If he thought she could be made to love him by any means, he would carry her off from the island; off into the woods. But it was no good. . . . He strode away, flourishing his arms above his head. Then I noticed an old negro, who had been sitting behind a pile of cases, fishing from the wharf. He wound up his lines and slunk away at once. But he must have heard something, and must have talked too, because some of the old Garibaldino's railway friends, I suppose, warned him against Ramirez. At any rate, the father has been warned. But Ramirez has disappeared from the town."

"I feel I have a duty towards these girls," said Mrs. Gould uneasily. "Is Nostromo in Sulaco now?"

"He is, since last Sunday."

"He ought to be spoken to—at once."

"Who will dare speak to him? Even the love-mad Ramirez runs away from the mere shadow of Captain Fidanza."

" I can! I will!" Mrs. Gould declared. "A word will be enough for a man like Nostromo."

The doctor smiled sourly.

" He must end this situation which lends itself to——I can't believe it of that child," pursued Mrs. Gould.

" He's very attractive," muttered the doctor gloomily.

" He'll see it, I am sure. He must put an end to all this by marrying Linda at once," pronounced the first lady of Sulaco with immense decision.

Through the garden gate emerged Basilio, grown fat and sleek, with an elderly, hairless face, wrinkles at the corners of his eyes, and his jet-black, coarse hair plastered down smoothly. Stooping carefully behind an ornamental clump of bushes, he put down with precaution a small child he had been carrying on his shoulder—his own and Leonarda's last born. The pouting, spoiled camerista and the head mozo of the Casa Gould had been married for some years now.

He remained squatting on his heels for a time, gazing fondly at his offspring, which returned his stare with imperturbable gravity ; then, solemn and respectable, walked down the path.

" What is it, Basilio ? " asked Mrs. Gould.

"A telephone came through from the office of the mine. The master remains to sleep at the mountain to-night."

Dr. Monygham had got up and stood looking away. A profound silence reigned for a time under the shade of the biggest trees in the lovely gardens of the Casa Gould.

" Very well, Basilio," said Mrs. Gould. She watched him walk away along the path, step aside behind the flowering bush, and reappear with the child seated on his shoulder. He passed through the gateway between the garden and the patio with measured steps, careful of his light burden.

The doctor, with his back to Mrs. Gould, contemplated a flower-bed away in the sunshine. People believed him scornful and soured. The truth of his nature consisted in his capacity for passion and in the sensitiveness of his temperament. What he lacked was the polished callousness of men of the world, the callousness from which springs an easy tolerance for oneself and others ; the tolerance wide as poles asunder from true sympathy and human compassion. This want of callousness accounted for his sardonic turn of mind and his biting speeches.

In profound silence, and glaring viciously at the brilliant flower-bed, Dr. Monygham poured mental imprecations on Charles Gould's head. Behind him, the immobility of Mrs. Gould added to the grace of her seated figure the charm of art, of an attitude caught and interpreted for ever. Turning abruptly, the doctor took his leave.

Mrs. Gould leaned back in the shade of the big trees planted in a circle. She leaned back with her eyes closed and her white hands lying idle on the arms of her seat. The half-light under the thick mass of leaves brought out the youthful prettiness of her face ; made the clear light fabrics and white lace of her dress appear luminous. Small and dainty, as if radiating a light of her own in the deep shade of the interlaced boughs, she resembled a good fairy, weary with a long career of well-doing, touched by the withering suspicion of the uselessness of her labours, the powerlessness of her magic.

Had anybody asked her of what she was thinking, alone in the garden of the Casa, with her husband at the mine and the house closed to the street like an empty dwelling, her frankness would have had to evade the question. It had come into her mind that for life to be large and full, it must contain the care of the past and of the future in every passing moment of the present. Our daily work must be done to the glory of the dead, and for the good of those who come after. She thought that, and sighed without opening her eyes—without moving at all. Mrs. Gould's face became set and rigid for a

second, as if to receive, without flinching, a great wave
of loneliness that swept over her head. And it came
into her mind, too, that no one would ever ask her with
solicitude what she was thinking of. No one. No one,
but perhaps the man who had just gone away. No ; no
one who could be answered with careless sincerity in the
ideal perfection of confidence.

The word " incorrigible "—a word lately pronounced
by Dr. Monygham—floated into her still and sad immobility. Incorrigible in his devotion to the great silver
mine was the Señor Administrador ! Incorrigible in his
hard, determined service of the material interests to
which he had pinned his faith in the triumph of order
and justice. Poor boy ! She had a clear vision of the
grey hairs on his temples. He was perfect—-perfect.
What more could she have expected ? It was a colossal
and lasting success ; and love was only a short moment
of forgetfulness, a short intoxication, whose delight one
remembered with a sense of sadness, as if it had been a
deep grief lived through. There was something inherent
in the necessities of successful action which carried with
it the moral degradation of the idea. She saw the San
Tomé mountain hanging over the Campo, over the
whole land, feared, hated, wealthy ; more soulless
than any tyrant, more pitiless and autocratic than the
worst Government ; ready to crush innumerable lives in
the expansion of its greatness. He did not see it. He
could not see it. It was not his fault. He was perfect
—perfect ; but she would never have him to herself.
Never ; not for one short hour altogether to herself in
this old Spanish house she loved so well ! Incorrigible,
the last of the Corbelàns, the last of the Avellanos, the
doctor had said ; but she saw clearly the San Tomé
mine possessing, consuming, burning up the life of the
last of the Costaguana Goulds ; mastering the energetic
spirit of the son as it had mastered the lamentable
weakness of the father. A terrible success for the last

of the Goulds. The last ! She had hoped for a long, long time, that perhaps—— But no ! There were to be no more. An immense desolation, the dread of her own continued life, descended upon the first lady of Sulaco. With a prophetic vision she saw herself surviving alone the degradation of her young ideal of life, of love, of work—all alone in the " Treasure House of the World." The profound, blind, suffering expression of a painful dream settled on her face with its closed eyes. In the indistinct voice of an unlucky sleeper, lying passive in the grip of a merciless nightmare, she stammered out aimlessly the words :

" Material interests."

CHAPTER TWELVE

NOSTROMO had been growing rich very slowly. It was an effect of his prudence. He could command himself even when thrown off his balance. And to become the slave of a treasure with full self-knowledge is an occurrence rare and mentally disturbing. But it was also in a great part because of the difficulty of converting it into a form in which it could become available. The mere act of getting it away from the island piecemeal, little by little, was surrounded by difficulties, by the dangers of imminent detection. He had to visit the Great Isabel in secret, between his voyages along the coast, which were the ostensible source of his fortune. The crew of his own schooner were to be feared as if they had been spies upon their dreaded captain. He did not dare stay too long in port. When his coaster was unloaded, he hurried away on another trip, for he feared arousing suspicion even by a day's delay. Sometimes during a week's stay, or more, he could only manage one visit to the treasure. And that was all. A couple of ingots. He suffered through his fears as much as through his prudence. To do things by stealth humiliated him. And he suffered most from the concentration of his thought upon the treasure.

A transgression, a crime, entering a man's existence, eats it up like a malignant growth, consumes it like a fever. Nostromo had lost his peace ; the genuineness of all his qualities was destroyed. He felt it himself, and often cursed the silver of San Tomé. His courage, his magnificence, his leisure, his work, everything was as before, only everything was a sham. But the treasure was real. He clung to it with a more tenacious, mental grip. But he hated the feel of the ingots. Sometimes, after putting away a couple of them in his cabin—the fruit of a secret night expedition to the Great Isabel—he would look fixedly at his fingers, as if surprised they had left no stain on his skin.

He had found means of disposing of the silver bars in distant ports. The necessity to go far afield made his coasting voyages long, and caused his visits to the Viola household to be rare and far between. He was fated to have his wife from there. He had said so once to Giorgio himself. But the Garibaldino had put the subject aside with a majestic wave of his hand, clutching a smouldering black briar-root pipe. There was plenty of time ; he was not the man to force his girls upon anybody.

As time went on, Nostromo discovered his preference for the younger of the two. They had some profound similarities of nature, which must exist for complete confidence and understanding, no matter what outward differences of temperament there may be to exercise their own fascination of contrast. His wife would have to know his secret or else life would be impossible. He was attracted by Giselle, with her candid gaze and white throat, pliable, silent, fond of excitement under her quiet indolence ; whereas Linda, with her intense, passionately pale face, energetic, all fire and words, touched with gloom and scorn, a chip of the old block, true daughter of the austere republican, but with Teresa's voice, inspired him with a deep-seated mistrust. Moreover, the poor girl could not conceal her love for Gian' Battista. He could see it would be violent, exacting, suspicious, uncompromising—like her soul. Giselle, by her fair but warm beauty, by the surface placidity of her nature holding a promise of submissiveness, by the charm of her girlish mysteriousness, excited his passion and allayed his fears as to the future.

His absences from Sulaco were long. On returning from the longest of them, he made out lighters loaded with blocks of stone lying under the cliff of the Great Isabel; cranes and scaffolding above; workmen's figures moving about, and a small lighthouse already rising from its foundations on the edge of the cliff.

At this unexpected, undreamt-of, startling sight, he thought himself lost irretrievably. What could save him from detection now? Nothing! He was struck with amazed dread at this turn of chance, that would kindle a far-reaching light upon the only secret spot of his life; that life whose very essence, value, reality, consisted in its reflection from the admiring eyes of men. All of it but that thing which was beyond common comprehension; which stood between him and the power that hears and gives effect to the evil intention of curses. It was dark. Not every man had such a darkness. And they were going to put a light there. A light! He saw it shining upon disgrace, poverty, contempt. Somebody was sure to . . . Perhaps somebody had already . . .

The incomparable Nostromo, the Capataz, the respected and feared Captain Fidanza, the unquestioned patron of secret societies, a republican like old Giorgio, and a revolutionist at heart (but in another manner), was on the point of jumping overboard from the deck of his own schooner. That man, subjective almost to insanity, looked suicide deliberately in the face. But he never lost his head. He was checked by the thought that this was no escape. He imagined himself dead, and the disgrace, the shame, going on. Or, rather, properly speaking, he could not imagine himself dead. He was possessed too strongly by the sense of his own existence, a thing of infinite duration in its changes, to grasp the notion of finality. The earth goes on for ever.

And he was courageous. It was a corrupt courage, but it was as good for his purposes as the other kind. He sailed close to the cliff of the Great Isabel, throwing a penetrating glance from the deck at the mouth of the ravine, tangled in an undisturbed growth of bushes. He sailed close enough to exchange hails with the workmen, shading their eyes on the edge of the sheer drop of the cliff overhung by the jib-head of a powerful crane. He perceived that none of them had any occasion even to approach the ravine where the silver lay hidden, let alone to enter it. In the harbour he learned that no one slept on the island. The labouring gangs returned to port every evening, singing chorus songs in the empty lighters towed by a harbour tug. For the moment he had nothing to fear.

But afterwards ? he asked himself. Later, when a keeper came to live in the cottage that was being built some hundred and fifty yards back from the low light-tower, and four hundred or so from the dark, shaded, jungly ravine, containing the secret of his safety, of his influence, of his magnificence, of his power over the future, of his defiance of ill-luck, of every possible betrayal from rich and poor alike—what then ? He could never shake off the treasure. His audacity, greater than that of other men, had welded that vein of silver into his life. And the feeling of fearful and ardent subjection, the feeling of his slavery—so irremediable and profound that often, in his thoughts, he compared himself to the legendary gringos, neither dead nor alive, bound down to their conquest of unlawful wealth on Azuera—weighed heavily on the independent Captain Fidanza, owner and master of a coasting schooner, whose smart appearance (and fabulous good luck in trading) were so well known along the western seaboard of a vast continent.

Fiercely whiskered and grave, a shade less supple in
his walk, the vigour and symmetry of his powerful limbs
lost in the vulgarity of a brown tweed suit, made by
Jews in the slums of London, and sold by the clothing
department of the Compañia Anzani, Captain Fidanza was
seen in the streets of Sulaco attending to his business,
as usual, that trip. And, as usual, he allowed it to get
about that he had made a great profit on his cargo. It
was a cargo of salt fish, and Lent was approaching. He
was seen in tramcars going to and fro between the town
and the harbour ; he talked with people in a café or
two in his measured, steady voice. Captain Fidanza was
seen. The generation that would know nothing of the
famous ride to Cayta was not born yet.

Nostromo, the miscalled Capataz de Cargadores, had
made for himself, under his rightful name, another
public existence, but modified by the new conditions, less
picturesque, more difficult to keep up in the increased size
and varied population of Sulaco, the progressive capital
of the Occidental Republic.

Captain Fidanza, unpicturesque, but always a little
mysterious, was recognised quite sufficiently under the
lofty glass and iron roof of the Sulaco railway station.
He took a local train, and got out in Rincon, where he
visited the widow of the cargador who had died of his
wounds (at the dawn of the New Era, like Don José
Avellanos) in the patio of the Casa Gould. He consented
to sit down and drink a glass of cool lemonade in the hut,
while the woman, standing up, poured a perfect torrent
of words to which he did not listen. He left some money
with her, as usual. The orphaned children, growing up
and well schooled, calling him uncle, clamoured for his
blessing. He gave that, too ; and in the doorway paused
for a moment to look at the flat face of the San Tomé
mountain with a faint frown. This slight contraction of
his bronzed brow, casting a marked tinge of severity upon
his usual unbending expression, was observed at the

Lodge which he attended—but went away before the banquet. He wore it at the meeting of some good comrades, Italians and Occidentals, assembled in his honour under the presidency of an indigent, sickly, somewhat hunchbacked little photographer, with a white face and a magnanimous soul dyed crimson by a bloodthirsty hate of all capitalists, oppressors of the two hemispheres. The heroic Giorgio Viola, old revolutionist, would have understood nothing of his opening speech ; and Captain Fidanza, lavishly generous as usual to some poor comrades, made no speech at all. He had listened, frowning, with his mind far away, and walked off unapproachable, silent, like a man full of cares.

His frown deepened as, in the early morning, he watched the stone-masons go off to the Great Isabel, in lighters loaded with squared blocks of stone, enough to add another course to the squat light-tower. That was the rate of the work—one course per day.

And Captain Fidanza meditated. The presence of strangers on the island would cut him completely off the treasure. It had been difficult and dangerous enough before. He was afraid, and he was angry. He thought with the resolution of a master and the cunning of a cowed slave. Then he went ashore.

He was a man of resource and ingenuity ; and, as usual, the expedient he found at a critical moment was effective enough to alter the situation radically. He had the gift of evolving safety out of the very danger, this incomparable Nostromo, this " fellow in a thousand." With Giorgio established on the Great Isabel there would be no need for concealment. He would be able to go openly, in daylight, to see his daughters —one of his daughters—and stay late talking to the old Garibaldino. Then in the dark . . . Night after night . . . He would dare to grow rich quicker now. He yearned to clasp, embrace, absorb, subjugate in unquestioned possession this treasure, whose tyranny

3²

had weighed upon his mind, his actions, his very sleep.

He went to see his friend Captain Mitchell—and the thing was done as Dr. Monygham had related to Mrs. Gould. When the project was mooted to the Garibaldino, something like the faint reflection, the dim ghost of a very ancient smile, stole under the white and enormous moustaches of the old hater of kings and ministers. His daughters were the object of his anxious care. The younger, especially. Linda, with her mother's voice, had taken more her mother's place. Her deep, vibrating " Eh, Padre ? " seemed, but for the change of the word, the very echo of the impassioned, remonstrating " Eh, Giorgio ? " of poor Signora Teresa. It was his fixed opinion that the town was no proper place for his girls. The infatuated but guileless Ramirez was the object of his profound aversion, as resuming the sins of the country whose people were blind, vile, *esclavos*.

On his return from his next voyage, Captain Fidanza found the Violas settled in the light-keeper's cottage. His knowledge of Giorgio's idiosyncrasies had not played him false. The Garibaldino had refused to entertain the idea of any companion whatever, except his girls. And Captain Mitchell, anxious to please his poor Nostromo, with that felicity of inspiration which only true affection can give, had formally appointed Linda Viola as under-keeper of the Isabel's light.

" The light is private property," he used to explain. " It belongs to my Company. I've the power to nominate whom I like, and Viola it shall be. It's about the only thing Nostromo—a man worth his weight in gold, mind you—has ever asked me to do for him."

Directly his schooner was anchored opposite the New Custom House, with its sham air of a Greek temple, flat-roofed, with a colonnade, Captain Fidanza went pulling his small boat out of the harbour, bound for the Great Isabel, openly in the light of a declining day, before all

men's eyes, with a sense of having mastered the fates.
He must establish a regular position. He would ask him
for his daughter now. He thought of Giselle as he pulled.
Linda loved him, perhaps, but the old man would be glad
to keep the elder, who had his wife's voice.

He did not pull for the narrow strand where he had
landed with Decoud, and afterwards alone on his first
visit to the treasure. He made for the beach at the other
end, and walked up the regular and gentle slope of the
wedge-shaped island. Giorgio Viola, whom he saw from
afar, sitting on a bench under the front wall of the cottage,
lifted his arm slightly to his loud hail. He walked up.
Neither of the girls appeared.

" It is good here," said the old man in his austere,
far-away manner.

Nostromo nodded ; then, after a short silence :

" You saw my schooner pass in not two hours ago ?
Do you know why I am here before, so to speak, my
anchor has fairly bitten into the ground of this port of
Sulaco ? "

" You are welcome like a son," the old man declared
quietly, staring away upon the sea.

" Ah ! thy son. I know. I am what thy son would
have been. It is well, *viejo*. It is a very good welcome.
Listen, I have come to ask you for——"

A sudden dread came upon the fearless and incorruptible Nostromo. He dared not utter the name in his
mind. The slight pause only imparted a marked weight
and solemnity to the changed end of the phrase.

" For my wife ! " . . . His heart was beating fast.
" It is time you——"

The Garibaldino arrested him with an extended arm.
" That was left for you to judge."

He got up slowly. His beard, unclipped since
Teresa's death, thick, snow-white, covered his powerful
chest. He turned his head to the door, and called out
in his strong voice :

" Linda."

Her answer came sharp and faint from within ; and the appalled Nostromo stood up too, but remained mute, gazing at the door. He was afraid. He was not afraid of being refused the girl he loved—no mere refusal could stand between him and a woman he desired—but the shining spectre of the treasure rose before him, claiming his allegiance in a silence that could not be gainsaid. He was afraid, because, neither dead nor alive, like the gringos on Azuera, he belonged body and soul to the unlawfulness of his audacity. He was afraid of being forbidden the island. He was afraid, and said nothing.

Seeing the two men standing up side by side to await her, Linda stopped in the doorway. Nothing could alter the passionate dead whiteness of her face ; but her black eyes seemed to catch and concentrate all the light of the low sun in a flaming spark within the black depths, covered at once by the slow descent of heavy eyelids.

" Behold thy husband, master, and benefactor ! " Old Viola's voice resounded with a force that seemed to fill the whole gulf.

She stepped forward with her eyes nearly closed, like a sleep-walker in a beatific dream.

Nostromo made a superhuman effort. " It is time, Linda, we two were betrothed," he said steadily in his level, careless, unbending tone.

She put her hand into his offered palm, lowering her head, dark with bronze glints, upon which her father's hand rested for a moment.

" And so the soul of the dead is satisfied."

This came from Giorgio Viola, who went on talking for a while of his dead wife ; while the two, sitting side by side, never looked at each other. Then the old man ceased ; and Linda, motionless, began to speak.

" Ever since I felt I lived in the world, I have lived

for you alone, Gian' Battista. And that you knew! You knew it . . . Battistino."

She pronounced the name exactly with her mother's intonation. A gloom as of the grave covered Nostromo's heart.

" Yes, I knew," he said.

The heroic Garibaldino sat on the same bench bowing his hoary head, his old soul dwelling alone with its memories, tender and violent, terrible and dreary —solitary on the earth full of men.

And Linda, his best loved daughter, was saying, " I was yours ever since I can remember. I had only to think of you for the earth to become empty to my eyes. When you were there, I could see no one else. I was yours. Nothing is changed. The world belongs to you, and you let me live in it." . . . She dropped her low, vibrating voice to a still lower note, and found other things to say—torturing for the man at her side. Her murmur ran on ardent and voluble. She did not seem to see her sister, who came out with an altar-cloth she was embroidering in her hands, and passed in front of them, silent, fresh, fair, with a quick glance and a faint smile, to sit a little away on the other side of Nostromo.

The evening was still. The sun sank almost to the edge of a purple ocean ; and the white lighthouse, livid against the background of clouds filling the head of the gulf, bore the lantern red and glowing, like a live ember kindled by the fire of the sky. Giselle, indolent and demure, raised the altar-cloth from time to time to hide nervous yawns, as of a young panther.

Suddenly Linda rushed at her sister, and, seizing her head, covered her face with kisses. Nostromo's brain reeled. When she left her, as if stunned by the violent caresses, with her hands lying in her lap, the slave of the treasure felt as if he could shoot that woman. Old Giorgio lifted his leonine head.

" Where are you going, Linda ? "

" To the light, padre mio."

" Si, si—to your duty."

He got up, too, looked after his elder daughter ;
then, in a tone whose festive note seemed the echo of a
mood lost in the night of ages :

" I am going in to cook something. Aha ! Son !
The old man knows where to find a bottle of wine, too."

He turned to Giselle, with a change to austere
tenderness.

" And you, little one, pray not to the God of priests
and slaves, but to the God of orphans, of the oppressed,
of the poor, of little children, to give thee a man like
this one for a husband."

His hand rested heavily for a moment on Nostromo's
shoulder ; then he went in. The hopeless slave of the
San Tomé silver felt at these words the venomous fangs of
jealousy biting deep into his heart. He was appalled by
the novelty of the experience, by its force, by its physical
intimacy. A husband ! A husband for her ! And yet
it was natural that Giselle should have a husband at some
time or other. He had never realised that before. In
discovering that her beauty could belong to another, he
felt as though he could kill this one of old Giorgio's
daughters also. He muttered moodily :

" They say you love Ramirez."

She shook her head without looking at him. Coppery
glints rippled to and fro on the wealth of her gold hair.
Her smooth forehead had the soft, pure sheen of a priceless pearl in the splendour of the sunset, mingling the
gloom of starry spaces, the purple of the sea, and the
crimson of the sky in a magnificent stillness.

" No," she said slowly. " I never loved him. I
think I never . . . He loves me—perhaps."

The seduction of her slow voice died out of the air,
and her raised eyes remained fixed on nothing, as if
indifferent and without thought.

" Ramirez told you he loved you ? " asked Nostromo, restraining himself.

" Ah ! once—one evening . . ."

" The miserable . . . Ha ! "

He had jumped up as if stung by a gadfly, and stood before her mute with anger.

" Misericordia Divina ! You, too, Gian' Battista ! Poor wretch that I am ! " she lamented in ingenuous tones. " I told Linda, and she scolded—she scolded. Am I to live blind, dumb, and deaf in this world ? And she told father, who took down his gun and cleaned it. Poor Ramirez ! Then you came, and she told you."

He looked at her. He fastened his eyes upon the hollow of her white throat, which had the invincible charm of things young, palpitating, delicate, and alive. Was this the child he had known ? Was it possible ? It dawned upon him that in these last years he had really seen very little—nothing—of her. Nothing. She had come into the world like a thing unknown. She had come upon him unawares. She was a danger—a frightful danger. The instinctive mood of fierce determination that had never failed him before the perils of his life added its steady force to the violence of his passion. She, in a voice that recalled to him the song of running water, the tinkling of a silver bell, continued :

" And between you three you have brought me here into this captivity to the sky and water. Nothing else. Sky and water. Oh, Sanctissima Madre ! My hair shall turn grey on this tedious island. I could hate you, Gian' Battista ! "

He laughed loudly. Her voice enveloped him like a caress. She bemoaned her fate, spreading unconsciously, like a flower its perfume in the coolness of the evening, the indefinable seduction of her person. Was it her fault that nobody ever had admired Linda ? Even when they were little, going out with their mother to Mass, she remembered that people took no notice of

Linda, who was fearless, and chose instead to frighten her, who was timid, with their attention. It was her hair like gold, she supposed.

He broke out :

" Your hair like gold, and your eyes like violets, and your lips like the rose ; your round arms, your white throat. . . ."

Imperturbable in the indolence of her pose, she blushed deeply all over to the roots of her hair. She was not conceited. She was no more self-conscious than a flower. But she was pleased. And perhaps even a flower loves to hear itself praised. He glanced down, and added impetuously :

" Your little feet ! "

Leaning back against the rough stone wall of the cottage, she seemed to bask languidly in the warmth of the rosy flush. Only her lowered eyes glanced at her little feet.

" And so you are going at last to marry our Linda. She is terrible. Ah ! now she will understand better since you have told her you love her. She will not be so fierce."

" *Chica !* " said Nostromo, " I have not told her anything."

" Then make haste. Come to-morrow. Come and tell her, so that I may have some peace from her scolding, and—perhaps—who knows . . ."

" Be allowed to listen to your Ramirez, eh ? Is that it ? You . . . ."

" Mercy of God ! How violent you are, Giovanni," she said, unmoved. " Who is Ramirez . . . Ramirez . . . Who is he ? " she repeated dreamily, in the dusk and gloom of the clouded gulf, with a low red streak in the west like a hot bar of glowing iron laid across the entrance of a world sombre as a cavern, where the magnificent Capataz de Cargadores had hidden his conquests of love and wealth.

" Listen, Giselle," he said in measured tones ; " I will tell no word of love to your sister. Do you want to know why ? "

" Alas ! I could not understand, perhaps, Giovanni. Father says you are not like other men ; that no one had ever understood you properly ; that the rich will be surprised yet. . . . Oh, saints in heaven ! I am weary."

She raised her embroidery to conceal the lower part of her face, then let it fall on her lap. The lantern was shaded on the land side, but slanting away from the dark column of the lighthouse they could see the long shaft of light, kindled by Linda, go out to strike the expiring glow in a horizon of purple and red.

Giselle Viola, with her head resting against the wall of the house, her eyes half closed, and her little feet, in white stockings and black slippers, crossed over each other, seemed to surrender herself, tranquil and fatal, to the gathering dusk. The charm of her body, the promising mysteriousness of her indolence, went out into the night of the Placid Gulf like a fresh and intoxicating fragrance spreading out in the shadows, impregnating the air. The incorruptible Nostromo breathed her ambient seduction in the tumultuous heaving of his breast. Before leaving the harbour he had thrown off the store clothing of Captain Fidanza, for greater ease in the long pull out to the islands. He stood before her in the red sash and check shirt as he used to appear on the Company's wharf—a Mediterranean sailor come ashore to try his luck in Costaguana. The dusk of purple and red enveloped him too—close, soft, profound, as no more than fifty yards from that spot it had gathered evening after evening about the self-destructive passion of Don Martin Decoud's utter scepticism, flaming up to death in solitude.

" You have got to hear," he began at last, with perfect self-control. " I shall say no word of love to your sister, to whom I am betrothed from this evening, because it is you that I love.   It is you ! " . . .

The dusk let him see yet the tender and voluptuous smile that came instinctively upon her lips shaped for love and kisses, freeze hard in the drawn, haggard lines of terror.   He could not restrain himself any longer. While she shrank from his approach, her arms went out to him, abandoned and regal in the dignity of her languid surrender.   He held her head in his two hands, and showered rapid kisses upon the upturned face, that gleamed in the purple dusk.   Masterful and tender, he was entering slowly upon the fullness of his possession. And he perceived that she was crying.   Then the incomparable Capataz, the man of careless loves, became gentle and caressing, like a woman to the grief of a child.   He murmured to her fondly.   He sat down by her and nursed her fair head on his breast.   He called her his star and his little flower.

It had grown dark.   From the living-room of the light-keeper's cottage, where Giorgio, one of the Immortal Thousand, was bending his leonine and heroic head over a charcoal fire, there came the sound of sizzling and the aroma of an artistic *frittura*.

In the obscure disarray of that thing, happening like a cataclysm, it was in her feminine head that some gleam of reason survived.   He was lost to the world in their embraced stillness.   But she said, whispering into his ear :

" God of mercy !   What will become of me—here— now—between this sky and this water I hate ?   Linda, Linda—I see her ! " . . . She tried to get out of his arms, suddenly relaxed at the sound of that name.   But there was no one approaching their black shapes, enlaced and struggling on the white background of the wall. " Linda !   Poor Linda !   I tremble !   I shall die of fear before my poor sister Linda, betrothed to-day to Giovanni—my lover !   Giovanni, you must have been

THE LIGHTHOUSE

mad! I cannot understand you! You are not like other men! I will not give you up—never—only to God Himself! But why have you done this blind, mad, cruel, frightful thing?"

Released, she hung her head, let fall her hands. The altar-cloth, as if tossed by a great wind, lay far away from them, gleaming white on the black ground.

"From fear of losing my hope of you," said Nostromo.

"You knew that you had my soul! You know everything! It was made for you! But what could stand between you and me? What? Tell me!" she repeated, without impatience, in superb assurance.

"Your dead mother," he said, very low.

"Ah! . . . Poor mother! She has always . . . She is a saint in heaven now, and I cannot give you up to her. No, Giovanni. Only to God alone. You were mad—but it is done. Oh, what have you done? Giovanni, my beloved, my life, my master, do not leave me here in this grave of clouds! You cannot leave me now! You must take me away—at once—this instant—in the little boat. Giovanni, carry me off to-night, from my fear of Linda's eyes, before I have to look at her again."

She nestled close to him. The slave of the San Tomé silver felt the weight as of chains upon his limbs, a pressure as of a cold hand upon his lips. He struggled against the spell.

"I cannot," he said. "Not yet. There is something that stands between us two and the freedom of the world."

She pressed her form closer to his side with a subtle and naïve instinct of seduction.

"You rave, Giovanni—my lover!" she whispered engagingly. "What can there be? Carry me off—in thy very hands—to Doña Emilia—away from here. I am not very heavy."

It seemed as though she expected him to lift her up at once in his two palms. She had lost the notion of all impossibility. Anything could happen on this night of wonder. As he made no movement, she almost cried aloud :
" I tell you I am afraid of Linda ! " And still he did not move. She became quiet and wily. " What can there be ? " she asked coaxingly.

He felt her warm, breathing, alive, quivering in the hollow of his arm. In the exulting consciousness of his strength, and the triumphant excitement of his mind, he struck out for his freedom.

" A treasure," he said. All was still. She did not understand. " A treasure. A treasure of silver to buy a gold crown for thy brow."

" A treasure ? " she repeated in a faint voice, as if from the depths of a dream. " What is it you say ? "

She disengaged herself gently. He got up and looked down at her, aware of her face, of her hair, her lips, the dimples on her cheeks—seeing the fascination of her person in the night of the gulf as if in the blaze of noon-day. Her nonchalant and seductive voice trembled with the excitement of admiring awe and ungovernable curiosity.

" A treasure of silver ? " she stammered out. Then pressed on faster : " What ? Where ? How did you get it, Giovanni ? "

He wrestled with the spell of captivity It was as if striking an heroic blow that he burst out :

" Like a thief ! "

The densest blackness of the Placid Gulf seemed to fall upon his head. He could not see her now. She had vanished into a long, obscure, abysmal silence,whence her voice came back to him after a time with a faint glimmer, which was her face.

" I love you ! I love you ! "

These words gave him an unwonted sense of freedom ;
they cast a spell stronger than the accursed spell of the
treasure ; they changed his weary subjection to that
dead thing into an exulting conviction of his power. He
would cherish her, he said, in a splendour as great as
Doña Emilia's. The rich lived on wealth stolen from
the people, but he had taken from the rich nothing—
nothing that was not lost to them already by their folly
and their betrayal. For he had been betrayed—he said
—deceived, tempted. She believed him. . . . He had
kept the treasure for purposes of revenge ; but now he
cared nothing for it. He cared only for her. He would
put her beauty in a palace on a hill crowned with olive
trees—a white palace above a blue sea. He would keep
her there like a jewel in a casket. He would get land
for her—her own land fertile with vines and corn—to
set her little feet upon. He kissed them. . . . He
had already paid for it all with the soul of a woman
and the life of a man. . . . The Capataz de Cargadores
tasted the supreme intoxication of his generosity. He
flung the mastered treasure superbly at her feet in the
impenetrable darkness of the gulf, in the darkness defying
—as men said—the knowledge of God and the wit of
the devil. But she must let him grow rich first—he
warned her.

She listened as if in a trance. Her fingers stirred
in his hair. He got up from his knees reeling, weak,
empty, as though he had flung his soul away.

"Make haste, then," she said. "Make haste,
Giovanni, my lover, my master, for I will give thee up
to no one but God. And I am afraid of Linda."

He guessed at her shudder, and swore to do his best.
He trusted the courage of her love. She promised to be
brave in order to be loved always—far away in a white
palace upon a hill above the blue sea. Then with a
timid, tentative eagerness she murmured :

"Where is it ? Where ? Tell me that, Giovanni."

He opened his mouth and remained silent—thunder-struck.

"Not that! Not that!" he gasped out, appalled at the spell of secrecy that had kept him dumb before so many people falling upon his lips again with unimpaired force. Not even to her. Not even to her. It was too dangerous. "I forbid thee to ask!" he cried at her, deadening cautiously the anger of his voice.

He had not regained his freedom. The spectre of the unlawful treasure arose, standing by her side like a figure of silver, pitiless and secret with a finger on its pale lips. His soul died within him at the vision of himself creeping in presently along the ravine, with the smell of earth, of damp foliage in his nostrils—creeping in, determined in a purpose that numbed his breast, and creeping out again loaded with silver, with his ears alert to every sound. It must be done on this very night—that work of a craven slave!

He stooped low, pressed the hem of her skirt to his lips, with a muttered command:

"Tell him I would not stay," and was gone suddenly from her, silent, without as much as a footfall in the dark night.

She sat still, her head resting indolently against the wall, and her little feet in white stockings and black slippers crossed over each other. Old Giorgio, coming out, did not seem to be surprised at the intelligence as much as she had vaguely feared. For she was full of inexplicable fear now—fear of everything and everybody except of her Giovanni and his treasure. But that was incredible.

The heroic Garibaldino accepted Nostromo's abrupt departure with a sagacious indulgence. He remembered his own feelings, and exhibited a masculine penetration of the true state of the case.

"*Va bene*. Let him go. Ha! ha! No matter how fair the woman, it galls a little. Liberty, liberty.

There's more than one kind !   He has said the great word,
and Son Gian' Battista is not tame."   He seemed to be
instructing the motionless and scared Giselle. . . . " A
man should not be tame," he added dogmatically out of
the doorway.   Her stillness and silence seemed to dis-
please him.   " Do not give way to the enviousness of
your sister's lot," he admonished her, very grave, in his
deep voice.

Presently he had to come to the door again to call
in his younger daughter.   It was late.   He shouted her
name three times before she even moved her head.   Left
alone, she had become the helpless prey of astonishment.
She walked into the bedroom she shared with Linda like
a person profoundly asleep.   That aspect was so marked
that even old Giorgio, spectacled, raising his eyes from the
Bible, shook his head as she shut the door behind her.

She walked right across the room without looking at
anything, and sat down at once by the open window.
Linda, stealing down from the tower in the exuberance of
her happiness, found her with a lighted candle at her back,
facing the black night full of sighing gusts of wind and the
sound of distant showers—a true night of the gulf, too
dense for the eye of God and the wiles of the devil.   She
did not turn her head at the opening of the door.

There was something in that immobility which
reached Linda in the depths of her paradise.   The elder
sister guessed angrily : the child is thinking of that
wretched Ramirez.   Linda longed to talk.   She said in
her arbitrary voice, " Giselle ! " and was not answered by
the slightest movement.

The girl who was going to live in a palace and walk on
ground of her own was ready to die with terror.   Not for
anything in the world would she have turned her head to
face her sister.   Her heart was beating madly.   She said
with subdued haste :

" Do not speak to me.   I am praying."

Linda, disappointed, went out quietly ; and Giselle

sat on unbelieving, lost, dazed, patient, as if waiting for
the confirmation of the incredible. The hopeless blackness of the clouds seemed part of a dream too. She
waited.

She did not wait in vain. The man whose soul was
dead within him, creeping out of the ravine, weighted with
silver, had seen the gleam of the lighted window, and
could not help retracing his steps from the beach.

On that impenetrable background, obliterating the
lofty mountains by the seaboard, she saw the slave of the
San Tomé silver, as if by an extraordinary power of a
miracle. She accepted his return as if henceforth the
world could hold no surprise for all eternity.

She rose compelled and rigid, and began to speak
long before the light from within fell upon the face of
the approaching man.

"You have come back to carry me off! It is well!
Open thy arms, Giovanni, my lover. I am coming."

His prudent footsteps stopped, and with his eyes
glistening wildly, he spoke in a harsh voice.

" Not yet. I must grow rich slowly." . . . A threatening note came into his tone. " Do not forget that you
have a thief for your lover."

" Yes ! Yes ! " she whispered hastily. " Come
nearer ! Listen ! Do not give me up, Giovanni !
Never, never ! . . . I will be patient ! " . . .

Her form drooped consolingly over the low casement
towards the slave of the unlawful treasure. The light in
the room went out, and, weighted with silver, the magnificent Capataz clasped her round her white neck in the
darkness of the gulf as a drowning man clutches at a
straw.

CHAPTER THIRTEEN

ON the day Mrs. Gould was going, in Dr. Mony-gham's words, to " give a tertulia," Captain Fidanza went down the side of his schooner lying in Sulaco harbour, calm, unbending, deliberate in the way he sat down in his dinghy and took up his sculls. He was later than usual. The afternoon was well advanced before he landed on the beach of the Great Isabel, and with a steady pace climbed the slope of the island.

From a distance he made out Giselle sitting in a chair tilted back against the end of the house, under the window of the girls' room. She had her embroidery in her hands, and held it well up to her eyes. The tranquillity of that girlish figure exasperated the feeling of perpetual struggle and strife he carried in his breast. He became angry. It seemed to him that she ought to hear the clanking of his fetters—his silver fetters—from afar. And while ashore that day, he had met the doctor with the evil eye, who had looked at him very hard.

The raising of her eyes mollified him. They smiled in their flower-like freshness straight upon his heart. Then she frowned. It was a warning to be cautious. He stopped some distance away, and in a loud, indifferent tone said :

" Good-day, Giselle. Is Linda up yet ? "

" Yes. She is in the big room with father."

He approached then, and, looking through the window into the bedroom for fear of being detected by Linda

33

returning there for some reason, he said, moving only his
lips :

" You love me ? "

" More than my life." She went on with her embroidery under his contemplating gaze and continued to
speak, looking at her work. " Or I could not live. I
could not, Giovanni. For this life is like death. Oh,
Giovanni, I shall perish if you do not take me
away ! "

He smiled carelessly. " I will come to the window
when it's dark," he said.

" No, don't, Giovanni. Not to-night. Linda and
father have been talking together for a long time to-day."

" What about ? "

" Ramirez, I fancy I heard. I do not know. I am
afraid. I am always afraid. It is like dying a thousand
times a day. Your love is to me like your treasure to you.
It is there, but I can never get enough of it."

He looked at her, very still. She was beautiful. His
desire had grown within him. He had two masters now.
But she was incapable of sustained emotion. She was
sincere in what she said, but she slept placidly at night.
When she saw him she flamed up always. Then only an
increased taciturnity marked the change in her. She was
afraid of betraying herself. She was afraid of pain, of
bodily harm, of sharp words, of facing anger, and wit-
nessing violence. For her soul was light and tender with
a pagan sincerity in its impulses. She murmured :

" Give up the palazzo, Giovanni, and the vineyard on
the hills, for which we are starving our love."

She ceased, seeing Linda standing silent at the corner
of the house.

Nostromo turned to his affianced wife with a greeting,
and was amazed at her sunken eyes, at her hollow cheeks,
at the air of illness and anguish in her face.

" Have you been ill ? " he asked, trying to put some
concern into this question.

Her black eyes blazed at him. " Am I thinner ? "
she asked.

" Yes—perhaps—a little."

" And older ? "

" Every day counts—for all of us."

" I shall go grey, I fear, before the ring is on my
finger," she said slowly, keeping her gaze fastened upon
him.

She waited for what he would say, rolling down her
turned-up sleeves.

" No fear of that," he said absently.

She turned away as if it had been something final,
and busied herself with household cares while Nostromo
talked with her father. Conversation with the old
Garibaldino was not easy. Age had left his faculties
unimpaired, only they seemed to have withdrawn somewhere deep within him. His answers were slow in coming, with an effect of august gravity. But that day he was
more animated, quicker ; there seemed to be more life
in the old lion. He was uneasy for the integrity of his
honour. He believed Sidoni's warning as to Ramirez's
designs upon his younger daughter. And he did not
trust her. She was flighty. He said nothing of his cares
to " Son Gian' Battista." It was a touch of senile vanity.
He wanted to show that he was equal yet to the task of
guarding alone the honour of his house.

Nostromo went away early. As soon as he had disappeared, walking towards the beach, Linda stepped over
the threshold and, with a haggard smile, sat down by the
side of her father.

Ever since that Sunday, when the infatuated and
desperate Ramirez had waited for her on the wharf, she
had no doubts whatever. The jealous ravings of that
man were no revelation. They had only fixed with precision, as with a nail driven into her heart, that sense of
unreality and deception which, instead of bliss and
security, she had found in her intercourse with her

promised husband. She had passed on, pouring indignation and scorn upon Ramirez ; but, that Sunday, she
nearly died of wretchedness and shame, lying on the
carved and lettered stone of Teresa's grave, subscribed
for by the engine-drivers and the fitters of the railway
workshops, in sign of their respect for the hero of Italian
Unity.   Old Viola had not been able to carry out his
desire of burying his wife in the sea ; and Linda wept
upon the stone.

The gratuitous outrage appalled her. If he wished to
break her heart—well and good.   Everything was permitted to Gian' Battista. But why trample upon the
pieces ? Why seek to humiliate her spirit ? Aha ! He
could not break that. She dried her tears. And Giselle !
Giselle ! The little one that, ever since she could toddle,
had always clung to her skirt for protection.   What
duplicity ! But she could not help it probably. When
there was a man in the case the poor feather-headed wretch
could not help herself.

Linda had a good share of the Viola stoicism. She
resolved to say nothing. But, woman-like, she put
passion into her stoicism.   Giselle's short answers,
prompted by fearful caution, drove her beside herself
by their curtness that resembled disdain. One day she
flung herself upon the chair in which her indolent sister
was lying and impressed the mark of her teeth at the
base of the whitest neck in Sulaco. Giselle cried out.
But she had her share of the Viola heroism. Ready to
faint with terror, she only said, in a lazy voice, " Madre
de Dios ! Are you going to eat me alive, Linda ? "
And this outburst passed off, leaving no trace upon the
situation.   " She knows nothing.   She cannot know
anything," reflected Giselle. " Perhaps it is not true.
It cannot be true," Linda tried to persuade herself.

But when she saw Captain Fidanza for the first time
after her meeting with the distracted Ramirez, the certitude of her misfortune returned. She watched him

from the doorway go away to his boat, asking herself stoically, " Will they meet to-night ? " She made up her mind not to leave the tower for a second. When he had disappeared, she came out and sat down by her father.

The venerable Garibaldino felt, in his own words, " a young man yet." In one way or another a good deal of talk about Ramirez had reached him of late ; and his contempt and dislike of that man, who obviously was not what his son would have been, had made him restless. He slept very little now ; but for several nights past, instead of reading— or only sitting, with Mrs. Gould's silver spectacles on his nose, before the open Bible—he had been prowling actively all about the island with his old gun, on watch over his honour.

Linda, laying her thin brown hand on his knee, tried to soothe his excitement. Ramirez was not in Sulaco. Nobody knew where he was. He was gone. His talk of what he would do meant nothing.

" No," the old man interrupted. " But Son Gian' Battista told me—quite of himself—that the cowardly *esclavo* was drinking and gambling with the rascals of Zapiga, over there on the north side of the gulf. He may get some of the worst scoundrels of that scoundrelly town of negroes to help him in his attempt upon the little one. . . . But I am not so old. No ! "

She argued earnestly against the probability of any attempt being made ; and at last the old man fell silent, chewing his white moustache. Women had their obstinate notions which must be humoured—his poor wife was like that, and Linda resembled her mother. It was not seemly for a man to argue. " Maybe. Maybe," he mumbled.

She was by no means easy in her mind. She loved Nostromo. She turned her eyes upon Giselle, sitting at a distance, with something of maternal tenderness, and the jealous anguish of a rival outraged in her defeat. Then she rose and walked over to her.

" Listen—you," she said roughly.

The invincible candour of the gaze raised up all violet and dew, excited her rage and admiration. She had beautiful eyes—the *chica*—this vile thing of white flesh and black deception. She did not know whether she wanted to tear them out with shouts of vengeance or cover up their mysterious and shameless innocence with kisses of pity and love. And suddenly they became empty, gazing blankly at her, except for a little fear not quite buried deep enough with all the other emotions in Giselle's heart.

Linda said, " Ramirez is boasting in town that he will carry you off from the island."

" What folly ! " answered the other ; and in a perversity born of long restraint, she added, " He is not the man," in a jesting tone with a trembling audacity.

" No ? " said Linda, through her clenched teeth. " Is he not ? Well, then, look to it ; because father has been walking about with a loaded gun at night."

" It is not good for him. You must tell him not to, Linda. He will not listen to me."

" I shall say nothing—never any more—to anybody," cried Linda passionately.

This could not last, thought Giselle. Giovanni must take her away soon—the very next time he came. She would not suffer these terrors for ever so much silver. To speak with her sister made her ill. But she was not uneasy at her father's watchfulness. She had begged Nostromo not to come to the window that night. He had promised to keep away for this once. And she did not know, could not guess or imagine, that he had another reason for coming on the island.

Linda had gone straight to the tower. It was time to light up. She unlocked the little door, and went heavily up the spiral staircase, carrying her love for the magnificent Capataz de Cargadores like an ever-increasing load of shameful fetters. No ; she could not throw

it off. No ; let Heaven dispose of these two. And
moving about the lantern, filled with twilight and the
sheen of the moon, with careful movements she lighted
the lamp. Then her arms fell along her body.

" And with our mother looking on ! " she murmured.
" My own sister—the *chica* ! "

The whole refracting apparatus, with its brass fittings
and rings of prisms, glittered and sparkled like a dome-
shaped shrine of diamonds, containing not a lamp, but
some sacred flame, dominating the sea. And Linda, the
keeper, in black, with a pale face, drooped low in a wooden
chair, alone with her jealousy, far above the shames and
passions of the earth. A strange dragging pain as if
somebody were pulling her about brutally by her dark
hair with bronze glints, made her put her hands up to her
temples. They would meet. They would meet. And
she knew where, too. At the window. The sweat of
torture fell in drops on her cheeks, while the moonlight
in the offing closed as if with a colossal bar of silver the
entrance of the Placid Gulf—the sombre cavern of clouds
and stillness in the surf-fretted seaboard.

Linda Viola stood up suddenly with a finger on her
lip. He loved neither her nor her sister. The whole
thing seemed so objectless as to frighten her, and also
give her some hope. Why did he not carry her off ?
What prevented him ? He was incomprehensible.
What were they waiting for ? For what end were these
two lying and deceiving ? Not for the ends of their love.
There was no such thing. The hope of regaining him
for herself made her break her vow of not leaving the
tower that night. She must talk at once to her father,
who was wise, and would understand. She ran down
the spiral stairs. At the moment of opening the door
at the bottom she heard the sound of the first shot ever
fired on the Great Isabel.

She felt a shock, as though the bullet had struck her
breast. She ran on without pausing. The cottage was

dark. She cried at the door, " Giselle ! Giselle ! " then
dashed round the corner and screamed her sister's name
at the open window, without getting an answer ; but
as she was rushing, distracted, round the house, Giselle
came out of the door, and darted past her, running
silently, her hair loose, and her eyes staring straight
ahead. She seemed to skim along the grass as if on
tiptoe, and vanished.

Linda walked on slowly, with her arms stretched out
before her. All was still on the island ; she did not
know where she was going. The tree under which
Martin Decoud spent his last days, beholding life like
a succession of senseless images, threw a large blotch
of black shade upon the grass. Suddenly she saw her
father, standing quietly all alone in the moonlight.

The Garibaldino—big, erect, with his snow-white
hair and beard—had a monumental repose in his immobility, leaning upon a rifle. She put her hand upon his
arm lightly. He never stirred.

" What have you done ? " she asked in her ordinary
voice.

" I have shot Ramirez—*infame* ! " he answered, with
his eyes directed to where the shade was blackest. " Like
a thief he came, and like a thief he fell. The child had
to be protected."

He did not offer to move an inch, to advance a single
step. He stood there, rugged and unstirring, like a
statue of an old man guarding the honour of his house.
Linda removed her trembling hand from his arm, firm
and steady like an arm of stone, and, without a word,
entered the blackness of the shade. She saw a stir of
formless shapes on the ground, and stopped short. A
murmur of despair and tears grew louder to her strained
hearing.

" I entreated you not to come to-night. Oh, my
Giovanni ! And you promised. Oh ! Why—why did
you come, Giovanni ? "

It was her sister's voice. It broke on a heart-rending sob. And the voice of the resourceful Capataz de Cargadores, master and slave of the San Tomé treasure, who had been caught unawares by old Giorgio while stealing across the open towards the ravine to get some more silver, answered careless and cool, but sounding startlingly weak, from the ground.

" It seemed as though I could not live through the night without seeing thee once more—my star, my little flower."

.   .   .   .

The brilliant tertulia was just over, the last guests had departed, and the Señor Administrador had gone to his room already, when Dr. Monygham, who had been expected in the evening but had not turned up, arrived, driving along the wood-block pavement under the electric lamps of the deserted Calle de la Constitucion, and found the great gateway of the Casa still open.

He limped in, stumped up the stairs, and found the fat and sleek Basilio on the point of turning off the lights in the sala. The prosperous major-domo remained open-mouthed at this late invasion.

" Don't put out the lights," commanded the doctor. " I want to see the Señora."

" The Señora is in the Señor Administrador's cancillaria," said Basilio in an unctuous voice. " The Señor Administrador starts for the mountain in an hour. There is some trouble with the workmen to be feared, it appears. A shameless people without reason and decency. And idle, Señor. Idle."

" You are shamelessly lazy and imbecile yourself," said the doctor, with that faculty for exasperation which made him so generally beloved. " Don't put the lights out."

Basilio retired with dignity. Dr. Monygham, waiting in the brilliantly lighted sala, heard presently a door close at the farther end of the house. A jingle of spurs died out. The Señor Administrador was off to the mountain.

With a measured swish of her long train, flashing with jewels and the shimmer of silk, her delicate head bowed as if under the weight of a mass of fair hair, in which the silver threads were lost, the " first lady of Sulaco," as Captain Mitchell used to describe her, moved along the lighted *corrédor*, wealthy beyond great dreams of wealth, considered, loved, respected, honoured, and as solitary as any human being had ever been, perhaps, on this earth.

The doctor's " Mrs. Gould ! One minute ! " stopped her with a start at the door of the lighted and empty sala. From the similarity of mood and circumstance, the sight of the doctor, standing there all alone amongst the groups of furniture, recalled to her emotional memory her unexpected meeting with Martin Decoud ; she seemed to hear in the silence the voice of that man, dead miserably so many years ago, pronounce the words, " Antonia left her fan here." But it was the doctor's voice that spoke, a little altered by his excitement. She remarked his shining eyes.

" Mrs. Gould, you are wanted. Do you know what has happened ? You remember what I told you yesterday about Nostromo. Well, it seems that a lancha, a decked boat, coming from Zapiga, with four negroes in her, passing close to the Great Isabel, was hailed from the cliff by a woman's voice—Linda's, as a matter of fact—commanding them (it's a moonlight night) to go round to the beach and take up a wounded man to the town. The *patron* (from whom I've heard all this), of course, did so at once. He told me that when they got round to the low side of the Great Isabel, they found Linda Viola waiting for them. They followed her : she led them under a tree not far from the cottage. There they found Nostromo lying on the ground with his head in the younger girl's lap, and father Viola standing some distance off leaning on his gun.

Under Linda's direction they got a table out of the cottage for a stretcher, after breaking off the legs. They are here, Mrs. Gould. I mean Nostromo and—and Giselle. The negroes brought him in to the first-aid hospital near the harbour. He made the attendant send for me. But it was not me he wanted to see—it was you, Mrs. Gould! It was you!"

"Me?" whispered Mrs. Gould, shrinking a little.

"Yes, you!" the doctor burst out. "He begged me —his enemy, as he thinks—to bring you to him at once. It seems he has something to say to you alone."

"Impossible!" murmured Mrs. Gould.

"He said to me, 'Remind her that I have done something to keep a roof over her head.' . . . Mrs. Gould," the doctor pursued in the greatest excitement, "do you remember the silver—the silver in the lighter— that was lost?"

Mrs. Gould remembered. But she did not say she hated the mere mention of that silver. Frankness personified, she remembered with an exaggerated horror that for the first and last time of her life she had concealed the truth from her husband about that very silver. She had been corrupted by her fears at that time, and she had never forgiven herself. Moreover, that silver, which would never have come down if her husband had been made acquainted with the news brought by Decoud, had been in a roundabout way nearly the cause of Dr. Monygham's death. And these things appeared to her very dreadful.

"Was it lost, though?" the doctor exclaimed. "I've always felt that there was a mystery about our Nostromo ever since. I do believe he wants now, at the point of death——"

"The point of death?" repeated Mrs. Gould.

"Yes. Yes. . . . He wants perhaps to tell you something concerning that silver which——"

"Oh no! No!" exclaimed Mrs. Gould in a low

voice. " Isn't it lost and done with ? Isn't there enough treasure without it to make everybody in the world miserable ? "

The doctor remained still, in a submissive, disappointed silence. At last he ventured, very low :

" And there is that Viola girl—Giselle. What are we to do ? It looks as though father and sister had——"

Mrs. Gould admitted that she felt in duty bound to do her best for these girls.

" I have a volante here," the doctor said. " If you don't mind getting into that——"

He waited, all impatience, till Mrs. Gould reappeared, having thrown over her dress a grey cloak with a deep hood.

It was thus that, cloaked and monastically hooded over her evening costume, this woman, full of endurance and compassion, stood by the side of the bed on which the splendid Capataz de Cargadores lay stretched out motionless on his back. The whiteness of sheets and pillows gave a sombre and energetic relief to his bronzed face, to the dark, nervous hands, so good on a tiller, upon a bridle and on a trigger, lying open and idle upon a white coverlet.

" She is innocent," the Capataz was saying in a deep and level voice, as though afraid that a louder word would break the slender hold his spirit still kept upon his body. " She is innocent. It is I alone. But no matter. For these things I would answer to no man or woman alive."

He paused. Mrs. Gould's face, very white within the shadow of the hood, bent over him with an invincible and dreary sadness. And the low sobs of Giselle Viola, kneeling at the end of the bed, her gold hair with coppery gleams loose and scattered over the Capataz's feet, hardly troubled the silence of the room.

" Ha ! Old Giorgio—the guardian of thine honour ! Fancy the Vecchio coming upon me so light of foot, so steady of aim ! I myself could have done no better. But the price of a charge of powder might have been saved. The honour was safe. . . . Señora, she would have followed to the end of the world Nostromo the thief. . . . I have said the word. The spell is broken ! "

A low moan from the girl made him cast his eyes down.

" I cannot see her. . . . No matter," he went on, with the shadow of the old magnificent carelessness in his voice. " One kiss is enough, if there is no time for more. An airy soul, Señora ! Bright and warm, like sunshine— soon clouded, and soon serene. They would crush it there between them. Señora, cast on her the eye of your compassion, as famed from one end of the land to the other as the courage and daring of the man who speaks to you. She will console herself in time. And even Ramirez is not a bad fellow. I am not angry. No ! It is not Ramirez who overcame the Capataz of the Sulaco Cargadores." He paused, made an effort, and in a louder voice, a little wildly, declared :

" I die betrayed—betrayed by——"

But he did not say by whom or by what he was dying betrayed.

" She would not have betrayed me," he began again, opening his eyes very wide. " She was faithful. We were going very far—very soon. I could have torn myself away from that accursed treasure for her. For that child I would have left boxes and boxes of it— full. And Decoud took four. Four ingots. Why ? *Picardia !* To betray me ? How could I give back the treasure with four ingots missing ? They would have said I had purloined them. The doctor would have said that. Alas, it holds me yet ! "

Mrs. Gould bent low, fascinated—cold with apprehension.

" What became of Don Martin on that night, Nostromo ? "

" Who knows ?   I wondered what would become of
me.   Now I know.   Death was to come upon me unawares.   He went away !   He betrayed me !   And you
think I have killed him !   You are all alike, you fine
people.   The silver has killed me.   It has held me.   It
holds me yet.   Nobody knows where it is.   But you are
the wife of Don Carlos, who put it into my hands and
said, ' Save it, on your life.'   And when I returned, and
you all thought it was lost, what do I hear ?   ' It was
nothing of importance.   Let it go.   Up, Nostromo, the
faithful, and ride away to save us, for dear life ! ' "

" Nostromo," Mrs. Gould whispered, bending very
low, " I, too, have hated the idea of that silver from the
bottom of my heart."

" Marvellous !—that one of you should hate the
wealth that you know so well how to take from the hands of
the poor.   The world rests upon the poor, as old Giorgio
says.   You have been always good to the poor.   But
there is something accursed in wealth.   Señora, shall I
tell you where the treasure is ?   To you alone. . . .
Shining !   Incorruptible ! "

A pained, involuntary reluctance lingered in his tone,
in his eyes, plain to the woman with the genius of
sympathetic intuition.   She averted her glance from the
miserable subjection of the dying man, appalled, wishing
to hear no more of the silver.

" No, Capataz," she said.   " No one misses it now.
Let it be lost for ever."

After hearing these words, Nostromo closed his eyes,
uttered no word, made no movement.   Outside the door
of the sick-room Dr. Monygham, excited to the highest
pitch, his eyes shining with eagerness, came up to the two
women.

" Now, Mrs. Gould," he said, almost brutally in his
impatience, " tell me, was I right ?   There is a mystery.
You have got the word of it, have you not ?   He told
you——"

" He told me nothing," said Mrs. Gould steadily.

The light of his temperamental enmity to Nostromo went out of Dr. Monygham's eyes. He stepped back submissively. He did not believe Mrs. Gould. But her word was law. He accepted her denial like an inexplicable fatality affirming the victory of Nostromo's genius over his own. Even before that woman, whom he loved with secret devotion, he had been defeated by the magnificent Capataz de Cargadores, the man who had lived his own life on the assumption of unbroken fidelity, rectitude, and courage !

" Pray send at once somebody for my carriage," spoke Mrs. Gould from within her hood. Then, turning to Giselle Viola, " Come nearer me, child ; come closer. We will wait here."

Giselle Viola, heart-broken and childlike, her face veiled in her falling hair, crept up to her side. Mrs. Gould slipped her hand through the arm of the unworthy daughter of old Viola, the immaculate republican, the hero without a stain. Slowly, gradually, as a withered flower droops, the head of the girl, who would have followed a thief to the end of the world, rested on the shoulder of Doña Emilia, the first lady of Sulaco, the wife of the Señor Administrador of the San Tomé mine. And Mrs. Gould, feeling her suppressed sobbing, nervous and excited, had the first and only moment of bitterness in her life. It was worthy of Dr. Monygham himself.

" Console yourself, child. Very soon he would have forgotten you for his treasure."

" Señora, he loved me. He loved me," Giselle whispered despairingly. " He loved me as no one had ever been loved before."

" I have been loved too," Mrs. Gould said in a severe tone.

Giselle clung to her convulsively. " Oh, Señora, but you shall live adored to the end of your life," she sobbed out.

Mrs. Gould kept an unbroken silence till the carriage arrived. She helped in the half-fainting girl. After the doctor had shut the door of the landau, she leaned over to him.

"You can do nothing ? " she whispered.

"No, Mrs. Gould. Moreover, he won't let us touch him. It does not matter. I just had one look. . . . Useless."

But he promised to see old Viola and the other girl that very night. He could get the police-boat to take him off to the island. He remained in the street, looking after the landau rolling away slowly behind the white mules.

The rumour of some accident—an accident to Captain Fidanza—had been spreading along the new quays with their rows of lamps and the dark shapes of towering cranes. A knot of night prowlers—the poorest of the poor—hung about the door of the first-aid hospital, whispering in the moonlight of the empty street.

There was no one with the wounded man but the pale photographer, small, frail, bloodthirsty, the hater of capitalists, perched on a high stool near the head of the bed with his knees up and his chin in his hands. He had been fetched by a comrade who, working late on the wharf, had heard from a negro belonging to a lancha that Captain Fidanza had been brought ashore mortally wounded.

"Have you any dispositions to make, comrade ? " he asked anxiously. "Do not forget that we want money for our work. The rich must be fought with their own weapons."

Nostromo made no answer. The other did not insist, remaining huddled up on the stool, shock-headed, wildly hairy, like a hunchbacked monkey. Then, after a long silence :

"Comrade Fidanza," he began solemnly, "you have refused all aid from that doctor. Is he really a dangerous enemy of the people ? "

In the dimly lit room Nostromo rolled his head

slowly on the pillow and opened his eyes, directing at the weird figure perched by his bedside a glance of enigmatic and profound inquiry. Then his head rolled back, his eyelids fell, and the Capataz de Cargadores died without a word or moan after an hour of immobility, broken by short shudders testifying to the most atrocious sufferings.

Dr. Monygham, going out in the police-galley to the islands, beheld the glitter of the moon upon the gulf and the high black shape of the Great Isabel sending a shaft of light afar, from under the canopy of clouds.

" Pull easy," he said, wondering what he would find there. He tried to imagine Linda and her father, and discovered a strange reluctance within himself. " Pull easy," he repeated.

.   .   .   .   .   .

From the moment he fired at the thief of his honour, Giorgio Viola had not stirred from the spot. He stood, his old gun grounded, his hand grasping the barrel near the muzzle. After the lancha carrying off Nostromo for ever from her had left the shore, Linda, coming up, stopped before him. He did not seem to be aware of her presence, but when, losing her forced calmness, she cried out :

" Do you know whom you have killed ? " he answered : " Ramirez the vagabond."

White, and staring insanely at her father, Linda laughed in his face. After a time he joined her faintly in a deep-toned and distant echo of her peals. Then she stopped, and the old man spoke as if startled :

" He cried out in Son Gian' Battista's voice."

The gun fell from his opened hand, but the arm remained extended for a moment as if still supported. Linda seized it roughly.

" You are too old to understand. Come into the house."

He let her lead him. On the threshold he stumbled

34

heavily, nearly coming to the ground together with his daughter. His excitement, his activity of the last few days, had been like the flare of a dying lamp. He caught at the back of his chair.

" In Son Gian' Battista's voice," he repeated in a severe tone. " I heard him — Ramirez — the miserable——"

Linda helped him into the chair, and, bending low, hissed into his ear :

" You have killed Gian' Battista."

The old man smiled under his thick moustache. Women had strange fancies.

" Where is the child ? " he asked, surprised at the penetrating chilliness of the air and the unwonted dimness of the lamp by which he used to sit up half the night with the open Bible before him.

Linda hesitated a moment, then averted her eyes.

" She is asleep," she said. " We shall talk of her to-morrow."

She could not bear to look at him. He filled her with terror and with an almost unbearable feeling of pity. She had observed the change that came over him. He would never understand what he had done ; and even to her the whole thing remained incomprehensible. He said with difficulty :

" Give me the Book."

Linda laid on the table the closed volume in its worn leather cover, the Bible given him ages ago by an Englishman in Palermo.

" The child had to be protected," he said in a strange, mournful voice.

Behind his chair Linda wrung her hands, crying without noise. Suddenly she started for the door. He heard her move.

" Where are you going ? " he asked.

" To the light," she answered, turning round to look at him balefully.

" The light ! Si—duty."

Very upright, white-haired, leonine, heroic in his absorbed quietness, he felt in the pocket of his red shirt for the spectacles given him by Doña Emilia. He put them on. After a long period of immobility he opened the Book, and from on high looked through the glasses at the small print in double columns. A rigid, stern expression settled upon his features with a slight frown, as if in response to some gloomy thought or unpleasant sensation. But he never detached his eyes from the Book while he swayed forward, gently, gradually, till his snow-white head rested upon the open pages. A wooden clock ticked methodically on the whitewashed wall, and, growing slowly cold, the Garibaldino lay alone, rugged, undecayed, like an old oak uprooted by a treacherous gust of wind.

The light of the Great Isabel burned unfailing above the lost treasure of the San Tomé mine. Into the bluish sheen of a night without stars, the lantern sent out a yellow beam towards the far horizon. Like a black speck upon the shining panes, Linda, crouching in the outer gallery, rested her head on the rail. The moon, drooping in the western board, looked at her radiantly.

Below, at the foot of the cliff, the regular splash of oars from a passing boat ceased, and Dr. Monygham stood up in the sternsheets.

" Linda ! " he shouted, throwing back his head. " Linda ! "

Linda stood up. She had recognised the voice.

" Is he dead ? " she cried, bending over.

" Yes, my poor girl. I am coming round," the doctor answered from below. " Pull to the beach," he said to the rowers.

Linda's black figure detached itself upright on the light of the lantern with her arms raised above her head as though she were going to throw herself over.

" It is I who loved you," she whispered, with a face

as set and white as marble in the moonlight. "I! Only I! She will forget thee, killed miserably for her pretty face. I cannot understand. I cannot understand. But I shall never forget thee. Never!"

She stood silent and still, collecting her strength to throw all her fidelity, her pain, bewilderment, and despair into one great cry.

"Never! Gian' Battista!"

Dr. Monygham, pulling round in the police-galley, heard the name pass over his head. It was another of Nostromo's triumphs, the greatest, the most enviable, the most sinister of all. In that true cry of undying passion that seemed to ring aloud from Punta Mala to Azuera and away to the bright line of the horizon, overhung by a big white cloud shining like a mass of solid silver, the genius of the magnificent Capataz de Cargadores dominated the dark gulf containing his conquests of treasure and love.

THE END